Āndrōmakhê

An Epic Novel of Troy and a Woman's Triumphant Valor

Andromakhe Cycle, Volume One and Volume Two

(Lands of the Morning ™ Series, # 6)

By

Kristina O'Donnelly

In memory of Louise Halley Forshaw,
who laid the groundwork.

BooksForABuck.com and
Rose International Publishing House

U.S.A

ĀNDRÕMAKHÊ © KRISTINA O'DONNELLY

ISBN: 1-930574-59-2

Author's websites:

www.kristinaodonnelly.com – www.trojanenchantment-novel.com

Publisher's website:
www.booksforabuck.com

From the Lady of the Unicorn in Keltia, to Mevlana Jelaleddin Rumi in Anatolia,
Do not let the light go out!

Author's Note: As in my other novels in this series, *Āndrõmakhê* contains a lot of mythological/historical background woven into the story. Advised by some to delete these parts on account of that "the Readers' eyes will be glazing over," I have chosen to let you decide. Yes, dear Reader, I believe that it is *your* prerogative to either make notes to return later, or skim through, or skip altogether, those paragraphs that do not hold your attention.
I live to learn, and *to tell;* my soul's urge is to be the conduit of news and knowledge – so let the information be available, and it is up to you what to make of it. "From Keltia to Anatolia, do not let the light go out."

Warm regards,
Kristina O'Donnelly

Table of Contents

Āndrōmakhê

"The end of Troia will never end ... The flame that consumed it, will itself never be consumed." [G. K. Chesterton]

Discoveries made at the beginning of the 21st Century A.D. on site in Chanakkale, Turkey, provide strong new evidence of a sophisticated Bronze Age city and fierce armed battles in the right area, at the right time. Simply put, archaeology and mythology support each other to a surprising degree. For example, many of the towns and locales mentioned by Homer, obscured during the time he wrote the *Iliad* (circa 8th Century B.C.) are now proven as real Bronze Age settlements; 13th Century B.C. tablets recently unearthed in Greece list names of women abducted from Troy, and Hittite tablets from the era, mention a Wilusian nobleman/king in hand-to-hand combat against a rival. In the *Iliad,* the Olympian gods were closely involved with the affairs of the warring parties, and the original Homeric tale, in its core, is of Gods and Men, and of how they manipulate each other for their respective agendas.

Foreword

Author Kristina O'Donnelly creates a respectful, but different vision of the immortal story of Troy as told by Homer and the Greek playwrights. For over three-thousand years, Hector and Andromache have symbolized the archetypical, loving husband and wife in Classic literature. O'Donnelly takes us deeper into their relationship. Also, rather than the male-centered heroics of Homer, she tells of the women they leave behind—of Āndrōmakhê (Andromache), Kassandra (Cassandra), Helen, and Hekabe, Priam's Queen and the mother of so many children killed in battle. O'Donnelly's research brings an added dimension to the story that reaches beyond The Iliad—and to its magic. Mythology, history, conquest, fate, prophesy, talking animals, and reincarnation all play a role in this richly textured, powerful novel.

Caught in a world being transformed, Āndrōmakhê still worships the triple goddess, but patriarchal gods and patriarchal lines of descent are overcoming the older ways. Haunted by flashes of a previous life in a land called Shardana, Āndrōmakhê has a mysterious bond with Alexis (Paris) Prince of Troy. Admired by the legendary Memnon, King of Ethiopia, who comes to Troia's aid to win her as prize, to Pyrrhos Neoptolemos, son of Akhilles, who enslaves her and loves and hates her at the same time, to Hektôr's brother Helenos, a warrior, seer, and priest of Apollo, men battle gods and fates to win Hektôr's widow, whose heart remains faithful to him even beyond his death.

Through the story, no matter how great the hardships and humiliation in the hands of her captors, Āndrōmakhê never gives up her hope of finding her lost son, Skamandrios Astyanax, and her dream of creating a new home for her people, and all her sons. Set in a time of heroes, O'Donnelly fills her story with not only the Homeric characters of Achilles, Agamemnon, Helen, Hektôr, Odysseus, Telemachos, and Paris, but also with the figures that came afterwards—Hermione, daughter of Helen, her cousin Orestes, legendary King Memnon, also King Peleos of Thessaly (father of Akhilles), and with the earlier myths, recounted as recent history during the story.

O'Donnelly's retelling of these myths includes an understanding of the battle between Goddess-worship and the worship of Olympian gods, which increases our sympathy for the women of the age who were often fighting for their traditional rights.

Rob Preece, Publisher

9

VOLUME ONE

The Mysteries, The Blessing, The Tragedy

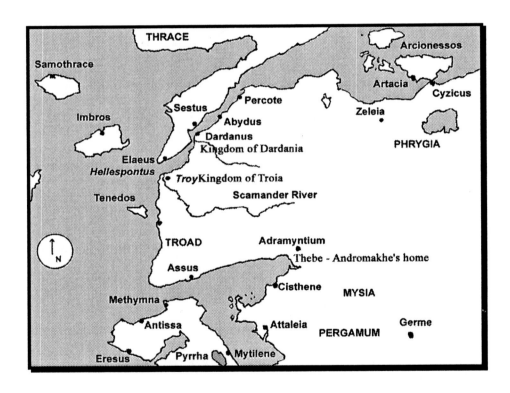

PART I: The MYSTERIES

"The life I have given you, bear with courage; and take upon yourself the sufferings I see fit to bestow upon you," the Goddess had ordained for Āndrōmakhê, "in the end, your sorrows will lift you upon a pillar."

Āndrōmakhê

Prologue: January 1, 2006, dawn hours.

"Goodbye, Viktor, farewell, my beloved Priam," Rosemary Thompson whispered, standing upon the hill facing the frosty dawn inching to light up the Trojan Plain in Hissarlik, Turkey. She was a tall woman clad in a dark purple robe, her long, russet hair flapping around her face and shoulders. The wind howled, tossing around everything that was not nailed down. Viktor Berk had faded away at midnight, and as the world at large had been out celebrating the New Year—his breath barely stirring the air around his lips, his hand in his son's hand, his head facing Rosemary. Presently his body was being washed, prayed over, and wrapped in white linen, thus prepared to lie in state in the center hall of the Berk estate, and she had stepped out for a few moments in the brisk air. On the verge of collapse from fatigue, she fought hard to keep body and soul together; there was so much she had yet to do, so many people depended upon her, including Olivia, the pregnant mother-to-be of Viktor's first grandchild.

When a hand landed upon her right shoulder, she turned around, facing Somer Berk*, Viktor's younger son, and Olivia's husband. His tousled blond hair fell over red-rimmed blue eyes swimming in tears, and his tall form, clad in a black pullover and jeans, looked unsteady. With a choking voice, he announced, "My brother phoned from Rome, he'll be here in the afternoon. His wife too is on her way, taking the same plane as Olivia's parents; but as you know they're traveling from New York, so it will take longer for them to arrive."

"Naturally we will postpone the burial until the whole family is present and accounted for."

"Naturally."

"Viktor will be buried in a closed coffin," Rosemary spoke up, "you know this was his request."

"No, it's *your* wish, Auntie, but don't worry, we shall abide by it. You know that we'd not have opposed you even if you had demanded that we cremate him and scatter his ashes upon this plain."

"God bless you for understanding me, Somer."

"You are the one who loved my father most and sacrificed most," Berk continued, "yes, you loved him even more than my mother did. My mother, your sister...."

"Yes, I loved him very much," Rosemary stated simply.

"Would that he'd married you, instead of her."

"I know we shall meet again," she murmured, "one last time."

"I wish I had your strength of belief, Auntie."

"But you do! If you hadn't, you'd not have been reunited with Āndrōmakhê."

Despite his aggrieved state, Berk had to laugh. "So, Olivia is not just an author obsessed with her subject, but was in fact Āndrōmakhê?"

"Is it not a comforting thought?"

"Then, tell me, who was Priam's wife, Hekabe? You, or Brigit, who'd been your twin sister in this lifetime?"

Tears stormed down Rosemary's face, her reserve torn open with grief. "And I the aged, where go I, a winter-frozen bee, a slave, Death-shapen, as the stones that lie, hewn on a dead man's grave; I...that was Queen in Troia."

He paled. "Queen Hekabe's speech...by Euripides."

Rosemary turned and looked at him, the window into her soul without a defense in the world. She then sobbed in short bursts, unable to lift her hands to wipe her eyes.

Berk remained silent. He had never seen Rosemary so unabashedly vulnerable, and did not know how to react, what to do. When he found his voice, "This is all fanciful talk, Auntie."

Through the curtain of tears, she managed a nod, but when she replied, sounded calmer. "Yet it's hopeful too, isn't it? I will find your father again, just as you have found Āndrōmakhê. Death is never the end, only the beginning—like circles and spirals, which begin from where they end."

He stepped forward and stood next to her. "Talking about Āndrōmakhê…" he began, "I read Olivia's novel about her yesterday, while I was sitting in dad's room, keeping him company…he had asked me to read it aloud to him, and only when I finished did I realize that I'd been at it for eight hours straight…and he was wide awake, listening to every line; I'll never forget how his eyes remained focused on me."

"Olivia's Āndrōmakhê is different than the one we know from the familiar myths, isn't she?"

He shrugged, then reddened, and nodded agreement.

"Did she surprise you with her insight into the era?"

"Yes," he replied simply. "The more things change, the more they remain the same."

Rosemary fumbled for his hand, gave it a gentle squeeze, and then held it. Together they watched the dawn, now in full swing.

*Viktor, Somer, Olivia Berk, and Rosemary Thompson, are the protagonists in the contemporary suspense/travelogue 'Trojan Enchantment,' Book V in this series.

Chapter 1: Ma Kybele

Anatolia/Asia Minor, ca. 1300-1200 B.C.E

A new scream ripped through the air, more agonized yet, and I jumped, tears stinging my eyes as I envisioned the blood pouring out of my mother while she writhed on the birthing chair. How many times had I felt so terrified, waiting at the births of my younger brothers? Trembling like a leaf on the wind, I was standing at a window in my father's palace, watching tall masts spearing the blue sky above the farthest olive groves. Those masts, playground for noisy seagulls, tilted gently as water lapped against the stone quay of our port-town.

Strangled by helplessness, I had had to flee from the screaming— my mother's.

Another scream exploded, like the howl of an animal, sending me racing for the doorway. I paused there as my father's field-boots thudded up the stairs and along to the birth-room.

Moving softly, I looked out and observed with terror that he was about to break taboo by entering that room. I crept down the stairs, sped to a dark corner of the Hall near the entrance, and crouched down.

A harshly efficient female voice struck my ears, "Stop worrying, Lord! There is olive on the front door, isn't there? No evil spirits are about; the pitch is safely on the lintel, isn't it? You hurry and make those sacrifices, Lord! I'm busy." Having had her say, Nurse Mykale whipped the door to his face, its noise striking me like a sling-stone.

Rising on tiptoes, heart thumping in my throat, I took a few steps, craning my neck to get a better look. In the center of the Hall, Father was pacing around the firepit. Now he paused, a gigantic, kind-faced, red-hair and bearded man with sea-blue eyes, King Êetiôn, ruling from holy

15

Thébé, south of Troia and Mount Ida, resting a scarred hand on the family altar beside the firepit.

When he let out a ragged sigh and blinked rapidly, I suspected tears. I burned to offer comfort, but did not dare; he would not want me to see him so vulnerable.

After a frozen moment, he regained momentum, strode past me without seeing me and out through the door, hurrying to the shrine atop Plakos Hill, as bidden. A warm smell of loam lingered in his wake; he had been out with his men at the plow. Now he must beseech the Goddess to protect his beloved wife. Once again, terror grasped my shoulders, shaking me violently. Nurse Mykale had often grumbled that this pregnancy was not as normal as all the previous six had been. Was the Goddess indeed angry? I knew well about divine anger because of my own horoscope. It had been foretold at my birth that I must beware of a blessing that would bring a tragedy upon me.

Footsteps from an inside passageway announced Althaia, a thin, dark-haired, servant girl. She was carrying my brother Thoon on the crook of one arm, a large purple bruise on his little white rear. He was only just out of swaddlings and getting into trouble as he crawled around or tried to stand up on his own.

Althaia stood him beside me. "Everything male must get out of here or your mother's pains will get worse!" she screamed, "Take him away and chase out all the dogs and ganders—and your brothers, too, if you see them. They're to be no closer than the outer courtyard."

Hurrying to the hearth, Althaia bent and retrieved a ceremonial pot of silver. She then scrambled back to where she had come from, without another glance.

I ambled to my feet with clenched fists, determined to protect my mother. Her agonized screams were filling the palace again. Oh, Holy Ilythia, Goddess of Childbirth! Help her! Mother was going to be killed by the dangerous process of giving life!

Thoon howled his protest as I grabbed his pudgy little hand, dragging him as fast as I could, into the courtyard. Anger mingled with fear as I struggled with my tiny brother through the doorway—anger that I was not allowed to see and comfort, Mother. With only thirteen summers to my credit, I was not yet old enough to trap the child's spirit in my womb. Really, Mykale was a tyrant, always asserting her rights as the Queen's nurse from her childhood days in Miletos.

Dragging Thoon into the bright sunlight of the inner court, I scowled up at the smiling Helios, Sungod, riding the noon sky in his chariot; hah, he need not be so cheerful.

I then came upon my oldest brother, eighteen-year old, redheaded, freckled Andros, absorbed in training a clumsily playful puppy to heel, with little success.

"The taboo, Andros!" I cried, "The males of everything have to leave immediately! Go, go *now!*"

One terrible scream silenced me and paralyzed my brother.

I streaked back to the door, leaving little Thoon to wrestle with the play-barking puppy.

At last, an ominous silence was followed by the tentative cry of a newborn.

I dropped to my knees. "Oh, thank you, Goddess!" Glory be, my mother had performed another miracle with Her help.

Streaks of reddish light tingled through my arms and fingers, and I smiled triumphantly on Mother's behalf: Nothing could be more wonderful than being female, and giving new life.

* * * *

Rose and saffron edged the entranceway as I wakened. I lay a moment, motionless, smiling to myself—a smile of determination. No one must know of my plan about finding Helenos, son of Priam.

Eager to start the day, I sat up, pushing back tangles of strawberry-blond hair from my face. My fellow initiate Lanassa's slicing tongue had already told me that Helenos had been detained at Sipylos because of his bloodguilt. It was customary for boys and girls to be brought here for puberty initiations, and now I, with other daughters of princes and kings, was here, for instruction in the duties of oncoming womanhood.

I left my bed and went to the opening, looking out into the horizon. My body tingled and sang as excitement rushed through my veins. I drew back my shoulders, straightening my spine with pride. Indeed I was about to defy one of the strongest of all taboos! Fearless only daughter of King Êetiôn, I would let nothing interfere with my plan.

One sun-bronzed hand grasping the coarse black fabric of the tent I shared with three other girls, I stared across the lake. My attention centered on that enormous rock on the mountain, rising in dark outline against the air: a woman's face shaped by wind, rain and the hand of Ma Kybele, the Goddess, our Great Idaian Mother, or Great Kind Mother. My mother Latmia was a priestess of hers.

Stone against space, the divine profile reached out for me.

I lifted my arms in homage, breathing deeply of the evergreen-scented air. My heart struck another wild chord, echoing in my throat, causing me to swallow hard with apprehension. The bloodguilt attributed to Helenos was not just, and he should know that even though everyone thought so, *I* knew he was innocent. However, because he was an outcast, if anyone should witness me talking to him I would suffer the same fate. Ahh…but surely Great Kind Mother would understand my need to right a wrong.

My memory tripped and I recalled the day when I had first felt the power of Her infuse my veins, glowing in red streaks down my arms and emanating from my fingertips. It had been two months ago, on the day of my newest brother's birth.

Presently a fresh sense of urgency brought me down to earth, propelling me to fly out from the tent to join the other girls assembling along the lakeside.

I waited with my group of girls while a priestess chanted invocations, her sharp glance roving around the forbidden area: *Good,* she seemed to declare, *no sign of any male except those eunuch priests guarding ships by the seashore.*

The invocation ended and we separated from each other.

Standing alone, panic gripped me as I stared into the lake's depths, where shadows of the lost city were sometimes seen. I shivered. Would spirits pull me into those drowned palaces and suck the breath out of me until I was as lifeless as ancient stone?

Swallowing nervously I unfastened the clasps at my shoulders and dropped my gown, the cool breeze raising goosebumps all over my naked body. There was no point in delaying the inevitable, it had to be done. I reminded myself that this was my thirteenth summer on earth, and the ritual dive would restore me to the purity in which I had been born of my mother.

As I slid down a high, craggy rock jutting into the lake, waves clutched at my toes like fingers of the unburied dead.

Trembling, I dove into darkness, watery sheets closing icily about me. Down and down and down I swirled, sinking to the craggy bottom, raising clouds of sand around me.

Once more memory intruded the present, reconnecting me with my mother's painful ordeal, a clear reminder of our common destiny—the deadly perils of giving new life.

Shaking my head fiercely, I forced myself to remain in the moment. Lungs almost bursting, I thrust upward, surfacing in a foamy rush, floating back to the shore.

When my feet touched the sandy bank, I sighed with relief, bent and lifted the fresh robe a priestess had spread for me on a tamarisk. My hands made gray mud-prints as I pulled it over my shoulders.

Then I felt the eyes. Turning, I saw the face.

A boy's face, one near manhood.

Tallish and wide-shouldered, he stood framed by tamarisk fronds. His long-lashed blue eyes held mine. He had sandy hair, his black robe and the black goat's pelt fell from neck to ankles. Hmm, another one under the taboo of bloodguilt.

He stepped forward, declaring hoarsely, "Ãndrõmakhê Êetiônis, you have forgotten me."

Recognition exploded from my tightening throat, "And you are Helenos Priamides!"

Shocked at my failure to recognize him, I bit my lips, drawing blood. This was not how I had planned our first meeting after three years. I drew back, no longer defiant of the taboo.

Helenos seized my shoulders, pulling me against himself. "I've dreamt about you this morning," he whispered, "you were mine to do with as I wished."

One of my immature breasts was crushed against the ridge of his chest. Numbed, I became rigid. "Let go at once, Helenos!"

Nevertheless, his free hand began working to release the brooch at my other shoulder. The catch held. His breath was warm on my cheek, his lips burned my neck. Then his mouth was crushing mine and his hand fumbled at my breasts. I felt a mysterious excitement, confusing me. He was three years older than I was, and under a taboo. Surely, he was aware of the restrictions; surely, he would not attempt an act that would bring death upon us both!

Then, anger won, "Outcast!"

He held me even closer, whispering, "I knew you were coming here for the initiation, Ãndrõmakhê. I expected you, searched for you. But I was not ready for your beauty."

Sensing that he was about to dare couple with me, I reached up, slapping his face. He broke away and plunged out of sight through the profusion of tamarisk and galingale—all rough-edged leaves, reddish spikelets, and aromatic roots. I watched the feathery branches and long spikes sway behind him. My knees went weak and I almost dropped to the soft earth. I had not only talked to him, but also been touched by him, and the latter might just be the death of me. Yet why did I not feel any real fear, or regret?

Furious at myself, I stripped off my robe and leapt back into the lake. Now my heated skin welcomed the cool water and its power to wash away his touch. I swam further up, then dove to the very tops of the sunken towers below, freezing mid-motion as I observed a nude female presence float up next to me. Unnerved, I swam away from her. My gaze searched the shimmering liquid depths housing massive, moss-encrusted stones. The skin and muscles of my arms and legs stretched and tingled. There was something strange about this other swimmer! Her long dark hair trailed her substantial body, she was pendulous-breasted, with wide hips and globe-like buttocks that had a pearly sheen. She did not look like anyone in my group of initiates, nor any of the priestesses. Must be one of the locals, disrespecting the taboo of entering the lake during the ceremonies. Or, was she a guardian Nymph, watching over the secrets of the ancient, sunken city?

A bolt of hot light struck me, searing me all over, but even though my mouth fell open, I did not swallow water.

Awe captured me. This swimmer was no ordinary Nymph! Could she be the Goddess in the flesh?

Like a moth drawn to flame, I swam toward her. Then I found myself turning cartwheels in the water as the air left my lungs in bubbles blurring my vision. Indeed something eerie was afoot!

I steeled myself against the panic demanding I leave the water. Did the Goddess come to punish me for talking with Helenos? Did She ordain my death by drowning?

If so, then so be it.

I would accept Her judgment with grace, for I was no coward. I had faced up to the chimera of fear for as far back as I could remember; dark undercurrents had always swirled about my father's hearthside, stirred by the chanting of minstrels. Yet I had loved the twanging of their chatty lyres with tales of heroic deeds. Alas, of late, many of them sung of deathly skirmishes in places where peace had held for many years. Less often they repeated the old epics of Mysian Thébé, the holy city of King Êetiôn, and still less of Mother's home at Miletos ....

So, I let myself float. The mysterious woman lifted her arm, tossing something in my direction. I reached instinctively, and it landed in the palm of my hand, as naturally as a sinking feather. It was a milky-hued pebble, round, shiny, the size of a large pigeon's egg.

When at last I regained control and came up for air, still clutching the pebble, I was no longer a child. The Triple Goddess Kybele Ma Sipylene was with me as Maiden, not yet Woman. Mystically reborn, my childhood had sunk gently downward like a lost veil in the lake....

20

* * * *

Dawn was turning from gray to pearl when I joined the other white-robed worshipers at the lake. An elderly eunuch priest, torch flaming, led the procession along the shore, followed by three priestesses in a slow dance timed to their sistra. I kept step with the bevy of swaying girls along the Sacred Way. Lions carved from living rock stood guard at intervals as we ascended the mountain. The pebble, round, smooth and warm, remained folded in the palm of my hand.

Gold touched the colossal shaft of Ma Sipylene—Mother of All Gods and Men—just when our group formed before it.

I shivered as light moved up the incredible face, softly shadowed by its triple crown. The column, covered with globelike breasts, glowed as the eastern sky shimmered from gold to rose to silver. It became touched with pink and yellow, heralding the oncoming dawn: Helios, Divine Son, and the Sungod. The stone became flesh before my very eyes. For a brief moment, I was sure I heard the Voice.

Beginning as a low moan, the Voice rose to a howl; then, silence.

Helios leapt as a ball of fire, claiming superiority by reducing Ma Sipylene back to stone.

Tossing back our gossamer veils, we moved to sit on flat rocks around the altar-table. Eunuch priests with blank expressions served stew of goat cooked with asphodel roots from a great black kettle steaming over a brazier beside the shaft. Asphodel, a food preferred by the dead and thus planted near tombs, was a plant that grew to three feet in height, sported large white flowers and radically long, numerous flowers. It gelatinized the stew and gave it a strong, acrid flavor, sticking to my throat, causing thirst. However, there was plenty of unwatered wine to wash it down, strong enough to send a careless drinker into a deep sleep.

My hold on the present was fragile to begin with, and provoked by the lingering vision of the mysterious woman in the lake as well as the copious wine, scents, asphodel, and smoke whirling in the air, my mind leaped backwards again, to the day of my youngest brother's birth.

My mother's screams echoed in my mind, rising and falling in tandem with my own heartbeat.

The priestesses finished their invocation and the brief silence tossed me back to the Here and Now.

Blinking rapidly, I felt my cheeks burn, fearing they would know I had been here only in body, but not in spirit.

I joined in as the group continued to partake of the food served in gray pottery dishes. Priestesses chanted hymns in honor of the Goddess as Girl, Woman, and Crone.

Afterward, two novices collected and tossed fragments from the meal back into the pot.

Slowly shaking their sistra, the old women beside the cauldron hummed an incantation. All of a sudden, a figure began emerging from the pot. I gasped, my skin turned cold and roughened with bumps. It was happening right in front of my eyes: The Divine Son, eaten as Goat, was being restored to human form!

The golden arc of his head appeared; then neck, shoulders, torso, dark and solid against the sky.

The naked male figure posed a timeless moment on the rim of the kettle. The tempo of the sistra increased dizzyingly when he sprang onto the altar-table and paced with slow grace, eyes closed, around its outer edge. As he passed by me, chills ran down my back and I swallowed with horror: *This was NOT Sungod! This was ordinary human flesh framed by the light.*

Numb with shock, I was looking at Helenos.

I left the group and drifted off alone. The thought raged in me: It was impossible to continue with my false initiation! I had never felt so cruelly used, so deceived. Yet…was this not a place of deception in order to teach? On that same spot, ancient King Tantalos had eaten his son Pelops in such a ritual.

Something nudged me to open my palm, and I stared at the pebble. Its shine was stronger now, pulsating, flashing with fire, emanating a heat that almost scorched my flesh. Squinting my eyes, I brought it closer; this was no ordinary pebble, but an opal. I turned it around and around in my fingers, its iridescent colors flashing or changing according the angle of light. Prickles ran through me, from scalp down to neck and back. It was believed that opal, opallios, which meant to see a change of color, bestowed its owner with the powers of foresight and prophesies.

I was last to approach the initiation caves. A breeze sang through the pines as I turned onto one of the paths leading around the caves. I followed it until I came to sit on a flat rock. Here I was concealed by young myrtle and oak. Still clutching the opal in one hand, I bent over, massaging my bare feet with the other, feet bruised from sharp stones along the Sacred Way. I then pulled off my veil and peony wreath. Settling my robe around me, I breathed deeply of the aromatic air, trying to calm down as I fingered the gemstone. Opals were also linked to invisibility and astral projection, and used to recall past lives, each color representing a different past life.

My mother's image reappeared in my mind. Even as love warmed my heart, I trembled violently, unable to stop memory from imposing itself upon my surroundings.

The door to my mother's room opened with a click and Mykale appeared. I scuttled back to my private corner as the nurse came down the stairs with the baby in her arms. Naked, the newborn glistened with oil. Mykale's white robe was covered by a trailing black veil, appeasing powers of sky and earth.

Three nude priestesses followed, carrying wet laurel branches.

The child's lusty screams proved that no evil spirit possessed him. Placing the child on the bare floor to draw strength from it, the priestesses whirled in a dance of incantation, sealing him from evil.

Father entered. Striding to the child he lifted him and swung him thrice toward the hearth-fire, and away, then placed him in Nurse Mykale's arms. Now the child belonged to Humankind, anyone killing him after this would suffer bloodguilt.

Bloodguilt.

My thoughts returned to Helenos and *his* bloodguilt; I had been nearby, and witnessed when he had accidentally killed Chaon.

Only one night before Chaon's death, my father Êetiôn, and Chaon's father, Priam, had agreed on a marriage between Chaon, one of Priam's younger sons and me. In celebration of the pact, a great hunt was held and Helenos joined his older brothers. He was put in charge of Chaon. Nine-year old Chaon, with a bow and arrow of his own, snuck away and hid in a thicket, hoping to bring down a hare to impress me with his skill. Helenos and his brothers, in hot pursuit of a boar, mistook Chaon's rustlings for that of the prey. It was Helenos whose arrow pierced Chaon's heart. Afterwards, Helenos sat stiffly with his older brother Hektôr in the wagon as it bumped back into the city bearing Chaon's body. I saw the flood of tears he was holding back, broke free from my mother's hold, and scrambled into the wagon. "Helenos," I spoke warmly, and his sweaty, trembling hand clutched mine like a lifeline.

Something had stirred deep within me then, and stirred again as I remembered it all now. I had planned to find him today, defying the taboo of his bloodguilt, and tell him...*what?*

The plan that had seemed so easy before was now so impossible. I had wanted to tell him that I knew he was innocent, as much a victim of the Inevitable as young Chaon had been.

The sound of sandals padding on stone startled me. Turning, I saw, through frilly myrtle blossoms, an old priest and a young man stop nearby. The priest spoke a few words, then, twitching his red-and-green striped robe, strode on down the mountain. The young man stood, fists at sides, head high, defiant.

My eyes remained fixed on him.

Sungod made mortal—yes, yes, he was Helenos Priamides...and I had come here to be deceived in order to be taught a vital lesson.

Pulling aside branches I leaned forward, calling out his name. He rushed and stood in front of me, a muscle in his square jaw working.

I pointed to the gray robe he wore. "It's not black."

"I have partial absolution from the Goat Dance this morning." His blue eyes glowed golden in the green shade. "Forgive me for how I behaved earlier."

I said coldly, "You pretended to be the goat we ate."

"That is a mystery of the Goat Goddess." His voice deepened, man from boy. "She cleansed me of taboo, for now."

"You are free now to go home?"

"Priest Merops told me—just now—that I am to train at Apollo's shrine in Perkote, to become a healer-priest. Merops will foster me."

Hmm, so he was going to be trained at Perkote. I knew that the priests of another Apollonian shrine had taught Helenos and his twin sister Kassandra. Apollo had blessed them with the gift of foretelling the future. "Tell me, is Kassandra at the Thymbra shrine as well?"

"Yes. She is seeress there now."

"*Seeress*...to be able to see beyond the veil thrown upon our eyes by the Fates...."

"A burden not to be envied!"

I nodded. "For how long will you stay at Perkote? That's not far from Troia, is it?"

"Yes, not far. I shall study at Perkote until Father sends me on to the shrine at Sparta."

"Sparta? Why? Will you be taking gifts to a princess?"

"No! No bride-gifts to Lakedaimon—Greater Sparta, from Troia." He swung around to leave, and then faced me again. "But when *you* are ready for bride-gifts, Āndrōmakhê, I will bring such riches for you that your father cannot refuse."

He moved off, striding down toward the dark, unlit lake below.

Helenos would come for me.

The promise hummed like lyre-strings in my heart.

Helenos, noble son of Great Priam, Helenos, who would one day become Chief Hierophant at Thymbra, would come for me! Here was the sign I needed to complete my initiation. The revelations I would receive today were important—to both of us.

Back inside my tent, I placed the opal in a pouch, anchored it around my wrist by tightening its string, then collected an ivory stylus, a stack of soft clay tablets and a bowl of tepid water to wet the tablets, ready to record the visions I felt sure would come. The tablets had convex-shaped backs, easily fitting into the palm of my hand. Rare among my peers, I had been schooled by Wise Kiron, our resident scribe, in a script comprised of wedges and hooks that represented sounds or abstract thoughts, as well as pictograms. Born in Krete to noble parents, Kiron was a survivor of great calamities, first captured by Phoenicians at age ten, years later sold to a Hittite merchant, and then sold to my father. He knew well the Kretan and Hittite manner of writing, and taught me to the limits of my ability to learn.

Now I took a bunch of dry twigs and lit a fire in the stone-ringed center-pit, then tossed in laurel leaves to flavor the smoke and speed me along my journey.

Sitting on a cruciform couch, I drank deeply from a white alabaster cup waiting beside it on a low table. The too-sweet wine was laced with drug made of the soma poppy. At first, however, I felt restless, thoughts racing around in my head. Helenos had called me beautiful. Was I? Really? Driven to rise and rummage in my travel-chest, I took out a polished copper mirror, studying myself critically. I then retrieved a dainty gold wreath with drops of amber hanging from it on slim gold chains. Placing it on my head, I stared at my shining reflection. My strawberry-blonde hair, though smoothed back behind my ears, looked unkempt against the artistry of the wreath. The amber drops blended into the long strands of my hair. I examined my eyes, nothing like my mother's pink-tinged albino ones, but an azure-blue shadowed by red lashes. I tried to smile, hoping that there was indeed promise of a beautiful woman. I had naturally arched thin brows, and they peaked now with a worried frown; my straight, narrow nose was too long to be beautiful; my mouth, like Mother's, was rather large, red, and wide.

Feeling dizzy and nauseous, I flung away the mirror, lay down on the cruciform couch with arms stretched out on each side, and waited for the visions that would give me a share in the Mysteries that Helenos already knew.

On the brink of trance, fear reined me in.

Kiron's white hair and bearded face appeared in my mind: *What are you doing, Ãndrõmakhê? Have I not taught you the value of patience and caution? Are you strong enough, mature enough, to...?*

Yet the first notion that came to me, with urgency, was that our world was changing—fast. As rolling waves of foreign traders and warriors crossed our land, our beliefs, ways of life, even our language, would fade away.

Then another thought struck me: The Great Mother was under siege! A pantheon of new gods with their rules and demands were pushing their way into her breast, tearing her apart from inside out!

Panther-toothed terror clasped its jaws around my throat.

I fought to shake it off, struggled to sit up, desperate to pull myself out of wherever I was going.

However, it was too late to stop the journey.

More visions rushed in, one after the other. I saw water in blues and greens as the opiate guided my mind. The Great Mother appeared as Eurynome the Creatoress, wide-wandering Moon, born of Khaos. She danced on the primeval ocean of rainbow colors. Into the circle of her dance glided the purple fertility serpent, Ophion, encircling the whirling Goddess. Eurynome became a white Dove floating, her delicate pink eyes shafting light into darkness. She laid a blue Egg; it floated and halved, releasing the Son as Hyperion. He illuminated the dark waters.

Another spin and I was on a ledge upon a sun-splashed mountain, among granite rocks oddly shaped by the wind, overlooking a dark-blue sea breaking along the sandy coastline. Beached on the shore was a slender ship, light hulled, at its mast a carved white swan, the Eye of Her painted on both sides of its prow so it could see where it was going, and on the ground by its side sat a stone anchor. Above me, canopied the blue sky, below me, green fields speckled with flowers of summer, yellow, white, red, and purple.

I breathed in deeply, loving the warm scent of pine—pungent, invigorating. I stood within a female body, mine, yet not mine; I was a girl-child, barefoot, clad in a shift of soft yellow kidskin. Around me, towered magnificent trees, chestnut, wild yew, myrtle, oak, juniper, all of them taller, greener, with brown trunks thicker than I had ever seen in my life...in my life as Ãndrõmakhê.

Shardana.

My heart leapt: I was on an island kingdom called Shardana!

Now my thoughts were a clear stream, I knew that just a swift run down the slope, I had a home built of stone, shaped like a truncated cone upon a circular base. Dwarf palm trees and shrubs of oleander, heather, rosemary and dyer's green weed, surrounded and protected it from prying eyes. There I lived with Nurziu, my older brother, so named because he was fortunate, and Gatto, a spotted-yellow lynx cat.

I wanted to start walking to return home, but could not; my feet were rooted to the ground. I pushed my body forward, but was stopped by an invisible wall.

Everything changed again, and I was in a terraced city engorged in flames, black smoke destroying the skies and creating dark streaks of reflection on a fast-running river of foaming blood. Countless warriors, stripped of their armor, bleeding profusely and howling with pain, were crawling around on the ground, among mud, blood, gore, hacked off limbs and trailing entrails.

Screaming with terror, I hurled myself forward, landed on the outside of the defense walls, observing a long procession of keening-women pouring out from the city to hold the wake.

Wake?

Whose?

The women swayed under their white veils as they beat their breasts, wailing. Conch shells sounded, and minstrels joined in playing throbbing lyres and wailing flutes as priestesses added heartbeat sistra [1] and sobbing bagpipes.

At once, my drugged vision faded away. Gasping for breath, I woke, alone in the dark. I sat up, terrified, trembling, chilled, my eyesight blurred, still nauseous, yet excited and gratified.

Shardana as well as the burning city and keening women were eclipsed in my memory as images of the Great Kind Goddess returned, her strength flowing through my skin and bones.

Forgetting to record my visions, I leapt to my feet and hurried to dress and mask for the Dance of the Dove. It took me a while for I kept bumping into things, and twice lost balance and collapsed on the ground in a heap.

However, when I collected myself and joined my group on the lakeshore, the short, sharp, rhythmic pulses of the sistra aroused me to movement and activity. The Dance of the Dove commenced, followed by the Mystic Spiral. Barefooted, we threw off our masks and tunics, baring our nubile selves to the elements, whirled and leapt, faster and higher, scattering around the seeds of time, healing and fertilizing the earth.

Time sped away like fleeting clouds. The dancing ended at moonset, and only then did the Chief Priestess accept us as women.

We were now Creatoresses like Mother Eurynome, meant to nurture the seeds of men, and bring upon new life.

[1] Sistra (plural of sistrum): or rattle, an ancient percussion instrument consisting of a thin metal frame with rods or loops attached that jingle when shaken. Its close modern equivalent: the tambourine.

Chapter 2

Bright morning sun draped young bodies in multi-colored flounced skirts, tight girdles, and vests displaying budding breasts, as we boarded homebound ships. The slender hull was straining against hawsers in the undulating water when I joined Astynome, auburn-haired, blue-eyed, beautiful daughter of Chryse, Theban Priest of Apollo, at the rail, glad to be among familiar faces. Brunette, green-eyed, playful Lanassa, daughter of Teuthranian King Telephos; Briseis, blond and blue-eyed, willowy tall, daughter of Priest-King Brisos of Pedasos, who served Zeus; almond-eyed, curly-brown haired, spirited, pretty Diomede, daughter of King Phorbas of Lesbos, were at the head of the gangplank, giggling as they watched men hand-walking barrels, earthen jars and wicker baskets up and into the hold.

Astynome, my close friend from childhood, moved on, trying to keep order among other girls fluttering and chattering about.

The whine of thunderstones alerted us.

Rushing to portside as the sounds crescendoed to a thundering roar, I stared toward the shore. Novice priests stood along the Sacred Way, their yellow robes rippling as they swung the thongs that held the stones. Whirling and whistling, the stones sounded the call of mating bulls, shattering the air. Then, hanging over the bay, the roaring crashed into silence as young men released the thongs that dropped into serpentine coils. They raced to the clearing where naked women lay on their backs with open legs, and fell upon them, coupling with them in a frenzy of ecstasy.

I shrunk within my skin. I had heard that this was part of the rituals, yet felt violated as if I were one of those women. The feeling did not make sense for they were willing participants, here to serve the Goddess by fulfilling their duty as potential mothers.

Lanassa, behind me, hooted delightedly.

Astynome glared, "Hush! This is sacred! Don't you know, these women are childless wives on pilgrimage to Ma Sipylene?" She looked solemn, soon to follow her father's example and train as a priestess. "Those young men are giving the last of their seed for life in the bodies of these dedicated women. Tonight, at the Creation Dance, they will emasculate themselves in honor of the Creatoress."

Concerned, my eyes searched for Helenos. The gelding of priests dedicated to Kybele went back to the mists of time, when She fell in love with Atys and made him Her priest. Nevertheless, before he took his vows, he could not resist a final affair with Sagaritis, the Nymph. Kybele punished him and drove him temporarily insane. When he recovered, Atys was mortified to discover that he had castrated himself during his insanity. He wanted to kill himself, but Kybele turned him into a fir tree. Afterwards, all priests in Her service had to castrate themselves, and the fir tree became holy. Helenos must be exempt though, for he was serving Apollo, and not Kybele.

Diomede came up beside Astynome and we watched the sun-drenched mountain recede into lavender distance as the ship smoothly drifted seaward.

Our ship docked at Lesbos Island just as the moon was scattering stars over the waves that seemed decked with the mane of galloping horses. Beyond the wharf, I saw the spread of Bresa where Diomede's father, Phorbas, was king. Oars were run out and the ship hove to for berth. Men grabbed ropes flung ashore and secured the vessel to stone bollards.

Astynome, Briseis and I followed Diomede and the disembarking crowd. Diomede led us to where Lanassa was already seated on pillows in a decorated, covered wagon harnessed to a pair of bullocks.

Having arrived in Phorbas' palace, something made me look back, and I saw another ship docking. It was a large vessel, flaunting two purple-and-white sails billowing in the wind.

"Visitors from Troy," Diomede explained.

Queen Rhene embraced her daughter after Phorbas had officially welcomed their guests. She settled us in rooms along the upstairs gallery near Diomede's chambers.

When the men had brought their travel chests and gone, Queen Rhene said, "It is a privilege to have the daughters of Êetiôn and Telephos with us! Oh, Lanassa, my dear, your father sent word that you are to stay with us until your brother comes for you. Water is warm and maids will serve all of you in the bathing area."

Lanassa dropped her clothing and chattered, "Who do you think that man from Troia is?" She took one of the towels from a chair. "You know, my mother is not only Queen of Teuthrania but a Princess of Troia." Wrapping the towel around herself, she left the room.

"She never lets anyone forget who she is," I muttered, dismayed. Lifting a brush from the dressing table, I went to the window. Pulling my long tresses, I brushed leisurely.

Briseis came in, loosening her hair from its myriad tiny plaits. "Forget Lanassa! I'm to marry Mynes, and be Queen of Lyrnessos next year," she announced, laughing. "Priam is sending a man to captain the fleet Mynes will build for him in his shipyards. Ordering the finest timber of Ida mountain cedar, too."

I cleaned my brush of clinging strands of hair, rolled them into a ball and placed it aside for burying later to avoid harmful magic. "New ships?" I asked, "What for? Does he not have enough ships left from that fleet he had sent to Achaia with Antenor? I mean the time he had tried to get his sister Hesione [1] back?"

"Priam does not believe that she prefers to remain where she is," Briseis replied, "after all, she does have a son, Teuker, by Telamon."

Silently I reviewed what I knew of King Priam. I had heard ballads about his tragic boyhood, of how Herakles, son of Zeus and mortal woman Alkmene, teamed with King Telamon, and attacked Troia. "Telamon received Priam's sister as battle-prize," I wondered aloud, "besides, she must be an old woman now. So why, after all these years, demand her return?"

"We may soon find out," Lanassa snipped as she came in, lancing me with a sharp look.

Ignoring her, I continued, "Telamon was one of the Argonauts who accompanied Odysseus on the quest for the Golden Fleece—"

"The Golden Fleece! Bah!" Lanassa shrieked with laughter, "Get your facts straight. That was not Odysseus, but *Jason!"*

I slapped my forehead, humiliation flaming my cheeks.

"Odysseus' sole claim to fame is to be the King of Goats!" Lanassa went on laughing.

"Don't talk like that!" Briseis scolded, "He is King of Ithaka, and his wife is the beautiful Penelope, niece of King Tyndaros. Father says that Odysseus is widely respected for his wisdom, eloquence, cunning, and resourcefulness. *And* he is a loyal and loving husband."

"Ithaka! Bah!" Lanassa chortled. "A tiny island so rocky that only goats can grow there. No wonder he ekes out his fortune from pirating his betters." She opened her travel chest and pulled out a ruffled skirt.

Turning to me, "I'll have more treasure—when my time comes for courting, more than anybody. More than that nobody in Sparta."

"What nobody?" I demanded.

"The nobody who's heiress to Lakedaimon."

"Her father is King Tyndaros," Astynome said.

"Yes, *that* what's-her-name," Lanassa scoffed.

"You mean Beautiful Helen, *Queen* of Lakedaimon." Astynome skewered her auburn hair, then went out, headed for the bathing room.

I said to Lanassa, "Did you know that Helen was just twelve when King Theseus saw her dancing in the temple of Artemis, and carried her off. He brought her to Attika, and—"

"Ah-ha, so she was first pawed and despoiled by grizzly old, toothless Theseus!" Lanassa laughed triumphantly.

Briseis pursed her lips. "Not according to what I heard. Her twin brothers Castor and Pollox raided Attika while Theseus was at sea, and took her back home. But I also heard that they captured Theseus' mother, Queen Aethra. She has become Helen's servant."

Lanassa scowled. *"What?* Theseus did not move heaven and earth to free his queenly mother? I am soo disappointed! He is a coward, and the stories about his heroism, about having slayed the Minotaur in his maze in Krete, are nothing but a bunch of lies."

"Theseus couldn't free his mother," Briseis said, "because he was forced into exile and took refuge on the island of Skyros, which is ruled by King Lykomedes. And there, he was murdered."

"Well!" Lanassa was furious for being shown as uninformed. With a jerky move, she retrieved a red silken vest from her coffer. "Helen or whoever, is still a nobody—"

"She is now the wife of Meneláos, King of—"

"And *I* am niece to King Priam of Troia!"

Nevertheless, I shall be the one marrying Priam's son, I thought, biting back a smile of satisfaction.

* * * *

Dawn-lit east was tipping the masts with fire when I dismounted from the wagon to reembark our vessel. I was still groggy and nauseous from the odor of sacrificial blood and heavy incense of this morning's sacrifice at the altar. That poor bull! He had refused to cooperate, bucking against the priest's knife severing his neck from ear to ear. Sacrificing animals as a bribe to various gods in return for their favors was not a practice that sat well with me.

Astynome grabbed my arm, pointing ahead. "Look! That's the ship we saw docking last night!"

The majestic vessel was berthed next to ours', and bore the figurehead of Troia, white horse-head with mane flowing on the purple-stained sail and prow. The tall, blond, very handsome young man boarding was obviously of consequence, for the captain was unctuous, unlike Priam's captains' usual behavior.

I smiled when I realized who this was: Alexander Paris Priamides. I remembered well the charming herdsman, who had joined the Games accompanying the Trojan Fair and the unexpected funeral for Chaon. I had liked him at first sight. Moreover, I had rooted for his victory, screaming encouragements until I was hoarse, clapping my hands until they hurt. Had it really been three years since that day? Now at the age of twenty, he was an aristocrat, with a sleekness defined by bearing and mien. He wore his air of imperiousness as casually as he wore his embroidered leather vest, left open to reveal jewel-hung gold chains on his bronzed chest. Sunshine caught his shoulder-length, curly golden hair on fire.

"What a prize!" Lanassa breathed, blushing, her arms stretched in his direction, fingers clawing the air. "He could carry me off any day."

Briseis spoke wryly, "Our captain says that Priam is going to send Prince Alexis to Salamis to bring back Hesione."

"Oh? I can't believe my ears." Astynome looked disturbed. "Priam can't try *that* again! Not after the way Telamon threw Wise Antenor, Priam's previous envoy, off his island."

While the others went on gossiping, I recalled last night's talk at King Phorbas' banquet. So, that messenger from Troia was Alexander, Alexis for short. Much gossiped about Alexis, also known as Paris, the wild mountain-man. It was said that Queen Hekabe dreamed he would be a torch setting Troia afire, and Priam, with a heavy heart, ordered him abandoned on Mount Ida. But Fates intervened: Arkelos the chief-herdsman found the baby swaddled in purple cloth, and brought him home to his childless wife. When he first presented the babe dangling within the long cloth, his wife cried out, "Oh, what a beautiful little purse!" Thus, they named him Paris, meaning Little Purse. Blessed with good looks, strength and intelligence, from early on he stood out amongst the common folk. At the age of ten, after routing a band of cattle-thieves with his bow and arrows and recovering the cows, he earned the honorific, Alexander, Defender of Man. At seventeen, he entered the Trojan Games and bested everyone, even heroic Hektôr. Then Hektôr's tempestuous brother Deiphobos, angry at defeat by a shepherd, drew his sword to kill him. Alexis fled to the Altar of Apollo for sanctuary, where Kassandra, a priestess of Apollo, recognized him as her brother. Then Priam and Hekabe accepted him as their son, and gossip and dire oracles erupted like wildfire.

I looked from Lanassa to Astynome. "Alexis already has a wife and child. His wife's name is Oinoné, and she is skilled in the arts of medicine and healing. It is said that Apollo was her teacher."

Lanassa grinned wickedly. "But she's just a stupid mountain girl. Imagine, she claims to be a Nymph! Calls herself Daughter of the Rivergod Kebren, no less!"

Astynome said, "Oinoné was born on Mount Ida, the seat of our Goddess Kybele; her father was a priest serving Kebren, that's why she is called Daughter of the River."

Lanassa stared her down. "But as a Prince of Troia, Alexis needs a high-born wife. His heir's legitimate birthright to the throne should never be contested. Her very name, Oinoné, means Wine Woman, surely she dances at the rites celebrating Dionysos! Who is to say her child is *really* Alexis's?" Her smile turned cold. "I would not mind being his second wife to start with, for I can get the upper hand. Trojan royalty have several wives, not to forget concubines. And if he's the eldest son, he'll be inheriting..."

"Hektôr is heir," Astynome interrupted decisively.

Lanassa stiffened. "Humph! Something has to be done about him."

Disturbed by the course the conversation took, I left them, strolling along the rail. Yes indeed, what about Hektôr? Hektôr was the most beloved of Priam's fifty sons by three wives and twenty concubines, and his undisputed heir. Renowned as a tamer of horses, Hektôr was also an unrivaled warrior. I then recalled Hektôr's efforts to prevent Alexis's acceptance as their brother. Hektôr had joined their sister Kassandra in resisting identification of him. Considering that Kassandra had recognized him at onset, how strange her change of heart! Priam made sure Alexis was given and taught all due to a royal prince. Today Alexis seemed as arrogant, wealthy, and cultured as any of his brothers.

Well, no wonder. Troia ruled a large part of the eastern Aegean coast and Thrakia, thus was more powerful than all of our small kingdoms here put together. Its riches came from its harbor, positioned at the mouth of the Strait of Dardanos [2]. At the height of the season for maritime trade, a northeasterly blew against all vessels entering the Strait. In addition, a powerful current swept down from the Marmora to the Great Green—lately renamed Aegean, in memory of the tragic death of King Aegeus, father of Theseus. Thus, the wind and the current combined against oared and sailing ships, forcing them to anchor at harbor. Some dragged their galleys up onto the beach and camped until the wind changed, waiting days or weeks. Meanwhile much cargo would load or unload, fresh water and supplies collected. Troia, the Port Authority that was perched high over the coast, always aware of everything and everyone, profited. Collecting tolls, imposing tariffs, supplying victuals, trading goods, and services of pilots able to navigate in these tricky waterways.

I heard the humming of thongs as the sails strained against them. Looking up I watched the masts dipping in the wind as sweaty rowers shifted oars. We were out into the Aegean Sea, avoiding the jagged coast, heading north.

I smiled to myself. Glory be! I had completed all rituals required at puberty, and would soon be a woman. In due time, Father would announce my readiness for marriage. Suitors would bring gifts. Among them would be Helenos. I would reject all others.

[1] There are two myths regarding the princess offered to a sea monster as sacrifice: Princess Hesione of Troia, saved by Herakles, and Princess Andromeda of Ethiopia, saved by Perseus. Andromeda went willingly to the monster, Drako, to save her parents' life and kingdom. Andromeda's legend is from an earlier time than Hesione's and thus possibly its origin.

[2] The Dardanelles Strait (Strait of Dardanos) is the outlet for all the great rivers of the interior (the Danube, the Don and the Dnieper) that pour into the Black Sea. The water flows through the Bosporus, down the Sea of Marmara. As the land narrows, the westward current surges through the Dardanelles averaging three miles per hour. The current is often driven by a prevailing north wind that can hold for weeks and months at a time. For light and relatively small Bronze Age ships under sail and oar to make a successful run of the Dardanelles required a perfectly timed approach.

Chapter 3: Alexis

King Priam, handsome in long-sleeved purple tunic edged with gold, sat in his chair at the head of the long table, a narrow slab of cream marble on legs of wrought iron. His hair was a thick gray-blond mane tamed by a serpentine gold band encircling his brow, and his short-bearded face was deeply bronzed, scarred and lined. Placed on a gold-painted base behind him towered a marble statue of Zeus the Thunderer. Facing him stood his son Alexis, in leather armor upon a white tunic and arm and leg grieves, the smell of the outdoors still clinging about him. His contemplative sapphire-blue eyes fastened on his father's, which were of a similar shade.

I pressed my back against the wall to feel its hard cold surface. But I had no weight, no substance, and seemed to disappear into its smooth stones. With growing horror, I banged my head backwards, repeatedly, and still felt nothing. Last I remembered I was clutching the opal in my hand, spitting my lungs out in a bloody fit brought on by the coughing sickness, and then floating up towards a white light that promised me peace and eternal love.

From a great distance, I heard Priam speaking gruffly, "Something is wrong between you and Oinoné, my son. You have lived here and been taught by my wisest elders. I have given you and your family all that is due a son of mine, yet you and she are not happy."

"Oinoné is the ideal wife for a mountain man," Alexis replied. "We *were* happy. I did good work, but was a man of no consequence. True, Arkelos is your chief herdsman. When I believed I was his son, other men respected me. However, I have an important position to maintain now. Oinoné will always remain a free-spirited, beautiful nymph, who prefers woodlands and mountains to palace intrigues."

I opened my mouth, trying to call out to them, to get their attention, no sound came out. Incredibly, these two were talking as if they were alone. Yet *I* was here, in the room, with them....

And yet...this could not be! I was tossing and turning in my bed at home, in Thébé. The sickness had sneaked up on me, full-blown, days ago, and I could hear worried whispers about my impending death.

36

Feeling burning hot and freezing cold at once, I looked down at myself, and saw that I was still in my white nightshift, patched with large stains of perspiration, and soaking wet.

"I am beginning to realize that," Priam continued. "I wonder if you would be happier back in the mountains with her. Archelos is an old man and you could take over from him."

Alexis remained silent.

I am standing in Troia, I reminded myself, *I am far up to the north of Thébé and Lesbos Island.*

My eyes scanned the premises. The room was rectangular, off a short passage into the palace from the courtyard, lit from an arched window and an open door to the terrace. The walls were fitted with shelves holding clay and wax tablets and rolled papyruses, probably treaties with neighboring kingdoms as well as accounts of lands, livestock, and treasure.

Priam motioned his son to sit. "Princes are herdsmen, too, Alexis; Ganymedes herded for his father Tros before Zeus stole him away."

"Oinoné belongs there, not I!" Alexis remained standing.

Priam rose and went to the window opening into the courtyard. He was very tall, like my father, with wide shoulders, barrel chest, and trim abdomen. I floated behind him and peered over his shoulder. The Hittite ambassador, a dark-haired, squat, beefy man decked in splendor, was hurrying toward the Temple of Athené, with Hektôr—who towered over him—at his side.

"Then you are ready for an assignment I have in mind," Priam declared, "it will get you away from here for a spell, and give Oinoné more time to adjust."

Alexis came and glanced through the window, but Priam returned to his chair, standing with arms folded across its high back.

Alexis burst out, "You're sending me away with him!"

"No. To Salamis and Sparta."

"Salamis I was expecting to be sent to; but Sparta? Why?"

"First and foremost, to cleanse yourself of the bloodguilt you have acquired by causing the death of Antenor's little son. You will do so at the Temple of Apollo in Sparta."

"Father! You know it was accidental! I did not kill with *intent* to kill, but while I was fighting—with bow and arrow—against those bandits who fell upon our hunting party. I felled three of them with my arrows, but another arrow was deflected and struck Antenor's son hiding in the bushes. But in the end, I did force the bandits to flee and saved the rest in our group."

"Yes, I know. *Of course,* I know! Hazards of hunting; happens to the best of us, and too often. Nonetheless, your bloodguilt is the same as that of Helenos, over Chaon's accidental death. There is no escaping it, son; you *must* be washed free of its stigma. Meneláos will permit it, of course. We gave him the same courtesy when he needed to pray at the Thymbraean shrine of Apollo to cleanse Sparta of the plague. Brought upon Sparta by *his* bloodguilt, I might add."

"Father...why do I sense that you have another motive for my journey to those lands?"

"I have long planned revenge," Priam replied calmly. "But before I strike, I must be sure they cannot lay claim to Troia through my sister, Hesione. The citizens there still observe the ancient rule of queens, and their kings are not beyond taking advantage of that."

Alexis drew out a straight-backed chair and sat down, eyes fixed on his father's blond-bearded full lips.

I really am here, in Troia, and not in my own bed, in Thébé, I thought, shaking from head to toe, struggling to draw each breath, sweat still pouring from my body, dripping down my legs. I looked down and gasped: there were wet footprints on the floor...mine.

Priam continued, "You are the perfect envoy to follow what Antenor began. My sages have taught you not only writing skills and ciphering, but use of the mind. You need to appeal to the queens' sense of sisterhood with Hesione, to influence their husbands in our favor."

"Do you believe they will hear what is beneath my words?"

Priam looked his son up and down, replying flatly, "Use your charm to convince them that I am only a sentimental old fool."

Alexis smiled. "I can do that! Yes, Father, I can do that building on your easy acceptance of me as your son."

Priam went on carefully, "Alexis...while there, remember that Agamemnon at Mykene and his brother Meneláos at Sparta control all the lands between. Agamemnon, as descendant of Tantalos who once ruled a wealthy kingdom to our south, where the Sipylene shrine draws pilgrims—and what a *profitable* draw it is!—is both a challenge and curiosity to us all...."

As Priam's voice drifted off, I envisioned ships that anchored in the harbor, and caravans pouring in from inland, waiting to be identified for admission or to pay tolls at the mighty block-towers squaring the ornamental gates. Oh, yes, pilgrimage was a profitable business, and Priam wanted more of it for his already bustling empire. I could imagine colorful groups of men and women fermenting along the ancient tan-dusted roads, surrounded by clinking pack-donkeys and onegers and bullocks plodding their way, drawing after them wagons of wicker and wood, bumping along on creaking wheels bright-painted in reds, blues and yellows, piled high with goods, and canvassed over against the elements.

"You *must* gain Helen's attention," Priam declared, "because Helen is the true queen of Lakedaimon, and can influence Meneláos in Hesione's favor. If Helen allies Meneláos and Agamemnon against Telamon, Telamon then will be forced to free my sister, or face trouble with his allies."

"Helen of Sparta." Surprise seemed to widen Alexis' eyes, and he clenched his fists at his sides, as if he needed a moment to let his father's words sink in.

Priam continued, "You will, of course, visit more than Salamis and Sparta, but negotiate trade agreements with as many kings as possible. I must also have updated military reports about each kingdom you visit. I have eastern allies who are interested in this, mainly the Hittites."

Alexis stepped back, flashing a set of white teeth. "Gaining the attention of Helen...? That should be easy."

"Be careful, be thorough. If they refuse treaties, we will invade. By that time, the kings might suspect there is more to your mission than sentiment demanding the return of my sister. They must *never* land on our shores. I want to avenge the destruction of my father's city."

"Do we have the military capability for this revenge?"

"We are preparing, with my vassals and allies. We already have more than Pelops did when he took settlers across the sea after his father's kingdom at Sipylos was destroyed. Now Pelops' descendants hold the thrones at Mykene and Sparta. It is important to learn whether they plan to retake these lands, which are now allied to *me.*" At a nod from Alexis, "I've received secret reports that Agamemnon and Meneláos are preparing to seize the territory around Sipylos."

"You did?" Alexis bit his lips, adding with an embarrassed smile, "I've shamed my calling as a shepherd, Father! I've been sleeping on my watch while wolves are out stalking the flock."

"My claim to Sipylos is stronger than theirs', for it comes through my mother Plakia, based on the old manner of queenship. Plakia was a daughter of King Atros, father of Agamemnon and Meneláos."

"Meaning, your mother and these two were siblings? Therefore, they are your uncles? Many would say they have equal claim."

Priam's voice gritted, "I said my claim is greater based on the *old manner of queenship.* Agamemnon and Meneláos were of his Achaian wife, Aerope. I *will* stop the first of their ships to sail eastward."

"But Father…are we to invade across the sea without hordes of settlers, such as Pelops took over to Achaia? He had enough people to subdue an entire region now called Pelopenese, including Mykene, Korinth, Argos, and Sparta."

Priam laughed. "You are an ardent pupil, Alexis, your teacher has earned the gold I've been paying him! I am pleased. You cannot succeed as a ruler unless you know everything about the territories under your control. That aside, let me tell you this: I am renewing the old treaty we had with King Muwatallis the Second, at the time I fought with him at Kadesh, ten years ago, against Egypt. Surely you remember the details of that campaign."

"The battle of Kadesh [1]; yes of course I do. Fought on the Orontes River, in Syria, it was the largest chariot battle ever fought. The horses we contributed to the Hittite forces made a positive difference in its outcome. Hektôr was with you and at only fifteen, he commanded an entire battalion, and performed as well as you did."

Priam's face glowed with unabashed pride. "Yes, so he did. In addition, I like the manner with which you just spoke of your brother. You do not begrudge him his skills, or his fame. I know he is fond of you too, and trusts you. He will be able to count on your support when he becomes king, one day." He smiled. "I am indeed blessed by Father Zeus; I have good, strong sons."

Alexis' face flushed with emotions, and he looked away.

Priam continued somberly, "Getting back to the treaty with the Hittites. True, henceforth we will pay them even more tribute, but the iron-based weapons and added detachment of soldiers they will provide us with, is substantial. The Ambassador is here from Hattushash; he arrived an hour ago."

Alexis nodded, relaxing. "With my shepherd's flute and my lyre, I will enchant the Achaian queens." Determination shone in his blue eyes. "I will finish what Antenor began."

Priam moved away from his chair. "Be friendly with all those of Pelopid descent; appeal to their ancient kinship with us. Their alliance to protect the throne-claim of Meneláos over Helen's lands is a hostile military alliance against Troia, to take away our control of the traffic through the Straits. But the people are loyal to *her,* not him; the Pelasgian element there still accepts only the matriarchal heritage." Priam frowned. "Pay full attention to what I am telling you now: As long as my sister stays on in Salamis, Telamon *can* claim Troia by right of her heritage upon my death."

The king paused, contemplative as his white eyebrows drew together tightly.

I floated in the direction of the farthest wall, and stood, my gaze searching for the footprints. Still there, but fading away, drying in the gentle breeze from the window. Their sight frightened me even more, adding a twist of reality to my dream-state, and I recoiled.

Priam spoke, "You know of course what had happened between my father, Poseidon, and Herakles."

Alexander nodded.

Priam turned aside, staring at the piece of sky visible from the window. "Herakles saved my life. He killed my father; he killed three of my brothers...but saved me. Because I was the youngest, because my sister begged him to ransom my life, the ransom being that she would give herself to him willingly. And Herakles, instead of making a display of violence against a weak enemy, showed mercy. He spared my life and told me: "Take the reins and rule your state, sitting on your father's throne, but wield the scepter with better faith."

"And you do, Father!" Alexis cried out impulsively.

Priam laid a steady hand on his son's shoulder. "Did you know that my real name was Podarkes, meaning swift-footed?"

"No...I did not."

"On the day he spared my life Herakles renamed me Priam, which means *ransomed*. And in honor of my sister, I promised myself to wear this name with pride, to bring it glory, and have it remembered as that of a man who made a difference in the great scheme of things."

"Father...if my aunt offered herself to Herakles, why did he hand her over to Telamon?"

Clouds darkened Priam's face. "I can only speculate, Alexis! Herakles was on his way from Hero to Immortal and, as a man of conscience, shied from taking a mortal woman. Unions between the Immortals and Mortals are known to produce calamity."

"Conscience," Alexis spoke wryly, "is a rare attribute among the Olympians. They order us to live by the rules they set out, but they themselves honor nothing but their own caprices."

When Alexis left the room, I studied Priam as he moved around. I was intrigued by the news that Priam and Agamemnon were related by blood. Yet, it made sense that a great ruler like Priam would have a cousin called King of Kings. Then I willed myself to follow Alexis, and was surprised at how easy it was.

Alexis sat on a stone bench at a shaded spot on the wind-swept, crenellated parapet of Troia's twenty-foot thick, Cyclopean walls.

Loosening the bonds of his breastplate, he placed it aside, reached into a bag he had stashed there and retrieved his flute and lyre.

After playing a few notes on his flute, he spoke without looking at me, "Who are you?"

"You can see me?!"

"No, but I can feel your presence."

"Oh."

"I saw your footprints."

"Oh."

"You smell. Are you very ill?"

"I smell? What of?"

His nostrils flared for a few seconds, then, "Blood. Sulphur. Yes indeed, you must be very ill."

"Not only ill, but I fear I am dead...."

"No, you are not." Another pause, then, "Though you might, soon. Have you no healer nearby?"

"I do, but he doesn't seem to be able to help."

He looked troubled. "What do you want from me?"

"Nothing."

"Herbs? Potions? Incantations?"

"No, none."

"You are a woman, yes? No, not exactly a woman, just a girl. I am sorry. But if it's your ordained time, there is nothing I can do for you."

"I don't want anything."

"Then why are you here?"

"I wish I knew!" After a lengthy silence, "I like you, Alexis, son of Priam. I don't know why, because I don't know you; not well enough, that is, yet I do like you."

"Oh. Why, thank you, how kind of you."

"But I find this puzzling! I don't mean you are not worthy of being liked...it's just that...I don't even *know* you."

"Oh." His eyebrows drew together, and he too looked puzzled.

"I remember the first time I saw you, Alexis, at the Games three years ago. I looked at you, and the thought crossed my mind: He protected me, he saved my life, and he gave me his food and went hungry."

Alexis turned in my direction, but his eyes were not focusing, so I knew that I was still invisible to him. "Just *who* are you, little girl?"

"I don't know!" I cried out, "I don't know how to explain this to you, but...I...I...know who I am, yet...I don't know who...who...is that girl who thought she knew you."

He gave a casual shrug. "I'm not one for riddles."

I blinked, my sight blurring, my head on the point of bursting from a throbbing pain.

After a while, he spoke with a distant tone of voice, "Oinoné had warned me against entering the Games. But I did not listen. "I am the son of Priam's chief herdsman, and as good as any of those arrogant champions invited to the contests," I told her proudly, and tethered the best bull of the royal herds."

"Do you regret it now?"

No reply. Laying down his slender flute, Alexis lifted his ivory-and-silver inlaid lyre. His fingers searched the strings for tender chords. As he began to play, he smiled again. Watching him sway in tune with his music, I sensed that there must be so much more to him than what the gossipers were crediting him.

I hugged myself, feeling cold, colder. Strength deserted my limbs and I sank down, perched on my knees at a distance from him. I willed myself to leave, to return home to my warm, safe bed, but I could not. I must be dead. *Dead!* But this was not Hades, or the Elysian Fields. Indeed Elysium was the abode of the blessed. Situated at the end of the world, it was the resting place of the souls of the heroic and the virtuous, which I was not. Was I then perhaps under some kind of a conjurer's spell? If so, why was I able to see, hear, think, and wonder?

My sight blurred again, everything around me went in and out of focus, and I felt colder still.

When Alexis began to speak, I heard him as if I were beneath the waters of the ocean, "My assignment to meet and charm Helen means that Aphrodite is finally at work; she is fulfilling her promise to me. Perhaps I should let Father in on the secret. Surely, this is the right thing to do! Alas though, Aphrodite ordered me not to, never, ever, under no circumstances."

"Aphrodite? The Goddess?"

"Yes. And I know well the fury of mortal women when crossed, so there would be no end to the fury of a goddess! What matters is that with her help, I might charm them all, win Helen over to our cause, and do right by Father, too. I bear no grudges against the old king who ordered my death so long ago, and I'm grateful for the chance to prove my devotion."

"You do, do you?"

No reply. I wondered if he could still sense my presence, or was the spell, or whatever it was that had brought me here, fading away like my footprints.

Turning his face up to the wind, he closed his eyes as he spoke, "Ever since the truth of my birth was revealed to me, dread has poisoned my existence. It is a horrific burden to live knowing that my mother dreamed of me as the torch that will set this kingdom afire!"

I knew the nagging pains of living with a frightful birth-oracle, and nodded in sympathy.

When he went on, I realized that he had forgotten about me and was merely talking to himself, "Before I was made a prince of Troia, my life was simple but happy, deriving joy from music, the landscape, and the seasons. My happiest time was when Oinoné chose me for a lover. Oinoné is not only beautiful, but matches me in wits and bedsports alike. Together we herded flocks and hunted. I carved her name on the bark of trees with my knife. Then, one day, Zeus gave me the task of choosing the most beautiful among three goddesses, a task so difficult that even the all-mighty Zeus hadn't felt up to it.

"On that fateful day when I spotted the three luscious women approaching me, I tried to run away. However, my friend Hermes the Swift-footed appeared on the roadside and held me back, claiming Zeus himself gave the orders. According to him, the goddesses had gone before Zeus, to ask for his opinion. Alas, poor thing, Zeus was in a delicate position: one of the contestants was his wife, Hera, another one his sister-daughter, gray-eyed Athené, and the third, his daughter Aphrodite. Therefore, Zeus had no choice but to wash his hands and send them to Mount Ida, where I, the lowly shepherd Paris, had to decide what Zeus could not! Trapped, I sat down and listened as each of them talked about herself in glowing terms. My task was hard to begin with, but it was made harder when Hermes said they should all undress, so I could judge better. They agreed, dropping their clothing, robbing me of breath. They were all magnificent in a voluptuous, earthy way, making me doubt their divinity. Could these be ordinary women playing a trick on me? Thinking on my feet, I offered to split the golden apple three ways, but Hermes said it was not possible. I *had* to choose only one goddess, Zeus had commanded it so.

Each of the women compounded my misery by promising lavish gifts, should she be chosen: Hera offered dominion over all Asia, Athené wisdom, and victory in all battles, while Aphrodite promised as wife the most beautiful woman on earth: Helen. Have you heard of Helen, little girl? Helen, who is the Queen of Sparta? Rumored to be a daughter of Zeus, her parents are the Spartan King Tyndaros and his wife, Leda. Zeus, supposedly, came to Leda as a swan while Tyndaros was at sea. And Aphrodite is not only the goddess of love, but also of beauty, desire, sexual rapture, and matters pertaining to all passions and wedlock. Also, she *really* was the most beautiful among them! Nevertheless, I hesitated before saying so; I was afraid of enraging the others. Aphrodite then manifested Helen's likeness in my mind. I actually saw Helen…taking a bath, walking in the garden, playing with her children, standing by the window and looking up longingly at the sky…."

Alexis stopped, a ragged sigh leaving his throat.

Even as I wondered about what he meant with the golden apple, I gave in to the weakness engulfing me. I could no longer remain sitting, and turned around, lay down on the ground, curved into a ball, knees pulled up to my chest. My neck hurt for lack of a pillow, but as soon as I thought of it, a pillow appeared beneath my head. My discomfort ebbed somewhat, and I returned my attention to Alexis.

"Helen is beautiful," he was saying, "I have no doubt that what Aphrodite showed me is the truth. Why, Helen is more than just beautiful! She is warm, caring, and so very lonely…and she is unhappy with Meneláos. Her life is in danger too, for Meneláos beds many women. All of them resent her unique beauty and high standing; there are many plots to kill her, and I fear one day, one of them will succeed! Nevertheless, Helen is the wife of Meneláos; it is unseemly for me to interfere. And I told so to Aphrodite. She laughed, revealing that some time ago, Helen had invoked her, on her knees, begging her to bestow upon her that which she lacked most, *love,* and Aphrodite promised to grant her wish. And *I* could be the fulfillment of her wish. *That* did it for me! I chose Helen, above all the wisdom, victories, and dominion offered by the other goddesses, and declared Aphrodite as the fairest who deserved the golden apple."

The golden apple again! I thought, *what golden apple?*

He continued to speak to himself, "Yet…today, the prospect of meeting beautiful Helen, troubles me. This means I really did meet the three goddesses in person. A rare, yes, but not unique occurrence. The Olympians do walk among us whenever it suits them…and while I have pleased one goddess by judging in her favor, I've earned the wrath of the two others."

Silence ensued. His shoulders slumped, lost in deep, dark thought.

Struggling to breathe, I reviewed his account of the goddesses. I believed him. After all, I, too, had an encounter with the divine. Ruling families, especially kings, claimed blood kinship or otherwise close ties, with the gods. And no wonder! Zeus, Master of Olympos and Earth alike, was reckless as he swooped from one beauty to the other, leaving many a godling in his wake.

45

Then I recalled Kiron teaching me Troia's history: Herakles captured Troia and killed Laomedon, Alexis' grandfather by Priam. There were several versions as to why, but Kiron believed the one told by a priest at Thymbra. Apollo and Poseidon, jealous of the attention Laomedon received from Zeus, decided to test Laomedon's worthiness. Assuming the likeness of mortal men, they offered to fortify Troia's walls for wages. When the work was done, King Laomedon, who ran out of funds because of an ill-fated trade venture, could not pay. Believing the two gods to be mortal men, he invited them to return later to pick up their purse. However, the gods did not believe him and accused him of cheating them.

Apollo sent pestilence, and Poseidon dispatched Drako, the sea-dragon that snatched away the people of the plain. The oracles foretold deliverance if Laomedon offered his daughter to be dined upon by Drako. Laomedon refused; Drako made huge waves that flooded the plain, which left salt on the crops when the waters ebbed away. Famine came, and the people rioted, wanting to slay Laomedon and his wife.

Finally, Princess Hesione was dragged to be fed to Drako, and was chained to tall rocks protruding from the sea.

Herakles promised to save her, but only if Laomedon paid him with the mares in his stable. These were immortal mares, given by Zeus to Laomedon's grandfather, Tros, in recompense for the abduction of Ganymedes, Tros' favorite son. Captivated by his beauty, Zeus had snatched him up to Olympos, where he had raped him, then appointed him cupbearer to the Gods. But Tros would not quit lamenting his son's fate. Zeus would not free Ganymedes, but he gave Tros six immortal mares and a gold treasure.

Therefore, Laomedon agreed to give these unique horses to Herakles, and Herakles slew Drako after a lengthy battle. Alas, when Laomedon went to fetch the horses, he could not find them, because frightened by Drako's ear-splitting screams during the battle they had trampled down the stable doors and bolted away.

Herakles did not believe Laomedon's story and accused him of cheating once again. Clearly, it suited Herakles' agenda to call the King a liar and thus have the excuse to ravage his city and carry off his treasures. In addition, usurp command of the waterway to lands rich in metals and other bounty. Herakles left and returned with Poseidon to wreck the Trojan walls. Built by Immortals, only Immortals could tear them apart. Poseidon raised his trident and shook the earth, tumbling them down, and Herakles, with only a small army contributed by his ally King Telamon, sacked the city. Impressed bards described Herakles' deeds with colorful phrases: *He stretched a girdle of blood about the walls of Troia* [2]. He then slew Laomedon and captured three horses. And Hesione, while rescued from Drako the Sea Monster, was given to Telamon as battle prize.

Considering its terrible past, the power and prosperity of Troia, today, inspired awe. And all due to one man, Priam-Podarkes, son of Laomedon, King and First Magistrate of his realm, but also diplomat, warrior, and shrewd negotiator/tradesman par excellence.

Alexis rose to his feet, murmuring, "Action and reaction...."

How true, I thought.

I felt sorry for the Trojan Prince. Even a kinship because of our equally mystifying, respective birth oracles. Aphrodite was a fickle Goddess, vicious when crossed, and of course, he could not rule against her. We all knew what she did to Medusa, who had been more beautiful than Aphrodite. The jealous Goddess of Love and Beauty turned Medusa into an ugly, old Gorgon, with snakes forever wriggling in her hair. Yet Hera and Athené were dangerous goddesses, too! Could Alexis' judgment favoring Aphrodite, bring about the predicted calamity to his people?

[1] The Battle Kadesh was fought around 1275 B.C.E.
[2] Euripides.

Chapter 4

In sunny Thébé on the Adramyttion Bay, north of Sipylos and south of Troia, I was weaving my bridal sheet, bordered with purple grapes and green vines. For the umpteenth time, I weighed telling Mother about my dreams that begun last month, during my brush with death. I did not understand why I could not share them with her, though I had confided in Kiron the Wise. These dreams did not feel like dreams, but unbidden forays out of my body, hurling me through vistas in strange lands— Shardana, Epirus, Illyrikon. Thankfully, upon awakening, their details did not linger long in my memory.

Kiron believed in that we lived many lives, returning to flesh to pay debts incurred in a previous life, or to reap rewards for past good deeds, or to begin a new cycle of existence; thus, he said, I might have lived in mysterious Shardana before. The opiate I had consumed during my initiation at Sipylos was the kind that allowed a seeker to receive glimpses of the past as well as a possible future.

Unlike Kiron, who had been a scribe under the Babylonian King Hammurabi [1], recording his Code of Law, and talked about it in detail, I had no memory of a past life in Shardana, or for that matter, of anywhere else. Just a few scenes within dreams. Kiron said that in Babylon he had kept accounts of trade with Shardana—*Shard Ana.* Shardana had been a thriving outpost of the golden Empire of Atlantis; Babylonians had sailed to and from Shardana through a strait between Libya and Sicily. In those days Shardana was a beautiful island, full of game animals, dwarf elephants, hot springs, baths, sacred wells and temples, buildings shaped like beehives, and its people worshipped the Goddess Dea Madre and the Bull God [2]. Alas, a catastrophe had sunk Atlantis, and then devastating earthquakes and tidalwaves had divided Shardana into two islands [3].

Stopping to weave, I stood up and looked over my handiwork on the loom. We had two looms in this room, one for Mother, and one for me. Each stood upright with a frame attached to the wall and the weaver standing or sitting, in front. As the work progressed, the sheet would wind up in a roll at the top. We used small clay weights to weigh down the ends of the warp. My smaller workstation was against the wall by the window, Mother's larger loom stood on the wall angled next to it.

Satisfied with my progress, I sat back on my three-legged round stool and continued weaving. Something quickened in my mind's eye, and a spotted-yellow lynx with black tufted ears, crept through the bush, trailing a fox that carried a limp bird in its jaws. Even though I had never seen one of these solitary big cats up close, I found myself smiling. What a beautiful animal was this lynx! It had pronounced cheek ruffs, long legs, and a black-tipped short tail. Another scene appeared in my mind: that same lynx chasing and killing the lost fawn of a roe deer. My smile disappeared and I found myself screaming at nothing, "Bad boy! You should not have done that! You too were a lost baby when I found you and took care of you."

Horrified, I jumped to my feet, throwing a worried look toward the open door. Pheeww! What a close call. The last thing I needed now was to be caught by Althaia or Mykale, or worse, by one of my brothers, arguing in an empty room. There would be no end to the teasing.

I sat down again, but could not pick up my work. I stared at my hands, angry at their willingness to stay idle.

Not knowing what to do with myself, I thought of Alexis.

Yes, I did care for him, and felt a kinship of destiny with him. Also, I wondered why, of all the people I knew, I had dreamed about him with such clarity. Even though he had not realized it, he had revealed to me, Āndrōmakhê, his great secret: The Judgment. That he had to decide on an issue Zeus himself dared not, was ominous. I suspected that this Judgment had demanded of him a choice between three possible lives, like the Choice of Herakles [4]. Hera had promised royalty, Athené victory in wars, and Aphrodite, love. Could I fault Alexis for choosing love? Even though he already had a wife? Besides, he did have the right to take another, or several, wives. Led by Priam of the many wives and concubines, Trojan custom was different from ours', here at Thébé. My father would never look at another woman, let alone consider bringing home a second wife—not even if it were politically expedient.

We lived on the Aegean shores of Anatolia, lands of the morning, a near-rectangular peninsula surrounded by the waters of the Great Green [the Aegean], the Mediterranean, the Propontis, and after navigating the Bosporus Strait, the Somber/Black Sea. Hittites ruled the central region, a high, arid plateau. Our peninsula was a landbridge for blond and red-haired Keltoi from Europa, red-haired Phrygians from Thrakia, and dark-haired Acadians, Assyrians, and Babylonians.

I found living on the crossroads exciting; it brought knowledge and exotic people. Our language was Luvian [5], yet all of us spoke, or had an understanding of, several other tongues.

However, our interaction with the peoples across the Aegean Sea, called Achaians, Argives, Danaans, and Dorians [6], with their alien dialects, gods, and customs, was altering us. They were more warlike than us, choosing the easy gain by the sword to the lengthy harvest earned by the plow. Their small city-states fought and plundered each other all the time, unleashing bloody grudges that lasted many generations. They believed death in battle lead to honor and glory, and Glory was more important than Right and Wrong. To us, they were the locust, sweeping down to feed on the fruits of our hard work, and either slaughter us or appropriate us as slaves.

Why, according to my mother, a devotee of Kybele, even the names and attributes of our gods had been changing! Theirs' were the Olympian gods and goddesses, a family forming the third generation of divinities born from the union of Earth and Sky.

Kiron had drilled me often, yet I had to think hard now, for there were just too many of them. I lifted the clay tablet on a small table beside me, looking over my cuneiform script that resembled drunken chicken feet, for the names.

Suddenly Athené's image with her helmet, spear, and shield, appeared in my mind and filled my mouth with bile—bitter and sour.

I feared I would throw up.

But why?

Athené was the Defender of Heroes, and Champion of Justice. She presided over maidens preparing for nuptials, household arts and crafts, spinning and weaving, and textiles. She invented the flute, the plough, the ox-yoke, the horse bridle, and the chariot.

Alas, the more I considered her now, the greater mushroomed my fear of her. Oh, Great Kind Mother, why?

Athené had sprung fully-grown and armed from the head of Zeus, because he had swallowed his pregnant first wife, Métis, she who was the most knowing among all beings. Athené was her father's favorite. She alone possessed the keys to his thunderbolts, and was entitled to wear his magic aegis—a goatskin breastplate fringed with snakes, that produced thunderbolts when shaken—and to carry his shield.

Anxiety and nausea continued to claw at my senses, growing in weight until I burned to scream and vent it all out.

Finally, I switched my mind to Helenos, and as I calmed down bit by bit, I fingered the opal suspended on a gold chain on my throat.

I had told my mother how I came to it, and she had agreed that I must keep it, for it was indeed a divine present. She did not think that it had been the Goddess, but a guardian Nymph, the same one she had encountered there during her own initiation, years ago. When I had asked for details about this, she had changed the subject.

Ahh, much too much thinking, and here came the familiar, skull-splitting headache!

Exasperated, I resumed casting my shuttle and pressed each thread before drawing another from the oil-jar beside me. The brightly painted clay weights clattered gently near the wood-veneered floor. The golden afternoon sun slanted through the eastern window between green vines framing it, reflecting hued patterns all around me.

I smiled. It was once more season for the Trojan Fair; ships sailed northward to the Strait of Dardanos. Their merchandise was endless, copper, tin, gold, amber, myrrh, ebony, cedar, wine, cloth, exotic animals, and exotic people. Often ships stopped for exchange of cargo at one of the three cities along the Bay of Adramyttion, where Thébé sat. Our herd of prize cattle, seven-thousand heads and growing, drew many a captain who needed onboard meat supplies.

I lowered my aching arms and looked longingly outside to where rivulets of water sparkled down the Hill of Plakos. Ahhh, to be out there, riding Iris, my rambunctious mare! Father had named her after the Goddess of the Rainbow. Iris was my age; her dam had birthed her around the same time I had entered this world. Hers was the color of chestnuts with a flaxen mane, a star-shaped white mark between her eyes, a flaxen tail, and matching socks.

"I hoped you'd be doing your woman's work!" My mother's voice startled me. She breezed into the room clad in a belted red chiton with a long overflow, in her arms Leukon, a swaddled infant.

I looked at my baby-brother where he lay in the curve of Mother's arm. Leukon was still so small, scarcely able to keep his mouth on the clay nursing-bottle, dribbling milk of sycamore-fig over Mother's full breasts. My heart swelling with tenderness, I took him and placed him in his wicker basket. Caressing his satiny cheek, I said, "I only stopped for a bit, to rest my arms."

Her tone softened, "I'm proud of your speedy return to good health, Drommie. You gave us quite a scare!"

"Not as much as to myself," I blurted out.

She smiled, and then pressed her lips together as she tried to look serious. "I trust that you have learned a lesson. I warned you about that the coughing sickness felled many people in the area, and that it is contagious. But no, you would not listen to me; you had to scurry from one sickbed to another, to—"

"But they needed medicinal herbs and food!"

"And we have trained healers and priests for this task!"

"Oh, Mother...."

She came and stood by my side, inspected what I was doing, then spoke warmly, "Remember this, my daughter: No man will boast of a wife without skill in her work. You alone must weave that bridal sheet; there is so much still to make for your marriage-chest."

"I don't feel like a woman," I replied hesitantly, "I am confused by so much they taught me at Sipylos."

"Don't fret, Drommie," she patted my head, "you will understand as you mature." She went and sat on a stool before her loom, preparing to finish the last rows of a large red cloth for my oldest brother's wedding. She began casting her shuttle. "I went through a more strenuous time there than you did."

I remained silent, casting my own shuttle in tandem with hers. My heart tightening with love, I reflected on the joy of seeing her alive and well. Her translucent skin glowed with the good spirits of childbirth that still protected her. That beautiful hair, in a white loop about her head, framed the clear straight lines of nose and forehead, the fullness of red lips. I threw her a sideways glance and smiled at what I saw: Good, she had not forgotten to wear the protective amulet, a little globe of amber with sprigs of wormwood twined about its gold chain.

My mother continued, "You know I was trained as lay priestess." The look in her unique silver eyes with the pink cast was gentle.

I miscast and made a sound of frustration.

She pushed wisps of swan-white hair from her forehead. "When someone is born without color as I was, she belongs to a sky deity. My father Nomion sent me to Sipylos from Miletos for training, but *your* father changed that." Her mouth curved in a warm smile.

My shuttle hopelessly caught, I turned on my seat. I knew the great love my parents shared. Its aura blessed our home, people, and lands. "Do you know when Helenos will finish at Perkote?" While unable to tell her of my strange dreams, I had told her of my feelings for Helenos. "When am I to marry him?"

"Priam sent Herald Idaios here while you were away in the shrine to give thanks to the Goddess, but nothing is settled. You are trained to become queen somewhere, Drommie; not to be a mere priest's wife."

"Mere priest? Helenos? *Priam's* son Helenos?"

"Dear child, we are concerned for your welfare, given that birth-oracle of yours." Rising from her seat, she went to a chest placed against the wall and retrieved a dark blue vest and a little bag of beads.

"Oracle!" I flared with dismay. "I am to be given a *blessing which will bring tragedy.* How can something good, so good that it's called a *blessing,* lead to tragedy? I do not want to believe it, Mother! I want its shadow wiped off my life...."

"Sometimes I forget you are a girl-child," she spoke thoughtfully, "you are so stubborn! You remind me of defiant Antigone."

Antigone's name sent a rash of feelings through me. "Yes! *Yes!"* I exclaimed, instinctively grasping my opal that began to vibrate against my skin, "Antigone was right in trying to bury her slain brother Polynikes, against the order of King Kreon, who wanted Polynikes to be fodder for dogs and vultures."

"But as punishment for contravening Kreon's order, she was taken to the desert and walled in a cave alive! And she, a bride-to-be."

"True, but she died *gloriously,* Mother! She martyred herself to loyalty to her brother. And chose her own time of death, proudly, for something she believed in. Yes, Antigone was the master of her own destiny. So, there! And I am tired of doom-saying horoscopes too. Let us take Leukon's. When it was cast, it indicated he would die young—"

"Not unusual for a man-child," Mother interrupted me calmly, "for if he is proven brave in battle, an early death will bring him eternal fame. Don't you remember that Leukon did not scream when the sacramental water and blood was dripped onto his head during his name-ceremony?"

"Yes, of course I remember," I replied, shame-faced now, "just as I remember being told that during mine, I screamed loudly and long, which taken with my horoscope, terrified you and father with concern for my future."

"I will help you with the shuttle later," she changed the subject, leaving her seat and coming to me, "here, try putting these beads on for me," and handed me the thick-woven material. Because Mother was an albino, her eyesight was weak, yet it was remarkable how well she could weave, embroider, and perform many other chores. She said that she could see with her fingertips, the small hairs on the back of her neck, and even with her nose, for she had a very keen sense of smell.

Returning to her seat, she declared casually, "My brothers think you would be better off married to an Achaian prince."

I bit my lips hard. She was avoiding the real issue: *Helenos.* Inserting gold thread in an ivory needle, I began threading the beads along neck and armholes.

After a moment of brooding, I let out a hiss, "I'd rather be dead!" Blood rushed to my head and my fingers crushed the cloth. I stomped my feet. "No, no!" and a few beads slipped to the floor.

Mother took up her ball of gold thread and focused on the fringe to border her finished work. "My brothers are convinced that, as unsettled as relations have been since Priam—"

"I don't want to hear this! Like you, I am descended from a long line of ruling queens! I will marry Helenos, or no one else." I leapt up from my seat and kicked the loose beads across the polished wood floor. "Mother! You named me after Queen Ãndrõmakhê, the fearless Amazon who fought against Herakles. Like her, I shall always be armed with the courage of my convictions."

"Don't take your name as license to be foolish!" she snapped at me with an unusual sharpness, "Yes, Ãndrõmakhê was very strong, brave, and noble, but also hot-headed, which made her leap first and look later. Don't forget, Herakles slew her in the battle between her people and his pirates."

I sighed, deflated. "O Mother. Now you made me feel like Ikarus. Here I was, soaring high, soaring happy, and you brought out the sun in full force and melted down my wings."

She ignored my contrition. "Idaios also told your father that a new alliance between Troia and Lakedaimon is being planned."

"Let Priam send one of his own daughters to seal the treaty with marriage to a Spartan!"

"Better marriage than war, Drommie! Those Atrides brothers, Meneláos and Agamemnon, united, are as powerful as Priam. They have a cousin, a bit older than you are; his name is Aigisthos. Your father thinks it might be well for you to consider—"

"Never!"

"Listen. Helen took to husband Meneláos of Sparta; her sister, Klytemnestra, Agamemnon of Mykene. If you wed Aigisthos, you would have powerful Achaian relatives, Drommie."

"No! I told you Helenos and I are promised to each other."

"You're idling, Drommie. Get back to your work."

"Mother! Have you forgotten what Agamemnon did? Huh? Have you? Agamemnon was not Klytemnestra's *chosen* husband! She was first married to...uh, what was his name? Tantalos...and they had a baby son. Agamemnon raided their land, murdered her husband and the baby, and claimed her as property from the man he defeated. Because Klytemnestra was Queen of Mykene, Agamemnon became King. No heroic relative to be proud of, is he, Mother?"

My mother sighed and looked away.

I had found my second wind, "And while we're on the subject, Mother, let's discuss Meneláos! Like Agamemnon, who rose to kingship because of his wife, Meneláos too became King of Sparta because of Helen, because through her mother, *Helen* is the rightful Queen of Sparta. Meneláos did *not* make Helen a Queen, *she* made *him* King!"

Mother broke out laughing. "Lower your voice; you really are hurting my ears! Your father and I have spoiled you, haven't we?"

I looked down, once again ashamed for being so ornery. "I mean no disrespect to you, or to Father. It's just that…I want to be like the two of you. Happy, that is. *You* chose to marry my father."

Her pink eyes twinkled. "We chose *each other.*"

I nodded, and then whispered, "Mother…uh, you and I…could…could we have met in a previous life?"

She pursed her lips. "What makes you say that?"

A scrape of boots at the door kept me from replying.

My father Êetiôn entered, his expression somber. The baby woke up and Mother slipped her hands under him. Êetiôn stood looking down at his wife and child. His gaze was so tender, he smelled of the earth, and wheat-chaff clung under his nails. My father, a strong and just king who was as good with the plow as he was with the sword, but loved working the fields better than conquest.

He said, "Latmia, a messenger is here from Telephos." He began pacing the room. His muscular body almost glided from step to step.

Telephos, of course, was my friend Lanassa's father, and my ears stood at attention, waiting for my father to say more.

Mother stood up with the baby, pressing him to her breast as she asked with a trembling voice, "What's happened?"

"That Achaian upstart, Tlepolemos of Rhodes, has invaded our neighbor Karia, and set up base near Miletos."

"*Miletos?* What of my people there?"

"I have no news from Nomion, your father. However, Telephos' message is urgent. I must draft men and go to his aid immediately. Andros will follow me with more troops."

"Andros?!" My mother cried, "But—"

"As my heir it is time he shared responsibility," he reminded her. "Skirmishes at our borders have given him some experience. If these invaders are not stopped now…."

"I know." She bowed her head and sighed agreement. "A mother of sons must expect their lives to be short."

He touched her shoulder.

"I'll see to the ordering of supplies," she said calmly, then looked at me, "take Leukon, Drommie, and give him to Nurse Mykale."

"You will rule during my absence, Latmia." He followed her to the doorway. Their voices faded along the gallery and down the stairs.

I glanced at Leukon. He was so tiny, but had a new-old look to him. Tears welled in my eyes. It seemed unlikely that he would grow to acquire the stature of a warrior. If his horoscope should be proven accurate by his death at a young age, it would not be due to a heroic battle in the field ...I fingered the opal and tried to envision Leukon as a grown man, but all I could see was blackness.

Nurse Mykale came in as if she had sensed I was off daydreaming again, threw me a condescending look, and took Leukon away.

I remained sitting, staring at the patterned sheet I was supposed to continue weaving. But my fingers were not willing.

My swirling thoughts leapt back to Antigone, daughter of King Oedipus, who had lived in the namesake of my city, Thébé, on the Achaian mainland.

Presently, as I contemplated her life, I felt disturbed, for it seemed Antigone's fate was cast before her father's birth. Like the Trojan Prince Alexis-Paris, Oedipus too had been left to die on the mountain because of a dire oracle. Like Alexis, Oedipus' life was saved, flowing along a seemingly pre-determined course until he killed his father, wed his mother, and thus fulfilled that awful prophecy.

Whether the fact that Alexis was saved from death on Mount Ida, would culminate in him being the predicted torch that would burn Troia to cinder, was yet to be seen....

[1] King Hammurabi: 1728 - 1686 BC. He wrote the Code of Laws (Hammurabi's Codex) to please his gods. Unlike many earlier and contemporary kings, Hammurabi did not claim to be related to any god, although he did call himself Favorite of the Gods. His Codex is the first example of the legal concept that some laws are as basic as to be beyond the ability of even a king to tamper with or to ignore. By writing the laws on stone, they were made immutable. This concept lives on in most modern legal systems, and has given rise to the term *written in stone*.
[2] Oldest version of Goddess and Bull (Her consort) worship dates to Chatalhoyuk, in Central Anatolia, around 8,000 B.C. Possibly, this belief spread from there across the Aegean and Mediterranean.
[3] Shardana: Today's Sardinia and Corsica.

[4] Choice of Herakles (Hercules): Herakles was a Hero who became an Immortal. He had to perform Twelve Labors to earn immortality. One day, while still a mortal, he was invited by two beautiful women, representing Pleasure and Virtue respectively, to choose between the easy path of pleasure and the rocky uphill path of virtue. He chose Virtue.

[5] Achaians, Argives, Danaans, Dorians: Tribes that later formed the Greeks. The name Achaia/n is cross-referenced in Hittite records of the era, spelled as Ahhiyawa or Ahhiya, and is probably based on Achaiwia, the reconstructed Mycenaean-Greek for Achaia.

[6] Luvian/Wilusian language: Hittites help us determine the Trojan language. Place names in cuneiform texts such as *Wilusiya* and *Taruisa,* can be identified with Ilium/Ilion, and Troia. In addition, a "Wilusian" king mentioned in one of the Hittite texts, Alaksandu, is similar to the name of prince Alexander/Alexis (Paris) of Troia.

Chapter 5: Helen of Sparta

My father and two-thousand warriors headed south into the thick of battle against the invaders. Grapes purpled, and my brothers and I pitched in as they were gathered to make wine. Olives too were gathered and the best saved for winter stores, others pressed into oil.

Harvest festivals led into winter, and Mother ordered the looms brought down to the Great Hall for warmth.

I perfected my spinning and could twirl my spindle as expertly as Mother did.

One evening, our resident bard Ialemon chanted nostalgic tales of Troia and Thébé. His voice entered my heart with urgency, echoing even in my sleep. Compelled to leave my bed, I dug into a bronze-bound chest, retrieving the sword I had stashed in its bottom. It was a crude one cast of bronze, more a dagger than a warrior's sword, but I had practiced with it when I brooked no difference between my brothers and myself. As I grasped it now, its hilt felt good in my hand. Nimbly passing it from one hand to the other, I lifted it above my head, slashing the air in wide arcs. The unexpected fluid strength in my arms was a pleasant surprise.

"Haiiiaaa!" I shouted, imagining myself mighty like Ãndrõmakhê, the Amazon. "For life!" I added, getting excited, "For sunshine, and my parents, and my seven brothers! In addition, for love, and flowers, and horses, and cats, and spring lambs, and birds! Most of all, *against* cruelty and injustice! Haiiiaaa!"

Strangely, though, the opal I wore heated again, vibrating against my skin. My head spun as reddish streaks ran down my body. I rose on tiptoes and while I was continuing to whirl, my gaze drifted to the open window, and I was mesmerized by the brilliancy of the stars in the sky.

"The life I have given you," spoke a woman's calm voice, "bear with courage; and take upon yourself the sufferings I will see fit to bestow upon you."

I froze mid-motion, the sword dropped to the floor with a clank.

"In the end, your sorrows will lift you upon a pillar."

Holding my breath, my widening eyes swept the pearlescent semi-darkness. But there was nothing, no woman, no fleeting shadow, and no more words were spoken.

* * * *

Days passed, stringed with anxiety and wonder. I did not doubt the experience, the Goddess had spoken to me and *I* was a Chosen One! That She had ordained suffering for me did not frighten me anymore. There must be a reason, a greater goal, the nature of which would be revealed to me in good time.

One morning after a disturbing dream involving a golden-haired warrior, I sought out Kiron for advice. The details of the dream had turned hazy in my mind, but I recalled bits about a golden apple, and an oath sworn upon the blood of a sacrificed horse.

Mother gave me shocking news: On the night before, Kiron had begged for leave to visit his birth-town in Krete, and she had granted it. Not only had she given him permission, but also enough gold to live out the rest of his days in comfort. Wise Kiron was a good man, deserving of such a boon, and I should rejoice on his behalf. But selfish that I was, I could not. He had been more than my teacher, but my friend, the only one in whom I could confide the mysteries that were boggling my mind, and I would miss his counsel sorely.

Then the Feast of Pots was held. Stored wine was opened and left overnight for dead relatives to savor.

When the solemn time ended, still my father Êetiôn did not return. He was ensnared fighting along Lanassa's father, King Telephos, against waves of raiding Achaians.

I found it disturbing that Telephos, who claimed Herakles as his father, could not destroy his enemies without my father's help. Also, I worried about Lanassa; for all her pettiness, she was a bright girl with a sharp sense of humor, and I was fond of her.

I went on dividing my time between womanly spinning and manly training with the sword. Daily I grew in height as my breasts filled, jutting upwards, while my hips curved with a swinging gait.

* * * *

It was a glorious day in early spring, with nary a white cloud marking the crisp blueness of the sky. A white chariot approached from the wharves at Troia, drawn by two white horses, bearing two people. At the shore beyond, apart from the black-hulled Achaian ships with lion-pennants and carved gryphon and ram-heads rising from their prows, stood another ship, its masts being released from sail. On second look, I recognized that the sail boasted an image of Aphrodite.

Priam and his queen Hekabe rode down the ramp in their gold-plated chariot. Behind them Hektôr, strikingly handsome in jewel-encrusted light armor, drove his own vehicle. Polites, one of his younger brothers, rushed in from Bateia's Mound, which stood midst the Plain and was used as lookout, and exchanged words with his parents.

Then one single exuberant word was shouted from many throats,

"Alexis!"

Hektôr dismounted and assisted his mother to the pavement as Priam leapt from the chariot.

The white chariot forded the river, and then slowed to a stop before the bronze-plated city gates.

I was in Troia accompanying Father and my brother Andros, who were finally back from war, and here to consult with Priam. We stood on the viewing platform atop the Skaian Gate, the main entrance to the city. Kassandra, Helenos's twin, stood by my right, swaying and moaning about thousand ships sailing in to destroy Troia. Realizing that no one was paying attention to her, I felt uneasy. But the clear horizon was free of any approaching vessel that might trigger concern.

Alexis leapt down from the chariot, saluted the city, and then turned back. He lifted the woman down, removed her goldthread veil, and his parents, stepping forward, seemed thunderstruck. In the bright sunlight, this woman looked golden, Aphrodite in the flesh, wearing a yellow, bee-waisted skirt over ruffled green silk trousers, tight-fitting vest and gold-threaded girdle, Kretan-style exposed full breasts covered with the flimsiest frontpiece. Her tiara was richly bejeweled, and her amber hair a darker flame than the flashing gold of Alexis. In his white brocaded tights and gold embroidered green vest, Alexis, Prince of Troia, was Earth to her Celestial glory.

Alexis, an arm about her slim waist, led the breathtaking beauty to stand before his parents. "My wife Helen, Queen of Lakedaimon."

As a confused wild buzz erupted among us gathered, the couple knelt, touching a knee of each parent, then rose as Hekabe and Priam, though pale-faced from shock, embraced them formally.

At once, a stunned silence stopped words of welcome as Oinoné broke through the ranks down at the gate, and ran forward. Flinging her supple form against the unyielding figure of her husband, she covered his face, neck and arms with frantic kisses.

Helen frowned, and Alexis pushed Oinoné from him.

Priam's lesser wives, Laothoe and Kastianeira, stepped forward and gently took Oinoné's hand. Her expression frozen like a mask, she lifted her chin, and went silently with them up into the city.

My eyes trailed her. *Do not let pride destroy your claim on your husband!* I thought with sympathy. This was Troia, headed by Priam, renowned for his many wives and concubines, chosen not always for their beauty, but also for strategic or political gain.

That night during the banquet in Priam's rectangular *Megaron*— Great Hall—lined with nine-foot tall marble statues of Zeus, Hera, Aphrodite, Apollo, Artemis, Athené, and Hermes, many of the guests seemed pale. Even in this brightly lit opulent Hall, with Priam's gold and ivory throne set on a dais, exotic dancers flashing jewels upon oiled, naked bodies as they whirled, leapt, shook and contorted to flutes, drums, and castanets, one could not forget the Achaian ships in the bay, bobbing up and down in the yellow glow of harbor lamps. The rich variety of wines, honeyed mead, barley beer, roasted meats, fried fish, octopus, giant shrimp, syrup-dripping pastries and fruits spread on the tables in exquisite ceramic dishes, decanters, and gold and rockglass goblets, served as the stark reminder of possible famines ahead. The wafting aromas of garlic, olive oil, fresh herbs, lemons, and spices bonded with the smells of human sweat, clouds of frankincense and essences of lilacs, musk, and roses in the women's perfumes.

Beneath the polished bronze chandeliers and red-yellow fires on tripods casting orange flickers upon noble men, women, and various weapons and shields displayed on the walls, whispered gossip buzzed around: Helen of Sparta ran and wrestled, naked, with boys; she had been an athlete, beating young male contestants in the Games; she was much older than Alexis; she had left her three sons behind, for, at ages six, seven and eight, they were being trained as warriors; she had left her little daughter Hermione, as well, to hold their claim to the Spartan throne; but she had brought along a huge treasure.

I sat at one of the two rectangular tables set against the full length of opposite walls, flanked by Father and my brother, Andros, with the dancers and musicians performing in the open center.

Hektôr appeared, nodding to me with a warm smile, sat down, and faced red-haired, freckled Andros. As the night progressed, Hektôr ate and drank little, rising often to circulate among guests, talking, laughing, all in measured tones. I felt drawn to watch him, but as befits a fourteen-year old, chastely, from beneath lowered eyelashes. And I worried about my flaming cheeks. He truly was a handsome man, though not as refined as the slender, gem-blue eyed, blond Alexis. Hektôr was clad in sleeveless, short purple tunic gathered at the waist by a wide leather belt holding his sheathed dagger. His vigorously muscular, confident warrior's presence demanded obeisance—by men and women alike. A scabbarded knife was looped over one shoulder, and a turquoise charm carved like a horse's head, hung about his neck, on a heavy gold chain. Gold bands engraved with galloping horses circled his biceps that bulged with power, and bands of gold-studded leather guarded his strong wrists. His clean-shaven, bronzed, oblong face was bluntly featured, shoulder-length blond-brown hair had sun-bleached strands, his bushy eyebrows and green eyes were the same shade as those of his mother, Queen Hekabe, and his skull was broad, his brow and nose salient, and his wide mouth curved easily as he smiled. When he glanced over at Alexis and Helen, his expression was unfathomable. Occasionally his guarded green gaze roamed in my direction; then my throat dried and my breathing turned erratic, I fretted about the state of my hair—were the elaborate ringlets drooping due to humidity, was I wrong in choosing a crimson silk Kretan outfit that left my breasts jutting above the halter-vest, breasts which though round and firm, were tiny compared to Helen's bounty, and how did my unpainted complexion stand up in the flickering, smoky lights.

Tonight, Priam sat not on his throne, but on a high-backed chair at the head of our table, Hekabe on his right and Antenor on his left, and Alexis and Helen next to Hekabe. Andros sat next to Hektôr's younger brother Deiphobos, who was big, blond, blue-eyed and handsome in his own raw-boned way. Deiphobos had huge hands that could make hammers when clenched into fists and crack open any man's skull. Quickly Deiphobos and Andros got deep in their cups, gulping down undiluted wine, and began to pit the virtues of Helen's creamy breasts, against all the other women's. Soon they got so boisterous and silly that both Priam and Father demanded they tone it down, or else Hektôr would remove them to the soldiers' quarters. They grumbled apologies but went on chuckling and gawking at Helen.

Alexis and Helen told of their journey from Sparta to Troia. Before they embarked at the Spartan port Gythium, Alexis had dedicated a sanctuary to Aphrodite-Migonitis in appreciation for her assistance. Then they had stopped at the island of Cranae, on the Laconian Gulf, married under the auspices of an Apollonian priest, and consummated their marriage. But when they put back to sea, terrible storms had thrown them far off course. They had anchored at Sidon, a coastal city of Phoenicia, to wait an entire month for auspicious weather. There Alexis had purchased magnificent jewelry and silk robes which he tonight presented to his mother.

The newlyweds sat practically in each other's lap, eyes shining, hands touching, their love displayed for all to witness. They looked so young, aglow with happiness, imbibed wine from golden goblets shaped like pomegranates, and dined using gold utensils.

I overheard Antenor, older brother of Queen Hekabe and husband of Priestess Theano, question a remark by Alexis, "Then you believe that the future lies in Achaia?"

Alexis smiled. "I am now King of Lakedaimon—Greater Sparta, and no blood was shed. When I return there with Helen, her people will welcome me in place of Menelaos."

"No doubt," Antenor clipped wryly, looking away from him. "But Menelaos has a powerful ally in his brother; Agamemnon is not called King of Kings for nothing. Look at the crowded harbor, and the surrounding countryside! The real war has not begun, yet already there are casualties on our side."

Although several seats removed, I could hear them clearly and listened attentively. Antenor and Theano hated Alexis, who had killed their son accidentally, while fighting off bandits, and I worried Antenor would oppose anything that might place Alexis in a favorable light.

Alexis' glance swung from Antenor to Priam. "Hear this: You know of Katros' death and that many kings went to Keftiu for the funeral games. Menelaos invited me to remain in Sparta until his return. However, while he was away, Helen chose me as King to replace him; she did so after the Pelasgian custom. Menelaos was detained in Krete far beyond the requirements of the funeral, for he was loitering there with a temple-dancer. Of course his Kretan dalliance was not the first time Menelaos has amused himself with other women."

"I heard of a considerable treasure you've brought along," Priam said curtly, ignoring the subject of Menelaos' dalliances. After all, Priam himself presided over a harem. Marital infidelity was a sin only when committed by wives.

Alexis replied, "Yes, we did. Waiting under heavy guard on two of my ships. Helen has brought all the wealth of her bride-gifts."

Nervously Antenor moved in his seat, gleaming dark gaze roving around. He was tall and slim, black-haired, pointy-bearded, and dressed austerely; he had a pale face, sharp cheekbones, slanted green eyes, and his nose reminded me of a falcon's. With an icy voice, he grated, "You were a trusted, honored guest in Menelaos' house, Alexis, but you robbed him of his wife and treasure while he was gone. You broke the sacred code of hospitality."

Alexis scowled. "This treasure is Helen's dowry! She severed her ties to Meneláos, and has the right to take it back. We will offer half of it to King Telamon, for Hesione's release. I trust it will be accepted. After her return here, Helen and I will go back to Sparta."

Antenor's eyes narrowed into slits, and then he faced Priam, "I would *urgently* advise my King to encourage Helen of Sparta, to—"

Priam silenced him with a raised hand, "Enough!" His speculative gaze swung from Antenor to Alexis, then back to Antenor. "You forget, Antenor, that without Helen, Meneláos cannot claim the Spartan throne." He looked at his son, "You have earned a rich kingdom, and I will support your claim. Thanks to you, Alexis, my fleet will carry merchandise, and not warriors, across the sea."

As the night progressed, Father remained quiet, but from his eyes, I discerned that nothing escaped his attention. The same happened with Hektôr, he too spoke only when he had to, but I felt sure he saw and heard everything. *They seem so alike*, I observed, *two uncommonly strong and skilled warriors, yet at heart, men of peace, who loathe gossip, greed, and pettiness.*

The banquet, music, singing, and dancing went on and on, spiced with an erupting fistfight here and there.

I thought of Helenos, feeling sad that we could not meet. Our visit had been impromptu; I had had no time to find a messenger trustworthy enough to send to him at Perkote.

Mother had drilled me on how to comport myself in her absence, and I was not touching wine or mead; but my throat kept drying and I drank copious amounts of pomegranate juice, sending me to the privy-chamber often. To reach it, I had to skirt my way among bands of drunken noblemen at their worst behavior with the dancers and the slave girls, and soon it turned dangerous for me. My long skirt flared from my tightly laced waist, and the halter-vest emphasized my breasts, reminding them that I was initiated into womanhood and must be ripe for the taking.

By then Father was sequestered somewhere in the Palace with Priam and Antenor, Kassandra, Hekabe, Alexis and Helen had left too, and dear Andros, charged with the task of taking me safely to our assigned sleeping quarters, had lost the drinking contest to Deiphobos, and was snoring under the table. Deiphobos was not in good shape either, gloomily studying the bottom of his wine cup, slobbering, and growling that Helen was comelier than Aphrodite.

Hektôr came to rescue. Escorting me away from the banquet and after guarding the door of the privy-chamber, he brought me to the guest-wing, removed a burning torch from its wall bracket near the door and stepped in. Using the torch to light the sconces and the tripod, he checked the corners to make sure no one lurked in the shadows, and then that I had enough water for drinking and washing in the morning.

I looked around, liking what I saw. A spacious wing, thoughtfully arranged with three sleeping-niches separated by folding screens.

"I am glad you came to visit us," he said, "Troia is younger and more beautiful with you here."

His compliment was unexpected; I looked at him wide-eyed, and only with great effort I kept my jaw from dropping.

"Good night, Āndrōmakhê." Briefly, he touched my flaming cheek, smiled, and turned to leave. I thought that in the wake of his massive, vigorous presence, the room would shrink and darken.

"Hektôr..."

He looked over his shoulder with a warm smile, "Yes?"

"May I pose an unseemly question?"

"Unseemly?" He laughed, "Oh please, don't hesitate!"

"Were you surprised that Alexis brought Helen?"

"Surprised, no, Alexis is a charmer of women; but am I worried? Oh, yes. Very much."

For some strange reason, my knees buckled and I collapsed into a chair by the bed I chose for myself. "Please, explain."

He hesitated, approaching me with a troubled expression. "If I had known of this from the onset, I would have opposed him. Antenor was right when he pointed out his breach of the rules of hospitality. Alexis had no right to spirit her away while Meneláos was gone—especially because Meneláos had left his queen and his treasure in his care."

"But they are so in love with each other..."

"Alexis is in love, I am not sure about Helen."

I could not help bristling, "Have you been blind tonight!?" Biting my lips, I looked away. "I am sorry; I shouldn't raise my voice to you."

"Don't fret, Āndrōmakhê, I understand. You are still young and unable to grasp the whole picture. You see, as a Prince of Troia, my brother's first consideration has to be Duty and Honor, and not Love. Helen is married to another man, a powerful king. Whether Meneláos is an ugly brute, or an uncouth lover, is irrelevant. A king is what he is, and his wrath affects the lives of many. Therefore Alexis has sinned twice: first by betraying the time-honored rules of hospitality, and second, by dismissing the possible consequences of his lust."

65

Looking at it from Hektôr's viewpoint saddened me. "But with Helen, he brought you the claim upon Lakedaimon."

"But it's not an enforceable claim."

"Why? *Helen* is the Queen of Sparta! *She* made Meneláos a King, and she has the right to unmake him."

He shook his head. "In theory, yes. But not so in reality."

"But…of course these claims are valid! What about your aunt, Hesione? I know Priam is worried about that because she is his wife, upon his death, Telamon will use her right of inheritance to claim the Trojan throne."

"He might try, but would not succeed. That said, Hesione was his legitimate prize for winning the war against us."

"An unfairly won war! Herakles wrecked your walls, and Poseidon dispatched Drako, the Sea Monster. A bride won by trickery, does not make a legitimate wife."

Hektôr frowned, and then sat down on the bed, facing me. "Tell me, how would you know of my father's concerns about Telamon's possible claim on Troia?"

I certainly could not tell him that I heard it during my out-of-body excursion into Troia, so I just pursed my lips. "Everyone knows of how your father has tried to get Hesione back. She is no longer young, and by all accounts, content as Telamon's wife. Yet tonight Alexis spoke of offering half of Helen's treasure for Hesione's release. Meaning there is more at stake here than a brother wanting his sister returned home."

"Ah," he said dryly.

"Hektôr…women, married or not, and be they queen, princess or slave, are carried off all the time; that's a tragic fact of life. Why is Helen's case so different?"

"Would that Alexis had won her in battle! But he was a guest in Meneláos' house, and—"

"*Helen's house!* Helen is *Queen* of Sparta, and they lived in the palace built by *her* parents. And she was not stolen; she *wanted* to leave with your brother."

He rose to his feet. "I must go now, dear Āndrōmakhê. True, we are having quite an interesting conversation here, but the hour is late."

I smiled and nodded. I knew that his concern was not the late hour, but my reputation, and I thanked him.

Briefly touching my hair, he turned and left without looking back. I watched the heavy, ornamental door close behind him, then listened to his boots thudding down the corridor until they faded away.

I fell asleep as soon as my head hit the rolled pillow.

When I awoke mid-morning, I knew I had dreamed sweetly, but recalled no more than that Hektôr and I were riding on a purple-draped chariot through vast green fields, and somewhere at the end of this journey, the Lynx was waiting for me to come home.

Later on that day, I watched ebony-haired, almond eyed, lovely Oinoné, in a gold-embroidered white chiton, embrace Hekabe at the Dardanian Gate. A wagon waited, loaded with her things.

Alexis was conspicuously absent.

"You are like my own daughter," Hekabe mourned. Her expressive eyes, green like grapes reflecting the gold of mid-summer sun, went to the small, blond boy toddling toward the onager hitched to the shaft. "And I will miss him, too."

"It is better so, my queen-mother. We both know that I have never belonged here."

"Alexis is merely infatuated with Helen," Hekabe tried to comfort her, "but *you* are the one he loved first! Remember, *your* son is his heir. Priam, too, has other wives, but I don't cherish him any less."

Oinoné bit her lips and moved away. "This intrigue-ridden, stuffy court life is not suited for a daughter of Kebren."

She stepped through the bronze-plated Skaian Gate, lifted her son into the wagon, and then turned back. As tears stormed down her cheeks, she raised one clenched fist toward the sky, "May you live long with Helen, dear Paris, until the day you send for me! On that day you will die full of pain, regretting the wife you had cast aside."

She climbed into the wagon and grasped the reins, leaving Troia without a single, backward glance.

Chapter 6: Akhilles and Hektôr

On a morning about two weeks after Alexis had brought Helen of Sparta to Troia, I woke up full of zest, with no warning of anything unusual about to occur. The sun was not yet out when I washed up with cold water, slipped into a short, belted tunic woven from the fleece of our own sheep, clasped a blue cape around my shoulders, and hurried down to the stable, to Iris.

She greeted me with a cheerful whicker, eagerly chomping down the apple and handfuls of high-energy barley I fed her. Then she whickered again, rearing on hind legs, signaling readiness for adventure. Iris was a light horse, graceful with long legs, fifteen hands tall from the ground up to the withers, the highest point on her shoulder. Leaping onto her chestnut back, I held on to her flaxen mane and as the joy of freedom pumped in my veins off we went galloping into a morning smelling of woods, grass, and a promising future. Spring flowers had budded in a riot of colors, and fields were green around Thébé.

I brought Iris to a stop only upon reaching the grove at the end of our woodlands. Fed by a playful brook, this was a particularly green corner, carpeted with tufts of tall grass. I jumped down, took off my cape, dropping it on the ground, and let Iris free to roam, knowing she would never wonder off. We had grown up together and Iris was as faithful as any of our shepherd dogs, with an acute sense of smell and direction. And the fact that she was born at the same hour as me made her my star-sister.

But as I perched on a smooth-topped tree stump, enjoying the rosy hues filtering through the trees forming a canopy above my head, my heart gave a wild thump. The downy hairs on the back of my neck and arms bristled, my opal pendant heated and vibrated against my skin—a warning? I did not move, holding my breath. Narrowing my gaze, I scanned my surroundings. But all remained quiet, and there was not even a mild breeze on the air.

Moments passed; I relaxed, focusing my attention on a pair of plump squirrels who chased each other up and down the oak tree ahead.

They rustled leaves and shook branches, triggering a shower of gray-brown dust as the weaker, dryer ones broke off and fell onto the ground. The rest of the inhabitants of the grove woke up as well, and soon the air was bursting with the racket of cicadas, frogs, birds, insects and the splashing waters of the brook.

It was then that he stepped out from the thicket of brushwood on my right. The grove fell silent again. He stood at a distance from me, shoulders erect, chest forward, clad in a light leather armor over a plain sailcloth tunic, one hand on his belt from which dangled a short sword, his feet shod in sandals laced calf-high. There was something eerie about him, and I wondered if he was an apparition. He was of heroic height and built, his straight white-blond hair hung free around his shoulders, his somewhat narrow face with its high forehead was clean-shaven, and he seemed young.

I did not move, torn between the urge to bolt away and the need to find out if he was flesh and blood.

"Ãndrõmakhê," he spoke after a while.

I noted that it was not a question but a declaration.

I nodded. "And you are…?"

"Akhilles, son of Peleos of Phthia and Thessaly."

I did not blink. "I don't believe I know who you are."

"Ãndrõmakhê," he repeated, "Ãndrõmakhê Êetiônis." He took a few steps toward me, and then stopped.

I remained quiet, and so still as if frozen in stone. He must be a cattle thief, lucky for having bumped into the daughter of King Êetiôn.

"You knew I was coming for you," he said quietly.

Some of my reserve left me. "How could I?"

"Because you are able to see beyond. Like Kassandra and Helenos."

"And you are not an apparition, but flesh and blood."

He smiled. "Indeed."

"Who are you? How did you get here?"

"Easy. I sailed into harbor, jumped ashore, mingled with traders, merchants, soldiers, and at dusk, walked in through your gates."

"Why?" *To hold me for ransom,* I thought with a sinking heart.

He shook his head as if privy to my mind. "No, Ãndrõmakhê, not for ransom. I am a warrior. Nevertheless, I intend to offer peace and prosperity to your father, Êetiôn. There are other kings in the region, such as Phorbas and Telephos, with lovely daughters. I like what I hear of Êetiôn; he is brave and just, his people speak well of him. That is why I will let him know that the House of Priam is doomed, just as surely as the walls of Troia are doomed to fall. But Êetiôn's fate is not yet cast, and he ought to enter a treaty with me."

"How so?"

"I would take you to wife."

Now I remembered bits of the dream I had wanted to talk to Kiron about, last month. The golden warrior, the golden apple, and the oath of the horse. However, what did *he* have to do with any of these things?

Akhilles smiled, taking another step. "Kiron was ship-wrecked before he could reach Krete; I rescued him from Poseidon's clutches."

I leapt to my feet, "Kiron...*what?*"

"Do you wish to ransom him, Ãndrõmakhê?"

"But of course! Name your price."

"The opal on your neck."

I gasped, outrage searing through me like lightning.

He pursed his lips. "You are transparent, Ãndrõmakhê. Learn to shield your thoughts from those able to scan them. You see, now I've learned that this opal is special for you."

I sat down, placed my clenched fists on my lap, looked up at him and spoke coldly, "I hope you have treated him well! His back is injured, he cannot do heavy work. And he's losing his teeth; he cannot eat much, only bread soaked in milk, stewed figs and apples, and—" I stopped, troubled by the grin spreading over his face.

Akhilles then shifted his gaze and cleared his throat. "No need to fret, he is not starving."

"If he is, I'll find the means to make you sorry."

"Ãndrõmakhê!" He chuckled. "Good. A man likes a wife who has humor. So, what is your offer for Kiron's life?"

Bravado was not helping me. "I have other jewelry, more prized than this opal. Care for a serpentine gold bracelet?"

He did not reply.

Nervously I probed, "Or a set made of unusual red amber? It's a triple-stranded necklace with a pendant, bracelet, and ring. The pendant is bigger than my fist, clear in the center, set in gold, with leaves and a tiny dragon caught in it."

His eyes widening, he exploded, "You really would pay *that* much for this old goat?"

"Well, I have never negotiated with a thief before. So I'm not familiar with the going rate for a man's life."

He let that pass.

When he spoke, he sounded kind. "I know that Kiron is a scribe, and has taught you. He told me he is proud of you, that he never had a pupil such as you. But he is old and sick. What with the war going on, markets are glutted with skilled slaves. You could purchase two of his kind, younger, with more years to serve, for three milk-cows and two sheep."

"Kiron is not only my teacher, but my friend. I shall give you the amber set *and* three milk cows."

"But not the opal?"

My hand flew to my pendant; it felt cool to my touch. Strange. Just a little while ago it had been afire, vibrating against my skin. Did this mean the Goddess would allow me to trade it for Kiron's life?

"No, she wouldn't," Akhilles spoke, shaking his head.

"You are toying with me! May the pox get you! I will up the milk cows to four. I want Kiron freed! Just tell me what you *want!"*

"Hmm. You care deeply for him."

"Obviously yes, I do."

"My teacher too, is named Kiron. He is a Kentaur."

"A Kentaur? Really?"

"Really. A good man he is, pious, incredibly wise, taught me all about herbs, potions, and the art of healing, but also to ponder the universe, and play the lyre."

"You can play the lyre?"

"Why are you surprised?"

"Alexis, Prince of Troia, plays the lyre."

"So?"

"Did you ever meet him in person?"

"No. But I've heard plenty about him."

"Anyone ever tell you that you two look like each other?"

"He could *not* look like me! He is a milksop."

"Milksop? *Alexis?* I don't think so. The point is, you do resemble each other. Same color of hair, though yours is not curly as his, eyes, eyebrows, shape of your face and high forehead, straight nose, even the shape of your chin...but you are taller. Without seeing you two side by side, I'd hazard a guess that you're taller by about...a hand's length."

Frowning, he waved dismissively. "You want Kiron back. And I will accept the cows for him; that is enough. Thank your Goddess I am not demanding the opal, or your pet, Iris. I shall send Kiron tonight."

"Good, it's a deal. How do I get the cows to you?"

"They will be gone from your herd as soon as I leave here. Now let us return to the subject of the treaty between us."

"The subject is moot; there shall be no such treaty."

Akhilles spoke softly and slowly, "Telamon, who battled with, and subdued, Laomedon of Troia, is brother of my father, Peleos. Thus, he is my uncle. Telamon, as you know, is also the husband of Priam's sister, Hesione. And King Priam's fate was sealed when Eris, Goddess of Discord, tossed that golden apple." He paused.

"Go on," I said impatiently, "go on, have your say!"

"Eris is also called Nemesis, Goddess of Divine Retribution."

Another pause. And it lengthened.

"Enough of this teasing!" I burst out, *"Have your say!"*

He shrugged, bent forward, looking at me closely. He then pulled his sword from its scabbard, came closer and sat on the grassy ground, laid the sword aside, pulled his knees up to his chest, winding his arms around them, and faced me.

He is so beautiful! I thought, frankly amazed.

"Akhilles! You are getting too comfortable. Don't you fear that my brothers might show up?"

"No, not for now. They are busy chasing off a bunch of would-be cattle thieves." He winked, "Just a few of my men, pretending to be a whole lot. I planted them for a diversion so that we can talk without being disturbed. No, do not worry; nothing will happen to your brothers. You have my word."

I looked into his eyes, and believed him. Yet I asked, "Just who are you that I ought to take your word?"

"I am Akhilles," he repeated, then added, "I am the son of Thétis, the Nereid [1], and King Peleos, of Thessaly."

"Son of a mortal and an immortal. Are *you* immortal?"

His face reddened, but he held my gaze. "I am not sure. To be truthful, sometimes I wish for it. I don't want to die and turn to dust, for I love the rush of being alive. But immortality is not what the oracle prophesied for me. I was given two destinies, two paths to choose from. One was a peaceful long life, the other short but glorious, with certain death on the battlefield and my name remembered for all times."

"You chose glory," I said dryly.

"For all times," he added.

Like Alexis and the three goddesses, I thought.

He laughed, "I warned you! You should cloak your thoughts! However, yes, you are right, like Alexis-Paris, and his Judgment about which one among the three is the most beautiful. This is where the Golden Apple comes in. The Apple of Hesperides [1]. It all happened on the day of my parents' wedding. Eris—Discord!—was not invited to attend. She felt snubbed and decided to take vengeance. She threw a golden apple, inscribed with 'to the fairest', in front of Athené, Hera, and Aphrodite. All three attempted to claim the apple. An argument ensued.

Then they asked the guests to decide on who should get it, but no one dared. They asked Zeus, but he too had no courage. Years passed—on Olympos time doesn't flow forward as it does here on Earth, and the Olympians have no Yesterday or Tomorrow, they simply exist in an endless Here and Now—so the three goddesses continued to hate each other over the apple, and nagged Zeus for his opinion. Finally, Zeus gave up and assigned the burden to Paris. Whom you know as Alexander."

"But why would the Great Zeus pick a lowly shepherd for such an important decision?"

"Because he had gained a reputation for fairness, because during a competition, he had judged in favor of a bull—he had declared it the winner even though it had trampled to death his very own, prize bull. Alas though, this time Alexis could not remain fair! Aphrodite infused him with a nagging lust for Helen, and he accepted her bribe and gave her the golden apple."

"He chose love above all!"

"So he did, so he did. And I chose the glorious life of a Hero. I know I have to die one day, but not *when.* Meanwhile, my life is one splendid victory after another, made even sweeter by the risks I take."

Another silence.

I too remained silent, unsure if I wanted to hear more.

Finally, curiosity got the better of me, "What do you *really* want, Akhilles? If you are hoping to trade peace for my hand, you should let your intention known to my father."

He laughed. "But he is loyal to Priam."

"Then why bother meeting with me? If you can read thoughts, then you know my answer as well. I am promised to another. But even if I weren't, I would not take you to husband."

"I know that, too. Nonetheless I wanted to try to win you over."

"I see no reason why you would."

"I wonder if we could alter Destiny."

"How so? Would our union save Priam and his House?"

"No, for their fate is already cast and sealed in place. But your father's is not. Neither is yours, unless you choose to step into the web the gods have woven for Priam, his sons, and Troia."

"I don't believe you, Akhilles! Besides, even if it were true that the House of Priam is doomed, *you* are not who I want."

He gave me a long, speculative look. Then, "When Alexis left for Sparta, he knew nothing about the Oath of the Horse. I will tell it to you now, so you can make an informed decision. Yes, Helen is very beautiful, and every Achaian king came to ask for her hand in marriage.

They were willing to kill each other to that end, heedless of the chaos that would result. Then Odysseus, whose wits I respect, offered a solution: All of Helen's suitors, just before the winner of her hand was announced, should swear on the blood of a sacrificed horse to protect the right of the winner from any challenger—just in case someone carried her off afterwards. The oath was sworn, Meneláos won her, and now, these kings are gathering an army. To capture Troia and restore Helen of Sparta to her husband."

"Troia is strong," I bristled, "and Troia has strong allies."

"But Troia's enemies have engaged *me*, Ãndrõmakhê, for Troia shall fall when their armies are headed by me."

"Yet another prophecy?"

"Yes."

"And you are sure that Troia's and Priam's fates are sealed?"

"Hektôr's as well." He pulled out a blade of grass and took it in his mouth, playing with it.

"What about Helenos?"

"His renown as a seer is growing, and will grow more."

"So his fate is cast and sealed too?"

He shrugged and remained silent.

"But you just talked about wanting to change Destiny."

"Ah. I can hear your thoughts again! So, is this your decision? That you will refuse me and still try to change Troia's fate, on your own?"

"I hadn't thought it out this far, but...yes."

"Hektôr..." he said mildly, "Hektôr...he is brave, and the gods like him. Would that I did not have to fight him."

"Then, don't!"

"I have to. The one-to-one battle I will wage with him one day is ordained to be my *Aristeia [2]*. Hektôr will lead me to the glory I seek."

Akhilles fell silent, looking at me with his bright blue eyes. Slowly he rose to his feet, bent and retrieved his sword, sheathed it, and looked at me again. "I have to leave now, Ãndrõmakhê."

I nodded.

He turned his back, walked to the edge of the grove, turned and looked at me again, hesitant, thoughtful. "Are you sure, Ãndrõmakhê? I have asked you to align yourself with me."

"And I have decided not to."

He sighed. "Then, Ãndrõmakhê, I have decided *not* to take you as my wife. You and I, today, have made our decisions freely."

"Yes, *freely.*"

Akhilles disappeared among the trees. Iris appeared, neighing softly, chestnut coat shiny under the rays of sunlight, came with a slow trot, and nuzzled my face. I leapt upon her back and we cantered home.

My brothers returned that evening, in good cheer, boasting about how they had fought off a band of at least fifty thieves.

The three milking cows were never taken from the herd, and neither was Kiron heard from again.

Afraid of that Mother would curtail my freedom and I would no longer be free to ride out with Iris, I kept my encounter with the mysterious, blonde young man called Akhilles, a secret from her.

* * * *

First grain sprouted. It was time for the festival to honor the Triune Goddess at Her cave near Lyrnessos, south of Mount Ida.

My mother attended the three priestesses, called Gorgons, who lived in the womblike cavern. I arrived with Astynome, serving as acolytes. Our friend Briseis had married King Mynes during the midwinter bridal season, and was our hostess. Briseis' father King Brises, who hailed in from Pedasos, together with visiting Alexis, offered up sacrifice on this third night of the vigil. At the moon's meridian, the Son of the Goddess would be born.

The banquet had ended in Mynes' hilltop palace. Now Brises was examining the offering for an omen. Tall and gaunt in his yellow robe and goatskin apron, he bent over the cooling mass of red-splotched, gray intestinal tubes heaped upon the small altar near the hearthfire.

"He saw a bad omen from the entrails, and doesn't want to tell it to us," Briseis speculated, sitting down between her husband and myself Mynes. He was young, reasonably handsome, and treated her kindly, and she seemed to be in love with him.

"Perhaps it will be better after the Rebirth ceremony," Astynome said, sounding doubtful. She was on my other side.

Briseis frowned. "I'm sure the omen concerns Alexis."

"No." Astynome was firm. "It is about the ships."

Mynes stirred in his seat. "Silence is best when the prognosis is doubtful. He can take another oracle when Alexis leaves the cave." He motioned impatiently, and King Brises stepped to the chair meant for him. Briseis leaned across her husband and spoke a few words to her father. Brises moved his head negatively.

Herald Idaios rose from his seat. He bowed to Mynes, and then faced the gathering. "I have word from King Priam." He turned back to

75

Mynes. "In reward for furnishing such fine ships for his fleet, my lord has sent his own shipwright, Danaos." He nodded toward a swarthy, red-faced, portly man enjoying his meal a few chairs away.

The man grinned, lifting his drinking-pot in salute.

Beware the Oath of the Horse, a voice spoke in my mind. I almost choked on the piece of apple I had bitten into, and turned around, trying to cough it out in a dignified manner.

Idaios continued, "Shipwright Danaos will oversee the facilities here. Equipment and supplies will come from the Skamander yards. The lumbermen of Pedasos are already hauling timbers from the best stands on Mount Ida."

The clattering of cups on tables applauded, and Idaios sat down.

I glanced at Briseis. She was smiling her approval. I looked away, disturbed. For the span of a heartbeat, a dark specter had hovered behind her back.

* * * *

It was after midnight when the moon rode high. Ten circles of twelve young women in diaphanous tunics, were dancing to bring out the new moon from a shielding cloud. The baleful old moon was dead; the life-giving new one would soon emerge.

My mother remained in the Cave where she had been for the past three days, awaiting the birth of the Son/Lover. No male but the Son dared enter the awesome place of female mystery. Only he might touch those guardian Gorgons of the Triune Goddess, as the Divine Child.

As I spun and leapt on arched, winged feet, I got a glimpse of the shadowy figures of sun-masked young men, in brief white loincloths, symbolizing the Sun, waiting to join us. When we whirled to a stop, they ringed the dance area. Acolytes began passing around moon-masks, attaching them to the heads of gracefully swaying bodies.

One of the masked, near-naked men, taller and more muscular than all the others, the gold bands on his sculpted biceps resembling those Hektôr had worn at the banquet, claimed me with a sudden move, and held me tight against his body. *Helenos, here at last!* I thought, giddy, *but he has grown, and he is so strong....*

The music changed from sistra to flutes as moon-girls swung in the arms of sun-boys to the humming of hymning voices among the trees. He freed me, flutes rose to unearthly wailing as the pace increased and I rejoined the dance, with the masked man in tandem with me.

When the freewheeling dance ended, the tall man pulled me against a tree, his eyes gleaming behind his golden mask. Now I noticed that on his barrel chest he wore a turquoise charm on a heavy gold chain, carved like a horsehead. I felt alarmed.

He laughed when I struggled to free myself, then pushed my mask off and dropped his own. I had to gasp: his craggy but handsome face could never be mistaken for Helenos'! And his shoulder-length hair, darker at the roots with sun-bleached streaks atop, was thick and wild.

"Have a care, Ãndrõmakhê, remember me!" He chuckled, though he was breathing hard. "It hasn't been *that* long since we met last!"

"Hektôr!" I tried to move away from him but got entangled in my own feet. To my dismay, joy grew wings, lifting my heart. The music around us hushed to a low whimpering sigh and the deep-toned throb of a kithara matched my pounding heart. I felt free, wild, and strong.

"How enchanting you look when you dance," he whispered. "I could watch you and dance with you all night long. I am glad that when I heard you were coming here, I joined Alexis at the last minute."

The sistra gained new momentum, rippling through my blood, and I pushed him away, began whirling to the mystical Dance of the Maze, and Hektôr kept pace with me. The ground was marked in a circular maze pattern, the lines fading away beneath our swiftly moving feet, and we danced in labyrinthine evolutions with measured steps to the added accompaniment of harps. In this dance, our twists and turns mimicked the unfolding of life—not knowing what happens next—with death and rebirth in the center. We worked through the maze in a series of nested loops, from the outside to the center. Hektôr's moves were so very graceful for a man of his height and bulk.

Alarmed at my bone-deep awareness of him, I paused mid-step, and then leapt aside to give way to the other dancers, among them Briseis and Astynome.

Hektôr followed me. As a fresh gust of wind buffeted everything around us, my gaze swept the surroundings. "Where is Helenos?"

"Still at Perkote. Why do you ask?"

I lifted my chin defiantly. "Surely you know we are pledged to each other."

His heady burst of laughter was shocking. "You are no priest's wife, beautiful Ãndrõmakhê! You need a king's hand."

I stared at him, feeling skittish. "Why are you here?"

"I told you why, already; I heard *you* were going to be here."

"I see." The news made me uneasy, but I knew not why.

"Are you not glad to see me, lovely moon-maiden?"

I was, but could not admit it to him. I tore myself away from Hektôr, left the leaping, whirling dancers behind, stumbled over a protruding serpentine root, and he caught me back to him. He caressed my hair, his hand gliding down the waves along my back. His large, calloused hands were surprisingly gentle and warm, his smell pleasant, so earthy. And his arms! Strong, hard, knotted with muscles from wielding various weapons, shields, and reins. I had thought of him often since that night in Troia, nonetheless I felt ashamed to admit—even to myself—that I enjoyed his hard body touching mine.

"You are beautiful, Āndrōmakhê. My lovely moon-maiden." His voice was a honeyed breath in my ear. His touch was nothing like the boyish fumbling of Helenos, and I quivered violently.

Akhilles' blond image and his talk about the House of Priam and of sealed fates, popped up in my mind. "Have you heard of a warrior by the name of Akhilles?" I asked tentatively.

"Akhilles…?"

"Yes, he is the son of King Peleos from Thessaly."

"I know of Peleos, but don't recall a son by this name."

I wavered, unsure whether I should tell him more. Then, "I met a young man who said his name is Akhilles, and that one day he will battle with you, one-on-one…."

Hektôr laughed. "Ah, he has to get in line, and wait his turn, for there are many so inclined." After a silence, he spoke with a darkly troubled look on his face, "Wait…indeed I've heard about this man! Peleos had sent him to be raised at the court of Lykomedes, in Skyros—not one of my favorite places, I tell you, because King Theseus, who had taught me how to wrestle when I was a boy, was slain there—so Peleos sent his son to Skyros, and for whatever reason, disguised as a girl. But he couldn't keep up the pretense for long and bedded Deidameia, Lykomedes' daughter, and she gave him a son."

"Well, Akhilles is no longer on Skyros."

"How would you know?"

Wanting to tell him about the encounter and Akhilles' proposal, I hesitated. Then I decided to reveal the gist of it. "Akhilles is interested in an alliance with my father."

"Military?"

"What else?"

"Are you sure?"

I shrugged and did not reply. Then something made me blurt it out, "He offered a peace treaty to be sealed by our marriage."

"Of course Êetiôn turned him down!"

"Father never got to hear it," I said honestly, angry with myself for having brought it up at all.

"Your father did not hear it, but *you* did. How so?"

"Because…Akhilles spoke to me directly."

"Of course you turned him down."

Hektôr's tone was casual; he was not taking me seriously. Perhaps he assumed that I had spun a tale just to tease him. I felt relieved; better so, I was spared further explanation and possibly, lie, to hide the fact that I had kept it from my parents.

Hektôr tightened his grip around my waist, and bent his head, his warm moist lips seeking my mouth. I swung my head aside and he had to kiss the top of my head. "Your hair smells good," he whispered.

"What is it you want from me, Hektôr?" I asked suddenly.

"You don't know?" he chuckled, pressing me closer to his body, "You don't feel it, you can't guess?"

"Helenos…."

"Yes? What about Helenos?"

The wail of a conch-shell horn called the worshipers.

I grasped the opportunity to spring away. "I have to go," and I ran without looking back.

The young men, masked again, stood along either side of the Sacred Walkway. Beyond the restricted halfway mark, the girls waited. There was plenty eye contact and smiles full of promises.

The new moon beamed pearlescent light on the white-haired Priestess Latmia who emerged dancing down from the cave. I watched her smiling, proud that I was her daughter. To the rattling incantation of gourds, she moved in slow precision, balancing a breast-shaped pot on her uplifted palms. Beautiful and light as the moon on earth, she moved to one of two columns, poured a dark liquid so that it trickled down the shaft. Leaving her pot upside down on the earth, she took another from behind the column and added a white liquid to drench the ground. Thus, the blood of childbirth and milk of sustenance announced that the Son was born and chosen as Abductor of the Maiden, Lover of the Matron, and Son of the Crone.

The Gorgon-priestesses appeared at the Cave's entrance, masked as Dove, Goat and Mare, striking awe and terror among the worshipers. I could not help trembling, for those women were never seen except during the four holy turnings of the year.

Then Prince Alexis, a triumphantly reborn man of golden fire, emerged. His long blond hair was arranged in sunrays about his head, and tiny gold sun discs glinted over his white robe. In the dim light, he was a blinding flame. He held a large golden quince in both hands as he moved down the path. Feeling proud and protective at the same time, I watched him. The Son as Sun, shining in the beautiful person of Alexander Paris Priamides!

Girls followed him down the path, dropping flowers as if his feet had coaxed them from the earth. At the end of the path, handsome young men lifted and held high fast-clicking thin slabs of olive wood. Alexis offered the quince to Latmia, who returned slowly to the cave. One of the Gorgons stepped forward, accepting the gift.

At this point, I, as acolyte, straightened my back, lifted my head high and shouted the ritual words my mother had taught me, "To the most beautiful form of our Great Mother, Queen of Love and Youth, your Son offers the prize that no woman can refuse!"

Flutes and lyres thrummed and shrilled as the chorus was silenced. The three priestesses retreated into their cave.

"The Goddess accepts him," Astynome whispered, touching my hand. "He will now choose which of the Lady's gifts to honor."

"Beauty, Wisdom, or Wealth," I whispered.

Astynome spoke in her priestess' voice, "He never existed until now. At long last he is a full Prince of Troia."

Minutes later Hektôr was clasping arms with Alexis as King Brises concluded a short ceremonial speech, "May the Maiden and Matron bless the laying of this, the first keel of Priam's new fleet."

Alexis's voice rose high, "The Triune Goddess welcomed me into her Cave. In her three forms, she offered me my full heritage as Son of Priam. I could have only one destiny: the oracle of kingdom, of wisdom, or the love of a beautiful woman. I chose the last, my wife, Helen. Thanks to the Goddess, I may also earn other rewards. But at this time my duty is to my father and his plans for the future."

Well-wishers surrounded him. I smiled, glad that this dedicated young man would one day be my brother by marriage.

* * * *

One late summer day I was carding wool, seated against the cool house-wall on the balcony outside our workroom. The day was sultry, though a breeze occasionally rippled the cloth in my lap. Goosebumps rippling my skin, I was thinking of Hektôr, this past spring in Lyrnessos. He had stirred me in such a different way from the touch of Helenos! And during the dance, our moves had complemented each other's with a fluid familiarity as if we had been partners for many years. But how could this be? I loved Helenos! Yet, just recently, an ache had shot through me when I had heard Hektôr was about to marry Princess Sigeia, beautiful sister of King Polymestor in Thrakia.

I placed the comb on the raw wool piled in a basket beside me, and was cleansing my fingers of lanolin on the cloth when the sound of several running feet and excited voices echoed from inside. What had happened?! I hurried inside and onto the gallery. Looking into the Great Hall below, I spotted my mother talking to a travel-soiled messenger near the hearthfire, a Karian by his dress. My heart sank with dread. It must be about Father! He had had to depart again last month, and there had been no word since.

My younger brothers streaked in from the courtyard, shouting up to me, "Victory for us! Father is in Miletos now, triumphant!"

Mother sailed in then, face aglow with relief and joy. She took hold of my hand, led me to the balcony and declared in a singsong voice, "Your father will be home soon!"

I collapsed onto the bench while she sat down beside me and wound a tender arm around me. "And Father...is he all right?"

"Yes, the messenger says he is well."

With a huge noisy sigh of relief, I got up and trembling all over, leaned against the wall of the balcony.

My mother straightened, announcing calmly, "You are to have a sister, Drommie. Andros will marry Lanassa next summer."

"Ah, Priam wants this marriage. He marries Princess Laothoe to get fuller control of Pedasos. He sees to it that Briseis marries Mynes, drawing Lyrnessos to Troia." Then a more personal realization struck me, "Lanassa will be queen here...."

Preparations began at once to welcome the victorious return of King Êetiôn and his three older sons. When their ships were sighted, I rushed into the courtyard to order my chariot. The boys were to follow in a wagon drawn by their favorite onager. Taking my own reins, I stormed out through our gate.

Women in doorways and at the center fountain stopped gossip or laundry to stare as I streaked by. The village was made of granaries, storehouses, homes for the stevedores and other watermen, several wineshops, potteries, and canvassed-over stalls doing brisk business with seafarers passing through. Vine-frosted houses touched with blooming red and purple bougainvillea, sun-browned children playing in the runnels from hillside streams, men hauling burdens, all flashed by as I whipped up speed. Through the orchards I raced, where roseate blooms gave way to green balls of young fruit. I slapped reins across Iris' back

81

and whirled to the wharves, where I drew rein and stared at tall masts fringing the sky.

Dismounting, I patted Iris on her neck, whispered thanks for bearing with my uncouth speed, then threw the reins to a village boy and walked onto the stone wharf. Jetties were built into the water for safe anchorage. Trade goods were being unloaded from my father's many vessels. His own ship was just tacking into anchorage beside the goods-bearer. Dropping anchor, the gangplank was run out and I raced to him as Father started landward. He strode to the quay and grabbed me in a crushing embrace, then was besieged by the younger boys scrambling from their wagon.

"Oh you are safe, safe!" I cried, sobbing, unable to stop.

The war-chariot was brought from the other ship with his steeds, and the boys rushed to it.

"So are your four brothers." He gave me a hug, and I turned toward the boys—so much matured now, I observed—and ran to them.

Our mother met us in the outer courtyard, where she had ordered the laying of a crimson welcome carpet. My brothers immediately joined up with those who had been left behind. They all rushed up the stairs, while I stayed and made sure everything was ready for the welcome-feast. When satisfied, I went up to my room to arrange my hair in a ponytail, put on a gilded wreath, then donned my best bee-waisted cream-colored dress with its wide ruffled skirt and stiff bodice.

After the meal, Father's cupbearer carried around the point-ended pourer of white alabaster, filling each flagon. Minstrel Ialemon struck up triumphal chords on his kithara and chanted the tale of victory. My mother's father King Nomion of Miletos and her brothers had joined Father and Telephos in driving out the last of the Achaian raiders.

Firelight flickered on Father's craggy face and on Mother's soft white hair. As Father chanted, I thought of Helenos, revisiting my long-ago dreams about how we would share something like this one day. Then, the rugged face, booming voice, and tall, muscular, vibrant body of Hektôr eclipsed the slender image of his brother in my mind, and my cheeks burned.

"Never again." Father's words brought me back to where I was. "Trojan allies are not to be interfered with! I was in Teuthrania when Hektôr arrived. Truly, he is one of the best warriors, ever! He'll see that neither Tlepolemos nor Althaimenes will dare attack ever again." He glanced at Mother. "Fact is, Priam has long coveted Rhodes. Now the Fates are on his side against those upstarts." He shared a tender look with my mother, and then turned to me. "Next year, Daughter, I will invite bride-gifts for you. Nothing has come on behalf of Helenos, so I am not obligated. Perhaps we'll consider Eurypylos of Thrakia for you."

I winced and my mother touched my suddenly ice-cold hand. "Rest easy, Drommie, we will not force you. Nothing is decided yet."

She gave Father a warning look.

* * * *

One evening, during a visit by the Hittite Ambassador, my ears pricked and I spurred myself to pay attention to the topic of new treaties in our region. As a future Princess of Troia, it was vital that I grasped the historical and political aspects of our world. Hattusilis the Third, had just taken over the Hittite throne, and was forging alliances with the neighboring kingdoms and us. Ten years ago, his brother King Muwatallis had battled Ramses the Second of Egypt over control of Syria. Priam and Hektôr had fought there alongside the Hittites. It was the largest chariot-battle ever fought, with five-thousand chariots, and the exquisitely trained, giant-sized battle-horses brought by the Trojans had tipped the odds in favor of the Hittites.

The Hittites were vital allies, our source for tools and weapons made of iron. They kept the process of how they worked the metal, secret, yet of late, as their loosely federated empire strained under constant attacks by the Thrakians, Egyptians and Assyrians, some of their smiths migrated to serve customers elsewhere.

Would the past continue into the future?

[1] The Apple of Hesperides: Gaia, or Mother Earth, presented a tree bearing golden apples to Zeus and Hera on their wedding day. Guarded by Ladon, a serpent who never slept, the apple tree was in the garden of the *Hesperides*, daughters of the Evening Star. As time passed, these golden apples spawned many tales of love, bribery and temptation, from the abduction of Helen of Troy, to the defeat and marriage of Atlanta, to the apple that Adam and Eve munched on in Paradise, and consequently, were thrown out of there. The sexual and romantic connotations of the apple might be the powerful reasons of why apples were served as dessert at the end of the meal. They not only tasted heavenly and were salubrious, but also were regarded as a transitional aphrodisiac for the pleasures that followed.

Chapter 7: The Three Kings

Mopping the sweat off my brow with a cloth, I left the loom and stepped out onto the balcony. The room was too hot and my arms ached from long hours at work. I was busy with an embroidered coverlet for my bridal bed, waiting in an uncertain future. As I leaned against the house-wall, the jutting roof shaded me from the late morning sun.

My gaze shifted to the fresco running along the outside of the building, bright with red lilies and blue flying birds. The border was a design of black swastikas [1] sacred to Troia. My father's father, Lykos, had this done to commemorate his entering the Confederation of Assuwa and Arzawa as an ally of Troia.

Troia!

I winced as Hektôr's vigorous image flooded my mind, he who would be king over Helenos and me. Often he entered my dreams, doing the things couples did during festivals celebrating fertility—but with *me,* and oh, with such sweet abandon! I woke up from these dreams torn between delight and guilt. I had heard nothing of Hektôr's impending marriage to Princess Sigeia, though they said she was living with him in his chambers at the palace. A sharp stab to my heart made me wince. Jealousy? Certainly not!

Envy…perhaps. But why?

I loved Helenos and waited for him…did I not?

"Drommie!" My mother came onto the balcony, her expression solemn. "News is here from Priam."

"About Helenos?" My heart gave a thump.

"I only know Hektôr's bringing an important document. We have nothing new about Helenos."

I cringed. I did not want to set eyes upon Hektôr, fearful of something within myself. "I won't be here; besides, he's to see Father, not me. I'll be in the town of Chryse."

"You must not insult Priam's heir." Her mouth hardened.

I moved toward the workroom. "Surely he will understand my seeking an oracle."

Having decided to ask the oracle about my and Helenos' future, I felt a renewed sense of purpose. In my room, I changed into a knee-length, full-skirted driving dress. I then went out and ordered Iris harnessed to my chariot.

When it was readied, I climbed in and took the reins. Driving at a brisk trot, I wondered why Hektôr, and not Helenos, was coming. Yes, indeed, I *needed* an oracle.

When I reined in short of the sacred precinct, my eyes took in the shrine with its backdrop of rich yellow fields. The sound of threshing was in the air as humble folk, wielding wooden pitchforks, went about their work. Field mice, sacred to the god, had not despoiled this year's harvest. Thank you, my Goddess.

Leaving Iris and the vehicle in charge of a stableman, I went to the squat red-stone altar set between two astral columns. I glanced up, lifting my arms in respect to the dove atop one, and an eagle carved on top of the other. They seemed to float, gold against the clear blue sky. I took from the front of my dress a lock of hair I had cut while dressing, and laid it on the altar.

Astynome, followed by her servant, came running, flinging herself into my embrace. "Why are you here? Isn't Hektôr just now in Thébé?"

"I need an oracle."

Astynome backed away. "Ah, of course," she laughed knowingly, "Hektôr or Helenos, that's the question!"

"Hektôr *or* Helenos? Humph! You are being frivolous! The question is about Helenos and Helenos *only!*"

She winked, "Perhaps I know something you don't know."

Frowning, I grumbled, "I'm not in the mood for silly games."

She winked. "Sure, sure. By the way, I already have my own answer about marrying Presbon, your brother. However, it is vague. Says I will have more than one love. So much for your brother being the sole lord of my heart!"

We turned toward the Speaking Oak but were interrupted by a hurrying woman, "Achaian ships are entering the bay!"

Astynome shrugged. "More pilgrims. You will stay over, of course, Drommie. Your oracle will not be ready until tomorrow, now."

She led the way into the house and the room we shared whenever I spent the night here.

Astynome was perfect hostess with her father Chryse when the guests came from their ablutions. Bathed and freshly dressed, the four men looked appreciatively at the fat calf roasting over the firepit. One of the men, red-blond, freckled, big and commanding, strode in as though he owned the sacred precinct, his purple cloak whipping around his ankles. Rawboned and hawk-nosed, clean-shaven, dressed in gold finery, he lifted a muscular arm in salute to his hosts. Golden spirals encircling his biceps shone in the glancing light. I noticed the greaves about his legs, fastened with ankle-clasps of silver and gold. Even though this was an Apollonian shrine and thus a sanctuary, he carried a sword. That sword, studded with bosses of gold and boasting a silver scabbard with a chain of gold securing it to his wide belt, added to his air of unbridled menace.

The second man was shorter, fleshier; his shoulder-length hair was similarly red, his sunburned, blue-eyed face equally freckled, deeply lined. He too was clean-shaven, bejeweled, richly attired and armed, his purple cloak ankle-length. It was easy to see they were brothers.

Their companion was short, wiry-limbed, and burly. He wore a plain brown leather vest over a cloth tunic roped at the waist, and leggings with threadbare sandals. His manner was courteous, but his green eyes carried icy glints of speculation as he surveyed the premises, and he was darker than the other two.

The fourth man, seeming as if he could barely endure the presence of his three companions, was the youngest, curly dark-haired, tall and slim, with big, black-brown eyes. He was quite handsome, clad in a thigh-length belted tunic of white linen, green cloak, and gem-studded, high-knotted sandals that contrasted the rest of his plainer attire. He wore a dagger and leather wristbands. As he surveyed the premises, his expression remained detached.

Once they were seated, and small tables rolled out to the chair of each, Chryses introduced them. "Agamemnon, High King of Mykene, and his brother, King Meneláos of Sparta." The Priest paused, cleared his throat, adding, "Their friends, Odysseus Laertides, King of Ithaka, and Prince Akamas, son of Theseus of Athens. We are honored that such distinguished men seek oracle at our shrine."

Though surprised to meet Agamemnon and Meneláos in the flesh, I kept my expression blank. Men of wide renown, they did not bother to cloak their warlike nature. However, Odysseus of Ithaka, referred to as King of Goats, was a different matter and more dangerous than his companions, for he was full of hidden layers.

Akamas was the one who intrigued and excited me. Son of the legendary Theseus! Theseus, who beat the Minotaur at his own deadly game, and who, among his countless deeds of valor, showed kindness to the blind Oedipus, at Kolonos. Akamas was his son by Phaedra, the Kretan Princess who had fallen in love with his older son, Hippolytos, born to his first wife, Antiope, Queen of the Kolchian Amazons. My namesake, Ãndrõmakhê, had been their queen before Antiope. Later in life, Theseus had fallen to foulplay, was exiled and then on the island of Skyros, King Lykomedes had killed him.

Astynome mixed wine and filled their cups while servants served the food. Wrapping a bit of marrow in sesame bread, I ate it delicately with an onion. Through lowered eyelashes, I watched the two brothers gnaw their fleshy ribs of beef, and observed the glint of lust in Agamemnon's eyes as he fixed them on slender Astynome. When she filled his cup he put a large hand over her dainty one, but she ignored it and moved on. Agamemnon's eyes followed her slim form, and I had the horrific notion that he had marked her as his own.

Odysseus spoke, "Treacherous rocks lie under your waters, Priest! Your winds brought us here, though we had set sail for Trojan Ilion."

Treacherous. Treachery. Sailing to Trojan Ilion.

It had begun!

Dread ran sharp knives down my back, and the opal burned upon my skin; but I remained calm, seeming impervious to what was implied with this revelation. I knew that Agamemnon should not be taken lightly as an enemy. King Aegistos, who took possession of the throne of Mykene and ruled jointly with his father, Thyestes, had murdered his father Atros. During this period, Agamemnon and Meneláos had found refuge with Tyndaros, King of Sparta. There they took to wife Tyndaros' twin daughters, Klytemnestra—widowed by Agamemnon's hand—and Helen. Then Agamemnon, with Meneláos' assistance, recovered his father's kingdom. He extended his dominion by bloody conquest and became the most powerful force in Achaia. However, Agamemnon's family history, dating to legendary King Pelops, was marred by incest, murder, treachery, and outright cannibalism.

Meneláos dropped his gnawed-down bone and wiped his battle-scarred fingers on a hunk of freshly baked sesame-bread. "Our ancestor Pelops was once master of Troia, before he crossed over to Achaia. I would visit the city now, since my beloved wife Helen has seen fit to stay with Queen Hekabe overlong."

"Perhaps you will direct us," Agamemnon said to Chryses. "I have an account to settle with Priam. His defiance is intolerable. He has broken his treaty with Herakles, who set him on his father's throne as vassal. Herakles only spared Troia because of Priam's sworn allegiance to Telamon. Hesione came as a pledge of faith."

"Pay heed to what I say: *I am not a party to any of this,"* Chryses declared sternly. "And I prefer to stay that way. Consider that Priam has strong alliances eastward, including the Hittites. In addition, his half-brother Tithonos is husband to Kissia of eastern Ethiopia, and rules from

Susa. And his wife Hekabe harkens to the Amazons at Kolchis, the land of the Golden Fleece, on the Black Sea."

"No, no, Hekabe is pure Thrakian, daughter of Dymas," Meneláos interrupted him curtly.

"And her mother is daughter of the Rivergod Sangarios, Sangarios being the principal river of Phrygia," Odysseus added to the argument.

Chryses spoke wryly, "Either way, King Priam is not someone to be antagonized, my Achaian friends."

Agamemnon had flushed a deep red. Drawing in a deep breath, he opened his mouth, but Odysseus silenced him with a dark look of warning. "We are here only to escort Queen Helen back home."

"Our young daughter Hermione needs her mother," Meneláos added equitably. "We shall continue north after the oracle speaks. Our admiral should be here in a day or so."

Agamemnon took a long pull of his wine and glared. "We leave in three days, Akhilles here or not. He might stop in Lesbos forever, lost in dancing women and wine."

Akhilles! That blond young warrior in the grove. And still no word of Kiron's fate in his hands....

"Akhilles gave me his promise," Odysseus said to Agamemnon, "I know he will join us. Besides, it is ordained, the oracle does not lie."

Akamas, silent all this time, shrugged. "Be warned, Agamemnon. Akhilles *is* a godling, not to be manipulated by the likes of you."

Raising clenched fists, Agamemnon rose from his seat as if to pummel him, but Odysseus pushed him back.

I found it noteworthy that the King of Kings would pay heed to the King of Goats.

It was late before I could escape the disconcerting table with Astynome. We climbed outside stairs to the rooftop, where pale roses were opening to the moonlight and perfuming the air from pots along the perimeter. The air vibrated to the song of a nightingale.

"Father says Agamemnon spoke for me on behalf of a cousin, named Aigisthos," Astynome began. "He plans a kingdom in Asia for this Aigisthos. But I love your brother, Drommie, and don't want to marry anyone but Presbon."

"Then don't accept this suit!"

Astynome looked crestfallen. "I fear Father considers Aigisthos a better match...for his own, greater purposes." She sighed. "He is a good father, Ãndrõmakhê, but he is also my master. He can dispose of me as he wishes. Daughters like us don't marry for love, but to do right by our fathers."

I was shocked into silence. Wholeheartedly I wanted her to rebel against accepting anyone but the one she loved, and I too had said so to my own parents, yet...if Father really ordered me to...declaring it was for the greater good....

Trembling, I whispered, "I hate to admit it, but yes, daughters like us marry to seal treaties."

"Well, what did you think of the famous Goat King?" she asked then, and the forced lightness in her tone hurt my ears.

"Seems like a good man," I replied hesitantly, and then the words poured out my mouth, "I know the real reason of why he has joined Agamemnon and his brother on this trip!"

"Yes of course, to implore Helen to return—"

"Not just to implore, Astynome! She will refuse Menelãos, and I understand why. Helen has reached for what you and I are afraid to reach; she has left the husband forced on by her father, for the *husband of her own choice.* She is in love with Alexis just as much as Alexis is with her. I saw it; I was there when he brought her from Sparta. But unfortunately this will lead to all out war."

"Ah, don't fret. Neither Agamemnon nor Menelãos are a match to Troia's power."

"But this will be a war led by *many* kings! I've heard that Helen's past suitors had committed themselves to defend the right of the King who would win her hand in marriage." Ticking off one by one with my fingers, I recited the rollcall of Helen's past suitors: "Odysseus, son of Laertes; Ajax, son of Telamon; Ajax, son of Oilos; Akamas, son of Theseus, Ascalaphos and Ialmenos, both of them sons of Ares, God of War; then Diomedes, son of Tydos; Antilokos, son of Wise Nestor; Agapenor, son of Ancos; Sthenelos, son of Capanos; Amphimachos, son of Cteatos; Thalpos, son of Eurytos; Meges, son of Phylos...."

Early on the following morning the Achaian quartet of kings received an oracle and departed with their retinue, expressions surly, clumping up the gangway so that it swung beneath them.

One more day of waiting, and my own oracle came too, and it was almost the same as that given at my birth: A blessing followed by a tragedy; but after that, *glory.*

* * * *

Hektôr was in conference with Father when I returned home. My heart chimed with guilty joy: Hektôr was still here!

I ran up the path to my favorite spot on Plakos Hill, behind the palace. Sitting on a bench near a grotto from which one of the many streams issued, I dabbed my fingers in the sparkling pool and hoped Hektôr would not leave soon so that I might steal a look at him.

A branch snapped and a hot flush of expectation rose from my neck to face. Clad in an armless white tunic that barely reached his muscular thighs and a leather girdle tight around his waist, Hektôr approached me. He came and sat beside me and I nodded, giving him a smile of courtesy.

He asked, "Did you have a good oracle at Chryse?"

"Yes...a familiar one." What else could I say?

Silence stretched between us, until Hektôr spoke up, "I have come to an agreement with your father. When you are ready for bride-gifts, you will have mine."

I surged to my feet. "What about Helenos? He promised!"

"He dedicated himself to Apollo, at Thymbra, as a healer and seer priest, and intends to stay there. He has no room in his life for a wife." He looked searchingly into my face. "How old are you, Ãndrõmakhê?"

"Almost fifteen."

He looked away, whispering beneath his breath, "Old enough...."

I knew better than ask for what. Biting my lips and tapping my foot, I waited for him to continue.

After a long silence, he faced me fully, and spoke warmly, "You will honor me as my esteemed wife, as Queen of Troia, and in sharing the overlordship of Achaia."

Helenos...dedicated to serve Apollo. So be it!

I pulled my veil around me and stood up. "You honor me, Hektôr, noble son of Great Priam."

I stepped before him down the path, and to my great surprise, there was no sense of loss, but a shining sense of determination: I, Ãndrõmakhê, would change Troia's fate, to the better!

Sun and shadow slanted along the path ahead of us. It was like an omen. Perhaps the marital blessing I had hoped for with Helenos would have brought along that curse. Thus, by accepting Hektôr in his stead, I might be turning the oracle around.

[1] Swastikas illustrated the solar-key pattern.

Chapter 8

Finally, the war came to a decisive end in Teuthrania. King Telephos sent runners to light signals from peak to peak of the mountains in between. He had slain Thersander, son of Polynikes—Antigone's brother Polynikes—and routed new invaders led by that upstart Akhilles, whose fame was growing in leaps and bounds. Tales about Akhilles were colorful; they said he was invincible, moody, exuberant, unforgiving, generous, and trailed by many women who were desperately in love with him. On the brink of victory against Telephos, he had heard of his father's failing health, left everything, and hurried back to his side. Interesting that he would drop Glory, for Father. Therefore, he was a good son. Yet, he was a sacker of peaceful cities, killer of men, and enslaver of women. I made a mental note of the lesson learned: A good son did not necessarily make a good *man*.

* * * *

The clatter of my loom quieted and I sat before it in silence.

Inarticulate thoughts buzzed around in my head, and my senses heightened. This was a strange phenomenon, occurring often lately. If I should let my guard down, I would be smelling blood on the wind instead of grass and flowers, and hear the cries of the dead or displaced, instead of bird songs.

I thought of Hektôr, missing him, his beloved face always in my thoughts, and daily prayers for his good health and long life. I was hoping that my Goddess would watch over him, deflecting the spears, swords and arrows thirsting to take his noble life. Moreover, I feared that Athené would be his downfall. Our wedding day was yet to be set. Nevertheless, I made good use of this time of waiting, schooling myself in matters that would make me a better wife. True, Father had taken the oracle at Chryse for a favorable one. However, I could not forget the talk with Astynome—deeply in love with my brother Presbon, who loved her just as deeply—about daughters like us marrying to seal treaties. And here I was, primped for that very same fate....

Hektôr had just sent me another chest full of betrothal gifts. But his most important gift was the set of clay cuneiform tablets he had brought back from Hattushash, about the Epic of Gilgamesh [1]. I had told him that I was trying to find out more about a distant land called Shardana, and he had promised to help. He had sent these tablets hoping they would do, which they did not. The setting of this epic was ancient Mesopotamia, while Kiron had said Shardana was close to the Pillars of Herakles in the Mediterranean. The script was in an older form of what I knew, and I could not decipher it all. However, I understood enough to appreciate the moral of the story. The great hero Gilgamesh had lived a thousand years before my time, and built the fabulous city of Uruk. During his youth, Gilgamesh had been a cruel oppressor. His people had called out to the sky-god Ani, to deliver them from his bloody rule. In response, Ani created a wild man, Enkidu, out in the forests surrounding Gilgamesh's lands, to challenge him. Yet, in time, Enkidu became Gilgamesh's friend as the King regretted his bad deeds and went with Enkidu on a journey of enlightenment. The twosome lived through exhausting quests, heroic battles with monsters, supernatural beings, and natural forces. From what I could decipher so far, the Epic of Gilgamesh was the story of a man who faced his destiny, and rose to every challenge with courage and determination.

So like my beloved Hektôr....

Now I recalled the day when Priam's herald, Idaios, had brought word of how Agamemnon, Meneláos, and their entourage were ordered out of Troia after seven days of arguing, and sailed home in disgrace. Just as I had expected, Helen had refused to leave with them, further endangering Meneláos' hold on the Spartan throne. It was no secret that the people of Lakedaimon rejected him as king. Helen was due to sail for Sparta next spring, and present her people with their new lord Alexander Paris Priamides.

Priam had summoned my father and told him that the new Trojan fleet would soon be loaded and ready to sail. As Father recounted to us later, midst their talk word came that King Telephos had been grievously injured by Akhilles, and all this time the wound had refused to heal. Telephos then had sailed to Delphi seeking a cure, and the oracle determined the wound could only be healed by rust from the sword that caused it. This meant Telephos had to find Akhilles and entreat him for the cure.

"Telephos is likely entering the port of Aulis now," the messenger had concluded, "where Achaian and Danaan leaders are camped."

Listening to these things in the safety of my father's palace, the uneasiness that had nagged me ever since meeting Agamemnon and Meneláos, sons of Atros, at the shrine at Chryse, had returned full force. Yes, without a doubt, there had been great danger foretold in the overt sureness of those two brothers.

Leaving the workroom, I went downstairs, in search of my mother. I found her in the kitchens, busy as always, not only supervising but also performing many of the chores herself.

"Do you think Lanassa will still marry Andros even if Telephos doesn't recover?" I asked her.

She set a bronze kettle on firedogs to melt fat. "Of course, dear." She rubbed sand on the spit to clear it of burned grease.

I laid out ivory spoons on the firewall and began wiping at a tarnished spot on a silver ladle.

My mother added, "Telephos will have recovered by then."

"But should he trust an Achaian seer?"

"Everybody knows the cause is also the cure, Drommie." She bent to poke at the sizzling fat with a large earthenware spoon.

Andros and Presbon came in, laughing at a private joke.

"I have the heifer ready for sacrifice," Presbon announced. "Good, I see you've already cleansed the spit."

That evening, a wandering bard arrived with news of yet more bloodshed, from Phrygia to Karia and Lykia. The killings, rape and pillage continued as hit and run skirmishes. It was blamed on Helen, the bard reported, because the Pelasgians were demanding her speedy return with Alexis, and the ousting of Meneláos. Priam had ordered all land and sea routes under his control tightened. No trade was exchanged between Achaian merchants and those of Kolchis and Tauris in the east. Their contact was also virtually cut off with peoples of the Herkynian forest northwest of the Ister River. Troia's Customs Patrol at the Strait of Dardanos set prices higher, defying even the formerly friendly merchant-princes of Orkomenos.

On the next day came swift-footed Polites, son of Priam, with urgent demands from Priam. Agamemnon's fleet was outgrowing Priam's, which was still at anchor in the Lyrnessos yards. Every day new Achaian chiefs arrived at the Achaian port of Aulis, honoring the Alliance they had agreed to when Meneláos had wed Helen. Thus, Troia needed ever more seafaring vessels, cattle, and timber.

Then, only one week later, Polites returned with more news that struck horror, anger, and dread throughout the region:

Full-fledged invasion! Merciless slaughter!

Where the Skamander emptied winter torrents and summer eddies into the Strait, and along the Aegean coast southwestward, gratings of war sawed the lavender air. Hitherto unknown Achaian dialects muttered against ears of the Coast Patrol when they investigated. They were cut down under arrows from every ship that sailed into the narrows. Rowers defied wind and tide as the ships passed swiftly, their sides hung with round war-shields.

After this, the vast Trojan Plain echoed ceaselessly to the trample of horses, rumble of hostile chariots, and thudding feet of troops. The grunting of dying men and screams of wounded horses blended with the stench of putrefying flesh.

Akhilles, back from Thessaly and in the thick of battle, also attacked the southern cities of Cymae, Phocaea, Smyrna, Clazomenae, and Colophon, making off with slaves, treasure, horses, and cattle. To steal horses was even more important than cattle, for the Achaians lacked horses. What they had were mostly ponies, nothing like the swift, tall, strong-boned stock raised and provided to their allies by Priam and Hektôr.

Often I deserted my loom and sneaked out to practice with my dagger and the leather-bound wooden shield I had pilfered from my brothers' stash. Then I laid down more flowers and filled the oil lamp that I kept burning at my small altar to the Great Kind Mother.

Polites brought more news: Cured by Akhilles, Telephos had been forced aboard Akhilles' ship to Troia, and sacrificed within sight of Troia as an offering to Poseidon for safe passage into the turbulent Strait of Dardanos!

Hektôr led a deftly executed bloody counterattack that forced the invaders back into their ships.

* * * *

As another summer progressed through harvest, minstrels reported that the enemy, pressed for supplies, had dispersed. Some had settled to farming the Chersonesos region of Thrakia. King Polymestor, husband of Priam's daughter Ilione, had ignored this occupation of his land, as if to spite his wife's father. Other hordes of Achaian and Danaan raiders stalked mountains and rivers, seizing sheep and cattle. Priam sent his prize herd of Laomedon Whites to graze near Alybe under charge of his concubine's son, Demokoon.

During the winter, minstrels sang of Priam and Hekabe's daughter Kreusa, and her marriage with Aeneas, Prince of Dardania, and some said plotter for the Trojan throne.

Laodike, another daughter of Priam, renowned for her doe-eyed, full-figured beauty, was married to Helikaon, Antenor's son.

Long ago, I had sent inquiries to Krete seeking news of Kiron, and finally replies came: Indeed his ship had been rocked by storms, and among those lost at sea, was Kiron. Now I knew for certain that Akhilles had found him. However, why had he broken his promise of returning him to me? By all accounts and there were plenty of those, Akhilles was a man of his word. Thus, the only conclusion I could draw was that Kiron had died before he could be released.

I mourned for my old teacher. Helped by my brother Presbon, I built a small tumulus in the garden near the cottage he had lived in, and added a stone carved with his name and deeds.

* * * *

On a warm, early-spring day two years after Alexis brought Helen to Troia, I was sitting with my spinning beside the pool. Geese hissed around me as I made a mental inventory of all the fine cloth I had made and stored in my marriage-chest. I was twirling my spindle and watching the bobbin rise when I heard a chariot rattle into the outer courtyard and stop. Putting aside the tufted spindle as my father's boots thudded toward me, I realized it was followed by a heavier tread.

I looked up, and Hektôr stood beside Father.

Ah, at last!

Hektôr, green eyes sparkling, was magnificent in rich clothing, gold ornamenting on chest and arms. I could scarcely hear my father speak, for the dazzle of this man.

"We welcome Hektôr, who is here to claim you, Ãndrõmakhê. His brother Deiphobos will stand with him."

I rose unsteadily, and then lifted my head high. "I welcome you with pleasure, Prince Hektôr."

Father took my hand and placed it in that of Hektôr. "There is a brief spell of peace now in the region, and it is expedient to seal my treaty with Priam."

"The war has ended?" I drew back my hand.

Father smiled with satisfaction. "Hektôr tells me that the invaders' ships are almost empty of men."

Hektôr leaned forward and touched a stray curl on my forehead. His touch sent quivers through me. "Beautiful Ãndrõmakhê, I could have no greater honor than you, for my wife and queen."

In my room that night, I leaned against one of my bed's four tall posts, protectors of my childhood, guarding the four directions of wind and seasons. In the light of the small lamp, the tiny blue faience beads set into their ivory finials glinted.

For only a few more nights....

My thoughts switched to Helenos. Hektôr had told me of his dedication to Thymbra. Now, that time back in Sipylos, along Lake Salai, felt like a dream, a dream that had catapulted me from childhood to the border of womanhood. Joy spread through my veins. The Goddess had paved my way to the man I truly loved, and that man was Hektôr. Yes, oh yes, I loved Hektôr.

Then, pride raised its head. To be Hektôr's wife and Queen of Troia, and perhaps save the House of Priam, was worth any sacrifice. Hektôr's eyes had been sparkling with affection when he looked at me today. Love might grow in his heart as well? I was young, and though skilled at cloth-spinning, writing, estate management, and even swordplay, there was much that I lacked. I knew duty, but nothing of sensuality, neither was I as beautiful and voluptuous as Helen, or from what was rumored, as his concubine, Sigeia, sister of King Polymestor.

Moving to the window, I tilted my head backwards, and gazed up at the dark sky, invoking the Great Kind Goddess for guidance. Thoughts formed in my mind: Beauty was heaven's gift, few could boast of it, and the heart of a good man like Hektôr, would not be won by beauty, but by character, and by being useful to him! I had to continue to learn everything that was important to him, be vigilant in all matters pertinent, and be wise enough to give counsel if needed—as did my mother with my father.

Once again, I reviewed what I had learned of the complicated origins of Hektôr's realm: King Ilos had founded Troia upon the visible remnants of an ancient city, magnificent in the days of old, and named the new city Ilion, after himself. Ilos was son of Tros, and grandson of Eriktonios, a son of Hephaistos, God of Fire. Eriktonios, a blond and blue-eyed giant who had hailed in from Keltia, with the protection of the goddess Pallas Athené, became King of Athens. Kiron believed that this Eriktonios, Erik for short, had been a godlike king not from Keltia, but from around the Baltic Sea, and treaded down the Amber Road. As King of Athens, Erik had celebrated the Panathenéan festival in honor of Athené. Erik was the first man putting horses to chariot, cultivating the earth with plough, and teaching people to use silver, which was a more important metal than gold.

When Erik's son Tros—also a blond giant—had grown, he moved on to rule Dardania, an ancient city on Mount Ida, near Troia. Dardania was founded by Dardanos, which meant 'burner up'. Dardanos came to our shores from Makedonia.

When Ilos, son of Tros, yet another blond giant, came of age, the King of Phrygia awarded him fifty youths and maidens as a wrestling prize. Further, as advised by an oracle, the king gave him a spotted cow, told him to let the cow roam and then found a new city where it should first lie down. The cow chose the Hill of Ate, so named for the old Anatolian Goddess. Here Ilos marked out the boundaries of Ilion. Ilos then prayed to Zeus for a sign and saw the Palladium, a black wooden statue of Goddess Athené, drop from heaven and land in front of his tent. However, he was blinded for the impiety of directly looking at the image. He regained his sight after making offerings to Athené. He raised a temple in her glory atop the hill of the older goddess, Ate. Time passed, Ilos preferred his new city to Dardania, and left his brother Assarakos to rule Dardania.

Laomedon, father of Priam, succeeded Ilios, and Troia became the dominant of the two cities because it controlled the trade route of the Hellespont.

And so went the illustrious lineage of my husband-to-be, Hektôr Priamides, renowned Tamer of Horses. Being the great-great-grandson of the blond giant King Erik, he who first put horses to chariot and taught his people how to work the plough and silver, no wonder Hektôr had carried on his trait to handle horses!

Presently, my gaze fastened upon a fast-moving cloud, I swore that I would never pit my own pride against my husband's, and would even love his mistresses for his sake. Thus, by being a congenial and unfailingly loyal companion, I would draw him to me. Further, I would never fail in taking care of his beloved horses, those superb creatures that faithfully drew his chariot, and feed them solicitously sweet grain and wine.

In the end, constancy and trueheartedness might bring about the kind of love that still warmed my parents' marriage bed....

* * * *

[1] Gilgamesh: There was a real Gilgamesh, a king who ruled some 2700 years before Christ lived and the Romans consolidated their vast empire. The character and exploits of this king were preserved in the form of stories that circulated for millennia after his death.

PART II: The BLESSING

Chapter 9

On my last day in my father's palace, I stood by the window, my posture straight. Soon I would be leaving my home behind. My gaze shifted to the harbor where tall masts fringed the farthest olive treetops shimmering silvery in the sun. Those masts tilted gently in the brilliant light, beckoning me to dare venture into the unknown—as they had done so from the earliest days of my childhood....

Suddenly shouts and singing rose from beyond the courtyard gate. The citizens were already out celebrating my marriage, announced by a red leather phallus attached to the heavy, nail-studded door.

I smiled. All this excitement, because of me!

My mother entered, motioning to me. "Come to your loom now, daughter, I want Hektôr's brother to witness your good work."

I followed her to the room where we had shared so many years companionably spinning and talking, sat at my loom, and began tying off the last row of cloth.

Footsteps came along the gallery and tall, robust, blond and red-cheeked Deiphobos stood in the doorway. He smiled as his deep voice boomed, "Is there a daughter preparing for her marriage here?"

"There is indeed," my mother replied, following the ritual.

"Hektôr Priamides asks that Ãndrõmakhê Êetiônis marry him on this fine day." He backed away with a huge grin and a deep bow.

I stood up, legs weak. The inevitability flooded me with shock. The long expected, was suddenly unexpected.

Mother continued the ritual, "My beloved daughter, now is the time to go into your own home. Prepare yourself."

Deiphobos bowed again and moved away. Astynome entered and unpegged my cloth, folding it for packing away.

Back in my room, I stood frozen at the threshold, looked around, observing that the rest of my familiar things were already removed: my treasure of clay tablets, reed and ivory styluses, handsomely carved cedar clothes-chest, had all been loaded on the ship, leaving a bare oblong under the empty clothes-rail. The enormous tapestry my mother had created with her adept hands was down from the wall as well.

A sharp knot formed in my throat at sight of the bridal gown of red Egyptian linen lying across the bed, crusted over with intricate gold and silver embroidery, a golden tiara, and a diaphanous white veil.

My mother came with Althaia, helped me sponge myself with warm water, then unstoppered jars of myrrh and violets, smoothing scent over my skin. Astynome slid the dress over my head and adjusted the stiffly embroidered apron. Mother tinted my bare nipples with silver. When I sat down, faint with insecurity, my mother brushed out my bridal hair, plaited it into long slender tendrils, and fastened the golden tiara around my head, enhancing it with dangling earrings made of golden spirals. She worked fast, and quietly, her lips trembling, tears shining in her eyes like pearls. She kept them from pouring down her cheeks, and when my own eyes welled up, I did the same.

Coming out onto the gallery all decked out in bridal splendor, I smelled the heady aroma of beef and wine that rose from where my brothers tended the herbed roasts, and mixed wine for the impromptu banquet. Unlike my mother, they were laughing and joking raucously. Nevertheless, I knew them all too well, and approved of the lighthearted facade they were presenting to the world.

Then breath caught in my throat. Hektôr was standing in a light-beam from the clerestory, resplendent in a yellow doublet and white ankle-length trousers embroidered with gold. His brown-blond hair was dressed in Trojan moon-horns, and he was beardless. Beside him were my solemn-faced father, and Deiphobos of the twinkling eyes. As I slowly descended the semi-circular stone steps to the Great Hall, Hektôr's proud green eyes washed over me appraisingly, so that my cheeks burned. What a wonder that this splendid man would be my husband! Then I pinched myself inwardly, lest I lose sight of why this was happening. Hektôr was taking me to wife only to seal the treaty between our respective fathers, and in his brother Helenos's stead, for Helenos had chosen a different path. Unlike that of Alexis and Helen, our union was rooted not in idyllic love, but in filial duty.

I held my head high. I was sworn to be a loving and loyal wife, and would give him no cause for regret.

My father's voice spoke ritual words in his priestly role. "Have you made a firm choice, my daughter?"

"I freely marry while the moon is new," I gave the required answer. I glanced at my mother who, just down the steps, moved up to her place beside her husband. It was only now that I noticed the Megaron packed with our neighboring friends as well as all the members of our household and farms.

Mother took my right hand, Father took Hektôr's, and they joined our two hands together and then bound them with a silken cord.

Father concluded the blessing: "In the name of Immortal Father, I bless this bride and this groom. May Destiny give them the full joys of peace and happiness in this life, and through all ages to come!"

He released us lingeringly, a muscle erratically jumping on his clenched jaw. Hektôr and I knelt, touching his knees with our hands. Deiphobos offered wreaths and my mother crowned me with white peonies, Hektôr with pink.

Seated at last, we waited while servants thrust flaring torches into polished bronze sconces attached to columns. Father moved among guests, of which more were streaming in. I looked at him and saw a sun-toasted, burly warrior clad in a short purple mantle and gold-belted long white robe, smiling, proud of the distinguished marriage of his daughter. Then the clothing worn by people from many places dazzled my eyes. The oil-soft gleam of Egyptian cottons and the muted tints of Milesian wools and brocades filled the hall with color and form. Bone-stiffened bodices lifted breasts high, girdles with stiff aprons of fur and gold leaf emphasized women's generous hips, hips that signaled fitness to bear strapping children. Not for the first time I worried about mine, slim like a boy's upon too long legs. Fire reflected from torches shone on the men's tubular gold or silver circlets confining their hair. Their bare torsos were draped with necklaces of rare gems and metals. Lights mirrored, thread by thread, down their richly embroidered kilts.

Then it was time to share the love potion and end the feasting. Astynome, my friend and sister of my heart, brought the cup, and held it as Deiphobos filled it with undiluted wine mixed with honey. Hektôr took one handle, I took the other, and together we drained the cup.

It was near midnight when my father, at feast's end, lit a huge torch from the family hearth-fire and gave it to Hektôr.

"My life and this fire burn for my wife and our hearth," Hektôr responded to Father's prompting, and then handed it to Deiphobos for safety during the long journey northward, which would require the rest of this night and a day.

As we left the hall, care was taken to avoid an ill-omened stumble at the threshold. Young men ran cheering alongside Hektôr, while teasing girls accompanied me during the long procession to the harbor brilliantly lit by countless torches.

Aboard ship, we stood at the rail, side by side, for last farewells. Our union had happened in haste, and my parents were not able to accompany us to Troia. However, they promised to visit at the first opportunity, and spared four of my brothers to accompany me.

Realizing that my protected youth was forever gone, I felt a great, cloying sadness overcome me. Yet once again, I held back tears, held my head high, and surely did my parents proud.

The huge white sails bellied; the vessel weaved and creaked, and its ropes began to sing. As my parents, remaining brothers, including Leukon the toddler, and Nurse Mykale, Astynome, our guests, slaves, and citizens broke out in song to wish me happiness in my new life, the anchor lifted, and our ship moved slowly out into the starlit bay.

Hektôr kissed me then, sweetly on the lips. His mouth so warm, and the pressure so light. His eyes shone with what I hoped were desire, but he drew back, lifting my hand to his lips.

"Three days. And then we belong to each other." He strode away.

Shuddering with the fear I hated to admit, I thought of the Trojan requirement for royal brides: the Skamander River must be first to taste my virgin blood.

Then the winds and tides, all in auspicious concert, began sailing me to a glorious future. Soon I would see the murmuring Skamander and the plains of Troia, as my own....

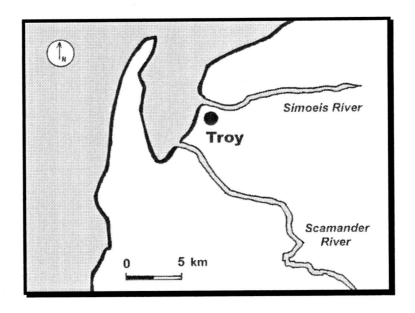

Chapter 10

Riding fast across the green Plain as the gems on our chariot horses' bridle glittered in the sun and the bells on their bridles rang, I saw Troia's towers rise like fists doubled on the high-prowed rock. The tan caravan road snaked ahead us, fording the Skamandrios River and bordering the battlemented walls. These were made even more impressive by coating the brick ribbon atop the stone walls with a varnish containing metal flakes that glowed in the sun like fire. They were sixteen feet-thick, strong, masculine—so like Hektôr.

My heart thumped joyfully, and I breathed in the salty breeze of the sea. I was approaching Troia not as a visitor, but as part of its very fabric. Troia, a diadem perched about hundred-and-twenty feet above the Plain, was magnificent with broad, paved streets, white mansions on terraces with courtyards, a town hall, an auditorium, and buildings for storage and commerce. Athené's temple sat on its peak, near Priam's Palace, visible from a great distance.

The outside walls encompassing the Lower City were fortified with a horseshoe-shaped ditch cut about fifteen feet wide and twelve feet deep, hewn into limestone bedrock, full of sharpened stakes to break chariots and impale invaders. This outer wall was eighty feet high, and twenty feet wide at the top, paved with flagstones. The battlemented walls furnished with towers, two or three-stories high, communicated with each other by arched doorways. These towers were at distances, on the average, of the cast of a javelin, but varying according to the exposure of each part of the wall. Hundreds of archers were on constant lookout among the battlements. Machicolations, those projecting galleries around the outer and inner citadels, supported by corbelled arches, contained openings in the floor to throw stones and boiling liquids on the attackers.

Discreetly placed sally ports, hard to locate from outside and easily defended from within, allowed scouts to survey the surrounding area during a siege.

Travelers raved that Troia was an acropolis unparalleled in the world, unmatched by the Hittites and Egyptians. Scattered upon the walls sat statues of round-eyed owls, one of Athené's symbols. There were springs and wells inside; also, an underground cistern transmitting water with a three-hundred foot long canal, giving Troia enough to drink and feed gardens and orchards. Beyond the outer walls stretched a cleared wide area, making a sneak attack on the city impossible. It had five entrance gates, the Antenorian, Dardanian, Ilian, Skaian, and Thymbran, topped by watchtowers, embellished with carvings and statues of Zeus, Poseidon, Apollo, Athené, Artemis and Hermes. Tens of thousands of men and women lived and traded in the city, outside its walls and in nearby villages. Fertile fields, vineyards, pasturage, orchards, textile-mills, potteries, metalworkers, scribes and artisans kept the city afloat. Despite continuous Achaian attacks and with victory swaying back and forth, Troia held on to its majesty.

At once, a dark shadow fluttered above my head and I looked up. It was a golden eagle, flying with a great swoop of wings from my left side toward Troia.

An omen!

My trembling hands gripped the curved wood rail before me. Our purple-draped bronze chariot, drawn by Hektôr's favorite stallions, Xanthos and Aithos, bumped and rumbled, threateningly churning my insides. Deiphobos followed us with the shielded torch, in his own chariot. Iris, carrying two large leather packs of my most personal items, trotted next to him. Behind them, my four treasure-wagons, canvassed over and flanked by four of my brothers, lumbered to the pull of bullocks. Two-thousand head of cattle was part of my dowry as well.

They were brought in separately, under heavy guard. To avoid bandits, they took an intricate, secret land route.

Next to me, Hektôr's sun-darkened hands switched fluidly between reins and rail. Hektôr! My heart contracted anew in my breast. How I loved him, wanted to take care of him, and looked forward to our future....Helenos came unbidden into my thoughts. What kind of a future would I have had with him? A redundant ache touched my heart. Then it was replaced by determination. I would strive to change Troia's destiny to the better. I should never forget that!

Now a dark blue strip of water beyond Troia came into view. Black hulks that were double or three-masted, boom-rigged enemy ships with the mystic Eye on both sides of the high-curved prow, hunkered there like leeches. Because of the growing danger they posed, we had disembarked before dawn, at the little town of Larissa, preparing to complete our journey over land.

The warm late afternoon wind whipped my goldthread veil against my face. The chariot slung out from the last clump of oaks, slowed for one more hillock. We reached the Skamander Ford and I drew in a sharp breath. Was it here I must shed my first blood?

I glanced aside at Hektôr; he turned his face to me and blew a kiss as people began pouring in from the gates. The wheels roiled through the shallow sacred river of yellow clay hue, and he drew rein near the rough-hewn foundation stones of the outer wall. Deiphobos drew up and dismounted, continuing to shield the hearth-fire torch.

The ornamental timber and bronze gates, folded back on either side against the inside wall, were beamed with great logs. On each side of the gates, gigantic stone statues of Athené and Apollo stood guard.

As we approached the main gate, men and women, old and young, spilled out, ran down the ramp, surrounding us, tossing flowers. The thrum and lilt of lyres and whistle of flutes colored the chanting voices raised in bridal paeans. It seemed that all citizens of the realm were here, their laughing faces lining the upward-curving broad street from the Gate to Pergama, the summit citadel of Troia.

Hektôr sprang down, lifted me to the pavement and led me to the gate where his parents, resplendent in purple and gold, waited. As we stepped onto the ramp, my eyes lifted to the enormous lintel that I knew was the sarcophagus of Ilos, Founder of the city. On the pylon-towers it joined were carved rampant horses.

Two men of about Hektôr's age, stepped forward, gave a formal bow and introduced themselves as Polydamas and Misenos.

Hektôr whispered in my ear, "My good friends. Polydamas is also my levelheaded second-in-command. He tempers my fire with the cool breeze of his wisdom."

Inside, I noticed that the beams that locked the gates when folded, sported horse-head finials of how Priam had loved, courted and won Hekabe Dymaseis. Everything looked so new today, so different! My gaze searched for familiar faces, and recognized King Anchises, ally-cousin of Priam and father of Prince Aeneas. Antenor was there, and Alexis, Helen, and Priam and Hekabe's daughters Kreusa, Laodike, Kassandra, Polyxena, and others I had met at other times.

All around us, cymbals, lyres, and flutes played, their sweet sounds blending with the clatter of castanets, and clear-voiced girls sang a holy wedding song. Wherever I looked, I saw shining faces.

Now the older women raised a joyful shout, and men sent forth a high-pitched cry, calling on Paian the far-shooter, renown for his lyre, and then praised their godlike Hektôr and his nubile bride.

During the festive banquet in the Great Hall brimming with richly dressed guests, and gold, silver, ivory, and faience trappings, aromas of roasted meats, fruits and honeyed pastries mingled with the scents of myrrh, cassia and frankincense.

When the meal was over, Hektôr strode to the hearth-fire in the center, and lit a fresh torch, offering it for me to hold it with him. From here, we were escorted into a spacious wing of the palace set aside for us. In our own hall, we lit our own hearth-fire, blessing the new home.

Now the singing around us took on a wilder beat.

Hektôr's sisters, among much laughter and jangling of bracelets and earrings, grabbed my arms, rushing me outside to a prepared wagon. As night darkened the sky, we rode through the Dardanian Gate as far as Thymbra, where Queen Hekabe was already waiting. There was a low bank with a small stone platform set into the water.

The girls slowly undressed me according to ritual, handing my wedding finery to a small dark woman, named Thalpia, who carried everything back up into the city. Completely naked, I stepped from the ramp into the chilling river. Waist-deep in the slow-moving ripples, I shivered involuntarily, from its cold as well as dread over what was about to be done to me.

At first, they laved my body with soft, perfumed sponges, calming me so I could recoup my courage. Then the girls pulled me backward, supporting me flat on the rocking waves. Hekabe waded toward me, wielding the sharp ritual knife, its obsidian blade glinting in the pale moonlight. The queen bent over as my trembling legs were pulled aside.

With a wildly racing heart, I opened my eyes wide, invoking the Great Kind Mother as I fixed my gaze upon the shining firmament above.

Just as a shooting star blazed high across the cloudless sky, a quick, sharp pain stabbed from loins to brain.

I bit my lips and tongue, and choked back a scream.

The girls helped me to straighten up and stand on my feet, waiting for my virgin blood to stain the river. It did, in copious red rivulets turning dark as they widened in circles. Suddenly weak all over, I shuddered with the throbbing, fierce pain rising from pelvis to throat, and though I'd have preferred to walk on my own, with dignity, I could not protest when the girls supported me as I left the water.

Queen Hekabe remained by my side, first wrapping a large woolen cloth around me, then keeping me straight with her arm on my waist. She was a tall, brown-haired woman with expressive green eyes, high cheekbones, full mouth, and her body strong and firm despite the many children she had given birth.

Drawing in a shaky breath, I turned back toward the river, and spoke the necessary ritual so that I would soon bear a child:

"O Skamander River, take my virginity!" I glanced at Hekabe, and her smile reassured me that I had done well.

When we were back in the palace, Helen sauntered in and handed me a long veil shimmering with the colors of the rainbow. With Hekabe, she arranged it so that it flowed over my hair and face, and then, smiling, said it was a gift from Aphrodite.

Singing and dancing girls led me to the bridal chamber where Hektôr waited at the door. Hekabe preceded us to unroll the bedding upon the bed frame on the elevated dais, and then retreated.

Thalpia appeared and led me inside, whispering ritual instructions as to the warding-off of evil. As she withdrew, young boys thrust Hektôr into the room. Deiphobos followed, gave Hektôr the key, and went out. I caught sight of Polydamas, introduced as the one whose wisdom cooled Hektôr's fires, flush of face and so drunk that he could barely stand on his feet.

Hektôr slammed the door to the shouting and antiphonal singing of his friends and locked it after himself.

"May fertile Skamander give Prince Hektôr early fatherhood!" young male voices chanted outside.

"Fruit from the glory of this night, the richness of love from bridal tears!" the girls shouted back.

Now it was time—the last moment.

Exhaustion and the continuing sharpness of prickly pains kept me still. I looked into his face as he moved close. I swayed as his eyes blurred; his hands cupped my face, lips came down on mine. I reached up and twined my fingers about his wrists. Then his flesh sweetened against mine. I closed my eyes tightly, yet started to shake, violently, and he clasped his arms about me. With a small sob, I pressed my face against his broad chest and the clean male smell of him was good, soothing, reassuring.

Hektôr held me until I was calmed enough to stand alone. "I will not hurt you, my delicate flower." He paused. "I know your pain, and will not bring evil into our marriage."

At last, the strange numbness left my mind. I realized he was being careful of me, and thus my lingering pain from the deflowering knife, lessened. Joy danced within my soul. I reached up and unfastened his golden brooch so that the fabric glided down to reveal the hard-muscled planes and roundings of his body. What a strong man he was! Despite the fear of what was yet to come, my eyes swept his face, neck, down his chest, and then, as fresh terror engulfed me, further below.

Hektôr moved and unfastened the hook-and-eye closures of my girdle, then released it and my hair. He threaded his fingers through the long strands and set his hand behind my head, gently lifting my face to his. A low, involuntary laughter released itself from my throat, floated like golden bubbles toward the moon. Then his lips took me soaring on a plane of unimagined closeness.

He gave a low moan, and the urge to please him rose high within me. He was my prince, my lord, the owner of my heart. I would perform my duty no matter how wrenching the pain. I would bear him children, the heirs to his noble soul, and when the time came, gladly follow him to the Elysian Fields and beyond.

He began kissing my breasts, pushing down my robe, and I ran my fingers over the ridged muscles on his back.

"Oh wife, my tender wife!" he whispered into my mouth.

I arched to meet him and knew that I had begun to love this man with a womanly intensity that could never end.

Chapter 11

I stretched luxuriously as I opened my eyes. Morning light splintered on the blue-tiled floor and walls frescoed with blue sky and sea, seagulls flying, dolphins leaping, men rowing in boats, nymphs swimming and dancing. The lower part of the wall was entirely a blue-green sea with a silhouette surface that rippled all round the room. The top border of the walls was livened with horizontal ribands of color, red, black and gold, and blue and primrose.

My gaze met Nefru's blue eyes. A black-masked, white bodied, slim cat with black paws and long black tail, brought here from Egypt, Nefru sat perched on a pillowed chair near my side of the bed. Smiling, I reached and gently patted the cat on its elegant head. Slinking forth from the shadows as soon as I had set foot in our bedchamber, Nefru had appointed himself my loyal companion.

The moon had rounded and become Artemis' bow twice since our wedding. My husband and I loved each other deeply, and were aware of, and grateful to, the blessing bestowed upon us by the gods.

Priam ruled from a sprawling palace, on the highest point of his hilltop city. It had a broadly sweeping view all around, and was fronted by marble colonnades and a wide marble porch. In the main building were fifty apartments of polished stone; his sons lived there with their wives, including Hektôr and myself. Priam's daughters and their spouses occupied wings on the other side of the rectangular courtyard filled with exotic trees, flowering plants, statues and a private temple. A two-storied house with one wall attached to the main palace, its own small courtyard, an altar for my Goddess, and a bath-chamber boasting an oval pool, was being built for Hektôr and me. I looked forward to our impending move.

My eyes swept the room. Hmm, my husband was already out this morning, most likely feeding his horses, and together with Polydamas, making a routine inspection of the ramparts and his soldiers. The Achaians, having sent two more emissaries demanding Helen's return, had not yet dared an all-out attack upon the walls. They flexed their muscles and postured to intimidate and wear us out. Hunkered down in tents and shacks visible from every corner of our walls, they waged a war of nerves by pillaging the countryside and fighting us only when we swept down in reprisal. They were sure the hardships of siege would bring internal strife and dissension. Moreover, they were right. Spearheaded by Antenor and Theano, the Council pressed Priam and Alexis to relinquish Helen and her treasure in return for peace. Nevertheless, Priam refused, pointing that Helen was an excuse and not the real cause of the siege. Thus, we had no doubt that deadly fighting would resume.

Meanwhile we newlyweds made the best of this interlude, and I enjoyed getting to know Hektôr better. Though inclined to quiet thought, mystical, he was not. He was a man of compassion, piety, and integrity; he cared deeply about his family, his soldiers, the citizens of Troia, and his horses, those magnificent, intelligent animals that indeed looked like a gift from the gods. He ran a horse-farm in the remote countryside, its perimeter fortified by tall stonewalls and protected by a sturdy contingent of his veteran soldiers. Allowed to retire there with their wives and enough copper and silver to live well, these were fiercely loyal men. The breeding and training of these horses was the closest to Hektôr's heart, he loved every dam, stud, and foal, treating them tenderly yet when needed, with a very firm hand.

We had a favorite place for a stroll, where the Simois River flowed into the Skamander. Hidden behind mossy stones and green shrubs, we made love, and then perched on rocks and discussed various subjects, laughed at gossip, second-guessed decisions made by the grumpy members of the Trojan Council, and savored the fragile peace. Agamemnon's newest fleet was delayed at harbor in Aulis due to inclement weather, ranging from lack of winds to terrible storms.

Meanwhile Priam sent everywhere for stores, his artisans and smithies tirelessly produced more bows, arrows, swords, daggers, axes, armor and helmets. Citizens had their own man-size clay jars dug into basements, but he also kept vast areas stocked with grains and wine. These would be opened to all, in the event of famine.

Every week Hektôr and I rode across to Dardania where Kreusa and Aeneas already had an infant son, Askanios. I wondered when I would bear a son for Hektôr. Sometimes Oinoné joined us in Dardania with her own son, Korythos. Now and then, she would ask wistfully about Alexander, whom she still called Paris.

"You are worried!" I cried out presently, seeing my husband storm into the room, his expression troubled. "What is it?"

I sat up in bed; he came and placed his hands on my shoulders. "Polites sent a message from his post that the Achaians sealed an

111

agreement with Polymestor, in Thrakia. Polymestor ceded them farmland enough to supply their army."

"Such treason! How could he do that, wed to your sister?"

"Polymestor is shrewd; wants to keep both alliances going. I never did trust him, and when Sigeia went back to live with them...."

"Sigeia." Dread nearly stopped my heart; beautiful Sigeia was the woman he had almost married. Would Hektôr take her as his second wife? My throat tightened. Like Hekabe, I had to accept lesser wives and concubines. It was the royal Trojan custom, as in Egypt. Indeed this was a fate I had prepared myself to deal with, without complaint. Yet the prospect hurt....

"Ãndrõmakhê." His touch on my cheek was tentative. "I want no one but you." He sat next to me on the bed, pulled me gently and held me close. "I am concerned, though, over what Sigeia might do at Polymestor's." He drew me closer. "You can believe me when I say: Sigeia is not part of my heart any longer."

I bit my lips, mutely accepting this morsel of comfort.

Nefru made a black and white streak as he leapt up to perch on the dressing table. Watching us locked in embrace, he purred.

* * * *

Later that night, upon returning home from tending to his horses in the stable, Hektôr reminded me, "You will see less of me in the coming days, my love; I must make sure our fortress is strong enough to withstand any kind of attack the Achaians will mount." His voice hardened, his face grim. "Groups of Achaians have been attacking our allies in the east. We are sending fresh troops to protect towns in danger of total butchery."

"Oh, Great Mother!"

"I am riding out to see to better garrisoning and the strengthening of weak plates in our walls. Ah, wife. Agamemnon wanted an excuse to wage war against us over control of the Strait, and Alexis handed it to him on a silver platter. Agamemnon can now unite all the other kings under his command—kings who used to constantly wage war against each other—forging his own agenda of expansion."

"But it's happening at a slower pace than he had planned for."

"Yes, of course. Some of those kings are smarter than he credits them. Not all of them are forgiving of his past transgressions against them. They salivate at the thought of plundering Troia, but also admit this will be a costly and bloody campaign. So they are weighing future gains versus upfront loss of men, weapons, and ships."

"So there is hope. And we are not alone in this conflict."

"Sure, we have warriors and allies; but allies can be depended on only to the extent of our usefulness to them. If the winds of war blow against us, how many will stay on with us to buck the tide?"

Polites met us at the gate. "Father has dispatched a contingent led by Aeneas, to—"

Hektôr interrupted him, "And who is protecting his own citadel?"

"Brutos, his lieutenant," Polites replied uneasily.

"Brutos! A nobody." Hektôr turned to me. "Go home and don't wait up for me." He dropped a kiss on my cheek and left.

* * * *

Two days later, as sunlight filtered softly over our wide bed, I was wakened by a strange odor. Hektôr was gone, not unusual. Yet something was terribly wrong. Nefru was on the windowsill, hissing at something with narrowed eyes.

I sat up, dread drying my throat. Small puffs of air fingered the tapestry my mother had made where it hung on the opposite wall. Quickly I pushed down the covers. That unpleasant odor wafted in again. Acrid, stinging my nose. Sliding from the bed, I crossed to the window, stood there with Nefru and looked out.

Eastward, mists joined earth and sky where the Ida Mountains jagged against dark clouds, concealing the eagle-circled throne of Zeus.

Southward, fertile Dardania sprawled among trees and orchards bordered by rivers and roadways, fringed by outlying farmhouses among the lower foothills.

Realizing that a smoke-like haze was obscuring the Dardanian hills, I blinked rapidly to clear my sight. Oh, Great Mother! Indeed something was wrong! So terribly, terribly, wrong....

Uneasiness wafted in on the air, echoing voices and sounds just beyond hearing. Fear squeezing my heart, I glanced inside at the clothesrail: good, Hektôr's clothing still dangled in the knot where he had thrown them last night. A second look told that he was in his boots, his heavy fighting boots; the thick leather jerkin was gone as well.

Ice cut through my spine as I hurriedly pulled down my blue housedress and a short white veil. Raking an ivory comb through my hair, I had just slipped into the dress when Thalpia, the servant Hekabe had given me, entered.

"What's wrong?" I asked quickly.

"Wrong, lady?" The dark little woman's smile was uneasy.

"Yes, I said *wrong*. Tell me. *Now!*"

Thalpia silently took the veil and laid it aside, then began winding my long hair into one long curl for the front of my left shoulder. Tapping my foot irritably, I watched in the mirror as Thalpia's sepia-hued fingers fastened my hair in place with amber-headed bronze pins and arranged the veil. Thalpia's almond eyes were heavy-lidded with long black lashes, her red lips full, her touch gracefully impersonal, and though around thirty, she looked older.

"All right now, Lady," she declared and faced the door, her face pinched. "Lord Hektôr is leaving for Dardania, and Lady Hekabe said you are to come to her in the Agora."

Nefru at my heels, I rushed down the shallow stairs, out through our small courtyard and across Priam's big court. I reached the altar, then the huge oaken door on its wide stone dowel, and then the pavement outside. Each side of the doorway behind me could admit a chariot-and-four or a wagon with mules.

I came to a stop on one of the flat, oblong stone blocks. The crowded Agora was seething with raised fists, echoing to the roar of shouted commands.

Hektôr, in his hand his bronze-tipped spear made of ashwood, towered next to Priam and Anchises upon a stone platform near the City Hearth. A slow hot wind slapped at the long robes of the two elderly kings, tall men with broad shoulders and strong bodies, testifying to their mutual ancestor's heroic stature.

That dreadful, sickening stink seeped through the air again.

Nefru let out a distressed, loud meow, and then curved himself protectively around my ankles.

Hektôr lifted his arm wielding the spear for attention, big muscles flexing on his biceps as he gestured, and the crowd subsided to shuffling and muttering. "My fellow soldiers and esteemed citizens! Prepare to avenge Dardania!"

Howls and clanging weapons gave approval, and there was eager stamping about.

"We will attack Achaian allies as they have attacked us!"

The din of spears and weapons clanking on shields, and furious shouts, beat upon my ears as fists slashed through the air. Men began stamping about as they gathered more weapons. Hekabe appeared, touched my arm, drawing me along in a quick, decisive manner that made her seem younger than her years. Nefru hissed, but ran ahead, flashing in and out of the crowds.

Back in the Great Hall, we sat on a bench and Hekabe explained, "The Achaians attacked Dardania during the night. Anchises and Kreusa arrived here at dawn. We do not know where Aeneas is, though there is report he escaped south with some of his troops. We suspect the enemy is still at Dardania. Akhilles is leading the enemy raid."

"Dardania!" That malevolent odor...of burning wood and flesh. Blood pounded in my forehead. I swallowed the spiky knot forming in my throat. I was stunned, could not accept it all. That ominous sordid smell, the people so near....

"Hektôr will drive them off," Hekabe continued calmly, "we will then attack Rhodes."

"Rhodes?" I thought I misunderstood.

"Our southern allies must be protected, child! The King of Rhodes is supplying Agamemnon's armies. They reached an understanding during the time Akhilles attacked Teuthrania."

"My father said that Rhodes is a key to the safety of the southern kingdoms," I spoke slowly.

"Your father is right, of course. Priam has already dispatched Polites to alert the bay cities, so your father will be prepared. Aeneas will be there with enough Dardanians to defend Mysia. Rest easy, your father is well garrisoned at Thébé."

The roar outside increased manifold, then slowly faded as the crowd broke up, buzzing and clattering.

Hektôr came in, towing Priam and Anchises. The morning sun flared gold over the high knot of my husband's hair and clean-shaved face as he passed through the doorway. His green eyes were aflame with determination, and he wore his reinforced battle-leathers and arm-and-leg greaves. Priam's blond head seemed grayer, and he held it low.

Hektôr strode towards me and took my hand, drawing me aside. My gaze dropped to the stains and ridges from armor-straps marking the brown leather sculpted with bronze at his chest and waist.

He touched my brow with his lips, then grasped my arm and led me to the other side of a pillar that supported part of the clerestory roof. In the ridges of the wood, spears rested, ready for use.

"I have to leave you now," he said, regret clear in his tone, "I know you have not lived with war before—"

"But I have! I am King Êetiôn's daughter, remember? I will do what I must, husband, you can count on me."

"I know I can. And your part is here."

I lifted my head to him, failing in my smile. My eyes burned and I closed them tight. One of his hard, calloused fingers carefully brushed away a tear.

"Hektôr…" *I must not sob, no, I must not.*

"Ãndrõmakhê," he said softly, and took my lips in his mouth. His fingers bit into my shoulder, my breast. He pressed close, the length of him molded to the length of mine. My heart spun.

"Hektôr, I was telling Anchises…" Priam's voice boomed, and then stopped as Hekabe shushed, "Priam!"

We broke apart, Priam clipped on, "Alas, time is short! Hektôr, you must take my place; I'm getting too old for these expeditions."

"Father, I will act for you in every way needed." He turned back to me with hollow eyes. "I have to go as far as Rhodes."

I straightened, determined not to show the dread I felt. "My father will not let the enemy pass Thébé."

"Polites went ahead to alert Êetiôn," Priam said gruffly. "You need not worry." He turned away and moved to the hearth.

Hektôr led me into our corner of the courtyard, walking with that smooth roll he had learned from taming colts. His breath fanned against my face, and the wind pulled a loose strand of his sunbleached hair. My skirt billowed ahead of us as we went to sit on a jade bench near the altar. Hektôr had a tiny kitchen garden made for me between this bench and the altar. Young herbs grew near our feet, tender to ripeness. I waited, sensing that he needed quiet. Around us, the strong breeze whirled the burnt fumes of Dardania. Hektôr sat hunched down beside me, and carefully I reached to touch his arm. He stirred and pushed his other hand across his face. "The people in those ruins…."

"Surely not…burned alive? This is not the smell of the flesh of funeral pyres."

"No. This was once *living flesh.*"

"Oh." My mouth turned sour and my stomach floated. I swallowed hard. That city, now a pyre of the living, yet even older than Ilion, great in the lore of minstrels….

"Girls I danced with and bedded," he whispered, "boys I roped colts with…it is they and their children who are burning." His jaw clenched tighter. "Our spies report that some might have escaped, with Aeneas. South. Perhaps to Larissa where King Lethos and his son will grant shelter until we arrive. We *must* follow the Achaians as far as Rhodes. Besides, we have a score to settle there."

"My father will never let them pass Thébé," I repeated.

Later I kept close to Hektôr as he went and joined his brother Kebriones, who, acting as charioteer, brought out the great-crested war helmet. I took and held it in both hands with all my strength, praying to the Great Mother to keep it safe on his head. Its rich red plume prismed through the tears I fought back.

Hektôr reached for the helmet, smiling grimly down at me.

It was then that courage and dignity deserted me. "Let me go with you, my honored husband!"

"I am a soldier, Āndrõmakhê. You are the future Queen of Troia. Your place is here, at home."

"Let me go with you as far as the mountains, then."

"I travel by sea from Larissa." He studied me grimly as he took the helmet from me and secured it on his head.

"I must be with you a while longer!"

"Keep our hearthfire bright while I am away."

As my husband stepped away from me, a great eagle flew low on the left, its scream eerily appalling.

Kassandra came running in from the street, calling to her brother. She was wild-eyed, her dark-honey blond hair in long tangles around her shoulders and waist, her dress hung away from her body. Hekabe rushed and tried to calm her but she flailed her arms toward an eagle flying overhead, toward Hektôr, toward Mount Ida.

Green eyes staring, she broke from her mother, lifted both arms to the circling eagle, and screamed, "Look, look on your left, Hektôr! See how Zeus-Badogios warns you, keep away from Larissa. Don't enter Thébé; keep away from Pedasos; turn your back to Lyrnessos!"

"Kassandra, this is war," Hektôr reasoned with her.

"Leave the Achaians to their foraging," she went on as though not hearing him, "keep away from the sea!"

"I can't neglect our allies, Kassandra!"

She began breathing heavily, screaming each word, "Troia MUST LIVE! Holy Father, send your eagle to sit on the right hand of Hektôr!"

"The eagle is now on my right, look," Hektôr spoke calmly, turning and pointing.

"You can not fool and change Fate! The Inevitable will be. O, you are all blind, deaf." Kassandra doubled over, hands to her face.

Hektôr strolled until he climbed in his chariot beside Kebriones, and Priam gave his blessing. Polydamas rode in on his own horse.

Then Kassandra screamed, "The black shadow of death!"

I looked up and saw that blackness was indeed flowing over from the mountains, casting a dark pall over the land. Above the shadow was a huge, heavy cloud forming with uncharacteristic suddenness.

The last hour came.

I felt Hektôr's big hand under my chin as he leaned down from the war chariot. Tenderly he pressed his lips upon my fear-scorched ones. "My little darling," he whispered, "I must go. Wait for me."

"I will!" I handed him his war helmet. "All my life…forever."

The chariots wheeled and clattered down the street.

* * * *

Time died slowly through summer heat, veiling the crenellated towers with transparent waves that rose, height on height, above the waiting plains. Sharp breezes blew cooling odors from day-baked tamarisk, from the musky river evaporating, and from white, red, and yellow flowers blooming in multiple patterns. However, I could no longer take Iris out for free-spirited rides through the countryside. My freedom was totally curtailed because marauding bands snatched men and women for ransom or rape and slavery.

Our new home was finished at last; I moved in, helped by Thalpia, Hekabe, and Helen. We pretended to enjoy ourselves, yet Hektôr's absence was felt by all. Our house was two-storied, with six rooms, including that bath-chamber with the pool I had looked forward to, centripetal courtyard with a jade bench, marble fountain, altar for my Goddess, and an herb-garden. Most of the furniture was built-in, arraigned with colorful, soft pillows, thick carpets would cover the polished stone floors in winter, and windows in the porticoed bedroom and family room had shutters inlaid with palm-sized squares of rock-glass leaving in the light when closed. Walls brimmed with frescoes of abundant outdoors, brooks, meadows, the yellow-spotted lynx of my dreams, luxuriant vines, and deep blue seas, alabaster sconces, and on other places ornaments, garlands, double-headed axes made of jade, and on tables and corners sat alabaster figurines, faience vases, sculptures and potted lemon trees.

O, my husband, please come home soon!

As I sequestered myself, studying clay tablets and scrolls brought by Hittite merchants, filled with information about the world we lived in, summer passed into those days when, of old, Trojans had gathered harvest from peaceful fields. Now the grains were taken at night by

Achaian men, from what fields the Trojans had not fully gleaned by day. Thus, I passed my sixteenth summer on earth.

Hekabe and Priam's youngest son Polydoros came for a visit from Thrakia, where he had been staying as a guest of King Polymestor. However, worried about the danger around Troia, Priam and Hekabe dispatched him back posthaste, laden with gifts for his hosts. As well, they sent a wagonload of gold for safekeeping, which, if ever Troia should fall, would be used to ransom family members.

I wondered if this was such a good idea. We all knew that King Polymestor was doing business with the Achaians. Nevertheless, because he was married to their daughter, Ilione, Hekabe considered him reliable. On the other hand, why had Priam, whom I witnessed to be a sharp-eyed, adept ruler, not objected?

* * * *

Polites returned from his mission. He reported that Achaians were hauling stones by ox-cart from the ruins of Dardania. As the remains of Anchises' beautiful city diminished stone by stone, a high, stone-and-timber stockade rose around the Achaian camp, protecting it from Trojan approach. There was festival along the shore by night as though some great event was celebrated, and the rocking black-hulled ships gleamed in torchlight.

Slowly the fields beaten down across the Simois River during that fourth year of fighting greened again. Time passed and there was no outright attack, other than daily skirmishes, on our besieged city.

I went often to the walltop with the other royal women, standing in the tower above the Skaian Gate, to watch or to sit below it, between the crenels, and spin in the sun. Swallows with glossy-blue backs, red throats and long tail streamers flapped their wings as they flew above me, or dove down to pick on the breadcrumbs and seeds I placed on the walls. The sweet song of their 'tswit, tswit, tswit,' or 'weet-a-weet' often echoed in the pattern of my designs. Nefru, impervious to their presence, would snooze by my feet, or perched on the wall, watch the world go by.

The Skaian Gate was the principal entrance to Troia and faced south, giving me a good view of the river, the harbor, and comings and goings. The city's population was greatly increasing as more refugees sought protection inside the walls. Shacks and stalls clustered every available space in the Lower City, rooftops sprouted huts and tents for friends and relatives whose homes were destroyed by the raiders. So, we added new enclaves, and built more walls. Tanners, weavers, and dyemakers thrived with this extra pool of ready laborers. Traders continued to bring in raw material for dyes such as woad, which was of the mustard family grown for the blue dye harvested from its leaves, also saffron, acorns, seashells, red beetles, and murex.

Akhilles was now renowned everywhere as 'Sacker of Cities.' He had become the great leader of the Myrmidons—ant-people—a Phthian tribe from Thessaly. They were indeed hardy as ants, and completely loyal to him. Rumor said that Agamemnon and Akhilles feuded often, for Akhilles refused to kowtow. The King of Kings desperately wanted to end his dependence on Akhilles, but could not. He had urged Odysseus to recruit him because of a prophecy by the seer Kalkas of Megara, in Korinth: Troia would fall only to an army led by Akhilles. Everyone believed Kalkas, for he was called the best of bird-diviners, knowing past, present, and future.

Though mention of Akhilles unnerved me, the mushrooming stories of his origins were captivating. Embellishments were served up daily. His mother Thétis, the Nereid, habitually intervened in the affairs of both gods and mortals. When Zeus cast Hephaistos from Heaven, Hephaistos fell into the sea and Thétis saved him. When King Lycurgos of the Edonians persecuted Dionysos, he sought refuge in the sea with Thétis. Even Zeus received Thétis' assistance; when Hera, Poseidon and Athené plotted to dethrone Zeus, Thétis averted the coup by summoning to Olympos two of the Hekatonkeires, who frightened the rebellious deities away. Being the children of Uranos, they were enormous in size and might. Impressed, Zeus wooed Thétis, but she refused him. Infuriated, Zeus decreed she had to wed a mortal man, noble Peleos, King of Phthia in Thessaly.

Thus born as the son of a brave, independent-minded Nereid and a human father respected as a fair and brave king, Akhilles unleashed death and destruction upon our lands in his quest for eternal glory.

* * * *

Time of festival came, celebrating a formal truce. It was the feast of the Triple Mare Goddess, Ate-Kybele in her dread aspect. We watched from the walls as, far off, colts bucked and pranced under the boys sent out to tame them. I imagined Hektôr, always foremost, winning fame in his youth as Tamer of Horses. He had tamed and bridled the very same horses that now drew his chariot.

By night, the festival changed to age-old breeding-rites honoring the Great Mother. Led by Priam's son Laokoon, a priest of Poseidon, priests held broodmares against the wind for divine coverage before sending them to the impatiently rearing stallions. Unmarried girls ran down the high terraced street and out the gate to couple with their lovers among late-blooming flowers near the Skamander River. The streets echoed to laughter, the shrilling of Phrygian melodies on ivory pipes, and the strumming of bass lyres.

However, our eyebrows rose as word circulated those Achaian men came inland, joining the festive orgy. Many a lonely matron was pushing secretly through the postern gates to meet the heavy-set blond men of Achaia, enemy by day, lover by night.

Then, to my great dismay, I heard it whispered that one of those women was Priam's beautiful dark-haired daughter Laodike, married to Antenor's son Helikaon, but consorting with Akamas, son of Theseus. They had a young son, so that as troubled as I felt about this, I decided it was better to turn a deaf ear. It might well be malicious gossip! Laodike was not just beautiful, but possessed a sharp mind and equally sharp tongue, often offensive to those who did not like hearing the truth, thus her detractors were many.

* * * *

On the final day of truce was a pilgrimage to the throne of Zeus, to offer sacrifices for Hektôr's victorious return with his men. I was restless, sleepless, constantly worried about him, and was happy to participate, eager to pray with all my heart, on my knees.

As we set out in a procession flanked by soldiers, I focused on the peaks of Gargaros and Sarikis. Rising in high, white marble, they were touched with snow most of the year. Below them, the plains were purple with thistle and blue with flowers. As we moved along, raising dust smelling of sandalwood, we passed clumps of trees, oak and evergreen, with hillocks of nettle trees and dwarf oak.

The Sacred Way followed the Skamander to its source below the throne of Zeus-Badogios. Frogs of early evening croaked their concert amidst the marsh where lotus, tamarisk, and willow grew.

I turned my attention to the venomous snakes, flipping back, or caught beneath the wheels, as the wagons and chariots thumped along, while cicadas whirred in the trees and birds chirruped. The snakes heightened my awareness of what might be lurking in the forest. This pilgrimage was a daring act, for there were roaming bands of bandits not bound by truce, and would love this opportunity to pounce upon us— especially with the King of Troia and his womenfolk present.

At last, the blue-white mountains neared and enlarged. Their marble glowed like a saddle between the twin peaks where clouds of dew folded about crests reflecting gold sunlight before my eyes. We dismounted where the river splashed down as a small brook. The pungent odor of pine stung my lungs as I began climbing with the group. The lower areas of nut and fig trees yielded to high conifers, and then the ground became slick and sinking with brown needles. Rocks gnarled across our way, and sunlight filtered through, spotting us with dancing rays as we climbed.

Several times, I sensed someone following me from between the trees. Here and there, I caught a flash of blond hair, or the glint of metal. However, the group of soldiers I sent to reconnoiter the trail returned with nothing suspicious to report.

It was late when we reached the sacred precinct under Kassandra's guidance. Kassandra, though moody and unpredictable, was a woman I yearned to get to know better; alas, she spurred all my cordial advances.

Presently our group achieved the lower peak, Sarikis, where the Father of Gods sat at pleasure to oversee the welfare of his Trojan peoples. We stood before His throne in awed silence; Kassandra chanted a ritual hymn praising Him. Tradition said Titans had carved the throne eons before, and indeed, it was a perfect chair with a footstool, fit for a gigantic figure. Of mica slate, a mosaic of delicate wildflowers surrounded it.

I stood silently with Hekabe, Priam, and their daughters Laodike, Kreusa and Polyxena, worlds of mysteries weighing upon us all. From the barest whispers and fleeting misty shadows in the air, I could discern the divine presence, as though He had just now risen from the chair and stepped upon his great storm cloud that carried over Ilion and away to Mount Olympos, northeastward beyond Alybe. Strangely, my opal pendant heated, so much in fact that I had to discreetly unclasp and remove it from my neck, sliding it into a pouch attached to my double-wound belt.

When I at last looked about, I saw the entire Troad region like the design on a shield: the rivers like silver streaks, the fertile green plains, the distant blue Strait and seas, Thrakia and the nearby islands with their snowy mountain peaks. Below me stretched the Skamandrian Plain, with Troia rising lofty and wide amidst, overspreading a hill. Close to one side of the Gargaros was the blackened rise where Dardania had ruled the land for centuries—now not one stone remained atop another.

My gaze traveled westward, to the Aegean Sea with the island of Lemnos, and rising above that from beyond, the conical top of Mount Athos. South and southwest was Issa with the Gulf of Adramyttion.

From my spot here, I could not see Thébé—Thébé where my beloved parents and brothers looked after their people, fields, and herds. The area was covered by darkness, as of cloud.

Thébé! Yearning squeezed my heart with an iron hand. Hektôr would have joined his cousin Aeneas there by now, and Father would sail with them to Rhodes and once again stop Tlepolemos. As I looked, I heard an eagle scream above me, wheeling to the left.

I froze. What evil omen did this mean, or should I turn around as Hektôr had done, mocking the very Fates?

I glanced at Kassandra, but she was sitting on the great footstool, leaning forward like a little girl, hands folded on her knees, perhaps having visions. At last, Kassandra moved and brought forward a few hyacinths she had gathered earlier. Leaving her seat, she came and presented them to me, then turned to lead us downwards.

We were to camp overnight at the quarry, on the saddle between Sarikis and Gargaros. Slaves and well-armed soldiers had been sent ahead to put up tents, and a cow and two sheep roasted over great pits in the stone.

Onetor, the Hermit of Gargaros, cut and served the meat, sprinkling the portions with barley-meal. Priam offered libation, and Hekabe saw to the proper mixing of water with the honeyed wine. We ate heartily, for in the morning we were to go up fasting to witness the fiery glory of the great god's return.

When the meal was over and remains cleared away, Hermit Onetor summoned Kassandra and led her up to the cave where he lived a short way up to the slope of Gargaros.

As I watched them go, I noticed Kassandra moving ahead of her companion. A figure met her at the dimly visible opening to Onetor's cave, and they blended into one.

With a loud cry, Hekabe rose from the rock where she had been sitting and ran forward; Priam, joining her in a rush, stood with her while both watched the scene above. Then Kassandra turned and together with Onetor, escorted the newcomer down the path.

"Helenos!" Hekabe cried his name. Leaving Priam, she rushed to embrace her son.

Priam moved forward and Helenos, after embracing his mother gently, reached his father in a few steps and knelt to clasp his knees with both arms. Priam lifted him up, kissed him ceremonially on face, neck, and shoulder. Then, together with the hermit, his parents led Helenos to our group. As he moved in the flickering torchlight, I noted that Helenos had acquired a certain maturity. Clean-shaven, his eyes were low-lidded and secretive as he bent his head before me in turn, walking among the assembly, looking strong and calm. Unusually tall and raw-boned from years of self-discipline and training, his sandy hair hung about his face with carelessness that Kassandra shared. The lines around his mouth were deepened by torchlight.

Hermit Onetor spoke, "The lost is restored after this long time. Priest Merops has sent Helenos to me, to witness his final judgment. Divine Apollo-Helios will judge when he returns to his throne at dawn. Should his fullest glory be dim, Helenos must remain here and serve. But if He returns in burning fires, Helenos is indeed free, and may rejoin his family and live as seer or soldier, however the Fates decree."

The two men walked up the path together and entered the hermit's cave.

That night, in my deepest sleep, I woke to sudden, full awareness. I sat up, confused, for I was sure I had heard Kiron's voice calling me. I was on a pallet in a tent shared by the royal women. Instinctively I reached for my cape and tiptoed out into a pearly darkness, punctured by the sentry's fires and gleaming weapons of the patrols.

I walked a few steps and paused facing the forest. Something in me told me that here I was to wait, and so I did, without knowing for what.

Now a shadow quickened, hurled something in my direction, and as a parcel fell at my feet with a dull thud, vanished.

I bent and lifted it. Wrapped in cloth, it was small and light. I unwrapped it with trembling hands. Moonlight and the probing of my fingers was enough to recognize its nature: a letter, carved on beeswax, on an ivory-hinged wooden panel holding the wax in its recess.

Kiron! I rejoiced with a thumping heart, *he is not dead; he has managed to send me word.*

Nevertheless, why in secret?

I looked around, realizing that some of the sentries had noticed me and were forming a protective circle. Holding the parcel to my breast, I acknowledged them with my free hand and returned inside. I dared not light a candle to read the contents, and rolled it in the fold of my pallet.

At last the stars showed approaching dawn, and the careful pilgrimage climbed the path without lights. The precinct included the top of Mount Gargaros, where the naturally level area was further smoothed and enclosed by a low wall. The flat area enclosed a rudimentary temple where Onetor waited at the altar with Helenos. They were joined by Kassandra, and near them stood the other priestly members of Priam's family, so that the small roof barely covered them. Incense rose into the sky with the eagle-sacrifice for Zeus, amidst prayers and chanted hymns.

124

I was overwhelmed, enfolded as I was by clouds that gave a sense of remoteness from the earth and everything mortal. There was only the clear, sharp air, and mists enfolding everything below. Then the sky began to glow, reflecting the approaching presence of divinity. First, between the astral columns standing on either side of the temple, a roseate glow graduated in intensity until it was a great ball of fire. The fire spread and glowed along the horizon until it rolled into consuming wheels that rested upon all the surrounding mountain peaks. The red intensified to amber with streams of green and lavender, at last heightening to brightest gold shot with silver. The presence of the god was so intense that only the initiates dared look. At last, when the fiery splendor was so intense as to consume the sky, it faded toward the peak of Sarikis and was at last dimmed before the solid ball of the sun*, charioting Apollo-Agdistis for another day. Father Badogios had come to his seat above the Troad, and blessed the return of Helenos to his family and destiny.

*Author's note: This phenomenon has been described by ancient as well as modern travelers.

Chapter 12

The grinding wait stretched into the fallow heaviness of autumn. Despite the blockage, days were alike in Troia. Priam was always early of a morning, receiving ambassadors, councilors, commanders, or inspecting the Lower City where fortifications were strengthened and a second ditch, this time inside the wall, was being dug. Manufacturing and storing of weapons went on day and night. Hekabe was up and about soon after Priam, daughters and sons' wives in tow. They began each day under the guidance of Priestess Theano, with morning prayers and honors to Pallas Athené in her shrine. The temples were reached from the Palace through an underground passage constructed by King Laomedon, during the siege by Herakles. In good weather, we went to the temples by stepping onto the inner citadel's wall, upon which the Palace was partly built.

That parcel delivered at night by the mysterious shadow had indeed been from Kiron. It was brief, telling me he was alive, treated well, teaching Akhilles' son, and would never forget me, his favorite pupil. He wished I would not neglect my studies, and prayed for my health and safety. I read it repeatedly, caressing the etchings with my fingers, weeping and rejoicing at the same time.

Often I brought my spinning or embroidery to the ramparts where I could sit and gaze through a crenel toward Mount Ida, beyond which Thébé sat. Nefru, always by my side, would curl up nearby, purring in tune with my hand movements. Would that I could bring Iris to sit with us! I visited her daily, feeding and grooming her along with the two horses Hektôr had left behind. Afterwards I took her on short rides inside the city walls; in her own way, she let me know she missed our freedom of bygone days.

On the occasions when I glanced up from work, the mountains gently undulated across the horizon in purple, blue, and gray. The broad level plain was scattered over with tortund, thick-foliaged trees. It was peaceful to observe the gleaming Skamander flowing through in smooth, winding curves, dwindling off into the mountains. On either side toward the denuded site of Dardania, foothills rose close to the river. On the southwest opposite, hillocks sloped to the water in a wide horseshoe arc; trees speckled into groups where flat banks flooded as if smoothed back by a Titan's hand during winter floods.

I became used to the strong winds, keeping my hair and dress in disorder unless I wrapped the full length of my veil about me. During the summer days, this was a relief from the withering heat. As I gazed over the Lower City, I could watch the ever-increasing red clay rooftops, tents and shacks, and sadly wondered how many more could be crowded into the area. People milled about like ants through the narrow alleyways in their daily work. Sometimes I spotted a wedding party throwing flowers, singing and dancing as they crossed the central Square. Then I would think of my own lack, for my monthly blood still flowed and I could not yet boast of a child for Hektôr. I would have another year after his return; or else, Hektôr must take another woman to second wife and mother of sons for his inheritance.

Footsteps announced visitors nearing my corner on the wall, and Nefru slinked away. Chilled without knowing why, I called out silently, *Come back, do not leave me!*

The cat paused, threw a backward glance, a soothing message in its blue eyes: *There is nothing to worry, dear friend.*

I stiffened; the needle slipped and stuck me in my right forefinger. This was not the first time I had found myself conversing with the cat, yet I felt as taken aback as ever.

Priam together with Deiphobos, Helenos, and Alexis, came into view. They stood apart from me, studying the horizon as they spoke with animated gestures.

"Before attacking Rhodes," Priam declared, "Hektôr will enlist the aid of King Sarpedon of Lykia. He has my written guarantee with him that Lykia will enjoy equal privileges with us after the war. They were to go from the citadel at Melanippeon and cross to the island, which by rights belongs to us, through Altes and Pedasos. With the Mysians, Moesians, and Karians who will have joined him by now, and the two dozen ships I have deployed along the coast, Rhodes will certainly capitulate before winter."

"It is imperative that supplies continue, and Lykia is vital for contacts inland," Deiphobos agreed. "But we should attack and destroy the blockade in our harbor, now, before Agamemnon arrives. That will leave them no refuge for the winter."

"I don't like the eagle omens," Helenos spoke up, looking up to the clear blue sky.

"What eagle omens?" Alexis asked.

"We have had several," Helenos replied, "and even you told me of the left-hand flight the day of Hektôr's departure."

Alexis laughed. "Clever Hektôr turned and put him on the right."

"Fate is not to be mocked!" Helenos declared grimly.

The others stared at him, and fear rode my breath as I turned so as not to see them. I knew of other times when an eagle had floated above us on the left hand, and how Hektôr had refused the oracle. Then I thought of something else: on the day of pilgrimage, when I had looked from Sarikis toward Thébé, I had seen a great shadow over the gulf area. Smoke and fire? No! No. Only a black cloud....

Gathering my needlework, I rose, went into the palace and hurried up the stairs to find Hekabe. I liked the warmth of her enormous, noisy family, and the gracious queen handled those pretty rivalries between wives and concubines deftly.

Hekabe was in the royal women's workroom, placing her shuttle to rest in the threads of her loom with an air of finality. She turned on her stool and motioned me to pull up another. However, I could not sit. With a respectful nod, I leaned my back against the doorjamb. I closed my eyes a moment in vertigo.

Hekabe asked gently, "Has anything happened?"

"I was on the wall and heard too much of the southern war. I wish Hektôr were safely back."

"You must not brood while he is away! I spent my early marriage alone here, waiting for Priam. Biding my time, I learned much that I needed to know later on. Just like you are doing now. Yes, I know of that you are studying the records in our archives, and asking for more. No, do not look worried—I am on your side! You remind me of myself, at your age. You are a quiet one, Āndrōmakhê; you keep to yourself, do not gossip, and are loyal and astute. I know you are doing right by my son."

Hekabe sighed lightly, and went on, "I bore Priam's children while he came and went about the business of renewing the city, and building ties with our allies. After Hektôr, came Alexis, and then Helenos and Kassandra. Alexis...Priam was here when Alexis was born...I should have never told him my dream of the firebrand, else he'd not have felt he had to expose the boy..." Pausing, she glanced around, and then whispered, "Aisakos, Priam's son by Arisbe, who was his first wife, read the horoscope that my baby would destroy our city. Pay heed to this: Yes, Aisakos, *Priam's son by his first wife.* Did he read it accurately, or did he make it all up to have a rival to the throne out of the way? After Alexis, I had my two divine ones, Helenos and Kassandra. I cradled those twins on the altar at Thymbra, and the temple serpent of Apollo coiled around them and hissed wisdom in their ears. They were both walking and talking by the time Priam returned from the south."

"It's not right that a woman must always wait, wait, and wait, for whatever might happen!" I burst out, then blushed, embarrassed.

Hekabe said kindly, "After more than thirty years, I have learned that such things must be."

"If I accept this, I would become a nothing!"

"Not if you are strong. Oh, before I forget, I know of your old sword, and of how, in the darkness of the night, you leave your bed and wield it as if warding off an enemy."

"But...how...could you?"

Hekabe smiled. "I am the one who set Nefru to watch over you."

My knees gave way and I sat down on the stone floor. "So it is true," I murmured, "Nefru can talk."

"Not everyone can hear him."

"Yes...he doesn't *really* talk, but sends picture-thoughts to me."

Hekabe pointed to my pendant. "Your opal. Surely, you know that it is more than a gem! It acts as a conduit between what you can see and hear, and what is veiled from ordinary senses. Tell me; was it a gift from your mother? Has it been in her family for long?"

My hand cupped the opal protectively, and I hesitated. Somehow, I could not mention the Guardian Nymph of the Lake. The lie came easily, "Yes, it's been in my mother's family for generations."

Hekabe nodded. "One day, your husband will be king as well as soldier, and you will sit with his counselors while he is away; you will keep his hearthfire bright, and care for his children."

"Shuttle, spindle, loom...."

"And sew, embroider, and wash swaddling cloths. Yes, these are things we need, in order to live. Strength and power are earned by the patient woman. In years to come, you will have other companions— Hektôr's lesser wives and concubines, and their children, to love. I trust you will care for them for *his* sake. Tolerance comes with love, Āndrōmakhê. Things are like this for a Trojan queen."

"Suppose I am childless?" I dug my shoulders into the wooden frame, and then stepped away.

Hekabe followed me, going with me downstairs and outside to the courtyard altar, round and massive in the afternoon light. The big stone enlarged as I neared it and began pacing round it. At last, I stood still and turned to the waiting queen.

"You *will* have children," Hekabe declared gently.

I glanced helplessly up at the sky.

Hekabe added, "The Mother Goddess will hear you."

"But if She doesn't, I cannot hope for respect in your family." I paced back and forth beside the altar. "The men out on that wall talked about Hektôr invading Rhodes, as if it were nothing. Helenos points out to the bad omens from eagles flying over to our left. I fear he is right! I remember, now, but did not pay heed then, when Hektôr and I came here, that first day—an eagle screamed and flew away on our left."

Hekabe remained silent. After a long moment she said, "Helenos' prayers mean much. His future is also propitious. Aisakos was chief priest from before Alexis' birth, and his death has left no one worthy. Laokoon is younger, devoted to Poseidon, and tries hard, but he is not successful. Priam wants Helenos to take Aisakos' place." Gently she took my hand in hers.

I found myself confessing, "I've been so lonely...and so very homesick...and frightened, that..."

"New Moon comes in a few days," Hekabe said comfortingly. "Try to get to know the other women of the family better, Āndrōmakhê. I had hoped Thalpia would encourage you to go about in the city. I gave her to you because she is very efficient; never tires of hard work. In addition, she is *wise,* more a companion than servant. I would have freed her long ago, only there is nothing for her out there. Kolchian horsemen had killed her parents with most of her villagers in an attack. They kept her alive because she was pretty, and they used her body. Priam bought her ten years ago, in Miletos. She had been ravaged, passed from camp to camp, and now the trader had stashed her among farm animals, not expecting anyone to buy her. Priam had stopped for supplies and noticed her. The quiet grace she carried herself with touched him, and he purchased her to free her and send her home. But she had no home left to return, and I have had no reason to complain about that."

"I thank you for such valuable gifts as Nefru and Thalpia," I said sincerely, with a slight bow.

Together we strolled across to the courtyard entrance. I then asked, "But what of the New Moon?"

"At the turning of the moon we celebrate with parties and entertainments. Helen is hostess for this night, and you must join us. The whole family will be there."

On my way home, something she had said earlier, about the oracle that Alexis would be a firebrand, rang in my mind: *Aisakos, Priam's son by his first wife, Arisbe. Did he read the omen accurately, or did he make it up to have a rival to the throne killed?*

130

Yes, yes, of course Aisakos would interpret Hekabe's dream in a manner that served him! If so, Troia could survive this siege and prosper far into the future. Ah, the sweet opiate of hope....

* * * *

Helen's Feast of the New Moon concluded with her solo whirling dance. I came out into the Pergama—the inner citadel—breathing in the cool midnight air.

After the dance, Helen had stood at the family altar, graciously welcoming each guest. The white lamb's-wool trim bordering her hoop-skirted blue dress had swayed and bent with her movements. She had braced herself with one hand against one gold-wrapped tip of the stone altar horns, lyre-shaped like those of the cattle Alexis had herded when a shepherd in the mountains, long ago. Her pale lavender veil was thrown back over her shoulders like a cape, accenting the richness of her red-gold hair that flamed around her face, and then tumbled into masses of long curls over her breasts and down her back. She had held her chin high as her eyes moved like arrows over everyone.

Presently light steps sounded behind me and Polyxena tugged at my hand. "Come on." She led the way to a bench just outside the Temple of Athené's gardens. "I have something secret to tell you."

We sat down. I was uneasy, for I did not like to be close to Athené. Then I looked at the eager girl, Hektôr's youngest sister, and smiled. The dark-haired, blue-eyed pretty girl was just past her puberty rites and was becoming interested in men. "What's so urgent?" I probed encouragingly.

"I know something important that will make the Achaians go home! They are not all our enemies." Polyxena touched her own shoulder as if in supplication, and then drew back at the sound of approaching footsteps. She put her mouth close to my ear, "One of them never wanted to come in the first place, and will go home, taking all his men, if my father agrees to..."

Kassandra appeared through the gate of the temple garden. Polyxena placed a finger over her lips, leapt to her feet and ran away.

Kassandra paused, her eyebrows drawn together. She then stepped toward me, and I rose in greeting.

"Polites has just sent a message," she announced calmly. "Hektôr and Aeneas left Pedasos and are defending Lyrnessos. Pedasos has fallen and Akhilles' men are razing the city."

"Oh no!" I collapsed back onto the bench. "Where is Briseis? Is Mynes safe? And what about my friend Astynome? You know that her father Chryse serves Apollo, just like you do."

Kassandra's calm shattered and her voice took on its familiar, prophetic moan, "Go and sleep while you can, Ãndrōmakhê! We must live through what the gods have willed for us."

I stood up, brandishing an imaginary sword. "Akhilles cannot conquer Lyrnessos or Thébé! No one will ever take Troia. Not all the thousand ships of Agamemnon can vanquish King Priam."

Kassandra threw back her head and laughed. "Don't fret! Akhilles will never set his conquering foot inside our walls." She whirled away from me, words trailing behind her, "Akhilles...Akhilles will never, ever conquer the Trojans!" She ran out through Priam's gate.

Pedasos had fallen....

Numb, I moved like a ghost into my own house. Thalpia came and helped me into bed. The soft clank of the door latch faded into silence when she left, and I was bleakly alone. Nefru appeared and leapt onto bed, curling up next to me. I hugged him to my breast.

In my lonely bed, I felt like a blank effigy before priestesses clothe it at times of festival. Once, as a small child, I had lain so for the first time in a great bed my father had built for me....

I envisioned the sunny walls of Thébé that gathered the city close against the hill. I could observe the grapes ripening on the hillsides in September, dragging at dwarf vines. My father and the city men always worked together on the common fields. Then, winter nights in Thébé when my mother brought the loom downstairs, where she would weave in the flickering firelight. Servants, chattering like cicadas, would help my brothers make cheeses in big hole-lipped jars; the smallest of the boys would climb all over our father as he sat back, teetering his chair against one of those fireside columns, bantering with them. In my memory, I watched the firelight flicker red and yellow on Father's square proud face and on Mother's soft pale hair. The littlest boys seemed happier than ever, their naked bodies squirming about Êetiôn as they pestered him for stories or a chant with his lyre inlaid with ivory. Oh yes, my fingers grew hot and sticky on those nights, learning to card wool so that I could one day oversee a similarly happy household, properly....

I turned onto my side and plumped up the roseleaf pillow. It was damp. Tears. Trickling down my eyes unbidden.

* * * *

An empty blue light drained of all warmth, hovered over the city early next morning when I went out to the high wall. Dark clouds hung over the twin crescent peaks of Mount Ida.

The wind carried the voices of Priam and Deiphobos, from beyond a bend in the wall, "The potters are alerted; kilns burn day and night," Deiphobos was saying. "Every house is assured to have at least three large, deeply held storage-pots."

"The Moesians should be arriving soon," Priam added.

"I like not the eagle omens." Helenos' voice repeated, and I stepped farther away. I did not want to see him; his penetrating eyes made me uncomfortable.

A scrape of sandals, and the men left.

"I am still Queen of Lakedaimon, and yet they ignore my advice," I heard a hoarse voice declare behind my back, and whirled around.

It was Helen, shoulders drawn back, chin high, dark shadows beneath her eyes, her unbound hair framing her head like a halo and cascading down her back. Obviously, she had not slept last night, and was thinner than when she had first arrived here. Yet she was beautiful, cloud-soft and granite-strong at once.

She continued, "Alexis *will* be king. My people need leadership in gentler arts, Ãndrõmakhê. I worry about them, for Meneláos is turning them into uncouth beasts, as bloodthirsty and greedy as himself." She sighed. "But I should be fair. Meneláos is not as bad as Agamemnon. What he is, however, is a mirror image of Agamemnon. He is not just influenced by his brother, but he is a reflection of him."

Helen paused; I remained quiet, hoping that my silence would encourage her to continue talking.

Helen flushed delicately, and hurried on, "During my father's time, Lakedaimon was a land of song, art, and beauty. My mother, as priestess of Zeus, helped him in this. We came upon sorry times after my first marriage. I did not want him; Agamemnon manipulated the events in his favor, so the two brothers can be Kings of Mykene and Sparta." She paused again, biting her lips. "I had to agree to choose Meneláos among the others. I *had* to choose someone; there was no way of avoiding it anymore. When Agamemnon charged Klytemnestra with the task of convincing me to choose Meneláos...I had to go along, because if I refused, Agamemnon would have harmed my sister. Just as importantly, I owed it to her. I owed to give her this victory."

"You owed it to her? Why?"

She gave me a lingering look through red-rimmed eyes that were haunted. Then she spoke up bluntly, "Iphigenia is my daughter."

I gasped, and stared at her, not knowing what to think or say.

"Yes," she said quietly, "Iphigenia is my daughter, by Theseus. You know of how Theseus kidnapped me when I was thirteen. The three months I spent with him and Aethra, his mother, in Athens, are unforgettable. I loved Theseus! He was deemed old at fifty, but he still had the unshakable courage and convictions of the true hero that he was. Everything they say about him now, so many years after his death, is all true. Also, he had really loved his Amazon wife. He had cared about his second wife, Phaedra, too, but she fell in love with Hippolytos, Theseus' handsome son from the Amazon. Too bad. I still feel sorry for Phaedra, because of how she killed herself, and of course for Hippolytos, who died because Theseus, in his hurt, cursed him and set Poseidon upon him. Hippolytos died while driving his chariot; Poseidon shook the earth, the ground opened beneath, and he fell in."

When she remained silent, I pursued, "But...how? I mean, how... and why, did Agamemnon think Iphigenia was his daughter?"

"After my brothers had brought me back from Athens—against my will, for I wanted to stay with Theseus—my father had sequestered me from the world, and only Aethra, and later Klytemnestra, who came to visit me, knew of my condition. And Klytemnestra *needed* a child! She had just lost hers in stillbirth, and was afraid to tell her husband about it. Therefore, she stayed on with me, at my chambers in our father's palace, the loving sister watching over her traumatized little sister, suffering from the effects of being kidnapped by Theseus...and well, everything fell in place. Aethra assisted at the birth of her own grandchild, while everyone else thought it was Klytemnestra giving birth, and then my sister took my daughter, and presented it to her husband as her own."

"O Helen...how you must have suffered...."

She gave me a long look, then, "I told Alexis about this. He is the only one who knows. And now, *you* know."

"But of course I'll keep your secret!"

"Yes, I know you will." She smiled. "You don't gossip. Also, you should keep silent for Klytemnestra's sake. My sister did not want this war; she is not an enemy of Troia. I miss my sons, though; and most of all, I miss Hermione. However, I do not care for the life I left behind. I am better off with Alexis; when at last our time comes, he will let me rule Lakedaimon. Incited by Agamemnon, Meneláos usurped my rights. He has two sons by other women who will also give trouble one day, though in my kingdom inheritance goes through the female line. My people know and love both me, and my daughter." Helen moved forward, desolately staring down the wall into the flickering smoky lights of the Lower City.

I could not help asking, "Is it true that you had begged Aphrodite, on your knees, to give you Love?"

Her shoulders moved as if startled, but she did not reply.

"I heard that She gave you Alexis as the answer to your prayers."

Helen's eyes gleamed. "Yes, I asked Aphrodite for Love. And yes, Alexis *is* a gift. I love him. As much as you love Hektôr."

Helen turned her back and moved down the length of the wall.

I watched her. It was not easy to be the most beautiful woman on earth! As it had been in Sparta, here too women were sickly jealous of her beauty, watching like a hawk to catch the first wrinkle appear on her face, the first sagging muscle in her jaw line; also, those who dared, used all their wiles to seduce Alexis to get back at Helen.

Most men were in love with her, or lusted after her. From what I observed, however, she did not elicit their lust deliberately, for she was simply being herself. She danced because she enjoyed dancing, dressed in the revealing Kretan fashions because this was how she dressed in her homeland, and not because she thought of her effect on men. Aware of her own beauty, she would not apologize to those less endowed.

Helen's charm was inborn; she was intelligent, with a keen sense of humor, and not as self-absorbed as gossiped. Among the servants she brought along from Sparta, was Aethra, mother of the late Theseus; until tonight, I had wondered at her treatment of the old queen, finding it strange. At times she was cruel to her, giving her chores the frail woman was unfit to perform—why, Aethra was in her seventies, a *very* old age indeed—and yet, at other times, with great tenderness. Stranger still had been that Akamas—Aethtra's grandson by Theseus—during his visit here with Agamemnon to demand Helen's return, had not asked for his grandmother's release. Now of course it all made sense.

Deiphobos was among the ranks of men in love with Helen. So too was Antenor. Hektôr said Antenor posed a problem, for Antenor's love was lust combined with hatred because he could not have her.

What about Hektôr?

Was he too beguiled by her?

I never saw any sign of it, perhaps because we lived under siege and he had no time to pay attention to her. On the other hand, perhaps, he was as unaffected by her beauty as I was by Akhilles'....

Alexis loved Helen more than anything on earth. Their lifestyle was opulent, she commanded—by her own admission—more servants, singers, dancers, silks and jewels here, than she had ever in Sparta. In Sparta, Meneláos' cavortings had placed her in constant danger from rivals who tried to murder her to take her place, and he had been impervious to it all.

So, for Helen, Alexis son of Priam, who played the lyre and sang songs, was completely faithful, protective, young, and handsomer than most men under the sun, was indeed a gift from Aphrodite.

Chapter 13

Leaping fire and billowing smoke signals followed by messengers carried shockwaves to Troia: Lyrnessos had fallen! King Mynes had died heroically, in one-to-one battle with Akhilles. Akhilles then had plucked the weeping Briseis from her husband's body at the gate, and thumbing his nose against Agamemnon's right to first choice, claimed her as his slave. The sorely undermanned defenders, led by Hektôr and Aeneas, were forced to retreat behind the defenses of Thébé. The invaders set up camp along the shallow-rippling Plakia River that flowed bayward from the city.

When night fell and the moon was out, I went to a far corner on the wall and wept as I thought of Briseis, and the fortress at Lyrnessos, of how it had looked when I saw it for the last time, with Hektôr, on my bridal journey. I had glanced up from the ship as it passed the town, walls far above the water, strengthened by square towers.

Presently my feet moved by themselves as I stepped back from the wall, down the steps, and through the courtyard gate to the altar of my Goddess. I was trying to brace myself; at any moment, there would be gut-wrenching pain. Kassandra appeared, clad in her usual, loosely belted white tunic, her long rich hair swinging down her back.

"Why isn't there news of Thébé?" I asked.

"Lyrnessos is next inland from Pedasos. Thébé is at the head of the bay. You know that...." Her voice had hardened. Seizing the bullhorns of the altar, she hung backward to stare at the moon.

"Surely with Hektôr and Aeneas to help, my father will break these sieges." I could not, would not, accept defeat. "Akhilles cannot destroy everything! Thébé is a sacred city, guardian of the shrine dedicated to Apollo. Achaians too worship Apollo; he would not dare trigger the Sun God's wrath." My teeth chattered nervously in the cooling night.

Kassandra said, "Herakles came against us with six ships, yet it was the earthquake sent by Poseidon the Earthshaker that gave him victory, not his own military prowess." She laughed. "Akhilles...will never conquer us!" She turned around, stumbled, and pulled herself up by the curved horns of the altar. "Akhilles...foremost champion of the Achaians...and the rest of those accursed, will *never conquer Troia!*"

137

I watched with mixed feelings as the lovely young woman's pale soft arms pulled again at the horns, and her slim body twisted with serpentine shudders. "I tell you what I know," Kassandra went on, "as I tell it to everyone; but no one believes me. Oh, how I curse this gift of mine! I curse it just as Apollo, who tried to rape me on the night I was alone in his temple, cursed me for fighting him...yes, yes, he cursed me to *prophesy the truth, and never be believed!*"

I had heard the rumor of Apollo versus Kassandra, but stayed with the general opinion, dismissing it as a tale of a wanton ritual-night in the temple. Now I felt guilty about doubting her.

Kassandra swung her head away, let go of the horns, and lunged across the courtyard with slow, staggering steps. Out through the gate, back to her gloomy loneliness.

Sickly, I returned to my own chambers. Hektôr and Aeneas *must* rout Akhilles; Agamemnon *must* relinquish his blockade of Troia. And Thébé with my parents *must* be safe....

Thalpia met me at the door, holding up a softly glowing alabaster lamp. "I was coming to meet you, Lady; you know it's not proper to go about unchaperoned."

"I was not alone, Kassandra was with me." Nefru nuzzled my ankles, and I laughed at the irony. "The cat, too, was with me, and he is as good a chaperon as any."

My legs were stones, my back a long sheet of ache, as I moved heavily toward the bottom of the stairs. When I reached them, they were thousands of feet high. Thalpia followed, the oil light casting reddish-black shadows ahead of us. I was barely able to undress, my clothes slipping in a puddled heap on the floor. The square of stars through the window guided me to bed, where I climbed in between covers.

Nefru quietly leapt onto the bed, nuzzling my face, purring.

I fell asleep, imagining Hektôr's head facing me on the pillow.

* * * *

Winter flowed into spring. Thébé and her environs held. Hektôr returned with three broken teeth, his body riddled with fresh scars, and laden with letters and presents from my parents and brothers. Even as I took care of his injuries, he gave me five glorious days, and was my sun and my moon. Many times, he proved to me how much he missed me while he was away. Meanwhile his favorite horse, Xanthos, broke through several doors in the stable, found Iris, and mated with her.

138

Then urgent news of yet another influx of raiders heading toward Thébé erupted; Hektôr collected his men, weapons, and horses, and sailed off with ten ships, ordering another contingent to follow on land with more weapons and horses.

Agamemnon and the full strength of his new fleet showed up a few days later, crowding the shallow Trojan Bay. Half of them navigated reefs and swamps, and beached their ships on its eastern shore near the mouth of the Simois River.

Agamemnon and Meneláos disembarked, displaying themselves with their lion-painted shields, prancing and preening along the shore, facing our walls. His helmet with the boar's tusks, and gold-embossed armor distinguished Agamemnon. We caught sight of Odysseus as well, though he was discreet, organizing his men to raise structures on the crowded grounds.

Shortly, large pavilions made of red, gold, and blue-painted leather with lion-pennants fluttering atop in the wind, distinguished the High King's residences.

Among the new contingent of soldiers were units of Epioi, misslemen feared for their formidable accuracy.

Spies told us the price Agamemnon had paid to be able to sail here: He had triggered the wrath of Artemis the Virgin Huntress by killing a stag sacred to Her. Artemis had held back the wind, grounding the Achaian fleet. After an endless wait, the seer Kalkas had divined that unless Agamemnon sacrificed his daughter Iphigenia to appease the Goddess, she would never release the wind. The High King then slit his daughter's throat on Artemis' altar, the wind blew up the sails, and he put in to sea to sack and loot our Troia.

On the following night, I came upon Helen in the battlements. She stood there, her shoulders shaking, weeping silently.

I could not help asking, "When Kalkas told Agamemnon to offer up Iphigenia...did he accept it because she was not of his own flesh?"

"No," she whispered, "I told you before, Agamemnon did not know; he really believed he was her father. Because he loved her, it must have been painful to kill her. But Artemis knew the truth, of course. Therefore, she would *not* have demanded the life of my child for a sin of *Agamemnon's!* Kalkas interprets omens in a way that suits his own agenda, whatever that might be at any given time."

"O, Helen, I am so sorry...."

I wanted to reach for her comfortingly, but did not dare. Her grief was too deep; the last thing she would want was my presence.

I turned to leave, but her words stopped me, "Āndrōmakhê, look at the size of Agamemnon's fleet! Consider how, with his own hands, he killed a beautiful young girl he believed was his daughter. Antenor and Polydamas are wrong in wanting to surrender me to Meneláos! Everyone with any sense knows this campaign was not launched just to restore Meneláos to my throne. Even if I should leave Troia tonight and join Meneláos in his tent, Agamemnon would not forsake his long-nurtured dream of conquest...."

* * * *

Spies helped us gauge the enemy's strength: As rumored, its fleet added up to a thousand vessels, though not all full-sized and sea-worthy, thus doomed to sink or rot away, soon. The number of warriors was over forty-thousand. The larger vessels could carry about fifty rowers each. Every vessel and dinghy was loaded to its brim with men, chariots, weapons, armors, slaves, concubines, tools, provisions, even sheep and cattle; clearly, they realized that days of easy pickings off the land were no more. Villages around us had been destroyed by their previous campaigns. Only half of the enemy force was dedicated warriors, the rest slaves, thieves, and renegades. They received no payment for services and lived on dreams of plunder. Nevertheless, they outnumbered us four to one.

Gossip in the Palace and Agora now included exotic tales about enemy kings and heroes such as Patroklos, Diomedes, Odysseus, old Nestor, and the two warriors named Ajax: Ajax the Greater, son of Telamon, King of Salamis, and Ajax the Lesser, son of Oilos, King of Lokris. King Nestor of Phylos was the oldest of the leaders, said to be a pious sage, and respected commander.

We noted that Agamemnon did not place guards along routes delivering supplies and soldiers from our allies. His hopes must be of a swift and easy victory....

* * * *

I did all I could to help. Besides making cloth, I helped collect fruits, herbs and roots. Even with Agamemnon eyeing us like a hawk, there was yet little danger outside the immediate city walls. Supplies of food and arms continued to flow into the city from allies. The men stepped up efforts of hauling lumber and stones from the mountains and diminishing ruins of Dardania.

Once more I took my carding or spinning to the wall, watching the horizon for Hektôr's return. I cast my shuttle and pressed down the threads, not allowing myself to stop no matter how vicious the pain of exertion in my fingers and wrists. The white threads ran together with purple as I dipped the oil and it slicked down the woof in tiny droplets.

Purple, lavender, violet, red.

The tightening Achaian' chokehold was forcing us to leave off murex, harvested from marine snails, and used oak dye. Sheets were purple, and babies' swaddlings often red. The freemôn gathered dye-acorns, bartered the raw stuff for food, and it was bought and used so we could all survive.

Purple, lavender, violet, red, I continued to spin.

We, the Trojans, all of us, were indeed royal in our famous color now! Even the street-repairers and blockade-runners were captured or escaped in this rare-dyed cloth.

Nervous impatience tore at me, and I miscast my shuttle. Beside me stood mounds of thread I had spun out from hours of sitting on the corridored wall. At last, I turned away from the loom, crossing my arms to massage my shoulders. My legs were stiff like columns. The opal burned beneath my throat like a piece of live coal.

With a start, Nefru rose from his nap, hissing and growling, his paws clawing at my sandaled feet as if to alert me.

I looked up into the horizon, and noticed something that I had not before: Many of the enemy ships, and rippling ranks of spear-warriors, swordsmen, bowmen, and slingers, were missing! Miles away and far below, mists rose from marshes, swirling in golden-ray vapors toward the delicate blue and lavender mountains, the colors reflected in the cloth I was spinning. The dark mouth of the pass was lipped in sun-yellowed green, a speck far off, seeming many leagues closer than it was. A few horses still grazed about like white and brown spots.

Though my arms were still numb, I reached for my distaff. The spindle-whorl fashioned of decorated terracotta fell from where I had left it on the nearby stool, and broke on the mottled stone floor. Bits of shard scattered. I stared at them. One lay near me with a word uppermost, the name Sigo from its dedicatory motto. Sigo, the dragon-slaying hero from long before Dardans and Trojans separated into rival kingdoms, from ages past while they were still tribes wandering about north of Thrakia.

Foreboding grasped me by the throat: this was a dark omen—*the breaking apart of a hero.*

No, no, oh my Kind Goddess, please, no!

Even if Thébé fell, my family must escape. Hektôr would see to that. I gathered my things and hurried back the distance home, twice tripping over Nefru on the way. There, I went to the chest where other unfinished work was kept. Ah, here, my new pink veil; it needed a hand's length of gold leaves to finish the hem. My ivory needle was still in it, gold thread through the eye. Picking it up, I tossed the big square backward over my shoulders so that the unfinished edging came down in front. Taking a handful of golden leaves, I dropped them inside the pocket looped to my girdle. Hurrying downstairs, I shortcut through the tunneled passage to the wall.

I made my way along the machicolations that opened in the battlement between me and the plain below. Winds whipped by, billowing my veil and straggling loose hair into my eyes. Glancing back, I caught Nefru and Thalpia following me. Nefru, I was used by now, but Thalpia! Ah, that incorrigible chaperone. Our eyes met as the wind whipped off the unfinished veil and it floated into her grasp.

Suddenly a faint sound of music tinkled nearby. Plink. Plang. Plang-plink. Then a delicate melody flowed in softly rippling cadences. I glanced about. Tan-leather sandals showed beneath a reddish-brown robe. The musician was sitting in one of the crenels, his back to the mountains. The lyre rippled faster, raising notes of melancholy. I moved closer. It was Alexis, his lyre propped on one knee.

"Lovely day." His playing continued, presently switching to a lighter tune, though his blue eyes remained hooded.

I stopped beside him. "That tune is beautiful."

"It's mountain music. I invented it during my days when I sat and watched the herd, in the mountains. Just now, I am working for a bit for the new baby. Kreusa's. She'll be having hers rather soon now."

"Let's hope Aeneas is safely back by then." I felt struck by my own selfishness. I had paid no attention to his sister Kreusa, wife of Prince Aeneas, who might give birth to their second child before her husband's return. Indeed Kreusa too was a young wife in love.

"I prefer music to fighting." Alexander said dryly. "Helen tells me the Lakedaimonians are very musical. I plan to open a school there for young bards and choristers." He changed to an ancient Phrygian melody from the days of Tantalos. His face took on wistfulness.

"But as king, how would you find time for teaching?"

"Helen wants me to bring her people the best of Trojan heritage in music and poetry. She wants to elevate austere Sparta to a shining center in mainland Achaia, such as Troia is in Anatolia." He bent over his lyre, drawing from it haunting melodies. "On the battlefield I'm no good except with the bow." He struck a final chord and began wrapping the instrument. His thoughtful eyes met mine and as a soft sigh escaped his throat, he stood up, drawing himself up to his full height. His tone changed. "Troia is a civilized power, Ãndrõmakhê. But the future, dear sister, is with those swords waiting on the beach." He turned sharply and strode away.

I retrieved the golden leaves I had stashed in my belt-pocket and flung them down the wall, as an offering to the Goddess. Those who were close below noticed and fell over each other to collect them.

Hours passed and still I would not abandon my lone sentry spot, sight glued to the horizon. Then, suddenly, the walltop began filling with people moving around excitedly. All eyes and fingers pointed toward where Polites was racing down the Mound of Bateia. I looked toward the Ida Pass; faint puffs of yellowish dust billowed slowly there, like smoke. Points of metal glimmered.

Hektôr?

A roar swelled up from within the city when Polites slammed through the Idaian Gate, closely followed by Polydamas. Shouting and screaming pressed against my ears. I felt grown into the wall for one long frenzied moment. Where was Hektôr? Were my parents and brothers with him? Then I realized Alexis was standing behind me, with Helen.

"Come away, Lady." Thalpia touched my arm with slender fingers. "Hektôr will meet you down there."

"And what of my father?" Blood rushed to my head. "Are you afraid of telling me that…that Thébé…has fallen?" I screamed the words and they echoed back from close walls.

"Come, Lady, come," Thalpia beseeched, reaching for me.

"Don't you touch me!" Weeping, I ran blindly down the stairs. Everything around me was moving—was it an earthquake?

Then I realized that my own body was shaking and I was not able to control it. Then a wailing sounded from the courtyard. I heard the name of Thébé and my father's name with that of Akhilles.

Priam stormed down the stairs, followed by Hekabe and Kreusa.

Desperate, I grasped Priam's arm. I was speechless, my eyes on fire as I stared at him.

"I see that you have heard," Priam spoke gently. "Thébé's fall is a terrible blow to all of us."

I gasped, "My family….?"

"The womenfolk are prisoners. Your mother lives."

With a throat-wrenching scream, I collapsed at the foot of the stairs. "My father…my brothers…."

Another loud scream voided the emptiness in me, needling my own ears as I doubled over myself.

The thud and slap of booted feet rushed upon me from above, Hektôr's strong hand lifted and steadied me against his body. I stood, shaking uncontrollably.

Then Hektôr freed me and placing his crimson-maned helmet under an arm, knelt before his parents. "Akhilles sacked Lesbos too. I heard that Diomede, King Phorbas' daughter, fell in love with Akhilles, and tipped him about how he could win."

He rose again, turned to me, and I flung myself into his arms. Briefly I thought of my old friend Diomede, wondering if her treachery would save her from slavery. Perhaps being a captive of Akhilles might be an easier fate than having Agamemnon as master.

With an easy swing, Hektôr lifted me into his chariot and sprang in beside me. Slapping reins over his stallions the car lurched forward, tore up the ramp onto the walls of the inner citadel. The pressure of the climb pushed me against him as the animals, already tired, frothed and their hooves sparked along the stones.

There Hektôr paused, winding an arm around my shoulders. His voice was tender. "We are far from prying eyes. You can weep now. The wind will carry the sound away from everyone."

I thrashed my head from side to side, but the horror would not leave. I had to know more, but could not bear it now. "Oh, Hektôr!" I drew a deep breath. "Where are they?"

His fingers traced my face and throat, his head lowered to mine. I felt his breath on my skin as his lips smoothed tender love over my face. Folding my hands in his, he spoke with care, "Latmia is safe because she is dedicated to heavenly powers. Akhilles personally paid her ransom and sent her to her father in Miletos."

"What of my father? And of my brothers?"

"They defended Thébé nobly; they are heroes."

"They are dead. By whose direct hand?"

"Akhilles."

I had known it all along. My father, and my seven brothers, all slain. SEVEN brothers I had, and now, not ONE was left! I turned my head away. If I had accepted Akhilles' proposal on that day in the grove, they might have been alive today. However, I had not, and Fates cast their doom. On the other hand, perhaps, my rejection of him had been pre-ordained too, in order to pave the way for their death. Emptiness entered my heart. Then everything turned black like the silence of death.

* * * *

It was a long time before I could feel beyond my own grief. Though I moved about, cast my shuttle and twirled my distaff, I knew only vague impressions from without, and an inner suffusion of unshed tears. The days of wailing and tearing of clothes had ended for me, yet I was suspended in the magenta darkness of grief.

At night, I was conscious of my face against Hektôr's shoulder, and knew the sweetness of that strong man's gentleness. During the day, when he went about his endless duties, I lay staring at the tapestry my mother had made. Sometimes I imagined I saw her pale hands fluttering over its red, blue and white figures twined with gold threads.

Then Nefru would come and jostle me out of bed with purrs, reminding me that I was still needed in the world of the living.

Trailing the survivors Hektôr had brought to Troia, refugees, freemen and slaves alike, arrived at our gates and were granted permission to enter. When their representatives addressed me as Queen Ãndrõmakhê, I realized that indeed I was their ruler by inheritance. These were my own people, expecting me to step in my parents' stead, and do right by them.

One of them, a leathery-faced seafarer by the name of Zibotes, brought me a gift: The Goddess, as an obsidian statue about the size of my hand. Zibotes said he had found her in a cave in the distant island of Shardana, near the Giant's Tomb; she was called Dea Madre. Bluntly carved, she had a large square head and eyes, a wide smile, small breasts, round hips and thighs. The sensations this little statue evoked in me were so formidable that, even though I wanted to question Zibotes, I could not unlock my tongue. Shardana. Dea Madre. Parents murdered by bald-headed, blue-painted, naked and screaming raiders. A gallant brother Nurziu, saving his tiny sister Kiara's life by hiding her in the deepest corner of the forest. A yellow-spotted, friendly lynx that hunted, and brought his prey, sharing it with them—keeping them alive during an unusually cold winter. The Lynx! *Loyal like Nefru...*

At last, I tore through my grief-induced stupor, resumed my duties and offered my dowry for purchase of fresh supplies and the care of refugees. They swelled the ranks of the already huge numbers of needy in Troia. Yet I was proud of them. Those who could bear arms joined the defenses, others helped with daily labor, cutting stones, carding wood, and hammering metal, and women and girls entered the textile mills that never stopped producing purple cotton and linen.

Hekabe went with me into the storerooms and looked over my treasures. There were gold cups and glaze-ware, silver ingots, rhyton, ebony, carpets and bowls and plates on shelves in the dark. Everything had been decorated by the best artists. I scarcely saw them as Hekabe inventoried them with the scribe. Chests of tapestries, linens and fine clothing of Egyptian linen and wool were checked; others held pillows and hides tanned to silken smoothness. There were huge jars of olives and olive oil and wine, still untouched, with grain sealed in others. Tears filled my eyes as my parents' image came alive in my memory, caringly preparing these assets that made me a woman of substance in my husband's house.

* * * *

On the following day, I sat with Hekabe in the royal women's workroom. Priam's lesser wives and concubines were scattered, some sitting on stools, others milling around. Their cedar looms stood high along the wall and their clatter was background to the women's talk. In the center of the room stood a great jar of oil, imported in earlier days when Troia traded freely with Krete under Minoan kings. About it were placed wide-topped baskets of gilded rushes holding huge mounds of thread, a different color for each basket. The purple and reds of the women's dresses reflected in the polished tile floor.

Laodike came to chat with her mother Hekabe about children and household matters. Enjoying their easy banter, I sat a while longer. Surrounded by my husband's family, I was filled with the need to know everything about the fate of my own. I must get Hektôr to tell it all, for I was stronger now, could endure the full truth.

I looked around at the other women. Two of them were Priam's wives, Laothoe, whose father Altes had died with the collapse of Pedasos, and Kastianeira, whose family was safe in Thrakia. Like me, Laothoe had no longer a family from which she had come.

After exchanging a few courtesies with the women, I stood and went out, hurried down the stairs and into the courtyard. The faintly damp greenness of the herb garden refreshed me as I breathed it in and sat down on the bench nearby.

"You look pale," Laodike's voice interrupted my thoughts, as she sat down beside me.

"I could no longer breathe in there," I replied honestly.

"If you'd just let go, Ãndrōmakhê, just scream and tear your hair, things would be easier for you," she said warmly. "I ought to know."

"I didn't know you had grief lately...."

"Not lately, but it's a constant one."

"Can you talk about it?"

Laodike looked at me strangely. "You don't know? You haven't heard the gossip?"

I shook my head.

"Then you are the only one, far and wide, who hasn't."

"You know I've always kept to myself, Laodike."

With a small smile, she said, "Surely you realized that my son Munitos doesn't look like Helikaon."

I sat up. "But…he does…same dark hair and eyes…."

She smiled. "Not the face or shape of the body. Not even his voice, or swagger! But of course, you were not here when Akamas came, so you never met him and—"

"What are you saying, Laodike?"

"Munitos is Akamas' son."

"Akamas is out there now, in the field, slaughtering our people!"

"He wouldn't have to if Alexis had not brought Helen here. We fell in love when Akamas came along with the Atrides brothers and Odysseus to fetch Helen, but of course, no one was listening to reason, least of all Helen. At the time, Akamas stayed apart from most of the talks, only a witness and not a participant. We fell in love. It was strange how easy, and how quickly! On the seventh day, we decided that no matter what, we would not be separated, and leave Troia together. Alas, just before we could do so, our love was discovered, and Alexis attacked and wounded Akamas."

"Oh, yes," I said dryly, "I had heard that Akamas quarreled with Alexis, and was hurt seriously. It took him a long while to recover. That's why he entered the war against us later than the others did."

My gaze was riveted to Laodike's face and downcast eyes. The pain I saw there was so great that I had to reach and hold her hand. "Does Helikaon know about this?"

"Yes, along with almost everyone else but you. Helikaon had loved me from long before, and when I realized I was pregnant, offered to marry me. Helikaon is a good man, Ãndrõmakhê. He does treat me and Munitos well."

Laodike left without another word, and I remained sitting.

My mind returned to dwell on my own grief. Indeed, it was time I urged Hektôr to tell it all. My whole being was immersed in blackness shot with the memory of unbearable loss and pain.

After the evening meal, as we sat in our own hall, I looked him straight in the eye. "Tell me now. Everything. How it was in Thébé. I need to go into the ritual of mourning, reciting the lives and virtues of my parents, and each of my brothers."

"Better leave it for a minstrel to recite their bravery."

"No, that is for future years when they will be remembered and honored by our children. This is from *you,* how it was, with you there. Come, tell me! I must meet the full truth and learn to live with it."

And so he told me. For long weeks, Hektôr and Father had mowed waves of soldiers along Adramyttion Bay, and burnt down their ships. But the enemy had recruited more and more runts and jackals. Then Akhilles had arrived secretly. In swift, silent action as he had used in Dardania, he had raided the fields by night. My seven brothers, out tending flocks and herds at the dark of the moon, had failed to return in the morning. Hektôr had led a scouting party. He had found them slain in the pasture; limbs and torsos hacked to pieces, lying scattered about in the grass, and all livestock gone. Gathering whatever could be found, he had seen to their burial.

Brave Andros, handsome Presbon, studious Aidan, playful Doran, bright Thoon, cheerful Almon, and Leukon, our mother's youngest, the one whose birth had almost caused her death, three years ago. All dead.

Afterwards, before the memorial-stone was atop their burial mound, Akhilles had broken truce and attacked Thébé.

Each citizen stood up to the invaders street by street. Women killed themselves while in the embrace of their ravishers, using knives or bobbins or sticks; others stalked men as they slept. Blood ran in the fountains and runnels of my beloved Thébé, choked by putrefying corpses and reddening every stone of the city.

My father was cornered with Hektôr in the Great Hall, defending my mother, Nurse Mykale, loyal servant Althaia, also Lanassa and Astynome. Akhilles and his cousin, Patroklos, rushed them together. Father and Hektôr stood back to back, one fighting Akhilles, the other Patroklos. Mother was with her daughters-in-law within a protective ring of Théban soldiers. She screamed when she saw Akhilles thrust his sword into my father's shoulder. Then the soldiers' line around her broke and Akhilles grasped the advantage, moving in on her. Father sprang to defend her, but was slashed to death at her feet.

Hektôr seized Mother about the waist, grabbing Astynome's hand. Lanassa followed them as they ran. In the courtyard, they were surrounded and, leaning my mother against the wall, Hektôr stood at her defense. When he at last beat back the attackers, the two younger women were gone. He reached for my mother but she flung herself away, running off.

Back inside, Hektôr found her weeping and blindly dragging at the fallen bodies that covered my father. She stared up at him with maddened eyes, "Sir, this is my husband, and he's sleeping. This is King Êetiôn Lykosides, beloved Overlord of all Mysia. He's an important ally of King Priam, and must not be wakened." Then she stood up and shrieked wild laughter. "All my seven boys will return and punish those evil men!"

Hektôr rushed for Akhilles but was held back by roaring flames licking down paneled walls, feeding on oil from the women's weaving-jars in the workroom. As he continued battling the enemy throughout the palace, the rest of Akhilles' men swarmed in, more intent on dragging out women then combing the fires for loot.

It was morning before Hektôr and his men found several hundred of survivors and brought them to Troia.

"Akhilles was noble enough to give your father a hero's burial and raised a large mound over him," Hektôr concluded now. "Your friend Astynome was allotted to Agamemnon as battle prize, but we expect that Chryse, as Priest of Apollo, whom the Achaians too revere, will manage to ransom her."

"Tell me about my mother," I whispered.

"Akhilles found her too. However, her father, King Nomion, ransomed her. Yes, Miletos survived the raids. It's battered, its treasure gone for ransoms, but free. And your mother's mind has found peace, for she believes herself a small child again in her father's palace."

I clung to Hektôr. "I have no one but you! You are now my mother and my father, and all my seven brothers."

"Dearest love, I will protect you with my life." He kissed me with lingering tenderness. Lifting me in his arms, he carried me up the stairs and to our bedchamber. My hands grasped his shoulders and I felt his bright solidity in a dark world where I was lost.

He unrolled the bedding and laid me there. I looked up at him and swallowed hurtful tears. "You are the reason for me to go on living."

"My sweet Ãndrõmakhê! I have loved you from the time I saw you at the welcome banquet for Alexis and Helen."

He stood up and kicked off his sandals, then climbed onto the bed beside me. At his touch, I trembled from knowing how deeply he cared. He held me, and I wound my arms about his body. A heady mixture of passion and tenderness uncoiled within me. I gasped as he traced a line of assurance from my mouth to my shoulder with his lips. My mind whirled, my body roiled in huge pulses from heart to toe. I was falling through space.

He shifted to loosen our clothing. "I love you!" I breathed, sobbing. The sweat of his body was sweet to me. I nestled my face in the soft curls of his chest. I had no other way to express my grief except in the shelter of my husband's arms.

Hours later, I was wakened by an indescribable clattering and crunching of wheels, the stamping of hooves on stone, that came in from outside. Could an Achaian have broken into the city?

Hektôr was already up, straightening his clothing.

"It's that Troilos," he ground out. "If he lives to age twenty, it will be a miracle." He strode from the room.

Quickly I pulled on a loose linen robe and ran after him.

His young brother Troilos was there in his new chariot, blond hair flying, face flushed. The horses were lathered from their run up the street. I could not resist a laugh as Hektôr seized the chariot-rail and shouted, "No more of this vagabond behavior, young man! You shall leave at once! The racetrack at Thymbra is good enough. You will be protected there by the god."

The boy carelessly waved an arm, wheeled, and drove back down the street. Hektôr turned back to me, grinning.

"Isn't there an oracle about him?" I asked.

"Yes. Ilion will never be conquered if Troilos lives to age twenty. Therefore, he has to be reminded of that now and then. Come." He led me back into our house.

I promised myself to weave a tapestry to continue the story of Thébé to its end. I would hang it near that of my mother, in the bedroom. Through my fingers, I would evacuate poisonous grief that seared my mind....

Chapter 14

Runners reported that Akhilles' troops were now torching the coast eastward from Troia. Sailing through the unprotected Strait, they had picked up more men at the Achaian camp. Troia's renowned herd of ancestral prize horses, watched over by Demokoon, a son of Priam, were in danger, penned in between the raiders and the ships. However, a pattern of confusion emerged among the enemy; were they afraid to attack Troia, or did they think to destroy all sources of supply first?

Then came news, specifically for me. My mother had died! She had lived like a silent child in her father's palace in Miletos, cared for by loyal Mykale whom Akhilles had freed without demanding ransom, until the Goddess had ended her pain. Even as I recited her eulogies of mourning, I was thankful that my beloved, proud, and beautiful mother was released of all earth-bound hurts.

More than ever, I longed to give Hektôr an heir. I offered gifts to Goddess Ate as Giver of Life. Upon the altar in our courtyard, I placed the Dea Madre, surrounding her by symbolic pots of red clover, licorice root, and wild yam. Nightly, as Thalpia poured thick oil of violets into my bathwater, I felt like an expectant bride on her wedding day. Finally, my body and mind were in concert, for I learned the meaning of womanly response to my husband's ardor.

Then, finally, I missed my monthly blood.

Hope rode high in my breast but I dared not speak of it until another month went by, and I could be sure.

* * * *

Every day I waited for Hektôr inside the Skaian Tower that overlooked a huge, ancient oak tree, when he left with Deiphobos for routine work on the walls or at the recruits' encampment. On hot days I welcomed the winds that somewhat cooled the air. When he would rush up the Skaian Stairs in the evening, grimy, sweaty, breathless, my hands grasped eagerly at his sun-browned, battle-scarred shoulders. As we strolled along the walltop, he would joke about how Agamemnon kept Meneláos idle at the beached ships while Akhilles ran loose like the overgrown boy he was. So, we laughed, as the Achaians, terrified of Troia on its great rock, searched for easier game. Occasionally Hektôr looked wistfully at the royal houses that rose up from the wall of the Pergama—the inner citadel. I knew he wanted a quiet home such as men have in peacetime, such as my parents had, a long time ago.

On another day, I was out with Thalpia to shop in the Agora. Among the marble temples, statues, and towering citadel walls, stalls of fish, fruits, and vegetables stood out among crowds of shoppers. To venture out of the city was dangerous, for stray Achaians often appeared in nearby fields. Along the shore anglers and divers worked by night, harvesting conch and fish.

It was quite hot today, the wind listless, and the stench of the tanneries in the Lower City hung heavy in the air. What was left of these tanneries, so vital for the making of leather armors and shields, were forced to move inside the walls and the oak, alum, brains, smoke, and grease they used in close quarters spewed out a dizzying array of smells.

After I sent Thalpia home with purchases, I spotted the group of Councilmen emerging after another one of those interminable meetings, and waited for Hektôr. He came, in his sweaty gray linen jerkin, as if he had been in armor all day. His shoes were laced up to the calf with high, military thongs. The bulge of his sunbleached hair looked dark about his head, still in its helmet knot.

We went to the wall-top for coolness, and he leaned against where the Skaian Tower joined the wall. Beyond him the black-hulled ships with the mystical Eye on their prows, threatened along the bright water of the strait beyond.

"What of the meeting?" I asked, seeing his drawn face.

"The usual frustrations. Come." He moved irritably into the tower room that crossed the gate. I hesitated, a faint nausea rolling in me.

Hektôr paused at his grandfather Laomedon's burial-urn. "Troia's Protector, hear me!" he muttered sourly. "Without our horse-trade, our silver-mines at Alybe and the tolls by land and sea, we shall fall into ruin without a single fight." He clenched a fist and pounded the stone, then stepped out onto the wall beyond.

"Was the meeting so bad?" I followed, standing beside him.

"Yes. We have to have a leader chosen, an Astyanax, Defender of the City. When I left this morning, Cousin Aeneas was bidding to be Astyanax." His teeth gritted. "He is a good strategist and brave warrior. But what right has he to be *Trojan* General? He couldn't save his own citadel!" He moved along, and I with him.

"Y*ou* are Priam's heir; *you* must be Defender." I noticed that we were near the wild fig tree that grew from an earth-patch below us, where the ancient abutment had never been completed. "Alexis goes to Sparta when this is all over, and Aeneas will have to find a new kingdom. *You* are Troia."

"I, Troia, without a son?"

I watched him slap at a nearby leaf and reached idly for another one. The wind blew it away from me.

Hektôr spoke again, "No one in the Council fully realizes what we are up against! It is clear that the Achaians are forcing openings farther and farther east and north. Antenor is for capitulation, as usual. Even my levelheaded Polydamas continues pushing to give up Helen. But Alexis and Father know the enemy, and they are for holding out." His laugh was grim. "Even though I quarreled with Alexis about taking Helen from Meneláos, I agree that her return will not bring a conclusive end to the war."

I stared down at the roots of the gnarled fig tree. Alarm sounded in my mind. Really, this spot was an invitation to scale the wall. "Why was this let go?" I pointed.

He looked down. "Peacetime. This is the fortress of Priam the warrior, warlord, and leader of all other warlords. I am keeping my troops busy on these abutments and strengthening our gates. It was not necessary to hide behind walls in the past; we were successfully busy with trafficking Achaian commerce."

"And yet, wouldn't those innocently toll-paying Achaians gone home as spies?"

"Yes, of course. I must admit Antenor deserves credit for having foreseen trouble! Years ago when Father dispatched him to Salamis to demand Hesione, he returned with warnings of dire times ahead. He recognized my aunt as the proud mistress of Telamon's palace; she was unwilling to leave, just as Helen prefers to stay here. Now Hesione's son Teuker is an Achaian archer, despite his Trojan name. Yes, Teuker, her son by Telamon! He has a Trojan name but is out there, a leader among the invaders. My first cousin, with arrows pointing at me! What an irony. And so is Ajax, that even greater archer, Telamon's other son by his second wife, Periboea." He kicked the stones in frustration. "As a warrior, Ajax is second only to his cousin Akhilles in strength and bravery. In addition, like Akhilles, Kiron the Kentaur trained Ajax. Kiron had also trained his father Telamon, and Akhilles' father Peleos."

I reached for an unripe fig. Missing it, I pointed again, "Those jagged stones are scaleable, Hektôr. A good arm, a rope, and a strong man could leap over this wall aided by the tree." I shuddered as a chill of fear cut through the heat of the stones. "Best to work here, first."

"Had I?" He pulled me up against him, laughing.

"Yes! And you'd better do away with that ledge down there, as soon as possible."

"Such a military mind you have my little strategist!" He held me by the bun on my neck and pressed his lips against mine. "If you're as good at having babies as you try to be at my work, we'll keep the Trojans free for many more years than have already passed over Old Ate's Hill."

"Oh, Hektôr! Seriously, this might be our weakest spot. I didn't have a warrior father and seven brothers without learning something from them." I laughed, dizzy from the searing heat. The sun had lowered but the stones were sending up wave after wave.

"Yes, of course," he chuckled, "let's talk to Antenor about it. Those two weak spots together should make a strong one! As the Achaians climb in, we could clip off their heads one by one."

Heat had begun forming mirages all around me, and now they grew more lifelike, countless disembodied heads dripping and spouting blood—and I was sick, so sick!

I clung about his neck, and then tumbled into a freefall.

At one point, I felt myself being carried by hands locked under me like a chair. The stair-rail slipped downward as the women struggled with my weight. Helen stood at the top of the stairs, one hand against the wall where the balustrade ended. Her golden eyes were dark as she answered Hekabe's question, "I have unrolled her bed, and it is ready." She turned and moved briskly along the gallery.

"Where is Hektôr?" Hekabe panted, reaching the top step.

"My lady, Prince Alexis has sent Helen to help." Thalpia sounded reassuring. The queen, together with the servant, worked their way along to the bedroom. Then I realized… it was *they* who were carrying *me*.

Helen stood at the door while other women placed me on my bed. Hekabe undressed me deftly while Thalpia pulled the covers about and smoothed pillows.

"She has not been herself lately," Thalpia said, and held a revival-herb under my nose. I sneezed.

"Surely you know what's wrong." Helen's matter-of-fact voice sounded nearby as she placed a small bottle of aromatics on the pillow beside my head. "And it's about time!" She stepped down from the bed-dais. "A child can pull a woman out through the darkest depths when she has nothing else to live for." Helen's voice came from the door, and then her sandals clipped softly away.

I drowsed as the scent of cedar from the paneling soothed me.

It was dark when I wakened with Hektôr's weapon-hardened fingers gripping my hand. "Āndrõmakhê?" His whisper was cautious.

"So tired." I felt him inch onto the edge of the bed. "But I have something to tell you." I nestled into the hollow of his shoulder as he held me, loving his strong male odor. "Our prayers are answered, my lord husband."

"Wife! Dearest!" His heartbeat quickened against mine. "Troia is safe now, and will have a Defender after me." He pressed his lips to my forehead, and then spoke with pride, "Laomedon returns to us. Remember, we were by the old king's urn when you turned weak with the child. His title will be Defender of the City."

"Our son. We give him the royal name." I smiled up into his eyes.

"I have long known the name of our son," he said slowly.

"Don't say it, not the name...you know the danger, until he is born we must not utter his name."

"Rest easy, beloved. Never, until he is born, shall evil spirits hear me call to him. No evil creature will deform our child. So I swear!"

The quietness of the room enclosed me like a friendly presence. A patch of the thick, white-figured red carpet had pooled near the door, where it was aglow by the late afternoon sun. I turned my head to see the darkness of my mother's tapestry, from ceiling to the floor. I breathed in deeply. Those times were ended, pushed into the past. Now the future must be everything.

* * * *

Priam was at our door early next morning. Hektôr, just back from his bath, invited him to sit in the cushioned chair in our bedchamber. I did not rise but turned onto an elbow to exchange morning greetings.

"My dear, the queen has just told me of our blessing." He glanced at Hektôr who, naked at the foot end of the bed, leaned over to pick up his clothing from the floor and toss it into the wicker laundry basket. He opened the clothes-chest for a fresh linen breechclout.

"The future of our land is assured now!" Priam boomed with pride. "I thank the gods to have let me live until this day." He shifted and his tone changed, "The Council is about to hold an urgent meeting shortly, Hektôr. You know you have to join it."

Returning to the chest, Hektôr sighed and pulled out his long ceremonial robe of purple wool.

I looked at Priam fondly. Stately even as he sat there, his blond hair turning snow at the temples, he was truly a noble warrior and king. His white robe embroidered in purple, and the belt of purple-stained leather, could not make him any more regal than he was by nature.

Priam was speaking, "No doubt the people will approve the Council's choice. Today I am demanding that they appoint you, Hektôr, as Astyanax. Only the heir may become Defender of the City." He then answered my question, "My dear, henceforth the enemy shall fight us on our terms. When we are ready. Yes, the Achaians have ruined us in the south. They are raiding our eastern allies. But we have other resources." A smile stirred his white beard.

"And you believe firm decisions will actually be made by this contentious Council?" Hektôr grinned, adjusting his belt of gold links.

"I do. The impatience of the young and the deliberation of age, show degrees of experience. Prophecies and omens have their place. So does battle. We are planning a new, surprise move. The Hittites had promised aid for our assistance in their wars with Egypt at the Orontes River. They have not forgotten the valor of my then fifteen-year old son, Hektôr! My queen Hekabe's father has sent men, and her other brother Asios will bring Phrygians. My half-brother Tithonos is powerful among the satraps of Elam, having built his famous city of Susa. He has a son your age, Hektôr, already known as builder of roads and beautifier of cities, his name is Memnon."

"Then we should soon be ready to attack," Hektôr said.

"One day, my son, you will be overlord of all Asia. The Hittites will join to challenge Egypt in Palestine. Who conquers in this contest, will rule all Asia. You are not only intelligent, Hektôr, but unrivaled with the sword. Yes, one day, my son, you will be overlord above the Phrygians and Hittites!"

"The Council knows of these ambitious plans, Father?"

"To some extent. I have schemed ever since Herakles thought to hold me as puppet in Anatolia. I have been patient. The Achaians and Danaans are determined, and impatient. But with you here, and one day Alexis in Lakedaimon, Troia *will* rule the world." Priam rose to his feet. "I am sending Deiphobos and Helenos to Hattushash and Elam." His eyes glinted with humor. "Perhaps Troilos as well, just to keep him out of trouble." He turned to me. "May blessings rest on you, dear child." He stepped to the bed and touched my hair as if in blessing. "You are the mother of Troia's future."

I smiled my answer, too emotional for speech. The old warrior looked down at me with moist eyes, turned away, and left the room.

* * * *

Spring again and mornings dawned with fiery gold, tipping the peaks of Ida and lighting the gray towers of Troia.

Sweet smelling from the rinse of perfumed water that ended my bath, I sat at the dressing table while Thalpia worked on my hair. The thump of Hektôr's bare feet went along outside toward the bathing room. I knew he had already been out with his men.

I was slipping into a crimson robe with a flax belt, gathered to emphasize my pregnancy, when he came in. Tossing his purple cloak onto the clothes-rail, he strode to the chest and retrieved his horsehide vest and white linen kilt.

When I sat down to tie on my sandals, he tossed his things aside and knelt before me. "Let me do that." He took the leather from me, laid it aside, and began caressing the contours of my instep, arch, and ankle. He drew his fingers from my heel all the way to my toes, and I could not help a responsive gasp. Startling sensual heat whispered all over my skin. "Stop that," I chided him, not meaning it.

He looked up, pretending surprise. "You don't like it?"

"Too much! But we have to be in Thymbra...."

He quickly tied on my sandals, then stood and finished his own dressing. "Always so much else to do," he muttered.

I put on my transparent veil. "Are you sure the Achaians and Danaans will respect this truce?"

"Yes! No one desecrates religious places; nowhere is safer than Thymbra. Why else would I insist that Troilos race the horses there and not at the Bateia track?"

"Hmm," I replied, not quite getting his point.

"We have learned from the Achaians," he grinned. "They've got Akhilles, a mere boy from—"

"He is *not* a boy! Not by a long shot! And you know that he is semi-divine! Son of Thétis, the Nereid."

"Still, a spoiled boy, who grew up with girls. Who would have expected him to become the brawn to Agamemnon's brains?"

"Meaning?"

"Troilos...the Achaians will assume he is merely prowling their encampment in the east, as boys will. They scarcely know his face, so no harm would come to him. That said, we really are better off sending him away, for he will be a problem when fighting starts decisively. We would never be able to keep him off the field."

I remembered Kassandra's prophecy about Troilos: *Troia lives if Troilos reaches the age of twenty.*

We went into the courtyard.

Out in the Pergama business had already begun. Shiny perch sat beside tuna looking round and pale; crusty mollusks and slick oysters in open shells glistened. One proud fisherman displayed a whole shark that covered his stall of sapling-logs. I realized how far this man had had to go for his catch to circumvent the blockade, and congratulated him, then turned back to ask Thalpia to buy it for that evening's meal, and pay him more than he would ask for it.

Those who still hunted offered boar, pig, and hare. Fish from the rivers was eaten only to escape starvation because of the muddy taste. Flower stalls near the temples were garlanded in flax and asters, marigold and medicinal peonies.

Hektôr strode off with Polydamas and Deiphobos, and Helenos came out with Troilos from Priam's palace. I smiled softly and watched Troilos swagger along beside his older brothers. As my own brothers had once been, Troilos was impatient for the adventure of war, dismissing the horror, enamored only of heroism.

Then, as once long ago, I felt eyes upon me. The tall figure of Helenos stared at me, his white robe and apron of dappled horsehide motionless. An air of deep asceticism cloaked him, quite unlike the equally ascetic but violently tempestuous religiosity of his twin, Kassandra. When his eyes met mine, dread fanned me like cold air, for his hooded gaze was afire. I smiled as formally as I could and held out my hand, which he entangled in his lean fingers. I felt his muscles strain as he bent down to kiss my wrist. I brushed my fingertips over the top of his sandy hair for no more than ceremony required. Momentary warmth glowed over me from him. He turned quickly from me to the others.

Polyxena came running, followed by Kassandra, and seized my hand. "Oh Ãndrõmakhê, I have to tell you..."

"We will be late." Kassandra took the girl's free hand and they went to join the other girls. I turned slowly to where other pregnant women were assembling.

The procession snaked down Ilion and across the plain where the famed white horses of Laomedon had grazed before Demokoon drove them to Abydos for safety.

Priam and Priest Laokoon led with Hektôr who, as Defender of the City, took equal precedence with his father.

The small village of Thymbra was adjacent to the Apollonian shrine. This was only a three-walled, roofed shelter for the altar. In front of it grew an enormous oak, nurtured from a seedling Dardanos, the ancestor, brought across Thrakia from the Herkynian Forest. A smooth lawn surrounded the area, cropped by sacrificial horses dedicated to Belen, the archaic deity of the land. Three low steps led to the altar itself, which was ornamented at either end by serpents of ivory. Today they were wrapped in dark red flaxen threads so that the subterranean powers would know to step aside, for the divine sun to nourish the hungry and thirsty dead.

Ilioneos the Priest had spent the night in rites summoning dead souls. The end of day would find bowls and pots of food and drink before each house for nourishing and appeasing dead ancestors, who would subsist on aroma from these offerings for the coming year.

Behind my group, walked childless wives, and after them young girls. Filing around the great tree three times with their offerings, their steps matched the rhythm of jingling sistra shaken by the Priestesses Kassandra and Theano. At each pause, one among them attached her offering to a branch.

I held my just-spun wool ready. Going around until a suitable gold-green leaf caught my eye, I lightly tossed my beige skein so that it loosened and tangled wispily among the sun-soaked branches. I joined the circle to go, in my turn, to the ancient altar. Behind me, the red and yellow dresses of childless wives swung rhythmically around the trunk in a dance inducing impregnation with some ancestor.

Ilioneos tied a black ewe and a white ram with red woolen threads to the altar-serpents. Helenos lit and held incense-cups while in the concealed background, young priests stamped their feet and shouted. The sheep were sacrificed and their blood drained into the earth. Ilioneos and Helenos then joined in a chant older than Troia as the girls began a whirling dance around the sacred oak. I watched them, swaying from side to side with the music.

When the ceremony ended, the girls broke apart to race with young men into the nearby shrubbery. I was to join other mothers in tying votive images to the tree. I selected mine from those piled in baskets near the altar. While I was tying mine, a sesame cake in the shape of a crescent, a flicker caught my eye and I spotted Polyxena racing alone toward the river.

Curious, I moved in that direction where the married women gathered wheat stalks in thanksgiving for their fertility. Reeds nodding along the bank, a rustle as I neared, and a low laugh…then a comment that a child conceived here would be half-divine.

I moved to turn away when a couple stood up.

Recognition set in: The girl...Polyxena!

And something familiar about the man's bright flowing hair, his height and wide shoulders.

Before I could adjust my sight, he sprang away to the mud-and-stone huts dating to the earliest days.

I sat on a mat of dry reeds as Polyxena came to me, walking jauntily. She tossed back her dark hair. "I hope he put twins to nestle in me," she said. "One for the divine river and one for Akhilles. Then perhaps my father will see how to end the war..."

"Akhilles!" I breathed in sharply. I should have recognized him! "But when...how...is this the first time?"

"No. We first met on the night of the Triple Mare Goddess. I wanted to tell you that time of Helen's New Moon banquet. If Father will let me marry him...oh, Āndrōmakhê! The war could end."

"Tell me about it." I encouraged her calmly.

"He was up from the south to reconnaissance. He looked so glorious, so divine in the moonlight, among the flowers, laughing at our boys while they bred the mares. It was a night of LIFE."

"I see. Akhilles has been spying on us." I could not bear seeing the love that glowed from the girl's eyes for Akhilles, he who had slain my father and seven brothers. My voice trembled, "You, Priam's daughter, hoping for an Achaian's child?"

Polyxena rose to her feet and made a little dance. "I'd die rather than marry anyone but Akhilles!" She then blushed deeply, glanced at her feet, adding with a small voice, "But the child is just wishful thinking, Āndrōmakhê. We never went any further than kissing. I told him that I am a Princess of Troia, and my virginity belongs to the Skamander River. So he agreed to wait until the time is right and we can be married properly."

Akhilles agreed to wait? I wondered, *this ruthless murderer has honor?* I glanced back toward the shrine, where torches were being lit. And I had only a few stalks of wheat on hand. "We must go back."

The blush of morning ended the Feast of All Souls. I moved through the growing light, retrieving my empty pots from my threshold. The omens were propitious, they were empty; my parents and brothers had taken the cheese, wine and sesame cakes.

Hektôr, standing at our hearth, watched me set down the vessels. He left off turning the spitted hare and reached for my hand.

"Everything has been taken," I told him, and his face relaxed. "Troilos will be safe."

"Deiphobos and Helenos should succeed, then, among the Hittites. Perhaps the Assyrians will revolt against their Mitanni overlords and also send us men."

I suppressed a bitter laugh, thinking of Polyxena and Akhilles. We hade the freedom to hope, plan, and devise, be prudent and consider the many odds, yet the Fates had their way of thwarting us.

Hektôr said, "We know the Achaians are still afraid of us. And perhaps other plans can be made to end the siege."

"By the way, what about that unfinished section of the wall?"

"I didn't forget! I am working on it. But you know more refugees are streaming in daily, and this makes it necessary to put up additional defenses around the Lower City."

"Let me warn you again: *That is a dangerous spot by the fig tree.*"

"Other places come first. A herd of horses could be sent through some spots in those outer defenses. These have to be strong enough to hold until we get the main fortress wall reinforced."

We took seats in chairs against the wall, soft skins covering us warmly in the morning chill. Thalpia set tables with food, then filled her own plate and sat at the hearth to eat. Nefru appeared, leapt upon the table, demanding his share of delicacies. Gently I placed him down on the ground and gave him a bowl full with rich, meaty tidbits.

"The Achaians may be hoping for such an earthquake as let Herakles into the city," Hektôr spoke. He picked up a roasted chestnut, dipped it in marrow paste, and placed it between my lips. I laughed, ate it and handed him a crunchy skin.

A cheerful voice from the doorway startled us. Young Troilos stood there, dressed for travel in boots, leather jerkin and cloak. "We must leave before the Achaians' watch."

Hektôr pushed back his small table and stood up.

I jumped up, quickly bundled a loaf of bread, cheese, salted meat and figs for the travelers, and followed.

Troilos spoke while we were walking, "An Achaian was seen yesterday at Thymbra. No one knows who it was, but if Akhilles is back from Alybe, we'd better get there while we can."

I almost staggered, my cheeks burning. I should have reported what I knew! But how could I also protect Polyxena?

Hektôr's voice interrupted my concern, "I'll go part of the way with you, Troilos." He strode easily, one hand on the boy's shoulder.

Priam, straight-backed, in gold tiara and long purple, waited at his hearth. With him were Antenor and Anchises. Aeneas, Alexis, and Laokoon were to one side.

161

Troilos turned to Helenos and Deiphobos, also dressed for travel. Hektôr moved to Priam while Hekabe motioned me to a chair beside her. Helen and Kreusa sat on stools at a hearthside column.

Priam spoke to Hektôr, "As Chief Defender—"

Aeneas stepped forward, scowling. Not for the first time, I noted his resemblance to Hektôr. Priam silenced him with a look. Aeneas growled something, his eyes smoldering.

Helen hissed through her teeth, "I'm sick of all this Trojan snarling and indecision!"

"You know how to handle the situation in Karduniash," Priam was concluding his remarks. Helenos and Deiphobos nodded. "Meleshipak is expecting you. I've had no answer from Dudhalia, but such an opportunity to foil Egypt should appeal to him."

Helenos and Deiphobos knelt with Troilos for their father's blessing, then rose and went out. Troilos, to whom I handed the bundle with provisions, was to join Demokoon at Alybe, and see to the salvaging of whatever silver ore remained.

From the wall, I watched the envoys' party flow out from the city, following the old route along the coast to Larissa. There the road turned eastward for Babylonia and lands of the Hittites.

Hektôr returned, ran up the tower stairs, breathing heavily with angry concern. He stopped beside me and stared after the dust of Troilos' chariot, swearing under his breath. The boy had swept off toward the Achaian camp and swerved away, as if in challenge. "That fool brother of mine will get us all killed yet! He's got to learn that bravery is more than flexing muscles in front of the enemy." He tucked my arm under his. "We have much to do if Akhilles has returned as Antenor said."

"Hektôr...I'm sure I saw him. At Thymbra."

"What?"

"While I was gathering wheat-offerings. An Achaian was running away from the river. I...think now...it was Akhilles."

"Do you know what you are telling me? That the danger to Alybe was a false report? If he is here secretly, he had to give up the attack. If their leaders have become spies, it would not be the first time."

My heart leapt to my throat. Ah, perhaps I could help Polyxena without betrayal! "Akhilles could change the war." His startled look made me pause. Then I drew in a deep breath for courage, and blurted out, "Suppose he was to marry one of us."

"Akhilles? He is betrothed to Menelos' daughter, Hermione. She's in Tauris now, waiting for him." A frown made lines between his eyes. "Surely none of our women would have him. Besides, only my full

sisters would be important enough; and all are married except Kassandra and Polyxena. Kassandra is promised to Koromikos, whether she likes it or not—Koromikos joined us to win her heart, and we do need his troops."

"Yes, but there's Polyxena. True, she's barely of marriage age, but she'd be happy…" I caught myself in time. "To help the cause."

He straightened and we started along toward the Tower Stairs. "You think too much, Ãndrõmakhê. I have work to do outside. That wall has to be finished before the winter rains arrive."

"Mull it over, Hektôr…about Polyxena and Akhilles."

"All right. But we know that he already has a son, a boy called Pyrrhos, by Deidameia of Skyros. Meaning, my poor little sister will have two women of royal blood to grapple with."

"A son by Princess Deidameia? Bah! What else, when he grew up with King Lykomedes' daughters! Consider it this way: he has only *one* child by all of them." I laughed. "Why not discuss it with your father? By now the Achaians might welcome the excuse to get out of this stagnant situation on our shores."

"Perhaps." He dropped a kiss on my forehead.

"Also see about that place by the fig tree. It frightens me."

Chapter 15

I felt—already—widowed, but to the walls of Troia. Hektôr spent long days and nights working at the fortifications, his trusted lieutenant Polydamas always at his side. Sometimes he came in only long enough to sketch ground plans and defense areas on soft clay tablets that he left lying about in the courtyard to harden in the sun. He moved stones and chiseled away rough corners until calluses formed on his hands. He sang and cursed with his men, laughed uproariously at his own mistakes as well as theirs'. Tirelessly he drilled them in military defense. Spear-throwers, shield-bearers, swordsmen, charioteers, and archers were kept hardy and fit, on their toes, but always well fed, compensated, and armored. He spared no one, chiefly not himself, and his men loved and respected him for that.

One morning, my beloved Iris died, while giving birth to Xanthos' equally gigantic son. Hektôr and I had spent the night with her, tending her, suffusing her with our own strength, and when she gave up her soul, I fell in my husband's arms and wept inconsolably. Born on the same day and hour as I, Iris had been my star-sister and her death robbed me of my last sibling.

Against all odds, or perhaps because as the descendant of Zeus' horses, Xanthos was part divine, the strapping foal survived, and we named him Phoenix. He sported Xanthos' richly golden coat, and Iris' flaxen mane, tail, socks, and playful good nature.

* * * *

Shortly before the winter rains, Demokoon returned to the city through a postern gate opened to his secret knock. He came disheveled into the Great Hall just while everyone was assembling for the evening meal. Dropping to his knees before his father, he sobbed as he embraced the old man's legs. "They are gone, all gone!" Demokoon raged. "Your entire fine herd; the sacred Laomedon. Whites as well, meant only for divine service. Akhilles raided by night while I slept and Troilos…he meant to watch, but…well, at least he is safe."

"So be it." Priam heaved a sigh. "What is done can not be undone. The day will come—Zeus be praised!—when we shall exact full reckoning from those thieves." He embraced his son and Demokoon stood up. "We rejoice in your safety."

Lykaon accompanied his half-brother to the bath.

When they returned, laughter and hopeful conversation made a festive banquet of the meal.

"What of the mines?" Hektôr asked them.

Breaking a brittle crust from the fried lamp chop on my plate, I chewed it without tasting. Then I used a small silver spoon to drip roseleaf preserve onto a bit of bread. There was mares' milk cheese and whey in small bowls beside my plate. I sprinkled roasted almonds over the whey. Images of pale-faced, hungry children in the Lower City, danced in my mind. My throat tightened and I could not swallow.

"Troilos is seeing to them," Demokoon answered Hektôr's question. "Much silver has been taken from storage and sent out singly in wagons, rather than the usual caravans, so as to escape the attention of bandits. Some should be here by now."

"We have had only two wagonloads," Hektôr said. "The rest must arrive before the rains."

"Speaking of winter rains," Lykaon interrupted. "There's little time to double our supplies of chariot rails before the best saplings break in the weather."

Hektôr warned, "Akhilles was seen about their camp!"

"We need twice as many rails as chariots," Lykaon reminded. "Rails are first to break in an encounter. Young boys have done what they could, but almost nothing is left after those night-raids. I've had to use fig wood a lot because the ash trees are nearly all gone." Not waiting for comment, he moved from his chair. "I shall go now. We left bundles in the farthest orchard today. Raiders will be out and could find them before morning."

Laothoe laid a hand on her son's shoulder. "This is too dangerous, after what you've been telling us. Stay in tonight."

He kissed her cheek briefly, gave her an impatient look, and strode from the great room.

* * * *

Lykaon did not return the next morning, and no trace of him could be found. After spending hours trying to reassure Laothoe, I went to join Hekabe in the Great Hall. I stopped at the door, not seeing the queen; but Hektôr was there. He stood near the hearth facing a young woman.

Angry words rested on the air. Then recognition slapped me in the face: The woman was Sigeia! Small and tan of skin, rich dark hair and eyes, she held a toddler in her arms. I sat on the absent guard's stool to wait. The woman had no right here; she had no claim on Hektôr....

Hektôr sounded furious. "I would have fostered the boy and made you my second wife, for his sake! However, there can only be one son bearing the royal name. Until you change that, or leave the boy for me to foster, I will have none of you. This child is *not* to bear the name Skamandrios! That name is given only to the heir."

Sigeia lifted her chin. "I will name your son as it is his right. He is your firstborn and will rule all the Trojans!"

"But he is not my *heir*. You bring evil into this house by forcing me to speak that name."

"So be it, Hektôr! Remember: You will never be rid of this child. I will be first wife, or nothing. Polymestor will protect my son's rights to the throne. I have no need for your queen's patronage." She put the child on his feet and led him into the courtyard.

Hektôr strode out passing me without seeing me.

* * * *

Later we heard that Lykaon, son of Priam and Laothoe, was taken to an island and sold into slavery. Then Alybe together with its silver mines fell to Akhilles. Troilos escaped to Priapos, where Arisbe and Hyrtakos hosted him. Just before the collapse of Alybe, he had had the foresight to dispatch wagonloads of silver to Troia.

The freezing nights of winter could not loosen the discipline that Hektôr maintained with his loyal men. I kept a charcoal brazier in my workroom. Thalpia and Nefru sat with me as I spun out fibers to be made into swaddling-cloths for our much-expected son. I took care of the herbs I touched, and ate, protecting my growing child from countless spells and spirits waiting to enter my body. By night, I was thankful to be able to nestle closer to my husband, and he never failed to draw me against him.

Chapter 16

Star of Hope

...a mere babe, the well loved son of Hector, like a fair star."
Homer: Iliad, Book VI A. T. Murray, Translator

The mystic rites of spring equinox were celebrated under Kassandra's leadership. Spies brought word that Lanassa was captive, but no one knew where she was held.

Spring greened the plains, flooding rivers and fattening tamarisk-needles. Achaian farmers remained across on the Chersonesos part of Thrakia, land of King Polymestor, where his wife Ilione, daughter of Priam and Hekabe, guarded her young brother Polydoros.

Kassandra assembled all the single girls of Troia for celebrations in the temple gardens of Apollo. Nightly, as the moon filled, I listened to fervor of dance and music; louder and louder came the clink of sistra and the tickling of castanets to the hungry crying of bagpipes, warding off evil. Nightlong we danced, barefoot on the pressed-down grass, working out intricate music against full-moon madness.

My own hour of fullness came during an afternoon, when, struck with nausea and vertigo, I collapsed on the grass.

Theano rushed and chanted over me, trying to postpone the birth until the appearance of tonight's new moon. Tension pressed more strongly within my body even as the priestess chanted and I was helped inside, to Priam's Great Hall.

Hekabe came to sit with me, and the tension inside me eased. I relaxed while women ran about, holding smoking pine torches to doors and windows that their pitch would keep out evil spirits.

I was glad Hektôr had left earlier that evening, for the bearing would be easier with no male in the house. I doubled over in pain in my chair and Hekabe leaned toward me. She and Theano got me up to my feet and walked me around the hall. A new pain gripped me and I twisted in their grasp.

"Bear down," the Queen urged gently. "It's almost time."

Pains tore through my body in ever-growing pulses as the hours dragged. Compelled, I stopped in front of the firepit, staring down and seeing Hektôr's image in the flames. I cried out.

Hekabe touched my wet hair tenderly. Theano, her dark eyes even darker, placed an inquisitive hand against my abdomen. "Let's get her upstairs, and send Thalpia to tell Hektôr to begin sacrifices to Ilythia, Goddess of Childbirth."

The women pulled me to my feet. The stairs before me were endless. Far away, the long narrow gallery. An earthquake; no, the bed under me. My abdomen bursting with flame and blood.

"Mother! Mother! Oh, Mother!" My lips twisted back over my teeth as terror returned with even more pain. Hands fluttered over my naked body. It was so dark; why didn't someone bring a torch?

Thalpia rushed about brandishing laurel branches as added surety against evil. Placed on the threshold of each door, they would trip harmful feet attempting to enter. Theano stood close, holding a stem of wormwood over my head, chanting spells for an easy delivery, for a healthy child. Hekabe forced a cool tart drink between my swollen lips. Compress made of cool water sizzled on my burning forehead.

Suddenly the moon melted pale silver over our marriage bed, and I imagined seeing my husband's oblong face.

The moon grew, grew, into a bright womb up in the velvet sky, rounding with life as was my abdomen rounded with the child. The moonbeams then shot arrows of life to earth. Hektôr's life and my own blended to bring back a powerful ancestor to fulfill Troia's need in the future. This new life, this hoped for young-old son to be, filling my heart with wonder and hope....

The brilliant moon shed stars over the sky, and I felt elated, so grand and proud in my own femaleness. Man guided the flow of life that ever circled the earth, into Woman's body, and Woman carried that life and brought it to movement in the hands of Humanity.

"This won't last longer!" Hekabe's voice. "Ready with the knife?"

There was a loud flapping of wings, a throaty cooing, and then... silence. Something warm and sticky ran from a feathered tube between my lips. Somehow, I managed to swallow the sacrificed dove's blood.

"The dove's soul has gone into her," Theano declared, "a soul for one born. Live, o Prince of Troia!"

A sharp slap. A wizened cry.

My son.

Our son!

"Hektôr—Hektôr...Hektôr." I could not stop crying.

"Thalpia! Let him in!" Hekabe's command.

"Evil will come to the child if taboo is broken." Theano.

"Defilement can easily be purified!" Hekabe. "She can't survive this way, weak as she is. We cannot let Hektôr lose her. I said *open the door, Thalpia.*"

Hektôr entered, stumbling up the steps of the dais, calling my name. He touched my forehead delicately with his lips.

His voice was far away, "My son, heir to all the Trojans, Defender of the City after me!"

* * * *

I had seven tender days to bask in the quietness of my secret woman's world. Day by day, my son grew rosy, plump, and strong. Timeless peace enclosed the two of us as I lay with my child, the only attendants Thalpia and Hekabe. No male creature, including Nefru, who feverishly scratched at the door for admittance, was allowed near me lest his influence hinder my recovery.

In all his waking hours my son nursed, his tiny pressing hands on my breast, his little body smooth with oil. I watched anxiously for any sign of evil that might prevent his acceptance into humanity, after which time there could be no fear of exposure. This, the much-coveted heir of Troia, must live, must become a man. Through me, this tender, delicate child would one day be a mighty warrior and just-minded overlord and defender of his people.

Then my days of dreaming ended.

Purified of taboo, my body cleaned by ritual, I feasted my eyes on Hektôr in Priam's Great Hall. He stood near the hearth, his big body resplendent in skin-tight purple trousers and yellow tunic. He seemed more royal, his hair gleaming in two horns above his forehead. He held his great tower-shield ready to cradle our son. Hekabe gave the infant to Theano and the cushion to Thalpia. The priestess, balancing the baby before her, raced around the hearth three times in the courses of sun and moon. Her bare feet thumped to the clink of sistra and the shriek of flutes, played by musicians.

Hektôr hefted his shield flat onto the hearth-wall, where Theano laid the baby. "My son!" He held him on the shield over the flames. "Be you Laomedon or Ilos, returned to strengthen the city and beat back our enemies, I now name you for your work in *this* life. Son of Hektôr and of Ãndrõmakhê, you are Skamandrios Astyanax, King and Defender of the City!"

His words clanged back from wall-hung weapons, whispered away to the flat-planted frescoes. He turned to me and I took from Thalpia the red swaddling-cloth I had woven with symbolic galloping horses, and as a whisper rustled through the hall, I began wrapping the infant as he lay on his father's shield.

Kassandra entered silently, dressed in loose-hanging undyed linen, her dark-honey hair in careless waves over her shoulders. She stood rigidly against the hearth-wall opposite us, staring across the fire at the child. In her hands, she held a large blue and white globe.

My heart danced with pride and joy as I tucked in the last ends of the cloth. Kassandra lifted up the ball. Hektôr kept the shield steady as his sister began her oracle:

"Skamandrios Astyanax. Your future is on the cusp with planets opposite, in the house of..." She gripped the great globe to her breasts. "I can only see, it is not clear, not finished...I have studied this all night, and I am telling you again... his horoscope is *not finished!"* She let out a howling laugh, thrust herself from the wall and whirling about, raced from the hall.

Watching her leave, I recognized the fresco upon which I had set my eyes. It showed Princess Andromeda standing on the sacrificial rock amidst tall waves, a grinning sea-dragon lifting its head at her feet. I felt myself trembling, losing control. Hektôr placed his hand over mine, and I noted its wetness, he had been sweating profusely.

Hekabe broke the stunned silence and ordered the start of feasting. Alexis and Sesamon joined with flute and lyre in the chanting of heroic songs. I sat beside Hektôr, my gaze on Skamandrios, peacefully asleep in his nurse's arms.

* * * *

Skamandrios was the first Trojan heir not presented at Thymbra upon naming, due to the dangers on the road. Spies reported that, when the Achaians got wind of Hektôr's newborn son, they began prowling the plains more diligently than ever before. To them, our son was the future of Asiatic power, a threat to their own expansion.

Our son was presented to Ate in Her Pergamene sanctuary. We walked to the cool, oblong temple, blue inside with wisping incense. Flowers gleamed over the stone floor and sneaked around the smooth columns. The great, round, lime-washed altar of slate granite was dim amidst incense that rose lazily to the clerestory above. Below this was the green slate through which sacrificial blood ran into the earth. At the altar's head stood stone horns where the neck of a sacrificial animal could be held firm. Between the symbols painted in yellow and red circles, solar crosses, dots, swastikas, and wheels with owl-eyes, ran the carved inscription in Trojan pictographs, a dedication of Ilion and the Simois River.

Above everything towered the ageless stone figure of Ancient Ate, sculptured to personify Athené, in her throne-chair. Fresh robes of white, yellow and purple covered her divine knees. Beneath her throne was the hollowed platform where the sky-fallen origin of Pallas Athené was kept.

Hektôr laid his son on a winnowing-fan at this base, where he must sleep for the next three nights under divine protection. But my pride and joy were marred by fear of what Kassandra had not told of our son's horoscope. Though no one else took Kassandra seriously, I could never overlook any threat of danger to my child.

Outside, I drew in a shaky breath, tasting the freshness in the air. The warm sun shone brittle-white through the lilac hazes that stretched to the Achaian ships, rocked at their moorings by the rising winds of early morning. Opposite at the inland mountains Helios's face gilded the cloud-crowned peaks of Mount Ida, bathed in lavender shades. The paving stones, white and flat beneath my feet, were warm already. My heart tightened as I gazed at the fields, no longer tended, yet quickening with delicate wheat interspersed with red and white patched grasses flowering with spring. A beautiful country, I thought, a blest land that Hektôr was ready to fight for and if need be, die for. Now we had a son who would love the land and rule and protect it after us.

Together we went through the cool, secret passage that led from the temple's site directly into Priam's Hall. Along the way points of light pricked where it connected with the city wall and the temples, then breached out into other courtyards.

As our group dispersed, I went in search of Kassandra.

Skamandrios cradled to my breast, I hurried up the broad steps, passing round columns mounted on square bases. Kassandra's room was at the end of the gallery where it ran along three sides of the Great Hall. This room had always seemed daunting to me, for none of the family ever entered it. The appearance of the nail-studded mahogany door almost discouraged me; nonetheless, I knocked loudly. I would have an answer! Out of nowhere, Nefru appeared at my feet, nuzzling my ankle. *Knock again, my friend, she is bound to let you in.*

I did as his voice in my head, suggested.

"Go away!"

"Please Kassandra. I have to talk to you." I shifted the baby to my other arm. "I must know Skamandrios' future."

"Must you indeed!" The door was snatched open and burning eyes stared among unruly hair. "Come on in, then."

I stepped in with Nefru; he leapt ahead, sniffing as he inspected the corners of the oval room. I noticed an abundance of aromatic leaves scattered about on the floor. On the wall hung a large amber cross in an ivory ring. Bunches of herbs were strung up at the top of each wall. Below, cut into the wood paneling, were hundreds of cabalistic symbols, the maze and the less complicated swastika. On the ceiling shone, in electrum inlay, the complete zodiacal wheel.

I went to the dais and smoothed out the tumbled skins and linens, and laid Skamandrios on the flattened roll.

Kassandra sat on a high-backed chair. In her lap, she held the globe [1] she had used at Skamandrios' naming. A magnificent aura shone above the globe, reflecting in the fuzzy lengths of her honey-colored hair as she bent forward.

Nefru leapt upon a chair near her, watching her intently.

I pulled up a chair and sat facing her.

"This is the world and the heavens," Kassandra ignored the cat's presence, then placed the sphere in my hands, pointing as she explained, "This line around the middle, divides night from day. When one-half is night, the other is day. Here are the four sacred points: these two where the sun turns in summer and in winter, these two where the first day of spring is, and the first of autumn. Twixt are the stars and the nine holy worlds where our gods live, with their constellations."

"What can you learn from this?"

"The future and plans of the gods. I calculate where the planets and constellations are at certain hours, and then compare that with what might happen in the world. Aisakos and Ilioneos taught me to interpret, with the inspiration of ancient Belen, Giver of Light." She took the globe back. "It takes years of hard study to know the inner Mysteries, and with them, the sacred numbers." She turned her gaze to me. "I know you've wanted to be friends with me. I am sorry I have not responded. But you are in the flesh, Āndrōmakhê. You love a man. I am in the spirit. I live on another sphere. My yearnings are beyond you. I have been a woman on earth so many times that I am no longer a woman...I chose to return this one more time to change the destiny of my people—something I know you've been hoping to achieve. There is no time left, for niceties. I must complete in this life what I have not finished in others. Then, only then, I can rest."

Spellbound, I listened without batting an eyelash.

"I did not forget your question about your son's horoscope." Her voice was a whisper when she rose to her feet, went to the bed-dais and bent low over the child, "Skamandrios Astyanax, King of the City!" She turned back to me, her green eyes, so alike her mother's, getting glassy. "I did not finish...because it...stops. There is *nothing,* if you must know. Atropos, one of the three Fates, cuts the thread. Do you know what it means to have no horoscope? Here, see, a crown in his hair, a crimson wreath—"

"Stop!" Rage and fear washed tears down my cheeks. I sprang to my feet and threw myself upon her. I found myself slapping and pushing her until, stumbling from the dais, Kassandra fell to her knees, looking up at me with dazed eyes as if suddenly wakened from sleep, sea-dark and dreamy.

She shook her head from side to side, speaking quietly, "I don't know what I just said to you, but I can't help what's there, because I see it happening. *I know.*"

Aghast, I stared from the sleeping Skamandrios to Kassandra. I could not accept her prediction! A child with no future was a dead child. But no, not mine! Skamandrios was the future of Troia, the glory of Hektôr, and would be the glory of my old age. In addition, Kassandra was living under a divine curse; she was to be pitied even if not believed. I lost all resentment against her, and then I noticed that Nefru was at her feet, nuzzling as if to comfort her.

"Oh, Ate, Great Mother!" Kassandra chanted, "Hold this child to your limitless breasts, and protect him, save him! Dear Lady, heavenly Virgin, guard your own young!" She rose to her feet and returned to sit on her chair. "Don't pity me, Ãndrõmakhê, who was once, long ago, known as Kiara Kupra! Just tell me this: How far were you initiated into the Mysteries, at the Cave of Ma Sipylene?"

"Only to the third degree."

"Life might teach you another nine. I spent many years learning these things at Thymbra. Strength comes to me in quiet hours of meditation; it may also be found after much trouble and tears and waiting...throughout a long life. But you—you will learn it—in another way. Look at Nefru, the Lynx: He knows who you were before, in Shardana, and who you *will be* in your next life."

"Kiara *Kupra?*" I whispered, "And Nefru, the *Lynx?*"

"Kupra is an ancient Shardanian nature goddess," Kassandra said slowly, "to have that added to your name must mean you had been dedicated to Her service."

"How so? Like a priestess?"

She shook her head. "Or, perhaps you were her daughter."

Kassandra was speaking in riddles again, too much for me to deal with right now, worried as I was over my baby son's future or the lack of it; still, I found myself repeating, "Nefru, the *Lynx?*"

She shrugged and did not reply.

I looked at Nefru, silently asking him if what Kassandra said, was true. He did not react, sitting there like a small, blue-eyed, black-masked, white statue.

No, I thought, *Nefru cannot be the Lynx, or else I would have recognized him on my own.*

Nefru purred, his eyes bluer than ever.

Kassandra said finally, "Does the name Kupra carry a familiar ring to you? Does it feel like it was your mother's name?"

I shivered. "My mother's name was Latmia."

"But it could have been Kupra, before."

"Before…?"

"Before, in Shardana. When you were Kiara; and your mother, perhaps… Kupra, the Goddess."

Cold rippled down my neck and the memory of a long-ago day with my mother, at home in Thébé, flashed through my eyes: *She pushed wisps of swan-white hair from her forehead and said, "When someone is born without color as I was, she belongs to a sky deity."*

"But how would *you* know about Shardana?" I asked nervously, "And the Lynx? And those names? How, and why?"

"Must be the depth of my training. I notice things, or things come to me. Does it matter how and why?"

"Yes, Kassandra, it does! If I truly did have a life before this one, *I* should be the one with its memories, and not you."

Kassandra turned her head away, signaling our talk was over.

I found myself unable to breathe.

I lifted Skamandrios carefully so as not to waken him. Keeping my back to Kassandra, I moved toward the door. Prophecy and horoscope be damned! Skamandrios would grow into a strong prince, and be the trusted arm to his father even as Hektôr now was to Priam.

[1] Author's note: Such a globe was found by Schliemann in the remains of Troia, and it was so analyzed by an astronomer before being informed of its origin. Schliemann: *Troja, Harper, 1894, pg.129.*

Chapter 17

"For Troia!" thundered Hektôr, "For our wives! Our children!"

The first gray of dawn filled the rockglass squares in my window with soft pearl. Something had wakened me…the closing of the door. Hektôr's side of the bed was still warm. I was used to his being gone when I awoke, but this was earlier than usual. I rubbed fingers across my eyes and sat up. Perhaps this was the day he would begin that long-planned attack.

A flash of light cut the sky, reflecting on Skamandrios' crib by my side. He was peacefully asleep. I rushed to the window, opening it wide. Light was forming wheels, rolling from crag to crag of the distant mountains. Wheel-forms flashed and burned, blinding even at this distance, as Helios' chariot rested shortly on the twin peaks. An omen of something significant!

Skamandrios awoke, gave me a toothless smile, and I picked him up, putting him to my breast, until he was full and let go. Thalpia entered, and I handed my baby to her, then dressed and ran downstairs.

The courtyard was full of hissing geese. Kebriones was at the stables, leading out Hektôr's horses, first Xanthos and then Pedasos. "Polites sighted Helenos and Deiphobos," he said. "We are to meet at the gate." He began hitching them to the chariot.

Thalpia came, breathless, her face flushed. "Alexis says Chryses is anchored off Sigeion and has gone to the Achaian camp. He has recovered enough from the wounds inflicted on him during the attack, to be able to stand on his own two feet, and project a majestic image as expected from a priest of Apollo. He now demands the return of his daughter, Astynome."

I clapped my hands. "This is truly a propitious day!"

"Chryses threatens pestilence if they refuse." Thalpia put a veil over my head and we started for the wall.

"But where is Hektôr?" I asked, "Kebriones has his chariot ready."

"In the bath chamber."

I turned on my heels and ran back into the house.

He was shaving in the steamed up room, in front of the silver mirror. "Thalpia says Chryses has come for Astynome!"

He smiled. "Good, they will have to let her go now. They'd not dare insult a priest, especially one who has given them an oracle."

"Perhaps I could visit her when she returns home?"

"I'll go see Chryses, if I can, while he is out there."

"Oh, I love you!" I threw my arms about his neck and hugged him, razor and all.

"Leave my throat for the Achaians to cut." He laughed, pushing me away, holding the razor aloft.

Back in our room, I pressed again, "Will you send Astynome a message for me?"

He pulled on thigh-length trousers. "This is wartime, Ãndrõmakhê. You know I cannot promise anything. But we'll break that blockade as soon as we get new men." He sat down to put on boots.

I saw that they were spotted with mud, and retrieved a cloth from a pile in a corner basket. He held out a hand to take it from me. I knelt and began rubbing at the smooth leather.

He scowled. "You're not to do slaves' work."

I laughed up into his eyes and flicked away the last bit of dirt. "For you, my lord, it's a queen's work."

Assembled for the welcome-feast in the Great Hall, I scarcely recognized his brothers when a manservant removed and put away their stiff-woven Hittite cloaks. On second look, Deiphobos' face was still the toughened oblong of a warrior. Helenos held my gaze. He stooped a bit in the shoulders, his lank body seeming just a gathering of bones. His mouth was heavily lined, but I sensed a strength coming from him, an aura of holiness. His hands clenched and unclenched on the arms of his chair. When I saw that he stared at me with an unnerving intensity, I looked away.

A frisson of warning went through me when I noticed how Deiphobos' eyes devoured Helen where she sat with Alexis. She returned his look with unblinking hatred.

"When may we expect troops from Hattushash?" Priam's rumbling voice stopped a cup to Deiphobos' lips.

"They were levying when we left," Deiphobos stated. "The King is having trouble on his western border. He also has to strengthen Karchemish against General Meleshipak of Babylon."

"We will get help as soon as these rebellions are put down," Helenos added reassuringly. "At the least, he has many Amazon warrioresses who are prepared to come to our aid if no other troops are available. Under a female general, one Penthesilea, I believe."

Priam looked pleased. "That is good news."

Helenos gave a warning grunt. "There is much unrest fostered by Babylon. Their Assyrian vassals grow more restless, and promote the claim of Meleshipak. Then, Elam grows stronger."

"Elam." Priam said, "Hmm. That sounds good for us, what with my brother Tithonos so powerful there."

Alexis spoke, "If the Hatti have their hands full with rebellions all over, they'll send us nothing."

"We met Memnon at Karchemish," Deiphobos chimed in. "He assured us that his father is still Trojan enough at heart that one day Elam and Troia will divide Asia."

Helen, leaving her place beside Alexis, put a fist on the back of my chair. "I'd have been better off dead in my mother's womb than involved with you, Trojans!" She started toward the courtyard, and then turned to me. "Come outside." Shocked at her untimely sentiments, I followed. She continued challengingly, "Do you, obtuse Trojans, know what you are fighting for?"

"We defend out homeland." It was dawn, and the cool air was refreshing where we stood near Priam's gate. "I don't get your point."

"If my people were not attacking yours, yours would be attacking mine. Everyone knows why Priam sent first Antenor, and then Alexis to Achaia. To spy! But the trick turned against the tricksters! I made a mistake coming here with Alexis. Now this has gone beyond war and kingdoms." Her tone softened. "I am enslaved to him, Āndrōmakhê; I can't live without him now." She stepped outside the gate and turned back. "I hear the cruel remarks women make about my marriage with Alexis. No one cares that Meneláos loves my land, and not me. Now, after the tender love Alexis has given me, I could not return to the crude pawing of Meneláos! But to my people, neither man means more than a defender of their queen's rights."

"If you would meet with Meneláos, surely they would negotiate."

"Meneláos has only me between power and exile. He was sent away from Sparta. Without me, his Pelopid dynasty is nothing in Lakedaimon.

In that, Alexander is a better man than Meneláos, he will let me rule while he develops his school."

"If you had parlayed with Meneláos when he and the others were here before the war, things might be different now."

Helen moved dismissingly. "The past is over with. I see through you, Ãndrõmakhê. You too are jealous. All the women of Troia tremble when their husbands merely glance at me."

I swallowed resentful words as Helen walked away, her head high. She entered the temple enclosure. I remembered that Helen and Theano had become close friends. Did Theano, a Thrakian through her mother, know secrets from the court of Polymestor?

Moreover, what of Sigeia, with a son bearing the name forbidden to any, but my son, the rightful heir to Troia?

* * * *

Terror spun my heart as I raced breathlessly along the northeast wall. Thalpia and Nefru followed full speed, Thalpia clutching Skamandrios in her arms. Every member of Priam's household was assembling to watch Hektôr leave through the great Skaian Gate.

Hektôr stood, in full battle armor and crested, shiny war-helmet with its curved cheek-guards, a hand on his chariot-rail, eyes intently scouring the troops. I could barely hear the tone of his firm, measured instructions to his men.

Alexis, at the far jamb, waited with his quiver of arrows slung back and one shoulder crossed by his bow.

Helenos and Aeneas, with Deiphobos, seeming without a care in the world, inspected their chariot-wheels.

Groups of more men took position along the street behind them, their line stretching up to the Pergamene citadel.

I gave in to my heart and raced down the narrow steps without rails. The soldiers parted before me as I ran silently to Hektôr. He turned toward me; I could feel the strain of his urgency. He pulled and kissed me briefly; the hard metal of his breastplate crushed my breasts, and then pushed me aside. "Go back up, Ãndrõmakhê. *Now.*"

It was a clear order, one that I had to obey.

Men seized the oiled wheels that unwound the knotted ropes raising the bolts securing the thick, bronze-reinforced gates.

My heart pounding in my ears, I scurried back to the top of the wall, stood straining my eyes for his appearance on the field outside.

At last, he emerged, on foot, at the forefront of his men, the stallions frisking so that Kebriones, his brother and charioteer, had to fight hard to hold them in check. At the same time, the charioteer had to keep the great oblong shield on its support before Hektôr. The horse emblem carved on the shield's front, at a forever-gallop, blazed in the brilliant sunlight.

Helenos followed closely in another chariot and after them trotted Deiphobos and Aeneas leading the right and left wings. Polydamas led the contingent right behind Hektôr.

Then, a glint of movement far off, at the crowded Achaian camp.

More of our foot soldiers emerged from sally ports.

Horn and conch-shell trumpets blared forth, calling for battle.

"For Troia!" Hektôr thundered, "Our wives! Our children!"

Our warriors' agreement made a thunder of equal strength.

Hektôr, his great sword sheathed across his back, at the left side of his belt a bronze dagger with a broad blade, counter-balanced by a double-headed axe hanging on his right, leapt into his chariot, grasping his spear and adjusting his shield while Kebriones raced Xanthos and Lampos out and away, down the steep hill.

Dust and mud-water sprayed as charioteers and infantry raged across the ford after him. My ears ached with the sharp twang of thousands of bowstrings and whizzing arrows as our archers on the battlements let loose their arrows.

The opposing armies poured behind their respective leaders, speed increasing as they turned around the bend of the river and closed in on each other. Royal officers led both sides in chariots, but the regular fighters ran on foot. While we had more horses, stronger and better trained than theirs', making good use of chariot power, the enemy held undisputed supremacy in manpower.

Metallic clanging and pounding drifted back to us women on the wall, clawing at our hearts with worry about our men.

I strained my eyes to keep my husband in sight.

First, the charioted warriors met in an explosive clashing that shook the earth. Even as the sun glinted and bounced off helmets, swords and shields, I could distinguish the crimson of spraying blood, a severed limb here and there, or a fallen warrior who roared for the last time in his life.

Then Hektôr emerged from the tangle, his vermillion-crested bronze helmet and armor gleaming, bypassing toward another chariot. Kebriones managed reins and shield while Hektôr broke into the thick of enemy ranks, slashed along, outward and down, striking with his two-handed Thrakian sword. Spears glinted, ready in their sconces at the back of his chariot. While a dark hailstorm of whizzing slingshots and arrows continued to churn the air, missing or striking targets, men on foot and in chariots slashed all around or tangled in hand-to-hand combat with thrusting swords. No man broke into another's individual bid for glory—his *Aristeia,* the fighting dividing about engaged groups like the river about an inlet.

I spotted Odysseus, Ithaka's King of Goats, rushing with spear in hand upon Deiphobos, and striking him on the shoulder with a downward blow drawing blood; then he struck a man I could not recognize in the loins under his shield as he leapt down from his chariot. Ajax the Greater, son of Hektôr's aunt Hesione's husband Telamon, sprang forward among the Achaians, and in the blink of an eye killed brave Doryklos, a son of Priam.

A shuddering moan from Helen behind me tautened my awareness. I turned to see her rush to the edge of the wall, pointing.

It was Meneláos of Sparta, his chariot gaining on Hektôr.

Hektôr then clashed with Meneláos, clanking metal against metal, while other warriors met in new clashes that splintered the air. Meneláos, sturdy but shorter than Hektôr, nonetheless fought well, not with skill and smarts, but stubborn fury.

Hektôr, throwing Meneláos off-balance with a lightning sword-thrust, broke from Meneláos, swerving toward another leader coming at him from the side. Another chariot, racing toward Hektôr, swung out of control. The warrior and his charioteer, arrows in their bodies, plunged headlong between their horses to be tossed and bloodied under their own wheels.

Below me, I spotted Alexis, swift as a fleeting colt, race behind an olive tree and draw his bow.

Helen shook her fists and screamed with all her might, "No! No! That is Meneláos! No! His blood should not be on your hand!"

Before Alexis could let his arrow fly to the thickset figure of Helen's concern, he was forced to swerve toward the beleaguered Aeneas on the Trojan right wing, leaving Hektôr in the knot where Agamemnon fought on doggedly.

Hektôr pushed Kebriones aside and whipped his horses. They drew the chariot at breakneck speed over fallen bodies and shields on the ground. I saw that his chariot's axle was bespattered with dark blood, and the rail round it was streaked with muddy splashes from the horses' hoofs and the wheels.

Hektôr thundered his way through to the center, handed the reins back to Kebriones and flung himself into the thick of the fight, wielding both double-edged sword and spear.

Akhilles whirled forth from the enemy like an apparition. Helios-bright in gold-plated armor with regal white-plumed helmet with nose and cheek-guards, his chariot sped toward Hektôr. I swallowed my breath and my knees turned loose as I observed Hektôr snatch a spear from his reserve and aim as the two titans thundered together. Luckily, way was not made for them and they were deflected.

I was able to breathe again.

But terror continued to hold me in its jaws. Both were warriors of Ares-like physique and skill, therefore an even match, but their agendas differed: Hektôr, loving son, husband, and father, fought to defend his people from death or slavery. Cold-blooded Akhilles fought solely to kill Hektôr in order to grasp his *Aristeia,* prophesied to give him eternal fame. And I feared that his unbridled greed might strike down the Valiant Defender.

Aeneas, swerving right from a spear-thrust by Meneláos, headed for the center where Hektôr was.

Helenos, on the left flank, a priest who proved himself as good a warrior as any, cut his own arc toward Akhilles, raising clouds of gray-yellow dust from his chariot wheels. Yet, abruptly, the Trojan infantry panicked, racing about amidst screeching chariots and pounding hooves swelling the onrush of retreat. A press of howling Achaians stampeded toward the walls after them.

We, the women of the wall, roared warning as if from one body.

Aeneas wheeled back against the enemy.

Helenos brushed chariots with Hektôr, shouting words. Hektôr shook his fist toward the coast, raised his twelve-foot [1] long lance, and led his contingent away from the city, toward the Achaians' stockade, fortified with a freshly dug ditch.

Kebriones brought Hektôr's chariot swiftly to the front.

After this, everything became a mass of attacking and whirling chariots, cries, curses, and entangled feet as spears shot fire through the choking dust. The thought *Achaia given chase by Troia!* chimed in my mind. Wild flowers matted down into a bloody carpet, muddying the dusty earth. The Plain of Troia became splotched with dead and wounded men and horses, broken chariots, fallen weapons and sections of armor.

Ally King Sarpedon of Lykia was now fighting bravely, axle-to-axle with Hektôr, while Deiphobos and Helenos returned to lead their respective wings. Amidst the organized fighting, ally King Asios and his nephews led their Phrygians in irregular raids through the enemy lines. Priam's other sons were scattered everywhere. In three small groups, contingents of my Kilikians fought under Chronis and the seer Ennomos, and the Paionians.

The battle surged back toward Troia and away on the great plain, raging like the moon-drawn tide. When the fighting once again neared the city, our shouts and screams sent our men out with renewed fervor. Horses bereft of drivers dragged their chariots around, bleeding, neighing with pain and confusion, trampling the wounded and the dead, regardless of friend or foe. Repeatedly our defenders regrouped, reformed broken lines, drew breaths, and charged back into the ceaseless waves of Achaians.

At long last the sun rode low over the isle of Lemnos in the horizon; Achaian and Trojan drew apart, each to gather as many of his own dead as possible in the brief twilight, and to rest for that night.

Only the dead and dying had the right to judge the worth of that day's savage combat.

My husband's chariot stopped at the gate for the infantry to rush by, soldiers meeting their womenfolk in the Lower City. He stood there, sweaty, bloodied, breathing hard, yet softly and patiently talking to those questioning him about the fate of their fallen men.

I handed Skamandrios to Thalpia and breathlessly raced along the wall, homeward, stopping only long enough to watch him start up the high street. Kebriones leapt off the chariot, melting into the fermenting crowds as Hektôr took the reins and returned to the Pergama.

I ran on, meeting him in the Agora—the marketplace and administrative center of our city. Pulling me into his chariot, he kept one arm around me while holding the reins with his other hand. The narrow floor of the chariot bounced and jagged beneath my feet, almost breaking my toes as I tried to keep my balance, and I wondered how he had kept his balance and fought on, all those hours in the battlefield.

"I sent many brave men into darkness this day," he told me grimly, bitterness burning through his lips.

Later, while Thalpia and two helpers brought water and lit braziers to heat it for his bronze bathtub, I leaned over my husband where he slumped in a deep chair, elbows on knees, head on both hands.

"I've grown soft," he growled.

He stood up, loosened the straps of his bronze armor, discarded the greaves protecting his arms and legs, and I followed him to the bathing-chamber. He had forbidden me to light the kind of fire needed to heat the

183

large, deep pool with the hypocaust, a system imported from Krete, to conserve wood. While the bronze tub was filled with water from hand-carried buckets, Thalpia brought in Skamandrios to see his father. He playfully tested the infant's biceps and legs, lifted him, swinging him high above his head, laughing aloud at the look on my face. Then I laughed too, but took the child away and handed him back to Thalpia.

With a ragged sigh, Hektôr dropped the rest of his armor and stepped into the warm, soothing water. He closed his eyes and blew me a kiss as I laved him with the sponge.

After the evening meal, Alexis and Helenos came to our door, Priam behind them. Helenos said, "You'd better have Kebriones keep your chariot wheels well greased! This is not over yet."

"We did poorly today," Alexis declared calmly. "I was prevented by some fool from shooting down Meneláos."

Hektôr invited them to sit. I served wine in rock-glass goblets.

"The situation is serious," Priam admitted. "But I feel proud of how bravely fought Aeneas, my nephew, along with all my sons."

"We have all winter to wear down the enemy." Alexis' voice was calm, his eyes low-lidded. "With Helen, I gave Troia a valid claim on Lakedaimon. Remember that!" He shoved his table with the emptied cup aside and stood up.

Priam said, "There has to be a middle way, something that would make Meneláos save face in front of his men and other kings."

Draining his goblet of wine, Helenos rose to his feet. "I've an errand to Ilioneos, but will be back before morning."

"Sleep here tonight," Hektôr said. "You should not be fighting out there without a night's rest."

"Don't worry about me. No harm can befall me in Thymbra. After all, Thymbra is my mother-shrine, from the first night our mother left Kassandra and me there and the sacred serpent whispered in our ears."

Later, finally alone in our bedchamber, Hektôr took my wrist and kissed the palm of my hand. "Helen will never go back, and I am fine with that. Because regardless of what she does, I know the war will go on. Agamemnon is not pressing his chiefs to the limit for nothing."

I took his cup to the mixing bowl and refilled it with one quarter of wine to four quarters of water. Hektôr did not like wine when he had to go to battle on the next day, believing it would cripple him, make him forgetful of his courage. But I figured that just a little would help him relax and sleep better.

He spoke grimly, "Today's fighting was just a scuffle."

I spoke before I could reconsider, "I would rather be dead than live without you."

"No! You will always have Skamandrios! He is our future, to go on beyond us." He dropped his fist heavily on the arm of his chair, and I saw his bone-deep weariness drift through. "Death does not frighten me, my love. What terrifies me is the thought of what happens to you, if I fail in my duty. You, my delicate Ãndrõmakhê, my soulmate, in a foreign land, bedslave to some evil man whose wife will slap you with insults and hard work! And people will point to you and say: there goes the wife of Hektôr, he who was champion of the Trojans when Troia was conquered."

"Hush, my husband," I touched his hand, "please, let's not speak of what we fear most! Neither will I worry you with tears. My work is here at home, and the cloak I am making will be ready for you when victory is yours. I'll not leave it to idle on the walls."

He sighed. "When I look up to the walls and see you, it gives me courage. Your time is not wasted there. Today, whenever I came close to defeat and heard your voice shouting encouragement, I remembered what it means losing a war, and my strength returned manifold." He then drew me onto his lap. "Ãndrõmakhê. I love you with all my heart, dearest wife. We are two halves of a whole, but *you* are the better part of that whole."

[1] In the *Iliad*, Homer cites Hector's lance as measuring twenty cubit in length, which would make it 30 ft. During reenactments by fans as well as anthropologists, 30 ft. proved to be impossible to cast, especially in such close combat.
Although Hektôr—better said the real Bronze Age man whose characteristics begat the legends—must have been a warrior of well-above average stature, a more conservative figure ought to be assumed.

Chapter 18

On a day of mist and chilly rain, Chryses, Priest of Apollo and father of Astynome, made a straight cruciform figure on Sigo's Hill, and spoke his curses. He chose the spot sacred to us Trojans, because ancient Sigo had killed a dragon there before he ever built the first human hut on Ilion's hill and called it Xanthé. Chryses called on dread Badogios-Bronton of the Thundering Voice, and on his own shrine's patron, Apollo-Agdistis, to send the Achaians pestilence. He aimed to punish them for their continuous refusal to release Astynome, still ravished by Agamemnon, from his clutches. Then Chryses folded his arms and returned with trailing steps to his ships.

After him the night-rains and early day-mists fell softly and continuously into those swamps where the three Trojan rivers flowed together and parted again. Here the dark green meadows spread for our sacred herds—no longer there. Now they neighed, gamboled, and whinnied on the fields of Chersonesos, where King Polymestor's Thrakia was lush with peace. The rains and floods did not worry us this year because we no longer had fields and orchards to fence in and drain. Presently hungry Achaian soldiers prowled around for supplies. The city gates were bolted shut, posterns sealed, thus no watery seepage came in to threaten Lower City houses.

Hektôr's horse-farm, which, due to its off-the-beaten track location had been safe until now, suffered a massive attack. Though the raiders could not win, they slaughtered half of the defending force and carried away one hundred prize animals.

Time crept by as the Achaian army shivered and sopped about in floodwaters. Scores of Achaians died of disease, with full credit given to Chryses' curse. At last came spring, but it brought more floods, for Ida's peaks melted of snow that avalanched in roaring thunder down the creek-beds and gulleys. As the swamp waters crept into the Achaian tents and huts, it brought along malaria and respiratory infections.

We the besieged rejoiced in the continuing power of Chryses' curse upon the Achaians.

Still, Agamemnon did not return Astynome to her father.

186

Battles continued. My husband, along with our walls and warriors, endured his share of the battering, his body riddled with bloody gashes, bruises, broken bones, constantly building new scars upon the old ones.

Seagulls and swallows came and left, figs, apples, and almonds bloomed, gave fruit, and wilted. The plains were pressed and beaten down with blood on wilted petals. Field and swamp became so choked with dead that wheeling vulture-eagles, black and glossy, screamed plague warnings. Stripped naked by their victors, blackened and picked by vultures and scavenger-dogs, little remained of the dead to tell apart Trojan or Achaian. All were mixed as to their blondness or darkness, be they nobles or lesser men. So it was that enemy joined enemy in the task of gathering putrid fragments that had once been lively comrades.

Inside Troia, the diadem that sat upon its own great rock, ruled by Priam, the codes of civilized life were never slackened; quarrels were restrained, courtesy to opponents was shown, and kindness to the weak was the order of the day.

On days when burial truce was called, the gatherers of the dead would stay to sleep outside on grass and rags so that their grisly task might resume at dawn. Many were the nights when roaming bands of hunter-dogs prowled, scavenging bones from rotting bodies ripe for burial. Then smoky pyres would roar skyward; one near the city, one by the sea. At sunset after such a truce there would begin the piling of another heroes' mound, over the ashes circled in a nest of protective stones. In their homeland across the sea, the Achaians were not in the habit of cremating their dead, rather, they buried them with pomp, but they did not want them to rot on foreign soil, therefore mowed down a wealth of our trees for their pyres.

During each battle, all of Priam's sons who were of age rode two brothers to a chariot, always in the thick of fighting. Many fell in the course of duty, among them Doryclos and Gorgythio. Ironically, Princess Hesione's son Teuker's arrow brought down Gorgythio in front of our eyes.

Yet I felt hopeful. It seemed that the poisoned arrows of Apollo-Agdistis would conquer the enemy with endless disease.

As fighting raged, I often caught Helen's haunted eyes burning through intervening space while she paced the wall searching, always searching, among the enemy, for Meneláos. He, fighting from his chariot, forced himself ever closer to the tall walls of Troia. I observed her pass and pass, and pass again, weariness in her step. She seemed to live between two men by day, returning to Alexis every night.

On the walls also was Polyxena, dark and quiet, beautiful, but no longer young of face. She sat with her distaff, flax uncarded in her basket. Looking through space and men, she watched only the flying assaults and forceful fighting of gold-armored Akhilles. Her eyes never wavered to a brother or fellow-Trojan, but stayed as if in trance upon the flashing commander of the Myrmidons.

On occasion I realized that I was completely wrapped in Hektôr and Skamandrios, without much thought of how and what the other women felt. Lonely, sensitive, misunderstood Kassandra, whom I liked and admired; dreamy, sad-eyed Polyxena, who lived in her own world the way I lived in mine; and what about faithful Thalpia, always there like a shadow, never, ever, complaining about her lot. At least as far as Thalpia was concerned, I was a kind mistress, providing her with a wing of her own, the pick of helpers she needed for chores, as well as good food, clothing, and in the event of my death, enough gold which would support her comfortably in her old age.

Sometimes I brought Skamandrios to witness his father's heroism. Then I would let him down to crawl about or stagger in his sack-suit with holes for legs and the drawstring tied across his chest. His adept hands had learned to investigate; he would get underfoot, or try to play with older naked children who lived in his ever-expanding world. Kreusa would be there with Askanios and his nurse, a year older than Skamandrios and the leader of the two. Nefru followed him with the same loyal diligence he showed me, enduring much abuse as the little boy pulled his tail and ears.

Hekabe often came and sat with her daughters. While men below slaughtered each other, she shared intricacies of motherhood. Oh, yes, we women had to do our duty, bear sons for the next generation of soldiers. Ares the God of War and his earthly-counterparts needed them as fresh fodder.

Priam sat with old Anchises of Dardania in the nobles' corner at the Skaian Tower, comparing their sons' actions below. In those moments, when I observed the look in their eyes, sorrow churned my heart, for I seemed to eavesdrop to their thoughts: *We are all fighting in a hopeless cause, for our generation and we will pass away and be of no more account than the fallen leaves of the forest.*

* * * *

Hektôr and I lost our second child, one boy who gave up life after only ten days on earth. Thalpia whispered that I was at fault, for I did not eat enough to nourish him while he was inside me. I bowed my head. She was right, as I went by with a bit of bread, piece of cheese, and a few figs. Food was scarce now and all of us women, with husbands battling the enemy daily to uphold our freedom, allotted whatever bits of fortifying morsels could be had to our gallant defenders.

Then a son was born to Alexis and Helen.

The glow of their happiness warmed us all, filling our hearts with hope for a new future.

* * * *

This year, fevers and agues plagued the enemy worse than ever before. Surely, the curse of Chryses was the cause. Yet Agamemnon would not return Astynome to her father.

Akhilles kept both Briseis and Diomede in his tent. According to rumor, Briseis was the woman he loved, and Diomede the one he protected until she could find a lover of her own choosing.

While the Achaian camp lay quiet and sick, an occasional Hittite caravan brought food to us by the old Dardanian Road.

From Alybe and the salt flats of Aisepos, came some silver and salt under Troilos. Also came Lykaon, ransomed from slavery and sent home by an ally of Priam.

* * * *

On an opulent evening, foretasting of summer, news arrived about a possible downturn of fortune at the Achaian camp. There had been threats of an attack on their homelands by redheaded settlers from the Ister River. These settlers had allied themselves with Jebusites and Keftian Philistines against Egyptian encroachments into Palestine. They named their newly won territory Galilee, and were strong enough to hold back the army of Ramses-Siptah. Calling themselves Galatians, they were moving northward, toward the shores of the Aegean.

After evening meal, I took Skamandrios into the courtyard. The air glowed as if Helios shook gold dust from his chariot, laying a spell over the city. Hektôr came, and told more news, "Ramses-Siptah has sent fresh troops against the Galatians from Egypt. Yet shiploads of their men are noted sailing north to Achaia!"

We held hands, the three of us, smiling at each other. So grew our hope for a diversion of enemy forces.

* * * *

189

The mote-filled light from the doorway dimmed as two silhouettes entered Priam's throne-room. First was Herald Idaios, still tall and strong, though no longer young. He wore his purple robe of office with its white overall pattern of running horses edged with owl-eyes. His white-streaked brown hair, waxed into a horse's crest on top, ended as a loose horsetail behind his back. The man coming after him was younger, slender, with strong muscles bulging his official robes of Achaian blue, embroidered in red bullheads front and back.

Idaios presented the younger man to Priam. "My lord, I bring Talthybios, herald of Agamemnon."

The Achaian spoke, "I come under truce, Lord Priam."

Priam bent his leonine head in acknowledgement. "We welcome you in peace."

Hekabe ordered watered wine and a chair for the guest.

Seated, clutching his goblet filled with wine, Talthybios stated, "I bring a marriage-bid to end the war. From Agamemnon, the King of Kings, on behalf of Akhilles Peleosides, Prince of Thessaly. As a recompense for Helen, and other considerations."

I leaned toward Hektôr and touched his arm excitedly. Perhaps now was the time I could help his love-struck sister, and end the war as well. "Polyxena! Offer Polyxena!"

Hektôr frowned slightly, started back, and then faced the herald. "A marriage-bid for whom?"

"Akhilles mentioned Polyxena," the man spoke stiffly.

I drew in a too-loud breath of relief. Light at the end of the tunnel!

Priam hesitated. "This needs to be discussed by the Council."

"My lord, Akhilles is not for wasting time."

Priam exchanged a quick glance with Hektôr. Then, "Tell King Agamemnon we will consider this."

"Then I can report that you are favorably inclined?"

Yes, yes! I screamed silently.

"Depending on other matters," Priam replied imperiously. "We shall send details with Idaios." He moved a hand in dismissal.

Talthybios bowed and strode from the hall.

"What do you think of this offer?" Priam asked Hektôr.

"We must accept it!" I burst out, unable to wait.

Hektôr gave me an amused look. He whispered, "When you rule with me, I'll see that you have equal power." Quickly kissing my earlobe, he patted my hand.

Priam ignored our byplay. "We must give Polyxena a large enough dowry so he'll keep her as first wife, even if he later marries Agamemnon's daughter."

Priam looked at his other sons. "What do we have left, now that much of our treasure has been paid out in ransoms? Only one wagon of silver could be brought from Alybe with Troilos."

"We can offer that land north of Polymestor," Hektôr suggested. "That is not too far from Akhilles' own territory. I suspect he has quarreled with Agamemnon. Send word that you will give him Polyxena if he withdraws his forces and takes along as many allies as he can. The Achaian troops are just as tired of this war as we are; they will be glad of a legitimate excuse to return home. Akhilles is not here to defend his country, neither was he a suitor of Helen bound by the Oath. This is not *his* war."

Priam turned to face me. "Would you bring in Polyxena? I will not sacrifice her against her will."

I hurried to fetch the girl, but Hekabe stepped forward from under the steps and caught my hand. "Come here first," she whispered, leading me into the storeroom. She closed the door behind us, and stood before the first row of wine and grain jars that reached to her waist, their lower halves sunk deep into the bottoms of older jars broken away. The strong, damp odor of wine, grain and dried fruits stung my nostrils pleasantly.

Hekabe spoke, "I know how Polyxena will reply."

"So she confided in you?" I smiled, relieved.

"I haven't reared nineteen children for nothing," she laughed, "but I am wary of her close friendship with Theano. That woman, my very own brother's wife, is a hidden enemy to us. I know of secret plots Antenor has made with Odysseus of Ithaka. Odysseus, he who used to call himself our trusted friend! My point is, a woman in love can be influenced by such traitors. What do *you* think, could a marriage like this lead to peace without betrayal?"

I did not know how to reply, and remained silent.

She said with a small sigh, "Go, now. Do the best you can."

I found Polyxena working several shuttles through her cotton-strung loom. "Your father wants to talk to you. About marriage with Akhilles." I smiled at the girl's gasp.

"Akhilles?" Her hands made fists at her sides.

I told her of Talthybios' message. Also, Hekabe's concerns, though I presented them as my own, mention of her mother's name might bring her back up.

"Marriage! Antenor came through for me!"

"Antenor? Oh, Polyxena...."

She bristled, "Don't fret! I am aware of where his help might lead! I am careful. I only tell you that I am not helpless."

"Come, dear Polyxena, your father is waiting for you." We walked from the room together.

"My beloved child." Priam took her hand when she sat beside him. "Akhilles, son of Peleos, has asked to marry you. But I will not force you to accept him."

"But I will be so happy, Father! If that stops the war, of course." Her glance at me glinted with restrained joy.

"I pray he'll be good to you," Priam said awkwardly.

She looked him full in the face. "Thank you, Father." She stood up and moved toward the stairs.

Later, I found Hektôr in Priam's conference room. He was clumsily holding a bronze stylus over a folding-tablet filled with beeswax, and began erasing with the blunt end.

"Are you any good at cuneiform?" he asked, preoccupied.

I replied quietly, "You might remember that I was taught by Kiron of Krete. But you need a wedge. What are you writing?"

"Our terms. I can't write Achaian, and they don't read us."

"Do not fret, everyone reads Babylonian," I said.

He held the stylus firmly, making oddly shaped wedges. "Idaios usually does this kind of thing." Straightening, he flexed his fingers.

I went to the other storeroom behind the stairs and found Priam's all-purpose stylus in a pile of others on the desk beside scales and an ox-shaped gold ingot. Returning, I began writing the terms as he read them out to me.

When we were done, he folded the tablet, tying it with red wool. "I could never manage Troia without you," he said softly, glancing at me as he rolled wax to softness in his palm and pressed it onto the knot. "You'll be more queen than I am king," he added warmly, and pressed his signet ring into the seal. It was a rearing colt with rider, in a cartouche of Trojan writing that told his name and title.

I smiled, my heart aglow with pride that I was able to help him.

* * * *

Kassandra raced through Priam's courtyard to the temple of Athené, with Helenos striding briskly after her. "Woe, woe!" she cried, her voice echoing after her. Helenos turned aside to where I stood at the municipal fountain with Laodike and Helen.

"Talthybios brought Agamemnon's answer," Helenos told us as we surrounded him. "A refusal. Akhilles will not pull out his troops without Agamemnon's consent, and that depends on Meneláos."

Laodike shot Helen a hard look. "With a husband each on both sides of the sea, what will you do now?"

"It is really not up to me, is it?" Helen asked coldly, and then whirled around followed by the nurse who was holding her baby son, strolled toward her own house.

Despite the coldness she projected, I knew it was forced; she was trying to save face, and felt a rush of sympathy for her.

"Priam and Meneláos decide for her," Helenos agreed. "But there will never be a solution."

"What did Akhilles expect us to do, hand Polyxena over for nothing?" Laodike's voice was harsh.

"Idaios reports that Akhilles meant to take Polyxena home to Thessaly, but leave his Myrmidons under Agamemnon. He is worried about his father's health and plagued with urgent messages from his mother. But Agamemnon will not allow even that."

I thought of Polyxena. Like Helen, Polyxena was being dangled between the agendas of two warlike men.

Troilos came from the stables, leading his chariot, hitched to only one stallion, Hektôr's Aithos. Helenos turned to him. "Do not go out today, Troilos. The omens are not good."

Troilos gave his brother a truculent look. "I always exercise afternoons after I've worked with Hektôr all morning. And I am only taking Aithos now. No one will attack me at the Thymbra track." He sprang into the chariot.

Helenos reached for the reins, "I said *not today!* Akhilles has been seen ranging farther from camp than usual."

"Helenos, I'm a man now, and am tired of waiting to prove it. You better worry about Polyxena!" He slapped reins over the stallion's back and banged away down the street.

Later in the day, I sensed anguish in Polyxena. After the news, the girl had paced about, with a tortured determination in her eyes, and then disappeared from sight for several hours.

I approached her upon her return, while she sat silently over a bowl of untouched whey with milk. She met my eyes with a look of fear. "Polyxena," I urged her gently, "tell me what's on your mind."

"Ãndrõmakhê, I'm afraid!" she burst out, "I want you to know that I never loved Troia any less because I love Akhilles so much! But today, when I heard Agamemnon's reply...."

"You sneaked out to meet him?"

"Yes! I went to meet him beside the Thymbra River above the swamp where it joins the Skamander. And then I spotted his chariot." She paused, sighed, shaking, and then went on, "Akhilles passed me by—he went to the shrine. I don't think Troilos could have seen him before he left, from where he was on the wall."

"Perhaps Troilos will force him to an agreement about your marriage," I forced myself to speak in an even, calm tone.

"But Troilos was angry when he went out, Ãndrõmakhê, and I'm afraid he guesses more than he's been told."

"Well, let's look at it this way: Thymbra is a shrine where the pursued can find sanctuary from an enemy; so, surely neither Troilos nor Akhilles would come to harm there."

Would that I could believe my own words, I thought, feeling dread.

* * * *

Helenos remained in Troia that night, so it was early next morning before Kassandra's cries alerted me to that something was wrong.

I found Helenos in the Great Hall with his parents and his brother Polites, horrified words ringing from Polites' lips, "From my post at Bateia's Mound, I spotted Akhilles racing away from Thymbra at dawn. He had with him..." He gulped air. "Troilos' shield was in his—the Achaian's chariot."

Hekabe's unearthly scream echoed back from the beamed ceiling. Priam turned pale as a corpse. Helenos stood rigid. I stared at him, unwilling to accept the full implications.

Priam asked, "Did you follow him?"

"First, Lord Father, I went to look for my brother!"

"Where—where is he?" Hekabe whispered.

Polites seized her convulsing figure in his arms, holding her with gentle force. He replied, "So I took my chariot and set out to Thymbra. Then I discovered Troilos on the shrine's altar, lying across the horns, beaten and stripped naked for sacrifice...He was pierced in the throat, and his blood had poured down the trough to those souls below." His tone hardened. "Priest Ilioneos had heard loud voices, but was praying in his quarters and thought nothing of it until the sounds of a quarrel. When he came out, Akhilles threatened to kill him." Polites' eyes shifted to Polyxena, shooting arrows.

Staring at her brother, the girl crumpled to the floor.

Polites went to the mixing-bowl, dipped a cup of wine, and drained it. He refilled it and turned to his father. "So," he said. "This time Kassandra was right."

"But where..." Priam's voice was strained. "Did you bring...?"

"I passed Hektôr at the wall. He has gone to fetch honey and wax for the embalming, which Ilioneos will oversee. Troilos shall have a shrine in the precinct."

I rushed to comfort Polyxena where she lay motionless, eyes open, staring. Later would be time for the full mourning of a city for its prince and an endangered future. However, most of all I worried about Hekabe, once upon a time mother of nineteen, so many times hence mourning a child. How terrible a vacuum her life after each son or daughter preceded her into the flowery Fields of Elysium....

PART III: The TRAGEDY

Chapter 19

The Plain of Troia disappeared under a renewed flood of struggling infantry. Attacking, wheeling, turning chariots crushed spring-fresh grasses into brown dust and mud. Pain stabbed my eyes as I watched from the wall, Skamandrios weeping in my arms. I made him look at the scene below. "See your father! Become a warrior like him! Kill—kill, the enemies of your people!"

My poor child, breathless with terror, stared at the ghastly scene. His lips trembled, and then he cried louder, with hiccupping sobs. Trembling, I pressed him against my heart. I held and kissed him until he quieted. The women around us sent servants to bring distaffs and wool or flax, so the day of watching would not be wasted. Thalpia and other servants brought noontime bread, cheese, and figs and we sat together worrying, and forgetting the food.

The sun's last rays speared an early dusk, and I rushed homeward as Hektôr drove to the gate. He met me in the Agora as usual, and pulled me into his chariot, weary, battered, but his eyes warm as he kissed me on the brow.

By midsummer fighting slackened when the Achaians began staying closer to camp. Spies reported with satisfaction that new fevers harassed the men, though it was not the season for such illnesses.

* * * *

Poseidon the Earth Shaker struck Helen and Alexis. During a sudden, terrible earthquake around dawn, a boulder fell upon their little son, peacefully asleep in his cradle.

Helen refused to surrender the baby for proper rites, weeping day and night. Finally, Hektôr, lovingly patient in his speech, managed to wrench him from her arms and the child was laid to rest.

Alexis remained silent, dry-eyed, but a whirlwind of fury in the battlefield.

For reasons unknown to us, Helen and Alexis had never told us the name of their beautiful little boy. In my heart, I named him Apollo.

* * * *

Some time later, all of us rejoiced over the news that Odysseus, the wily Ithakan King of Goats, was sent away with Astynome, sailing to the shrine at Chryse.

However, shortly after I was sobered when we heard how Chryses, in gratitude for the return of his daughter, had offered sacrifices on behalf of the Achaians!

Agamemnon, to save face for having surrendered Astynome to her father, ripped Briseis from Akhilles. As the High King, he declared, he must own the greatest-ranking prize of conquest.

Akhilles, rumored to love her deeply, was enraged. He quarreled bitterly with Agamemnon in front of all their men. When the rest of the leaders supported Agamemnon's claim on Briseis, Akhilles refused to fight any longer and pulled his loyal Myrmidons off the field.

Akhilles was my husband's greatest enemy, here to earn his *Aristeia,* by slaying him in battle. With Akhilles gone, I could breathe a sigh of relief. No one else among the Achaians was my Hektôr's equal.

That afternoon, standing at my loom to follow the rhythm of the victory pattern, I held three shuttles at a time to cast and press, to draw, and twist. The rise and fall of shouting from the walls blended in with my white threads on the purple, and the lines of yellow with green dots. I thought of this morning's short-lived victory when Hektôr had provoked the Achaians to fight without Akhilles. He had successfully fought his way through the throngs, leapt from his chariot to cross the ditch, exploded through their barricade and reached their ships, and was throwing flaming spears on their decks when our army had turned and fled for unknown cause. Yet when I had come down from the wall at noon, the looks I had caught fleeting between Helen and Antenor had sent ice cascading through my veins.

The sound of fighting stayed a steady roar; the armies had clashed beyond the river where men were scarcely distinguishable from the wall. Then the noises stopped, as if an old potter's wheel had ceased turning for a completed bowl.

I held the white shuttle for a breath; all the women on the wall were silent. Something new was happening, something to silence even the war. Thalpia appeared by my side, opening her mouth to speak.

"Where is Skamandrios?" I interrupted her, dropping my shuttle and its thread unwinding.

"I've just put him to nap. But go watch Alexis."

"What are you talking about? Why Alexis?"

"Oh—you'll not believe it, he went out to challenge Meneláos! To single combat! Helen and her dowry shall go to the victor."

I stood up, whipping the veil over my head so that it covered my entire body from the high winds, and Thalpia attached a close-fitting circlet on top. "Pray, Thalpia! Pray with me that this will end it all."

I turned and hurried in the direction of the Skaian Tower, the ground seeming to slide back beneath my flying feet.

At the Tower more of the cool dry winds whipped our clothing in the blistering sun as the rest of us women reassembled, like spectral images, to watch. Waves of heat rolled up from the field below.

Leaning over, I saw Hektôr speaking with Alexis, holding his spear crosswise for truce. Meneláos waited apart, his spear also horizontal. Hektôr moved away from his brother, giving him a punch in the ribs.

Alexis, smeared in blood and sweat, laid down his bow and quiver and sling-bullets, the muscles rippling in his bare arms and shoulders. Opposite him, Meneláos stomped about like a bull, big and beefy, straining with knotted muscles and brawn. His red hair straggled out from its wad at the back of his ox-hide helmet with bullhorns; his thick-fingered heavy hands seized spear and sword together, the great round shield leaning against his left hip.

Hektôr raised his horizontally held spear high, and Agamemnon, opposite him, lifted his own, also horizontal. The armies began removing their helmets and sitting down, like a surge of the river undulating to the ground.

Hektôr strode forward and faced Meneláos; his voice fluttered to us on the wall, "If your men pledge to stand aside, then Alexander, son of Priam, challenges Meneláos, son of Plisthenos son of Atros, to single combat for possession of Helen, rightful Queen of Lakedaimon, with all her dowry and her treasures. And Achaia shall leave Troia in peace, regardless of who wins."

Hekabe stood near me, her hand on Priam's shoulder where he sat, tears glinting below her lashes. Polyxena, sitting a little way off, leaned forward, tense, and looking so very young. Kreusa was quietly restraining little Askanios who was tugging at her hand, while her eyes searched the field below for Aeneas.

"Alexis is no sword or spearman," Helen muttered, looking drawn and worried as she came up beside me.

Howls and clashes drowned her next words.

"We accept on one condition," Agamemnon declared, "Priam himself must join the oath."

Swift-footed Polites raced up the stairs to Priam, and they stepped aside for low-voiced words. The old king, hesitating, glanced down onto the plain below.

Hekabe approached, "This is right and proper, Priam, let it be! Now our firebrand son will torch the enemy, and not Troia."

"We could end the war today!" Polites' eyes gleamed.

Hekabe touched Priam's shaking hand. "Make such an oath as no man will dare break! The Sacred Oath of the Horse."

"I will," Priam agreed grimly, then turned and went away to don his ceremonial robes.

Thalpia hurried and brought Skamandrios, fretful from sleep. His tender skin was flushed from heat as I took him onto my lap. About us, the dry winds swirled across through the blistering sunrays. Where we sat, early afternoon shadow spread out from the tower. What spare benches remained along the battlements filled as the rest of the women heard of the truce and arrived with their spinning and embroidery. We made a mere show of work, for all eyes followed the crucial action down below. Waves of heat rose from the quiet battlefield.

Polites emerged with a black ewe and a white ram to honor Earth and Sky, followed by Laokoon and Theano with jugs of wine and cups. The Achaians led forth a young black bull for Zeus.

I looked in vain for the sacrificial horse.

Antenor was with Priam when he rode down from the citadel.

The king wore his long purple robe under the full hide of a white horse, tied about his waist by the front-leg skins. His conical tiara of beaten gold was wrapped about with sacred woolen threads, and his long white hair hung in a club down his back over the empty head of the horse. Antenor drove carefully down the ramp, out onto the plain, splashed across the low part of the river, and drew up on neutral ground where the dueling area had been paced off.

Hektôr crossed after them and helped his father dismount.

Meneláos and Odysseus stepped forward behind Agamemnon, who was preceded by Talthybios carrying a double-spouted gold cup on both hands. He announced, in officially floral words, the terms of the duel.

Herald Idaios accepted in likewise elaborate language. He then held up Priam's enormous, ornamented goblet, which his ancestor Dardanos had brought long ago from Tyrrhenia, by way of Samothrace. The heralds mixed water and wine in a great Achaian bowl of tan pottery, and then poured holy water from the river onto the hands of Alexander, Meneláos, and the others.

Agamemnon, big, brawny, and gleaming red-blond, cut hair from the heads of the sacrificial animals and gave it to the heralds, who divided it between their respective leaders.

Priam slashed the palm of his hand with his knife, and then lifted both arms in prayer, blood flowing down from his palm, and facing Mount Ida. Meneláos lifted his arms toward Sigeion Hill. Agamemnon slit the sacrificial throats expertly, and laid out the sheep and the bullock on the ground. Wine was poured to seal the agreement.

Priam, still dripping blood from his deep wound, climbed back into his chariot with Antenor, and returned to the windswept high walls. First, he went in to divest his ceremonial attire and came back in his usual long white linens, with his injured hand tightly bandaged.

On the field below, Hektôr and Odysseus paced off the duel area again, while armies engaged in silent prayer.

When prayers were over, Hektôr stood in the middle of no-man's-land holding his great war helmet upside down in both hands.

Alexis Priamides and Meneláos Atrides threw in their lots with ostentatious carelessness and Hektôr, turning his head away, shook the helmet until one pebble fell to the ground.

Odysseus picked it up and handed it to Alexis.

Slowly Alexis took his stance, while Meneláos impatiently shouted something unintelligible. Alexis's face flamed red as he cast with grim determination. The spear struck Meneláos' shield and fell harmlessly to the ground. Alexis raised his oblong shield while his rival coolly took aim and let go with such force that he pierced the metal-plated ox hides and grazed his thigh. Then, letting go in a quick fury, Meneláos beat Alexis to the draw of swords, and crashed his own down on Alexis' helmet, so fiercely that the weapon broke.

Cheers, cries, and sobs rose in concert, ringing to the heavens.

Before Alexis could rally Meneláos grabbed him by the horsehair crest of his helmet and swung him around, then dragged him, as Alexis kicked and resisted with all his might, toward the Achaian camp.

At once, a hot gale blew in, raising a whirling, high, dark tunnel of dust, and the combatants disappeared from our sight.

The opal that hung suspended on my throat, for the first time in a long time, turned very hot and vibrated.

It was then that I saw her—Aphrodite!

I stared, frozen, unable to blink or breathe. I could not believe my sight, yet it had to be her: tall, slim, magnificent hair of spun gold, of unearthly beauty with high full breasts, wrapped in a cloud of fiery sparkles and iridescent light beams.

Now the dust cleared and settled, revealing Meneláos, stamping about, roaring, cursing, and kicking at Alexis' empty helmet with its dangling broken strap.

Alexis had disappeared into thin air.

Hektôr stepped forward, and both men began searching for him. At last, they faced each other, Meneláos with legs apart, arms wheeling about in angry jerks. I could hear enough of his roar to know that he demanded Helen brought to him immediately.

Hektôr replied with words I could not hear, and then Meneláos turned and stomped away.

Night came swiftly around the towers, and the armies separated. I went to meet Hektôr at our own gate.

Hektôr's voice sounded above the thud of his boots. "Alexis! Tell Helen to wear her best for Meneláos tomorrow. You lost the duel, brother; you have got to return her to Meneláos."

Alexis entered my line of vision, bleeding from wounds on his face and neck. "Meneláos knows he cannot best me in archery, but do so with the sword. Therefore, he used a trick with the lot, to force me to a sword fight. I'll not give my wife away on such terms."

"Collect her treasure from whatever fools you bribed to take you off the field, and have her at the gate tomorrow. This is an order."

A muffled curse was Alexis' answer. His footsteps thumped along the beaten earth of his courtyard.

I slipped through the gate unseen by either man, and reached the stables where Kebriones was feeding the horses.

"I'll take over now," Hektôr spoke, entering the stables, lit by one smoking torch giving out shadowy yellow flickers.

I watched Hektôr's dim figure, shoulders hunched with weariness, as he rubbed down his steeds. Xanthos, the lead-stallion, whose mating with my Iris had caused her death while birthing his foal, snorted and tossed his head when Hektôr laid a hand on his golden mane. He had tamed these animals and shared a love with them that was a deep, private, communion between close friends. He moved to Lampos, and the other two, Aithos and Podarkes, stamped and whickered. I looked at these horses and as always, admired their strength, and beauty. They were such huge animals that only someone of Hektôr's extraordinary physical stature could handle them. According to rumor—which Hektôr never bothered to deny—Xanthos was the offspring of Zephyros, the West Wind, and of a Harpy.

I went to Xanthos when he leaned over a bin, and he gently nuzzled my neck in greeting. Lampos half reared, tail high.

Hektôr moved away, picked up a stiff brush from the floor, and began grooming Aithos. "This war has to end, Ãndrõmakhê, no matter what the terms are. We cannot hold out another year. I will see to it that Meneláos gets Helen. Later on I can help Alexis reclaim her; if he'll only be patient."

"Aphrodite saved Alexis today," I said quietly.

"Oh?" He gave me an amused look.

"I saw her, out there, in the field."

"Hmm. But why are *you* the only one who saw her?"

"Does it matter? I am telling you Aphrodite saved your brother's life. Therefore, the story that she was the one who brought them together is true. At least we have one goddess who is on our side!"

"Only one?" He laughed. "You forget Athené."

"No, I don't. But she is *not* on our side. I fear that because of the golden apple, she has turned her back to Troia."

"And so here we are," he said wryly, "caught between a goddess who bears a grudge, and Achaians who slobber over our trade routes and beautiful city."

"You don't take me seriously."

He sighed, weary. "If divine help is what we need to persevere, then we are truly in sorry shape. Yes, in the battlefield, many times I have heard the Achaians call upon Athené for victory. Be that as it may, other than Aphrodite, we still have Apollo, or so Helenos and Kassandra assure me."

Hektôr leaned against one of the posts, and I drew out a measure of spelt—fodder made of wheat with lax spikes and spikelets containing two red kernels—and handed it to him. As he poured it into the feeding trough, pale torchlight hollowed shadows in the drawn lines of his face. Breath caught in my throat as the memory of glittering sunlight on bronzed iron, scorched my insides. I stared at my husband, in my ears the echo of screaming, dying men, and of dying horses wallowing in their own blood and spilled entrails.

Hektôr paused and burst out laughing, "Before I forget…ah, I have something interesting to tell you! Do not preen assuming Nefru is the only animal who talks in our household! My Xanthos too can be a chatterbox when he wants to…and today, he just would not stop…."

He dropped what he was holding, took me in his arms, squeezing me hard as he pressed me against him. "You're still mine, today," he said when he let go, his voice breaking. "I cannot blame Alexis for not wanting to give Helen up. I wouldn't surrender you, Āndrōmakhê, not even if the whole world thundered at our gates."

"Always, husband…. The two of us." A lump stuck in my throat.

"You will never be taken captive while I live," he said gruffly.

Quickly I turned and reached for the barley, clover, and wheat. Then I fetched the wine jar and poured plenty to the horses' water. Let them enjoy the bounty of gods.

"Darling, you're being wasteful!" Hektôr chuckled. "They're like children, they'll eat everything even after they had their bellies full; yet we still have thousands of people to feed before supplies arrive."

We left the horses to their feast, and returned home together, arms about each other, laughing, staggering with sudden joy.

Skamandrios rushed to meet us, leaving Thalpia smiling on the stairs. "Papa! Papa!" shouted the boy, and Hektôr leapt forward and caught him in his arms, swinging him to his shoulder.

"You weren't afraid of the Achaians today, were you, son?"

"Papa, Papa, oh, my dear Papa!" Skamandrios laughed, bouncing and flailing his arms about his father's neck.

"You're too strong for me," Hektôr grinned, tucked him under one arm, and then reached out for my hand.

Aghast, I scolded him, "You mustn't hold him like that!"

"I forgot," he winked, and set the boy down on his shaky two feet. "I'm so used to carrying my war helmet there."

* * * *

"I must see Helen before this goes any further!" Meneláos stepped ahead of his brother, Agamemnon.

I was on the wall again, positioned in a good spot between the crenellated parapets, along with all the women of Priam's family. From where I stood, I could see across the gate to the wild fig tree, waving and fluttering its leaves in wind currents. I shuddered as I looked at it, caught in nameless dread as, for a moment, the tree took on the shape of some horror.

Below us, the group of men stood stolidly, Trojans near the gate, Achaians across the river. The two heralds began setting up a folding table between the two groups, decked with soft clay tablets, stylus, and cylinders for rolling words into the clay. Talthybios added wooden blocks of Achaian pictographs.

Meneláos lifted one hand. "We will see Helen first!"

"Alexander is bringing her," Priam reassured him as Idaios stepped back from the table to bring folding stools. "Aeneas, Deiphobos, and Sarpedon of Lykia are seeing that my order is carried out."

Meneláos grinned, satisfied.

"Now to settle other terms," Agamemnon proffered.

"I agree to a reasonably lowered percentage for your merchants in tariffs to Kolchis, Kimmeria, and other areas of that region," Priam stated quietly.

"And I no longer demand free passage or a share in the tolls," the King of Kings conceded.

"Then we understand each other," Priam nodded. "Idaios, draw up the terms with Talthybios."

"Make a duplicate treaty in our language!" Agamemnon directed.

Meneláos interrupted just as the Achaian herald was setting down blocks of Achaian pictographs beside the Trojan cylinders. "I must insist on seeing Helen before any of this is drawn in clay! Lakedaimon is that part of her dowry I can only get with her."

"Go then," Priam said, turning to Hektôr. "Find out what's taking them so long."

Hektôr raced up the ramp into the city, and I moved along the wall, watching him progress as far as the Pergama. There he met Sarpedon who was coming in through the agora at a run.

Glancing about, I noticed Alexis walking nearby on the walltop. He slowed down and sat idly on a bench as if he had not a care in the world. Aeneas and Deiphobos appeared, springing upon him from either side, speaking rapidly. Alexis shrugged them off; they left him and passed me to stand at the top of the Tower stairs.

Hektôr appeared, cursing, followed by Sarpedon. He then towered over his brother, demanding grimly, "Are you bringing Helen?"

"No."

Hektôr reached out and plucked him to his feet. Alexis shook himself free, and then swung a sharp left to Hektôr's jaw. Hektôr sprang back, one hand to his blood-trickling mouth. I dared not come forward.

Hektôr grated, "Any man striking you would hit a woman! Bring out Helen, you traitorous dog!"

"Meneláos will never see her as long as I live."

"Alexis! *Our father gave his word!* Shame on you, brother!"

Alexis turned his back and streaked away.

Hektôr raced directly to Alexis' house abutting the inner citadel's high wall, while the others went after Alexis who began circling back when he reached the Dardanian Gate, then down the steps.

Agamemnon laughed loudly, watching them hurtle toward the assembled forces outside. Alexis reached where Priam stood with Meneláos and Agamemnon, smiling confidently.

"I don't see Helen!" Meneláos roared.

Alexis laughed, "She is at home, like every respectable wife."

"Son!" Priam seized his son's arm. "You know the oath! My word! I have never broken my word! Bring Helen here at once!"

"Your oath means nothing now, Father! And it wasn't *your* place to swear an oath that involved the return of *my* wife." He shrugged his father's hand away. "The duel was unfair, and inconclusive."

From my spot on the wall, I noticed our ally Pandaros of Zeleia slogging down the street with his famous bow made of sinew-backed goat horn and quiver of arrows. I screamed and pointed, but no one noticed. The man streaked through the gate and out of sight before I could point him to Thalpia.

Alexis shouted, "This is Troia's answer to Achaian tricksters!"

The twang of a bowstring ricocheted on the still air.

Meneláos howled, grabbed his belly, and doubled over. Blood seeped between his fingers clamped around the implanted arrow by the time Agamemnon was able to reach his brother.

Fate, stronger than man, was turning the stream of peace back toward the rushing river of war.

Deiphobos forced his father back into the city as a gigantic surge swept both armies against each other. Meneláos disappeared behind his own lines, supported by Agamemnon and the physician, Machaon.

Our Trojan warriors were uncontrollable as they leapt and hacked the enemy. Hektôr, behind his shield in the chariot as Kebriones drove, pounded into the unrestrainable melee.

Weariness stabbed through me like thorns. Slowly I returned home to my loom, rotting-sick inside myself. Horror at the future twisted in my abdomen as I worked on my husband's victory cloak, wondering if he would ever get to wear it.

When Hektôr returned at day's end, congealed blood was caked on his neck at the left shoulder. "Only a scratch."

Furiously drawing back from my ministering hands, he rushed upstairs to his bath. "Duel with Ajax Telamonides," he explained later, as I was swabbing another cloth with healing salve, around his wound.

"Ajax the Greater!" I gasped, well acquainted with his reputation.

"We've pledged to fight until one of us is killed," he continued, "Helenos suggested that it would be good if I took Alexis' place today and challenged one of the Achaian leaders."

"Helenos suggested *what?*"

"He had cast my horoscope and knew I would not die yet."

"So—your aunt Hesione's stepson took up the challenge."

"My spear struck his shield, but his came through and struck me in the neck. Hey, hey! Easy with that cloth!" His flesh quivered, but he looked up at me still defiant of the pain.

"Behave yourself!" I scolded him, "I've got to get that old blood out! It's black all around, clear down over your shoulder."

"I rattled him to his core, Ãndrõmakhê! We battled for a long, long time, with spears, fists, and swords, wrestled in the mud on the ground, until finally Talthybios stopped us." His words rushed on, a tense denial of the bulging veins on his forehead. "It was too dark for much else, so we made our pact, to meet again tomorrow. He gave me his belt, and I gave him my sword as token for our good will. I suppose I gave it to him to kill me with it, since I was carrying that good Thrakian two-hander today."

"Hektôr! What would Skamandrios and I do without you?"

"Don't remind me of defeat. It is bad enough this way. Getting back to Ajax…he was one of Helen's suitors, remember? Bound to fight on Agamemnon's side by the Oath of the Horse."

"The Oath of the Horse…" I whispered. "The one that your father swore yesterday, was not how it's done, was it?"

"No, it wasn't. Agamemnon had demanded Phoenix to be sacrificed, and because he is your beloved Iris' son, Father offered his own blood in his stead. He slashed the palm of his hand so deeply, in order to make it acceptable, that he might never again be able to hold a sword with it."

"Why would Agamemnon ask for Phoenix?" Priam's sacrifice on my behalf was so great that I could not bring myself to speak of it.

"I don't know," he shrugged. "They must have spies among us."

I finished dressing his wound, my tears dripping into the minty-smelling ointment.

* * * *

The meeting that night was prompted by a vicious riot in the Agora. The elders came in a body, closing around the speakers' stone where Priam used to make pronouncements.

"Alexis! Alexis! We demand Alexis!"

The chant began as a lone voice, and then united in a rhythmic chant of many. Word had spread of his use of Pandaros to strike Meneláos during the signing of the treaty, and they demanded his blood.

When he could be heard, Priam agreed to compromise. Troia would give up claim to Lakedaimon and return Helen's dowry, but Helen would remain with us.

Grumbling but pacified, the crowd was trickling away when I found Hektôr talking with a young shepherd.

"I am Korythos Alexanderides," I heard the young man say. His eyes flicked to me as I took my place beside Hektôr.

Priam came forward. "We welcome you, my boy."

"I am here as a suppliant. Where is my father?"

"You are near his door," I pointed.

Hektôr stepped to Helen and Alexis' gate just as it was flung open from inside.

"What is all this?" Alexis came out, staring from Hektôr to his father, and then noticed Korythos. "What can you want?"

"My mother needs you. If you return to her now, you will avoid the evil she foresees for you."

"Oinoné wants me back?" He laughed without restraint.

Korythos went on urgently. "She will bring about your destruction if you do not give up that woman."

"Helen is my wife and Oinoné is shameless. Tell her I hope never to see her again."

Korythos ignored him, "Fate is against you here! My mother saw visions! Evil and horror will come to you if you ignore her warning. Mother can save you from your own fate if you act now while there is still time. Kassandra will confirm this!"

"So she still goes to the mountains, that gloomy sister of mine!" Alexis growled, and then shoved the boy back from his gate. "Return to your sheep, boy, and tell Oinoné to cool herself with another man."

"I'll not hear my mother insulted for such a woman as Helen!" He struck out blindly at his father. "My mother did not send me. *I* came without pride, for I have watched her unhappiness for too many years." He spat on the pavement. "As for me, I hate you!"

Rage contorted Alexis' handsome face. One step forward, an upper cut to Korythos' jaw. A rapid left from the side.

The boy staggered back, his head striking the post with a loud crack. He slid down and lay limply.

Alexis strode back into his house.

I stared in horror. When Hektôr lifted him, the boy's head fell back, blood dripped slowly.

Kassandra emerged from Athené's temple, shaking her fist toward the house of her brother. "Accursed firebrand! Destroyer of men! Alexis, Murderer of Troia!"

Alexis rushed back out, this time with Helen, and stood at his gate, lips white as he took in the scene. "Dead! I've murdered my own son!"

His eyes rolled upward and he fell heavily.

* * * *

Priam had Korythos' body embalmed in honey and wax, then set out in state for three days. Afterward he sent it with honor to Oinoné in the mountains. Alexis was placed under taboo, but because of the war and every able-bodied warrior was needed, he was not sent away.

Distracted by this tragic turn of events, no one thought of giving up Helen's treasure to the Achaians.

Hektôr's wound had turned a blotchy yellow when fighting resumed once again. He laughed at my worry. "We can win now that Akhilles refuses to fight," and he grinned at me while taking up his helmet. "Even though Meneláos has already recovered."

"Hektôr," I whispered, "this bravery of yours will never end... but you have to think of your little boy and your loving wife whom you will make a widow soon."

He looked away, his face paled, and he spoke, "Ah, dearest wife! May the dark earth pile deep upon my dead body before I hear you weeping as they drag you off as prize for an Achaian chief."

* * * *

The morning came when Hektôr was obligated to meet Ajax Telamonides in the agreed upon duel.

After he embraced and kissed Skamandrios and me, I presented him his great war helmet, deftly securing its chinstraps. Then I went and stood near the fig tree to watch Kebriones drive him out, skirting beyond the Skaian Springs with intent of surrounding the enemy forces. Last night I had burnished his helmet, his armor, and arm and leg grieves with my own hands, proud of my skill, assuring there were no cracks or chinks, and especially that the thick, leather-covered padding inside his helmet was intact. This was a vital portion of his defenses, the padding absorbing the impact of most blows.

As Hektôr neared the front, an Achaian chariot detached itself, clouding its own trail with puffy dust, and hurtled inland, while behind it the enemy forces rallied to an advancing line.

It was Ajax, son of Telamon.

Hektôr, slowing his charioteer, stopped north beyond the ford of the river and dismounted. The high-blowing fig leaves kept switching before my sight, and I grabbed for them. Below, the two men faced each other on foot. Ajax was as tall and bulky with muscles as Hektôr. Slowly they raised spears above their shoulders, Ajax with his round shield in front of his chest supported by his left arm, Hektôr propping his oblong tower shield on the ground before him so that he could rest his chin on the top while steadying his spear. They stood apart the length of their spears— each spear the length of two men—made of heavy ash, and tipped with metal.

Please, Aphrodite! I saw you here, on the field, the other day, surely, you must be here again, somewhere... please, please, watch over my husband!

His wound was still inflamed, his neck, back, and arms bruised...if only he would raise his shield a little, or stop...I squeezed my hands until the nails pierced my palms.

Hektôr made the first move. Ajax staggered before his throw, shield and spear crashing to the ground. Recovering quickly, he threw a huge rock that hurled Hektôr away from his shield on contact, felling him with a banging crash of iron and bronze.

I clung frantically to the battlement.

Ajax lifted his spear in victory, and the howling Achaian troops surged forward to strip Hektôr for dead. Aeneas and Sarpedon thundered over in their chariots, savagely heading off the enemy. Our troops rushed after them, driving back the Achaians.

Polyxena, Laodike and Kreusa hurried to me, but I forced myself to stand tall without support. Hektôr could not be dead—he dare not!

Polyxena pointed and called out, "Helenos and Kebriones are bringing him in!"

Thalpia rushed back to the house with Skamandrios while I flew down the Tower stairs. Hektôr's chariot clattered in between the open-folded gates and I screamed to Kebriones. Helenos, supporting Hektôr in both arms and barely gripping the chariot-rail with one half-free hand, shook his head *No* at me. Kebriones lashed the horses, sparks hissed as their hooves banged the cobbled pavement up the incline.

Skittering back to the walltop and along to the palace area, I forced my collapsing legs across the courtyard as the chariot thumped into the Agora. Hekabe and Priam emerged from their door into the area as Kebriones leapt from the chariot.

I turned and ran home to prepare his bed, and a quick backward glance showed Helenos sliding my husband down from the chariot to Kebriones. Upstairs at last, I breathlessly unrolled and smoothed the bedclothes, my own voice shrilling as I worked, "Thalpia! Polyxena! The rest of you! Fetch water! Herbs! Salve!"

Finally, Hektôr was brought in and laid on the bed. I reached out, cradling his head in my hands.

Hekabe, flying in, clutched Kebriones' arm, "Is he—will he live?"

"Only Apollo the Healer knows," Kebriones answered. "I've got to get back—the Achaians are overwhelming us." He stared silently at Hektôr, and then went out running.

Hektôr breathed! I placed his head on the pillow and sobbed my relief. We began cleaning the blood from his face, neck, and chest. The old wound was broken open, bleeding into the new chest laceration that alone could have killed a weaker man.

Helenos arrived with more salves and medicinal potions. Together with Priam, he removed Hektôr's armor and jerkin.

Hekabe fastened laurel on the door as a summons to Apollo.

When done with his part, Helenos waited at the door, his gaze steady on Hektôr. Night fell around us suddenly, and we were in the dark until Thalpia brought a single-wick alabaster lamp. Helenos left.

Deiphobos stepped in with Skamandrios in his arm, hushing the child as he reached for his father. Deiphobos then stood motionless, eyebrows pinched into a frown.

"Pray to the Paionian God of Dardania!" Hekabe moaned.

Deiphobos went over, leaning down to kiss his mother.

Skamandrios began screaming, "Papa! Papa!"

Before I could soothe him, Deiphobos waved at me, and then left the room with Skamandrios in his arm.

I sat and watched over Hektôr through the night. Dimly I heard Hekabe and Priam talking, rehashing happy days from Hektôr's childhood. Such a great horseman he had been. At the Trojan Fair, he had always won the horse taming and riding contests. Not cut out to be a warrior, though, Hekabe stated. Priam, stiffening, pointed out how eagerly the boy had taken to military life, and how determinedly he had wanted the Defendership of the City. At heart, he was a man of peace, but stood tall in the heat of war and fought better than everyone.

So, I thought, *I must raise Skamandrios to be soldier first and a man of peace, second. He must not be quite as tolerant as Hektôr, for he would have much to guard, now that Achaians see Troia as weak.*

I promised myself that I would see to it—never again must the Achaian states presume to set claim to our soil! Priam had been stronger than Laomedon, and wiser. Now Hektôr the Defender, and after him Skamandrios the Conqueror, would be stronger than any of their ancestors. Not Achaia *and* Troia, but only one or the other would rule while the other vanished from earth.

* * * *

Hektôr lay unconscious for two days, and then began a low muttering. I bent over him, breathing my love and life into his nostrils. He felt around his neck with one hand, so that his fingers became sticky with the ointment.

"Clean that off! Troia needs me," he shouted. Covers slid to his feet as he forcefully pushed himself to the edge of the bed. He stared at me, swaying where he sat. "I've no time for bed."

I tried to hold him but he stumbled from the dais. "My soldiers need me!" He then collapsed in a heap on the floor.

I choked back the screams building up in my heart.

Deiphobos and Helenos sprinted in and heaved him back into bed. Helenos gave him a soothing drink and he subsided into sleep. I lay down curved against his body. I dozed fitfully, beset by strange dreams.

I was in a chariot, frantically racing around the walls of Troia, with Ares, God of War, at my heels. Then I was merged in Hektôr's body, standing at the outside walls of Troia, while Priam and Hekabe looked down and beseeched us to return inside, to safety. Hektôr and I, one body-one soul, gazed up at the bright blue sky, searching for Atropos, she with the gleaming shears that cuts the thread of our lives, beseeching her to give us more time. Athené showed up, helmet and armor blinding in the sun, and I screamed and screamed, alone in an endless chamber of echoes, begging Dea Madre to come and strike down the jealous Olympian.

* * * *

When fighting resumed next morning, there was no holding Hektôr back. His wound was still raw and sword arm seriously weakened by the injury. I begged him, begged him on my knees, sobbing, screaming, kissing his hands, pulling out my hair in bunches—dignity be damned—to recuperate for just one more day. He paid me no heed. He embraced Skamandrios and me, whispered endearments to us, rushed to the stables and ordered Kebriones to bring his chariot from where it was waiting, tilted, shafts upward, against the wall.

I pulled myself together, held my head high, and went to watch from the wall as he came out in his chariot, shouted his battle-cry, thundering onto the vast plain.

Alexis followed at a stroll with his bow and arrows.

The Achaians were pressing a forward advantage, but were thrust back when the Trojans rallied at sight of my Hektôr. As when heaven sends a breeze to sailors who have long prayed for one in vain, laboring at their oars until they grow faint with toil, so welcome was the sight of Hektôr to his men. The fight had gone badly without him, for, even without Akhilles, the presumed death of the Defender had given the enemy courage.

More of our warriors flew out through sally ports, bull-hide shields held in front. From the battlements, others hurled huge stones upon the approaching enemy groups.

Now a shout of dread tore from our collective breasts: Above the host a screaming eagle circled, in its talons a crimson serpent. The two creatures fought in the air, wounding each other. But as they flew over the hostile ranks, the serpent struck at the eagle with his fangs, and the eagle, gashed in the breast, dropped the serpent. Our warriors froze up as they saw the blood-red serpent lying across their path, for they believed it was an omen from Zeus.

They wanted to turn back, but Hektôr pressed them on, "One omen I know is to fight a good fight for our homes!" He pointed with his great sword, "Run forward, my friends! Bring the battle to those ships that came to our coast against the will of the gods!"

With that, Hektôr and Kebriones flung toward the camp, Hektôr raising repeatedly the dread-cry of battle, inciting them to fight on while scattering Achaian foot soldiers and chariots like chaff. When the enemy realized that the Champion of Troia was still alive, they fell back as before a ghost. As his splendid body with the gleaming armor fleeted in and out of the enemy ranks, I thought of the sun, covered by and freed from, dark clouds as it travels in the sky.

Hektôr thundered for the beached enemy ships, flew over the wide protective ditch, and landed in front of their fortifications. Kebriones was struck by a slingshot on the head. Dazed, he dropped the reins, the chariot shook, swerved, and Hektôr tumbled down; I screamed like a thousand furies, terrified he would not be able to get back to his feet, but he did, grasping on loyal Xanthos' neck. Hektôr lifted up a rock, as great as not even Herakles could raise it from the ground, and flung it at the main gate. The rock broke through hinges and bars, and the great gate caved in under its impact.

Hektôr leapt across its remnants with a spear in each of his hands. No warrior could withstand him now as he scattered camp-slaves and smashed tents.

Recovering, Kebriones pulled the chariot aside, quickly looking over both horses and wheels. Polydamas rushed to his side, helping.

Cowed by Hektôr's one-man scourge, the rest of the enemy was hemmed in at their ships in fear of him; when they rained javelins upon him, he still fought on with the force and fury of a whirlwind.

I let my tears flow freely as I watched him, Hektôr Astyanax, a mighty lion wreaking havoc in the camp of jackals. However, his high spirit might well be the death of him....

I began chanting, "Long live Hektôr! Hektôr Astyanax!"

The whole of Troia joined, "Long live Hektôr! Hektôr Astyanax!"

Many a time did he charge at his pursuers and scattered them. Meanwhile arcs of brilliant fire fingered the swinging throw of torches onto the listing decks beyond. The enemy raced for water with anything they could find.

Presently I spotted Ajax Telamonides cast at Hektôr a huge stone used to prop one of the ships, striking him on the breast, over the rim of his shield. The blow was so fierce that my beloved husband spun round like a top. Despite the distance, I heard the bronze of his shield and helmet clanging loudly as he fell on the ground. The Achaians swarmed to where he lay, ready to tear him apart limb by limb. Led by Polydamas his comrades placed their shields around him and drove back the enemy pressing round. They lifted him into his chariot, and Kebriones drove him away.

Sudden pandemonium broke out among Trojans nearer the city; Akhilles' golden armor, specially made by Hephaistos, flashed toward the Achaian front.

My knees weakened. Oh, no! Akhilles was back in the fight!

I joined my hoarsened voice to those screaming warnings that rose skyward. This time it was *our* warriors who were panicking at the sight of a rising hero, Akhilles. As if one body, they turned and fled back toward the safety of the walls.

The flood of fleeing men divided to pass an Achaian knot forming about the body of noble Sarpedon, who fell before Akhilles' onrush.

Once again, Ajax Telamonides raced for Hektôr, but Hektôr swept aside and continued toward the city.

At the city wall, Hektôr turned in his chariot as Kebriones slowed, lifting his spear crosswise for truce.

Agamemnon drove forward and accepted, holding his own spear crosswise in answer. The two men dismounted, exchanged words, and then shouted orders to their respective troops.

Hektôr remounted and rode into the city.

I stared out to where noble Sarpedon had fallen, growling enemy soldiers fighting each other to strip his armor to keep as prize; much was lost today with Sarpedon's death.

I raced down the stairs and met Hektôr at the ramp. He stopped for me, as always, and I climbed in beside the two brothers. Blood seeped in thick crimson rivulets along his upper arm, and I just could not help screaming, again and again. Kebriones drove on up to where Hekabe waited on the Pergama.

"You are wounded again!" I tried to pull him from the car with me as I slid to the pavement.

"It only rubbed a little," and he grinned down at me. He looked at his mother. "Please lay your richest robe upon Pallas Athené's knees, in her shrine, and get all the women to offer sacrifices too," he told her. "This day, I duel for victory." He faced me. "Pray to your Anatolian Goddess, and to your Dea Madre, and all the rest of the gods."

I was beside myself, screaming and pounding his chest with my fists, "No! You mustn't duel with Ajax today!"

"Sarpedon must be avenged," he replied brusquely. "He is close kindred to *your* people, Ãndrõmakhê, and his shade demands that I take next kinsman's duty."

"At least keep away from Akhilles!"

Hektôr laughed, shrugging. He then gave me a dark look, "Go with Mother to Ate's Temple. For me."

"But your injury," I resisted, "you really are not fit for fight!"

"My beloved wife, listen: the Moiras [1] have long ago determined everything about me: when my life began, when it's supposed to end, and what happens in between. Clotho spun the thread of my life, Lachesis measured it and cast my lot, and Atropos will decide when to cut it with her shears. Nothing I do today or any other day, will change what is already ordained. However, Helenos' divination predicts victory for me, *today,* if I take due precautions. I need your prayers. Prove your faith in me by staying away from the walls for the rest of the day. Your part is to keep our home and hearth, and pray for victory. Mine is to go out and do my duty to you and our citizens."

He turned and spoke to Kebriones, and they quickly wheeled back down the street.

I spent the following hours on my knees, in ceremonial prayers with Hekabe and all the other women of Troia.

At day's end, darkening night separated Trojan and Achaian.

I joined other women at the well in the inner citadel, and though we had a spring in our own courtyard, drawing water for our returning husbands. I was halfway up our stairs holding a pail in each hand when I heard Hektôr's boots at the door.

My heart thudded when I met him; this was the first time in these many years that I had not kept watch on the wall.

Without stopping for my clutching hands, he swaggered into our hall and set an oval Achaian shield with a leather fringe hanging off its bottom, against the wall with a clang. Then he glanced around as if seeing me for the first time.

I clung to him, dusty and bloody though he was. My breath burned in my lungs as he gave me a gentle push, stepping away to stand tall, a proud grin splitting his face. "See my new armor!"

It was so covered with mud and reddish brown stains as to need hours of cleaning. Then I realized that this armor was not his own. Gold engraved concentric circles shone through among the blood and dust-smears, and were certainly not of Trojan design.

"Patroklos, Akhilles' cousin and friend, has fallen in battle!" he announced quietly, "And this is Akhilles' armor; he had worn it to fool and scare us. He did, at first. I took him up on direct combat assuming he was Akhilles. See the blood on my boots? Patroklos's guts."

I did not know whether it was safe to cheer.

His face darkened. "I regret that it was Patroklos and not Akhilles I battled. But I am sure this will bring him out from his hole." Hektôr began loosening the straps of his armor, favoring his wounded shoulder. "Āndrōmakhê, they'll never get the best of us."

I unfroze my limbs and helped remove the last of his armor.

"I shall terrify his Myrmidons in this outfit!" His eyes sparkled feverishly. "When it's cleaned, they'll think Patroklos' ghost has joined us, against them." He went to the stairs with me at his heels. "They are great in resorting to tricks, my love. They camouflage everything. But tomorrow I'm going to hit them with their own trickery."

I paused on the step above him. "No! You are *not* to return to the battlefield tomorrow! You need to rest..."

"Troia will not suffer for a silly wound of mine!" he roared at me. Rotating his arm to prove his strength, a fleeting grimace showed me his pain. "Hah, I can still show Akhilles who is the better warrior. I would only need one arm for that. Keep to your work, Āndrõmakhê, and I'll keep to mine."

Chastised, I remained silent. He hurried to take his bath, and I followed to help, feeling humble. A pious man was my Hector, he would never offer libation to the gods with unwashed hands, nor would he pray while bespattered with blood and filth.

* * * *

"Brother!" Helenos warned Hektôr early next morning as we stood by the Skaian Gate, "Father Badogios has sent his eagle to the left, this is not a good omen. Take off your armor and your war helmet, and return home. Don't go out to the field of battle today."

"It's not a good omen for the *Achaians,*" Hektôr spat. He was clad in Akhilles' golden armor, and held his shield as well. "You know I won't shirk my duty. For hours now Akhilles has been standing at our walls, howling his dread battle-cry, challenging me to single combat for my sin of having slain Patroklos."

Then he turned to me, his smile confident, "Promise me, dearest one: You will not idle the day on the walls. Today, knowing you are safe in our own home, diligently working at your loom, will strengthen me as I grapple with the enemy."

Skamandrios was standing next to me, clutching my hand as he looked up at his father. Hektôr gazed at him, his green eyes ablaze with love and pride. I was compelled to rest against him for a moment, my breast against his hard, harsh, breastplate. His arm went around me, his free hand touching the shoulder of our son. Tears pooled on the rim of my eyes, but I held them back.

I bent and lifted Skamandrios in my arms, grasped his chin and turned him to face his father. "My lord husband," I said, ashamed that my voice was trembling but unable to steady it. "Look at our little son. Do not leave him fatherless! And do not make me your widow. Please heed Helenos' advice and stay home today."

Gently he touched my hair, my cheek. Smiling, he said, "My one and only, wife. Remember that no man, be he coward or brave, can fool and thus escape his destiny."

Something strange overcame our son. His eyes widening, he stared at his father's familiar great-crested war helmet, and screamed as if frightened by its sight.

Hektôr bit his lips, but took the helmet from his head and set it gleaming upon the ground. Taking Skamandrios from me, he kissed him, dandled him in his arms, praying aloud, "Holy Father Zeus! Grant that my son may be even as myself, chief among the Trojans; let him excel in strength, and let him rule Troia with might and wisdom. May they say of him as he returns from battle, 'Far greater is he than was Hektôr, his father.' And thus let his mother's heart be glad."

He put the boy down and looked at me, speaking quietly, "My dearest love, do not take these things too bitterly to heart. Go, then, Āndrōmakhê, go within the house, and busy yourself with your daily duties, your loom, your distaff, the managing of stores and servants; for war is man's matter, and mine—above all others born in Troia."

Lifting his helmet from the ground, Hektôr turned to his waiting chariot. Alexis arrived in his bronze armor, driving alone, being his own charioteer.

"Hektôr Astyanax!" shouted Alexis, saluting him, "I report to duty. I hasted as fast as my horse would take me! I hope you will find me worthy of fighting close at your side."

"My brave-hearted brother," Hektôr replied, "you fight nobly, and I have always appreciated your efforts in battle. However, you are often careless, and willfully remiss. It grieves me to hear the ill that our people speak about you, for they have suffered much on your account. Let us be going now, but we shall make things right hereafter, should Father Zeus vouchsafe us to set the cup of our deliverance before ever-living gods of heaven in our own homes, when we have chased the enemy from Troia."

I swallowed my growing terror, clung to my son's hand, and went in the direction of our house.

But when he was out the gate and sounded his cry to battle, "For Troia! For our wives! For our children!" I left Skamandrios with Thalpia and ran back to the wall despite his order that I do not.

Only for a while, I told myself, *until I get a sense of how the day will turn out.*

Akhilles, who had howled and carried on for hours near the Skaian Gate, was nowhere to be seen.

Towards mid-morning, a big black cloud cut off from the mountain and raced coastward by the winds. It hung over the crenellated towers and the mingled flat and gabled roofs of the city. At noontime, lightning snapped to the ground, then crackled in bright bunches among the clouds. I touched my opal, and it felt cool to my touch. Good! Nefru sat by my feet, black-masked blue eyes serene, purring.

Presently resounding bangs of thunder crashed through sudden torrents of rain that blinded sight of the plain ahead. Hektôr was compelled to rush for the Skamandrian Gate, troops streaming after him. Earlier, he had foraged among the enemy, driving them steadily back. Now the citizens ran for shelter and the gates opened for returning soldiers who entered the barracks for shelter.

Confident that fight had ended for the day, I ran home at a fast clip, and sat by my loom, wanting to show him that I obeyed his wish and worked at home today.

I smiled to myself. I could relax now; Akhilles was not around, and the Achaians had been on the verge of defeat.

Nefru showed up, turned around and around himself, shaking off the rainwater soaking his white coat, and then came and leaped on a nearby stool. After watching me for a lengthy moment, he began to groom himself, sometimes pausing to give a little purr.

I became engrossed in the cloak I was weaving for Hektôr, and did not notice the sun come out. It filtered in through the open window with a greenish translucence, and fresh green odors wafted into the room. I smiled to myself. Just so had I sat on spring afternoons as a child, when my brothers would be free to roam the fields. Sullenly, my sweaty hands had labored under Mother's well-meaning instructions.

Suddenly hot tears stung my eyes; Mother...Father...seven robust, good-natured, loving brothers...all gone. Seven brothers whose only partial remains could be found for burial, one father in tumulus with honorable relics about him, placed there in respect for his bravery by the man who slew him. Akhilles. And my mother—be she named Latmia, or Kupra—a child again, never remembering that she had been a woman cherished by her loving husband and eight children, dying as a child dies, as she wandered in her father's polished halls....

All, all, gone.

Akhilles!

All of a sudden, the opal turned fiery on my throat, so much so that I had to grasp, tear it off and throw it against the wall. Why, just the memory of Akhilles' deeds, was maddening me!

Nefru leapt down with a flash, retrieved the jewel, holding it in his mouth, its gold chain loose, looking as if he were holding a mouse with its tail dangling.

Ignoring him, I bit my lips, determined to pull myself together. I had to prove Hektôr that I had kept to my household duties. And I so wanted to finish this victory cloak for him!

By the time Skamandrios scooted in, I was casting and pulling with flying fingers. He was playing with sling-bullets, and Thalpia stood and watched from the doorway.

Dim shouts and clashing of arms tugged the edge of my consciousness. Strangely, I imagined I saw Ares, God of War, in the battlefield, looking more fearsome than in any of his statues, and then the vision melted and metamorphosed into Athené, fully armored, diverting someone's flying spear from its target.

I was glad when Thalpia took Skamandrios away for his bath.

But I was no longer able to continue my work, Athené's vision too lively in memory for comfort. She was out there, casting mischief. Then I reminded myself that the fighting had stopped for today, with my own eyes I had seen the men pass through the gate.

I rose to my feet and went to look at the sun-clock lying in the field-side window. An hour to darkness.

I hurried back and out to the gallery, "Thalpia! See that water is heated for your lord's bath!"

I had not meant that sharpness in my voice. I stood in the middle of the room, hugging myself with arms across my breasts. A freezing coldness drifted in, whipped across my shoulders, and was gone. Racing to the bedroom, quickly I changed into a loose-flowing green tunic with white veil and silver chaplet, went back to my loom and carefully dipped oil from the jar, sponging it to run down the threads and soak in. I would not weave again tonight. At any moment, Hektôr's boots would echo from downstairs, signaling he was coming home.

Then, my son's toy chariot, caught in some vagrant draft, rolled into the corner near me, clicking softly against the wall when it stopped. I smiled, listening to the chatter wafting in from the outside. Other sounds intruded; vague, screaming sounds. A spate of rain slapped the windowsill, and I stopped cold.

At once, an avalanche of screams from the walls rent the distance with despair. Wailing and commotion spread throughout the city.

A white butterfly flew in from the window, fluttered around, then lit upon my loom. Butterflies were a symbol of the soul. I thought of Hektôr with a clear, bleak shock.

I whirled and flew downstairs. Breath strangled in me as I raced along the wall. I almost fell against Hekabe who was swaying, staring ahead as if blinded. My own eyes refused to focus. Hazy forms began taking shape. Hekabe screamed with all her might, "Merciful Ate!"

Why? Why?

My sight cleared, and Akhilles was on the field below.

No...Hektôr had gone out in Akhilles' armor; it must be he I was looking at. Yet the chariot was Achaian, not Trojan, driving at top speed across the plain. Something long and pale, dragged behind it, streaked in red.

Then I noticed something else…a head? Banging along, leaving tracks in the bloodied mud…darkly blond hair flying....

Priam rushed down to the gate like a madman. His scream unearthly, he tried to push through the crowd. He fell on the wet, cobbled street, but struggled up to tear at the bolts. Deiphobos and Polites held and lifted him on his feet. Hekabe, her sobs full-throated, raced down after her husband.

I stared out again to the field below. The golden chariot tore back toward Troia with its burden, groaning, bumping, across the rough ground. Recognition stabbed my eyes: Akhilles' chariot! Its axle, made from trees of Mount Pelion, in Thessaly, trembled with an attached weight.

But what *was* that weight?

I blinked forcefully to gain sharper focus and leaned forward.

At once the thousand-fold shafts of iron swords ripped through my throat and heart: It was the stripped naked body of a massive warrior, dragged feet first.

Hektôr!

Somewhere in the distance, sounded Skamandrios' joyous cry, "Papa! Papa won! He is victorious!"

Another cry rose up, from far, far, below, "Trojans! See your Hektôr! He who most deeply wounded my soul, he who slew my dearest friend, Patroklos! O you lost Trojans, look down, and witness the price your wretched Defender has paid for his crime!"

I felt the blood drain out of me, hardening like stone in my feet. The red glow of evening bled over me, and flashed into night.

[1] The *Moiras:* Weavers of Destiny, Daughters of the Night, personifications of the inescapable destiny of Man. They are assigned to every person as his/her fate—or share—in the scheme of things. Clotho the Spinner, appears as a maiden, and is the Thread of Life; Lachesis the Apportioner, also Chance/Luck, appears as a matron and the tool of her trade is a ruler; and Atropos (also Aisa-Destiny) she who severs the Thread, appears as a crone. They arrive with Ilythia, Goddess of Childbirth, at the moment of birth, divine a person's whole destiny, and then return to be present at the point of death.

Chapter 20: Penthesilea, the Amazon

During my days of madness, wailing and weeping, forced to consume potions by Kassandra who feared I would harm myself, I lost track of time. Still, some details about Hektôr's death, details I could not bear to know about, seeped into my ears.

According to Kassandra, worn down by the entreaties of Thétis and Athené, Zeus had decided that Hektôr must lose. However, from the onset the odds were stacked against Troia's Champion, for the armor Akhilles wore in battle, built by Hephaistos, made him invulnerable. Only Akhilles, not anyone else who would wear it in his stead—thus it had protected neither Patroklos, nor Hektôr. As the owner of the armor, Akhilles had known precisely where it had a weak spot, and been able to strike it for deadly damage to Hektôr.

I remembered one of Hektôr's last comments to me, that only Atropos would cut his thread of Life. Ahh! So we had no say in our own affairs, in how we led our lives, or when to face death? No free will, at all? Were we just puppets dancing in the hands of the petty-minded, capricious gods?

True, Akhilles had killed Hektôr and won the *Aristeia* he had been thirsting for. However, certainly not for *true* valor!

When compared to my Hektôr, who had no divine help but only his own manly strength, skill, and honor, Akhilles was the lowest, meanest, cheat. And Zeus, Father of All Men and Gods, was an amoral weakling who appointed Alexis to judge in an issue He had no stomach for, and then favored one flawed godling, Akhilles, against a mortal man of blameless, noble character.

Now sudden voices and other sounds flew about my ears with no understanding. Words of anger, words of horror. "Akhilles…Hektôr.."

The haze in my mind began to clear. I recalled with a most painful stab to my heart, seeing…before I had fainted again…around, around, and around the tomb of Patroklos….

Akhilles had pierced the tendons at the back of Hektôr's feet from heel to ankle, inserted leather straps made of the belt Ajax had given as a gift to Hektôr, and thus bound him to his chariot, leaving his head to trail behind. He then raced the chariot around Patroklos' tomb, and in front of the walls, and round the city, for all these past days, while my beloved husband's head tumbled against the ground, and dust, dirt, blood, and small critters filled his open mouth, nostrils, and ears.

No! No! Such a ghastly act—it could not have happened! Torture for the dead warrior's soul, still not released by decent burial. No!

My feet moved of themselves and I left my bedchamber without knowing where I was going.

Dry-white sun sluiced over the pebble mosaics of the outer court. Shadows confused themselves in dreamlike movement. I recognized Thalpia, holding Skamandrios' hand as she walked him to the herb garden. I saw Skamandrios, eyes red and swollen from constant weeping, following her obediently. Wanting to call him, I could not, for I was inexorably pulled in the direction of voices.

I saw Deiphobos and Helenos, bending over a heap of dust-covered clothing; it moved, and they lifted their father to his feet.

Priam, mighty King of Troia. A legend in his own time. His nails torn and bleeding. I could see where he had scratched up the beaten pebbles that paved the yard, blackening his face with mud, veiling it from evil spirits that brought death and pain. I watched helplessly as his sons leaned him against an end of the small altar. His hoarse cries went on and on: "Revenge! My son, o precious Hektôr! Revenge!"

I ran to him and pulled his falling cloak around him to cover his torn robes. Then I glanced at the two brothers. They stood, faces stiff and eyes dark with helpless rage.

Lined up along the stable alcoves, were the few remaining of Priam's fifty sons. Alexis stood apart with Helen. Where was their laughter, the proud exuberance of those lost young men?

A nervous twitching in the aged body against mine, and Priam lifted his head. I moved away as he stared about, staggered a few steps, and then snapped erect. His voice was still strong, "We have stood by for twelve days, witnessing him insult Hektôr's body! Enough! I will go to Akhilles now, and ransom my son! Get out the wagon and hitch mules!" He flung off his cloak and strode to the door of his palace.

Hekabe staggered to him from inside, her voice rending the air: "You can't go alone, you can't trust Akhilles!"

He looked at her. "It is better to die today, trying to bring my son home, than live to see the destruction of my people. Zeus gave me the strength to bring my heroic son home." He disappeared inside, and she rushed after him.

My throat dry and tight after days of screaming, I could not speak. My eyes flicked around the place. Indeed Hektôr's bier was not set anywhere. Then it slammed me again: Akhilles dragging Hektôr's body around Patroklos' tomb and the Cyclopean walls of Troia. Akhilles refusing, repeatedly, all our entreaties and ransom offers to release him to us for proper funeral rites. My head floated in a red mist. I steadied myself against the altar, grasping a horn. Not to give up now...no, not until I had wrapped his beloved body for the pyre with my own hands. His soul must be freed of corruption and agony.

Blazing hatred streaked through me. To touch Akhilles, to make him suffer...I felt myself falling. Helenos supported me, holding me up. Then I heard concerns about if we had enough gold left to persuade Akhilles to relinquish Hektôr's body. His love for Patroklos had been so great that his fury at Hektôr drove him to demonic cruelty.

Priam's shout broke into my confusion, "Where's that wagon? Idaios!" Pointing the amber globe of his regal staff, he thundered, "And somebody load that ransom! If he doesn't deem it enough, I will beg him on my knees to take my life in lieu of Hektôr's body."

"Father!" I shouted, leaping to my feet, "Wait! Let me go collect my jewels to add to his ransom!"

Priam nodded. I ran home, looking over my gold and finery to give him the best. In a silver box, my mother had stored a great diadem of elaborate construction, and explained—prophetically!—that it was worth a king's ransom. Composed of four rows of heart-shaped leaves of gold connected with fine wire, it was fringed on each side with a row of larger, rose-shaped pendants. It was about the breadth of my forehead, and when clasped round my head with my hair bunched above, the tails would cascade below my shoulders. I also had elaborate earrings; rich necklaces made of gold rings strung together, thick bracelets of twisted gold, and a gold eagle-shaped ornament the size of a child's head. I had to laugh. Of special interest to Akhilles ought to be the gold bands with engraved designs used for protective blindfolding of the dead! At the last minute, I also added the amber pendant-necklace and bracelets I had offered Akhilles as ransom for Kiron on that long-ago day in the grove.

Finally I grabbed a drawstring bag made of soft leather and filled it to bursting with the jewelry as well as obsidian, jade, and marble artifacts I could get my hands on in such short notice.

When I returned, the wagon frame was pulled from its shaft-up lean against the stable wall. Two brothers lashed on its wicker body while others crawled under and smeared the axle with lanolin for soundlessness, using uncarded wool. Others got out the traces and hitched a pair of strong mules.

"Father," I entreated him quietly, "may I come with you?"

"No, Āndrōmakhê!" Seeing the desolation in my eyes, he added with a softer tone, "You are Hektôr's widow, my dear, and therefore the greatest of all battle prizes. Akhilles will never allow you to return to us. Would you forsake Skamandrios?"

Achaian watchfires were glimmering along the shore by the time Priam climbed into the treasure wagon beside Idaios. The eagle of Badogios flew ahead of him, showing the way. Idaios drove, cautiously negotiating the steps from the Pergama into the Lower City. The crowd of family and citizens followed as far as the Skaian Gate, and then the wagon rolled on down the ramp and out to the Skamandrian Ford.

We stayed late that night, for Priam did not return. I was among the last to bed in the royal complex. I kept Skamandrios with me this night. He slept sweetly beside me, Nefru curled up by our feet. I slept, waked, dozed. Our son must grow to manhood; he must avenge his father. In addition, he must rule the land—wisely, and justly. I would see to it that Akhilles suffered, I would not let him rejoice in the glory of having slain Hektôr Astyanax, Hero of Troia. My sheets twisted into knots as my hands burned to put a dagger through Akhilles' dark heart.

Before dawn I left the bed and glided like a ghost around our home—our sanctuary. Everything was still here, all the little things he had taken pleasure in, still solid to my touch, yet…Hektôr….

First mauve of dawn glowed in the sky when Kassandra breezed into the courtyard, startling me, for she was quite a sight with her loose long hair and flowing white dress. "Father just left Akhilles' tent," she whispered. "It will take them a while to arrive here. Would you like me to sit with you for a bit?"

"Yes I would, thank you."

"Are you feeling a little stronger?"

"I will, once Hektôr is home."

"Of course, I understand."

We sat down on the bench by the herb garden, listening to the sounds of the playful fountain, cicadas, and a distant nightingale.

"I still don't know what led to his death," I said. "The last I saw, fighting had stopped due to the torrential rain, and our troops were streaming home. Hektôr had told me that I should work at home, instead of watching from the walls. Of course I had not listened to him; but when I saw everyone leaving the battlefield, I rushed home to pretend to him that I had...."

"Surely you realize that he knew he would die and tried to save you from seeing it with your eyes."

"But if he knew, then why...?"

She held my hand. "I will tell you all I saw, Āndrōmakhê. So, yes, the fighting had stopped, and our troops poured in through the gate. Hektôr did not join them, even though Kebriones went in. Only after the gate had been bolted shut, did we realize that he had remained outside, closer to the Achaian camp than to us. He stood, alone in his chariot, looking up at the sky. Then Helios was freed from his cloud-cover, its shine brilliant. Hektôr was too distant, and the helmet shadowed his face, but I wager he was in a trance. Perhaps he inwardly debated whether he made the right decision. Our father leaned over the wall and called to him, ordering him to come home. Hektôr shook himself back into awareness, and shouted back, 'I don't want to postpone this any longer, Father! I *have* to face Akhilles in single combat, as it was ordained long ago.' Father shouted even louder, 'Akhilles is son of a goddess, he is stronger than you! Come back! We need you here! If the Achaians breach the wall and pour into the city you have to be here to protect our lives and honor!' Hektôr remained motionless, returning his gaze to the sky. Then Mother added her entreaties to Father's. She reminded him that his wound had not healed and he was too weak to be at his best. Now Akhilles entered the field, and something strange happened: Hektôr saw Akhilles, began to tremble, so much so that we could all see it from the wall—"

"Ares!" I cried out, "Hektôr saw Ares in Akhilles' stead!"

"What makes you say that?"

"I had a vision that Ares showed up, in his most frightful persona, confusing Hektôr. And then a vision of Athené, protecting someone."

Kassandra nodded, "Ah that makes sense. I did not see Ares, but I *did* see Athené. But before all that, I saw Hektôr whip his horses, Xanthos and Lampos, and tear away at full speed, with Akhilles behind. They went three times around the walls, until, as they were nearing the spot by the fig tree, Zeus lifted his golden scales and weighed their fates, and Hektôr's side came down—surely he tipped it in Akhilles' favor!—sealing my brother's doom. Up to that point Apollo had protected Hektôr, but looking at the scales, he deserted him. Now Athené, to hurry up Akhilles' victory, assumed Deiphobos' shape, appeared in Hektôr's chariot, telling him they would face Akhilles together, side-by-side. I shouted with all my might to warn Hektôr. He paid me no heed; or perhaps Athené had rendered him deaf."

"Did you actually see Zeus and the golden scales?"

"I did. As with some of my visions, it had a fuzzy quality to it, like a gray-tinted scene on a white cloth with torn edges."

Kassandra paused, sighed deeply, then noticed the tears running down my cheeks, and her own eyes welled up too. "This is how my noble brother faced up to his end. He brought his chariot to a halt and leapt down. He turned to Deiphobos, but of course, Deiphobos was not there, and realized that he had been tricked. With a small laugh he drew his spear and let if fly at Akhilles—"

"But Athené diverted his aim!"

"Yes. When Akhilles took aim at Hektôr, he did not fail. Mortally wounded in the neck, my brother fell backward. When he was on the ground and Akhilles stood above him, Hektôr, with the last of his breath, asked him not to give his body to the dogs, but allow us to ransom him. Akhilles roared in laughter, kicking him on his face. Xanthos, who had turned and pulled Lampos and the chariot close to Hektôr's body, spoke to Akhilles, 'Pause before you act! The gods will remember how you treated Hektôr—first among all warriors—when your turn comes one day soon, and you are slain at the Skaian Gate, by Alexis and Apollo."

"So that's why Akhilles ran his sword through Xanthos…"

"Yes. Xanthos did not just prophesy his ignoble doom, but tried to trample him to death. And then Akhilles claimed Lampos for himself."

"Kassandra…it wasn't Akhilles who murdered my husband, but the gods. Yes, *they* are the guilty; I call *them* to account!"

"Such is the way the gods spun for us, but the gods themselves have no sorrow." Her gaze was warm with empathy.

"But this is not *just!*"

"Alas, Fate and Justice are not related. Fate deals with those things that cannot be controlled. Justice deals with the choices that *you* make. The idea of justice is to punish when choices are bad."

"Akhilles who chose Glory by slaughtering people—like my father and seven brothers, who never did him any harm, and like Hektôr, who fought against him as Defender and not Aggressor…Alexis who chose Love by taking Helen who had asked Aphrodite to give her Love, and thus the two of them caused this extended bloody war by their choices…"

I shook my head, ever more infuriated yet confused, "So, either they are not guilty because they did what they did because it was their destiny, and therefore we should not seek justice, for they—and every

one of us—are only playing roles assigned to us at birth...or...or..."
Needing to clear my thoughts, I paused, forcing myself to breathe in and
out calmly, to no avail.

"Ãndrõmakhê, I've been wondering about this for a long time. I
have been studying, listening, asking questions. I gather that we do have
choices that can be made, even though they are limited. You just said
that Alexis and Akhilles made the choice to—"

"But Akhilles had Thétis for mother, and was told he had the choice
of two destinies! Therefore, he took the one that suited him best.
However, Alexis was left blind. If he had known that he would cause so
much death, even the death of Hektôr—of whom we both know he was
very fond—I doubt he would have pursued Helen."

"But I warned him. I told him not to sail to Sparta!"

"And he did not listen because so it was ordained! Therefore
Alexander Paris, son of Priam, is blameless."

"Let me tell you a cautionary tale my teacher in Thymbra told me
once: A group of flies were attracted to a jar of honey which had been
overturned in a housekeeper's room; placing their feet in it, they feasted
greedily. Their thin little feet became so smeared and weighted down
with the honey that they could not use their wings, for they could not
release themselves, and so they were suffocated. Just as they were
expiring, they exclaimed, 'O foolish creatures that we are, for the sake of
a little pleasure we have destroyed ourselves.'"

"Very nice, very smart, but it's not relevant to Alexis. He could
have chosen Dominion and Wealth, but he chose Love."

At once spasms shook Kassandra's body, her eyes rolled back,
leaving the whites. I wound my arm around her shoulders trying to
steady her. Finally, she drew herself together, "Hektôr...quick, get
ready, Father is approaching the gate with Hektôr."

I rushed home and struggled into my clothes.

Nefru emerged, dangling something from his mouth; he pawed at
my legs to draw my attention. I looked down: he was holding my opal,
which I had thrown off on the day of Hektôr's death.

I took the pendant, clasping it back around my neck.

Leaving Skamandrios in Thalpia's care, I raced with Kassandra to
the Agora where screaming crowds divided just enough to let the wagon
through. Priam crouched in the front, with loyal Idaios, immovable, not
looking at anyone.

I scrambled from hub to wheel-top and over the side, and then slid
down beside the motionless form lying beneath a richly embroidered
cloth. I touched his soft hair. A chilling tremor went through me from

the marble skin. It was impossible that he was dead, yet here I sat on the wagon-bed and cradled his lifeless head on my breast.

From the other side, Hekabe threw herself over the body, keening. Idaios quickly called for help to carry Hektôr's body inside.

The bier was already set up in the Megaron, and Thalpia had just finished putting on the mattress when the wagon drew up in the courtyard. She handed me my bridal sheets and Hekabe assisted in spreading them over the mattress of furred skin. Thalpia went out to bring back bunches of violets—for immortality—from the garden, for Hekabe to scatter over the bed.

His brothers carried in Hektôr's stiff body and settled it there. I went to him and admitted that Akhilles had done honorably by him. The body was like a statue under a shining white linen robe, clean and preserved in waxy honey. Pushing aside his robe at the neck, I saw, worse than his damaged shoulder and chest, how a great gash there had ripped out his noble life. His face, as I stared at it, was fixed in a strangely proud, half smile that not all the days of Akhilles' dragging chariot had erased. Tenderly I combed out his sun-streaked wavy hair and spread it over the linen head-roll. Then I leaned down and kissed the blackened wound where Akhilles' spear had pierced him.

Deiphobos spoke bitterly, "Akhilles' spear was longer than my brother's sword. After…when he was…dead…then…*brave* men came at him with more spears and swords." I moved to shift his covering but Deiphobos' hand stayed mine. "Best not to see."

Kassandra whispered in my ear, "Akhilles dragged him around on the field for twelve days, and at night left him out for dogs to gnaw on, and yet he is completely intact! Look, he is still wearing his turquoise horse charm around his neck, too! Because Aphrodite and Apollo protected his body from corruption."

"Would that they had protected his *life!*" I screamed.

Skamandrios came running and stared wide-eyed at his father. Hatred rampaged through me. "Skamandrios, see your father! Akhilles Peleosides tortured and defiled the greatest of all Trojans. Avenge him; avenge your noble father, Skamandrios!"

The petrified child stared with trembling lips, screamed, and left us sobbing loudly. Thalpia hurried behind him.

Hekabe handed me a knife. Taking it, I observed the beautiful, ancient, engraved obsidian blade, the multi-generational mourning-knife of the House of Priam. It was for me now. I raised it high above my head and seized a bunch of my hair in my other hand, stretched tight, pulling at my scalp. Scattered sparks of pain raced over my scalp, the hair loose in my hand, spread out on Hektôr's heart. Another bunch. Another. I cut again and spread again until long bright hair covered my husband's chest like a shield.

I returned the knife to Hekabe, who did the same, then passed it on to Priam. One by one our family cut their hair, draping full long locks over his heart: gold, brown, honey, white, black, red.

Helen, after laying her locks on him, spoke as tears slowly ran down her pale cheeks, "I mourn you, Hektôr, dear friend and honored brother, you, with your loving kindness and gentle speech, you who was always cordial and fair...these tears of sorrow are both for you and for my lost self...."

Later word came that Akhilles personally slit the throats of twelve young Trojan prisoners, and then threw them in Patroklos' funeral pyre, together with the corpse of loyal Xanthos.

Upon being told of this, Priam expressed surprise, "Akhilles is a man of bewildering contradictions! I came to him unexpectedly in the dark of night, yet he treated me with respect, even affection. He offered me and Idaios food and drink. After we spent hours talking about many things, including his own father, he urged me to rest on a comfortable bed, until dawn. Then he helped us slip away from camp unnoticed. Surely the gods torment him as much as they torment us."

* * * *

Feet toward the door, Hektôr remained in state for twelve days.

For twelve days, Games in his honor were played in and around the city, joined by scores of Achaians, who, when they deserved it, received substantial prizes from us, the besieged Trojans. Indeed, we were fair to them even though they waited for the chance to murder us.

By night, I slept near Hektôr, my head on the marble-like, motionless breast, refusing food and drink—for the last times with my husband and on my bridal linen. Awakening in the night, I would pray desperately that I might become pregnant of his spirit. No other woman of childbearing age was allowed near, lest she catch the disembodied soul in her womb.

* * * *

Dawn was bloodred when Hektôr's surviving brothers, to the wail of conch-shell trumpets, carried the bier with his body to the top of the great pyre they had built for him. I had wrapped him in my bridal sheets, a crown of grape leaves on his hair, the sword he had trained with as a boy beside him on the bier. In the palm of each of his hands, I tied a gold ring with silken cords, to pay old Charon, the old ferryman, to row him across the River Styx to the Underworld. On top of it all, we placed a pall woven of violets for immortality. Herdsmen held sheep and oxen in a circle around the pile while Priam walked amongst them and expertly slid their throats so that the blood enriched this earth.

The last of Hektôr's beloved horses, Aithos and Podarkes, also were sacrificed, to ride with him on the Elysian Fields.

I offered the slender throat of Xanthos and Iris' only son, my sweet-natured Phoenix. Unable to watch him die, I turned my back, moved away, and gazed up at the red-streaked sky.

The same hot wind that used to whip my veil about when I watched from the walls, lashed the torches to wide flames as men threw them arcing upon the dry-wood pile. Alexis lifted his flute and played a single tune of unearthly beauty. Then he switched to a conch shell horn, and I knew he sent his brother's soul on his way to the Elysian Fields, accompanied with all our love.

I stood stock-still and watched his pyre burn for hours, ferociously screaming at anyone who dared come near me.

Nefru kept returning, even after I gave the poor creature such a vicious kick that he flew a good distance in the air. Landing on four feet, he briskly shook himself to recover from the shock, rushed back and curled himself around my bare feet.

By sundown, the blaze was still howling skyward above reddened timber and blasting heat. Brothers and comrades ringed the fire as closely as possible, weapons reversed against the ground.

Kassandra and her fellow priestesses flitted among shadows, their mourning voices echoing from the sky.

When daylight returned, only a dry bunch of white bones and pale ashes remained in the center of that circle. His brothers gathered these and washed them in holy water that Helenos dipped and blessed from the river. I dispatched Thalpia to clear my loom of Hektôr's unfinished victory cloak. Then I took the purple cloak in my arms and tossed it like a sail down to the field, letting it soak in the scent of the wind and earth. His brothers gathered it and wrapped therein his charred bones.

His sarcophagus was a house-shaped box of gold, wrapped again in heavy black mourning-linen, and laid in a hollow at the midst of ashes. His weapons and best armor, his favorite food in jars, were then placed in a circle inside the small tomb. Then all the men of Troia heaped earth over the immense blackened circle.

That night I discovered that once more Priam had spared Phoenix, declaring that Hektôr's shade spoke to him, ordering Phoenix to be kept alive so that he could serve me until he died of old age.

Three days passed before the cone-shaped tumulus rose above the gate. On top, a big flat stone supported a red sandstone phallus.

I came down from the high wall to climb the mound, touching the monument to ensure fertility in future lives. Around its base artists had carved linear pictures of Hektôr in his chariot, with an inscription in Trojan pictographs giving his name as Hektôr, Tamer of Horses, and achievements as a warrior and master of horses.

Later, I sat next to Hektôr's vacant chair at his funeral-feast, so that my husband's ghost might preside with me, albeit free at last. I must eat double, once for myself, once for him. Yet it was all dirt and grit in my mouth. If not for Skamandrios, I would have slashed my throat upon my husband's grave.

At last, the meal ended, my husband's spirit was fed, and I retreated to our bedroom. Staring at the bed, empty in the orange torchlight, I dropped the black dress I wore and got upon the dais. Collapsing across the sheet, I wept until released by sleep, Nefru curled up by my pillow.

I woke up late morning. The sun shone across the bed, my face was hot and feverish, my arm numb. I drew it back slowly from the other side of the bed where Hektôr no longer slept.

* * * *

I could not return to the wall. Now that valiant Hektôr, Defender of Troia, was gone, whom could Priam appoint to lead his people?

One morning word spread through the city that three-hundred men, women, and children, fifty of them Mysians, had left during the night. Their leader was Brutos, and I had heard him often at Council meetings, disputing with Alexis. He left messages that those who wished to join him could gather at the coast of Teuthrania, where he would be stopping with permission of Queen Astyoche to build ships. They intended to sail up the Adriatic with hopes of reaching and settling in the far-off Tin Islands [1].

Through the days that followed, Alexis surprised everyone by the decisive way he took command. If only he had shown such prowess beside Hektôr! Yet no progress was made in the daily battles. Dissent within our walls continued to grow, fueled by Antenor and Theano. Hardship went on as well, the poor suffering the worst. Soon it became clear that Antenor and dozens of wealthy citizens hoarded food, buried treasure in underground vaults, or smuggled it out to be stored elsewhere. Achaians received plenty of bribes as well, for safe-passage to the wealthy who deserted Troia.

Skamandrios asked me often why his father was no longer among the living. Sometimes the child looked at me with an expression so like his father's, that certain bright glance with a smile in it, that I would hold him close and weep until he struggled to be away.

The aroma of roasting wild boar—a rare boon—filled Priam's Hall when I went to sit with Hekabe. Thalpia brought Skamandrios and sat near the hearth to feed the child on marrow and blood-soup.

Alexis' booming voice startled me from where he stood with Priam and some others. "I'll show that arrogant Aeneas who's in charge of defending Troia!"

Silence answered him; his reputation as a warrior, though he was an excellent archer and never shied away from a battle, was not stellar. This was unfair, for in battle after battle I had witnessed, swift and sharp-eyed Alexis had been as valuable as Deiphobos, or even Aeneas.

At once, I noticed that among the group was Sigeia. *Sigeia?*

"Aeneas came to Polymestor for help," she spoke up, "but my cousin is not joining in a lost cause."

"Aeneas?" Priam growled.

Alexis snickered, "He'll do anything to get control here."

"Aeneas is not a traitor to you," Sigeia said harshly. "But I am here to ask you to escape while you can. There is nothing for any of you left now. We have important, strong Achaian friends in Thrakia. And you, Āndrōmakhê, without Hektôr, and no father to ransom you, have no one to champion you."

"That is not so!" Alexis thundered. "She is my sister, through marriage to my slain, noble brother, and I'll not let my widowed sister without a champion, *ever!*"

Sigeia gave him a challenging look, and turned toward me. "You had best persuade Priam to see reason. Polymestor is protecting your dead brother Andros' bride. Yes, Lanassa is with us, Āndrōmakhê. Mark well where your best interests lie."

I stared at her coldly and did not reply.

Deiphobos spoke, "Cowardice is not the Trojan way."

"Polymestor wants you to know your city is doomed." She faced Priam. "I have a son, the firstborn of Hektôr. My son is heir to Troia, by treaty with Agamemnon."

I would not flinch. Of course, the woman was here to scavenge, now that a father no longer protected Skamandrios. However, I *would* find a means to safeguard my child's future, especially from the threat of that false Skamandrios.

Priam spoke, "Your son has no place here, Sigeia. Keep him with your father, for he may well need an heir some day."

Sigeia's laugh was harsh. "Hear this, you, the old King of a soon to be ravished kingdom: Polymestor is a stronger ruler than you are."

Calmly, with a smile, I said, "Hektôr's widow does not abandon her son's inheritance to others." Although betrayed by Zeus and Athené, my Goddess would protect this holy Trojan city, I hoped. She had to! In addition, my son would honor his father's memory by rebuilding the empire at whatever cost to myself.

Deiphobos growled, "Hurry back to that treacherous Polymestor, Sigeia. Let him look elsewhere to find a kingdom for your whelp."

Priam's stern voice stopped Sigeia's movement toward the door, "Polydoros is safe with his sister; Ilione is protecting him along with her own son. My son stays there and will be safe until the war ends. He, at least, will survive. Polymestor would not dare betray a fosterling. I order you to never, ever, do anything to interfere with that, Sigeia!"

"Polydoros too has no future," Sigeia spat. She swept her arm to include everyone, "You are all doomed! Fate is on *our* side. Ask Kassandra! I go now. Your choice is death, mine is victory."

No one moved or spoke, and she went out.

* * * *

The rivers of hot summer were trickling low in their beds when word of aid came from Hattushash. A contingent of Amazons was on their way from Kolchis! However, Trojan military leadership was not yet resolved. Intense arguments and discussions veered between Alexis, Deiphobos, and Aeneas to be appointed Defender.

One week later, I was back on the wall when I caught the rising of dust around Ida, the glitter of metal, the heads of perhaps one hundred horses, and the rumble of chariot-wheels.

One figure at the head, dismounting to walk across the river-ford. Taller than the others...a woman?

Presently, a rainbow spanned the wide sky.

There had been no rain for a while, and the fields were parched. Therefore, the rainbow and the quickening wind tasting of rain, together with Penthesilea, must be a good omen.

Pointed cone-helmet, bronze-enforced leather tunic, and gray knit jerkin; carrying an oblong shield head-to-foot length, her sword sheathed in a scabbard of ivory and gold. Striding up the ramp clanking a scimitar—a woman, yet fiery masculine. Coming along in step like a wave, marched other women in well-trained precision; mass moving, not scattered and uneven-paced like Achaians. I stared at them, awe-struck. If women could be so trained, could not I, and other Trojan women, also show the Achaians strength, and wreak our own vengeance? Could I not hope for a future with my son, in my own right? There was pressure behind my eyes, and my head ached. Even as I rejoiced in the idea that women could be as good a warrior as men, I turned back with the others to go in and welcome our gallant visitors.

Penthesilea, Queen of the Amazons, was assigned quarters for resting, bathing, and changing into fresh clothing. She had not brought the hoped-for numbers of warriors, nevertheless we felt uplifted by this show of support. In the meantime, details circulated about her among the courtiers: Some years ago, she had killed another Amazon, her cherished friend, Hippolyta, during battle. Today Penthesilea intended to request that Priam, King of Troia, purify her of this bloodguilt. Then she would be able to fight on our side.

Penthesilea was to appear at sundown, after the feast was prepared.

While Thalpia dressed my hair, I heard the sounds Skamandrios made playing with his toy chariot, its clicking and rolling tapping pleasantly against my ears. Then I put on a purple dress in the older fashion, wasp-waisted, with high white collar.

I said to Thalpia, "The Achaians will certainly be surprised at the battle field! It's to our advantage; think of the shock!"

Thalpia threw a gossamer white silk veil over my head and placed a gold-fringed circlet on top. I slowly untangled a silk thread from a bangle of my gold earrings, which drooped down over my shoulders.

Penthesilea was feminine enough to wait until all were assembled in the throne-room before making her entrance. Her burning eyes took in everything with the appraisal of a strategist. She had the beauty of an almost mad, fiery determination. Undeniably strong, taller than many of the men here, her large-boned frame was even larger than that of her troops. Vivid green-eyed with sun-browned skin, her blue-black hair hung in a straight plait down her back. She wore a short white tunic embroidered in red, with white laced-up boots.

Penthesilea saluted smartly at the throne of Priam, presenting her credentials, "Lord Tudhaliyas has no men to spare from his borders. But I and my Amazons, kin of Queen Hekabe, we who are fighting Priestesses of our Goddess Artemis, are stronger than any man."

Priam bowed his head courteously. "You will command beside my son Alexander, henceforth the chief Trojan warrior," he declared.

Gripping the arms of my chair, I told myself to stop staring at the warrioress. Nevertheless, ah, the thought of joining her and avenging Hektôr's death with my own hands felt so sweet! If Penthesilea would recruit women from Troia, I would be among the first volunteers....

* * * *

I slept better that night than for a long time. When I awoke to the sound of trampling feet and clanking arms, I hurried out, and was shocked to find Penthesilea and her warrior-priestesses armed in the market place. Fighting, already? But she had not even gone through the ceremony for purification of her bloodguilt!

I then saw her whip her team of horses. She flung off down the street, leading her troops—wearing golden belts and brandishing spears, swords, and crescent shields—at a brisk clip from terrace to terrace into the Lower City, and out.

"What sort of men are we to let women go on the field ahead of us?" Deiphobos shouted.

"Penthesilea didn't even have time to orient her troops!" I shouted back. "Yes, we should all go out with her!"

Deiphobos moved, crossed before me with Helenos, faces set in stone as they swung into their chariots. Alexis sauntered from his gate with bow and quiver of arrows. Men began trickling out of the assembly and homes, those without weapons stopping off to gather them.

Women rushed to the wall. My body stirred with desperation, hope and awe. *Women against Achaians!*

The wall seethed with women screaming encouragement to their men, and to those brave Amazon warriors. I joined them with my old dagger hidden in the folds of my cloak. My hands twitched as Laodike and Kreusa screamed beside me.

A sharp, grating sound cut down from above. My heart thumped sharply, and then nearly stopped. Before I even bothered to look closer, I knew it was an eagle, and that, like others at important moments, it would be circling on the left. I looked up anyway: the eagle of Badogios was indeed to the left of Troia—this time carrying something small in its beak. It was a white dove of Ate! From the dove, red drops fell on the ground.

Horns blared, chariots rattled, and weapons clanked.

Priam's loud prayer sank under the people's moaning.

Those priestesses were women, and I was a woman, still young at the age of twenty-three, and with a son to protect. And I was *Hektôr's wife*. I could lead the women of Troia to support those brave Amazons just as my husband had led our men. Suddenly I found myself leaping and standing on my bench, brandishing my dagger and screaming orders, "Women of Troia! Mothers, daughters, and sisters of Trojan warriors! Arm yourselves and come with me!"

Hekabe stood up, a hand at her throat. Priam stared. I raced along the broad walltop, continuing to exhort the women to arms.

"What do you think Penthesilea is doing out there?" Some strange female voice shouted at me, "Is she just having a social chat with them? The Amazons are trained for war from childhood!"

A scream of derisive laughter rose, and Sigeia ran forward. She had not returned to Thrakia after all. "Man's way is not the way of Woman," she stated above the sudden silence.

Hekabe appeared with Priam; both grasped my arms, tore me down the wall, loosened the dagger from my grasp and held me captive between them.

Below in the field, the Amazons were closely followed by the Trojans. I thought I saw Kassandra, armed with a thrusting sword, a bow, and quiver of arrows, blended among the Amazon warriors, but could not be sure. Clouds of dust began rolling inland from the ships, flecked with metallic glint showing the smooth outward undulation behind Penthesilea and Deiphobos' chariots.

The two armies met like thunderclouds above Mount Ida, moving with the crack of lightning and the roar of conquest.

Then I realized that Akhilles was not in the enemy lead.

The Amazons were winning us a victory!

Even from here, I could see what fine warriors they were; it showed in their movements, in how Penthesilea's gleaming chariot pursued, attacked, and wheeled away, her incredibly strong arm and curved scimitar slashing with precise, deadly, enthusiasm and accuracy.

Animated again, I freed myself of my well-meaning captors and streaked in the direction of my house. Kassandra was out there, and heedless of her own safety, drawing blood from the enemy. What an inspiration!

Entering the chamber where the last armor of Hektôr was kept in trust for Skamandrios, I checked his shield. Taller than me, it was impossible to use. However, his breastplate was big enough to protect my entire torso. My dagger had been lost on the wall, so I grasped his light Kretan thrusting sword; it was plenty to disembowel Akhilles.

In the Agora, women still rushed around.

I had to lead them, and by my Goddess, I would!

No organization was possible, but I began calling to them. At last, as I ran down the street with the breastplate in my hands, many began to follow me. I felt proud. Ahh, our brave women of Troia! Though lacking in skill and training, they were as spirited as the Amazons were.

By now, my arms and chest ached from the weight of the breastplate. I used one hand to tuck my skirt up around my knees by blousing it above my belt. The other women did the same, and there was soon a forest of bare legs rushing along the wall and down the steps to the inner ramp.

Through the tight crush of hundreds of women at the gate, I came face to face with Theano. Spread-eagled against the bolt, the Priestess looked supernaturally tall. "You chicken-faced women are not going outside these walls!"

"We will have our revenge!" I screamed furiously. "The Achaians won't dare fight women!"

"You think not? You fool! Look how they attack Penthesilea and her lieutenants!"

I was beside myself, "Then all the more urgent that we help her! She is fighting *our* battle!"

"Fools, I say again! Akhilles is out there now. If Hektôr couldn't kill him, how can a bunch of silly women?"

"Akhilles!" My eyes ceased to focus.

"Get back, you rabid cows!" Theano was a raging inferno of hatred. "Get back to where you belong! Be mattress to your men!"

"Let us through!" swelled the shouts behind me. "Step away from the gate, Theano!"

"Princess Kassandra is out there, too!" I announced, "No warrior training had she, yet she proves her noble Trojan spirit!"

Theano laughed. *"Kassandra,* you say? Praised be the day when her doomsday-prattling mouth will be shut forever!"

With all my strength, I pushed against Theano, who stood there, unbreakable like the gate itself. She had turned into a demon, for mortal flesh could not be so hard.

I lifted Hektôr's sword, touching its tip to her throat. "You heard the will of the women of Troia, Theano! Make way for us!"

Theano seemed to broaden, her eyes like marble.

More of us at the front pushed against her and struggled to grab the wheels and bolts holding the gate shut.

Then Priam's commanding voice thundered like Zeus, "Women of Troia! Get back! Ãndrõmakhê! Free Theano! Return home!"

The crowd, who had been so determined before, stepped back as if one body. Priam was still the King, and they could not disobey.

Priam grasped my arm with surprising strength and began pulling me along forcefully. His scowl was dark, set in stone.

I found myself going with him, dragging my feet, the breastplate clanking after me. My body stung all over from humiliation. I had to give up, but I was not vanquished. Yet Sigeia had spoken truth, for Hektôr too had said, 'Leave war to those who are men.' My work was in the making of cloth, the caring for my child.

Hekabe was waiting in my courtyard. Priam pushed me in her direction and left.

The Queen said kindly, "A woman can wait nine months to see the child she carries, can wait years to see her son a man. Ãndrõmakhê, my daughter, you are a strong woman, but you are not a man." She drew something from between her breasts. "Keep this for Skamandrios." She placed Hektôr's signet ring in my palm. His cartouche, the royal seal of the Defender. "Idaios slipped it from Akhilles' dressing-table while my husband was negotiating for our son's body. Hektôr was wearing it that day when Akhilles felled him at the bottom of the wild fig tree."

I held the ring to my lips reverently. Then the meaning of what she said, struck me, "At the fig tree? Did you say at the *fig tree?*"

"I have another thing for you," she added, ignoring my question, "I was waiting for just the right occasion." She bent and lifted a hefty bundle from the ground, handed it to me. "This is your jewelry. Priam said that Akhilles stared at the amber set, as if recognizing it, and then asked to whom it belonged. When Priam told him it was you, he refused to take anything. He explained that he had met you when you were still a young girl, had respected your spirit, and feels remorse over that he had to kill those you loved. He added that if ever you fell in the hands of an Achaian other than him, you need only to send word and he will have you ransomed."

I stood frozen, Hektôr's breastplate dropping from my slackening grasp. He slays my parents, my brothers, thousands of my Theban citizens, and finally my husband, then plays gallant by returning the ransom and offering me protection—from men of his own ilk. I stared at my hands, hating myself for not being able to take him on in combat.

My knees buckled and I collapsed on the ground, sobbing.

* * * *

Three days later, Thalpia came with the news: "Lady! To the wall! Akhilles and Penthesilea will meet in hand-to-hand combat."

To the wall. To watch again.

I held Hektôr's cartouche ring tightly in my fist. Hektôr's cloak, unfinished, was now ashes in his tomb; but at least one important duty still left for me: To raise Skamandrios. The hope of Troia rested upon my little son.

Thalpia chattered as we rushed to the wall with Nefru alongside us. "Akhilles is like a thunderbolt," Thalpia said. "He's already killed so many of Penthesilea's army that she is determined to fight him to the death, to avenge her comrades. The first one to fall today was her lieutenant Kleonie, and then her childhood friends Bremusa and Thermodosa; he even struck down Alkibie and then Derimaka. All her best lieutenants, I am told."

Once again, we witnessed the forward plunge of the Amazon Priestesses, Penthesilea enclosed by the last of her star fighters, Antandre, Polemusa, Antibrote, and Harmothoe. Each engaged in turn an Achaian warrior. They were slaughtered one by one, after lengthy, vicious, and tricky, struggles.

After an hour of fighting and mowing down scores of Achaians, Penthesilea ignored the rest and thundered head-on to attack Akhilles. She flung a spear before her but it glanced off her enemy's shield. She then lifted a gleaming battle-ax, ululating mightily while whirling it above her head, and pursued him with such focused, aggressive determination that it was breathtaking to witness. Their chariots locked onto each other's while their swords clashed. It was obvious that her wrath surprised and perhaps intimidated, Akhilles, who tried to elude her by riding away in an arc. She caught up with him, maneuvered close, and threw her battle-ax. He evaded it with a shrug of his shoulder, then stood in his chariot and exploded in uproarious laughter. She grabbed another spear and flung it, and this time her spear held to his shield. His charioteer reached and knocked it off.

Then Akhilles cast.

Penthesilea plunged forward, headlong over her horses, holding on to them with each arm; her helmet slipped, spilling out some of her hair. From the direction of the Achaian spectators, flew another arrow, striking her somewhere at her side. Her horses reared, neighing, and ran wild, dropping and dragging her between them, her head banging on the ground like Hektôr's had.

Akhilles tried to stop their stampede, to no avail.

Finally, she fell on the muddied grass, his spear loosening from her body. Akhilles leapt down from his chariot and hurried to her. She struggled to rise, got on one knee, and one of her warriors threw her a sword. She faced her adversary, swaying. The arrow stuck in her body kept her off-balance. Nevertheless, she raised her sword anyway, facing death as the mighty warrioress that she was.

There could be no contest. Akhilles, in his invulnerable armor by Hephaistos, versus a grievously wounded warrioress. One of the best, she was, alas, fully human.

However, later, some said that she had been a Daughter of Ares.

Just briefly, their swords clashed; even from where I stood, I could discern that he wielded his sword lightly, seeking only to give her the honorable parting she wanted, and down she went, backwards, lying motionless on the bloodied ground.

I glanced sideways at Priam, who slumped down on his bench, spreading knotted fingers over his eyes.

Akhilles towered over the slain Amazon leader for a long moment; then he knelt, lifted her head and shoulders onto his bare knee. Her helmet was gone, freeing her long black plait, swaying against the gold of his greaves—those shining gold, shin armors—sprinkled with dust and her blood. He bent his head, kissing the dead face, whispering in her now deaf ears.

The Achaian soldier who had struck her with his arrow, a bow-legged man with shoulders caving inward, ran forward, and stood arms akimbo, staring at the motionless body. Then he took off his helmet, whirled it around his head, jumped up and down as if in uncontrollable delight, then stopped and placing his hand beneath his jerkin, rapidly committed a most foul act upon sight of this nobly fallen warrior.

Then with a final bucking motion toward her, he laughed and turned to the crowds, arms raised, awaiting applause.

Akhilles dropped Penthesilea's body, swung up and cracked his sword through the man's skull from topknot to chin.

I leaned forward, forehead against the hot stone crenel. Acid mouth, cold currents rippling across my back. I was going to be sick. The hot sun was black, pressing on my head. Thankfully, my innards held on to their dignity. Time raced—onward or backward, I could not tell. At long last I looked up when Polites came stamping to Priam, breathing heavily from his run up the steps.

Priam straightened as Polites said, "Akhilles meant to give her honorable burial. He sincerely regrets her death, for she was a most noble warrior, one of the best he had the honor to do battle with."

"I'll send out a ransom for her body," Priam announced grimly, "it's the least we can do."

"There'll be no body, Father. One of the Achaians threw it to the eels in the river because they felt she had insulted them with her presence in the battlefield. In addition, they are angry with Akhilles for having slain Thersites, that ugly soldier who defiled her dead body. Thersites was an important man, son of King Agrios of Kalydon, in mainland Achaia. Even though everyone agrees that he had no business loosening his arrow upon her—especially while she was in personal combat with Akhilles—they believe Akhilles should not have felled one of their own. So, now it's Akhilles who's under bloodguilt."

"Ah." Priam turned away. "Go fetch Idaios for me. There are enough dead out there for a burial truce, with all the others of our allies who have fallen today."

Few hours later Idaios returned with a bundle, waxed and wrapped in linen. It contained what bones they could rescue from the river. Penthesilea and all her fallen comrades received a hero's pyre on the Trojan Plain. Her ashes were gathered into an alabaster box and placed in the Dardanian Tower, near Laomedon's, for safekeeping until they might be transported home with proper escort.

What was left of her fighting Amazons accepted whatever gold we could offer them in gratitude for their heroism on our behalf, and returned to their temples in the East.

[1] Tin Islands: Britain. Brutos/Brutus is credited as the father of today's London, where he had built Nova Troia.

Chapter 21: Memnon, Son of the Morning

Hope for breaking the Achaians' siege deserted Troia along with Penthesilea's troops. Nonetheless, Alexis held on the Trojan military leadership. His dedication was astounding. Kassandra's warnings were now the subject of amusement, for Akhilles did not reappear on the battlefield. They said that he had fallen in love with Penthesilea and would not forgive himself for having slain her. Strange man! Deeply passionate, cruel, and yet sensitive. Although merciless in sacking a city, he never returned to torment those who came back to rebuild. I had financed the recovery of the Théban shorefront, and it rose from the ashes and prospered.

Despite such irrevocable losses as Hektôr and Penthesilea, the kingdom of Troia persevered, a credit to Priam as a great ruler. Though devastated by the loss of Hektôr as well as his other sons, he remained clear-headed, sharp-eyed, just, and unwavering as a leader. Turkus, a Phrygian general who had joined us before Hektôr's fall but quickly distinguished himself as a brave warrior, talked respectfully about his keen stratagem.

I no longer stood at the wall to watch the fighting, but offered prayers opposite Hektôr's tumulus. Skamandrios would come, running from Thalpia to be caught in my arms. Then I would send Thalpia for my distaff and wool-basket to sit on a narrow bench and work apart from the other women.

One day Alexis surprised me with a wooden chair he had carved with his own hands. It boasted a tough, purple-stained sailcloth awning, a backrest fitting the curvature of my spine, even doubled as a rocker. He brought it with a huge smile and placed it near the crenellated walltop, angled so that Hektôr was always in my line of vision.

"Why do you stay here, Mama?" Skamandrios asked one day.

"Because your Papa is out there, safe now from the war. When his soul flies up from the tomb, he can see us."

And so I took up my spinning and weaving in obedience to my husband's last, living wish. My hair, shorn to the roots for Hektôr's pyre, grew out in a soft halo of curls twisting about my head, and Thalpia laughingly said that now she had more than one baby's head to caress. I smiled faintly and leaned back against faithful Thalpia, whose corded hands were gentle upon my shoulders.

Skamandrios' physical resemblance to Hektôr grew along with his height. He was already assertive and difficult to manage, as befitted a young hero. By the evening firelight, I would watch Priam and my son play or discourse together. Sometimes he would run around the firepit chasing after bratty Askanios, son of Kreusa and Aeneas. The thought that these two little friends represented rival interests for the throne of Troia, sat worrisome in my heart.

We were surer of victory now than for a long time, with Akhilles still off the field. He had sailed to Issa in the south, which sat out from the Bay of Adramyttion. His Myrmidons had sentenced him to seek penitence there for having struck down that vulgar soldier who had defiled Penthesilea. In Issa stood a shrine for Apollo. Thébé...inland from Issa; Thébé where I grew up with my cheerful brothers, godlike parents—glorified in my memory by death. Akhilles had murdered them. Apollo might absolve him of bloodguilt through farcical Achaian priests, but surely, *my* Goddess never would!

One day, Priam gathered the Council and invoked divine guidance for the proceedings. Alexis was given the title Defender of the City.

Alexis announced the latest news, "Tithonos, Lord of Susa in Elam, is sending his son, King Memnon, to our aid. Memnon brings a large contingent of warriors; due here in three months."

Oukagelon, one of the citizens, stood up, his aged face strained, "Our men are exhausted, treasury dwindled, and help comes too late. Our empty offers of wealth and patronage can lead to nothing."

His brother Hiketaon supported him, "Look at the enemy! They do not bother to fight us anymore. They wait for starvation to sink in and finish the battle for them. Then Agamemnon, Akhilles and the rest will be back at our gates for the pickings."

Antenor spoke up, "We were born to live, not to die!" He stepped forward to stand beside Oukagelon, "Capitulation, while we still live honorably with our city intact, is better than to die for those two!" He pointed to Alexis, and then to Helen, who stood by her husband.

"Hah! You cheap traitor!" Alexis spat.

Priam spoke in measured tones, "My friends, no Trojan yields to defeat. We live and die free! If we die, it shall not be as slaves, but with sword in hand to protect what we held dear in life. We will fight on because we have to, because there is no other honorable course. And you just heard that my brother Tithonos is sending his son, Memnon, renowned for his brilliant mind and bravery, to our aid."

Alexis faced his father. "As Defender, I will give Memnon equal command. But we still owe him treasure for his help."

Deiphobos pounded a fist on his chair-arm. "*I* should be Defender! Failing that, I, not Memnon, shall have joint command."

Alexis scowled. "I suggest we take inventory of what remains in our coffers before making rash offers to Memnon."

"That is already taken care of," Priam said quietly. "We will reward Memnon Tithonides with a queen. He has no wife yet, and we have the perfect one for him. Lady Āndrōmakhê."

Blood was ice in my veins. I stood as if turned to stone.

Helenos came in at these words. He strode to his father. "She must remain here as mother of Troia's future king."

"With no husband to protect her?" Deiphobos demanded grimly.

"I have decided," Priam declared. "Messengers leave for Elam today. Āndrōmakhê is to be cherished wife and queen of Memnon."

I stood and keeping my eyes downcast, left the Hall.

Hekabe came into my workroom afterward, speaking quietly, "My husband is renewing old ties with an even greater future for Troia when this war ends. Through you, my dear, he will unite these two lands against all others."

I was still numb. To be another man's wife? *But I was Hektôr's!*

"Remember your duty," she went on, "you married Hektôr because your father Êetiôn arranged it so. You shall marry Memnon because Priam, your husband's father and your son's grandfather, ordains it so."

"*Duty!* Therefore, it is my duty to be traded into slavery. I don't have the right to live in my husband's land, as his widow."

"Were you a slave to Hektôr?"

"Of course not! But I was lucky, because of the man he was."

"I know it will be difficult for you at first," Hekabe said gently. "But Memnon will be a fine husband, and you can give him heirs."

"Is there really no place left here for Hektôr's wife and son?"

Hekabe bit her lips, but went on firmly, "Āndrōmakhê! Listen! Memnon will protect you *and* Skamandrios. You know how necessary it is for a woman to have a man's guardianship."

"With Troia victorious, *Priam* will protect his heir." My whole body shook with fear and anger. "I have been Hektôr's wife, and am still. Until the day I die. I won't be wife to another man!"

Hekabe lifted a placating hand. *"Memnon* will protect your son. He will see to it that Skamandrios gets his heritage. With Memnon behind you, the son of Sigeia will be forgotten."

"Skamandrios leaves with me to a kingdom at the far ends of the earth, and will not lose his inheritance? Bah! Sigeia is no fool; she will use it to seat her son on the throne."

"True, and the best remedy would be for you to wed one of Hektôr's brothers—Helenos comes to mind. In ordinary times, you would be. But presently, there are other considerations involved."

"If Skamandrios leaves Troia with me, he loses his inheritance," I pressed. "Are you telling me that Priam gave in to Anchises? He will let the throne go to that branch of the family?"

"Āndrōmakhê! Don't you understand, if Troia and the Eastern kingdoms are to be united one day, Skamandrios could claim his Trojan inheritance more safely by coming from the East, than by remaining here, if the…Achaians…should…" She could not speak the words that Kassandra continued to shout.

After a pause, the Queen gathered strength and added, "Memnon is a blessing from the gods for you, and for all of us. Through him, Troia will live. With him, you will have a new land to rule and be the mother of future kings. Accept the inevitable, Āndrōmakhê. The righteous are those who endure what they cannot prevent. Priam is doing the best possible for you and Troia."

Pent-up rage exploded through my throat, "He is bartering me!"

"He is giving you a more secure future. What if the unbearable happens, and Troia falls? Would you rather be dragged off into the bed of an Achaian? Toil as the lowest of his slaves? And endure even worse when he tires of you? Listen: being a woman is no disadvantage if you use your abilities. You have been the kind of wife every hero dreams about. Beautiful, deeply loving, loyal, obedient, unobtrusive. I know that Memnon is aware of your qualities. He had expressed interest in you, based on all that he heard about you, and Priam considered, and then accepted his suit. You must now add to that the will to live, and the strength to rule. The earth about you is full of riches and glory, so stand tall and take your share."

"Yes, I have to be strong," I whispered, looking away from the gracious queen who was like a second mother to me. Memnon was still a long distance away, and there was always the possibility that things would change for the better. "For Skamandrios." I spoke calmly, "I will keep a place in the world for Hektôr's son."

* * * *

For three months I clung to the hope that a miracle would manifest; every dawn I came to the spot on the wall overlooking Hektôr's tomb, wishing him peace, for I did not want him to suffer from worry over my and Skamandrios' fate. Afterwards I rushed to my two Goddesses' altar and prayed, pouring libations, burning aromatic candles, exotic herbs, incense, and tending the flowers. I then hurried to Athené's temple, holding up an olive branch, barefoot to make it a harsh pilgrimage, always cleaning up the mess left behind by other supplicants, washing, polishing the floors, then begging her, on my hands and knees, to dismiss her grudge against Alexis and Troia.

It was on such visit that I heard a few faint words ringing within my head: *Aeneas. Empire. Hesperia. Fires and slaughter—Kartaj.* I held my breath, listening to the every-day noises around me, wondering how to tell apart a true oracle from the jumble in my thoughts. Minutes passed, no other pronunciation came forth. I must have heard the drift of some conversation outside. I rose and left the temple, dismissing the experience as inconsequential.

Outwardly, I remained calm, quiet, and strong, continuing to make myself useful. The battle went on, intrigues raged, brave soldiers continued to fall, many were the wounded and crippled, and I joined Polyxena, Kassandra, Kreusa, and the healer-priestesses as they treated the injured in a large wing opened on the grounds of Apollo's temple. Kassandra said that I had a warm smile and compassionate aura, and often assigned me to a wounded soldier who was about to give up his soul. When he did, I would close his eyes for the last time.

Women died too, and children in large numbers, some from disease, some from broken hearts, and many from outright starvation.

* * * *

When I emerged from my home on a sunny day three months later, Troia was festively decorated, and I was still a dead hero's wife, queen of looted Thébé and ruined Kilikia, about to be bartered to a foreign king for his help. Boughs from trees along the Dardanian Way were draped over doors and gateways. Greenery frothed the street and through the market place, thick to Priam's threshold. Gateways and columns were twined with flower garlands, and more were going up.

With the family I went to the walltop and toward Hektôr's tomb that stood between Troia and ruined Larissa. The sun, hanging low in the sea beyond Imbros Island, sent tower-shadows in long lines across the fields of trampled grass, acres of untended wheat.

Then puffs of air rose from the mountain pass.

Thousands of men, barely distinguishable as they spread across the plain, were coming. I recalled the flowers blooming lushly there on the day I had swung across in Hektôr's chariot as his starry-eyed bride.

Now I noticed one figure racing out before others in the oncoming group: Dark-skinned, ebony hair streaming loose in the wind. Rays of sun pinpointed the gleaming strips of gold and silver on his limbs. Red-white stripes for breechclout and belt, set Egyptian-fashion at his hips, square ends flapping. Glittering of wide gold about his slim waist. Closer, closer, he thundered. The greenish glint covering his chest was the padding of interlaced necklaces. He wore not a helmet, but a red and green Elamite turban. When his chariot slowed at the Dardanian Gate, I saw that his hair had been set in Assyrian-type long curls before the wind blew them into loose tangles.

Dismounting; meeting Priam at the gate; bows; long, formal speeches; embraces of welcome.

Into the city together, followed by a streaming rainbow of troops: white Elamites, yellow Assyrians, black men from farther India. Wild, untamed, fresh from victories, they stared hungrily at the city women. Amidst a protective circle of archers and swordsmen lumbered hundreds of heads of cattle, and heavy wagons, canvassed over and tied up with ropes. According to news preceding Memnon's arrival, as he had marched out from Susa, near Tigris River, he had been a firestorm, subduing all the peoples that lived between Susa and Troia.

As they passed below where the royal family stood, Memnon looked up. Hekabe acknowledged his courteous salute, and then she went to greet him at the Palace gates.

I beat a hasty retreat to my own courtyard, waiting beside the altar while Thalpia took Skamandrios upstairs to clean him up again.

If only I did not have to meet Memnon....

There was something unstable about this new miracle. Yet, why be afraid? This was no way to welcome a would-be savior!

When I joined our family in the Great Hall for the welcome banquet, Alexis was standing beside Memnon, at Priam's chair. Blond, slim, and pale, Alexis seemed delicate in contrast to the long-boned, sun-blackened Elamite, who was as tall as Hektôr had been. Memnon was indescribably handsome; in fact, I had heard endless praises of his physique and virility. He was said to be the most beautiful man alive. As he moved, gold bangles sparkled over his turban and flowing leopard-skin cape. While still a young general in Ethiopia, on the horn of Africa, he had simply overrun Egypt and conquered the East as far as the city of Susa, which he had surrounded by tall walls. Then he had built a fabled palace of many-colored shining stones, bound with gold, in the city of Ecbatana.

Skamandrios came in, half scrambling and half-swinging from Thalpia's hands, eyes fixed on the strange man.

Memnon grinned down at the child. "It doesn't grow on my head," he spoke in our Wilusian language, pointing to his turban.

I moved forward, taking my son's hand, releasing Thalpia from duty. Alexis stepped away and Memnon turned toward me. His startlingly brilliant blue eyes roved my hair topped with a slim, golden tiara, my face, and then my body, draped in a long, embroidered garment, so deep purple that it was almost black, covering my shoulders, breasts, arms down to my elbows, and tied at the waist with a belt of gold ringlets. I wore my opal and a bracelet, and no paint on my face.

"Hektôr's widow, the Lady Ãndrõmakhê," Priam declared. "And by right of inheritance, the Queen of Kilikia. My dear, this is Lord Memnon Tithonides."

"My Lady." Memnon bowed slightly.

I nodded, and then said proudly, "Hektôr is present here in his son, Skamandrios, who is the Heir to Troia."

"In you, young Prince Skamandrios, I salute my heroic cousin," he stated with a small bow.

Priam motioned the Elamite to a chair…*Hektôr's chair.*

"Do honor me, my gracious Ãndrõmakhê, with your company," Memnon said.

I went to sit beside him. My heart was a choking lump in my throat, for no one had sat there since Hektôr's passing. Alexis settled on the other side with Helen. Beyond them were Aeneas and Kreusa.

I looked aside into the brooding eyes of Helenos. He gave me a brief, reassuring smile. Skamandrios climbed possessively into my lap, staring at Memnon in a challenging manner.

Memnon's voice was low beside me as he spoke to Priam. "I see what you mean," I heard him say to Priam.

I wanted to ignore their talk, yet was curious to hear more. My thoughts clipped close on Memnon's next comment, "A glorious child! No price is too high, my esteemed uncle."

"Good, we understand each other." Priam straightened himself in his chair. "We can arrange final details later."

Priam motioned to Minstrel Sesamon. The old man took his place on a stool before his guest. He took care in settling the kithara on his knee. Richly flowing words paced by the rhythmically strummed strings told the story of Memnon's father Tithonos: how he had joined the Eastern wars before the siege of Troia by Herakles and Telamon. There, he had been victorious and taken in love by a veritable goddess, Queen Kissia, also called Eos [1], the Eastern Dawn.

Memnon smiled knowingly at certain fanciful turns in this tale, but overall he seemed pleased.

During the recital, I quietly fed Skamandrios, hoping to put a stop to his constant staring at Memnon. Then I capitulated and sent him home with Thalpia.

Memnon's voice, as he spoke with Priam during pauses in the story, was rich with confidence. I kept my eyes averted from his profile, as beautiful in outline as to appear godlike. His black skin was natural, not sun-browned as I had first thought. His black hair was straight and smooth, but coarser in texture than my own. Then he turned and glanced at me and our eyes met, his gaze shocking in its intense blueness. I held my breath.

"With you here, we can crush them before the winter rains," Priam concluded his answer to something Memnon had said.

Memnon spoke to me, "Dear Lady, do you doubt my ability?"

"No." I added after a brief silence, "I have hope now for the first time, in a long while."

"Woe! Woe!" Kassandra's hoarse voice rang through the Hall.

She was standing at the entrance, wide-eyed, staring ahead.

Priam motioned urgently for her to be quiet, and then turned to Memnon, proposing a toast. Memnon nodded, Priam placed both hands around the heavily ornamented gold cup of Dardanos, and Memnon drank of it with his uncle.

Kassandra turned away, leaving silently.

I had not heard the toast, but heard Memnon's words afterwards, "You have added double strength to my arm, by this promise, Uncle. Mark my words, in future years Troia, Elam, Babylon, and Assyria, will form a strong alliance."

After-dinner wine was being mixed with water in the great bowl, and the cupbearer brought the point-ended pourer first to Priam. When all were served, Priam rose. Holding the gold cup that Holy Dardanos had brought from Thrakia, he offered a last toast honoring their guest and troops, then made an announcement:

"The lovely hand of our Lady Āndrōmakhê will bring future greatness to Troia, in alliance with Elam, Babylon and Assyria!" He drank deeply and sat down.

My mouth was so dry that I emptied my cup without tasting the wine. Priam was laying the entire future of Troia upon my shoulders. Moreover, I had run out of hope; there was no way out.

When the meal ended, it was a relief to walk in the cool air of the courtyard. Minutes later, sitting on the jade bench beside the herb-garden's small pool, I was roused by warmth before me.

I lifted my eyes to see Memnon standing there, a black shadow against the cobalt sky. He touched my shoulder, gently, and then sat beside me. His body burned against my thigh. I could not breathe.

"Lady Āndrōmakhê," he spoke formally, "I respect your grief for Hektôr. Other sons I might give you shall not replace Skamandrios. I will see that he has his inheritance."

Gratitude softened my voice, "I thank you. As for me, I will serve you to the best of my abilities, Lord Memnon."

"Your reputation, your golden beauty and virtue, is as widespread as that of Hektôr's valor. No man of royal blood could hope to secure a more suitable wife to bear his sons." He paused. Then, "You, Āndrōmakhê, to gain *you* as a prize, are one of the reasons I came out on the side of Troia. Truly, I will be honored to wed Hektôr's noble widow. I swear before divine Astarte that you will be first among my women." He leaned closer and I held myself from moving away as he gently kissed me on the forehead.

First among my women...my heart jumped up and did a little dance. The thought of Memnon with a large harem full of beautiful concubines, felt so liberating! With a little luck, and if I could keep myself unobtrusive, I might be lost in there and forgotten....

Memnon stood up, looking down at me in the flickering torchlight. "Akhilles is back. He had been off raiding as far as Lesbos." His words were chipped ice. "We must camp out tonight as close to the enemy camp as possible."

I felt myself trembling. Dread drove spears through me. Hektôr's conqueror back on the fields. I shuddered with fear and looked up into Memnon's blue-eyed dark face. "Be careful. His mother is Thétis, the Nereid. And the armor he wears is made by Hephaistos."

Memnon threw back his head and gave a booming laugh. "Ah! And *I* am the son of Eos, Goddess of Dawn. In addition, Hephaistos made my armor, too. Yet, I am the better warrior."

I studied his expression and liked his unaffected manner. "I will offer sacrifices for your victory tomorrow," I said.

He dropped another light kiss on my forehead. "No need to worry about me." He strode purposefully from Priam's courtyard.

* * * *

Two weeks passed, Memnon rode thrice on the battlefield, people saying that he looked and led his warriors, just as Hektôr used to. The enemy ranks atrophied due to casualties dealt by Memnon and his men. But I was troubled by that he had not been able to rout them at first try. Memnon was indeed a keen strategist and heroic commander, with thousands at his disposal, yet the shock-effect that had benefited him on his way here failed against this firmly entrenched, battle-hardened enemy long starving for plunder and rape. Besides, even with Memnon's troops, the Achaians outnumbered us; many of them freshly recruited troops, mean-spirited jackals whose only hope for wealth was to confiscate the imagined treasures inside our walls. After years of scourging our shores, they were better familiar with the terrain than Memnon. Another trick their leaders used was to rotate men in ships, especially those tired and wounded, sending them on restorative spins up and down the coast, while our own fleet was decimated, and Memnon had none to give them chase.

With the cattle and other provisions they had brought along, his troops were self-sufficient; but also, Memnon was generous, offering substantial rations to our poorest citizens. Antenor and his likes, instead of being ashamed by his act of kindness, found ways to steal what they could and sell it for profit.

Memnon treated me with friendly respect. He would visit me at the end of a battle or strategy session, always bringing along an exquisite gift, asking my opinion about various things, also questioning about my parents and brothers, my likes and dislikes.

"I will fully rebuild Thébé for you, I promise," he said after he had listened to my story of its sacking by Akhilles, "and the Kingdom of Kilikia shall be great again. Yes, Queen Ãndrõmakhê, in due time, your son Skamandrios will rule Troia as well as Kilikia and Mysia, and prosper as he expands our empire far into Thrakia and Illyrikon."

One night, at a very late hour, Memnon surprised me on the wall, while I sat beneath a star-studded sky, watching Hektôr's tomb. Nefru slept in my lap, and tears slowly ran down my cheeks. Memnon stood by me, his hand placed upon my shoulder, his touch warm, comforting. "Do you dream of him often?"

"No," I replied truthfully, "and not once have I seen his ghost, or his shade. I am deeply worried. I fear he is lost wandering in the labyrinths of Hades."

"You could be right. He was forced to leave behind the two people he loved most on earth, and does not know where he is now, for he has not yet accepted his own death. Nights, just before you fall asleep— when the veil separating our worlds, is thin—try to communicate to him that you are safe, that you have a protector."

I nodded, touched by his thoughtful words.

Moments passed in silence.

Then Memnon made a shockingly thoughtful comment, "Beloved Ãndrõmakhê, be assured that once you are my wife, *you* will decide when to join me in my bedchamber."

"You amaze me," I said sincerely.

He smiled, gazing at Hektôr's resting place, which shone in the light of the bright moon.

"He was lucky to have known such enduring love," he whispered after a while, "I do envy him."

"Don't, my lord! You too will find it, if love is what you truly seek. Everyone has a soulmate."

Memnon laughed. "Alas, I fear it takes many lifetimes until you meet each other." He then changed the subject, "I heard that you can read and write, is this true?"

"Yes. Hittite cuneiform, Luvian pictographs and some Kretan."

"I have a rich cuneiform library in my palace," he revealed with twinkling eyes, "thousands of tablets about Law, diplomacy, politics, history, and legends. In fact when I was of Skamandrios' age, I didn't want to be a warrior, but a scholar."

I stood up and bowed to him. "You are offering me a boon, my noble lord! I shall be in your debt, always."

* * * *

On the following day Memnon and Antilokos, son of King Nestor of Messenia in Peloponnesus, locked in battle.

Antilokos was Old Nestor's youngest son, a brave, skilled warrior, and friend of Akhilles.

Memnon slayed Antilokos in a lengthy but fair battle.

Akhilles, as madly infuriated as he had been upon Patroklos' death, crashed upon the field like thunder, and the two legendary warriors confronted each other. Memnon slew Akhilles' charioteer and four of his lieutenants, but night fell and the battle remained a draw.

* * * *

Morning sun glinted brilliantly from the armor of men fighting near the Achaian ships. The paving was alive with heat under my bare feet as I stood on the wall, leaning as far out as I dared against the crenel, trying to pick out Memnon, whom I now perceived as Skamandrios' Champion and Hektôr's Avenger. I glanced at Hekabe; the old woman's face was sharply eager. Priam, nearby, held to the crenel-stones with white-knuckled fingers.

A sound of rushing pinpointed all thoughts back to the field.

A duel...it was happening! The death-fight!

Blond Akhilles, Black Memnon, both warriors fully armored and helmeted in gold. Rumors that Memnon's armor too had been made by Hephaistos were rampant, and I hoped that just the suspicion of it might give a tremble to Akhilles' arm, deflecting his aim.

The two warriors came together like two titans, on foot, and my own muscles tensed and strained with theirs' as they fought, endlessly, spear-to-spear, sword-to-sword.

Akhilles' blood on Memnon's armor.

Brilliant red drops on gold.

Beautiful!

No. They broke apart. Still on foot. Their respective charioteers raced by; they grabbed for the rails, whipped themselves up.

Memnon at head start; ebony-skinned, long black hair freed from helmet lost somewhere in the field, thundering toward Troia.

Golden Akhilles in pursuit, achieving casting-distance again.

They stopped, dismounted on more even ground; the flash of thrusting, slashing giant's swords like sunlit tears.

I howled like a she-wolf when the dark figure dropped to his knees. A silver point showing through at Memnon's back, facing me.

My ears hummed to the earthshaking rumble of defeat as the terrified Trojans pounded toward the quickly opened Skaian Gate.

Hektôr, my Love; Memnon, Defender of our son's future....

255

Both slain. By the hand of Akhilles.

Soon Memnon's body was covered by a growing pile of dead: defenders and despoilers together.

I wanted to leave so I could scream and sob, but couldn't, I had to stay and watch the contest for possession of gallant Memnon's body.

A truce for the dead was declared.

Akhilles burnt the armor and severed head of Memnon on the funeral pile of Antilokos.

Priam ransomed the burnt skull and rest of his body, and a second funeral pyre was lit for the noble Ethiopian King.

As the fires were burning and crackling furiously, we witnessed a most curious event: the smoke metamorphosed into a flock of white birds that rose and disappeared into the horizon.

Memnon was laid to rest in a grave by the Aisepos River, which flows from the mountains of Ida in the Troad.

The Ethiopian army disbanded. They packed up and left, with nary a backward glance. Yet those white birds returned time after time to Memnon's grave, sprinkling it with the water of the river from their wet wings. We called them Memnonides [2].

[1] Eos: (Dawn) was, in Greek mythology, the Titan goddess of the dawn, who rose from her home at the edge of the Ocean that surrounds the world, to herald her brother Helios, the Sun. As the Dawn Goddess, she opened the gates of heaven (with "rosy fingers") so that Helios could ride his chariot across the sky every day. In Homer (*Iliad* viii.1; xxiv.695), her yellow robe is embroidered or woven with flowers (*Odyssey* VI: 48 etc); rosy-fingered and with golden arms, she is pictured on Attic vases as a supernaturally beautiful woman, wearing a tiara, and the large white-feathered wings of a bird. Eos is the iconic original from which Christian angels were imagined, for no images were available from the Hebrew tradition, and the Persian angels were unknown in the West. The worship of the dawn as a goddess is inherited from Indo-European times; Eos is cognate to Latin Aurora and to Vedic Ushas.

[2] The Legend of Memnon: In Greek mythology, king of Ethiopia, son of Tithonos and Eos. In the Trojan War, he fought against the Greeks, and after he brought down Antilochos, he himself was vanquished by Achilles. The smoke of Memnon's funeral pyre is said to have turned into birds, some of which killed each other over the flames. These birds, called Memnonides, indeed returned on stated days every year to Memnon's grave, in a hill above the outlet of the Aisepos River, which flows from the mountains of Ida in the Troad region, and sprinkled it with the water of the river from their wet wings. Eos herself never ceased to lament the death of her handsome son, a magnificent king. The morning-dew, they say, is the tears shed by Her every morning, for the death of her beloved son. Yet it has also been told that Zeus bestowed immortality upon Memnon at Eos' request. He was supposed to have lived in Egypt,

and the Greeks gave his name to the great statue of Amenhotep III, at Thébés. This statue was said to make a musical sound at daybreak, at which time Memnon greeted his mother, Eos, Goddess of Dawn.

A good source for information on these subjects: http//www.answers.com

Chapter 22: Nurziu

I grieved for Memnon; I had known him as a uniquely noble man.

A few days later, during a lull in a rather listless battle, a cry from Thalpia attracted my attention to the tower buttress.

Alexis was standing there, partly protected. Black-feathered arrow nocked to his bow, head thrown back, he was laughing.

Out beyond, Akhilles heard and whirled toward him, topping the chariot just out of bowshot. He dismounted.

Unable to breathe, I pulled Thalpia with me to the edge of the wall. Akhilles lifted his spear, its length twice his own height, and drew it back across his shoulder, aiming.

Alexis drew his bow and let fly an arrow.

The quivering shaft pinned Akhilles's instep to the ground.

Akhilles cried out with surprise, bent to pull it out.

I laughed and sobbed at once, bursting with the glory of revenge, for I suspected that Alexis used poison on his arrows.

The feathered end projected from Akhilles' heel, and he could not remove it, though he lifted his foot from the ground.

Screaming hoarsely, Odysseus rumbled out in his own chariot and swept Akhilles away.

Alexis stood immobile, laughing, holding his huge bow casually in one hand. The Achaian army retreated.

Alexis strolled slowly back to Troia.

This time, I thought, *Aphrodite triumphed over Athené.*

I turned and locked eyes with Queen Hekabe. We shared a smile. There was hope for Troia! Yes, we had lost King Memnon, but without Akhilles, the Achaians were done and over with.

* * * *

Bereft of Akhilles' leadership, the Achaians were truly just a group of mangy dogs; when Alexis or Deiphobos chose to bestir the enemy there was only fitful fighting.

Then reliable spies reported that Akhilles lived. But he was just limping around camp, more ghost than man.

The news livened Polyxena, but struck me a near-death blow.

I could not eat, nor talk to anyone. I left home only to go and sit where I could embrace Hektôr's tomb in my sight.

Alexis came one afternoon and sat on a nook in the crenels, facing me. "Āndrõmakhê," he began quietly, "Akhilles will never return to the battlefield. And he *will* die. It is his fate. Take my word for it."

"I want to! I saw you drawing the arrow. I was sure you had tipped it with poison."

He shook his head. "Poison wasn't needed. Apollo told me Akhilles' secret: Upon his birth, Thétis, knowing that if he chooses to be a great warrior he would die at the walls of Troia, dipped him headfirst into the River Styx, to make him immortal. However, the heel by which she held him was not touched by the river and remained vulnerable. That is why I aimed to strike him on his heel. Yes, it is taking very long, for he is strong, far stronger than any of us, and Thétis is still beseeching Zeus to grant him immortality. But it will not happen. Zeus has tipped the scales too often in her and Athené's favor."

I stared at him, afraid to believe.

He rose and offered a hand, palm upward, motioning to place mine into his. I did. He held it gently, his touch warm. "Sister," he spoke warmly, "you are my sister, just as much as the others."

Sister…as the word vibrated in the air between us, Nefru appeared at his feet, sat on his hind legs, and purred. *He speaks the truth,* I heard him say in my mind.

What do you mean? I questioned Nefru silently.

He replied: *Before you two were Āndrõmakhê and Alexander, born in different places, to different parents, you were a brother and sister living on an island somewhere in the Tairenzee.*

I looked at Alexis, wondering if he could hear Nefru. But he seemed unaffected. He freed my hand and returned to his seat, looking out into the horizon. *A brother and a sister,* I thought, *yes, I had had a notion that I was a little girl, with a brother who took care of me, on Shardana. Nurziu and Kiara. Kupra's children.*

Nefru added: *And you had a cat, a keen and fearless hunter.*

"The lynx!" I cried out, "Yes, oh, yes, Nefru, Kassandra was right, YOU are the LYNX!"

"Nefru is a lynx?" Alexis chuckled, pointing.

"He was."

"Oh. How interesting. When?"

"I'm not exactly sure. But according to Kiron, who used to be my teacher and interpreted a vision I had, it must have been very a long time ago, when I lived on an island."

Alexis chuckled. "Hmm, I see."

I ignored his laughter, but brought up something I had not before, "There was a day about ten years past, when you sat on this wall, and spoke at length with a female entity. Do you remember it?"

His golden brows drew together as he searched his memory. Then he clapped his hands, "Yes, now I remember! The voice of a young girl...she was so very ill, and her shade was already out of her body; she said that she liked me, but could not understand why, for she did not *know* me...but then...how...oh! Ãndrõmakhê! She was you!"

"Yes, me. You are right, I had been very ill, and I recall flying up to the Light. I wanted to stay there, but some force pulled me back. I found myself with you and Priam, while you discussed your upcoming mission to Achaia. When you went out to the wall, I floated behind you. You were sitting and lost in thought, playing your lyre. But later you said that you could feel my presence, and talked to me. For years afterward I have wondered about why, of all the people I knew, it was you to whom I was drawn to while I was on the brink of death...." Nefru leapt on my lap, and I paused, caressing him on his pink nose and pressing him close to my heart.

Alexis remained motionless, his gaze swinging from me, to Hektôr's tomb, back to Nefru who was purring. At last he spoke, "Before you came to us Nefru was very close to my mother. She gave him to you because she said he has special powers."

"She gave him, yes, but Nefru chose to stay with me."

"I agree. Tell me this: have you found out why you paid me a visit on that day?"

"No, I don't know, not really. Nefru just said that you and I used to be brothers and sisters in a different lifetime. But—"

"But that doesn't explain why, on the brink of death, you would seek *me* out for a chat."

"True, it doesn't."

He fell silent again, studying me with a hooded expression.

I bristled, "You don't seem surprised at that we might have been siblings in the past."

He shrugged. "Somehow, I am not. However, I do not remember having lived before. Not as your brother, not as someone else. All I know is *this* life, and I was named Paris because the shepherd who found me wrapped me up in a small bundle, and when he handed me to his wife, she said: 'Oh! A little purse!' Paris means *little purse.* But when I grew up, I earned myself the title Alexander, meaning Defender of Man."

"But you don't doubt that you met the three goddesses, in the flesh, judged in Aphrodite's favor, and Helen is your reward."

"Of that I have no doubt. Though until the day Father told me I was to sail to Sparta and talk to Helen, I *did* doubt that they were *goddesses.* Or else, why wait four years to claim her as my own?"

"You don't regret it? Even though it has caused so much death?"

"I regret that I brought her *here.* I should have waited in Sparta until Meneláos had his fill of his lover in Krete, returned, and fought it out with him there. In Sparta, Helen was undisputed queen. The Spartans would have fought on our side against Meneláos. And with Meneláos dead, the Oath of the Horse would have lost its relevance."

"Yes but there'd still be Agamemnon to deal with."

"Him, too, I would have handled better in Sparta than in Troia. What empowered him to lead so many kings and soldiers is that accursed oath. But with Meneláos and the oath out of the equation, he'd have remained just another chieftain, bickering over small spoils."

"Yes, in hindsight..." I murmured sadly.

He laughed. "I lacked *foresight* because it was not meant to be. At the time, all I could think of was to claim Helen and bring her home, proud that I was handing the rights to the Lakedaimonian lands to my father. The gods had other plans for us."

"The gods!" I burst out, "And *their* plans! For *us!*"

Alexis' face darkened, revealing his nagging inner pain. "Who could have foreseen that this would go so far...Helen came with me willingly; besides, it wasn't the first time a woman has been abducted. Boras ravished Orithyia, daughter of Athenian King Arakthos, then whisked her away to Thrakia, and Athenians did not attempt to invade that country! Jason the Argonaut took with him, in addition to the Golden Fleece, the King's daughter Medea, and although the Kolchian fleet followed them, Thessaly was never invaded. And so I deemed the risks for retaliation as unimportant."

"The defining difference is that without Helen, Meneláos cannot rule in Sparta."

"Of course; that's why I regret that I did not battle with Meneláos on Helen's soil."

Nefru meowed, nudging my hand with his nose. In my mind appeared the vision of a sun-splashed coast. "Alexis...have you heard of a place called *Tairenzee*? Do you know where it is?"

"Tairenzee? No, I don't think so. Did you mean Tirenean Sea?"

I glanced at Nefru, but heard no reply.

Alexis continued, "If it's Tirenean Sea, yes, I know of it, but not enough to steer my ship toward it on my own. The farthest I have sailed is Messenia, on the Ionian Sea, down south of Sparta. The Tirenean Sea is beyond the Ionian Sea, westward, and then it stretches all the way to the Pillars of Herakles. Why do you ask?"

I smiled and tickled Nefru under his chin. "Nefru says you and I lived there before. On an island. I believe he means Shardana, whence comes my statue of the Dea Madre. My teacher Kiron had said that Shardana used to be two islands and part of the Atlantean Empire."

"Oh, is that so!" He threw back his head and laughed and laughed, patting his knee, stamping his foot.

"I am happy that I am able to amuse you, dear brother."

He winked. "Oh, yes! I just remembered Aeneas mentioning a race of immortal people around the Tirenean Sea. He wants to sail there one day and check it out for himself. Ask Nefru the *Lynx* if you and I were among those immortals?"

Nefru leapt down, stretched, meowed softly and streaked away.

Alexander watched him disappear. "What was that all about?"

We looked at each other for a few minutes, then he rose to his feet, repeated that I should rest easy for Akhilles would soon be dead.

"I've wanted to say something else to you," I spoke on an impulse. "You and Akhilles...look like each other. A lot."

His eyes widened and there was crack in his composure. "What do you mean? Surely not that *we were siblings in a past life?"*

I smiled at how offended he was by the prospect, reminding me of Akhilles' similar reaction when I had pointed this out to him. "No, no, nothing of the kind," I replied seriously, "besides, if you and I are an example of past-life siblings, considering that we don't resemble each other...I'd venture to assume physical attributes do not travel with the soul, but only with the bloodline."

Scowling, "Akhilles and I know exactly who our parents are!"

"Yes, but what if Erik...I mean the great, godlike King Eriktonios, he who came down from the farthest North, is ancestor not only to you, but to Akhilles as well? His father Peleos might be an issue of Erik's line, as is Priam. Hektôr was your brother, *undisputed* brother, but by the look of you, no one would have guessed that. True, Hektôr inherited his massive body from Priam, and from Erik the Great, his unique gift of handling horses. But his facial features, his deep green eyes, sharp cheekbones and prominent nose, were of your mother and not of Priam."

"This does not explain why Akhilles and I would look like each other! By the way, *you* are the only one who sees this resemblance. If Eriktonios is our common ancestor, then Akhilles was Hektôr's cousin also; and Deiphobos', and all the rest of us."

"*Distant* cousin, of course. Yet close enough to carry on Great Eriktonios' cartouche, so to speak. For reasons known only to gods, the personal stamp does not pass on to everyone. I remember Priam telling you that he and the Atrides brothers are related. Through Plakia, his mother, who was a daughter of King Atros. Agamemnon and Meneláos are Atros' sons from his other wife, Aerope, the Achaian."

Alexis sighed. "Sad-eyed Aerope, whom Atros drowned because she had loved his brother, Thyestes. He killed Thyestes' son by her, boiled him and fed him to Thyestes as punishment for having bedded her. Then he married his brother's daughter, his very own niece, not realizing she was pregnant because her father had raped her. Theirs' is not a salubrious bloodline!" His expression darkened. "The House of Atros is cursed by the gods. They are to be forever tormented by the Erinyes, terrifying, snake-haired Furies who punish those who killed their relatives."

He bent and kissed me on the brow. "Āndrōmakhê, when all is said and done, what matters is that Akhilles, cousin or not, murdered my brother, Hektôr; he did so unfairly, with the help of the gods and not his own manly skill. I am grateful I was the one who was given the honor of avenging noble Hektôr."

Briefly squeezing my shoulder, Alexis left.

I remained sitting with Nefru back on my lap, gazing at Hektôr's resting place until darkness fell and Skamandrios came running, scolding me for neglecting him.

* * * *

Alexis united with Aeneas and Deiphobos in strategies such as Hektôr had used, keeping our warriors off the field in hopes that the enemy would wear himself out smashing against our walls. Nine years was a long time to hang around any city, and they would have to break down soon, unless Troia fell because of starvation.

Winter rains and cold arrived, dismal both in the city and along the shore. Stored foods were depleted and hunger rode the day. Even Palace stores, kept in surplus for needy citizens, were low; each day more people arrived from among the refugees for grain.

When winter melted into spring, the last of Priam's herdsmen and some of my farmers from Kilikia brought in supplies.

Skamandrios was an energetic, bold child. Five years old now, soon he would begin military training. I decided to entrust him to Deiphobos, for he had loved Hektôr best among all the brothers.

Spies reported that Odysseus and Diomede braved rough seas, and sailed to the island of Skyros. Deiphobos lifted his head, his eyes narrowed. "The place where Akhilles grew up with a bunch of girls?"

"Indeed," it was confirmed. "They are to fetch his son, Pyrrhos."

"Akhilles' son?" Priam looked thunderstruck.

Alexis laughed. "He can't be older than fourteen or so."

Polyxena moaned. "That should have been my child!"

* * * *

Spring flooding from mountain snows created a lake of the inland marshes, and begun overflowing riverbanks when spies reported the arrival of sixteen-year-old Pyrrhos Neoptolemos among the Achaians. Gloom settled deeper over Troia. Akhilles' son Pyrrhos. Surnamed Neoptolemos—New Warrior—by the Myrmidons. This did not bode well for us.

As tall and strongly built as his father, Pyrrhos Neoptolemos led the next attack upon our city in a shattering nightmare. The howling Achaians poured from their camp after him, meeting us in a bone-and-chariot-crashing offensive. Agamemnon and Meneláos rushed their own forces in, seizing the offensive.

Swiftly falling night separated the armies.

Our warriors encamped along the Simois River, while the Achaians retreated to their camp.

From then on battles resumed at dawn each day. Fortunes veered between Trojans and Achaians with bewildering swiftness.

* * * *

Pyrrhos Neoptolemos dispatched his personal herald Alkibiades with demands: the surrender of Polyxena and me, with as much treasure as befits a Princess of Troia and Queen of Thébé, in return of his leaving with the Myrmidons. Priam refused to place this ludicrous request in front of the Council. It was wise that he did not, for I feared the Council would gladly hand us over as prize for a battle he had not won.

* * * *

One day I watched Deiphobos press toward Pyrrhos through retreating Trojans. He flung his men and my Mysian troops against the Myrmidons, whose advantage began to slacken. Archers on the wall rained burning tarred arrows onto the besiegers whenever our warriors were forced to divide before Achaian forays.

Alexis swerved in aid of Helenos, and Pyrrhos took after him. Deiphobos wheeled to help, and we, women on the wall, once again brandished our fists and screamed encouragement. Pyrrhos raised his spear high above his shoulder. Fearless, Alexis slashed his way nearer that raised spear, then sprang to the ground and came up with a small rock. He flung it and Pyrrhos staggered from his chariot, dropping his spear. In a flash their swords were slashing. When swords were knocked away, they used darts, stabbing and cutting. They wrestled and struck and pulled, sweat muddying the dust under their feet.

Pyrrhos left Alexis who was wounded and unable to rise, whirled around, and thrust a dart into the throat of advancing Eurypylos, a cousin of Alexis and brother of my friend, Lanassa, and one of our best fighters. He then snatched his sword from the mud, stabbing the Teuthranian to his heart.

Pyrrhos bent to pull out his crimsoned blade. He bent again to strip the body of its armor, and then remounted his chariot. The dead man's armor piled in with him, he rushed among the Trojans, dealing death as his father would have done. The naked body of brave Eurypylos was left to scavenger dogs and vulture-eagles to fight over.

Deiphobos streaked by like lightning and pulled Alexis up into his own chariot.

Pyrrhos pursued our warriors to the gate, which crashed shut barely before enemy arms battered against them. Frenzied Achaians, dragging huge logs, beat in vain against the multi-layered heavy wood and bronze. Our men and women ran to the wall, casting stones and fiery arrows onto those attempting to climb. Helenos organized the bringing of kettles of hot pitch.

Meneláos ordered men to start scaling at the wild fig tree. I pointed, screaming. Deiphobos immediately ordered pitch be poured onto them in burning streams, as arrows twanged and whirred across to stop fresh troops attempting to replace those scalded.

Alexis calmly directed the archers and slingers as red blood and black pitch massed with torn flesh below, clustered mainly at the buttress of that weak section below the tree.

Lucky for us, sudden sheets of rain boiled the Skamander over its banks, and the enemy was forced to retreat.

Pyrrhos Neoptolemos renewed his offensive at dawn.

Fear stalked us even as Alexis led his archers in sending sheets of arrows. Deiphobos' leadership rose to one of *Akhillean* madness as he charged over the dead, driving many an enemy soldier into the Skamander where the swollen waters were rusted with blood, and choked by flesh torn among squirming eels.

While his Myrmidons were dying at the river, Pyrrhos counter-attacked. Our warriors fled before his fury into thick clouds of dust, so that Deiphobos was left in the rear of a wild retreat.

Alexis sped down the Skaian Stairs. Forcing his way among the incoming men, he took stance behind a buttress and aimed at Pyrrhos. I leaned over the battlement and screamed a warning to him, my opal so boiling hot on my throat that I feared I was being set afire.

However, Philoktetes, chief Achaian archer, sent his shaft before Alexis could draw his bow and let fly.

Alexis shook blood from his wounded wrist, and reset his arrow, this time aiming for the archer.

Another arrow whirred from Philoktetes.

Alexis doubled over, dropping bow, quiver and arrows. He entered the gate at a limping run, the arrow protruding between thigh and groin. With a clank of breastplate and greaves, he fell forward in the street. His men lifted him and ran with him to his house.

I followed, supporting the wailing Hekabe.

Helen unrolled the bedding in grim silence. Helenos, bloodied from battle, strode in, dipped his hands in water held by Kassandra, and seized the arrow. Removing it, he bent and sucked out as much of the poisoned blood as possible, spitting into a cup held by Hekabe.

At one point Alexis struggled to raise his head and called to me, speaking excitedly but with a hoarse voice, "Āndrõmakhê! I saw the place Nefru told us about! Our house sat on a hill by the bay. Then, too, I played my flute, and hunted with bow and arrow. You were so small! Such a pretty little girl! You had a yellow-spotted lynx, faithful like a dog, and you roamed the hills with him, then came home and told wild stories of how you danced with a Kentaur and a Nymph. You shall return there one day, dearest Kiara, and live in peace—always. As an Immortal."

Alexis fainted from exhaustion and Helen threw me a cynical, cold look. *"Kiara?"*

I did not care for her expression and ignored her.

* * * *

Throughout the following days fighting continued under the pushing attacks led by Pyrrhos. There was no denying it anymore, fortune was turning toward a final Achaian victory. Aeneas and Turkus, from the walltop, took over the throwing of pitch. Helenos shouldered command of archers and slingers. Deiphobos forced his growing despair into unification of all our soldiers.

* * * *

Alexis panted in a final agony of exhaustion. His wound had festered. Helen did not eat, never left his side, held his hand, crooning softly, mixed medicines Helenos brought, and gave them to him in a quick touching of lips. However, the medicine lost its power quickly and Alexis lay wide-eyed in torment. Foam gathered at his lips and he screamed continuously, until no breath was left in him.

Priam, behind Hekabe, spoke through stiff lips, "Oinoné could cure him. The mountain people know relevant herbs."

Alexis' bleary eyes roved from his parents to Helen. "Oinoné? She would not! Not anymore." He strained, tossed, and turned for the drilling of yet another wave of pain. "Send for her!" he yelled then.

At one point, Alexis opened his eyes with a sudden move, sought mine in the room, and spoke, "Rejoice! Akhilles is dead! He is at the shrine of Apollo, where he had sacrificed Troilos, because Odysseus goaded him. Akhilles crawled there this morning, on his own, to beg Apollo's forgiveness for having offended him, but just now I witnessed his soul depart his body."

At any other time, I would have abandoned myself into a dance thanking my Goddess, but aggrieved as I was over Alexis' impending death, I let the news slide down my back like water on oilskin.

Within hours Polites was back from his mission to the mountains. "Oinoné refused to come," he reported ruefully.

We did not have the heart to tell this to Alexis. The stink from his wound became that of sure death, and the entire house smelled of it. The contours of his beautiful body became sharp and thin, the skin tight and blotchy with green shadows. Still he did not die, perhaps waiting for Oinoné, babbling of their carefree life in the mountains.

When Alexis at last gave up his soul, four of us were with him. Hekabe nestled his head on her breast. Kassandra held his hand, and I stood at his feet. Helen was at the head of the bed, blue eyes dark with the bleakest horror.

Then I sensed his soul return one last time into flesh, he reached a hand toward his wife, and her name faded on his lips into a low, moaning gurgle, "Helen...."

A last movement of sapphire-blue eyes, and light faded from them into blankness.

Hekabe kissed the departing soul through his lips, for Helen was not able to, weeping with gut-wrenching sobs, and Kassandra closed his eyes with trembling fingers.

The lying-in-state was short, for his body swelled as if to burst the embalming-wax.

His pyre was piled high on the third day. It was on that day when Oinoné arrived, lugging a large basket of herbs, demanding to see him.

"Oh, Oinoné!" I could say nothing more.

Hekabe went to her with open arms.

Oinoné indicated her heavy basket. "I forgive him, Mother. It was not his hand that moved to kill our son. I know, I saw the evil force that guided it. Let me see him now, for even at the very point of death, I could cure him." She stared as we covered our faces and turned away.

After a frozen silence, she let out a long scream, stepped back, tripped, and fell face down. Hekabe ordered maids to prepare a room for the grieving Daughter of Kebren.

By noon on the next day, Alexis lay upon a tall bier. After it was lit and smoky flames reached skyward, we saw Oinoné. Nimbly climbing up the burning wooden stairs, she threw herself atop Alexis, and was lost among the engulfing fire.

All of us kept watch, including Helen, hoping his departing soul would see us and take to the other side the knowledge of that he was loved, appreciated, and missed greatly, on earth. Saddened though we were by Oinoné's death, we were glad too, for she had joined him willingly. Freed from earthly hurts and grudges, henceforth the beautiful, free-spirited Nymph would be his companion as he played his music on the Elysian Fields. She had been the one who loved him best, while he had been a poor mountain shepherd, living in a rickety shed, owning nothing more than a flute and lyre. As well, the love he felt for her, had been his truest, from the wellspring of his own heart, and not due to an enchantment by a fickle goddess.

I also prayed that Hektôr—if at last freed from the labyrinths of Hades—would meet and guide him to Elysium.

As the burgeoning flames crackled and leapt, I also thought of Alexis as Nurziu, the brother whose face could not rise in my memory.

When it was all over, Alexis and Oinoné's ashes were mixed and sent to the mountains by Helenos' hand. He left them for the winds to scatter on the high peak where they had roamed and loved.

* * * *

Alexis' death left Troia without a Defender, and Helen without a husband/protector. Aeneas, Anchises, Antenor and Polydamas combined, raising their demand that Helen be returned to Meneláos, in one last effort to end the war. However, Deiphobos maintained that she must remain in Troia.

The Council awarded the Defendership to Deiphobos, who, to our shock, asserted his claim: "I have a brother's right to Helen and her lands. The Achaians will never make another agreement with us. I am Chief of Military now and I will beat them back." He turned to King Priam. "I demand permission to marry Helen at once."

"There's death if you touch that woman," Helenos warned.

Priam hesitated, and then looked at Helenos. "After Hektôr and Alexis, *you* are the oldest. Do you make a claim for this woman?"

"No. I speak only what I know."

Priam faced Deiphobos. "Marry her when you will, my son."

Helenos shot his brother a warning look. "That woman is a curse to any man who takes her."

Deiphobos laughed. "You don't fool me! I know you want her, cold priest though you are." He went stamping from the hall.

I rushed after him. "Deiphobos, wait!"

He paused, turned, and looked at me, his dour expression warming up. "Yes, my sister?"

"Please, indulge me for a moment…you have always been kind to me and Skamandrios and I know you loved Hektôr. I would trust you with my life. So please trust me, too. For what I'm about to tell you, I have no other motive than wanting what's best for you."

"I know that, Āndrōmakhê! Go on, have your say."

"I would ask you, no, not ask, but *beg* you, most urgently…to please… please…not to press your claim on Helen."

"What?"

I drew in a deep breath for courage. "Deiphobos, I like not the fear this prospect causes in my heart. Alexis and Helen were united because Aphrodite willed it so. Now, Alexis is dead. Aphrodite is finished with

Helen. Perhaps with Troia as well. If you take Helen to wife, you will enter uncharted waters."

"Uncharted only by gods!" He laughed. "Meaning, *I* will be the captain of my own ship, my own destiny."

I recognized the steely determination in his eyes and did not know what else to say.

His smile was kind. "Dear Ãndrõmakhê, I know you care for me. Accept my gratitude. But I shall do what is best for me."

I nodded and returned to the Council room, entering it just as Priam was concluding a statement to Helenos, "My son, do you truly not want Helen as your wife? I repeat, after Hektôr and Paris, *you* are the eldest, it is your right."

Helenos' hands made fists at his sides. "Father, I have loved another from long before I went to Perkote to train for priesthood." The name wrenched from his lips: *"Ãndrõmakhê."*

Priam turned thoughtful. "Perhaps it is well to consider your suit, Helenos. Yes, I will speak to her."

They were talking about me as if I were not here!

I bit my lips and prevented my outrage from exploding.

Helenos, Hektôr's brother and Priest of Apollo, stood rigid. "I know Skamandrios needs a father." He paused. Then, "I have become too ascetic to be a true husband to her right now. I made myself a dead man, turning all my urges toward the divinities. Otherwise I could not have endured...."

Priam laid a hand on his shoulder in silent sympathy.

"Father. I shall take Ãndrõmakhê to wife. I will tell you when, upon my return from the plains. I have reason to think the Achaians are building new ships. I suspect that is not all they are doing, and must go and find out."

"You may do so after Deiphobos' marriage. When you return, you can offer for Ãndrõmakhê." Priam dismissed him.

* * * *

Next day Deiphobos married Helen. She did not look happy, but neither did she protest when united with Deiphobos at the ivy-twined altar. Helenos stood as best man, speaking only the words required of him. When Deiphobos kissed Helen and led her away from the altar, her eyes flashed fire. She did not look at him and was quiet during the wedding feast.

Later, I went to bed knowing I must accept a protector for Skamandrios or leave Troia and hide in a distant land until gods settled Troia's destiny. Helenos as husband was a kinder prospect than anyone else Priam might sell me to, for a treaty. I had loved him once and could care for him again. However, love him as a wife should, I could not. Not after having been wife of Hektôr. But time was running out. I must accept Helenos or find a safe place, take my son, and leave!

Morning sun silvered to day-white by the time I found Helenos hitching his chariot for the shoreward expedition. He wore a breastplate over his priestly robes. "Helenos."

He looked at me, then away. His knuckles and nails shone white. "I never forgot Lake Salai. We were promised to each other."

I heard the bitterness in his tone. He had forgotten that he had been the one going back on his word, forcing his gallant older brother to step in to finalize the treaty between our fathers. I saw no reason to remind him. Instead, warmly, "I do not hold you to your brotherly obligation. However, I would want you to help me find a safe place for Skamandrios and me, lest Priam discovers someone else to trade me. I am still receiving messages from what is left of my own people, pledging support for when I resurrect my father's rule. But I must wait until this war is over, one way or the other, and then—"

"Rest easy, Āndrõmakhê. As for your future as Queen of Kilikia, yes, you need time to make plans and gather allies. In the meantime, I would be father to your son—even if you marry me just to have Skamandrios protected." He came around the chariot. "I will always love you more than you could ever love me. I could not speak out before, because I knew of Memnon's bid for you. He was a powerful king, Āndrõmakhê, his alliance of great value to Troia. My duty was to do what is best for Troia—not my heart. However, Apollo has shown me in my visions that Troia cannot be saved. In addition, you are in grave danger. I will protect you."

Troia cannot be saved.

My heart almost stopped beating. Helenos took me in his arms. I remained stiff, and ashamed of that he could desire me.

He let me go and leapt into the chariot. He stood tall, reins gripped, being his own charioteer. With a firm hand, he gave rein and thundered out through the Agora, and down to the Skaian Gate.

I stood motionless, watching his dust-trail fade after him as he headed for the enemy ships.

Returning home, I knelt at the altar of my Goddess. My mind was afire, my heart heavy. O my Hektôr.

* * * *

When Helenos did not return that night, Priam could not locate Dolon, the merchant, who was our most reliable source for news. Therefore, he sent Idaios and Polites to investigate.

"Odysseus captured Helenos," Idaios informed the king upon his return. "He's held in the camp, and I was allowed to speak with him only briefly."

My heart froze in my chest.

The herald glanced about uneasily. "Meneláos tried to force information from him...about how our city might be taken. He had him whipped, and tortured with fire. It was Agamemnon's outrage at the mistreatment of a priest that made him allow me to see Helenos."

I closed my eyes. Dignified, self-possessed Helenos, twisting under a knife-like whip, tormented by fire, in the tent of his enemy. The thought was unbearable.

Polites spoke up, "My lord, another news: Meneláos had Dolon killed. He went spying for us once too often."

Idaios added softly, "Helenos whispered to me...just before I was sent away...that he saw something suspicious. Larger than a ship, with such an enormous keel that only a giant could float. But that is all I was allowed to hear."

* * * *

Night winds complained against the frescoes of Priam's Hall as if jealous of their bright colors. Skamandrios was asleep at home, and Nefru purring on my lap. I leaned back against the soft skins covering my chair. Had Hektôr felt death's cold breeze on his face, on that last day, as he left me for the greater cold?

The heat of war and the cold of death.

I took a drink of spiced wine, and gave a bit of meat to Nefru. The cold current circulating the premises echoed my mourning.

Presently Theano's scream shattered the darkness of the deserted Agora beyond the walls of the Palace.

When Priam summoned her, she was hysterical. It was a while before Antenor, joining his wife, could get any sense out of her. "Just now, when I offered to the holy Goddess...oh Athené! Her true image, the Palladium, was missing from its place under the figure!"

"Do you mean the ancient one that fell before Ilion's tent?" Priam demanded thunderously. "You must have been negligent!"

Kassandra rushed in, screaming, "This is the end! A crack opened in the paving and the sacred python of Apollo left our temple." Her hands waved blindly before her. "Attack their camp with fire! Burn their huts, tents, burn their ships—and the greatest ship of all—burn it! Do it now. *Now!*"

Priam fixed his steely blue gaze on Theano. "Are you sure? You know Troia is doomed if the holy image of our Protectress is stolen from us. How did this happen?"

Theano drew herself up. "The Goddess herself must have taken her own image! For only *I* know of her secret hiding place. I keep the true one with several duplicates behind a stone under the chair of our great, seated statue. And now, it is not there! The Goddess has deserted us."

"Tell me exactly what you found," Priam commanded.

Antenor stood near his wife, staring at her, saying nothing.

Theano seemed to make a great effort to gather her wits. "While I was kneeling there, whiteness like a veil came over me and I fell faint. It was much later when I waked, lying beside the Goddess' throne. I looked into the secret place, but the true image was not there."

I saw the glint of triumph in Helen's eyes as she sat beside Deiphobos, rejecting his hand on her arm. Then I remembered having passed an old beggar—a refugee—on the street, yesterday afternoon. Now, thinking back, I found it strange how he had stopped Theano as if to beg, or ask directions. Helen had stopped too, but I had not, thinking nothing of it at the time. Yet something about the man had been familiar. As I replayed the scene in my memory, I realized that that beggar had resembled Odysseus, the King of Ithaka's Goats.

"You were negligent of your duty," Priam spoke presently. Raising his scepter, he uttered the ritual words removing the priestess from guardianship of Athené's shrine.

Kassandra, staring about, moaned to herself. Her muttering grew louder; and she repeated endlessly, "Burn it…burn its evil power…"

Antenor placed an arm about his wife's waist at Priam's final words of anathema, he led her to the altar.

Nefru leapt down, looked up at me with a soft meow, and left the Hall, his black tail held high, enhancing the white of his pelt.

"I suspect I saw Odysseus in the city," I told Priam, "I won't say I am sure of it, but we ought to investigate."

He gave me a brusque nod.

When I returned home, I found Nefru waiting for me on the bench in the courtyard. I sat down beside him.

My friend, I will be departing this life soon.

"No!" I cried, "No! You are not going anywhere!"

It cannot be helped. I am very old. I do not wish to drag it on, so I will go to sleep and wake up no more.

I shook my head, forced myself to laugh, and tickled him beneath his chin. "No, I won't permit you. And I do not believe you, either. We are not having this conversation! Cats cannot talk. Besides, you are *not* old! I have only known you…for…how long? Six years? Cats live much longer than that."

I was already old before they brought me here in a ship, from Egypt. I do not know why I was born there in the Pharaoh's Palace, and not in your father's. I am a cat. I always was a cat. But perhaps I will find you again, at another time.

I began weeping with hacking sobs. "This is crazy! The gods are playing with me!" Then I found myself screaming, "And you weren't always a cat! You were, are, The Lynx!"

My friend, calm yourself. There is an urgent matter I have to tell you. Tonight, take whatever precious gold and jewelry you possess, and bury them deep under the fountain here. I know this is a good, safe spot. Lay me on top of it. Then plant a rose bush above me and surround it with decorative stones. My bones will protect your treasure from robbers until you return home to dig them out.

"Until I return? Where am I going, Nefru?"

Get up now, and do as I say, my friend!

Nefru leapt down from my lap and I rose. Thalpia had heard my cries and was waiting at the threshold. Silently I went from room to room and did as my cat—Gatto, the Lynx—bid me. Nefru and Thalpia followed me, Thalpia lending a hand when I allowed her, Nefru keeping me close within his sight.

It took Thalpia and me several hours to dig a hole deep enough and wide enough to hold the bronze-bound chest we lowered into it, and then another two hours to fill the hole with stones and earth.

It was dawn when we were satisfied with our handiwork. Nefru was no longer around. My heart sinking, I tiptoed into my bedchamber, and found him asleep on the pillow atop my bed.

He never woke.

* * * *

Bereft of the holy image, reminder of Athené's covenant with Troia, there was no heart left among our fighting men. We lived from day to day, depleting the last of the stores kept in the city as well as the palace.

Refuse accumulated in the city, spewing noxious odors and enticing flies, bugs and vermin. Daily Priam heard from trembling lips how the sacred serpents of the city slid away into swamps and rivers. The python that kept promise of municipal life grew listless. I watched over my own garden snake with special care, but it remained.

Our people turned to Hektôr for comfort. His tomb was besieged by veneration and prayer.

Heavy rain fell for nine days and nights, without ceasing; the rivers Rhesus, Heptaporus, Karesus, Rhodius, Granikus, Aesepus, Skamander and Simois, which flowed from the Ida range, swelled and washed away fields. The united waters of these rivers reached the Achaian camp and swept away its wall, and debris blocked the narrow channels between the reefs and swamps in the shallow bay, so that these were no longer navigable.

* * * *

The pounding of racing feet throughout the city grew to loud shouts. Polites was still shouting when I raced into the market place. The Achaians were sailing away! From the wall, I could indeed see the billowing sails, filled with winds for Tenedos.

For I do not remember how long, I ran up and down all around the walls, with my little son breathlessly trying to keep up with me, scanning the horizon. Then I noticed a black hull, beached, without mast or sail, hauled to the promontory at Sigeion, behind the great tumulus, which hid the shore from view. The ship's bowsprit, shaped like the neck and head of a horse, resembled Odysseus', tempting me to hope that he had perished at sea. From this distance, I could not be sure.

That evening and night went by in waiting for certainty. The impossible seething of hope must be held in check until then. *Ah, Hektôr, beloved husband, are you here, can you tell me if our son and I, dare to hope? What about you, dear Nefru? Can you reach out from beyond, and show me what my eyes cannot see?*

By morning, no ship was in sight from as far away as Tenedos. The camp was demolished, stones broken into rubble, and huts burned, reported Polites. Deiphobos, going out to examine the matter with a few others, reported no sign of trickery either.

We nearly went mad with joy when Polites' reports were verified. Our people jammed the streets and narrow passages. I found myself wobbling, my muscles like pulp around my bones. The weight of freedom, the sudden release of the yoke that had been tight around my neck for so long, was too much. Then I had to laugh. It sure was amusing how freedom seemed to unhinge me!

At evening feasting, minstrel Sesamon sat with his kithara in glory, hands busy at the ivory crossbar adjusting pegs that held the seven strings. His heartfelt chant foretold the great future of Troia, and the heroic vengeance Skamandrios Astyanax, son of Hektôr, would exact of the Achaian chiefs.

"We've had so many false hopes," I said to Thalpia, "I am afraid to believe that they are really gone."

Presently, like morning sickness, the thought rose in my throat: *Hektôr was not here to share this deliverance with us.* All we had ever known together had been war, and the fear of it.

Thalpia was with me by my Goddesses' altar in the courtyard when Skamandrios came pattering, naked and barefoot from his nap, his blond curls bobbing as he hurried. I opened my arms to him. His soft little body was sweeter than ever in my arms.

At dawn, on foot and in what were left for riding, our people flooded onto the plain. Children ran wild, laughing with joy, climbing trees and splashing in the river, seizing handfuls of flowers and grass. It was a berserk carnival; everyone was out of control with happiness and relief. During a quick meal with Priam, Hekabe, and the last of their children, I noticed how much straighter Priam held himself, and Hekabe looked years younger. Priam reminisced about his youth, and of his rebuilding the city after its destruction by Herakles and Telamon. From this wreck, he had managed to build a kingdom surpassing his father's in splendor, and now he would do it one more time. Herakles had come with only six ships, but Agamemnon had not been able to conquer us with his one-thousand.

Minstrel Sesamon was called to bring his kithara. He sat in glory near the hearth, hands at the ivory horns of the instrument, adjusting the tuning pegs along the crossbar. Then all seven strings throbbed magically to echo deeply in the shell sound box as he chanted his recasting of Priam's epic. He ended his song on a prophetic note: The young hero Skamander would lift Troia to even greater glory, extending his realm over Achaia in retribution.

Deiphobos and Helen sat nearby; he, proud and victorious, she reserved as ever, eyes gleaming darkly.

Later, Priam mounted his chariot and Idaios drove, riding out to the clattering of hooves and banging of wheels over the Palace's courtyard doorstep.

I lifted Skamandrios into one of the women's wagons and climbed in with Hekabe and her daughters Laodike, Kreusa and Kassandra. My son screamed with delight as the wagon jarred its way through the Palace gate and down the street. We had a slow ride among the crowds of walking and running citizens drunk with relief of freedom.

To go beyond the walls and *not fear death!*

The three-mile ride to the abandoned campsite was a continuously festive parade. Citizens flooded out over the plain, boiling along in movement. Someone began a song of thanksgiving to the gods of sea and air. Soon the roar of it was pierced by the jangle of sistra and shriek of flutes, mounted like a great paean to the clear sky above.

Through it all Kassandra sat like a statue, shaken only in unison with the wagon. Her eyes were fixed and staring toward the wide sandy flats curving inland at the river's mouth. Scattered stones, broken-down walls, charred chunks of wood and cloth were what was left of the enemy. In departing, they had broken down again the stones they had torn from ancient Dardania.

The crowd divided as many moved to the flat-curving bay where the river flowed into the Strait, moving in faster current westward. For the first time in so many years, the people saw their own northern coast. The procession winded around ancient tumuli that hid the sea. Only masts at Sigeion had ever been seen from the city; and now those masts were gone!

Toward the left beyond Akhilles' tumulus near the Sigeian Mound, I noticed a dark mass, big and high like a ship. A howl went up as others saw it too, and then we noticed Priam's chariot start toward it. Even from some distance, I saw that it resembled a building on stilts, shaped like a boat. The sun shone on it obliquely, glinting against red and yellow colorings.

Priest Laokoon, son of Priam, raced his chariot ahead to examine it. As we all followed, I saw that its figurehead was a cedar tree with branches lopped to represent a horse's head. At the other end hung a tail of galingale. As the crowd surrounded it, Skamandrios ran to it with other children. I stared up at the monster. There was something fearful about its size and crude shape; yet it was like a ship caught in air at the crest of a tidal wave. Now I saw that the four supports represented legs, tapering down into blocks for hooves. It rested on a raft-like floor as if meant to be floated. Had the Achaians been unable to tow it behind their ships? Then I saw wheels along each side; ten chariots had been dismantled to provide for them.

Laokoon's voice sent shudders down my spine, "There are holy symbols painted and carved here, but this is no true offering to our Goddess, or to Poseidon."

"It is sacred to Athené," Antenor spoke up, stepping onto the platform with Theano. "We must accept such a fine gift."

"Achaians do not honor horses in the same way as we," Laokoon warned. "Remember how Akhilles ridiculed our sacrificial horses! Perhaps they will return for it. Or is it left to insult our sacred things?" He faced Priam. "This is no more to be trusted than are the Achaians; they do not make such gifts to their gods. But if we offer it by fire, all gods will be served."

Antenor countered, "No! We must accept this offering of peace."

"Destroy it!" Laokoon and Kassandra roared together.

Beware the Oath of the Horse, whispered a voice in me, and I wondered whence the connection to this wooden monster.

Two soldiers dragged a tattered stranger before Priam, "We found this man hiding on the riverbank," one said. "He's probably a spy."

The small dark man wrenched loose and fell, clasping Priam's knees in supplication, "My lord, I am Sinon." He cringed lower. "Agamemnon had meant to sacrifice me for a safe voyage, like he did Iphigenia at Aulis," he whined. "But I escaped, just as she did."

"Iphigenia escaped?" many voices asked, incredulous.

The man cringed lower, touching Priam's knees again. "Our shipwright made this in honor of Athené-Hippias. Agamemnon wanted to pacify her anger, because she is patroness of your city." Sinon shifted reverent eyes up to the image.

Priam summoned his counselors, who argued the gift must be properly set up in the precinct of Athena on the Pergama.

"Father, we cannot possibly get it into the city," Deiphobos said.

"My lord, King Odysseus ordered us to leave this by the sea in memorial to those of us who died here," Sinon said quickly.

Priam was determined. "Fine, then. We will take this trophy into our city; it will not stand here memorializing our enemies. And, Sinon, you will be my guest."

Laokoon came to stand between his father and the wooden horse. "Never trust an Achaian bearing gifts! This man is a spy. I will sacrifice this monstrosity, right here, by burning it, to Poseidon."

Kassandra, screaming all the way, ran along the sands. Flailing her arms and pointing from the image to the city, "There are men hidden in this who will kill us in the night!"

Laokoon seized a spear and cast it upward. Deep echoes and hollow groans sounded from the belly of the structure.

"That proves nothing," Priam decided. "Any ship has a hollow sound until loaded with cargo."

"Burn it! *Burn it!"* Kassandra cried hoarsely. "I see a row of air holes along the sides!"

"That is only pitch," Antenor dismissed.

I glanced at Helen and saw comprehension flare in her eyes.

Then I squinted up at the body of the thing and indeed noticed small round holes. I turned to Hekabe and pointed.

The Queen glanced up, and immediately seized her husband's arm. "Priam, we'd best dedicate it here and leave it."

Doubt rippled among the throng.

Priam laughed, moving away from his wife. "They must think we are fools. Fine, I shall listen to you and not take it in. It can guard us beside that part of the Lower City wall near the springs. We can build a bridge across for the priests."

I could see, even from here, the wild fig tree waving its branches in the wind, as if summoning death. Hektôr had died there, and now was this Achaian monstrosity to be placed on that very spot?

Deiphobos called his men to order, running to clear a space for the image near that weak spot below the tree. Others lined up, bringing cables of thong that they attached to the platform. The crowd was cheering and throwing flowers onto the platform. Throughout the long afternoon men pulled in turns, and the wooden horse slowly creaked across the endless-seeming distance.

Kassandra ran along tirelessly screaming doom and warnings. Marching with Hekabe, I shuddered with dread as the sky turned black and the air chilled. A strange warm breeze wafted across my face and after it a bellow from underground as of many bulls.

Signals of an earthquake! Poseidon was angered.

The procession stopped as the earth shook suddenly and violently. The high bulk of the offering seemed for an instant to gallop against the sky, and the tremors ended. I glanced shoreward where high waves were rolling. Laokoon was there, waiting while his sons brought a bull calf to sacrifice and appease Poseidon. Then there was a grinding roar from the sea, and waves lashed high. The earth trembled and I felt dizzy. The boys let the calf go, and ran to their father as the waves rolled inward again. Amidst a huge roller, something enormous and black flipped and slithered, descending from the crest of a horse-maned wave. The water boomed and receded. I caught an ugly gleam of flat-ended teeth, of a wide flat head and snakelike body. The strange thing crushed down over Laokoon and his sons, and then receded with the water. The sands glimmered, bare of man and boys.

A more violent tremor broke into the shock of the crowd. The tower at the ramp collapsed into rabble, tearing away the gates. The sarcophagus of Laomedon had fallen! Leaving unprotected the Skaian Gate that early men from Thrakia had built and named for themselves! The block containing the sarcophagus had split open, and I heard frightened calls saying that only dust was found within.

Shuddering, I looked back to the shore as others stared also. Their howling confirmed what I had seen earlier. There had really been a monster from the sea! Had it been Drako? That legendary sea monster to which Andromeda and Hesione had been offered as sacrifice?

"Divine judgment was passed against Laokoon!" cried the people.

Along the sands oozed out to sea a slick path of blood and slime, glistening in the late sunlight. Sprays sputtered along the shore as if beaten up by a tantrum of Poseidon the Earth Shaker's fists. And his devoted priest Laokoon's crimson blood crushed out to sea with that of his two sons'.

Another earth-shock rocked the spectators.

I felt the wagon lean against the ramp as I saw rubble slide down on either side of the wrecked gate.

The crowd roared, accepting Poseidon's will. Clearly, he was opening the city for that Achaian offering! Anyone who opposed him now would suffer Laokoon's fate. Men rushed to clear fallen stones before the great horse, and it was agonizingly drawn up into the city. Rubble was sliding everywhere as the tremors continued, breaking the walls of countless houses.

I felt faint, and pulled Skamandrios protectively into my arms.

Surely, it was not a Trojan god who had passed this judgment!

Chapter 23

"The whole complex associated with Troy, the Trojan War, and the Trojan Horse belongs to the oldest uninterrupted memories and effective components of European culture. The Trojan War in particular has become the symbol of war *per se* in art and literature – from Homer, Aeschylus and Euripides, through Chaucer, Shakespeare and Giraudoux. The imaginative reality this war produced has long bypassed the question of its historical reality. Yet the fascination emanating from the 'giant walls' of the citadel's ruin on the spur of Hissarlik ... still grips the visitor today." Joachim Latacz, *Berytus Archaeological Studies,* American Univ. of Beirut, 1986.

The earth settled as the wooden horse was painfully drawn up beside the temple of Athené. Kassandra stood rigid, staring in horror—at nothing. In the Agora full of fallen statues of gods and other debris, women were rushing about, bringing armloads of flowers and fine cloths to adorn the image. The gate was shut as best as possible, but there was no thought of repair. Few puffs of air and it would collapse.

Priam took his place before the altar in Poseidon's temple and made ready to light the sacrifice. His sons Pammon and Antiphonos brought in a playful colt.

When it was properly harnessed and crowned in woolen threads, I joined the festive procession into the temple. However, once on the altar with its throat slit, the sacrifice did not burn. The sacred coals and twigs smoked damply, but there was no spark.

A groaning of rocks rumbled up from beneath the floor, and two black snakes slithered wetly in, over the threshold. Tremors shook the entire hill of Ancient Ate, perhaps belatedly voicing offense at that she had been burdened by foreign gods, opening a fissure on the temple floor. I was dizzy again, yet dimly saw the twin snakes disappear into the crevice that snagged across the pavement stones. It closed over them, and wide cracks cobwebbed the floor, widening as if alive. Smoke rose from the pavement, but no fire from the altar. The slain colt lay in terrible quietness.

"No gods accepts this offering!" Kassandra declared, "Old Ate refuses Achaian bribery. Burn the wooden horse right now, and she will accept that."

Yet even as she spoke, the temples of Athené and Poseidon bloomed out in flowers from the eager hands of peace-thirsty wives, mothers and daughters.

The King and people of Troia ignored Kassandra and her prophecy, as ordained by Apollo long ago, once again.

Amidst boughs and garlands attached everywhere, Priam ordered the teeming Agora decked with tables and loaded with food for such a public feast as the city had never before seen. "There is no need to conserve provisions anymore," he announced, "in the morning everyone will be free to go out and gather fruits and grains, and to hunt beasts in our own mountains. So, tonight, no one shall go hungry!"

This was also time of the Summer Solstice, a time of celebration at any year, but sadly neglected of late. Priam's Palace and those of his ruling nobles were opened to any who cared to enter so that a constant stream of noisy, laughing people crowded in and out through the wide-tilted doors on their pivots.

I found a bronze bucket, filled it with linen-wrapped slabs of roast meats and cheese, and sent Thalpia home with Skamandrios. For the longest time Thalpia and I had been subsisting on bread and figs and she deserved some solid food.

Legendary Troia was a new city that evening as lights in windows striped the streets. Smoky orange torches were carried up the slope of the city like a trail of fallen stars, while above it all the dark sky covered the city like freshly dyed fleece.

Sinon the Achaian sat in Priam's Hall that night, eating well but drinking little. The sounds of flutes and lyres, the singing of joyous songs, echoed in through the doorway.

At once screams tore through the wine-fumed air. Kassandra raced in, wild-eyed. "Fools, blind Trojans! Doom and destruction! Ruin lies in that horse!"

She rushed to the wall where she tore down a broad-bladed Thrakian sword from among the weapons kept there. "There'll be no more loving after tonight! All the serpents have left our city."

"You're insane!" Antenor howled at her with raised fists, and she ran out into the Agora again.

The hall emptied through Priam's courtyard to see the wooden horse where it gloomed up into the black sky. Kassandra dropped her sword and snatched a torch from someone, and flung it up. It struck the belly and dropped to the platform where feet stomped out its flame. She retrieved the sword and swung it against a great hoof. A mob of women grabbed her, punching her, tearing her hair.

Polites rushed and dragged her back into safety.

With renewed vigor, the mob went on feasting and making love.

Skamandrios was asleep by the time I crawled in beside him, still wearing my tunic. But I was unable to relax in the hot, salty air, and became more wide-awake. At last, I left the bed, threw on a robe, slipped into sandals, and went out to the courtyard. Standing by the altar of my goddesses, I bent and patted the earth around the rosebush that covered Nefru in the ground.

From the shadows, the sound of distant voices sibilated. Then an urge took over my feet and I left the courtyard, slowly walking down to the Agora. That monstrous image, filling most of the square, towered like some grotesque ship atop a tremendous, frozen wave.

Then I saw them. Phosphorescent in their white clothing, Helen and Deiphobos were standing by the wooden horse.

Deiphobos was furious, "There are men in it, Helen! Do as I say!" He hauled her to the platform.

I crept after them, keeping close to the wall.

He demanded, "You will call Meneláos."

"No!" She tried to knee his groin but he slipped behind her.

"You will! You can speak in voices, you are good at it, and I've heard you do it for Alexis." He gave her a violent shake. "Call out to Pyrrhos in his mother's voice."

She pushed him and Deiphobos reeled, stumbling against a huge leg. He leaned against it, bent, and was thoroughly sick.

Sinon the Achaian emerged from behind the platform. "Go sleep it off, friend. This is a hard watch for you. I'll take your place."

Pale of face, purple shadows beneath his eyes, Deiphobos turned shakily and lumbered back to his house. Helen moved toward Sinon.

I sped back to find Thalpia.

She was already dressed, standing at her window. She turned, "I saw lights at sea."

I stared out. A gleam shimmered, brighter than the moon on water. Signal fire? Other flames began to appear. "Kassandra was right," I said, "Priam has to be told!"

First, take your old dagger and strap it beneath your cape, my friend. While you are at it, take with you Dea Madre, too.

"Nefru!"

I whirled around, searching wildly for him.

"But my lady…you know he is no longer with us…."

"I *heard* him, Thalpia! He spoke to me!"

She sighed. "What did he say?"

I did not reply, simply ran around until I gathered the things loyal Nefru—his shade—told me to gather.

Then I ran out again, Hektôr's cartouche ring thumping at my breasts, for I never took it off where it hung on the same chain as my opal. I started back as Helen ran past me, meeting a burly Achaian. Beyond them, I saw that a bonfire roared in the Agora.

"Let us leave here at once!" Helen screamed as Meneláos drew his sword, glaring at her.

My mouth fell open. Meneláos! Here, inside Troia!

Meneláos swung his sword toward her and she dropped to grab his knees, screaming, "I said let us leave here at once!"

He did not sheathe his sword, staring at her. "I did not hold the fleet beyond Tenedos to follow another whim of yours," he sneered. "Death will be your reward."

"O Meneláos! Forget Troia, let us go. Alexis is dead! What else is left here in this doomed city, to avenge yourself upon? You are not greedy like Agamemnon; you need not bloody your hands any further. When Odysseus came to steal that figure of Athené, it was I who persuaded Theano to reveal where she kept it." She turned frantic. "We have to escape *now!* Where are your ships, your men?"

"My ships have already landed. As for my men, Sinon is showing them the way. He lit the signal-fire as agreed. They are already torching the shacks inside the walls, below." He held her with his free arm and thrust against her. "Where is this fool Deiphobos?"

"Sleeping. I had made him drink unwatered wine laced with poppy juice; he won't be waking up any more." Her sandals slithered along, followed by his stamping tread. "Forget him, Meneláos, let's leave! I don't want you to have Troia's blood on your hands!"

"No! Not before I cut open his belly and spill out his bowels! As long as he lives, he will always try to claim you back."

"But he will not be able to!"

Sounds of scuffling, running, and screams of mortal terror rose up from the Lower City. I gathered speed, raced to the Palace, stumbling as I entered it. I began to climb up its winding stairs, red and yellow lights interspersed with blackness raced across the gaily-frescoed walls, reflections from the outside.

Thalpia, close behind me, was carrying Skamandrios. I grabbed for him and he yelled as Thalpia snatched him up again into her arms.

"Keep him for now, but stay close to me," I gasped, breathless. Reaching blindly toward the wall for support, my hands streaked across what turned out to be Priam's robe.

"Ãndrõmakhê! What's happening?" Hekabe came down beside her husband, a blind stare in her eyes. Around them, lit by torches, half-dressed sons, daughters, and grandchildren straggled from bedrooms onto the gallery.

Kassandra appeared, screaming and flailing her arms. Men dashed in from outside, seizing what arms they could from the stores leaning against fluted columns and hanging on walls.

Priam brushed past me to snatch his long ashwood spear from the wall while his armed sons ran out to the Agora.

Hekabe stopped him at the doorway. "You'll be helpless against those warriors!" she cried.

"I am King, I must lead!" He tried to pass.

Kassandra flung herself at her father, hair flying. "Quick, get into sanctuary! Stay at the altar!"

I crowded around him with the other women. He yielded to our begging but kept his long spear, and went with us.

Skamandrios struggled free from Thalpia's arms and tried to run to his grandfather. I snatched him up.

"But I want to fight like my Papa!" The child howled and kicked. Sounds from outside flooded in, louder and more deadly.

The invaders were at the very courtyard gates!

Brave Koribos, who had long ago joined our warriors in hopes of marrying Kassandra, entered and forced the great Palace door shut behind him and bolted. "Pyrrhos is here," he panted.

Other sounds behind the gate. Akhilles' son Pyrrhos. His infantry throwing firebrands onto the roof. Pounding against the oaken door.

Hekabe cried, "To the altar, our hearth, for sanctuary!"

"To the temples!" Kassandra ordered, "Our hearth means nothing to these beasts!"

She dragged open the bolted door. A hurled firebrand struck and caught above us at the clerestory. We spilled out into the courtyard. A roaring great wave of flaming smoke was belching into the sky. The Pergamene citadel was burning all around us, spewing red and orange cinders. The wooden horse, the gift of the Achaians, was a crackling and charring torch amid the conflagration.

Kassandra ran for the secret passageway to the temples, but it echoed with groans and shrieks of death and the clanging of metal on metal. Defense of the passage broke down with a roar and Aeneas came pounding through and onward to his own house. Behind him panted Antenor's son-in-law Eurydamas. Others poured out; firebrands began falling onto the stables. Horses screamed and men began pulling them out. My Phoenix! I had to find him!

Then I spotted him, he had been freed by some angel—perhaps one of the last of Hektôr's loyal soldiers. He galloped into a side street and I did not call him to a halt. I must consign him to my Goddess; she might help him better than I might, right now.

Other horses emerged; their hooves struck sparks as they clattered out and down the street with flaming manes.

Polites roared into the courtyard as the last of the horses vanished, to collapse at the courtyard altar. Blood poured from his side. Hekabe threw herself down to cradle his head and shoulders in her lap. Priam stood over them helplessly.

In the mouth of the passage before the Queen's eyes, lay prostate two of Priam's sons by his other wives: Antiphonos, and bright-eyed Pammon. Behind me, the loud wailing of Laodike told us the fate of her son Munitos, who had leapt over the dead youths, only to fall at the thrust of a slender sword.

She rushed to her dying son but his slayer grabbed her, stepping aside with her. Brutally he crushed his lips onto hers and she collapsed, he dragged her behind a column, and from her screams, it was clear he began raping her immediately.

I scrambled to the far side of the small altar with Skamandrios and Thalpia, my hand on the dagger beneath my cape. Firebrands fell near us, missing the palace roof. Achaian warriors roared into the yard, swinging their swords right and left.

Then Pyrrhos was there, flames burning reflections on his round shield, the bloody light further enflaming his red-gold hair. He was sweeping toward the altar, where Priam stood with his long spear, shoulders drawn back.

Pyrrhos' howl sounded above the din, "No use, old man, no use!"

Crouching in the shadow of a column, I shielded Skamandrios from sparks snapping like arrows from the roof. "Witness this," and I held the child to face Priam as he lifted his spear toward Pyrrhos. "Your noble grandfather, standing up to arrogance!"

My words faded on the ash-laden air. King Priam's spear clanked on Pyrrhos' shield and skittered to the beaten pebble floor.

"Well placed, old man, but weak like Troia!" Pyrrhos roared his scornful laughter, raising his sword as he leapt forward.

Winding his bronzed hand in the white hair of Priam, Pyrrhos dragged him around the altar twice. Hekabe leaned forward, wailing, striving to catch and protect her husband.

Pyrrhos gave a long, loud war cry. His sword-hand swung, his weapon a jolt of light striking beside my shielding arms.

Polites bled afresh against the whiteness of Hekabe's robe as the warrior withdrew his blade from her son's bowels.

Then Pyrrhos slammed Priam's frail body against the altar. "An offering to Akhilles, Old King," he shouted, kicking Hekabe aside.

Polites' life streaming in pools around his feet, Priam pulled himself to his full height by the altar urns. "So this is Neoptolemos the New Warrior," he spat. "Kill me to your glory, suckling-pig. Send me in death to all my sons you've slaked your father's thirst with." Pointing toward Mount Ida, he roared, "Father Badogios sits there in judgment with your god, Zeus. Let them see this, *your* god and mine!" The thin dry hands fell to his sides. "Now, Pyrrhos, prove you are not fit to wear your father's greaves! A glory-mad warrior he was, but at least he knew how to respect a king."

Pyrrhos' words ground out high above the noise: "Complain to him, you fool, Akhilles is dead," and slashed his sword through Priam's neck.

The white-haired leonine head of the noble King of Troia dropped at Pyrrhos' feet like a supplicant. Spurting blood, staring up at him with wide open, sapphire eyes.

Pyrrhos kicked the head against the altar-stones, then seized it by the beard and dashed it to halves upon the altar. He must have been spooked by Priam's frozen stare, condemning him forever.

His skull split apart like Troia's walls, Priam's blood spattered me, my son, and the prostrate Hekabe.

"Escape! Now!" Thalpia hissed to me. "No sanctuary here."

Hekabe was doubled over her dead son, her husband's headless body beside her. Kassandra and Laothoe were close by.

I held Skamandrios more tightly. Thalpia pulled at me, and at last, I rose and moved away.

The heat of roaring flames forced us back from the outer gate. Screams of captured women and groans of dying men slammed into our ears. The city was one great mass of fire, crashing with falling roofs and fire-belching houses, stables, temples and storehouses.

Kassandra appeared, grasped my hand. "To Athené's shrine!"

Skamandrios clung to my neck as we dashed out, stumbling around heaps of rubbish and contorting bodies. About a dozen Achaian soldiers emerged from Hermes' temple and blocked our progress. Fortunately,

Polydamas and Turkus showed up, engaging them with swords and axes, creating an opening for us to run through. We managed to gain the mouth of the passageway. A Trojan soldier rushed out and was cut down by an Achaian, his life bleeding away in front of my eyes.

We entered the deserted passage, and quickly emerged from its darkness into the temple precinct. Thalpia was at my back.

Hot wind whirled against my face, while below me fires were leaping from house to house. A man fell from the shadows beside me, watering the stones with blood from four hacked stumps.

"The child! Give me the child, Lady!" Thalpia demanded.

I held him more tightly. "Not now, he's last of Troia; I'll guard him until my last breath is drawn."

"To Ate! To Ate!" Kassandra's scream rang ahead of us. She was running, bare slim feet flying like white birds between writhing and leaping flames.

The brazen clash of metal pursued as we raced, with me continuing to shield Skamandrios with my arms. The market place was thick with lurching crowds of women young and aged. Hands tore at me from the paving as smoke urged me on. Then I found myself on the brink of madness. At the very door to Athené's shrine, a round lump of bloody placenta lay quivering by the torn remnants of a baby, lost by a mother who gave birth as she fled her will-be rapists.

I pushed into the shrine, unable to stop screaming. Kassandra had arrived there ahead of us, was now at the altar, but struggling with an Achaian. Her nails were digging against the stone. On the floor was the dead body of Koribos, holding his sword in a death grip.

Hiding beside the entrance, I stared in helpless horror as the man I recognized as Ajax the Lesser of Lokris, tore the clothing from the seeress' body.

"Lady Ate, help me!" Kassandra's cry cut short the laughter of the man. He forced her to the stones and crushed her under him.

Ah, the horror of it! Kassandra, Virgin Priestess of Apollo, a god revered by all Achaians, defiled at Athené's altar!

"Look on this too, my son, and remember," I whispered. But I knew we must get away before Ajax turned on me as well.

A clang of armor at the door and Pyrrhos stood there, legs gold from fire and red with blood. He saw me; there was no escaping his narrowing gaze. Luckily, what was happening in this sanctuary was foremost in his thoughts, and I was able to break into a fast run, passing him with Thalpia close behind.

The outer air was a furnace of flames and smoke. The howling and yelping of dogs, the whinnying of horses mixed in with screams and groans of pain seethed above my head from everywhere. Somehow, I had to make my way out of the city and hide among the tamarisk that fringed the river...

In the streets, Trojan men were wielding knives, women slamming pots or jars over the heads of their ravishers, all to no avail.

The clashing and screaming united in a deafening roar of despair. I forced my way back toward the covered passageway leading from palace to walltop. Maddened citizens around me were salvaging anything they could from burning houses and littered streets, then trying to escape under cover of the lurid glow of the firestorm. I passed one young man with a hatchet splitting open the face of an attacking Achaian, and then he began chopping off arms and legs. Others with knives pursued the enemy, and were in turn attacked and butchered. Bodies lay everywhere, some twisted, others in pools of blood or gobs of entrails and brains. What was left of those who had been hacked to death littered the paving and I had to leap over them in my desperate race. The firestorm blazed with all the fury that oil spilled from storage jars could give. Stinging smoke borne on wind almost blinded me while the stench of burning and death choked me.

We almost fell over another body, face-down in spilled wine, and I ran on, legs pumping, hampered by more bodies draped with a curious dancing grace over objects where they had fallen.

A boy child, with half a leg torn off, crawled screaming across my path and I stopped, looked back for Thalpia to help, then knew none was possible. A woman ran crouching from a burning house and snatched up the child, then raced between two fighting men and was run through by both swords. She stood a long moment, and then slumped to the street. The child dropped, silent.

I clutched my side, heart beating to bursting point. Doubled over with unbearable pain, I was forced to slow down and Thalpia snatched Skamandrios from my slackening arms. I looked up to see a lion's pelt on the door of an untouched house, standing alone amid the rubble. Antenor's! Would we find safety there?

Then shouts of pursuing men drove me on and breath sobbed in my throat when I at last stumbled to a terrified halt on the walltop. Smoke whirled across, sunk down to the far plain. I stared down, aghast at the mob incited to hysteria by the screams of their pursuers. All were trapped. There was no escape.

I took Skamandrios back into my arms and inched along, hoping to gain the Skaian Stairs and slip through the gate with those running counter to the inrushing Achaians. The space around us crowded with women and pursuing soldiers atop the battlement.

Many women leapt from the vast heights, yelling triumph as they fell into the freedom of death.

I looked down again. I was near that demonic fig tree.

"No time! Keep running!" Thalpia yelled hoarsely, trying to push me back into action.

An iron hand seized my wrist and the boastful shout of Pyrrhos rang through the flaming wind.

The eerie twin image of his father, he stood before me. "Hektôr's wife!" he boomed, "The first prize of Troia. I claim you as mine!"

Smoke whirled across the walltop and sank down to the far distance below. The big leaves of the wild fig bent and danced, spelling horror. Thalpia came up behind; I snatched back my child.

"So, this is Hektôr's seed!" Pyrrhos' mouth stretched. "The heir." He reached and I pulled away. Thalpia snatched a fallen knife from the ground and stabbed at him. Laughing, he struck it away and kicked her feet, she collapsed against me, and I lost balance.

He snatched Skamandrios as both of us fell. For endless seconds he stood there, the child dangling between his hands.

Slipping on the bloodied stones, I scrambled to my feet with Thalpia's hands under my shoulders. As I reached for my child, Pyrrhos swung him away from me.

I drew out my dagger from beneath the folds of my cape, raised my arm, "Free him Pyrrhos, or I will strike you down!"

Odysseus appeared from the smoke, streaked with dirt and blood, a frowning, malevolent specter. "Pyrrhos! Never mind the bitch! Throw him off the wall! He is the *heir!* You cannot let him live!"

Pyrrhos seemed to debate Odysseus' urging. Then, "I'm claiming Ãndrõmakhê! Father had told me to; he had demanded her from the onset, as war prize. She is not only a Princess of Troia, but Queen of Kilikia; the boy might prove useful in the future."

Odysseus screamed again, "You fool! Kalkas predicted Hektôr's son would avenge his father! And the soldiers voted to sacrifice him in a bonfire! Throw him off the wall! It will be more merciful! *Now!*"

Skamandrios' blue eyes were enlarged with terror, his blond locks glinted and his arms flailed toward me on the burning air. "Mama!"

"They would *burn him alive?*" Pyrrhos seemed incredulous.

"Yes!"

290

"But he is just a little boy…."

"Mama! Mama!"

My child's desperate cry stabbed me in the heart as Odysseus leapt forward, struck Pyrrhos on the arm with the butt of his sword, Pyrrhos staggered, losing his grip, and Skamandrios was hurled to the field far below, his screams disappearing into nothingness.

Odysseus laughed. "Troia's Astyanax is forever gone!"

"Skamandrios!" I moved to leap behind my son and catch him mid-air, but Pyrrhos pulled me back from the edge by grasping my hair, and I collapsed.

He forced me to rise, slapping my face against shock. He then moved along the wall, gripping my waist. Thalpia's keening followed us. I was a corpse still grasping the useless dagger in one hand as I was dragged by my captor down the Skaian Stairs, and out through the broken Skaian Gate.

I tumbled on the hot stones of the ramp, falling face forward. Screaming winds snatched flaming wood and cloth from collapsing houses above, dropping like oven-stones all about us.

Thalpia bent to cover me with her body, and Pyrrhos snatched at her. "Wise up, woman! Help me get her away, or I shove you both into the flames." His words hissed above the seething heat, barely heard amid howls from tortured people burning within the calcining walls. Behind us, huge flames roiled down the Skaian Stairs, tumbling and rolling with other women falling there, screams of their grasped infants drowned by the pursuing inferno.

I writhed on the pavement, hair in soaked streaks blinding me, soot and grime fouling my ripped garment, holding on to my dagger in a deathgrip. Thalpia tried pulling me to my feet. With one great heave, I broke from her hands and scrambled erect.

I faced Pyrrhos, my dagger and blood-rimmed fingernails like talons reaching for his eyes. "I will not die, Pyrrhos Akhilleides, until I have spilled your blood! Take me, and with me the Fates whose vengeance will tear out the bowels from your murdering body!"

"Your gripe is with Odysseus, not with me," he growled.

Then he kicked Thalpia aside, grasped my hands, wrenching my dagger. I fell against him as he yanked me forward. Half dragging me he hauled me away as the very earth heaved under our feet.

Poseidon the Earthshaker's bulls beneath the earth broke heavy stones to crash behind us, cracking the paved ramp. The hot wind roared, while in my mind I envisioned only the bleeding corpse of Pyrrhos. Goddess! Vengeance and its glory must be mine!

Poseidon's anger tore the earth again. The mob of citizens and warriors broke into a mad race for the shore.

I looked back once, and only once, to see the rock of Pallas Athené, Troia's treacherous Patron Goddess, with all its towers falling red and hot to ashen heaps upon the great Skamandrian Plain.

VOLUME TWO

The Diaspora, Sons, The Pillar

PART IV: The DIASPORA

… and did unfriendly men do thee hurt upon the land …?"
Homer: Odyssey, Book XI Lang & Butcher translation

Chapter 24: Skyros

Dark, tall waves washed the stony edge of the green island of Skyros draped with mists, sloshing back from shore to ship.

I dozed fitfully. I was in a narrow bed in a palace I had climbed a steep hill to on the evening before, high above the foaming sea. Yet I was not there; I was dancing naked, barefoot, in Hades, leaping over circles of flame—circles marking the Dance of the Maze—the Maze of Life.

A tall man's shade...somewhere in the maze, ahead of me. Hektôr? It is hazy, I cannot be sure. O my husband! The last time I had danced the Maze, was with you, and you were so good at it!

Where are you now? I need to find you, you must be here, somewhere, all alone, and doing your own Maze Dance.

As I leapt, whirled, bowed and contorted, flames appeared, roaring down the darkening, crumbling walls of Troia. At once thick, spiky bands of iron clasped my ribs, pressing against my lungs, strangling my breath. Gasping, I watched unquenchable fires consuming everything, flickering over gutted houses and broken towers aglow atop the hill, smoldering silhouettes black against the spreading light of dawn. From mountaintop to mountaintop across the sea, signal-fires began to broadcast victory—and defeat. Along the inward curving bay, myriad campfires embered. On a hillock near ruined Troia, Sesamon plucked out a chant with his lyre, mourning the fallen city.

Now I saw myself being dragged to the Trojan Bay, cluttered dark with black-hulled ships, fire-breathing gryphons with long curved necks topping their prows. Pyrrhos thrusted me into the large tent where Achaian warriors drew lots for captive women. I stood stiffly aside, hands clutching the Dea Madre concealed in a pouch beneath the folds of my cape, inwardly fuming over that Pyrrhos took my dagger away before I could cut him to ribbons. It was this boiling hot anger, this icy fury that kept me up on my feet, my dignity befitting Hektôr's wife and mother of his son.

O, Skamandrios!

A five-year old little boy who terrified the entire Achaian army.

It was not just Kalkas' prophecy of him one day avenging his father's death that had set them upon this small child, but the Cyclopean renown of his sire: Hektôr, Hero of Troia, that fully human, righteous Defender, against whom Akhilles, a demi-god, needed divine trickery to vanquish.

As I stood there, dry-eyed despite my gut-wrenching grief and the swirling, acrid smoke in the air, I swore upon Dea Madre that I would not grovel at any man's feet asking for mercy, neither would I, ever, no matter what torture and humiliation they would subject me to, allow any Achaian to witness my tears.

But despite the psychic and physical wounds knifing me, I was keenly aware of what was happening around me.

Hekabe stood facing me from the other side of the tent, ghostly pale but stoic, swathed from head-to-toe in purple cloth. Though as Queen of Troia, she constituted the greatest war-prize, Odysseus' offer to ransom her was accepted unanimously. Odysseus then came to her, bowed formally, gently held her arm, and together they left. She never looked at me, or perhaps had not recognized me.

Then I heard more.

Deiphobos, rendered helpless from the drugged wine Helen made him drink, was hacked to small pieces by Meneláos, in bed.

Meneláos and Helen had collected her dowry and already set sail for Sparta.

Antenor and Theano were spared by the enemy, their considerable possessions exempted from looting. Their son Helikaon, husband of Laodike, had been wounded tonight, but before being killed by the enemy, recognized by Odysseus and carried off to safety. Alas, Laodike had perished, raped to death by Achaian soldiers in the temple of Athené. Her son Munitos, whom I had seen run through by swords, though gravely injured, had survived, and claimed by his real father, Akamas, son of Theseus.

Among other survivors were King Anchises, Prince Aeneas, and Aeneas' son, Askanios, who had been my Skamandrios' playful friend and possible rival for the Trojan throne. Safe passage from Troia was granted for the three of them.

But Kreusa, wife of Aeneas and sister of Hektôr, had perished.

So had the two other wives of Priam.

With the exception of Helenos, whom they had captured before The Fall, no son of Priam was left alive. My heart leapt as I thought of Polydoros, Hekabe and Priam's youngest, in Thrakia, protected by their son-in-law, King Polymestor. Could it be that he too was killed?

More talk: Agamemnon had decapitated Ajax the Lesser atop Kassandra, midst raping her at Athené's altar. Though despoiled now, as Priestess of Apollo and daughter of Priam and Hekabe, she was indeed a most prestigious prize of war, and he claimed her for himself.

There was no clear word of the fate of the two generals, Polydamas and Turkus. However, some said that Turkus had saved a dozen of his men and many of the swift, strong horses who had been bred by Hektôr in his farm, and was on his way to the deepest parts of Asia. As I listened to them, Turkus' name chimed in my mind, and the assuring thought came to me that some day, his descendants would return to Anatolia with a horde of Kentaur-like horsemen, superseding the Achaians and Hittites.

Then the creeping gold of sunrise put sparks upon the water and yellow into the dark green of trees. Broad fields, their green trampled down long ago, stretched barren in the heat of early summer. Pale clouds piled up and crossed to the distant blue-gray Ida Mountains that were tipped with morning silver. Everywhere Troia's high wind swept along, carrying the moans of women and cries of children.

A boy...with flaxen curls, sobbing, screaming, falling...FALLING!

I tried to leap after him to catch him midair, but someone clad in gold held me back. I began trashing around, choking, weeping.

Painful consciousness slapped me in the face and I found myself back in a bed, on Skyros, outside my door hurrying footsteps slithering. I half wakened as other feet joined, with murmuring; the worry-sounds of trouble. The click of a closing door.

I braced myself against entering the Here and Now, needing to stay in Hades to find my loved ones. I dozed again and the searing heat and flames returned.

The scream of a little boy, then silence.

"I washed him in the river for you," Kiron's disembodied voice.

I fell against Hektôr's tower-shield propped on the pole of an Achaian tent, grasping the strap where the impression of Hektôr's hand still showed. Hektôr's gleaming bronze shield, the engraved horse forever galloping on its front, tipped aside, fell, and when I looked down, I saw what lay at my feet: a gold-embroidered purple cloth, covered with colorful field flowers.

Under it was a mass of flaxy curls and crushed bone where red blood seeped. Skamandrios!

"Calm yourself, he is not dead," Kiron's voice, gentle despite its gravelly sound. "But don't speak of it to anyone!"

I waked gasping and thrashing; hands pressed my shoulders. "Lady Ãndrõmakhê, I'm here," Thalpia said. "I will take care of you."

"What place is this?" I pushed her away, struggling to sit up. Dawn was brightening the sky, gilding the edge of a window. *"Skamandrios! Where is Skamandrios?"*

"Oh, my Lady…"

"Don't look at me like that, Thalpia! *Where is Skamandrios?"*

"You were there, you saw what happened…."

He is not dead…but do not speak of it to anyone.

Had someone—Kiron?—really said that, or…was it just a dream, sent as a cruel joke by the Fates?

Thalpia spoke now with deliberate formality, "Lady Ãndrõmakhê, we are in the palace of Lykomedes, on the island of Skyros."

"That accursed palace from where the noble Theseus was thrown down to his death?"

"That was long ago, Lady. Pyrrhos told me himself you are to be honored as his most valued slave, first in his household until he marries Hermione."

I fell back down. A fresh breeze wafted in. "I, Queen of Kilikia and Princess of Troia, to be honored as a slave."

"You are Queen of Troia, too," Thalpia said quietly.

"Queen of Troia? What about Hekabe?"

Hesitating briefly, she replied, "So you forgot that, too. She is gone to Elysium, by her own dispatch. After Polydoros' body was swept ashore with the tide. You were there, you saw it happen."

Shocked wide awake, I sat up with a cry, *"What?* Polydoros? Who was being watched over by King Polymestor, in Thrakia?"

"Polymestor murdered him to gain favor with the victors."

I let out a long shaky sigh. "Also to claim the treasure Priam had entrusted him with."

"Yes. But before she killed herself, the Queen blinded him."

"O my dear, noble Queen," I sobbed, "I trust your hand was steady when you brought your son's murderer to justice! And I hope Thanatos [1] was mercifully swift-footed when it came to take you."

"That he was," Thalpia replied with a small smile.

Sounds within the palace could no longer be ignored; they were not ordinary ones. "I'm going to find out what happened." Thalpia was dressed in an undyed sack-robe of coarse linen.

The door closed softly behind Thalpia as she left the room.

Shuddering, I looked around, noting the Dea Madre, placed upon an altar-like stand at the footend of my bed.

As my gaze fastened on Her small statue, I recalled last night's events bit by bit, and they took on a brutal clarity.

King Lykomedes had come in torchlight procession to welcome his victorious grandson Pyrrhos Akhilleides at the wharf. Pyrrhos had leapt from the ship, leaving his captives to follow under guard. I had walked uphill, in company of my old friends Briseis, Diomede, and Lanassa, Thalpia following me closely. I was then placed in this room, and was pacing its narrow confines when Thalpia had told me Pyrrhos expected me immediately in the Megaron.

The rectangular throne room had been lit by slender bronze torches blooming with white alabaster oil-bowls. Everything had shimmered before my eyes as light reflected upon gold and silver cups and the electron mixing-bowl. Through the dazzle I had barely distinguished the bulky king in his royal chair of ivory-inlaid ebony, swathed in multi-toned brocades. His white hair hung over his shoulders, held back from his brow by a wreath of gold leaves and amber drops. On either side sat his daughters draped in iridescent silk.

Beyond, I had seen Pyrrhos sitting with a woman, pale of face with unnaturally red cheeks, eyes shadowed by illness. Her blond hair had been in a net of gold threads. His mother, Princess Deidameia?

Thalpia had given me a tiny push forward.

"Now, Mother, here she is." Pyrrhos.

"So *this* is the wife of Hektôr..." Princess Deidameia, wife of the slain Akhilles, had examined me as Hektôr would a prize-breeding mare. "Turn around... slowly."

I had obeyed stiffly, the huge throne room prisming through tears of humiliation.

"Ah," Deidameia had smiled. "What a lady for you! And so tall! Wide though Hektôr's fame, we have also heard praise of this ideal mate for a great warrior. What more can the gods give? You can indeed boast among your friends. But you should free her before marriage, my son."

Pyrrhos had laughed. "Ah, you don't know my other news, you haven't heard. Meneláos promised to send Hermione for my queen, and that will give me claim to Lakedaimon."

299

Claim to Lakedaimon? *O dear Alexis! You so wanted to give it to your father Priam, to show your gratitude to him, he who had exposed you to die, yet rejoiced in that you did not, and took you to his heart.*

"So, the daughter of Helen as wife," Deidameia had spoken, "and the widow of Hektôr as concubine. My son, you have indeed brought home honors with you." Her eyes had moved over my face and body, their burning light showing the fevers of illness. "You must dress her suitably; she is your prize for valor. No one must say that you do not value the relic of your father's bravest enemy. See those smooth arms preserved so whitely from the sun's burn, that curve and fullness in the breasts that have already proven her fertility, and the—turn around Ãndrõmakhê—plumpness of those round buttocks—I said *turn around, Ãndrõmakhê!*"

"How could I not take her for me?" Pyrrhos, laughing. "Who could ignore those curves where Hektôr once slid his hands—"

I had turned and fled, Pyrrhos' voice fading behind me.

"Bring her back!" Deidameia had ordered.

"Enough!" Lykomedes had roared. "Would you have us appear crude before these Trojans?"

I had stopped, grateful to the old king. Then I had noticed the three other women being brought into the Hall.

Pyrrhos had turned to his mother, "This is Lanassa, daughter of Telephos and Astyoche; Telephos was a son of Herakles, and Astyoche daughter of King Laomedon, sister of Priam. Lanassa has a daughter of Andros, Ãndrõmakhê's brother."

Lanassa had stepped forward, pride in her eyes.

He had motioned her to step back. Then, pointing, "And this is Diomede Phorbas from Issa, which she calls Lesbos."

Diomede too had stepped forward and retreated, face blank.

He had motioned to the last captive. "Briseis, from Lyrnessos. Her father was Brises, chief priest to Zeus in Pedasos. She was married to King Mynes of Lyrnessos; my father sacked both cities, but she learned to love and comfort my father. For her sake, he left the battlefield and almost lost the war for Agamemnon."

"Ah." Deidameia had hesitated, her eyes on Briseis' face. Fondling the largest of her rings, one made of solid amber, she had said warmly, "Come here, Briseis."

Briseis had obeyed, kneeling before Deidameia.

Deimadea had removed the ring from her finger. "Tell me: Did you truly love my husband, or merely hate your own?"

"Both are true. I shed bitter tears when Agamemnon took me away from glorious Akhilles, slave though I was. And when he was placed upon his funeral pyre, I tried to join him, but your son held me back by force." Sighing, "And I love and serve your son for his father's sake."

Deidameia's thin face had lit up with a smile, dropping the ring restlessly from one hand to the other. "Indeed!" Her breathing ragged, she had added, "Take this, dear lover of the love of my life. May this ring bring you happiness." Leaning forward, she had taken Briseis' hand and pressed the ring in her palm.

"But I can't accept it!"

"Sure you can. With me, you share consuming love for a godlike man. Keep this, and think kindly of your master's mother. May this ring bring you good fortune with Pyrrhos."

"Mother, no! You may not do this!" Pyrrhos, shouting, was reaching for Briseis to retrieve the ring.

Deidameia, restraining him gently, "I no longer need it, son. My life is over, I am ill, and have nothing more to wish for now that you are safely home again. Briseis is young. I have heard directly from your father of his fondness for her, and her love for him. So be kind to her in memory of your father." She had smiled, her expression one of unconscious benignancy as she motioned the speechless Briseis away.

"But my father loved Polyxena, too," Pyrrhos had said coldly.

"Polyxena?"

"Yes, a younger daughter of Priam. She is not here; I sent her to him in sacrifice upon his tomb."

"Ah, yes. I had heard about it, but did not quite believe it."

"Why? Did you doubt my loyalty to my father?"

"No, not your loyalty. Only that you could be so cruel. You killed a noble young princess, who had been loved by your father, by cutting her throat from ear to ear."

Upon hearing Deidameia's last words about Polyxena's fate, I had collapsed on the floor. The last thing I had heard before being claimed by darkness was Deidameia's softly spoken command to their minstrel, "Sing to me of Akhilles, and sing to me of his sweetness before Odysseus came to make him a Hero."

The echo of the minstrel's chant had followed me through my entrance into Tartaros, below Hades, searching for Hektôr.

Now it was daylight, and I was fully conscious, in a world bereft of my loved ones.

Sounds of wailing and keening seeped in from the walls and door. I left the bed and slipped into my sack-dress. Someone had died—these were the sounds of mourning.

As I opened the door, I almost collided with Thalpia.

"It's Deidameia," she replied to my unspoken question. "She had been ill a long time, my lady."

"But she didn't seem close to death last night...."

"The gods allowed her to live until Pyrrhos's return."

"Too bad, Thalpia, for she seemed kind. Her death might worsen our situation."

Thalpia scrutinized my clothing. "You heard what she had said— you are to wear clothes denoting your rank. Go to the bath now and I will find something suitable. We are not called upon to share Pyrrhos' grief." She pointed down the stairs. "The bath-chamber is under here."

"Meanwhile, Thalpia, inquire discreetly about an old man named Kiron, a native of Krete. Of average height, brown-eyed and white haired, perhaps bald by now, no distinguishing marks other than a pair larger than usual hands. He used to be my teacher, and then fell captive to Akhilles. The last I heard about him, about four years ago, he was teaching Pyrrhos. If so, he must have lived on this island. And let's pray that he still is."

"You cried out his name in your nightmares," Thalpia said.

Tempted to tell her why, I did not. I had seen the purple-covered, inert body of my son, for Pyrrhos had him brought from the rubble he had been tossed into. But there had been no funeral pyre for him, neither had I been allowed to attend his burial. So, even though my eyes beared witness to Skamandrios' death, my heart preferred to cling to hope, however miniscule it was.

The bathing area was at the end of the long corridor, a vaulted, marble chamber with benches built around three walls and a table of cosmetics in one corner. Lanassa was already there, piling bits of charcoal into a firepan under the huge kettle that steamed on its tripod.

"You bathe after me," Lanassa announced, loosening the rope about her waist.

Briseis entered with a clay jar balanced on her head. She emptied it into the blue-glazed terracotta tub, and then went to the cauldron. "Help me with this, Āndrōmakhê," she said, taking one handle.

I seized the other grip in both hands and together we staggered to the tub and dumped the boiling contents into it.

Lanassa released the clasps at her shoulders and dropped her dress about her feet, revealing a figure still holding on to its firm, youthful voluptuousness. Trampling the crumpled linen, she kicked it aside and bent over to test the temperature of the water. "Be sure there is enough here for rinsing," she said over her shoulder.

Briseis went out. I stood silently for a moment.

Lanassa turned to face me. "Pyrrhos prefers me."

"I'm happy to hear that you are Pyrrhos' chosen bedmate, old friend." I sat on the massage-bench to wait. But I shivered as I noticed the shape of the tub—like a sarcophagus.

"Mama—Mama! I'm lost!" A curly red-haired small girl ran in, leaned against the tub, reaching for Lanassa's bare shoulder.

"Leave me alone, Okyone."

"No—Mama, no, don't abandon me to those people!"

Ignoring the child, Lanassa began luxuriantly sponging herself. "Hand me that oil, will you, Āndrōmakhê?"

"Whose child...?" I went to the table and among the clutter there found a small battle of scented unguent.

Lanassa snatched it from my hand. "Oh—your brother's. Can't you see the freckles? Born three months after his death."

"Andros' child! Okyone, come to me." I knelt, coaxing the child.

Okyone stood frozen, staring at me. "Who are you?"

"Your father was my very dear brother. Come." I leaned and drew the slender girl close to my breast.

"She is shy—don't maul her and she'll get used to you." Lanassa said. "I don't have any time left for her. Here, wash my back."

I took the proffered sponge just as Thalpia entered and snatched it from me, "Sit over there, Lady, this is not your work!"

I led Okyone by the hand and sat down, but the girl stood stiffly, staring back at her mother.

Lanassa spoke to her, "You'd just as well get used to that woman, little one, for I have to be with Pyrrhos; he is a more demanding master than his father had been."

Briseis and Diomede came in and emptied jars of cold water into the heating cauldron. Thalpia grasped a big ladle and poured rinsings over Lanassa. Diomede went for more water and Briseis gathered Lanassa's dress and hung it over the rail at the other end of the room.

Lanassa stepped from the tub and Thalpia rubbed her down with a rough cloth. Briseis went out and returned with fresh clothing.

"Briseis," Lanassa spoke imperiously, "pour some of that violet-oil on my breasts, and a bit musk—you know where. I want hyacinth for my feet and a tad of attar of roses on my hair."

Lanassa stretched out on one of the benches while Briseis slowly complied, massaging the various oils.

We used to be close friends, princesses of equal ranking...oh, my Hektôr, the many battles you fought, the broken bones and wounds you suffered, to spare me the life of a slave...

"Are there any others from home, who escaped?" I asked calmly.

"I've not seen any of your family since that horrible day," Lanassa replied fretfully, "all I could think of was how to survive, what with the endless fires and slaughter and raping going on. Akhilles left not one stone standing in Thébé. Or any woman unravished."

"I...was told they were all...gone. But perhaps...one?"

"False hopes are butterflies lacking wings," she said practically.

"Sigeia had told me that you were staying at Polymestor's. How come you ended up in Pyrrhos's hands? Did he betray you, too?"

"No, he did not betray me. After he had conquered Thebe, Akhilles was the one who had left me in Polymestor's care for two years. But then he came and reclaimed me."

"So Polymestor's betrayal of our trust goes back that far?"

"What do you mean *that far?* He never was on the side of Troia! Right from the beginning."

"But Ilione, a daughter of Priam and Hekabe..."

"She had no say in how Polymestor managed his alliances. And because I was property of Akhilles, Pyrrhos claimed me after his father's death. I am glad he did, for now I can look forward to a more secure future."

Rising, she allowed Thalpia to dress her, and then sat down for her hair to be coiffed.

"May I...take care of Okyone?"

"By all means! I thought I had made that clear. She'll be useful for errands. I've waited for the opportunity I have now, and she's not going to endanger my future with Pyrrhos. Just keep her out of my way." Lanassa hastened the fastening of her dress and flounced from the chamber.

Okyone ran crying after her.

I moved to follow but Thalpia reached for my hand. "Let her be. She'll come to you later. Come, your bath is ready now."

I slipped the sack dress from my shoulders, asking, "What are we celebrating? A funeral, or a marriage?"

Thalpia laughed sharply. "Perhaps both! It is a divine blessing that Deidameia is out of her misery; even Pyrrhos knows this. His mother was sick for a long time. When they found her around dawn, her face was drowned in a pool of blood that the merciful gods had drawn from her mouth." She caught my expression, and spoke with a curt voice, "My lady! You have enough grief of your own! Do not shoulder others' as well. So, now, your bath." She held up a tunic of turquoise linen bordered in white embroidery. "This is the best I could get my hands on. It will do until I get around better, and gather up things."

Later, I came out to the assembly hall where the princes were already preparing funeral meats on spits thrust over the firepit. Pyrrhos and Lykomedes were not there. I stopped to lift a small chunk of bread and some herbed bonemarrow paste and went out into the courtyard. Paid mourners were gathering, some beginning their dirges. Beyond the gateway, crowds of citizens came and went or stood and stared, some joining the cries of grief from within the palace.

I escaped through the town and went down to the shore, which was away from where Pyrrhos' ships lay at anchor. Passing through a grove of trees, I found a small but sandy beach where the sea washed up and away in soothing rhythm. I found myself smiling. No one had followed me, and for the time being, I was free.

Sitting on a log within sight of the waves, I ate my rations. Strange how, though all my loved ones were no longer in the flesh, my still earth-bound body demanded sustenance! Stranger yet, was that the Fates had tossed me upon this island, which, in the past, had often crossed my mind as the place where King Lykomedes had hurled noble Theseus to his death, from its sharp cliffs.

I had to sigh. Akhilles' name too was woven into these shores and hills, and it was poignant that on the night before her death, Deidameia had asked the minstrel to sing of his '*sweetness before Odysseus took him to be a hero,*' to be forever known as Sacker of Cities and Slayer of Troia's Champion, Hektôr.

I turned, gazing up at the soaring heights. Grim Thanatos, draped in black, beckoned me from the lofty summit. Excitement coursed through me. I was free for now, and if I could gather my strength and climb up, I could leap down into blissful release from bondage.

But I was dizzy from thirst, and decided to find water to strengthen me before I started the long upward trek. Rising, I went back into the wood where I found a clear stream flowing from a grotto. At the entrance was set up a small votive pillar crested by a crudely cut stone bird. I lifted my arms in homage to the Goddess, then knelt and scooped up miniature goblets of water in my cupped hands.

"Hello," said a small voice into my ear. Startled, I lost balance and plopped down on the damp earth. When I looked up, I saw Okyone staring at me curiously.

"O—hello," I replied, getting to my feet. "Are you alone?"

"Yes. No one plays with me."

I smiled. "Then *I* will." I reached out, but she moved back a step. Remembering Lanassa's advice, I added, "It's all right, sweetheart, I won't bother you." Evidently, the child did not know how to respond to affection, and therefore its display frightened her off.

Okyone stood straight-backed, looking at me with penetrating intensity, then moved toward the beach. "I need help!" she cried, and broke into a run.

I ran after her. We stopped beside a depression in the sand with a soggy mound beside it. Okyone lay down in the hollow.

"Cover me up," she said, and closed her eyes.

"Why?" I stood motionless.

"Because I am dead like the princess! They are going to put her ashes in a box and cover her with a hill. So I am dead, too."

I scolded her through the constrictions that roiled in my throat, "You are *not* dead!"

She kept her eyes closed. "I want to know what it's like. They say there is a field of asphodel to eat in Elysium, and I want some."

"No you don't." I sat down beside Andros' little girl, the daughter he had not lived to see, to love, and gently touched her shoulder. "You are full of life, Okyone."

"Do you have children?" She opened her eyes and sat up, staring at me intently.

I was silenced a moment by pain, then replied slowly, "I used to have one."

"A girl like me?"

"No—a boy. About your age."

"Where is he now?"

"With his noble father." Terrible grief rose in my heart and struck full force. Gasping, I had to turn my back to her and covered my face with my hands.

At once Okyone's small hands patted at my hair, and the young body leaned against my back. I reached around and seized the child; for a moment she responded, then pulled away. My mind chimed with the thought: Perhaps, for this lonely child, my little niece, I ought to stay alive a bit longer, to be of some comfort to her.

"I'll be his sister," Okyone said, "and maybe one day we can go to live with him."

I dried my tearing eyes with the edge of my tunic. Dear Andros' little daughter. "Yes, one day, we shall." I smiled through the tears. Standing up I held out my hand. "Come now—let's get some flowers for a garland."

"Yes, to put on the bier!" Okyone took my hand and skipped along with me.

"No, not for the bier but to wear them to celebrate our meeting. You see, we didn't really know the princess, and they don't want us among the mourners because we cannot truly mourn for her."

We gathered flowers as we went back into the copse. Okyone made a basket with her skirt, and it was soon filled. We returned to the shore where I taught her how to weave the stems together. By noon, we wore our wreaths, and Okyone had built a little house of sand and decorated it with the remaining flowers.

She is so pretty, I thought, *my Skamandrios would have loved running through the fields with her.*

With a happy laugh, Okyone declared, "This is for our welcome when we go visit your little boy and his father! Now let's go back to the palace and eat. I'm hungry, what about you?"

I thought of the succulent meats with an embarrassing longing, and then revulsion of the bier that would be set in the Hall. "No, you go," I replied, "I have to stay here awhile longer." I had had too much of death, and could not force myself to face those who mourned—or made a show of mourning—Deidameia's.

Okyone ran back to the palace on the hill without another word. I stood watching her, and when I was sure she had gone in through the gate, walked back and forth alone the shore. Whenever I looked inland I could see men bringing logs for the funeral pyre, but by late afternoon they had ceased. Would I be able to escape from captivity as easily as I now walked alongshore contemplating my own death, when the pyre was set aflame?

When the sun hung low to guild the sea, I got frantic. I must make a decision about my life. It seemed that his mother's death had caught Pyrrhos off guard, causing him to loosen his grip upon his captives. And I was failing to take advantage of that! Less painful than hurling myself off the cliff, was the option of simply walking into the sea and float out, until I tired and drowned.

Okyone.

No! Okyone was *Okyone,* and not Skamandrios.

And I had seen Skamandrios' broken body, lying inert beneath purple cloth and a pile of field flowers.

Yet…suddenly I felt hope.

Just the tiniest flicker, but hope, nonetheless.

I sat on the sand to rest before starting back to the town and climbing up to the palace. Fortunately, the acropolis was not as steep from this side as from where the ships had anchored last night at Lykomedes' private quay.

As I rose to my feet a few minutes later, I noticed a man in white robes, distinct against the trees, coming toward me. He must have seen me, for he stopped and looked toward me for a long moment.

I held my breath. I had recognized the priestly apron of white fleece, denoting dedication to the sky gods—it was Helenos.

We moved toward each other as if by signal and met at the sandy edge of the forest. His drawn face, marred by a purplish scar from his left eye down to his mouth, seemed lit by the burning of his blue eyes as he seized me, pressing me close to him.

My deep sobbing separated us, but then he leaned my head against the hollow of his shoulder. I felt his own warm tears damp on my cheek, my neck, and his head bent down over mine. Now he was not the self-controlled Priest of Apollo, but a man, demanding love. I was not able to return his passion, but responded to his tenderness. To my soul still captive in this flesh-and-bone frame, Helenos, the boy I had cared for before finding everlasting love with Hektôr, was a haven of sunlight.

When his sobbing lessened I drew back a little, and tried to smile, my eyes misting as I looked at his haggard, contorted face.

"Helenos, oh, dear Helenos," was all I could say.

He stepped back from me, holding my hands tensely in his own. "You—are you—all right?"

"Yes, considering the circumstances." Tears broke out again like tiny fire pins. "I did not know where you were. I thought you were taken by Odysseus."

"Yes he was my captor, but Pyrrhos ransomed me and sent me here." His eyes shadowed and a vein throbbed in his throat. He released my hands. "I was not there to defend you!" Stepping back, he gave me a probing look. "Pyrrhos will have to free me soon; he is obliged to! Priests are not slaves. He must let us marry because your husband was my brother."

I looked away.

Helenos turned and glanced toward the palace hill. "I must go. Pyrrhos summoned me from the Labraunda."

"But you..."

"I serve as he orders." Helenos drew aside his apron and showed me the ceremonial labrys hanging from his belt; it was a double-headed axe made of gold on a green diorite handle. This was to be used in the sacrifice honoring Deidameia.

Helenos strode quickly up the path.

* * * *

It was almost dawn when I went to my window. Stars were melting in the blue-gray sky. I could barely see the wharf where silvering waves crinkled, rushing over rocks and slowly receding. Beyond was Troia, the marital home I would never return to. Already ten days had passed since my arrival on Skyros. Thalpia had found that Kiron had stayed here, teaching Pyrrhos. In fact, Pyrrhos had been fond of him, respecting his skills and counsel. He had taken Kiron along to his campaign on our shores, but kept him under guard lest he escape. During the melee after Troia's fall while everyone was engrossed apportioning the loot and captives, Kiron had vanished. The timing of this fed my hope-against-hope that indeed I had heard his voice reassuring me that Skamandrios was alive, and no one was the wiser of it. If so, Kiron must have found a way to spirit him to safety. But... how, and to where?

Meanwhile Helenos was made Pyrrhos' official seer, and as such was in frequent demand during the mourning period for Deidameia. "Pyrrhos relies on him altogether," Thalpia had told me yesterday.

"Why would he trust an enemy?"

"His advice has always been good. But it's whispered that he told the Achaians the means of conquering us."

"No! He could not have been a traitor."

"Who knows? There is no question that he is held in high esteem by our enemies."

Tossing on a light veil, I crept outside and to the cliff-edge. Here, beyond the palace wall, I stared down, looking for a place away from Pyrrhos' moored ships. Spume-capped rollers gushed over rocky outcroppings, and between them, I saw sheltered beaches. What a different view than what I was accustomed! In Troia, I had sat in the rocking chair made for me by Alexis, embracing Hektôr's tomb with my eyes. And our little son had been with me....

Nimbly I went down the palace hill, carrying in a corner of my veil some bread and cheese left from the night before. Passing through a grove of wind-bent trees, I came out onto a smooth-sanded private enclosure where the sea washed in soothing rhythm. I sat down on a log within sight of the water, and ate my rations.

Then I went back to the grove, where I found the wellspring of a stream. Skyros was a blest island, rich with so many trees and streams. Beside the spring, a long-handled, double-headed ax leaned against a massive oak tree. I started back, fearful of desecrating the Labraunda – Place of the Ax. I lifted my arms in homage to the Bull-god, then knelt and scooped enough water to quench my thirst.

Back on the beach, Skamandrios was running.

Skamandrios?!

I blinked, and the emptiness of the beach affected me like a vicious slap on the face.

I could not move, or breathe.

A pelican landed farther along the beach, a small slim figure leapt forward: Okyone. I had to smile. A red-haired sprite she was, and sweet and lively as my flaxen-haired son had been—no, was *still.*

I paced along the shore feeling the soft arms of my son about my neck, seeing him hurled by those demons into fiery nothingness. Could he have survived the fall?

But I saw him with my own eyes...yet, what did I see, exactly?

A child's body, inert, covered with bloodstained purple cloth, a spill of flaxen curls visible from a corner of the cloth. Pyrrhos had prevented me from looking at his face. I had wept so loud and ceaselessly, violently thrashing against him to free me, that he had struck me several times; the last I remembered was hitting my head against the tentpole and collapsing into darkness. When I came to, Thalpia had told me that I had been unconscious for a full day and night.

Could Skamandrios have been in a coma rather than dead, and Pyrrhos complicit in keeping my son alive? But...why?

True, on the wall, he had resisted Odysseus' urgings to kill him, speaking of his value in the future—a notion quite likely put in his head by Kiron. Thus, it had been Odysseus' slapping hand that had loosened his grasp on my son. But if he did have the foresight to spare the life of a little boy for future gains, why not let me in on the secret?

The only answer I could produce was that if Skamandrios was still alive, it was no thanks to Pyrrhos but to a great feat by my old teacher.

I was spending most days with Okyone, who often left the other children and ran to me as I walked beside the sea. Flowers were always for the taking, and plenty good sand to build villages and grand palaces. All small pleasures I had never allowed Skamandrios to partake in, because of the constant siege! As Okyone and I twisted stems or patted down sand-walls, I would tell the child stories of Thébé, and of her father, Andros. The initial pain of talking about my brother soon eased the pressure of my own brooding.

Pyrrhos was a long time preoccupied with the ritual of his mother's death, whom he seemed to have loved sincerely, and during this time Lanassa took her place in a chair adjoining his, at meals.

Even though at first he ignored her, slowly he began to respond to her attentiveness.

This morning, as every morning for these past ten days, I sat on the sandy beach, played back Kiron's whispers about Skamandrios' having survived the attempt on his life, and waited for my little sprite of a niece to come to my side.

* * * *

"By Olympian Zeus!" Pyrrhos sprang to his feet while the last notes vibrated on minstrel Charops' lyre. "You bring bad news, old man. My father's father, driven from Iolkos by those sons of Akastos! I'll kill them all." Grimly he glared around, nostrils flaring.

"King Peleos is in refuge on the isle of Ikos," the minstrel said quietly, then bent over his lyre and crooned softly to it.

"He's not had enough of war?" Lykomedes spat.

"My song is not ended," the minstrel said, chanting the words into cadence of his narrative. He went on without stopping. He sang of old King Peleos, the king of Phthiotis and Thessaly, lands which Akhilles would have ruled today. He sang of Peleos' current exile at the court of his former friend Molon, King of Ikos.

Pyrrhos remained in his seat, with creased forehead and darkened eyes. He looked much older than his years, and if I had not known the truth, I would have judged him as well over twenty. The resemblance to his father was eerie, and at times such as now, I glimpsed in him the Akhilles I had first met in Thébé.

Charops continued for another hour until his tale was ended. The old man lovingly rewrapped his lyre in its linen coverings and picked up his stool, moving with slow deliberation back to his seat of honor and the well-earned wine awaiting him.

Pyrrhos nodded thanks to him, then to his grandfather, and strode from the room.

Lanassa remained in her chair, leaned toward Briseis on the other side, and said, "Now Pyrrhos will stay here."

"I doubt it. Pyrrhos would not take the coward's way by leaving the enemy to enjoy his gains."

"Then why not return to Troia, where he has already won a war?"

Briseis glanced at me with concern, watching me sit quietly with my wine cup untouched. I was then startled by Diomede's voice close to my ear, "I would prefer him to go back to Issa, and rebuild what his father wrecked at Bresa!"

"Useless talk," Briseis cut in impatiently. "He will go forth to claim his own heritage. He has to. People do not often inherit through their mothers anymore. Just wait and see!"

With a deep grunt King Lykomedes, forever etched in my mind as the murderer of Theseus, heaved his big body from the elevated royal seat. Glancing from one woman to the other as though we were household furnishings, he passed us in slow silence and went after Pyrrhos into the courtyard.

Pyrrhos ordered his ships made ready and the reassembling of Akhilles' Myrmidon troops. He sent for Helenos to make augury for a safe voyage under divine protection.

When Helenos came from the Labraunda, I started down the path with the other women.

"You are not to go about alone, Lady," Thalpia warned.

"I'm only a slave now, it doesn't matter anymore."

"You'd surprised," she clipped, a hard look turning her dark eyes opaque. "You are a female, a beautiful one at that, and I know Pyrrhos is a jealous master. He will not be for sharing you with anyone, now that his mourning has ended."

"He hasn't had me yet!"

"Thank the Dea Madre. So far, she has watched over you, but we are in a foreign place, Lady, their own gods also are powerful."

I bit my lips and resumed walking downward. She followed me closely. I found us a place to stand for the ceremony where I could see Helenos. His head was wreathed in ritual wool threads as he sacrificed a frisky white goat on Poseidon's altar. Its blood ran down a trough; as it flowed into the sea, he poured wine into it. Slitting the belly, he lifted out something and held it up before it dropped in two pieces.

Lowering his arms, he turned to Pyrrhos, "A warning. For three days, Poseidon allows no sailing northwestward."

"Akastos will not hold back his sons for my convenience," Pyrrhos growled. "Thunder in Hades!" He moved forward threateningly, but stopped. "Peleos might be dead even now, and dread Poseidon wants me to sit idle for three days?"

"The gods would protect you from disaster. Pay heed."

"What is this danger you speak of?"

Helenos' eyes turned inward, and when he spoke again, it was in blind trance, as I remembered so well of Kassandra. "We must remain here two days and three nights to avoid death. I see death, destruction, misery—behold, for the Trojan gods control these waters." His voice rose, trumpeting awe through the small group, seeming as if he were reading from invisible tablets. "Only few of my country's enemies will ever return whence they came; none will live in peace! There is an overflowing of warlike strangers into your Achaian lands—they bring along darkness that will last through many life times."

Pyrrhos waited in deadly silence as two of King Lykodemes' sons came forward and removed the sacrifice from the spits for cutting into roasts. Pyrrhos watched them unseeingly, and then whirled back upon Helenos, "How can I trust you, Priest?"

Helenos' stance was unbending. "I only interpret the omens of the gods, no more than that." He took an oval shaped black stone from the leather pouch that always hung from his belt. "I will try one more thing." He held the stone against his forehead. "I hear the seas roaring their anger."

Pyrrhos sneered. "That stone is no shell, you can't hear the sea."

"This is my Stone of Troia; it has its own soul, its own power." He replaced it in his pouch. "It fell from the sky just as did the Palladium, when Ilos took rein of Troia. If you put to sea now, you will never reach Peleos, for you shall be shipwrecked before three days have passed. Ignore the omen if you so choose." Helenos shrugged and strode away toward the Labraunda precinct.

Pyrrhos stared at the ships' masts where the half-furled sails billowed invitingly with a pleasant mistral, as if in defiance of Helenos' warnings. Then he strode to the nearest vessel and spoke to the captain. The man boarded, returning at once with a signal-shield for all men to see, first showing the red side outward, and then the white.

"Continue preparing my ships; seal in the food and wine against spoilage," Pyrrhos ordered as he strode from ship to ship, closely inspecting each.

I walked away, following the rocky shore with Thalpia, looking ahead into the misty distances embracing my loved ones' ashes.

Finding a sea-washed boulder, I sat down with her, forearms on knees, hands dangling. Memories of the sailing from Troia to here, with images I had so valiantly suppressed, began returning. I recalled that first stop at verdant Chersonesos, then the tragic scenes at burnt Kynosema. Now I moaned, hands on my ears; remembering more:

We were on the shore ready to embark for the far horizons, to lead us to enemy lands. A look of horror spread over Kassandra's face, and Hekabe, going toward Odysseus' ship, turned and looked.

The receding tide's slap against the shore was like lips vomiting the pale object lying among shallows. It was a naked male body. Howling like a she-wolf the aged queen lunged into the spray. "My son— Polydoros—my baby!"

Odysseus stepped forward to pluck her from the water; she bit his hand, tearing the flesh. "If Polymestor hadn't killed that boy, we'd have done it for him," he grunted, shaking his bleeding hand. "There must be no seed left of Priam to challenge us ever again."

"You beast! I curse you! You shall be lost forever in the seas!"

Seizing Hekabe by the hair, Odysseus yanked her to her feet. She kicked and clawed at him with inhuman strength, and flung herself back into the water, clinging to her son's dead body.

Polymestor appeared, striding towards us. When he reached the edge of the water, he stood staring at the Queen of Troia, lying in the water embracing her child. Bewildered, he spoke, "He was embalmed and left in a proper cave. Why is he here?"

She rolled away from the corpse, but stayed close and stared up at the Thrakian king.

Odysseus entered the water and plucked her to her feet. "Now you know, old woman! He killed Polydoros for the gold Priam had sent with him for safekeeping."

Queen Hekabe whirled around on her feet, and with eyes dilated to bursting and foam on her lips flung herself at Polymestor. She stabbed and gouged her fingers into his eyes until they hung from bleeding sockets, while he roared from shock and pain.

Odysseus grasped and flung her away from Polymestor, and she ran in widening circles, keening. Faster than Odysseus racing after her, she sped up a near cliff, opened her arms wide and sailed off onto the sharp rocks below.

"Lady Ãndrõmakhê, you are screaming!" Thalpia's voice shocked me back to the present.

Drawn back into the Hear and Now, I was blinded by tears.

"I stopped shedding tears years ago, for they helped nothing," she added gruffly. "But I can't bear to see you suffer as I have suffered."

"Oh, loyal Thalpia! We've come such a long way from home."

* * * *

When the last days of waiting ended, Helenos made another augury. Pyrrhos strode to him afterward. "I've had word that a ten-ship fleet returning from Troia was lost in a great storm; men and booty perished at those currents leaving the Strait." He lifted an arm in salute to Poseidon. "You saved me from destruction. And you, Helenos, you spoke truly. Never yet have you misinterpreted an oracle."

"My truth is from the Immortals."

Pyrrhos turned to face our group. Placing one hand on the shoulder of the seer, his face softened with emotion as he spoke, "I will not forget this, and your other services. One day you will have your freedom, when more urgent tasks are done and my grandfather returns to his rightful kingdom."

"Free Āndrōmakhê is all I ask." Helenos met him eye to eye.

Pyrrhos' face hardened. "You presume! Hektôr's wife is *mine* by right of conquest. You shall never usurp my place in her bed."

"Helenos holds no lascivious thoughts!" I protested, "But as my husband's brother, he has first right to claim me as wife."

Pyrrhos laughed. "Get to your duties, Priest! I swear by the Foam Born Aphrodite: Āndrōmakhê will mother no man's sons but mine."

The fragile cord that kept me bound to life, snapped, and I ran from him toward the sea, stopping on a boulder that overhung a small whirlpool. Both men raced after me and slammed by to struggle against each other at the edge.

"Step back, beast!" I shouted at Pyrrhos, "Hektôr will meet me in the Blessed Land."

The men fought as though I had made no sound, then I heard the splash, but in the dim light, I could not see which one was thrust down into the water. Worry for Helenos made me pause on the edge.

But Pyrrhos seized my arm.

I screamed, "You killed him! He is a Priest of Apollo! Murderer of Priam and Skamandrios, now you have killed Helenos too! Behold! Apollo will strike you down!"

"You shall die too!" He slapped my face with a ringing sound.

Just as my feet swung over nothingness, he caught and dragged me back. As his hands moved roughly over my body on its way below the waist, he pressed to kiss my mouth but I spat out against his lips and beat his massive shoulders with all the strength of my fists.

"You are most desirable in anger," he panted, breath seething from his nostrils. "If I'd cared less for Lanassa I'd have more time for you." He tore at my skirt, pulling it above my hips.

Rage sent my knee against his genitals so that he howled and had to let me go. While he struggled to regain his breath, I raced from the rock down to the water, and stopped as a figure darkened the ripples.

The sounds of dropping water and heavy breathing presented Helenos, climbing up the silvery boulders onto the sand. His hair scaled his neck and skull, gleaming wet in straggled ends over the wet, wrinkled tunic that molded his long, lean body.

Gaining the last rock, Helenos' eyes flashed toward me as he sprang through a receding wave and stopped erect beside me, bringing with him the creature-filled smell of land-washing water. He flung the wetness from his eyes and faced Pyrrhos, grasping in one hand the dripping bag that held his magic-imbued holy stone. His eyes flocked back to me in the dim light and I involuntarily stepped forward.

Pyrrhos regained his bearing and strode between us, his back to me. "Priest! Get on board and stay there."

Rebellion flashed in Helenos' eyes.

"Do as I say," continued Pyrrhos, *"now,* lest I toss Ãndrōmakhê over to my men."

As Helenos turned toward the ships, I raced up the hill faster than I had known was possible.

* * * *

The sky was blending with gold-tipped waves when I joined other women at the wharf. Pyrrhos' pilot ship was in berth, and I watched him lead Lanassa aboard. The old king had just given his blessing to Pyrrhos. The morning sun framed him in a nimbus as the captain greeted them.

For a heart-stopping moment, I admitted Pyrrhos Neoptolemos' beauty: Built like Wargod Ares, yet sun-golden like his father. He was sixteen years old. Overgrown though he was, how could such a boy be the same evil Neoptolemos who had decapitated Priam at his altar, and tossed Skamandrios away like a split wineskin?

"Now you know you must not go about by yourself," Thalpia had whispered after the three of us came from the palace door.

We went out together down to the ships, Trojan captives following after. Okyone ran to me, seizing my hand in both of her small ones. The child was crying loudly; I bent down to comfort her, kissing the heart-shaped, flushed face.

"Mama doesn't love me anymore," she sobbed.

"But I love you," I said soothingly. "You will be my little girl from now on." I smoothed back her damp hair while others walked by.

"Come *on,*" Thalpia hissed urgently. Each holding one of little Okyone's hands, we led her stumblingly down the hill, hiccoughing as she went.

As we boarded the vessel, I heard Pyrrhos' ironic Achaian greeting as he met his captain, "Rejoice!"

Sails cupped the breeze as ship by ship pushed from land, leaving wide-dancing wakes. I kept my back to the island and the beloved, lost land beyond it. Soon the vessels had swung away and the sails fattened on strong winds.

I was compelled to gaze into the horizon where the sky melted into the sea, and an unknown female voice spoke in my mind:

- Troia sleeps, but trust in that her people will rule again. There will be another name, as proud as ours', and in that name, Troia's conquerors will fall!

Holding myself stiffly, I went aft to the tent-cabin assigned to the women. At midmorning, the smooth motion roughened and the wind veered sharply. Sails were shortened, later furled, and oarsmen struggled while progress slowed. The wind was soon a gale and the six-vessel fleet scudded over surging waves. By afternoon, the northerly winds turned easterly, but it was evening before land was sighted. We dropped anchor in a bay between high bluffs.

On dry land, Pyrrhos summoned Helenos, "What of these winds?"

Helenos dipped seawater, and Pyrrhos ordered wine. Mixed in a silver ceremonial bowl, Helenos poured a libation to Poseidon. Dipping a finger into the remaining liquid, he held it to the wind. He raised his arms and face in prayer, "O Lord Poseidon-Hippios, sacred Horse God of Troia! Holy Sea-Mover, look upon me with favor! God Boreas, King of the Air, give us fair sailing!"

The wind whipped about his robe and teased sand-colored strands of hair over his face. Poseidon's answer was long in coming, but at last, he turned to Pyrrhos, and his voice trumpeted on the air, "Be warned! Sail in the direction to Athos."

"That is a longer course," Pyrrhos growled.

"I only know the warning." Helenos emptied the bowl in final libation. "Sail north and you will never see your father's land." He moved away with a brief shrug.

Pyrrhos swore and stalked to confer with his captain.

Diomede came shortly with an order signaled from Pyrrhos. "We remain on board with night, and return to land at dawn. He means to burn the ships."

"I don't understand…why?" Diomede did not reply. I pressed, "What is this place?"

"Pyrasos. [1]"

"Where is Okyone?" I stood up and looked around. Then I saw her under Briseis' watch, playing with the other captive children. Boarding the ship, I went into the women's cabin for a restless night. The last thought in my mind before I closed my eyes, was that I owed a debt of gratitude to Lanassa's skills in bed, for she kept Pyrrhos intrigued and away from me. I slept fitfully until the scent of perfume roused me.

"Smell what I found!" Thalpia exulted. "Come now, I'll freshen you. The men have already landed."

I stepped out and looked down at the water. Early mists swirled so that I could barely see the ripples, and land not at all. I leapt to the gangplank and dropped myself into the water. The chilling coolness revived me and I felt strengthened by the time I climbed out, heavily dripping in my shift. There were shouts of greeting and scrapings from the shore, and dim figures going about along the quay.

Following Thalpia into the cabin-tent where she removed my wet shift, I let her drape a yellow cloth about me and fasten it at the shoulders with enormous crystal-headed straight pins.

"No style!" I grunted, looking down at the flowing linen.

"Better than nothing, Lady; it's all I could find here."

"Where did these come from?" I wondered, fingering the point of one pin that protruded near my left breast. "Some noblewoman of Dardania must have worn these…."

"You'd better have a brooch instead," Thalpia said suspiciously, reaching for the pin.

I drew back. "No. These are friends! If Pyrrhos comes too near—"

"If you give me your word you'd not use them against yourself."

I nodded. Thalpia then secured the pin more firmly in the cloth, and we joined the other women going down to land. I drew my veil close like a wrap as I went silently down to the brown, warm earth, followed by Thalpia carrying our small possessions in a sack.

Okyone raced by laughing with other children, still overseen by Briseis. Helenos passed us from another ship, leading one of Pyrrhos' stallions into the sheltering grove of trees. Briefly, his eyes lingered over me but he said nothing. His pale skin was flushed, his lips and throat tensed as he mastered the big-boned restive animal. *Ah,* I thought with affection, *Hektôr's little brother, doing him justice!*

I then went and stood with the other women waiting for their tent to be removed from deck and set up on land. Some of the ships were ready for the torch, and Pyrrhos tossed the first flame.

I looked behind me, toward the inland mountains, beautiful and formidable, green with craggy peaks sharply serrating the sky. Before me seethed the gulf, fully as large as Andramyttion—my home.

Pain stabbed my eyes.

Diomede whispered softly, "I hear we must go south to Methone."

"Where is Methone?" I asked, not really carrying. Those flames from the burning ships…leaping skyward…

"A town near Iolkos," she replied. "Akastos holds court at Iolkos, and Pyrrhos has an ally king ruling in Methone—one Podarkes, brother of that famous Protesilaos the Achaians praised so much early in the war."

By now, the strange, eerie light of fire flickered crimson and orange against the tent, reflecting darkly as more ships began to burn.

Far across that sea in almost straight line, was deserted Troia. And my husband's tomb and my son's…body, in a grave I knew not where.

- *He is not dead,* Kiron's voice whispered in my ear, *but do not speak of it to anyone.*

- *Not even to Thalpia?*

- *Not even her; it's better so. What she doesn't know, she cannot reveal if put to torture.*

- *Torture! No!*

The flames turned taller, crackling, spewing smoke and cinder. Just as Hektôr's chariot had been burned ceremoniously after he brought me home to Troia to be his wife—as per ritual, to prevent me from returning to my parents' home—so now burned the means of return for me to my husband's home.

I must have revenge, I thought bitterly, *the gods must send justice.*

- *Divine justice exacts its price from all men.*

I sunk my teeth deep into my lips, restraining a gasp. Whence that voice? It belonged to a woman, but not to Kassandra, neither to the Goddess who had spoken to me years ago, in my room, in Thébé.

I want to see them all suffer, I replied silently to the entity, *for I hate them so! Yes, hatred breeds hardness, but I've had my time of softness, when I had the noblest man as husband, and was mother to his loving child.*

- Yes, you had that softness, as Hektôr's wife. Therefore, remember this: He was not vindictive.

- Who are you? I cried out in my mind.

- Once I was Kupra, Goddess of Nature, but am now a Spirit of the Sea. I live—exist—by doctrines that weave a slower but surer comeuppance.

- Kupra? YOU are Kupra?

- That I am, Ãndrõmakhê, once known as Kiara Kupra. Know that you possess great power, but take heed and do not abuse that power.

- WHAT power? My husband and my son are slain, my parents and seven brothers are long gone, and you talk to me of POWER?

- Ãndrõmakhê Kiara Kupra, you do have power; use it to bestow blessings, and never for curses.

I felt sharp prickles running through me, perceived the beach and the men through a red haze, and thought of the opal, in the pouch together with the Dea Madre. Then, for the briefest of moments, I saw Skamandrios, with Kiron, in a vessel rocking on an angry sea.

The world turned dark and I fell in a heap to the ground.

---

[1] Contemporary Piraeus, in Greece.

Chapter 25: Methone

While ships blazed one by one and sank, oarsmen busied themselves with wicker fibers and cutting of wheels from great logs. Two days later the last ship, transparent-red with heat and ash, guttered into the water. A row of two-wheeled wagons was propped for loading. The solid wheels had been hastily smeared with purple berry-stains so that evil spirits could not ride up the rims into the wagon. Pyrrhos' proud stallions were reduced to the ignominy of drayage.

The largest wagon waited for those favored among women, while lesser slavewomen must walk. My tent was collapsed, my companions stowed their sacks and climbed into their wagon. Helenos, with the other men, made sure that everything was in order. Okyone hung to my fingers, not looking for her own mother.

Soon enough I saw Lanassa come laughing with Pyrrhos, to ride in the chariot he had fashioned for himself.

I lifted Okyone into the wagon and climbed in after her. Thalpia and other low-caste slavewomen were given no choice but to walk alongside. Finally, the caravan got under way, rumbling and bumping along the old trail.

I was sleepless, exhausted battling insanity as inarticulate voices continued to roil in my mind, and perceived the journey as a jumble of scattered impressions. Countless mountains and hills, deep dark forests, clear streams and mossy stones mingled in my vision with the beauty of strange flowers of pink and white, lavender and blue—on vine and among grasses around boulders.

We pressed through Tempe to the Peneos River. The breathtaking beauty of this strange country, so different from lands I had known, was crested with white-foaming torrents that frequently broke the road we followed. There were gigantic oaks, immensely dark-foliaged, fat with the rich saps coursing through pulpy stems. We slogged onward, for Pyrrhos allowed minimal time for rest. He demanded food as tribute along the way from the Makedonians, Mygodian, and the Thessalian

321

peoples. Beyond Mt. Ossa were found the Myrmidons of Akhilles, and we entered the territories of Phthiotis and Thessaly.

During the last part of the journey, I was transferred to a different wagon, and sat on piles of goods—from the House of Priam. Vases, pots, and cups rolled as the wagon lurched, clanking against tripods and boxes of jewelry thumping about on the wagon-floor. Cushioned by rolls of linen, wool, and tanned skins, I recognized much that I had known. Sick to my heart, I remembered where each had belonged—the gold, the silver, the bronze and the iron—in my own household as well as that of Priam. My things, and parts of it from my dowry, prepared by Mother's loving hands—no longer my own.

Evening sun slanted across the Malian Gulf when King Podarkes welcomed us to his winter palace at Methone. We were as near Iolkos as Pyrrhos could get without engaging in open battle.

While Pyrrhos went with his host, the women were required to oversee the unloading of goods-wagons in the courtyard. Rooms opening from there were set aside for temporary storage of war treasure. I was assigned wagons bearing booty from Priam's enclave. Tripods, cauldrons, and mixing bowls came off first, followed by chests of clothing and boxes of jewelry. Last came cups and plates of silver and chunks of gold wrapped in rolls of linen and tanned skins, going into deep wicker baskets.

Shock galvanized me when a small gold cup dropped from a bundle. I snatched it up before the slave's hand reached it. It was intact, little winged children still dancing around the sides. I held it to my lips; it was the very cup from which Skamandrios had learned to drink.

Pyrrhos saw me and reached to take it from me, but I grasped it in both hands and silently stared at him. He swayed as if struck by a bolt of lighting from my gaze. He then shrugged, and turned away.

While Pyrrhos conferred with the king, I and the other women were taken to tiny rooms on an upper floor. I was grateful for the privacy after days and nights crowded with others aboard and on land. Thalpia had a room adjoining mine. Lanassa shared a large room with Pyrrhos, leaving Okyone out. Gladly I took her into my own room.

Thalpia entered and sat on the bedding, Okyone cuddling by her.

"Tell me more of your Trojan tales!" the little girl cajoled.

Taking on a somber expression, Thalpia launched a ghostly tale, of how the shades of slain Trojan warriors roared across the plain by night, devouring Achaian dead. The dim light of her oil lamp shadowed them, enlarging the child's awe-filled blue eyes. I began shivering toward the end of it; early winter winds had already iced chinks in the thick-molded rockglass windowpanes.

I rose, went out, and entered the vacant weaving-room. About a dozen looms stood against the walls, strung with cloth in various stages of completion, partially formed patterns wavering in the dim torchlight reflected through the open door. Jars of oil stood beside each, and the floor gleamed slickly from drippings off the lubricated threads. Baskets of wool and linen fiber stood waiting beside stools, distaffs stuck into them like spears.

Stepping gingerly, I went and gazed through the one large window that was left open, looking toward the Aegean Sea. Tears curtained my vision of the Hill of Ancient Ate. Ilos, son of Tros, had conquered it, making it a city greater in fame and power than it had been under Pelops, when he ruled there after escaping from earthquake-ruined Tantalis. Ilos had driven Pelops across the sea to Achaia. But Ancient Ate still hovered over that high rock, waiting, while Badogios-Papas brooded upon his Idaian throne. In my mind's eye, I could envision Troia, desolate, charred into rubble. And still no sign, not even the tiniest, to fan the ember of hope I cradled in my heart for Skamandrios....

A sound at the door startled me. Pyrrhos bounded in, putting a hand on my arm. "Podarkes is ready with his welcome-feast. You are to sit with me. I've ordered Thalpia to prepare your bath." He bent his head and nuzzled my neck, singeing kisses there.

I struggled to push him away, but he was a stone wall against my efforts, his desire a dagger against my groin.

"Proud woman, I need you." His voice was strained and deep.

"You need me?" I laughed a scream and slapped his face.

He stared at me. "I need not beg my own slave. You will obey me, Ãndrõmakhê." His voice strained and deepened.

"I hate you!" I pushed against him but he seized both of my wrists in a brutal grip, twisting them back behind me.

"I've waited a very long time to bed you, Ãndrõmakhê, wife of Hektôr."

"Never! The blood of Priam, of Skamandrios, and of Polyxena, cries for vengeance against you."

"None of that is of any consequence! And you belong to me."

I tried to knee his groin or kick his shins but he pressed until every throb and quiver of him pounded against my flinching body. He stared into my eyes, his own mirroring the dark of Tartaros, the abysmal region beneath Hades, where the wicked like himself, dwelled.

I went limp on purpose. Surprise loosened his grip and I was able to escape.

Later that night, after being inspected by King Podarkes like a prize mare, I sank back in my chair in the banquet room, unable to eat. Helenos was across the room, but did not look at me. Perhaps, after Pyrrhos left, we could escape. The thought helped, and I began to eat.

When the plates were removed and wine poured, Helenos tossed me a furtive look. I smiled at him, and then sensed hostile eyes.

Pyrrhos was watching, an ugly scowl on his face. I sprang up and hurried from the room. Running blindly, I streaked out through the courtyard, encouraged for no one was following. Light from the full moon slanted through trees in bands of silver, darkening the shaded portions of the grove. I sat down on a rough log, sensing the hush around me, and raised my face to the gently rustling leaves.

"Āndrõmakhê."

I turned my head sharply. "Helenos!" I lifted my hands to his shoulders as he sat down beside her, and clung to him as if clinging to one of my brothers. "I must kill him, Helenos!"

"And die a thousand deaths tomorrow, with your shade to forever wander without finding your beloved Hektôr?"

"But how can I submit to him? After Hektôr...?"

"I recall you accepting Memnon's suit," he said quietly, "you were not repulsed then."

"Helenos! Memnon and Pyrrhos cannot be compared! Besides, Memnon had promised that upon our marriage, he would let *me* decide if and when I would join him in his bed."

"Āndrõmakhê, do whatever it takes tonight, to survive."

"But why must he have me? He has Lanassa, Briseis, and Diomede. They care for him, and are always willing. Why are they not enough, why must he defile me?"

"Pyrrhos is young, hot-blooded, but also, he must assert his claim. You know that." His voice sharpened. "We both know there is no escape. You were blessed; you had a gentle husband with whom you shared a happy love. But now you *must* let his memory rest, and do what is needed to stay alive."

His bowing to the Fates heightened my terror. "What will happen to us, old friend?"

He smoothed my short curls, recently shorn again for offerings to my dead. "Pyrrhos is taking me with him to Ikos. He has received credible word that his father Peleos is prisoner, not guest there. We shall go as soon as the ships Podarkes is building for him are ready." He paused. "You and the others are to wait here."

My breath let out in a shaky sigh. "Can you not misread his omens and send him to his doom? If you don't care that he murdered your noble father, how can I forget that he killed Skamandrios?"

"I am a man of God. I live by teachings that work out a slower destiny, but bring retribution just as surely."

O Kupra! These are almost your words!

I leaned against him, liking the thought of retribution no matter how slow in manifesting.

He continued, "I must not abuse the power given me. My future is dark, my dearest, but there is hope for you."

We rose and I turned on him. "I care only that he suffers."

"And I only know that one day, you will be my wife."

He drew me against himself, his touch tender.

I could not help bristling, "You just said that your future is dark! If so, how can you know I will be your wife?"

"I know, as surely as I had known Troia will fall."

"Still you fought bravely," I admitted. "Tell me, when exactly did Pyrrhos send you to here?"

"After they had completed the wooden horse and pretended to sail away. I was put on the ship that *did* sail."

"So you were not there to see *The Fall.*"

"No. However, saw it all happen in my visions. And my parents' death and that you would be brought to Skyros."

"What about Skamandrios? Did you see what happened to him?"

"What is this?" Pyrrhos' voice roared behind us and I pulled away, but Helenos stood firm.

"My lord." His tone was respectful but unyielding.

"I told you, Priest, I warned you, this woman is for *my* bed only!"

I spoke quietly, "Have a care, Pyrrhos. Helenos explained before that as brother of my husband, he has first right to marry me."

Pyrrhos' laugh was icy. "And I too explained before that by the foam-born Aphrodite, you will mother no sons but *mine.*"

I whirled and raced up the hill, through the courtyard, into the deserted great hall, and collapsed onto the bed in my room.

Pyrrhos, son of Akhilles, did not find the time to rape me that night. I thanked Dea Madre for it.

* * * *

King Podarkes' best shipwrights were put to work under Pyrrhos, at the yards. They were in alliance for fear that Akastos' sons would turn southward once they had completed conquest of King Peleos' lands. On the night before embarkation, Podarkes ordered a splendid feast. There was minstrels and talk over wine afterward, but I had eyes only for Helenos, my hoped-for savior from rape and further degradation. Hunched over his wine, his own gaze gleamed concern to me.

When the minstrel's chant ended, Pyrrhos asked what news the man brought from up north.

"Your father's loyal tribesmen are now subject to Akastos' sons," the bard reported.

A growling curse from Pyrrhos, and rumbling words from his host. Then Pyrrhos' restive eyes flicked between Helenos and me.

I fled up the stairs and almost slammed into Lanassa who was standing at the door of Pyrrhos' chambers.

"I am to have Pyrrhos' child," Lanassa called, and went into the room, motioning me to follow her.

I did, moved to offer sympathy.

She continued, "I thought he'd want me for his queen now, but he rejects me!" She mounted the three steps to the bed. "The blood of Herakles and Laomedon flows in my veins, yet he holds to that child of treacherous Helen."

"Lanassa, Pyrrhos wants uncontested lands," I tried to soothe. "You know that with Hermione, he'll gain two kingdoms, not one."

"I've heard the people of Lakedaimon never accepted Meneláos; why would they let the true heiress go to far off Thessaly?"

"Meneláos has two sons by other women; the old ways are ended. Women no longer inherit when there are sons."

"Who cares?" Lanassa moaned. "I'm pregnant and my child *must* inherit the lands of Pyrrhos."

Unable to calm her, I returned to my room, now empty of Okyone and Thalpia, and prepared for bed.

It was pitch dark when I wakened with a start.

Footsteps?

My eyes strained into blackness as heavy breathing approached.

A heavy weight pressed my bed down.

"Pyrrhos! No!"

His hand burned on my flesh and his breath seared my face. He flung himself on top of me, fingers digging into my shoulders. His naked body was sweating and throbbing. His mouth smothered my screams. I kicked furiously, he grunted, slapped my face, hard, as I bit my lips and tongue. His arms twisted about my waist and I thrashed, tearing at his locked fingers. Breath shrieked from my throat and I stifled. Rage mixed with passion in him, panting as he held me, crushing me down. I spat in his face. Ah, if only I had my dagger! Nevertheless, even without it, I would show him that Hektôr's wife was a warrior, too, and the breaking of her would extract a terrible price, scarring and marking him forever. I was not afraid of death, but I would try taking him along down to Hades.

I flung at his face, fingers pressing in his eyes.

He grabbed my wrists and pressed me hard onto the bed. He was forcing his knees between my thighs, but I would not let up, for as strong as he was, and as fired with lust, I was strong too, driven by my love for Hektôr. I managed to wrench downward, out, under, across.

The door—bolted, but key still there. Seizing the great iron twist of rod in both hands, I wrung at it. Pyrrhos against me, his huge, bare body sweaty and throbbing.

"Stop!" I screamed. "You will regret it!"

Pyrrhos roared laughter, his mouth found mine, crushing my lips against my teeth. I opened my mouth, biting down hard. Grunting, loosening his fingers from my forearm, he slapped my face. I managed to get free, and off the bed. Inching along the wall…I knew the window let out over a high steep drop. Death! Release!

"Ãndrõmakhê." His voice a moan and hiss.

I found the corner, held my breath. His bare feet thudded as he groped about in the dark.

Breath piled up in me, pounding against my forehead. I must move, draw in air. A gasp, in spite of danger.

I ducked as he whipped toward me. He caught me leaning away, from the back, twisting his arms around my waist. Thrashing about, I tore at his interlocked fingers around my abdomen. Then I managed to turn and dig my nails into his face. Turning his head aside, he still held me, pressing ever closer. Breath shrieked from my throat, ending in a choking sound. Leaning against the wall, I directed strength into my legs, forced up my knee suddenly, missed, yet lurched forward into his soft underbelly.

His slackening hands gave me the momentum to whirl toward the pale square of window. Something hard cracked against my shin: the bed-dais. I tried to climb, reaching for the bed, pulling myself up by the footpost. Trying to pass the post, cross the bed, get at the window, crawl out, and fall into freedom.

But his hands were on me again. His rage battled his passion. "I will hurt you for this, my lame Queen of Troia and Kilikia!"

Crashed back against the bed, I reached up to choke him; his neck a bunch of ropes in my hands, unyielding, heavy with muscles. I drew up my legs on either side of him, managed to get my feet against his hips. Pushing hard, I employed every bit of my strength. Alas, I could not move him; this move had been a mistake.

Letting go of his neck, I snaked around with my hands. Seizing my wrists, he crushed them together in one fist, flung and pushed me farther onto the bed.

The question roared, "What did you do with Skamandrios?"

"You know very well I've sent him to his father!"

"*Where* did you bury his body?"

"Nowhere."

"Where is Hektôr's shield? Last I saw it, Skamandrios was on it."

"Damn you, Ãndrõmakhê! Both the shield and the boy are sent to where they deserved to go!"

"I swear by the River Styx that Tartaros' three layers of night will claim you! For ever and ever!"

He unleashed a storm of slaps and punches, and still I screamed through his violence, "Like Ixion, the murderer, you will spend eternity roasting, tied up to a wheel of flame! With the vile Odysseus for company!"

"No! *You* will be on that wheel with me!"

Finally, I had no breath left for further screaming. Desperately I tried squirming across the bed as I had done before. My muscles, now useless pains through my bones, cloaked a deathly exhaustion. If only I could twist my legs together, delay him until….

He dropped flat on top me, kissing me with hatred.

I scratched and bit him again and again, drawing blood, he mashed me down by hands on shoulders, kneeling on my kneecaps until I was paralyzed. A long slow convulsion incapacitated me as agony stabbed from groin through abdomen to heart and mind.

I lay as one dead.

* * * *

Late morning sun slanted in when I came around. Insistent sharp pain convulsed me when I rolled over to stare outside. I knew only that Pyrrhos had taken away the last of my right to think of, and feel one, with my Hektôr. To remember him now was worse than the loss of my last shreds of personal dignity. Nevertheless, avenge Hektôr's memory, I must. Now there was a reason to live for me, to kill this murderer and rapist with my own two hands.

I rolled onto my side, flopped back. Pain stabbed repeatedly. I inched over, easing myself carefully. Blood had dried beneath me, stiff and needling on the bed furs. Pulling a blanket over myself, I stared at the window. The window looked out at nothingness, for it was opaque light in my eyes, meaningless light.

The door opened to Thalpia. "My lady."

"Where were you?"

She replied in a hard, brittle tone, "Pyrrhos ordered me to satisfy men who will be leaving with him today." She stepped onto the dais.

"Thalpia! He demanded this from you?" Aghast, I propped myself on one elbow. Thalpia's face was bruised and swollen, and long-lashed black eyes were dilated, staring at the wall behind me.

After a long silence, her gaze fell onto my bed, the torn sheets, and she sighed. "He was terribly rough, my lady, you've shed enough blood for a month's flow, and you are not a green girl."

"I fought hard and was closed against him." I lay down again.

"After your bath you'll feel better. Come along."

When I got out of bed on spindly legs, it seemed that everything inside me would drop to the floor. In the bath, I winced as the water rose about my hips. Thalpia took a sponge and moved to bathe me, but I stayed her hand. Despite her immense self-control, I could read the wretched signs of trauma on her, her clenched jaw, her inner trembling; indeed, she was in as bad a shape as I was.

But even though I had prevented her from washing me, she would not stay still, busying herself with removing the bloody bedclothes, and replacing them with fresh ones.

When I left the tub after a thorough washing, I still felt unclean.

"After you empty the tub, prepare it for yourself," I ordered. "Your color is ashen, and neither are you steady on your feet."

Thalpia wrapped me in soft wool, and I returned to bed. "I'll be back," she said and went out, closing the door carefully behind her.

I pulled the covers over my head, wishing I could smother myself, yet willing myself to live on. If only I could have died, there upon the walls of Troia, together with my son, having known only Hektôr's love within the depths of my body!

At once, all the hitherto suppressed details of Polyxena's death, invaded my mind. Ah, to die like Polyxena! To mingle ashes with those of Hektôr … before now, before Pyrrhos had raped me, I was still as full wife to Hektôr….

I rolled myself into a ball, envisioning the many ways with which I was going to slay Pyrrhos.

Chapter 26: King Peleos

Days and nights passed for me like wisps of smoke, imprisoned as I was within myself. After the physical pain had healed, I was left with revulsion against my body that no bath could cleanse. Within the depths of my being, the violation scarred and flamed.

"You must think of other things, Lady," Thalpia would tell me.

But I could scarcely bear listening to her. Although Thalpia too was marred by rape, she had not known tender love. Was she better or worse for that? If only the Fates had allowed me to die with the fervor of my Hektôr still impressed within my body! Such had been the happiness of Polyxena, her body knowing only the drive of love, given with kisses; Polyxena, the free soul with Akhilles....

I had blocked thought of Polyxena's fate all these months, for it had been too horrible to relive. Yet now I recognized the glory in her death—Polyxena, this most fortunate of all of Priam and Hekabe's daughters. Hektôr's bright-eyed young sister, shiny haired, laughing, safe from the lusts of Ajax the Greater, who had demanded her for prize. While storms had held us captive along the Skamander River, Pyrrhos had stood before those jackal-faced, odious Achaian leaders, and somberly told of his father's wish for Polyxena to join him on the other side. Ajax had objected fervently, challenging Pyrrhos to a duel, for her life. But the seer Kalkas had screamed that storms would never cease with Polyxena alive among them. So Talthybios had been sent to fetch her—the same Achaian herald who had beaten a path to Priam's Palace in years past.

Now, as I relived the scene of her sacrifice, I watched the sun shine golden into her emerald eyes, fading through her body to come out as a lovely light on her smiling lips. "I am a proud Princess of Troia, and I shall die a virgin, because Akhilles had respected my heritage! Better to die as princess, than slave to the lusts of any of you!"

That serene look, like peace after orgasm…so had rested Polyxena, beautiful daughter of noble Priam and Hekabe, against the tomb of her bridegroom.

True enough, at the moment of her passing the winds had ceased and the Achaians had been freed to cross the Strait of Dardanos, to Kynosema.

* * * *

Throughout that long cold winter in Methone, I moved around as a dead body, alive only when I imagined myself standing over Pyrrhos' corpse, bleeding dagger on hand, calling on Hektôr to witness that I had avenged the murder of his father and our son.

Thalpia recovered physically, and I hoped that the extra duties she took upon herself kept her from dwelling on the brutality she had been dealt by Pyrrhos' men. Astutely she learned the ins and outs of the palace, its treasury, vast storerooms, slaves and overseers, gleaning information without anyone being the wiser, and was always on alert for news about Troia, Thébé, and Kiron. When she located some of my looted belongings in storage, she took the smaller items out one by one and we hid them in my chamber.

The northern winds pierced me to the very bone like nothing I had ever felt before. Shivering in the brazier-heated rooms, I was glad to gather of an evening with others about the hearthfire of Podarkes.

I had no comfort in my dreams either, for they were vacant of Hektôr. I used to dream of him wandering in the dark mazes of Hades, unable to see me or hear my entreaties, but now, not even that.

Had my husband at last accepted his own death, and found his way out and into Elysium?

And if it was true that Alexis had once been my Shardanian brother Nurziu, and Nefru, Gatto the Lynx, would I meet Hektôr again in another lifetime?

* * * *

It was early spring when Pyrrhos' ships were sighted on the horizon. I stood on a portico high on the outer palace wall, chill winds sluicing about me, when Thalpia gave me the news. Okyone huddled among my skirts and the length of my veil, having come to cheer me. It was now the child who tried to comfort the woman, bringing games and stories she had learned from other children. Indeed it was Okyone who kept me from losing touch with reality altogether. However, Briseis was in charge of all the captive children so that I no longer saw her every day.

I bent over the rail to better watch King Podarkes lead his retinue down to the shore. They offered sacrifice in honor of Poseidon who had seen them safely back from battle.

With a heavy heart, I went to the bath chamber and lingered long in the tub, not wishing to see the old man whose son had been so dead-set to murder my husband to win his Aristeia.

That night at the victory feast, Pyrrhos sat near the fire, a chunk of meat held in both hands. He looked like a reflection of the bright sun. His loose white doublet just touched bronzed knees, his hair glowed above that youthfully insolent face, square and rugged like a rock, barely softened by the short beard.

Podarkes sat in his throne-chair; the white-haired old man on his right must be Peleos, father of Akhilles. Hatred for him turned to bile rising in my throat. Of Priam's age, Peleos was still an impressive man, haggard-faced though he was. His very tall, robust body and clear blue eyes showed the unmistakable stamp of Erik the Great, the ancestor I suspected he shared with Priam. He wore a heavy robe of tapestry-work in red under a cloak of yellow knitwear. His hair was left free flowing, and his beard was long.

Scanning the premises, I noted that warriors and captive women were seated about the room, eyes shifting toward me when I was made to step forward. Thalpia gently pushed me, whispering, "Don't be reticent, my lady. They will interpret this as fear."

Peleos motioned me to come around the fire-circle.

Pyrrhos leaned to the old man, "Hektôr's widow, and my chief prize in honor of my father." Pride curled his lips. "Āndrõmakhê, bow to King Peleos of Phthiotis and Thessaly, noble father of my father."

"Father of Akhilles, I greet you." Then, unexpectedly, I recognized kindness in his face. Nevertheless, I refused to acknowledge it.

"Hektôr's wife." Peleos' words were deliberate. "My dear lady, your husband was a great adversary, worthy of my son. It would be more in his honor had he fallen by Hektôr in combat, than in ambush by Alexis Paris." He faced Pyrrhos, adding firmly, "Know that Lady Āndrõmakhê is not defeated."

Pyrrhos scowled, motioned me away, and I took a seat at the banquet table, placed close to theirs'. Thalpia set out food for me.

Peleos' next statement sent dread through my soul, "She will be a noble wife for you."

Pyrrhos laughed. "Oh, I have other plans, grandfather. Meneláos promised me Hermione. Through her, I will claim Lakedaimon. As for Ãndrõmakhê, she is already mine."

Lanassa entered, moving with grace, and stood before her master.

Peleos smiled. "Herakles' blood is in her veins. She can give your sons a fine heritage."

"She has Trojan blood as well," Pyrrhos boasted. "Her mother was Astyoche, sister to Priam." His eyes lingered on her swollen abdomen. Dismissed by a casual nod, Lanassa went to sit beside Pyrrhos.

"And who is this?" The old man fixed his eyes on Briseis now, who stood up and moved forward.

"She was my father's favorite; Briseis, Daughter of Brises."

Peleos stared at the large amber ring on her left thumb, given to her by Pyrrhos' mother hours before she took her own life.

Briseis spoke firmly, "I was wife to Mynes, and Queen of Lyrnessos. But I did love your son, Akhilles, with all my heart."

"That ring—he gave it to you?"

"His mother gave it to me."

"A precious token from my father to her when I was born," Pyrrhos explained.

Peleos smiled at Briseis, "And I had given it to Akhilles before he left for Skyros. Briseis, of course, will keep it now."

"I will never part with it," Briseis said, her eyes moist. Leaning forward, she kissed Peleos on the cheek and returned to her chair.

"And this one is...?" Peleos pointed.

"Diomede. A trophy of my father's from Lesbos."

Peleos' thoughts seemed to wander as he stared into his empty cup. With a ragged sigh, "You will rule with me, Pyrrhos. Then it will all go to you for division among your sons. Now that the threat of Troia is over with, we can build Thessaly into the greatest empire of all time. The future is yours! There is dissension in the north between the Makedonians and the Dardanians; they were divided against us in favor of the Trojans, but this disorganization will yield you rich victories." He put a hand on his grandson's, who still held his arm. "When Hermione gives you her mother's land in the south, you will be more powerful than Agamemnon."

"But before that, Akastos will regret taking advantage of the disorganization of your people," Pyrrhos vowed.

Helenos entered the Hall carrying a lyre, an Achaian one belonging to Podarkes' household. He glanced about uncertainly, then went to stand before Pyrrhos.

"A song, Priest!' Pyrrhos demanded. "Today you must be the minstrel; no other can tell the tale I want to hear. You know it best; you were with me, all the time."

"I am no minstrel, my lord."

"Then strum the lyre and *speak* the tale of the expedition to Ikos and the treachery of Molon, and how I freed my grandfather!" Pyrrhos roared laughing. "And Podarkes, my friend, see that your next minstrel learns the tale and sings it throughout these lands."

A stool was brought forth for Helenos and he sat, beginning to strum. He did not chant, but was good at keeping tune; like all priests, he had honed his skill for chanted portions of the Mysteries when he guided initiates. Soon he set a regular beat in rhythmic cadences and spoke in his natural voice, of how, with his best men gone to fight against Troia, Peleos had no warriors left to act for him now that age had weakened his sword arm. When sons of Akastos heard of Akhilles' death, they grasped the opportunity to attack and take his lands. The old king took ship to Skyros, knowing Akhilles' son was there; but winds drove him to harbor at the island of Ikos, where King Molon welcomed him. Then news came of Akastos' sons conquering the northward lands of Peleos. Molon imprisoned his noble guest, pending outcome of the war. Pyrrhos arrived disguised as a Trojan refugee with Helenos, and after many dangerous encounters, found the old man escaped and hiding in a cave along the shore. At this place, Peleos had first met Thétis, the Nereid, mother by him of Akhilles. The old king had gone there hoping to meet her one last time before he took his own life, but now he lived restored to freedom by his heroic grandson.

Finishing, Helenos left his minstrel's seat with lyre propped against it, and stood against the warm hearth wall. He looked keenly at the three chiefs, an opaque gleam in his blue eyes as though he saw things not visible to others. Yearning to talk to him, I dared not.

Sudden sharp voices and rough words veered my attention back to Pyrrhos. Lanassa stood before him leaning forward, reaching to him; then she turned and ran quickly past me, red-rimmed eyes staring, and stumbled up the stairs to her chamber.

Peleos said, "My boy, you needn't be so harsh."

"Well, after all, she is only a slave," Pyrrhos grunted.

"But now to be the mother of your firstborn," the old king chided. "You must acknowledge that."

"I do; with pride. But she is no wife for me."

Not waiting for dismissal, I went up after Lanassa. I found her in her chamber, on the other side of Pyrrhos' from her own.

"Lanassa," I spoke softly in the darkness.

Sobbing came from the bed, and sounds of thrashing. "Go away! Just do not think that you will ever be better off than I am now, Āndrōmakhê. I have heard from a merchant I used to buy goods from in Thrakia that there are plans to restore Troia. Of course, you know that Hektôr's son by Sigeia still lives. *He* is now the heir, for he has the royal name of Skamandrios, and Sigeia has everyone address him by the title Astyanax."

Pyrrhos's derisive voice boomed from the door behind me, "All *this* Astyanax will ever do, is to lord it over a few huts on a hill!"

I stood frozen. The prospect of that Troia might rise again, thrilled me for an instant. But not so for my son! On the other hand,…perhaps… the fact that Sigeia's son was known as Skamandrios Astyanax, might serve as cover for the real one… *if he was alive, that is.*

I whirled, pushed against Pyrrhos and ran out.

* * * *

In the morning, I remained upstairs, refusing an early meal with Pyrrhos when summoned. In the well-lit women's workroom, I warmed my hands at the brazier and went to the loom I had been using. Exchanging greetings with the others, I sat, smoothed oil from a jar onto the lower threads. Lanassa was spinning by the south window and did not answer when spoken. Briseis was rethreading her loom, while Diomede sat at her own loom finishing a pattern. I had just begun a new linen yesterday, having strung it with care and threading the new pattern across. I planned to sew the material after the old fashion, tight waisted, full-skirted, high-collared and décolleté to my diaphragm. Thalpia could make the button loops; she was good at such things. The native styles were easier to fashion, and I had worn similar loose-fitting garments sometimes in Troia, but they had been a necessity of wartime, brought over in King Rhesus' supply ships from Thrakia. Here in the north such a low neckline was impractical, where the long trailing sack-like dresses tied at the waist were warmer. It was already April and yet still cold.

Pausing for a while, I looked around me. Fresh oil jars stood beside each loom, reflected in the polished floor where drippings had pooled and soaked in from flax-threads. Baskets of spun flax wound into balls stood near each stool. Images of times I had worked like this with my mother and later with Hekabe flitted through my mind. Suppressing a sigh, I swallowed hard, took my shuttle and began casting it, standing on a low bench to reach the top edge. I had not been casting long when

King Peleos appeared in the doorway, wearing a blue, woolen shawl. "Come, child, I would talk with you."

I went with him onto the open gallery. Standing beside him at the balustrade, I shivered as I stared at the sheer drop below. Peleos turned to me with kind eyes and held out a length of woolen cloth.

"I'll not take your wrap, Old Father!"

"I'm used to the weather here and you are not."

He tossed the shawl about my shoulders and I could not help but grasp it eagerly, fastening its end to my brooch.

"Thank you," I said sincerely, resting both hands on the cold stone and leaning far over. Brown earth. Remains of last summer's garden mixed with winter debris. Delicate white and yellow flowers among pale shoots of grass and budding twigs of shrubbery.

Peleos too glanced downward then moved back pointedly and leaned lightly against the sidewall. The balcony was only a niche in the smooth façade of the building. He spoke, "Podarkes leaves tomorrow, and we will follow as soon as word comes from him."

"So—we wait to be carted elsewhere." My voice sounded harsher than I had intended.

He gave me a sharp glance. "Must you hate me so, Ãndrõmakhê? There is more cause for friendship than enmity between us."

"I regret any rudeness I might have shown you." My words came out stiffly. "But you are father of my husband's killer, and now am slave to your son's son. It's hard for me to put on a false face."

"Hatred is a poison working more against yourself than to others," he spoke gently. "Akhilles was my son, yet I only knew him as a young child. We sent him for fostering to Kiron at five years old, so that he could live as a warrior with the Kentaur tribesmen, and there he learned much and grew up to splendor feasting on the blood and marrow of lions. At age nine, his mother sent him to Lykodemes to live in protection as a girl. We had known of the planned war against Troia long before Helen left Sparta with Alexis, and Thétis would not have her son die young. Such was his oracle at birth, to die young but immortal in fame, or to live long and die unsung. However, Fate is stronger than a mother's love, and so I have known great pain and regret. I can tell you, Lady Ãndrõmakhê, bitterness is the worst of all poisons. I have at last rid myself of it in the joy of my grandson."

"Should I, then, forget how he snatched my child from my arms, a helpless little boy who could harm no one?" Sobs silenced me.

Peleos spoke firmly but kindly, "Pyrrhos did not kill *a* child, but a *future enemy*, and to prevent a future war. We all know how Herakles had trusted the young Priam! Herakles left him in trust as outpost between our people and the Hittites beyond. He was only a boy then, and not the most promising among Laomedon's sons at that! When Priam rebuilt Troia and forged strong alliances, he, like his father, betrayed a trust. It was debated among our chiefs, Pyrrhos tells me, whether once more to leave a Trojan heir alive; and he, a son of Hektôr! This time it was…a resounding no."

The scream left my throat before I could reconsider, "But Sigeia's son by Hektôr, lives! *He* might avenge his father yet!"

"Yes, but he is of Sigeia, not you. *Your* son was the outpour of not only his body, but also his heart. Sigeia's child will never amount to anything more than a shadow of his sire. I know it is hard for you now. But you are young and will have other children. You must accept what the gods decree: Pyrrhos, me, this land."

"Pyrrhos—the rape—oh Holy Goddess!"

"Pyrrhos is young and spoiled." His kindly voice turned urgent, "You are tempting—even to me, an old man. Consider this: You have had more consideration than most, and the only one he has waited for so long. Do not be foolish, respect his feelings for you. Once set in motion Life weaves a pattern that cannot be changed. You will destroy yourself if you fight the Fates."

"Old Father," I found myself whispering, "you shame me with your empathy. I can perhaps be a daughter to you…."

He turned toward the stairs, and I returned to my loom, his words ringing in my head. Children…sons. Sons of the murderer of my child, bred through my body! Oh, thunder in Hades! How horrible. Yet I knew that one night soon, Pyrrhos would return. To rape me again, to leave me wrecked! How long, how often, must I endure him? My hatred of him would always be there. Other sons. Could I perhaps rebirth Skamandrios? Or perhaps I could rear a son to defy his father, to inherit and rebuild Troia! My body as a vessel, a path to glory through horror, a means to destroying Pyrrhos…it was torture to live on knowing that there would be no sweet flood from Hektôr to cherish within my womb; only acrid residue of Pyrrhos, to expel and expel…to send forth a son from that robbed womb…my son….

At last, the long day ended. When I went up to my chamber after the late meal, Pyrrhos emerged. He stood in his short white linen kilt and brown leather sandals, staring at me intently.

I tried to push him out, but he grasped my arm and hurled me onto the bed. "Ãndrõmakhê, it has been a dreary winter. Don't make me force you again."

"No! Let me go!" I reached for the brooch at my shoulder to stab him with, but he snatched it and threw it away.

The dress slid down to bunch at my waist. He palmed one breast, sending storms of hapless fury through my entire being.

"I will have a son from you."

Darkness fell.

Chapter 26: Antron

Antron was a city within a double-coursed wall. Its center, the citadel, rose high with its own crown of palace and altars and mansions belonging to noble families. An inner wall ringed the citadel, for Antron had risen as a defensive outpost for mountain homesteads. Homes of herdsmen and farmers, of crude stone, clustered both within and without the walls. The stone-paved narrow streets that led from gate to citadel by circuitous ways were not as smooth as those I remembered from Troia or Thébé. The houses of the inner citadel were of stone as well, mostly two-storied, with glass-inlaid upper windows denoting wealth. The palace, in three levels, was cruder in design and workmanship than Priam's, or that of my father.

There was a shallow-roofed tunnel leading from the citadel to the courtyard, with openings in stone ceiling at intervals for light and air. Though designed for safety in time of attack, it was used now as part of the Sacred Way. There had been no unrest in the land for many years—not since the time of Peleos' youth—until Akastos.

Our party entered the main gate and rode along the cobbled street. Podarkes met us at the palace yard, proud victor and king in festive robes of yellow brocade. Weighted with gold spangles and red tassels, he seemed gigantic under the shadow of his hair arranged in horns with loose curls along his forehead. On his arm leaned an aged man beside whom Peleos looked vigorous in comparison.

"Welcome to my city." Podarkes bowed first to Peleos, and then grasped forearms with Pyrrhos. "This is my father, King Iphikles. Father, these are King Peleos and his grandson, Pyrrhos Neoptolemos."

The two old men clasped arms.

Iphikles spoke, "I have heard well of you, Akhilles' son. Men call you Neoptolemos for you are a new kind of warrior replacing the older ones. You will soon end the Phthian War for us."

Pyrrhos knelt for the old man's blessing, and Podarkes did likewise before Peleos.

340

"Noble Iphikles, may Zeus the Protector guard you and your people always," Peleos said.

Iphikles said quietly, "Podarkes rules for me in my old age, replacing my eldest, Protesilaos, who was first to die for our cause at Troia. Now, come."

I followed with the women and children as we were led into the palace. The palace did not impress me. The ground floor consisted of a maze of tiny storerooms with dividing walls supporting the floor above. Stables edged the courtyard, and a broad stairway led to the main hall. There were slots in the corners through which refuse could be thrown or kicked into pits beneath. The top floor was a beehive of small bedrooms surrounding one large area for the women's workroom. Slaves and servants wore crudely fashioned clothing made of sheep or goatskin; fine cloth linen, wool, and smoothly tanned leather outfits were in the domain of the wealthy.

After I quickly bathed and changed in the chamber assigned to me, I gathered along with the other refreshed visitors for prayers and sacrifices of thanks. Ceremonial speeches followed.

I located my chair near Briseis and Diomede. Lanassa, as usual, sat near the royal chairs.

Iphikles, acting as priest, helped spit the roasts, sprinkle them with barley meal, and moved to his seat beside Peleos.

Pyrrhos came and took my hands, urging me stand up. "From now on you sit with me and share my life," he said under his breath. His grip on my arm forced me to a chair beside his, so that he was seated between Lanassa and me. The food soured in my stomach, for I knew that my relative freedom was ended. I feared that I would explode out of my mind with hatred for him.

"Who is this lovely woman?" Iphikles asked, "I have not seen so sweet a face since my wife died."

"Queen Ãndrõmakhê, Hektôr's widow," Pyrrhos replied dryly.

"Ah! She is comforted for the loss of her husband!" The asperity of his tone deepened the insult of his words. "Trojan!" The old man spat this last word and turned away.

I felt myself go red, but Pyrrhos cautioned me with a look and said softly, "Have a care, do not anger our hosts. You will be subject to them after I leave."

When the meal ended, Pyrrhos pushed aside his wine cup signaling I was free to retire.

Thalpia was waiting in my room. "Lady, you are not to sleep here anymore. I've moved your things."

I stepped outside, glancing along the doorways with a sinking heart. Pyrrhos mounted the stairs. Dread dried my throat. He loomed above me, stopped, and stared into my face.

"You share my bed from now on. Lanassa must rest alone. Go in there, or in the name of Zeus, I'll drag you!"

He walked on, passing the room he had indicated for me, and entered the one for Briseis.

Numbly, I shuffled into his large chamber. An enormous bed was built into a corner. There were two pillowed chairs, a dressing table, and a pair of clothes chests; one was my own.

I dropped my clothes, left them on the floor, went up the dais and into bed. Grateful to be alone, I lay half-asleep. Then red light flickered over my eyes. A small torch flared in the heavy hand of Pyrrhos as he bent to look at me. I stirred, turning my head aside. The torch went out with a hiss in a water bowl on the floor, then came the thump and slither of his undressing.

His laughter was harsh. "Sleep on. I need rest for tomorrow." His weight pressed the bed. "I'll not touch you if I can forget how lovely you are in torchlight." He pulled the covers over himself and lay flat. "I will give you time."

He turned on his side away from me, then again onto his back. "Alas, I have something here that won't lie down."

He pulled me against his body.

* * * *

Pyrrhos did not remain idle in Antron. Like his father, he was a man of action and knew exactly what he wanted. He went about the territory calling up recruits, and after some weeks, he was ready to begin an offensive. I saw Pyrrhos only at meals. By night, he came into the room late, and left early. The nights were times of dread for me, but he did the unexpected, only slept beside me.

One morning he summoned a council in the Great Hall. "We march at sunrise tomorrow," he announced, and addressed each of his officers in turn.

When they had departed on various errands, the older men were shocked at such informality.

"War can not be undertaken without better planning than this," Iphikles remonstrated. "You must train these men."

"I have done that," Pyrrhos replied curtly. "It is not necessary to hold the usual lottery; I got enough men. Look at Agamemnon; if he hadn't been so slow, Troia would have fallen years sooner."

Thus, Pyrrhos pushed aside all criticism, though even Peleos shook his head disapprovingly.

On the morning of his departure, I remained in bed. Faint sounds of clicking metal and grumbling talk wafted in through the door and I drowsed, determined to miss the bloody spectacle of the sacrifice. Helenos would be there officiating, and I did not want to see again the pain in his gaze of seeing me as Pyrrhos' favored concubine.

Thalpia had told me that Helenos was studying the Achaian gods and adopting Trojan teachings to these new deities. He came to the palace only for the important ceremonials, for Pyrrhos had assigned him charge of the local shrine of the goddess Kallichora. Was Helenos becoming an Achaian in feeling as well as in practice?

The door clicked and Pyrrhos entered, dressed in short military linen kilt, with brown leather jerkin and boots.

I propped myself on an elbow, greeting him.

"Āndrõmakhê, I have to talk with you before I leave." He sat in one of the chairs and I pulled the covers over myself, leaning against the wall. "Have you no kindly farewell for me?"

I remained silent.

"I must drive Akastos from our land. If I should fail, you would have a master not so kind. Better make haste and pray for my victory." He rose and went to stare out the window. "You drive me mad, Āndrõmakhê, Widow of Hektôr! Thank the gods I haven't turned you over to the soldiers as some less patient man would have done." He faced me, his eyes burning into mine.

"No one would dare, because of who I am."

"Think not? Do not drive me to! You are the one challenge I have left over from Troia, and I shall overcome. I am worn out with that mewling Lanassa; but at least she is giving me a child. I took Briseis because she loved my father and then me, but she almost ate me alive with her passion. All women know what slavery is and how to control their masters, but I took three fools back with me from Troia! Have a big belly ready for me when I return! And pay heed: my father's father is to be obeyed while I am gone."

"He will be a kind master in your absence; I would have no qualms about showing him respect. As for you, Pyrrhos, I will gladly do heavy work; carry water, grind grain, store away beans. Anything. But no more of your bed."

"Hektôr's widow to work like a low-caste slave? Not while I have no wife to order you! You must be wife until I marry, then maidservant to my wife. When Meneláos and Helen return to Sparta from their visit to Egypt, he will send Hermione to marry me. Only then will you have the right to refuse me. But if Hermione bears me no sons, *you* must!"

"All this talk of bearing children…"

"While I am gone you will be subject to Peleos," he repeated in a weary tone. "Will you give me a blessing now? Hektôr's Widow, wish me victory *for your own sake!"*

Abruptly he strode to the door and out, not looking at me again.

Thalpia entered the room, hurried over to me, whispering, "My lady, there's been a sighting of Kiron, the man known as Pyrrhos' teacher, on Krete. He took passage on a ship bound for an unknown destination, together with a lame and blind boy—a dark haired, brown-complexioned boy."

I lurched to a sitting position. *"What* did you say?"

"Wise Kiron together with a dark haired, brown-complexioned boy. A bandanna around his brow to protect his blind eyes."

I stared at her, my heart pounding in its effort to explode out from my breast. "Skamandrios had flaxen curls and blue-green eyes."

"How better to protect his identity than covering his eyes, and dyeing his hair and complexion to a nut-brown? A paste made of henna and kaththa [1] gives a glossy dark shade."

"Oh, Thalpia…." Sobs bubbled in my throat. "I dare not…"

"Dare, my lady, dare! Hope. And after you are dressed and gone downstairs, I shall pour libations to Dea Madre."

Later, as Thalpia fastened the last button on its loop on my bodice, she said firmly, "Go down there and get control of *him."*

"I don't want him for my slave," I laughed sharply as I stepped through the door, pausing at the stairs. "I—can't."

"There is no other way, my lady. Remember that now you have cause to hope."

The steps I went down were not clean and polished with oil, as in Troia, and were closely built between suffocating walls.

Fifty men were assembled in the courtyard, Trojan captives whose freedom was ransomed. Peleos was winding white wool threads about the horns of a bull, which stood tied to a thick post. Pyrrhos, arms high, finished a long prayer for victory.

He took the sacrificial labrys and men bent back the bull's head. The animal gave a last forlorn bellow before the ax whacked deeply into his throat and blood poured down the square stone.

Helenos finished mixing water, honey and cheese in a bowl on a nearby table. He bent to catch the blood and his lanky yellow hair curtained his impassive face with that burn-scar. He wore the forepart of a horsehide tied about his waist by the empty legs.

Podarkes strode forward and sprinkled barley-meal from a basket, scattering it slowly over the altar as he prayed to the Dodonian Zeus. When the barley was thick over the sacrificed animal, men ran forward and unbound the bull. They heaved it onto the altar where Pyrrhos expertly flayed and gutted it with a sacred knife. He cut fat from the thighs while Helenos tasted the entrails for augury, and then wrapped them in double layer of fat. Pyrrhos butchered the meat into large roasts, which the men spitted and carried in for roasting over the fire. Helenos tossed meaty bones to the housedogs. Podarkes removed the hide for tanning and larger bones to be carved into implements. Helenos then lit the altar-fire where he laid the bundle of entrails to sputter and burn slowly, sending sweet smoke up to the divinities.

"All omens are favorable," pronounced Helenos. Having put aside the mixing-ladle, he blessed the watered mixture and each member of the household rinsed his or her hands in the holy liquid. Helenos added more wine, and then held the bowl for each to drink.

Pyrrhos motioned me to him, and then addressed Peleos. "The season is already late and I might have to winter in Pyrasos. If so, I will send Helenos to escort my household to Trikka, where he will train there in medicine."

Abruptly Pyrrhos entered the building, bounded up the stairs, and then paused midway to assist Peleos, putting one arm across the old man's shoulders. The others dispersed to where the meal was already being served. The thought of eating nauseated me, and I withdrew to one side, standing in the shadow of a stable roof.

At last Helenos came toward me as I had hoped, drawing me close. Clasping my hands behind his neck, I clung to him. My throat was tight, parched dry, and my words a sharp whisper, "You are not a warrior. Why do you have to go with him?"

"I must; he requires a seer."

"You were trained for this in the grove at Kallichora?"

"That and more, Ãndrõmakhê. This is only the beginning. I go now as his priest *and* his charioteer."

"You will advise him again? Well or ill?"

"You know I cannot betray my oath. I serve him well and he will be grateful."

"You are no soldier," I repeated.

"I fight if I must, for I'll not die before my appointed hour. I fought as a priest for Troia, and I may fight as priest here. But this time, Ãndrõmakhê, it will be for you."

"You serve the gods—why must you protect an enemy?"

"Why must you bear his children?" His eyes narrowed. "Thalpia has told me of you, my dearest."

I lowered my head. On an impulse, I grasped his hand and kissed it, and he withdrew it quickly. "Be careful, Helenos, my loyal friend. While you live, I believe there is hope for a New Troia."

Helenos held both of my hands. "Ãndrõmakhê, my sister through my brother, and my life-long love. I commend you to Ate-Kallichora, the One Divine Power."

Sobs racked through my body and I could not face him again.

"I must go now," he said firmly.

Pyrrhos's voice startled us, "Come to the chariot with me, my Trojan prize!"

He appeared behind me, and took my hand, forcing me along to the courtyard. Men shouting, horses stamping, and the banging of wheels nearly deafened me as Pyrrhos halted beside his chariot and kissed me on the lips. I did not resist him because my eyes were on Helenos, who leapt and took his place as his master's chariot driver.

Pyrrhos turned from me and squaring his shoulders went to Peleos. They embraced, exchanged a few words, and then Pyrrhos leapt into his chariot. Helenos, in leather body armor over his priestly robes, flipped the reins, and the stallions leapt forward. Podarkes had already taken leave of Iphikles and was lumbering along in his own chariot leading the baggage wagons. With last of the wagons came one of women and from it Diomede called to me, waving. I waved back. So she was chosen as most valuable—or expendable—of his captives.

Soon the women were beyond sight as they followed the line of men down through the citadel and away.

* * * *

When summer sharpened into autumn, I took to my spinning, carding or embroidery, and sat on the portico at the workroom. I was happy to teach Okyone cloth making when she was not required to run errands along with the other captive children. I wanted to teach her cuneiform and pictograms as well, but she rebelled so vehemently that I had to drop the project.

"It's getting cool, Lady, come inside," Thalpia said now.

"You still call me 'Lady'?" I let my work drop to my lap. "I am no more 'lady' now than you are, Thalpia. You owe me nothing anymore."

"Friendship has nothing to do with slave or free," Thalpia snorted. "As your personal servant in Troia, I was better off than all the others. Still I am so. You never demanded more than I was able to give. Before Priam had bought me, I had been trained to serve traders coming to do business with my master. Men arrived from everywhere, teaching me the magics of arousal and satiation. I would be made pregnant on purpose, for many of his clients preferred pregnant women; but also I was used like a heifer, to add to his stable of children for sale. By the time Priam saved me from there, I had birthed eight babies and been allowed to keep none."

Thalpia had never before told me details of the horrors she had had to endure in the past, and my heart ached for her.

It took a while to gather my wits, but then I voiced a concern I had been having, "Thalpia, I'm told it's not unusual here for a queen to loan out her maidservant to visiting dignitaries. Do you think Hermione will do this with me?"

"There'd be many who would want this, if for nothing else than to say they have bedded Hektôr's widow. However, I am sure Pyrrhos would not allow it. But you would be his chief concubine if Hermione bears him no children."

"I hope she'll whelp for him like a dog, and he'll leave me be!"

"Oh, his marriage to her will be a political arrangement. But I am not sure of its repercussions! I recall that Meneláos had first promised her to Orestes, son of Agamemnon and Klytemnestra. Considering that Hermione was raised by Klytemnestra during Helen's ten-year absence, I wager that she loves both her aunt, and her cousin."

"Yes…I remember that now. Strange how I had never thought of it before. Therefore, it is possible that Hermione is not a willing bride. I am not sure what this means for *me,* though."

"Time will tell. Pyrrhos loves you, you know that."

I had to laugh. "He is not capable of feeling love."

"In his own way, he is. I am convinced he would prefer you as wife to Hermione. But the lure of being King of Lakedaimon drives him to covet this union. He is not Priam; he cannot take you as second wife." She laughed. "Achaians defeat themselves by having only one wife among their rulers, though concubines are permitted. We Trojans had a more sensible kingship! How else but through the relatives of his wives in other lands could Priam have so successfully rebuilt the empire, and called in so many allies in his hour of need? How else to survive a blockade for so many years? Through these women!"

I thought of Hektôr, and how he had remained faithful all through our marriage. Never had he strayed from our marriage bed! Yet there had been plenty hints by Priam as well as others, and the pointing of this or that king's daughter. Nevertheless, even after I had told him that I would accept a second wife if he deemed it vital, he had refused it. "I serve Troia with my sword every day, but never shall I sacrifice the heart of my wife!" he had said....

Suppressing a sigh, I blinked back tears, gathered my work and went inside with her. I held my back straight and chin high. I was the wife of noble Hektôr, and would never neglect the dignity in carriage this epitaph deserved.

The welcome aroma of roasting meat drifted up the stairs, and we went down into the great hall. Suddenly very hungry, I went to sit beside Peleos and Iphikles. Before I could give greeting, I felt faint and rested my forehead on both palms.

"Are you ill, my child?" Peleos' voice was kind, and his hand touched my elbow.

"I am all right now, Old Father." I lifted my head even as a wave of nausea raged through me. What if I was pregnant?! Would I be bearing a son for the man who destroyed Hektôr's? For even if by some miracle, Skamandrios was still alive, what life did he have? Blind and lame, far away from his mother, and all those who loved him.

Perhaps I could die in childbirth. A way out from slavery! However, what of the child? A slave's child with no one to protect it, no one to teach Trojan lore, no one to foster vengeance against Achaian masters.

Lanassa came, rolling a table for the old king. I stared with new interest at her big belly. She was in her eight month of pregnancy. Pyrrhos' first child by Lanassa, mother of Andros' daughter, Okyone.

"What is it *now*, Ãndrõmakhê?" Lanassa's voice was high-pitched, grating annoyance as she glared at me.

She must have read my expression. "Nothing you'd understand."

"Oh, you!" Lanassa sniffed. "You might be a glory-prize, but my son will rule Thessaly."

"What if it's a girl child?"

"There'll be others!" Lanassa went to the hearth and heaped a plate for Peleos.

Sighing, the old man snorted, "Women!"

Lanassa returned with his plate and he nodded thanks, patting her hand. Silently I spread my chunk of bread with spicy marrow paste. I was too nauseated to enjoy food, yet was hungry, and perhaps this would satisfy the strange craving I felt.

So it went most nights. Lanassa made herself useful to both old kings; but I could not. Then I noticed Lanassa became frailer, as if all vitality were sucked into her womb.

Her time came during the bitterest cold, her terrible screams echoing throughout the building.

It was the following morning before the aged midwife-priestess carried a loudly crying, red-faced infant to Peleos. The old man accepted the boy on behalf of Pyrrhos, though no name-feast could be held until the child's father was present.

Lanassa remained a semi-invalid for the rest of that winter.

I clasped the opal pendant back around my neck together with Hektôr's cartouche ring, and found myself on the lookout for a small kitten, which might approach me on his own.

* * * *

In early spring, two bards brought tales of how Pyrrhos had taken Pyrasos and was besieging Pharsalos where Akastos was in refuge. I was in the bath when Thalpia told me of the news. Nausea washed through me again. Out of the tub, I waited while Thalpia smoothed oil of roses on my skin. I looked sideways at her. "I dreamed of Troia last night. I was in the Agora, and at my feet a great chasm opened up. I saw that this was a grave filled with bones and broken bodies. These were inhumed after the Pelasgian way, and must be properly cremated. Horrible vapors rose about me as if from a battlefield. Then I saw two separate heaps of ashes apart from the bones, one larger than the other. Horror winged to the sound of eagles and I was tossed out from the city's walls down to the Skamandrian Plain. Everywhere flowers were gloriously in bloom, white, yellow, blue, and red, softly cool against my bare feet. There were no graves. A rainbow hummed music across the roseate sky and silver lights winged across. Two figures came running to me—a man and a child, Hektôr following Skamandrios. I strained toward them but my feet would not move.

"Then Skamandrios was up in my arms, his silky curls bright and clean on my shoulder. I was glad that the blood was washed from them. He kissed my cheek with his soft mouth while Hektôr stood before me, smiling sadly. I reached out for him but was not able to break the otherworldly veil separating us. Yet I knew he was waiting for me, and knew about Pyrrhos. I stayed in the Elysian Field, enjoying the rich-blooming asphodel, whose roots feeds hungry souls, and beauty gives happiness. Then Skamandrios melded into my body and Hektôr faded into the flowers."

"My Lady! Do you realize what you just said? Skamandrios you were able to take in your arms, but you could not touch Hektôr because the otherworldly veil separated you. This can only mean one thing. The veil did not separate you from Skamandrios because *he is alive!"*

* * * *

Peleos came often to sit with me when I was in the workroom, letting me talk about Hektôr and our Skamandrios. In return, I said nothing against Akhilles. After all, Peleos and Thetis had loved their son and the kind old man had a right to keep his pride and grief. I was weaving Hektôr's figure into the cloth on my loom, and he only nodded and smiled when I told him so.

By the time I had finished this tapestry, I knew I had to embrace what lived and grew in my body. Yet I could not bear to think of it as a real child, nestling where my firstborn had grown.

It was on a day of warm breezes that Peleos entered the womens' workroom with joy in his eyes. "My dear, we will be in Pyrasos for the Mysteries of Kallichora. A messenger has come through the mountain snows with word that Pyrrhos has won back his city! Pyrasos, sacred from ancient times to Kallichora, and her daughter Basile."

"Kallichora? Basile? Pyrasos?" I turned on my stool.

"No one is a slave at the Mysteries of Kallichora and Basile! Kallichora is a gentle mother goddess. When her votaries attend you at the birth, you will be treated as a free woman. And you will learn what She means to us, here."

"New gods," I said, shrugging. "Only names. I will learn them, for I was taught enough at Sipylos to understand that all goddesses are manifestations of the One, Ma-Kybele. But who will care whether I join Her worship or not?"

"It matters, my dear, because you will need the protection of our priestesses at childbirth."

I laughed, "And you will suffer Trojans in your bloodline?"

"Every man needs sons to protect his old age and carry forward the heritage. I had the only one."

"I—yes." I looked down, reddening.

He smiled. "I will teach you what I know of our Divine Mother. I know more than many men, because of Thétis."

Bitter words hurled themselves out of my mouth, "I, Āndrõmakhê, daughter of godlike Êetiôn and widow of semi-divine Hektôr, now slave-concubine to Pyrrhos! Forced to bear Akhilles' grandchild at the shrine of Kallichora! Akhilles, who slew my noble father, seven brave brothers, and heroic husband!"

Sighing, he took my hand into both of his. "Listen now, dear girl. I will tell you of Kallichora."

Embarrassed of my outburst, I listened obediently to the soothing drone of his voice. Indeed this good man refused to let me hate him! And so he taught me to say Kallichora when at heart I meant Ma-Ate or Dea Madre, but otherwise there were few changes in the ritual of belief. Truly, it was the same Virgin Mother and Newborn Child everywhere in the world. Here, She was also addressed as Our Lady of the Sea, and together with flowers, freshly caught fish would also be placed upon Her altar. I could appreciate this; we all carried the sea within ourselves and the smell of the umbilical fish. All a man could do was to stir the ripening until a child swam out and was born.

The worship of Kallichora and her daughter Basile had centered at Pyrasos since time immemorial, and Pyrrhos Akhilleides was now lord of Her shrine, and city.

* * * *

At last, the weather had turned balmy and it was time for Kallichora's Seed Festival. One afternoon when the sun was warm Peleos asked me to walk with him to the little grove that surrounded Her shrine. I was glad to leave the town behind its stone wall, going from the palace through its private, shallow-roofed tunnel of corbelled stones that led to the citadel gate. The town sprawled around on lines of narrow ways connecting the houses like a school of fish in a net. The pasturelands were blue-green and yellow-green, rich with grazing cattle, sheep and goats. Northwest were piled the rockbound mountains, flat-sided and cornered, beckoning and defying at once with their up-thrust pointings.

We entered into the sacred grove, small but lush, bursting with moist color such as I had never seen in Thébé or Troia. There, the leaves were thinner and iridescent in early spring, shimmering silvery in the summer heat. Here, everything was moist the full year. Now, tender rays of golden light fingered young leaves, quickening them. The stone altar, a big iron-streaked stone as tall as I, had fallen from the heavenly throne of Zeus. It stood beneath a tangled bough. Kallichora's white statue was atop, holding in one outstretched hand the sacred red-painted flower from which Her son was forever reborn to fertilize the world. That flower—like a bursting womb of flowing blood, from whose petals a child emerged.

Like the child that grew in my own womb would break forth—but against my will, and unwanted.

I stared at Kallichora, my sight blurred by a sudden splash of sunlight that fell through the branches above. As a girl at Sipylos, I had identified with Ma-Ate as Maiden; as a wife in Troia, I had felt one with Ma Ate, the Great Mother. However, here I resisted and could not worship sincerely; nor at age twenty-four, could I identify with Ma-Ate, the Crone. For me, the Triple-Mare Goddess would never be Basile-Kallichora, nor Demeter-Persephone, but always the Great Mother/Dea Madre, in Three Persons, not two: Maiden/Mother/Crone Protectress of Children, Animals and Forests.

Skamandrios' image streaked through my memory, drawing forth a flood of tears. O my little son! Fruit of Hektôr's heart and mine! Far away, his body either thrown to predators, or alive but lacking sight and limb. Skamandrios, only a few times in his life to touch with his feet the fields around his home, never to run freely about as boys will, or play and muddy himself beside the Skamander River. Those verdant fields, wide rolling plains, brushed across with warm air bringing rich harvests for no one to gather...Ah, the wind-swept Hill of Ancient Ate, a high, wide mesa in the plain, black-topped from fire, spotted with unburied dead, pointing with broken towers and fallen houses to the leftward wheeling eagles of Badogios Papas....

Presently my sight cleared and I noticed, heaped upon the altar, a dozen or so, fish, still smelling of the sea.

Then I saw the yellow kitten.

It sat like a tiny statue upon the altar, among the fish.

With a cry, I leapt forward, grasping the little thing and holding it to my breast.

The kitten purred.

"Nefru?" I whispered, "Have you returned to me?"

The kitten stopped purring, but no reply came.

I lifted the small ball of lively fluff, his coat matted with dirt, searching its gaze. "Nefru? Gatto, the Lynx? What shall I call you?"

Silence.

"Strange critter," Peleos uttered, "it sat by the fish and did not touch it. Yet I think it's old enough to recognize a good meal."

"Because this is no ordinary cat!" I bit my lips, wishing to erase my words. It would be better not to draw any attention upon it.

Peleos patted me on the shoulder. "Come, dear, let's go back. Your little friend is so thin; you must feed it warm milk."

Your little friend, Peleos had said! And Friend was what Nefru used to call me. The kitten cradled in my hands, I bowed deeply to Kallichora, thanking Her for reuniting me with Nefru.

Chapter 27: Pyrasos

The Malian Gulf crossing was rough and I fell deathly sick, lying in the women's cabin-tent, cared for by Thalpia. At one point, I prayed for the strength to rise and throw myself overboard. Would it not be divine justice for the sea to claim this unwanted child, who was, after all, the great-grandchild of Thétis?

Lanassa and Briseis were also aboard with Okyone and the other children. Lanassa kept to the far corner with her baby boy and refused to let Okyone or anyone else touch him.

I had taken the frisky kitten along, and he bounced and climbed around on winged feet. He had not answered to neither Nefru, nor Gatto, but taken to the name Xanthos. Xanthos meant the golden one, befitting because of his yellow fur, which had a special, silky sheen—especially after I bathed him—but also, his name brought fond images of Hektôr's beloved stallion, Xanthos.

Naturally, the thought of Xanthos reawakened my yearning for and worries about, Phoenix. Last I had seen him was on the night of Troia's fall, when he broke free of the stables and disappeared galloping into the side streets. The Achaians had captured most of the horses afterward, but not Phoenix. This, even though Pyrrhos had offered a special reward for his capture. Indeed there had been many spies among us, for Pyrrhos had known all about Phoenix' parentage and that Priam had spared his life twice, the first time to his own detriment. Thus, he believed that Phoenix was as divine as his sire Xanthos had been, and would be a lifesaver as his chariot horse in battle. The one thing that I respected about Pyrrhos was that he did not attribute any super-human qualities to himself; neither did he boast about that he was grandson of the divine Thétis. Yet endowed as he was with such brilliant intelligence and extraordinary body—especially at such young age—minstrels were already singing colorful tales about him as a Hero of Herakleian stature.

When I could, I rose and crept to stand on deck, straining my eyes toward Troia. Seagulls glided above, following the ship like silent messengers from my home in the east. Were these the same waves that lapped the shores of Troia and Thébé?

Pyrasos, farther away yet, lay across the gulf, divided from the Aegean by an arm of land. Again, I was moving north and west, deeper into the territory of Hellas.

- *Oh Goddess, be you Kybele, Dea Madre, or Kallichora, won't you ever deliver me from this living nightmare?*

- *The life I have given you, Āndrõmakhê, bear with courage; and take upon yourself the sufferings I see fit to bestow upon you...*

At last, we approached land. Shouts and loud words made us hurry to where we saw Pyrrhos with his troops on the quay. By now, I was so ill that I felt beyond knowing or caring. I did follow Thalpia down the gangplank though. Pyrrhos rushed to Lanassa who was carried from the ship in a litter, the infant at her breast.

That evening, when Thalpia and I entered the crowded feasting-hall, Pyrrhos stood near the hearth with his grandfather. At seventeen, he seemed more a warrior than ever before. His weathered face was ruddy and his body appeared even bulkier with added muscles.

I stood aside, pulling the rich folds of my long cape around me. My sickness had abated and I was ravenously hungry, looking forward to heaping servings of roasts, peas, fresh greens and milk and cheese. Ah, this new child of mine! Skamandrios had not been so heavy, neither so demanding of food; I did not recall a single instance when hunger plagued me as much as it did now. Yet Skamandrios had been big at birth, strapping, healthy, happy. What was it that I was carrying in my belly? One thing I could be sure, this was no ordinary child.

Helenos came in from the courtyard, lank and straight as always, pink-faced from the cold. His blue eyes met mine and held. I noted that the scar on his face was fading in color, though not in size. As he strode toward me, his foot kicked aside a bone left by the yapping housedogs. He stopped, arms rigid at his sides. His gaze shifted briefly to my distended abdomen, his expression darkening. My throat constricted as his eyes locked once again with mine. Yet his time-tested love warmed me like the sun, and then he held me as I collapsed against his chest. Something broke inside me and my tears wet him.

"Release her!" Pyrrhos' voice tore through me. His hands roughly clasped my arms and removed them from Helenos.

"My lord!" Thalpia's tone was coolly firm with authority as she stepped in front of me. "Lady Ãndrõmakhê is six months along with your child."

His jaw dropping, Pyrrhos stared at Thalpia. Then his gaze lit upon my abdomen. His look of disbelief melted into a roar of laughter, and he cried out, "O, Ãndrõmakhê! A reward for both of us! My son!"

"My lord, you already have a son." Lanassa's voice sounded down the stairs as she preceded Briseis who carried the baby. "Lord Pyrrhos, this is the son to inherit your lands." Taking the child from Briseis, she lifted him on thin, trembling arms. Though puny at birth, the infant had grown healthy and beautiful; he smiled, sleepy from nursing.

Pyrrhos held him, kissing Lanassa on forehead, cheeks and lips. Raising her son above his head, he faced the household: "This welcome feast honors my firstborn!"

"Your firstborn son and heir to Thessaly," Lanassa spoke calmly.

He replied with a low voice, "We will see about that."

Lanassa gave me a triumphant look. I stared back at her, direct and clear-eyed. I was not at all jealous; I had other plans for my child by Pyrrhos.

The hours stretched interminably through the evening into night.

Torchlight filtered dimly through the building when, at meal's end, Lanassa came up the stairs behind me. "My son will inherit this kingdom," she whispered at her door. "Yours will be subject to him."

"My son can win a kingdom of his own."

"Dream on," Lanassa sneered. "Pyrrhos is ready for another son, and this, also, will be mine. Perhaps something is wrong with yours? We both know that evil spirits can change a child."

"I'll not have a monster; I've taken care against the Evil Eye."

"Hah! One small forgetfulness is enough. I have heard that at Trikka, to where Helenos is going, priests keep and study a thing born of a mother who cursed it—a heap of quivering flesh. If you don't believe me, ask Helenos, he can tell you all about it."

Terror did leap at me at her words, gnawing into my throat.

Lanassa went on, "But I will be remembered for all times as the mother of healthy children, of kings and heroes, for through me they will have the blood of Herakles and Akhilles! From you, Pyrrhos would only get a line from Êetiôn, and who, indeed, was he? No more than a glorified Phrygian farmer!"

I did not reply but entered my room and slammed the door.

Lanassa's silvery laughter sounded along the gallery as she went.

Xanthos, much like Nefru in behavior, had already made himself comfortable on my bed. Upon seeing me, he raised his head and purred his welcome.

"Dream about your child!" Lanassa's voice came back through the door. "No eyes, all neck and tiny body! Evil spirits reign supreme in this part of the world, Āndrōmakhê—the kind that mark children." Her sandals slapped sharply along the floor as she retreated.

My mind went blank.

When I came around, I stood naked in the center of the room. In the semi-darkness, I looked down the bulge in front me. What, indeed, was growing there? I knew tales of horrors that sometimes grew in a woman's womb; evil spirits exiled from humankind, yet found their way back through a woman. My love with Hektôr had brought a beautiful child, so now would my enmity with Pyrrhos bring a demon? A monster like the Kretan Minotaur had been?

The door flung open and Thalpia breezed in, holding a lamp, "I'm sorry I could not come right after you, my lady, but Pyrrhos is very excited about your pregnancy and held me back with questions."

"Thalpia...the air here is full of evil spirits. What if one takes possession of my child?"

"Not if you continue to wear your wormwood and keep dried peony at your door."

Pyrrhos' boots sounded coming up the stairs.

"Lady Āndrōmakhê," Thalpia whispered as she made haste for the door, "remember, even the gods are subject to Fate!"

* * * *

On the day that Lanassa's son was to be named, wine was already mixed with water when I entered the great hall. Pyrrhos sat with stiff formality, one foot barely showing beneath the hem of his green and red tapestry robe. His golden hair hung about his neck in careful curls and his eyes seemed looking inward. One hand clenched the chair-arm, the other balanced a heavy, gold cup. At my chair, I stood and turned my gaze to Peleos, so dignified and proud, carving portions from the sacrificial meat. His job completed, I sat down as he passed me and sat beside Pyrrhos. Lanassa was not to appear for some time yet, and Helenos later still, to make augury.

When a heavy silence shrouded the room, I looked up and saw Lanassa standing across the firepit, the baby on a white cushion in her arms. Her low voice carried clearly, "Pyrrhos Akhilleides, this is your son, heir to Phthiotis, Thessaly, and other lands you will conquer."

A murmur rose from guests who sat along the walls on benches. The fat rosy child sagged in her arms and Pyrrhos sprang to his feet, taking the infant. "I have given him life that you may have a son to honor you in your old age."

Suddenly his eyes roved to me, and dropped at the design edging my outfit. It was a white linen dress, hemmed in interlocking Trojan swastikas illustrating the solar-key pattern, at bottom, neck and down the side, embroidered in green by my rebellious hands.

Helenos came in and went to the hearth. Lanassa knelt before Pyrrhos. He hesitated, then spoke firmly, "I give this child the name my father had before puberty. Swift Akhilles was first called Ligyron." Licking dry lips, he paused, and then continued calmly, "My firstborn son will be King after me."

Helenos dipped an olive branch into the bowl of sacrificial blood and shook it over the baby and his parents, saying in chanting voice, "In the name of Apollo Protector of Boys, and of Kallichora Mother of Children, you are Ligyron Pyrrhosides!"

A cheer rose as from one throat while Lanassa got to her feet. "My son! He will be king!"

I knew their custom required that, with no marriage-borne child present, his first son from *any* woman must inherit the land. Ligyron, king of Thessaly! Lanassa, granddaughter of Herakles who had once conquered Troia, would now lord it over Hektôr's widow.

I heard the incantations of Helenos as theurgist. His holy stone in hand, he lifted one hand over the infant and began chanting the baby's oracle. I withdrew within myself and not one word penetrated my ears.

* * * *

I walked with other pregnant women celebrating the Mysteries of Kallichora. A long time ago, in a different lifetime, I had been proud, walking thus at Troia with Skamandrios growing strong in my body. Now I was called a Free Woman, but only for this festival.

An elderly priestess chanted before Kallichora's wooden statue, making incantations for the fertility of humanity and nature. Horror mixed with hope as I stared at Her, scarcely hearing the chants and responses around me. It was torturous to accept that my swollen womb belonged not to Hektôr, but Pyrrhos.

The bitterness would not leave, coiling and uncoiling itself in my soul like the greatest of all serpents.

* * * *

I took to slipping away from Thalpia's watchful eyes with some light needlework to the Grove of Kallichora. Diomede, Briseis, and Lanassa had formed a closely consorting clique, effectively shutting me out. I had no complains about that! Alas, because for some reason they kept Okyone from me, I missed seeing the little girl. Yet here at the Grove, I found peace. Sitting on a bench, I could see the priestly dormitory, gray stone through thick-foliaged trees. Helenos lived there with other priests and novices; beyond it lay the Labraunda.

On one such day with Xanthos in tow, I found the bench, sinking gratefully onto it. I was more tired than the walk justified and waited a while before starting my embroidery. For a pleasant moment, I watched Xanthos tackle the bushes, climb the tree trunks, and rattle the branches in search of prey that might be hiding. I had to laugh. While he would not talk to me as Nefru used to, he was just as loyal, and his hunting skills were so focused for a kitten that I could see the veritable lynx in him. Yet he did not hunt to kill, probably because he had enough food at home and still enjoyed lapping cupfuls of fresh goat's milk. Rather, he hunted for play, chasing squirrels, hares, and just as often, critters bigger than himself, making me think he did it simply to pit his skills against the others.

Drawing a deep breath, I settled the cloth and began picking at the last stitches. This was to be a wrap for the child, white designs over blue. Slowly I disengaged the bone needle from its safety-stitch. I had used this very same pattern for Skamandrios, symbols from Priam's family: owl-eyes and trefoil locked with the solar-key. Another day and it would be finished. I was using Achaian colors to placate Pyrrhos, but Trojan designs to please myself.

Hunger gnawed briefly, stirred by the wafting of the sacrificial smoke. Someone would be having a late meal after morning orisons! One of the novice priests, no doubt, who lived in that building with their instructors. But no, I was not hungry after all, only queasy. Had I made a mistake coming out alone, so near my time?

The crunch of sandals on pebbles made me look up, and there was Helenos. He spoke, "You should not be alone."

"Thalpia always finds me here. I have not seen you since Ligyron's naming." I wanted to embrace him, yet there was a barrier between us. Tears overflowed my eyes and he sat beside me, drawing me close.

"What are we living for, Helenos?"

"To conquer, Āndrōmakhê. The gods decree honesty among men, and I abide by that; but they also decree justice. Troia will conquer even in defeat. Remember that!"

"We wait and do nothing—and everything will change?"

"You are having a child very soon, and I am going to Trikka."

I noticed that he held himself stiffly, not touching me. I stared into his eyes as they met mine, naked and terrible in their loneliness and desire. His face was paler than usual, the scar standing out. "Pyrrhos will suffer," he went on, "just as everyone will who brought home a free Trojan as slave. You will rule, and overcome through his son."

I waved him off, "Lanassa's son is heir."

"The years ahead are long," he replied enigmatically. Placing one hand upon mine, he bent his fingers between mine, and held them. His touch was feverish, worrisome. "Āndrōmakhê, I love you, always have, and always will. No matter what happens." He turned his head toward the altar of Kallichora. "By the Goddess, if I could have killed him before—or even now..." He stood abruptly, slamming one fist into his other hand.

"What are you *really* going to do at Trikka?"

"More than what he sends me out to do! You may not have been told—but Trikka was a center of healing even before the Pelasgians came. Pyrrhos is Warrior-Protector of the shrine of Apollo-Asklepios in Trikka, just as your father Êetiôn was Warrior-Protector of the Apollonian shrine at Chryse. All he expects is for me to learn and represent him before the Healer-God. I am to be Chief Priest, which means I will be most powerful among the religious leaders in all his territories."

"Then it is determined that he will free you soon; he has to, for no slave has ever held such high rank."

"Now you understand my plan—in part. Slaves also have right to buy their own freedom, and I will be able to gather wealth as my share from among the offerings brought by pilgrims. I will buy you and free you if he does not free you before I am able to. As for Trikka, indeed I have something valuable to teach which they don't have—the laying on of hands, a power I developed during all the years of my training."

"And you are sure you can achieve so much at Trikka?"

"Even more! The shrine is in Makedonia, among the Thessalian people. To the north live our kindred, the Paionians and Dardanians. Farther west there is the Illyrian coast, and south, almost on a line with Trikka, is the country of Epirus, claimed by Pyrrhos. He has about three hundred Trojan refugees there, free men, on military call, who would rally to me."

"Why have you not told me of these things before?"

He looked at me thoughtfully, for a long time. Then, "One day I will take you from Pyrrhos, whether it be in war or by agreement."

I smiled at the thought of this gentle man as military conqueror, though he had shown steadfast courage around the walls of Troia.

He spoke again, "You know that the Makedonians were allied with the Achaians against us, but that the Paionians dispatched ship to aid our allies. The Bryges were also our friends. You'll remember that Kassandra…" he hesitated, his eyes moistened, then his voice firmed. "She was to have married Koribos of Mygdonia."

"Yes, I remember that. She did not want him, though. And the poor man died at our walls, fighting for the love of her."

"The Mygdonians in this region are the same who long ago sent colonists to Phrygia and Troia."

"You must succeed," I whispered, "o Helenos, you must! And we will work together." I dried my eyes on my veil. "Can you tell me—with your vision—if you know for sure Skamandrios is dead? Or do I have cause to hope?"

He stood up, his gaze on the shrine. "You will never again see Skamandrios, Ãndrõmakhê."

I leapt to my feet, "You mean he is alive! *Alive!*"

He sighed and pulled me close to him. "Yes I have seen the future, Ãndrõmakhê. The years ahead are long, but you and I must do what is decreed." He looked at me, pain flaring in his eyes. "I *will* buy your freedom, or fight to free you." He moved away as I reached for him, then stopped and turned back, facing me. "I have news of Kassandra, brought by one of my recent novices."

"Kassandra!" I tried to picture that proud girl in my memory, free as she had been, untouched by Ajax' rape at Athené's altar.

"She is with Agamemnon on Lesbos. It seems that Agamemnon gave up Mykene to Klytemnestra, who has a new king now after the old way; one called Aigisthos."

"So then Kassandra is Queen of Lesbos." I smiled with relief. "Agamemnon at least honors her." I visioned my girlhood memory of the island, a wreath of flowers on the purple sea, lush with thick olive groves, and the rare, delicate white roses opening to the moonlight.

"She has twin sons, mere infants yet." Helenos' gaze went bleak. "But I see only blackness around her. She is not queen there."

"What do you think we would find, returning to Troia?"

"My dearest, there can be no rebuilding of the past. Only the future is to be taken."

I shuddered as I thought of Kassandra. I had touched her hand as we stood on the wharf at parting. The beautiful seeress had seemed crumpled within herself. "I'll never see you again," she had spoken, "this is the last hour for us. Agamemnon takes me to Bresa tonight; we will be there a long time." We had turned away from each other, for to say goodbye was impossible. Never to see Hektôr's wild-eyed, lonely, tormented, yet magnificent, sister again…had Kassandra encountered the worst of a man in Ajax, as punishment for her rejection of the best man offered to her—Koribos?

"Oh, Helenos!" I lifted my face to him but he rose and strode from me back to the dormitory.

Only now, I allowed myself to consider the importance of what he had told me about Skamandrios. He had not reaffirmed his death, only said that I would never see him again. Therefore, the insistent memory of Kiron's reassuring whispers was true! Somehow, the Goddess had reached and cushioned his fall from the wall, saving his life.

- Oh Goddess, just let my little son thrive and prosper, and I gladly accept not being able to set eyes upon his dear, sweet face! Great Kind Mother, Ancient Ate, Dea Madre and Kallichora, I beseech You in all Your Names: here I lay my tortured, bleeding mother's heart as a burnt offering upon your altar, please accept it for Skamandrios Astyanax' ever-lasting health and happiness!

As tears ran down my cheeks, my throat dried to parchment and I began to tremble. I wanted to sing and dance with joy, but a sharp agony speared my abdomen, and I collapsed onto the bench.

Then terrible pain tore through my whole body.

"Thalpia!" I screamed, and everything went pitch black.

Chapter 28: Molossos, Son of Pyrrhos

I was wakened to the soothing massage of tender hands on my body. Thanks to Kallichora, those endless hours of being torn apart in the birth-chair were ended; I was in bed with Thalpia bending over me.

"Dear lady, you have a big, beautiful, strong and healthy son." A bundled heavy weight was laid on my arm near my breast. Hands placed one of my nipples into a tiny mouth.

My child! But not Hektôr's.

I touched the well-shaped head with its sapphire eyes and downy white hairs. Love flowed through my fingers. My heart too swollen for my breast to contain, I wept, offering thanks to the Great Kind Mother who gave me this new-old soul, to love, cherish, and protect.

Three days passed and the time came for naming, for Pyrrhos to accept his son.

Pyrrhos held him up before the guests. "This is my son, born to me by Ãndrõmakhê, daughter of King Êetiôn, and a queen of two lands by right. See my son and honor him!"

Peleos came forward carrying a shield in both hands, which he placed on the floor before his grandson, then spoke, "On this shield your father Akhilles was placed to receive his name and heritage."

Peleos then took a winnowing-fan from his servant, placing it in the hollow of the shield.

When he stepped back Pyrrhos laid the child on the fan within the shield, and Helenos came from the outside. Moving in slow dignity, he carried a lustral bowl of water and wooden wand. He set the bowl on the hearth-wall, and then thrust the stick into the fire.

Bowing to me, "Now, my lady, you must purify the water."

Taking the burning stick from the fire, I thrust it, hissing and smoking, into the water and held it there until it turned cold in my grip.

Helenos lifted the shield with its precious burden and balanced it on the firewall. I dropped the wand down into the fire where it was consumed with propitious cracklings.

I stepped aside; Pyrrhos took the bowl, and poured a splash over the sleeping child's head, speaking distinctly, "You are Molossos, son of Pyrrhos by grace of Kallichora and Apollo. I place you under the Protection of Zeus Molossos, God of the Sacred Fleece. The Fleece was brought back to Iolkos, where it belonged, by Jason from the Kolchians, who had no right to it. My people, see my son, and honor Molossos Pyrrhosides!"

Peleos whispered, "It will be propitious for this child to bear that name, for Iolkos is under my protection. Zeus Molossos is patron of Iolkos, the town that is second only to Orchomenos as our link with the East. Take comfort in that the name *does* have some association with your homeland."

"I thank you, Old Father," I nodded.

The baby's howls punctuated the long prayer that followed, and the exorcism against evil was pronounced by Helenos.

Taking Molossos, I turned to Thalpia who had waited behind me, and gave him into her arms, declaring, "Henceforth I appoint you Nurse Thalpia." I retreated to my own chair.

The new nurse, glowing with pride, took her proper seat beside the mother, and began to carefully swaddle the infant, her skillful hands moving in rhythmic regularity as she bound young Molossos. My heart shook with empathy for her. Eight children she had birthed when she had been a slave, and been allowed to keep none. Yet, now this was the second babe of mine to whom she was opening her heart to help me raise. When only his head, shoulders and arms were free of linen, she returned Molossos to me where his cries were quieted with milk from my breast.

Pyrrhos came to my side. Smiling warmly, I said, "I trust you will see to that my son has rights."

"*My* son!" he laughed, but added with soft tone, "no son of mine will be without rights or lands." He bent to my ear, "But will *you* change, Ãndrōmakhê, and allow yourself to care for me?"

"Of course, Pyrrhos, now that I have given life to your child."

Oh, Hektôr, my dear Lord and Husband. I am still your wife at heart, and I shall remain your wife always and forever.

* * * *

364

The Festival of Demeter was at hand with its ingathering of grains for storage against next season's planting. The days of celebrations were chill and damp as delegates from other regions filled the dormitories near the Sacred Precinct. Though it was less than ten days since I gave birth, I wanted to join the ceremonies, for I was eager to learn and practice. Kassandra's pronouncement on a long-ago day, that during my past life in Shardana I was either dedicated to, or been the daughter of, Kupra, a goddess, was ringing in my thoughts. Might I not find solace by dedicating myself fully to the Mother in All Names?

I had learned from the Chief Priestess here that women were the first to bring Demeter's celebration from Hyperborea, land of Boreas, the Northwind. There, neither illness nor wrongdoing existed, and the sun never set. But some said that Hyperborea was actually the Tin Islands. Far off, yet approachable if one knew the routes. Eons ago, the River God Inakos, son of Okeanos, had traveled there by land before the sea cut between, erecting temples set up in circles by magic, with stones larger than houses. And Brutos had taken hundreds of our Trojan citizens before the Fall, to lead them to the Tin Inlands. Their dark-haired women still crossed the sea and mountains to attend the ceremonies here; they wore white, and the sheaves they carried were larger than those brought by others.

Nevertheless, they were not the only women who braved such distances to worship and celebrate Demeter. The Laestrigonians sent golden-haired, buxom, giant-girls from the land where nightfall and morning were so close to each other that shepherds bringing in their flocks at night, were met by other shepherds driving out their flocks at dawn.

Pilgrims came also from the mountains where Prometheus the Titan first struck fire to benefit our kind.

The Priestesses of the Winds climbed from cave to mountaintop in performance of rites secret even from the initiated women. While the worshipers took part in these ceremonials of Demeter-Kallichora, the men prepared to honor Dionysos-Pseudanor. Dionysos oversaw the ceremonies upon reaching adolescence and the ritual disguises that accompanied them. Protector of both boys and girls, invoked as Agrios/the Savage, Epikryptos/the Very Hidden, or Pseudanor/the False Man, Dionysos was also attested as Zeus Hypsistos/the Highest.

Like seed-grains carefully stored within the pit below the cave, the Goddess as Maiden was taken to her subterranean chamber where she must await spring, living with her Lord in his jeweled kingdom, protecting the seedlings from decay and theft.

Our heads wreathed in rustling-dry peony leaves and carrying a distaff in one hand, with the other we led either a pig or goat, great with young. I followed the Chief Priestess of the Winds who was clad in rich purple and led us shaking a sistrum.

Beyond, on the dancing field, I saw maidens dancing themselves into a frenzy of identification with the pig and the goat.

The cave was bright with conifer branches and berries festooning the walls. I moved through the ritual, recalling a similar ceremony at Thymbra near Troia, before Skamandrios' birth. The memory rushed at me with such pain that set my opal afire on my breast, and thus unable to complete my part, I left the cave at a run. Seeking a quiet corner to regain my strength, I sat, wondering. The Goddess in the form of Kupra was strong on my mind; She seemed to disapprove of the blood-soaked manner with which Demeter was being celebrated.

I saw Pyrrhos, getting his men in line, helping them adjust their garlands of grape leaves over goatskins. Each carried an enormous red leather phallus in hand, preparing to attach it around the hips. Helenos, with one attached to the top of his priestly staff, began the chant launching the celebration of Dionysos-Pseudanor. They were to go far into the mountain for dances.

At Troia, similar rites had taken place by night, but here in this gloomy land sunlight was needed to impregnate seeds left by Dionysos among the vines as his death-blood splattered. The men implemented each other's potency through the magic of anal fertilization, so that their women are assured of young in the spring when Dionysos arose from death with blooming of the vines.

The rites of spring and fall in our part of the world revolved around the copulating of men and women. Here, it expanded to include men with men. I watched the snake-like procession of chanting men on the path to the mountain, contemplating how the same basic faith varied as interpreted by people in different regions.

* * * *

My eyes widened with apprehension as I observed Pyrrhos stride in through the courtyard door. Helenos, behind him, stopped at the entrance. His intense gaze locked with mine as I stared back. My body tingled with gratitude of Helenos' comforting presence when he turned and strode beyond my line of vision.

"We shall go to Pharsalos before winter," Pyrrhos announced to the crowded room at large. "But I will travel before then." He watched as individuals paused in their assembling for the evening meal. "I will have Architelos out of there, before summer ends."

He strode to where Peleos was sitting. Taking his own seat, he went on, "He sold out the Dorians and Herakleids, and dares to take over Mykene and Sparta." He accepted a cup of wine from Briseis. "But those cities will be mine by right, soon, through Hermione."

Peleos slumped in his chair. "Things will never be the same; the old days are ended, Pyrrhos. Perhaps we would have been better off if we had left the Trojans to their arrogance than leave our own lands undefended from jackals such as he."

The two men settled into low conversation.

Lanassa entered, and I noticed how pale and thin she looked, her beauty as delicate as to seem unreal.

"My lord," Briseis began softly, bowing to Pyrrhos, "must there be another war? Surely your kingdom is large enough."

"Not for the number of sons I will have," Pyrrhos grinned, looking toward me.

Let him look, I thought, *it is still too soon after birth, and by his own land's custom, he is not yet to use my body.*

"My lord," Lanassa spoke up from her chair behind Peleos, her voice low and urgent.

Pyrrhos turned smilingly to her. "I said your son will inherit."

"All my sons! I believe I am to give you another child. I can be sure in a few more days."

"So soon? Then praise the Goddess!"

She inclined her head, "I was careful not to nurse Ligyron too long, for I wanted to give you another son."

"Fool!" Thalpia muttered to me. "The Goddess gives no child to a nursing mother so that the flow of milk heals the body—only so the next child will be strong."

"She hasn't been well," Diomede whispered, looking angrily at Thalpia, her eyes cold with resentment. "We are all slaves here and this is the only way Lanassa knows how to protect her future."

"Tell her to rest easy;" I whispered back, "I am not contesting for favors with our master."

Diomede stood up and went to sit by Lanassa.

Thalpia harrumphed.

"Don't be angry at Diomede for my sake," I told her, "I'm only too glad Pyrrhos is in Lanassa's bed."

"But—the future—your son…" Her eyes flicked from Molossos to Ligyron, dark with concern. "My lady, Pyrrhos feels kindly toward you, though you have given him little cause. Don't endanger your standing in his eyes!"

Molossos whimpered, and Thalpia passed him to me to suckle. Voices rose around me from others in the room and the discussion centered on when Pyrrhos would start casting lots for military service.

Sated, Molossos drowsed, and I gave him back to his nurse. Then I rose, left the room and went up to the gallery after Helenos. He had been assigned to a room here for the night, since he was to leave for Trikka early the next morning.

His door was half-open and I stepped inside, closing the door after me. In the glow from one dim lamp he stood by his dressing table, which was turned into an altar, both arms lifted in prayer and face turned upward. He wore a robe of oiled white linen that gleamed as through irradiated, its folds uninterrupted from shoulders to feet. The flame-light brought out the strength of his beardless chin and made dark smudges of his eyes. "Helenos."

He wheeled from the improvised altar. "Ãndrõmakhê! You must not come here."

"Pyrrhos is down there talking about yet another war. And I am afraid I might not see you again."

"Don't be; I will never lose you." He reached for me, and then stepped back.

A pounding on the door, and Pyrrhos called, "I am ready for you now, Helenos."

"I'll be along soon, my lord," he replied.

Pyrrhos' sandals scraped about as if he turned away and then came back. "Who is in there with you?" and he flung open the door. "So!" he sneered, "And you claimed to be too holy to soil yourself with women, eh, Priest?"

"My lord." Helenos drew himself up and stood by me protectively.

Pyrrhos swung his narrowed gaze between us. Then his laughter deafened us in the small room. "Ah, I should rest easy…yes, you would not even know how, not even if she climbed into your bed!"

I cringed toward the door. His look turned ugly as he grabbed my arm. "Claws for me and tender fingers for him, is it? You will both die the day I find he's learned of your body."

Pyrrhos pushed at me roughly and I fled to the sound of his words directed to Helenos, "You'll serve me in my bath for this, eunuch! And then you will rub me down with your healing hands!"

I entered my room and Thalpia helped me into bed, then placed Molossos in his cradle.

When she left, I lay awake a long time, telling myself I must not brood. Xanthos gave an occasional little purr from his basket set in a discreet niche. Interesting how Pyrrhos resembled Akhilles in so many aspects! Filled with as many bewildering contradictions as his father, Pyrrhos was temperamental, merciless, yet capable of great and selfless generosity. He drove his men hard, but never cruelly, and was fond of animals of all kinds. He was especially tender with Xanthos. He never got angry when the kitten leapt on the table during meals, letting him enjoy choice morsels, played with him or cuddled him, and did not complain when he would join us in the middle of his deepest sleep. I had to smile in the dark. Xanthos too was fond of him. And did they not resemble each other with their strong, sculpted bodies and golden coloring?

Then I recalled how he had treated Helenos tonight, and wanted to kill him. My innards rebelled at the thought that driven by jealousy, he might enter at any moment, demanding use of me before sleep. No! I would not be here for Pyrrhos. I would crawl out and find the room Briseis shared with Okyone and two other little girls. He had not been using her lately, and I ought to be safe there.

My feet slid along the long gallery lined with doors, counting them. The oil-lamp that usually lit the place was out. A faint light appeared from the opening door of the bath chamber, and Pyrrhos' bare feet thudded toward me.

Panicking, I slipped into the first doorway, closing the door just as he passed. Then new fear shook me. I had lost count of the doors! So in whose room was I now?

There was no moon, but in the starlight I made out someone in bed. I turned to leave when Peleos' voice sounded, "Thétis? Has Hermes sent you to lead me below? Oh, blessed release!"

I saw, against the window, his hands move in the ritual sign of death. I stepped forward. "Old Father...the god has not sent for you. It is I, Ãndrõmakhê. Save me, pity me for this night! Give me sanctuary. I am still sore from the birth."

"Ãndrõmakhê, my child!" Sighing, he sat up quickly in bed. "Ah, yes, I understand." He moved to leave the bed. "My robe, please. Of course you shall sleep here."

"No, I'll rest in your chair." Tears flooded down my cheeks. "May the Great Kind Mother bless you! Forgive me, too, for any unkind thoughts I've ever had of you."

"You know I hold no grudge, my child."

When he was robed, I kneeled at his feet. "Old Father. I wish you and Priam had gotten to know each other before the war! He was a great warrior and wise ruler, just like you. You look like each other, too. Both of you have inherited Erik the Great's personal stamp!"

"Erik the Great?"

"I meant Eriktonios, ancestor of the rulers of Troia."

"I knew of Priam's tie to the House of Atros through his mother, Plakia, a daughter of Atros, but—"

"Old Father! If only you had seen Alexis Paris, you would have noticed the resemblance between him and your son, Akhilles! Their coloring, facial features…and it's not true what they say about Alexis now, for he was no coward. Not in the least! He always fought bravely on the front lines. After Hektôr's death in your son's hands, Alexis did a spirited job as Defender until Deiphobos took his place. Besides, in archery he was as good as any of your best swordsmen. Having known both Alexis and Akhilles, I had suspected that they must be related, but after I met you…and saw how alike Priam you are…"

"The Fates!" Peleos whispered hoarsely. "How they have played us against each other." Sighing, he added, "I know of that before you were spoken to Hektôr, Akhilles sought you out in Thébé and offered marriage. You turned him down. Why?"

"Because I loved Hektôr," I said truthfully.

Then I told him all, beginning with how Helenos and I, during the initiation ceremonies at Sipylos, had vowed to get married one day, and how I met Hektôr at the banquet for Helen and Alexis, and then fell in love with him during the Maze Dance, and later, when Helenos pledged himself to Apollo, Hektôr married me in his stead.

Peleos was sitting up in bed, one hand pulling on his beard, and he gave me an amused look. "I feel that Helenos did not voluntarily bow out of this marriage because of Apollo! No. Rather, he was made to step back because Hektôr was the better man for you."

"I had not thought of this before…"

"Well, Āndrõmakhê, Hektôr was heir of Troia, and your noble father Êetiôn Overlord of all Mysia, therefore a wealthy, strategically important king. Priam needed him at his side! Yet only marriage with the heir would do right by your station. When Hektôr made his interest in you known, I am sure both kings talked about this, and lucky for him, they agreed, and he won you for wife."

My chin trembled as tears blurred my eyes, "Lucky for Hektôr? Kind of you to say that, Old Father, but it was *I* who was lucky! What a unique, gallant man I had for husband! Pure of heart, uncomplicated, faithful, loving, kind." I stopped, afraid of breaking into sobs.

Peleos said softly, "Spread rugs for me on the floor, child. I've slept on many harder beds in years gone by." He left the bed and went to the clothes-chest, opening it.

Seeing that he was determined, I helped retrieve skins and lengths of heavy cloth, spreading them for him near the bed.

"How much do you know of your father Êetiôn, on the field of battle?" he asked, lying down.

"He was a warrior of extraordinary courage and skill. Many songs were sung in his name."

"Yes, that is true. But *what* do you know of how he fought?"

I hesitated, suspecting that he was hinting of dark things I would prefer not to hear about.

"King Êetiôn was a great warrior, indeed," he continued softly, "and victorious because he employed well thought-out strategies. Nevertheless, whenever he encountered an adversary as great and dangerous as Priam was, he did not hesitate to take his life, be it by running his sword through his heart or his neck—decapitating him. You do understand what I am telling you, don't you? If he were in Pyrrhos' stead, Êetiôn too would do to Priam what Pyrrhos did."

"But Priam was an old man!"

"Old man? Priam? By your own admission, a king the same age as I am now. Cut from the cloth of Immortal Phoenix, capable of rising from the ashes! No, Ãndrõmakhê, Pyrrhos could not leave Priam alive, no more than I, or Êetiôn, could, if we wore his boots."

"You speak of Mercy as if She were an enemy!"

He sighed, "Sleep now, child. You are safe here tonight."

"May all the gods bless you, Old Father."

"Your blessing is sweet in my ears and warms my heart."

When I awoke in the morning, Peleos was not in the room. I dressed quickly and found Thalpia standing with him outside.

"The Goddess be praised!" Thalpia cried upon seeing me. "Pyrrhos was raging at Helenos, and sent him off with curses."

Peleos gave a short laugh. "Send him to me. What can he say to an old man like myself?"

I went along to my room where the baby lay, freshly swaddled, waving his tiny arms. I took him up and put him to my breast.

"My lady, you smile." Thalpia, bustling around the room, looked at me sideways.

"I have found a grandfather," I said, fresh tears welling in my eyes. Then I told her of last night, looking down at Molossos' tiny face, squeezed with concentration as he nursed. Tender laughter bubbled in my throat. "He will be sung by minstrels in later years. A Trojan hero among the Achaians!"

Chapter 29: Pharsalos

We made camp when night overtook us near our destination. The road until now had been a series of unmarked mountain passes and steep valleys. White-foamed torrents frequently bisected the meager road we followed. Torches were lit from sparks tended all the way from the hearthfire at Antron. Now we were in a gorge where more white-foaming torrents roared in the quiet. I went into the tent where Lanassa lay under the care of Diomede. She had insisted that her pregnancy was not too far advanced for the journey; but the arduous trail had drained the strength of human and animal. The jolting and sliding had kept Lanassa moaning, but now she had sunk deeply into her pillows and was silent.

I had shared an ox-driven, tented wagon with Xanthos, Thalpia, Lanassa, Diomede, and the two babies. I had nursed both infants, for Lanassa had no more milk left in her breasts. The other slave-children with Okyone, and Briseis in charge, had traveled in another wagon and here they had a separate tent.

"Pyrrhos was a fool to take such a risk," Thalpia said, sponging off Lanassa's fevered body.

I did not reply, my mind on what Pyrrhos's last comments about Odysseus, just before we had left for this journey. "There is more that one way to victory," he had said, "for I learned much from the wily Odysseus of Ithaka."

Odysseus certainly had earned his reputation for trickery and hatred among us, Trojans. Hatred? Contempt, rather. I heard again the words of the priestesses at Sipylos, "The divine Moira moves among us; what she does, we do. Destiny may change, but not Fate! Destiny is but the road we take to meet our Fate. One day you will see that it is better to wait and not tempt Fate, for such acts can distort our Destiny, though not change Fate."

As I had watched Pyrrhos stand dark against the light, and then disappear into the sunlit courtyard, leaving Peleos in the doorway looking after him, I had wondered if I understood the riddle of Destiny and Fate. Had it been the Moira who threw Skamandrios from the walls of Troia, and not Odysseus' hand releasing Pyrrhos' grasp upon my child? And had this act set Skamandrios upon the road of his Destiny, blinded and with broken limbs...towards his Fate? But where was his Destiny taking him to, and to what ultimate Fate?

Hours passed, none of us able to sleep. My thoughts went on to linger on Odysseus. Traveling bards sang no less of him than of Akhilles, Hektôr, Priam, Agamemnon, Helen, and Alexander-Paris. However, the portrait they painted of Odysseus, the wily Ithakan King of Goats, was so different from the man I had known, that I felt I was listening to the exploits of a stranger. One news that gladdened my heart was that the curse Queen Hekabe had put on him, just before she took her own life, had been approved by the gods. Shortly after leaving Troia on his homebound journey, his small fleet and band of men had been lost at sea during an incredibly harsh storm. Now the bards sang of his deep yearning for Penelope, his beautiful and loyal wife, waiting for him all these years on Ithaka. I felt sorry for Penelope; I could believe that although he was a beast during war and had been merciless with my little son, he was a loving husband to her. Ah, and so were the two faces of Odysseus, and two opposing sides of his story...

When morning came, Lanassa was unable to leave her bed to continue the journey. She called Diomede to bring Ligyron and prayed over him, commending him to the Great Mother Goddess. She handed the child back to his nurse, and throughout the night, her moans and screams filled the tent.

I hurried to tell Peleos that we could not go on.

Behind me, Diomede ran to the old man, "We have to stay here! Lanassa is birthing."

Lanassa's gut-wrenching agony lasted all that day and through the next. On the third day, she lost the child, yet not fully formed.

With great effort, Lanassa managed to sit up in bed, calling Diomede to bring in Ligyron. Her lips trembling, she prayed over him and blessed him, commending him to the Great Ma Kybele.

An hour later, beautiful Lanassa, spirited proud granddaughter of Herakles and mother of Pyrrhos's firstborn, drew her last breath in Diomede's arms, while I held the crying Ligyron to my breast.

* * * *

Her passing pained me to the core. Yes, she had erred assuming I was a rival for Pyrrhos' affections, and had tried to break my spirit, but I had not hated her then, and mourned her now. With her untimely death, yet another thread binding me to my home was severed.

A runner was sent to Pyrrhos. He arrived with a fine bronze urn for the infant, and Lanassa's body was consumed atop a hastily gathered but suitably majestic pyre. His face frozen into a dark mask, Pyrrhos added a white stone on the mound where mother and child were placed at the juncture of three streams. He looked truly saddened by her death.

Snow was in the wind, and there was scarce time for proper rites. We passed Pherai and Pagasai, little towns that cut Pharsalos from the sea, while Molossos cried lustily, and Ligyron let out soft sighs, as if he were already aware that his mother had departed and there was nothing he could do about it.

The road we followed led as far as Larissa and beyond the lands of the Makedonians. Xanthos leapt from the wagon, disappearing in the surrounding forest. Hours later he returned carrying in its mouth a tiny wolf cub, its eyes not yet open, and whimpering. Laying it at my feet like a gift, he sat and looked at me challengingly. I looked at him, then at the baby, a female, and with a sigh, adopted her. It had a yellowish red coat, with black coloration on the nape and legs.

Grumbling, Thalpia climbed out, found the nanny goat we had taken along, and returned with a cupful of warm milk. We soaked a strip of cloth in the milk and soon enough the baby took to it.

It was late evening when we first alighted at Pharsalos, at the southeastern end of a great plain, the mountains looming beyond it. Herds of cattle tended by sheepskin-coated men grazed the fields. The saddle-shaped crag within the walls, topped by the royal fortress, was a welcome sight.

It began snowing heavily just as Pyrrhos dismounted from his chariot at the city gate. Townsmen brought torches to show us along the street to the sacred grove beside the palace.

I was given a room next to Pyrrhos' suite, with one for Thalpia, and Molossos on the other side of her. Beyond our master's room was Diomede's, where she was to look after Ligyron.

I had taken Xanthos' basket with us, and Thalpia found another one for the tiny cub. Naming her Lycosa, I cleaned her up and laid her amidst soft warm pieces of wool. The basket was spacious, and after watching me for a few minutes, Xanthos leapt in and curled himself around the little one.

"Where are all the children?" I asked that evening, taking my seat near Pyrrhos.

"Briseis will bring them when Mentes starts his chant," he replied.

"Where is Okyone? I never get to see her anymore."

"She'll be here with the others." He then turned to Podarkes. They discussed their next move against Akastos while they ate heartily. Podarkes had driven the usurper out of this city, and would depart in the morning to pursue Akastos despite the heavy snow.

The rustling laughter of subdued children sibilated through the doorway and willowy Briseis entered as queen bee, with her swarm to settle beyond the hearth. Two older girls carried the babies, and one went to Diomede with Ligyron while Okyone brought Molossos to me. The girl seemed so much older, I noted, and the brightness of her eyes was dimmed.

Taking my son, I bent and kissed her cheek. "Are you all right, my little niece?"

"Yes," she sighed, "though I'd rather be with you." With a longing look at Molossos, "May I be his nurse?"

"Thalpia is his official nurse," I told her, "you are young yet. But, when you are older, I'll ask for you as her helper."

"But I'm old enough to carry water and clean the floors," Okyone said. "I can card and spin and weave, too."

Now it was my turn to sigh. "I'm not free either, Okyone, and can only do what is permitted. I will always love you, and never forget that you are my dear brother's child." Then I thought of her carrying water and washing floors. "Tell you what: I will see about your helping Thalpia. Now go back to Briseis and wait for better days."

When the bard finished reciting tales of Peleos as a young man, Briseis collected her charges and shooed them into their own area. Thalpia grunted as she leaned down to take Molossos, "That's only an undivided storage area where she has to keep those children! No sunlight, and only straw beds along the wall, with a bath-pool in the center."

"No warmth for them?" I shivered involuntarily.

"Well, I spotted braziers, which are better than nothing of course. I'm told it's warmer there in winter and cooler in summer than upstairs where we are."

Thalpia looked across at Diomede, who held a terracotta nursing bottle to Ligyron's mouth.

Avoiding my gaze, Diomede said, "We're better off than Briseis; henceforth she has to sleep there with those children all the time."

"And she is the one so gone in love with Pyrrhos," I said. "Look, she still wears Deidameia's ring. Pyrrhos is not doing right by her!"

Diomede stared at me. "*You* could be queen, Āndrõmakhê. He need not marry Hermione. You are of higher rank than her, and while he might not get Lakedaimon without her, he will get claim to Thébé and what is left of Troia. And I don't doubt that you would be a better queen for me to bear with than Hermione."

"I've already advised her of her options," Thalpia intercepted. "Come, my lady, you are tired and it's late."

I glanced toward Pyrrhos for permission, and rose when he nodded to me, declaring, "Podarkes leaves early in the morning."

His eyes moved from me to the bowl of wine and water, and Podarkes held out his cup with an enigmatic smile. Ah, I was being given the official role of hostess.

Taking the cup, I filled it from the mixing bowl, and then spoke the customary words of farewell as I returned it to him.

"You would grace the home of any man," Podarkes said, "I must tell you that your fame as Lady of the Hearth had reached Achaia long before the war ended." He looked at Pyrrhos. "Landless though she is for now, does she not outshine Hermione in grace and poise?"

"I would give up neither," Pyrrhos replied wryly.

* * * *

All through that long, dismal winter, Pyrrhos kept active. Sometimes he took a body of men on hunting expeditions lasting several days. Lycosa was growing faster than normal, and he took her along, starting to train her for the hunt as if she were one of his dogs. I was pleased not to see him around and thrived under the kindness of Peleos. The old man kept to the great hall, dispensing judgment to those able to slog through the heavy mountain snow.

One day, while I was weaving, Xanthos came in with a strangely insistent, loud meow. He was not able to communicate his thoughts, but prompted by the warming of my opal, I rose, and he run ahead, his bushy tail high and waving like a golden plume. He led me to an unlocked storage building behind a copse of trees. Entering it, he scurried among chests, sacks, bins and parcels, and then stood meowing by a sack made of tough, oiled sailcloth. It smelled of must, weathered and stained from travel. Though securely knotted on top, it had tears on its side from which the tops of two objects protruded. Approaching it with a pounding heart, I bent and pulled out the first one, then the second.

A lap-lyre, and a toy chariot.

Recognition set in.

Alexis' lyre, and Skamandrios' toy chariot.

I fell on my knees, tears streaming down my cheeks as I gathered the precious objects to my breast.

Xanthos sat on his hind legs, purring.

* * * *

About mid-season Peleos told me in confidence that the year would soon be on hand when Assembly would be held. "They will choose Pyrrhos in my place; I am too old for such responsibility. I have ruled long enough and been reelected many times."

"At home our rulers are for life unless an act of Council deposes them," I said.

"We are chosen for seven or twelve years at a time, except in Mykene and Knossos where this is done after nine years. Helen's sister Klytemnestra married her new king when Agamemnon had been away that long." Peleos frowned. "Yes. Klytemnestra expected to revive the old custom, but I hear crafty Aigisthos has been reinstated after his nine years." Peleos chuckled.

In honor of Alexis' found lyre, I taught myself to use it, and when I played the haunting melodies of the mountains with such great ease, wondered if he reached down from Elysium to guide my fingers.

Skamandrios' toy chariot I set up on the altar, next to the Dea Madre. The significance of its reentry into my life must be that he was still leading a nomad's life, quite likely traveling on land, and perhaps calling out to me in his heart, for inner strength. If so, then I was here for him, with my Goddess.

Spring drew near, and mountain snows avalanched from high peaks into rivers that flooded the plain.

Our first visitor from the outside hailed from Sparta.

To Pyrrhos' impatient question the man answered, "Her brothers will not release Hermione until her parents return from Egypt."

Pyrrhos slammed his empty cup on the arm of his chair, glowering. "Egypt? So long? Why?"

"Word is that they are given so many honors that it is impossible for them to leave courteously."

"Ah. Of course, I cannot just sweep down and legally marry the daughter without due ceremonial gifts to her parents. And is Meneláos' brother still king on Lesbos?"

"Agamemnon went back to Mykene." The bard looked unwilling to say more. After a pause, he added, "Agamemnon is dead."

"Dead?" Pyrrhos half rose from his seat.

"The tale varies."

A shocked silence weighed over the hall.

"What of Kassandra?" I burst forth into the void.

"Kassandra and their children went with him."

"Give me the entire story," Pyrrhos demanded.

When he began his prelude, the bard's words took on the epic formula as it built within his mind.

Agamemnon arrived home with Kassandra and their twin sons, to find his wife had restored the matriarchy. Nonetheless, he proclaimed himself king, with Kassandra as his queen. Klytemnestra and Aigisthos, pretending acceptance, ordered festivities in honor of Agamemnon's return. There was the ancient ceremony of Agamemnon's rebirth in the Cave of Britomartis on Mount Ida. Then followed the ritual bath. Klytemnestra supervised filling of the pool below the Sacred Stairs. Aigisthos, as ceremonial father, escorted the King of Kings there for cleansing after ceremonial parturition. Later, Klytemnestra claimed to have found Agamemnon dead in the water, trapped by a net that usually hung above the lustral bath. She seemed to go mad when Kassandra descended the stairs with her toddling twins. Klytemnestra seized the boys together by their feet and hurled them against a smooth round column. Their heads smashed open, spattering blood and brains into the water where their father lay. Kassandra, trying to save them, slipped on her children's blood and fell into the pool just as Klytemnestra plunged a dagger into her back.

I covered my face with my hands, but tears would not flow.

- *Kassandra lives,* spoke a woman's voice in my mind.

- *Are you sure, Kupra?*

- *Apollo watches over her.*

According to the bard, at their funeral rites, the victims, namely Agamemnon, Kassandra and her twins, were given the honors due sacrificial victims. Because of this, the Queen had no bloodguilt in the eyes of her people.

"It was done in the manner of the old ways still respected by the Pelasgians, the Shore Folk," the bard concluded his tale. "Aigisthos is accepted as king. The lustral bath cleanses guilt."

"No! To us their old ways are ended, and this blood cries out for justice!" There was horror in Pyrrhos' eyes as he spoke.

The bard left the hall for the sleeping-room prepared for him.

Agamemnon was dead…killed, together with his children by Kassandra—twins, so most likely one of them was of Ajax the Lesser who raped her at Athené's altar—by Klytemnestra, whose first husband and son he had murdered to force her to marry him and take the throne.

Justice! Finally.

His death would not restore our world to its pre-Agamemnon era, neither did it bring back those tens of thousands Achaians and Trojans who had fallen as the result of his ambition. Nonetheless, he was dead. And I was glad that I had lived to hear the news of it.

I could not figure out how Kassandra's life might be spared, but now it was better to keep faith in the Voice.

It was late morning when I went down for breakfast. While I ate some bread and cheese with a spit-roasted onion, I heard Pyrrhos' voice in the courtyard. Another war? I had recognized his haranguing as military instructions. I finished and went to the doorway. He stood amidst chiefs of Phthiotis and Thessaly; they were receiving orders for the levying of troops.

Thalpia came with Molossos, and let the boy slide to the floor. Molossos tottered, fell flat, laughing with a clear, joyful sound. He ran to pull Xanthos' tail, and then to Ligyron, who was busy scraping designs on the stone pavement with a small dagger. When he proceeded to wrestle the dagger from him, Xanthos joined the fray, intimidating poor Ligyron with his hissing and spitting.

Pyrrhos turned and looked at the boys, then strode to them with Lycosa yapping at his heels. Swinging Molossos to his shoulders, he carried him back to me. "Don't look so troubled! It's never too soon for a man-child to learn war!"

Not for the first time I noted the striking likeness between father and son. Though Ligyron was the heir, Molossos was royal. The older boy was becoming ever more like my brother Andros, thoughtful, gentle, baby-faced. However, strong and husky Molossos had tried to walk at a much younger age than Ligyron. Now, howling with glee on his father's shoulders, he was a miniature Akhilles.

Pyrrhos dismissed his men and turned to me with bright eyes. "Oh Ãndrõmakhê, I know this child will be a great leader! I am right in my plans for him."

"What plans?" Fear iced me. He let the child down, who toddled off speedily after the departing warriors. "I will begin training him at the age of three, rather than the usual five."

"Ligyron is your heir," I spoke hastily. "Leave my son's training and education to me."

"That boy needs more than a woman's softness. I shall never take the scepter of Akhilles from Ligyron, but Molossos will be a greater king. Helenos will advise me on his future."

Pyrrhos left and I turned to Thalpia. "Bring my spinning," and I went out behind the palace where the hillside was cut into rows of seats leading down to a circular platform. Lycosa and Xanthos followed me.

I needed to think, think hard, and sat in a marble chair near the stage. Molossos ran before me and climbed onto the raised area. The animals sat by my feet.

Perhaps it was time to start speaking to Molossos about my dreams of resurrecting Troia. All along, I had been telling him stories of this civilized, golden kingdom. Also, he knew of Skamandrios; but as alive and traveling the Seven Seas with Kiron of Krete, who was as wise and holy as Kiron the Kentaur, who had taught his grandfathers Akhilles and Peleos. Thereby, I hoped, Molossos would grow up into the beacon drawing Skamandrios back home. And if I raised him right, gladly share its rule with the rightful heir, his half-brother.

"Someone is coming." Thalpia, holding my spindle, flax and distaff, touched my shoulder.

Pyrrhos and Helenos were striding down the bowl in our direction.

Pyrrhos put out a hand when I made to rise. "Don't go, our talk concerns Molossos."

I took my work from Thalpia, avoiding looking at Helenos, and began to spin. Pyrrhos turned to Helenos. "I did not order you back from Trikka for you to sit in that dank cell up there." He nodded toward the dormitory atop the hill. "I must have an omen about where Akastos is."

"My Voice does not speak on demand," Helenos replied.

"Fine! I'll find Akastos if I have to besiege every town between Argos and Laestrigonia."

"You should have left me in Trikka longer, to hear my patients. During a fever one of my pilgrims babbled of him, in a place called Opos. He is there with an old man called Menoitios."

"Menoitios! He fostered my father at Opos. He was King of Hellas, vassal to Peleos. And he deals now with Akastos?"

Helenos stepped back and drew his holy stone of Troia, from its pouch. Holding it to his forehead, he murmured, astonishingly, the eerie tones of a woman.

The sounds metamorphosed into coherent words, "You will overcome Menoitios and Akastos; cross westward for the lands of Molossos. You will find them where houses are roofed in wool and wooden walls are grounded in iron."

Pyrrhos exploded, "What kind of advice is this?" He stamped back and forth before me. "There are no such houses!"

Leaving us, he strode up the tiers and off to the royal palace.

I looked from Helenos to Molossos, "Is this war for the kingdom my son will inherit?"

"It will end a long-time feud." Helenos came and kissed me on the brow and cheeks while I clung to him. When we parted, I watched Thalpia on the stage with the child. "He will be all Trojan if I have anything to do with it."

Helenos moved his head in a sad negative. "Whatever he does, will be as son of Pyrrhos." He took my hands and put the stone in my palms. It was a rough cylinder, heavy, hard and black.

Helenos explained, "I told you this was given to me at Thymbra by Ilioneos, remember? It fell from heaven as a sign that the shrine belongs to Apollo. I bathe and swaddle this stone like a child, and it speaks to me."

The stone seemed to move in my hands and I nearly dropped it.

- Give it back to him, She spoke, *it is stamped with Helenos' signet, and your aura might interfere with it when he needs to consult.*

Helenos looked at me wide eyed. "It spoke to you!"

"No," I said, and handed it back to him.

"But from your expression…."

"My Goddess told me it's for you, only."

"Your Goddess?"

"Yes, my Goddess. Kupra."

"Kupra." He bit his lips, staring at me with such concentration as if he were trying to enter my soul in his quest to find Her.

"Alexis was my brother," I said now, "long time ago, when we lived on an island, in the Tirenean Sea. Kupra…was our mother."

Helenos' hands went to his ears as if not believing what he heard. "Why did you never speak of it to me before?"

"I don't know."

"Why did I not sense that you have the sight?"

"Because I don't! Not like…not like Kassandra. However, I know that Kassandra is not dead. Klytemnestra did not kill her, though she made everyone think she did. I don't know why."

"I tell you why. She didn't—couldn't—because they share a strong belief in the Goddess."

"And the Goddess must respect Apollo," I said, thinking of what Kupra's voice had told me, that Apollo watched over Kassandra.

"Probably. Kassandra is a pure soul; the gods respect that."

Pyrrhos returned with bouncing steps. Molossos was back riding upon his wide shoulders and laughed with delight.

"Ãndrõmakhê," Pyrrhos exclaimed, "this child is a true Akhilleid! Oh, how I admire you, Mother of Warriors! My sons with you will be sung by minstrels in the years to come!"

"Such is the blood of the Trojans," I replied quietly.

He did not take offense at that. "The best of Troia and Achaia will bring unending glory to our land, my queen. Your strength and mine are well matched."

"I would not agree with your assessment."

His eyes twinkled with assurance, "Oh yes, you do! Your very resistance is strength, my beautiful prize. It is well worth the struggle when such sons come of it. Fight me all you wish—the stronger you are the greater my own strength will grow. As for Molossos, he is so precocious that even I stand in awe in front of him."

- *Endurance is more effective than struggle, when used wisely.*

I shivered with foreboding.

Endurance.

More of that was required of me, for the rest of my life.

Endurance.

Oh, Goddess, how sorely you test me!

PART V: SONS

Chapter 30: Trikka

Sometimes, when I looked into my oval mirror of polished silver, I wished that my beauty were my ugliness; yet even if I were a veritable Medusa, Pyrrhos would still want me to mother his sons. I did not do anything to enhance my looks. Never used kohl to bring out the blue of my eyes, nor paint on my cheeks or lips. However, I did have one indulgence, more for protection against the elements than beauty, and that was a paste made of beaten together honey, almond oil, and an egg, which I slathered on my face and throat before a bath. There were other women, and always Briseis and Diomede, but Pyrrhos always came back to me. The very determination with which I resisted loving him, he said, would assure him of strong sons.

That I was seven years older than he, made me more desirable than younger women in his eyes, for I had the self-possession expected of a queen not to be denied.

By late summer, I could no longer deny I was pregnant again. Until then I had pretended to Thalpia that I was unwell for my usual three days each month, hoping to be mistaken.

I became short-tempered and snapped at Peleos when he reminded me that the more children I bore his grandson, the greater would be his— and mine—honor among the warriors of his land. Meanwhile the old king happily played games with Molossos, telling him stories of his own adventures and of Akhilles.

When I finally told him of the coming child, he agreed to assign Okyone to Thalpia for training as her assistant. Okyone took to her duties happily, learning quickly.

Soon I realized that Molossos, enthralled by his grandfather, was getting lost to me. In addition, the coming child, if another son, would be an Achaian rather than Trojan. Only with a girl could I expect to keep and train a child. Yet I could not wish for a girl, because she would be just another slave to some man.

Helenos—only Helenos—could help the future of a daughter of mine, by marrying me out of slavery. Strange how, his entire life, after the death of his little brother Chaon—the first son of Priam's to whom I was spoken for—had been that of an ascetic priest! Indeed, he was vastly different from all the other men I had known all my life.

"Pyrrhos would marry you," Peleos told me one day, "but he is too proud to say the word. He does not need to wait for Hermione to give him kingship to Lakedaimon; he is young and fiery, he can carve up an empire greater than that on his own. Besides, the people of your lands are waiting for your return, Āndrõmakhê. But with a strong king like Pyrrhos at your side. He can reconquer both Troia and Thébé from their present occupiers. However, he will not do so without you asking him first. Tell him you would be glad to be his wife, my child! Tell him while time is still at your side."

I bit my lips and looked at my feet.

To be official wife to Pyrrhos, son of Akhilles who slew my father and seven brothers, and then my husband with trickery, himself guilty of decapitating honorable Priam and not preventing the hurling of my son down Troia's walls...

Āndrõmakhê, Wife of Pyrrhos Akhilleides.

No longer Āndrõmakhê, Wife of Hektôr Priamides.

No!

I would not, could not.

I had to endure that he took possession of my body, but I did not have to surrender by giving him the honorific: Pyrrhos, *Husband* of Āndrõmakhê, Widow of Hektôr.

* * * *

It was near the time of first snow when Pyrrhos' household passed along the Peneos River to Trikka. The holy city lay on rolling ground beside the Selembria River. The winter there was miserable for me as my pregnancy progressed, and my tongue sharpened.

My new child decided to make its entrance into our world on a sunny, fresh-scented, day in spring. Attendant priestesses came from the Trikkan shrine and seated me on the bottomless birth-chair. Bracing myself against waves of pain, there I waited with straddled legs, my mother Latmia's face and voice lively in my mind.

At last, the infant, a boy, slid into the world and was bathed in oil by the most aged of the women.

Compared to Skamandrios and Molossos, he was an easy delivery. Smaller than Molossos had been at birth, and of colicky disposition. His cry was so like a squeal, that I laughed, "Until Pyrrhos names him I'll call him Smintheos. He is such a little field mouse."

He was small, and protectiveness sharpened the love I already felt for him. Peleos, wearing a protective amulet, examined the boy, basked in that he was flawless from head to toe, and accepted him on behalf of Pyrrhos. Though he could only be named when his father returned, Peleos' acceptance meant that the child was human and could not be exposed to death.

As the weather warmed, I got in the habit of walking with Thalpia, who carried Smintheos in a basket on wheels, to a grove of beeches and oaks that harbored a shrine of Paionian Apollo.

Encircled by a log fence, the shrine consisted of a stone altar with a pair of stellar columns, one supporting a golden disc, the other a silver moon. It stood against a tremendous beech whose yellow-green foliage shaded the area with mystic light. A clay pipe extended from a hollow in the great trunk and trickled water into a marble trough. Below this, the pavement of smooth slate glistened with damp. I often leaned on the fence to listen for an oracle, or a word of Kassandra, His priestess. I heard nothing except the soothing drip and rustle of water and leaves.

Then one day, I did indeed hear a word.

One single word: Zakyntos.

Zakyntos?

It chimed once more, and that was all.

Zakyntos.

Was this not a man's name?

Also, a distant place…an island. Tall, sharp cliffs, spilling into blue water. I began to tremble. Her image was alive in my mind; surely, this was a clue about her.

Oh, Kassandra! I so hope you are well…

When Thalpia and I returned home, I prayed for Pyrrhos' victorious return at the Dea Madre's altar set in my room. Though nothing would change that he had slain Priam, and Skamandrios had been in his grasp before being hurled into nothingness, he was now the sire of two of my children. Conceived against my will they were, but they were my sons, and he treated them fairly and lovingly.

As the summer passed, I got involved more and more running the household as well as his neighboring estates. Much to Peleos' pleasure, their profits began to rise.

* * * *

One autumn day, while I was upstairs nursing Smintheos, I heard a huge racket streaming up the stairs, namely Lycosa and Xanthos, yapping, howling, and meowing. I looked up to see Pyrrhos at my door, clad in light armor over short tunic, both animals at his feet looking up at him ecstatically. After a two-year long absence, Pyrrhos had returned unexpectedly, without any fanfare.

Rushing to me, he knelt before me, his hands placed on my knees as in supplication, staring at my face. I noticed that he smelled clean, and his short blond beard recently trimmed. I also saw the deep scars, some old, some fresh and still purplish, on his brow, cheek, side of his neck, and exposed parts of his arms. They left me cold.

Pyrrhos spoke chokingly, "You've given me a second beautiful son, Āndrŏmakhê! You should be my wife. Gods have blessed my victory. I have so much now—so much worth fighting for!"

"Then you have killed Akastos?" I replied calmly.

"Mentes, the bard, will sing of that," he said, rising.

The child dropped my breast and Pyrrhos took him from me, holding him against his broad chest. The little one screamed with a very loud voice, sounding like a much older boy.

He laughed. "What a voice! He will be another Stentor [1]."

I scarcely knew him at this moment as he glanced from the child to me, his expression so openly vulnerable.

Then he demanded, "Stand up with me! The mother of my sons must share this time of glory."

I stood and he returned Smintheos to my arms. "From now on, honored Āndrŏmakhê, things will *have* to be better between us." His voice trembled, as he looked at the boy, asleep on my breast. "You will bring him when I have bathed; his naming is long overdue."

"I call him Smintheos."

Pyrrhos laughed. "What kind of a name is that for *my* son? His name is Peleos."

Helenos made augury at the naming-feast.

Mentes sang a new epic of Pyrrhos when the meal was done.

The son of Akhilles found Menoitios in his empty palace at Opos, unharmed, but left to starve. Akastos had ransacked both palace and town, so that the king was forced to go out daily to scour the already ravaged countryside. Pyrrhos rushed onward in pursuit of his enemy, leaving a few men under the charge of Helenos to set things right for the old king. Pyrrhos clashed fiercely with Akastos in a narrow passage through the Pindos Mountains. Veteran Myrmidons who had fought with Akhilles, said later they could not tell who was leading them, Pyrrhos or Akhilles.

Most of the Magnates were slain in that fiery battle, and a truce declared long enough to gather and immolate the twisted heaps of men along the roads and among the rocks.

At dawn, Akastos was away with the remnants of his men. When caught again at Larissa, they were at the very borders of Magnesia north of Pharsalos. Days followed days of savage battle until, on a sultry afternoon, Akastos held his spear crosswise for truce. The two leaders met on a patch of earth before a cave where three rivers joined. At that holy place, they swore, over the halves of a horse, never again to invade one another's territory.

Pyrrhos was now undisputed regent over his grandfather's lands.

Then the bard's tale took on a new rhythm. Bypassing the Pindos range into Epirus, Pyrrhos found that tribesmen from the north had set up their own rulers. Here Pyrrhos spent most of the time he had been away, freeing his people from the invaders. He was welcomed as a savior, and chosen as Lord of Epirus. It was there that Molossos would rule after him.

When Mentes' chant ended, Pyrrhos called Molossos to him from play with other children. "My son, Ligyron, will rule here after Peleos, but for you I have a new kingdom," he told him gravely. "From now on, you shall be properly trained for rulership."

The boy held his own and stared at his father eye to eye.

"The land will be named for you," Pyrrhos concluded.

Sending Molossos back to the other boys, he turned to me. "You can thank Helenos for his prophecy, my dear. Near Dodona, I indeed found such a village as he had foretold for our son. The nomads were living in tents roofed in blankets spun of wool, held up by spears, with logs piled for walls." He leaned closer to me. "That boy will bring honor to us for generations in the future. You will be remembered as the Mother of Heroes."

I remained silent.

At a quick motion from Pyrrhos, Helenos stepped forward. I noted a new firmness in him as he stood before our master. His pale hair had darkened to a light auburn and was piled above his forehead in Trojan fashion, horns ending in a long plait down his back. He still wore the ceremonial wreath of laurel twisted with wool. His face was bronzed and creased by wind and sun. He no longer was clean-shaven but wore a short-trimmed beard after the Mysian fashion. His eyes glinted as he glanced from Pyrrhos to me and back again. It shook me as I sensed that it was Helenos, not Pyrrhos who was master at that moment. His spare, muscular body seemed, if possible, taller than before.

Pyrrhos spoke, "You have served me well, Helenos. You saw truth when you told me of the kingdom for Molossos."

"My duty is to speak only truth." His voice was quiet, yet sounded throughout the room.

"You will be Chief Hierophant here at Trikka," Pyrrhos declared, "Anakos is no longer able to serve, but will live with you in the high priests' house as Senior Advisor. You will have appropriate slaves, clothing and jewelry. The novices will be under your direction." He paused, and then added benevolently, "Also, you need a wife."

"Then I am a free man?"

Such a throb went from my heart through my body as to shake my chair, but I gripped the arms and did not look away from the two men. My hour of deliverance, at last?

Pyrrhos laughed, not unkindly, the joy of a man playing Zeus.

"Not yet," he replied, "though one day I will allow you to buy your own freedom. Until then you will serve me, so long as my lands are secure and my sons under age. Bur for now, that ascetic life of yours must end. I will find you a suitable wife."

"I need no wife."

"Is there none among the priestesses who has caught your eye?"

"No, my lord. The Goddess requires all my strength."

"The Goddess? But you serve Apollo Healer, here!" He pressed on after a short pause, "Some boy, perhaps? Or are you indeed a eunuch?"

"The Divinities absorb all my vital forces."

"So be it, then. But, if you ever want a wife, ask me. Any of my slavewomen. I brought several of noble blood! Young, comely, and fertile. Now return to your sacrifices and medicines."

When he had gone, Pyrrhos looked at me, a malicious gleam in his eyes. I kept my face devoid of any expression.

* * * *

I was short on patience that winter after Molossos reached his fourth summer on earth, and I entered my twenty-eight. The first time Pyrrhos took him in his chariot, he set him on the handrail, holding him with one hand while reining the horses with his other. Ligyron was already standing in the car, pretending to drive. Molossos kicked gleefully and almost fell while Pyrrhos restrained the restive steeds.

From that day on Molossos, taller than everyone at his age, was always around his father's chariot or horses. At such times when Pyrrhos took Ligyron instead, Molossos kicked and screamed, broke toys and fought other boys. Jealousy grew between him and Ligyron. Peleos the Younger, at three years, was no longer nursing. At last, Molossos accepted his younger brother, sharing with him the training his tutors gave him.

So, as time passed, my pride in my sons grew. I was already running his household and nearby estates, but in addition I deployed my skills at reading and writing, which I had not been disposed to do until now, and oversaw all the scribes in his employ. This resulted in more honest account keeping, increasing his wealth yet again.

To my dismay, though, Molossos' temper took a sudden uneven course, happy and fretful by turns. He clung ever more tenaciously to his father and became timid of me. His explosive temperament was daily more like his father and grandfather.

There were times when I studied little Peleos and found no resemblance to anyone. My pleasure in him was tinged with sadness, for I sensed that he would not be as brave as Molossos. Whenever he escaped from my helping hands and suddenly fell, he would cry and look around for help and soothing words, unlike Skamandrios, and later Molossos, who had been independent soon out of their swaddlings. I listened to his high-pitched voice babbling wordless sentences, and yearned for him, rejected him, and loved him.

Occasionally I weighed whether it would not be best to accept the inevitable and be more loving to Pyrrhos. It would only be common sense. Still, I hated myself to continue bearing sons to the man in whose hands Skamandrios had met an unknown fate.

Then one winter evening during after-dinner wine, Pyrrhos told Peleos, "I march to Sparta as soon as the weather warms. I have waited long enough for Hermione. Meneláos may keep Helen in Egypt forever, but Hermione is my promised wife."

"But the Spartan princes claim Lakedaimon."

Pyrrhos' laugh was harsh. "Nikostratos and Megapenthes were got by Meneláos on a slavewomen. Hermione, not they, is heir to the land. Who are they to break their father's oath to me?"

Peleos gave me a meaningful look, communicating that I should at last voice my willingness to be his wife, so he would drop Hermione.

I remained silent.

But before Pyrrhos' troops were prepared, pilgrims to the Trikkan shrine for healing brought news from Mykene.

Orestes, son of Agamemnon, had returned home with his blood-brother Pylados. Together with his older sister, Elektra, he had murdered Aigisthos, the usurper to Agamemnon's throne, as well as their mother, Klytemnestra, thus avenging the murder of their father. Klytemnestra had brought back the matriarchy to Mykene, but now through her own son's deeds, the road to patriarchy had opened. No more replacing of kings by queens after a few years laughed the men. Yet Orestes had left Mykene with Pylados immediately afterward, being refused the throne by an outraged public. The Princess Elektra was chosen in his stead.

"Chaos reigns supreme in Mykene," the pilgrim ended his tale.

King Peleos shook his head. "Will nothing be left for us, to enjoy our victory over Troia?"

Pyrrhos laughed with an ugly sound.

Peleos called an Assembly on the next day. "I must have a vote," he declared. "Pyrrhos Neoptolemos, as Conqueror of Epirus, holds that land. He rules for me here, in Phthiotis and Greater Thessaly. We must cede these lands of Akhilles to Pyrrhos after me, as overlord."

One of the elders stepped forward. "My lord, we are not clear as to this land of Epirus."

"It reaches from Hellas to the Western Sea, centered by Lake Pambotia, including the high oracle of Zeus at Dodona. If we do not harden our control there, those earth-roving chiefs will, threatening our own lands."

"So be it." The elders agreed, and the Councilmen rattled their staves on the floor in approval. "Hail, King of Epirus!" they shouted as one man.

Peleos spoke again, "The lord Pyrrhos is soon to marry the heiress to Lakedaimon, Hermione."

"Then all is well."

Pyrrhos seemed grown even taller as he towered beside his grandfather. "I rule under suzerainty of my father's father only. After me, the first Thessalian king will reign there, my son Molossos by Āndrōmakhê. Let the land be called Molossia for him, under the protection of the divine Zeus Molossos."

And so it was agreed. The Assembly broke up and Pyrrhos took Molossos into the courtyard. I followed as the boy rode his father's shoulders to where the chariot was being hitched. When he heard my footsteps, Pyrrhos turned, the blue fire in his eyes catching mine. He was so mature, and yet in a strange way vulnerable despite the muscles of his sun-browned body rippling as he moved. He was so beautiful in the sunlight just then that for one moment, I wished we had met under different circumstances and I could love him.

"I could marry you before Hermione, and you would be my First Wife," he spoke as if he had sensed my thoughts.

"This is not the custom," I smiled sweetly. "Besides, Hermione would never accept another wife."

"If any one, *I* am the man able to change customs!"

"But NOT in order to call Hektôr's Widow, your wife."

He gave me a long, dark look, and I held it unswervingly.

"You will regret your stubbornness," he said finally.

I bit my lips, the vise of foreboding squeezing my heart. My gaze traveled to Molossos, high on his father's shoulders. Both of my sons loved their father, and so did Xanthos and Lycosa. Pyrrhos meant for my sons to have kingdoms of their own, but what if he had other sons with Hermione? From what was being said about her, she was a woman of great ambition. Surely, she would manipulate her husband for her sons to get control of his lands. Yet, need I worry? Could I not, one day, turn such misfortune to advantage? Without heritage from their father, his landless sons would be forced to go elsewhere—and I could steer their course toward Troia....

Little Peleos ran out from behind me, with Okyone after him, playing nursemaid. Pyrrhos gave her a sharing-smile as the younger boy, fat and ruddy, held both arms to his father. Pyrrhos slid Molossos into his chariot and slapped the reins into his hands. "Hold the horses for a moment," he ordered, then swung the naked Peleos atop his head, chubby legs astride each cheek.

Laughing, he turned back to me, "What sons we have! One kiss, for them." He came to me and pressed his moist lips upon mine for an endless moment. I did not cringe.

"Now good fortune will promote our future," he said, returning Peleos into my arms. "Fill your breasts with lions' milk, my dear, so he will not fail us."

Then he turned to spring into the chariot. Just then, Molossos slapped the reins across the horses' backs, and the chariot shot away. Pyrrhos grabbed the mounting rail just as a hub caught against the jamb of the gateway. Leaping inside, he grabbed the reins from Molossos and rattled into the street and out of sight.

Peleos began flailing in my arms. Handing him to Okyone, I summoned Thalpia with a look, and following an inner call, set out for the holy precinct.

Helenos was there, beneath the Tree of Oracle, arms outstretched halfway around the trunk, forehead pressing against the trunk.

Motioning Thalpia back, I stood close against the log fence until his prayer ended. It was a long time until Helenos moved at all, and then it was as if a wind disturbed his robes about his body, though the air was still. His arms sank downward and he leaned his head sideways against the tree, eyes still closed. Time passed, and at last I stood close beside him, but he remained motionless. His face was pale, his breathing shallow.

"Kiron is dying," he spoke finally.

[1] Stentor was a herald of the Greek forces during the Trojan War. His name has given rise to the adjective "stentorian", meaning loud-voiced, for which he was famous. Homer said his "voice was as powerful as fifty voices of other men." Stentor died after his defeat by Hermes in a shouting contest.

Chapter 31: Passaron

Pyrrhos raised his cup and poured a libation, then drank deeply. He fixed his eyes on Helenos, who waited at the altar in the great hall. The augury for his military expedition had been favorable. I sensed that he was going to announce his departure to invade Lakedaimon. Pyrrhos' gaze moved from Helenos to me, then to Peleos and others who were sharing our meal at the long table. "Our time here is ended."

"But, my boy..." Peleos stopped, fingers gripping his cup.

"Father's Father, you will go to Pharsalos. I take the others to Passaron."

"Pharsalos? Passaron?" The old man suddenly seemed feeble.

"It is essential that you be protected. Trikka is only a medical center, not the seat of kings." He looked at Helenos. "You are to escort King Peleos and Prince Ligyron back to Pharsalos, and remain there to train Ligyron. You will have rooms in the palace."

"And freedom?" Helenos asked.

"What more could a free man ask than what I give you?" Pyrrhos' tone was sharp. "You are a Trojan, and I'll not have rivals in my land. Do as I order, and when the time is right you will be free, and I will give you your own land for your children to inherit. As for the present, I trust you more than others among your people."

"My boy," Peleos the Elder said, "I think you need not keep him, or Āndrōmakhê, any longer in slavery. You should free them and marry them together, and leave them both with me."

"And lose the inheritance for Ligyron? The gods forbid it! It is not a long march between Pharsalos and Passaron, if need be, I will be on call to defend you and my son."

"Pharsalos..." the old king quavered.

"Grandfather, Trikka is only a medical center and Pharsalos the chief city of your kingdom. I bid you to return where you belong."

He shifted his gaze to me. "You and our sons come with me to Passaron. When I bring Hermione, I will rule Molossia from there. Our first son will inherit there after me." He turned back to Peleos. "You will rule Hellas and Phthiotis, with Ligyron as your heir." He touched the old man's hand. "Helenos will be your protector."

Helenos stood in front of Pyrrhos. "What of my work here?"

"The shrine was holy long before Asklepeios, and will be here long after you. You will find a priest to succeed you. You are the son of kings, Helenos, and will now nurture kings for my people." He glanced at the other slave-women. "You, Okyone, will look after Ligyron."

"No! I beg! Leave my niece with me!"

He paused a moment. "Fine, so be it. Briseis will look after the other children as before. As for Diomede...she goes with Ligyron, for she had loved his mother, Lanassa. And at the proper time, she will teach him the proper use of women."

Pyrrhos turned to Helenos and spoke at length, his tone low.

I leaned toward King Peleos. "Old Father," I whispered as a sob rose deep within me, "you have been most kind to me. I love you as I never thought I would care for an Achaian."

"May the protection of Kallichora be always with you," he replied, placing his bony, wrinkled hand over mine on the chair arm. I raised it to my lips and kissed the fingers one by one, as hot tears streamed down my cheeks.

Helenos remained stiff as he listened to Pyrrhos with opaque eyes, his face expressionless.

What does he see? I wondered. His oracle about Kiron's death had been terrifying, for while it had affirmed that Kiron indeed saved Skamandrios' life, it had also attested to my son's utter loneliness now, traveling as he was in some distant land, so distant that even Helenos' vision had not been able to breach the gap of time and space.

* * * *

New land. Like a recurring nightmare, I was on the road again. The arduous journey seemed endless as our caravans passed from Phthiotis into Epirus. Xanthos and Lycosa were grown quite independent, and traveled on their own, though alongside us, at their own pace. Level plains gave way to the wild heights of Dodona. Pyrrhos took his entourage up the steep and narrow Way.

The tall summit above us was frightening in its awesome majesty, where rocks like teeth grinned above trees that seemed to wrestle themselves from the inaccessible earth. It was as if supernatural powers warned away human presumption on the climb to Dodona. Thundering torrents roared down from black clouds split with lightning, rushing down into gullets. As always, I called Xanthos and Lycosa inside when we paused for the night. Xanthos was now big-boned and strong, more a lynx than an ordinary cat. Lycosa too was big and strong for her age, and Pyrrhos joked that with these two animals I was as well protected as by two of his best soldiers. The first time that Pyrrhos took them to a hunt together with his trained dogs, they had thrown themselves into the thick of it with gusto, bringing down prey twice their size, and running to lay them at Pyrrhos's feet.

The next two days were bogged by heavy rains. We were slowed by black squelching soil miring wheels and hooves. The narrow mountain passes, rough with stones and threatened by overhanging boulders, seemed endless. Then, at last, we reached the Acheron River. Pyrrhos had sent Herald Tereos ahead, and he met us at the opened gates of a small settlement. Inside, a maze of tracks meandered between stone huts of the lower city. Arrived at the citadel, we found it built atop a small plateau jutting from the mountainside. Winds tore at us and struck like gongs reverberating into deafening echoes. Then I saw what made these sounds: a tremendous circle of bronze kettles in the midst of which was one larger than the others. This was straddled by the bronze statue of a man holding in one hand three chain-lashes that whipped in the wind against his kettle, roaring like mighty thunders as the sound echoed in the empty cauldrons around.

Barefoot priests conducted us to the visitors' inn where I collapsed into heavy sleep, surrounded with my sons and animal companions.

Awakening early, I stepped onto the terrace, and with Xanthos and Lycosa standing guard at either side of me, looked down into the sheer precipice. Bluish mists drifted there, hiding and revealing rocks, trees, and a rushing torrent. I felt warmth surge inside me, bringing along a familiar, old feeling. Compelled to raise my hands, I saw the reddish light sizzle and streak through my fingertips.

Palming my opal and Hektôr's cartouche that hung nestled between my breasts, silently I called out to Skamandrios, trying to envision his face, his body. Six years had passed since we had been torn apart from each other! Images lit up and eclipsed, yet none of them clear. Nevertheless, there was something. Stronger than ever, the certain sense of that Skamandrios was alive and making his way in the world. But, where? How? And with whom?

Pyrrhos came out now, took me by the arm and together we went outside, to where Thalpia met us. He left us to make offerings at the oracle of Zeus.

Leaving the boys with Briseis and Okyone, I took Thalpia and went to the shrine of Dionne, the Mother Goddess so named by the locals. The shrine was located on a high plateau at the foot of a still higher mountain. As I made my offerings on behalf of Skamandrios, priestesses came and went constantly about the deep-set grotto where the meteorite-image stood. On either side of the ancient figure slow-burning lamps glowed atop wooden columns on round stone bases.

You will never again see Skamandrios, rang Helenos' words in my memory. *Oh, Great Kind Mother!* I cried out inwardly, *just let him live...watch over him, protect him, do not let him suffer the pains of cold and hunger. And lead him safely to his destiny!*

I did not see Pyrrhos again that day, for he was keeping vigil for his turn at the oracle. The great oak tree of Zeus roared in the high winds, but the speaking of its leaves was understood only by the ascetic priests. It was the second dawn before we resumed our journey.

Pyrrhos handed me a leaden disc engraved with symbols.

"Zeus has favored me," he stated, explaining each pictograph as the priests had interpreted for him. "Our son Molossos will be welcomed in the land. The oracle foretells that he will father a long line of kings, and that they will control all the tribes of Hellas between Molossian Epirus and Thessaly, even far southward. Indeed, Molossos, your son from me, Pyrrhos Neoptolemos—and not Skamandrios, son of Hektôr Astyanax—who will keep your name upon the lips of men."

* * * *

Two more days along the trade routes through mountain passes and marshes were endured along the river before we could reach Passaron. Mountain tribes subdued by Pyrrhos earlier, gave surly hospitality to the party of their conqueror. Then at last, we were among the Suliots, strung out along the river and into Passaron. Their chief had perished at the hands of Pyrrhos, so they gave little resistance to his occupation of their land. I noticed that they were more like Trojans than Thessalian. The men here cut their hair to shoulder-length and wore trousers, some lightly twisted into elaborate creases, others full as skirts caught at the ankle. Their language too had a sweater sound to my ears, for the intonation was close to Trojan.

At last the city of Passaron, squeezed between river and mountains. There had been a heavy rain all day, black mud squelching succulently under wheels and hooves. Travel was through such laborious terrain that even Lycosa and Xanthos preferred the dry comfort of the tented wagon.

I looked out from under the damp skins that made a roof above us, and was relieved upon seeing the rough stone walls of human habitation. The Lower City was a maze of tracks between huts of mud-plastered stone with wooden beam-ends, where pale, pinched faces stared from windows or thin children clustered inside doorways. Above all, rose the fortified citadel, set as if by some Titan upon a small plateau jutting from the mountain.

The narrow plain along which we had traveled continued to one side of the city and narrowed almost to a pass as the caravan-route followed the river. Everything was shadowed by precipices and rocks like fortresses with dark chasms between. The raving Acheron River churned and foamed out from one of these gloomy gorges, rushed beside the city, and lost itself southward in the shallow Acherusian Lake. At the palace gate, Herald Tereos stood in welcome. Pyrrhos slighted and stood bareheaded, looking up at the sky, while the rain streaked his hair over his shoulders and down his back, splashing onto the cobblestones around his oiled boots.

So here we are, I thought, *we have brought our son, Molossos, to the threshold of his own future.*

* * * *

Autumn came and still Pyrrhos had not marched against the Lakedaimonians. The Enienes and Perraboans of the area did not readily accept their new ruler; these fierce tribesmen kept him busy on the wave between outlying villages. The Suliots, the strongest of the tribes, rebelled briefly, and were quickly subdued.

Yet, in the end, it was the Suliot priests, assembling for conference in the city who oversaw Pyrrhos' election as king.

I joined the ceremonies on behalf of my son Molossos. Tables were set up for public feasting in the market place, with one set beside a wooden throne-chair were Pyrrhos sat, richly robed. On his forehead, he bore the sacred tattoo of office, a circle surrounding a cross. Before him, long planks set on stones were piled with food where all were invited to feast.

The local Hierophant stood up, asking the ritual question: "What are the duties of a king?"

"He must be just, and honor the gods." Pyrrhos held up a round object as he spoke. "He must lead his men in war, and give protection to his tributary chiefs. He will levy men and supplies from those under him, as needed. At year's end, he will collect one-tenth of all produce for storage against siege, and provide shelter in the citadel at times of war. I, Pyrrhos Neoptolemos, Son of Akhilles, will do all this." He stood up as he finished.

The priest addressed the assembly: "We have a New Warrior among us!"

Cheers and clattering of weapons gave approval.

The priest turned back to Pyrrhos. "You are King of Epirus in the name of Zeus, of Hera, and of Apollo."

After anointing his head with oil, the priest presented Pyrrhos with a wand of black iron entwined with silver and gold wire. At the tip of this was mounted a large-crystal ball-veined in gold. Light from it struck into my eyes like needles. Oh, Great Mother, I knew that sphere! It was my father's symbol of power! I wanted to scream, grab and wield Pyrrhos' sword, to snatch it away from his hands.

Then Pyrrhos' words pierced my heart, "I, Pyrrhos Achilleides, name this land Molossia, for my son. By this scepter, I swear to honor the gods and be fair to my people. In witness, I have joined this symbol of two kingdoms—this land and that of the Trojans. My father took this globe as trophy from the scepter-head of Êetiôn, revered, godlike King of the Mysians."

Amidst howls of rejoicing, I sprang forward, screaming, flailing my arms as I pushed through the crowd to get near him, to take my father's treasure. All around me the crowd shouted praises, having mistaken my ardor for honor to their new king.

"My lady!" Thalpia's shout, her strong hands gripping my elbow, pulled me back.

"Thalpia, he must not keep that!"

We were at the courtyard door before I could hear Thalpia's repeated words, "You have Hektôr's cartouche ring, Skamandrios' cup and chariot. Pyrrhos is father of your sons, Lady, and they will inherit all of his that belongs to you. Therefore, Molossos will one day hold your father's insignia. Rejoice, your father King Êetiôn lives on!"

* * * *

Pyrrhos, as undisputed king, young, fiery, and enthusiastic, went about his territory seeing to matters of justice and tribute. He treated me with courtesy, allowed me free rein in household matters, let me supervise the scribes, and though his passion for me never waned, I saw the rise of a wariness in him that did not bode well. At last, I admitted to myself that indeed, in his own way, he had loved me for a long time, deeper than I had judged him capable. Now resentment that I did not return his feelings superseded his love.

Young Peleos was now more often with Molossos and the men than Okyone and Briseis. Molossos was so large for his age, and had developed such a Zeusian temper that I feared he might kill his younger brother as so often happened with destined heroes, but Pyrrhos laughed away my fears.

"Peleos is almost four, and it's time you weaned him from your breast," he declared. "You need another child to absorb your worries."

The last travelers of the season brought news of fresh turmoil in Lakedaimon and Mykene. The people, leaderless except for Princess Elektra at Mykene, were struggling to restore the old way and make her their supreme ruler. And travelers from Lakedaimon reported that sons of Meneláos ruled with iron fists. They had vanquished those who had wanted Hermione for their queen. All around the shores of the Western and Eastern Aegean Sea, Matriarchal rule was dying in favor of Patriarchal, which thrived on aggression, plunder, and rape.

Amid the first snowmelts of spring, a messenger from Sparta arrived. "Lady Helen sent inquiries to all her allies for the whereabouts of Prince Orestes. She has prepared Hermione for marriage, but the bridegroom has not arrived."

"*Orestes?*" Pyrrhos flared. "*I* am the bridegroom, and Hermione is to be sent here!"

"Helen promised Hermione to Orestes when they were yet children," the man explained, flinching. "The lands of Mykene and Lakedaimon will be united through them. There is talk of restoring the Queenship in Mykene."

"Inform their majesties that unless Meneláos honors his promise made to me at Troia, I will take not only his daughter, but all his lands as well."

The messenger straightened. "My lord! Know that Meneláos will not permit a return to the old ways anywhere. Helen's plan to unite the two lands through that marriage is not to be. This is my private message to you from Meneláos. He will see that Hermione comes to you, for he has sons to succeed him at Sparta."

Pyrrhos' reply rang with warning, "Inform their majesties I will wait only a reasonable time longer. But, when I have everything ready for my bride, if she is not here, I *will* take her."

When the messenger had gone to his room, Pyrrhos followed me to our chamber. "You have not conceded to be my wife willingly, therefore you will be my bridal gift to Hermione," he announced from the doorway. "Get Thalpia to teach you her arts. Your room will be next to this, where Hermione can call you easily."

He came in and seized my hand, pulling me to our bed.

Frozen, I stood while he pulled all clothing from me and removed his own. "But now, I will remember your beauty," he said. "You must give me the best we've ever shared, for today we will make our youngest son."

He clamped his mouth over mine, arms entwining me like serpents, as my screams were slaughtered in my throat. He pushed me back upon the bed and I stiffened.

It seemed to endure forever, but then at last he left me. I did not move. I was left bare upon the bed, aching all over. I let my mind turn blank, then drift, and roseate tints of sunset crept into the room.

A swirling white mist enveloped me and I was walking among trees. Everything about me was white as moonlight, frosty cold, yet beautiful. I walked among trees but they, too, were white as moonlight. When I reached for a pale grape in its cluster, I found it like marble; I touched a stony leaf, and then ran from one thing to another touching each, but everything was white as snow and hard as metal.

At last I came to a city—was it Troia, not fallen after all? It was white, still, and silent. No birds sang, no insects chirped, no people chattered. Silence pressed into my head so that tears were forced from my eyes. Then I was inside and everything was garlanded as for a festival; something was expected here yet did not arrive. The air was clear like crystal and without movement. Buildings were all great palaces of large smooth blocks from whitest marble. I reached the Agora and at last saw human figures; but they were of carved stone, each one with a great spread of wings. The deathly cold of still air came closer and closer until it turned as soft as a baby's breath.

As the only living thing here, I asked of the stillness why I had come, but no reply issued forth. Hektôr was not here, nor the laughter of Skamandrios. Then a series of pictures moved before me, of scenes I did not know, of things that were yet to happen.

I was in them, on a ship with a young man. Then I saw a picture of a scene I had lived through, and knew that it had not happened that way. Wise Kiron was standing atop the Skaian Tower at Troia, holding Skamandrios. He reached the child out over space and looked away. My son stared downward with wonder and terror in his eyes.

There were no colors; all was white.

I struggled to free my child, and waked.

The room was black. I lay naked on the bed in the chill night. Slowly I pulled the covers over and turned my back to the window.

"Skamandrios," I whispered, and slept.

Chapter 32: Hermione, Daughter of Helen

"So!" Pyrrhos slammed down his emptied wine cup.

The messenger repeated his words, "Meneláos, Son of Plisthenos, Son of Atros, King of Sparta and Overlord of Lakedaimon, sends greetings. Queen Helen has been unable to locate Prince Orestes, and has agreed to your marriage with her daughter."

"And saved herself from another war." Pyrrhos' laugh rang through the hall. "You will tell me more when you have rested. I see you have had a hard journey and I will not keep you standing here unbathed." He motioned to the bearer who was about to refill his cup. "Ask Lady Āndrõmakhê to see after this man."

"My lord, the princess Hermione is half a day's travel behind me. She is already your wife."

"Already my wife? And right behind you?" Pyrrhos thundered.

"King Meneláos ordered a full bridal for her, his son Menalippos standing in for you." The man breathed in deeply. "King Meneláos did this to assure his word will be kept. He mistrusts his wife when it comes to Orestes."

"Ah." Pyrrhos motioned the man away. His eyes shifted to me. "See that this man is properly looked after. All must be ready for my wife's arrival."

"Your *wife?*" I could not believe my ears.

"Yes." He looked away, but not quick enough and I caught the look of dejection in his eyes. Sighing, he added, "You are mistress here until Hermione enters that door. Look to your duties." He sprang to his feet and strode to the outer door. "Get my chariot ready." He returned, passing me and leaping up the stairs.

I nodded to the Spartan. "If you will come with me."

He was soon in the bathing room attended by slave girls.

I went to Pyrrhos' room, where he was rummaging in his clothes chest. "What is this about your wife? Am I to prepare for a wedding?"

He dragged a robe of Trojan purple embroidered in gold from his chest, tossed it onto the bed, and slammed down the lid.

"You did not hear?"

"I don't trust my ears, unless it comes from your mouth."

He shrugged off his clothes and struggled into his ceremonial robe. "While I am riding out to greet Hermione, you will see to our bridal feast."

"Yes, my lord."

He slung jeweled chains around his neck, and then seized my wrist, pulling me close. "Too bad you never stopped hating me, Āndrōmakhê. Resisting me for you mourned Hektôr, I understood, and lived with it. Resisting me because you are too proud to bend to my rule, I could live with, too. But hating me…without ever giving any consideration to the sincerity of my feelings..."

"Sincerity of your feelings," I repeated woodenly.

"No, I cannot accept this any longer! I loved you Āndrōmakhê, and love you still. But you are the property of Hermione now, and whatever happens henceforth, you have no one to blame but yourself."

Leaving me open-mouthed, he thumped down the stairs, and out.

I raced after him, stopping at the doorway when I saw Molossos. He stood in his father's chariot, reining in the horses.

Turning back into the hall, I ordered the preparation of food. At the last moment, I remembered to send for flowers and branches to garland columns and walls.

By nightfall, Thalpia was helping me dress in a loose robe I had fashioned from a length of Hekabe's purple cloth when the royal caravan clattered into the courtyard.

"Remember," Thalpia said sadly, "to do everything for her as I have for you." She tossed a veil of gold threads over me. I drew it around myself like a cloak, and Thalpia set a silver circlet over it to hold it in place. "That's good, now you are my highborn Trojan Queen again. You will always be, no matter who is mistress here."

She lifted the veil in front and tossed it over so that it trailed down my back. "Hermione must know to treat you properly," Thalpia said, opening the door. "You'd best see to things now."

By the time I returned to the hall, the bridal pair had already gone up to their room. Men were carrying kettles of water up to the bathing room, and I started back up to see after Hermione's bath.

This duty over, I came down to find Molossos feeding the horses. He was bent over a manger, and for a moment my heart thumped as fear shot through me. Hektôr's spirit was here! How often I had helped my beloved husband, after a day's battle, to reward his steeds for a safe return home! Then I took hold of myself; Molossos was Pyrrhos' son, and Hektôr's spirit was not here.

The boy stepped back from his task, patting a soft equine nose before he turned his head and saw me.

"Will you come in with me now for the feast?" I asked.

"Later, for the dance. Peleos and I eat in the barracks as usual." His smile twisted my heart. If only he were Skamandrios.

The aroma of baking bread, telling how efficiently the household was operating, drifted out and I went back inside to wait.

It was much later when the bridal pair descended the stairs. Pyrrhos, still in his purple, looked neat and smoothly coifed. Hermione's beauty was so like her mother's that I could not restrain the gasp escaping my throat. On her head was a mass of silver flowers mixed in with green feathers. Her hair hung down her back in sausage-curls, its color amber like Helen's, but her oval face had the ruddiness of Meneláos. She wore a green dress of the old fashion, the skirt in tiers of flounces edged in silver. Her silver-tipped breasts rested on a stiff corselet. When she glanced at me, I noticed her eyes gleamed like turquoises. She was of an age with Pyrrhos, though she seemed younger. Both were flushed, proving they had shared marital intimacy.

While the maids brought plates of food, Pyrrhos called me to the chair he shared with his wife. "My dear Hermione, this is my wedding gift to you, Hektôr's widow Ãndrõmakhê, Troia's queen by right, to serve you as befits *my* queen."

Hermione clapped her hands, eyes gleaming with pleasure, and she laughed. "What a wonderful present!" She looked me straight in the eyes. "My mother told me about you and Hektôr." She leaned on Pyrrhos' shoulder. "Oh Pyrrhos, everyone will envy me for such a slave as was the wife of Hektôr!" She laughed again. "Let me see you, Ãndrõmakhê; turn around! Do it now. Slowly. I need to know if you have any blemishes."

I did not move a muscle. Was Pyrrhos still as callous as that time on Skyros?

He shifted in his chair, seeming tense. "There will be time for that later, my dear." He laughed nervously. Indeed things were different now; I was the mother of his sons.

I turned my back to them and head held high, returned to my chair where Thalpia had brought food to my table.

The meal was over and wine poured when the strains of a flute whistled on the air. Bard Demos was still at his usual place, lyre wrapped. A glossy red-haired Spartan maiden leaned against a column, an ivory flute at her lips. A hushed silence pervaded the hall and Hermione left her seat. Twirling slowly, she outlined a circle around the hearth in time to the wavering melody of the flute. Twisting and turning ever faster, arms outstretched, she held one palm upward and the other with fingers drooping. The white feathers of her headdress bent to her gyrations as her skirt belled, revealing ankles, calves, knees. The flute shrieked into one wavering line of sound.

Memory shivered within my heart. Long ago Helen had danced like this, the snake-incantation of Britomartis.

Then Hermione slowed, arms drifting to her sides, and she slid to the floor as Pyrrhos stepped forward and lifted her in his arms.

* * * *

It was late the next morning when Hermione sent for me, her newest noble-born slave, her toy to command. "My bath. I'll be ready by the time you have the water heated." She was alone in the bed. "My nurse will be there with us."

I swallowed a sharp reply, and went out to follow instructions.

Steam was rising from the filled tub when Hermione entered and sank into the water with a sigh of relaxation. "The violet."

I brought a vial from the niche.

"All of it. I have to get rid of the stink of Pyrrhos' sperm." She lay back and laved water over herself. "But that should get me a child soon." She leaned forward, breathing in the perfume. "Were you sore after your first night with Hektôr?"

"I couldn't say." Was nothing sacred to this woman?

"You remember other times better?"

Was she trying to be friendly?

"My back, Āndrōmakhê." She leaned forward. I found a sponge on the bench and started smoothing it over the soft skin. Was this woman thoughtless, or deliberately cruel? "I'm filled with Pyrrhos' son."

She was gloating! How childish.

"I wish you motherhood many times over." I said quietly.

"Then you are not jealous?"

"I am grateful. You take him from my bed."

"But you have two sons by him."

"May you have twice as many!"

"Oh." Hermione lay back and took the sponge, smoothing it over herself. "This is wonderful." She laughed. "You, once Hektôr's wife, bathing me! I cannot boast enough of this."

"Indeed."

Hermione's Spartan nurse entered with perfumed oils and sumptuous clothing. She put these down and helped Hermione from the tub. While the woman dried her, I prepared the bench and laid out the oils for massage.

Hermione rested under a soft cloth and looked up at me. "I want to be friends even if you are a slave. You can tell me all about my mother in Troia. I suppose it must be quite dreadful to be a slave, when you expected to be queen." The Spartan nurse reddened as she laid out her mistress' dress. Hermione said lightly, "I'm really surprised how much I crave Pyrrhos even though I don't like him much. All my life I expected to marry Orestes, you know. He is closer than a brother, being the son of my mother's twin and of my father's brother. It would have been wonderful to unite both kingdoms as a queendom, exactly like my mother wanted."

A frisson went over my shoulders. The son and daughter of two brothers and twin sisters. Closer to siblings than cousins. Incest!

Hermione went on, "I know I'm safer here than in Mykene, with all those rebellions about whether Elektra is to be queen in the Old Way. Orestes would not be a very good husband anyway, if he runs off like he did after sacrificing his mother." She glanced at me. "But you do have ambitions here, don't you?"

"By the Goddess, no!" My dream was of Troia and Thébé, not Thessaly or Lakedaimon.

"I'd not tolerate a concubine," she declared with a softness I sensed was lethal. "I understand you Trojans have no scruples about multiple wives, either." Her eyes lit on her nurse. "Yes… the blue one," as the woman held up a veil.

"The fashions are different here," I suggested when Hermione stepped into a bee-waisted, ruffled skirt.

Hermione pulled her breasts above the neckline. "This is still the latest thing in Sparta." She draped the veil about herself. "Mother wanted me to bring my own dressmaker, just as she did to Troia. But I'll do as I please."

"Here you must cover your breasts or the people will not respect you," I said equitably. "The men will think Pyrrhos a fool for allowing you to go around like this—"

"Why do you care what men think of Pyrrhos?" she snapped.

"You must not shame their king, Hermione."

"Lady Hermione to you, slave!"

I bit my lips and did not take the bait.

"So Pyrrhos has been letting you play the mistress here, and not teaching you your duties! I have to see about that."

When we went downstairs, Briseis and Okyone were giving the younger children their breakfast.

"Where is my husband?" Hermione asked.

"He took the boys out long ago," Briseis replied. "I think they went down to the barracks."

"What boys?" Hermione looked around, "I see several here. Are all of these his children?"

"No. Some of the younger ones might be, but the rest are Trojan born."

"It's not easy to tell paternity with slaves, is it?" Hermione walked restlessly among the youngsters, examining their faces as they turned upward for her passing. Finally, she turned sharply to me. "Which of these curs are yours? And what of Hektôr's son?"

"Skamandrios is not here," I replied with a constricted throat.

"That child was killed," Briseis whispered to Hermione.

Turning my back to them, I went up the stairs to my room. Lycosa and Xanthos slinked in from different directions and sat with me.

It was after the evening meal before I returned downstairs. Wine was making its rounds among men. I went to the hearth and took some sesame bread and my favorite, herbed bonemarrow paste, adding a few roasted onions and cheese to my plate.

I no longer was to sit with Pyrrhos, so I was placed with Thalpia, Okyone and Briseis in the children's area across the hall from him.

Molossos and Peleos occupied a low bench near their father, sharing a table set before them.

I noticed Hermione was staring at them malevolently.

By the time the couple began to eat, I realized Pyrrhos had angered his wife. There was a long silence as Hermione flushed crimson and sat stiffly. Her eyes remained venomously on my boys, who were eating with hearty abandon and boasting to each other of what their father had allowed them to do that day.

"They're bastards!" Hermione's voice cut into the conversation in the room. She then turned her icy gaze to me.

"Molossos and Peleos are my sons," Pyrrhos said in a hard voice, as if not for the first time. "Molossos will inherit my kingdom, and this land is named for him."

"In preference to mine?"

Reddening, Pyrrhos replied, "Naturally, if we have sons, they will outrank these two."

"These bastards!" she repeated with open hostility, "I know what such can be, Pyrrhos, for I have two bastard half-brothers at home."

"Yes." Pyrrhos' hands were fists, on the table.

"You sent no bridal gifts for me," she said rigidly. "The rich dowry my father sent with me places you under obligation to me and to him. Remember that the old ways are not ended in Lakedaimon, for it was my mother who saw to it that I be independent of your control. Hers is the land, and my father merely her husband and defender. It is so, now, with you and me."

"My bride-gift for you was made the day your father promised you to me on the Trojan Plain. Otherwise, your people would have had no leader after my father's death. Without me, the war would have been lost. I gave more than treasure for you, Hermione. I gave my strength and arms and men for your father and uncle's victory!"

Hermione gave a short laugh, "And I am well worth it."

* * * *

Summer. Marauders attacked Molossian villages in waves. Pyrrhos marched north, using the men he had trained for his planned invasion of Sparta. While he was away, I realized I was pregnant again. It had happened during the last time he had taken me, on the day before Hermione's arrival.

Hermione was using me only as mistress of the bath, at other times ignoring me completely.

Yet mysterious things happened. First, a scorpion was found in my bed, among the sheets, and a week later, a deadly rattler made its way into my room. Xanthos was the one who sniffed them out before I came to harm. The dispatching of the scorpion was easy for him, but the snake bit his forelegs before he was killed. Thalpia and I sucked out and spit the poison as best we could, and a visiting healer priest did the rest. Still, even with quick intervention and good care, it took a long while for my strong and sturdy Xanthos to recover.

Soon I realized that I when I walked around the palace grounds on my own, a shadow or two would follow me. Soon after, a wild boar tore at me from the bushes, but was thwarted by Lycosa. She was a grown wolf now, her inborn skills honed by the training given to her by Pyrrhos, and while the boar was larger and more vicious, she was fleet-footed and big-jawed enough to get it dizzy and bleeding from her bites.

By the time the guards came running to see what the racket was all about, the boar had retreated to lick its wounds and nurse its injured pride. Hunters caught it in the end, and over an evening meal rich with its roasted succulent meat, everyone wondered whence it came, and how it managed to creep so close to the palace without being seen.

Pyrrhos returned at harvest-time, having once more pushed invaders from his land. By then Hermione knew that I, not she, was to bear Pyrrhos' new child. I hoped this would release me from the queen's presence; but no, Hermione devised small meannesses such as Pyrrhos would not notice. She objected to Lycosa and Xanthos' presence in the palace, even going as far as inspecting my room to make sure I was not hiding them there. Of course, she was not wrong, for I did keep them with me; they had their special way of slinking their way into my company. This was easier on Xanthos, but Lycosa, albeit slender and light-footed, was, after all, a wolf, and could not climb trees to leap upon rooftops and slide down to my window.

I began to fear Hermione. I offered up many prayers to the Goddess on the younger woman's behalf; anything to keep Pyrrhos interested in his childless wife. He did his best, though, bedding together by day as well as night, reminding me of how Alexis used to run for Helen, sometimes leaving the very field of battle if his desire for her became unbearable. Yet I could see that she did not love her husband. Nonetheless, she was desperate to get a son from him to take the inheritance from Molossos and Peleos.

* * * *

In the royal chamber one night, Hermione was at her dressing table while I removed gold pins from her hair. Smoothing the long gleaming locks, I noticed the malevolent stare reflected in the mirror.

"You are dismissed." The words hissed at me as Hermione stood to slip out of her skirt. "I'll not have you here, staring at me with your evil-eye."

"Very well."

"There's other work for you. I have used you long enough to please my husband. I know, you have another bastard there, so do not flaunt yourself. You scheme to have this land for your sons; but though my child be a girl, you and your young will have nothing. Nothing! This is the last you'll breed for my husband."

"I pray to the Mother you speak truth." I let my hands drop to my sides. "I never asked for these children, but they are here, their father honors their rights, and I will protect their future with my life."

"Your life?" Hermione laughed.

I held myself straighter. "You have no cause to hate me, Hermione. You know I am a slave and subject to his—and your—whim. Nevertheless, I was brought up to rule lands more powerful than Lakedaimon, Mykene, and Thessaly put together. My husband would have held allegiance from more men than Agamemnon ever hoped to claim, for the Hittites were only *one* of Troia's allies. Hektôr would have ruled north and south, west and east from Troia."

"A very good thing my people stopped yours, then! Even more misery for you, proud Ãndrõmakhê, wife of vanquished Hektôr, thinking on what *might* have been! I will no longer allow you to touch me with that…that *filth* in you, that *disease* sloughed off into you from my husband."

I flung out and to my room, where I dropped into the chair. If I could get rid of this child, I might be able to save my other two. But no, I could not even consider it seriously.

Strangeness came over me and I was no longer in my body. I was on the Pergama at Troia, and on the fields below, flowers covered the bloodied earth. Then I was down there, and two figures were running to me—Hektôr and Skamandrios. Once more Skamandrios melted into my body and Hektôr faded into the flowers.

My arms cradled the unborn child in my womb.

- *Skamandrios thinks of you always, Ãndrõmakhê, he has not forgotten your face. Neither has he forsaken his father's memory.*

Hermione's voice hissed from the doorway. "I know what you are! You will cease right now putting the curse of barrenness on me with your evil eye! This room is no longer yours; you shall sleep with the other slavewomen. Your boys too will be treated as the slaves they are." She turned, then took a sharp intake of breath. "Oh!"

Pyrrhos was behind her. "What is this about slave boys?"

"Hers. They are not to be with her any longer."

"Molossos and Peleos are already in the barracks as is proper for future warriors," he told her grimly.

"She has ordered me to go with the other slaves." I almost smiled, for to be away from Hermione was more a gift than punishment.

Pyrrhos stiffened. "No. I cannot allow Hektôr's widow to live with common flax-beaters and water-carriers. She has no land, but she is still a queen."

"I'll not have her putting the evil-eye on me! Āndrõmakhê is no replacement for my nurse who came all the way from Sparta with me.'

"Fine, you may have this room for her, then. But Āndrõmakhê will have the comforts due the mother of my sons."

"*I* am your wife, yet you keep her for yourself."

He frowned. "I've not touched her since you came to me."

"Then where did she get *that?*" She ran over to me, jabbing at my belly with her outstretched finger, "Is she promiscuous? Has she bedded with Helenos?"

Slapping her hand, I jumped back.

"I never knew...she did not tell me." He looked at my figure and pride lit in his eyes. "You have fulfilled my hope," he spoke kindly, "and yes, this is by all means *my* child, Hermione."

"Then you are not satisfied with me! Oath breaker!"

He gave a forced laugh. "I need no concubine with you, you're fiery enough. But believe of me as you choose."

"Pyrrhos! I do not have to endure these things from you. My father will come if I send for him. My mother mourns that I do not belong to Orestes as she and Klytemnestra had planned. You better make haste and please me, or..."

Pyrrhos threw back his head and laughed aloud. "Your beloved Orestes ran away! Come on now, wife, we can do better than quarrel over this woman. Perhaps I will give you a son this day."

They left, and a while later, Thalpia bustled in. "My lady, I'm to move your things into the room next to mine."

Chapter 33: Pergamos

Hermione did not come near me anymore, sending orders by message. Whenever Pyrrhos was absent, she would send me to fetch water from the fountain in the public square, or on innumerable errands, most of them trivial, but time-consuming and backbreaking. I walked, carried, stood, and waited until my feet burned and every muscle in my body was taut. Yet I kept my stubborn silence. I knew that Pyrrhos would protect me if I told him of these things, but feared Hermione's underhanded repercussions on my sons and my two animals. Thalpia and I had gotten wind of occasions when she ordered them trapped and killed, and we had rushed to save them. Lycosa could no longer show herself anywhere on the palace grounds for Hermione had men placed to kill her on sight. Xanthos too was in danger, but aware of Pyrrhos' special fondness for him, Hermione was more cautious in her moves against him.

On an early evening, she sent me out once again to fetch water, because I was so near my time. I fumbled my way along the stonewall; the light had changed from a misty pewter to sudden blackness. I shivered with cold, and then was suffused with heat. I was sick and gorged by turns. Wracked by sudden pains, I wanted to weep, but was hollow inside.

Another step...surely I was almost at the doorway...

Sharp agony shot through my body and, gasping, I dropped the jar I was carrying and grasped my abdomen. Cool water sluiced about my feet as the jar emptied.

"Ãndrõmakhê, why are you doing this?" Pyrrhos' breath was hot on my forehead as he lifted me.

I did not know why, but I fought against his hold, forgetting all pain, slamming my forearms at his chest and shoulders, scratching my nails across his face. He laughed, seizing my hands in his. Then a new kind of wetness poured down my legs, and I was helpless.

When I revived from a faint, old women were walking me around and around the room as I stumbled on wormwood spread there against the pain. They held me in a squat until the child appeared, and one knelt,

414

pulling the baby from me. The agony was so blinding that I sank into blank nothingness.

Hours later, "How is it with you?" Pyrrhos stood in the doorway, protective amulets around his neck. He entered and bent over my bed, touching his newest son's sleeping face. "He must be named soon."

"May I choose his name?"

He smiled. "I have named the others. Now that I have a wife, this child will be yours."

"Any name I choose?"

"Any *suitable* name. Such as a grandfather. However, of course, not Akhilles. My wife's son owns that name."

"I have a name!" Joy rushed into my heart as I looked up at him. Warmth flowed from me, gratitude that was almost affection. Indeed, I had a name that would make my son a Trojan, a name that his father would not recognize as such: the citadel of Troia.

"Pergamos," I murmured. "I will call him Pergamos."

"Pergamos?" He scowled, "What is that to you? I know your father was Êetiôn."

"It... it is a beautiful to me," I said quietly.

"I will consider it."

This son would be my long-dreamed of Trojan beacon, which would burn, lighting Skamandrios' way home.

* * * *

Pergamos was a year old, Peleos seven, Molossos nine, and Hermione still childless, when a stranger came into the great hall shortly before the evening meal.

I had gone upstairs to nurse the child, leaving Hermione nestling with Pyrrhos in their double chair. The queen had ignored me since Pergamos' birth. For the first time I began to feel secure in my plans for the future. This was indeed my Trojan son. With Pyrrhos' promise to leave him with me, I was sure the boy would one day avenge Hektôr and me and build anew the Land of Troia.

Pyrrhos greeted the traveler at his hearthfire, the man having been shown in by the door attendant. "Welcome to Molossia," Pyrrhos said. "Have my men seen to your horses and attendants?"

"They have," and his guest bent his head in thanks. "I am Telemakos of Ithaka, my lord, and come as a suppliant. My father Odysseus asks that you arbitrate for him in a matter of blood-guilt."

"So." Pyrrhos hesitated, courtesy forbidding more questions until Telemakos had been made comfortable. He called two serving-women.

415

"See that Telemakos Odysseides is bathed and given a sleeping-room." He touched the man's shoulder. "You will share our evening meal."

It was much later when, the meal eaten, Pyrrhos sat back to hear the man's story. "So you are from Ithaka," he opened, "where I understand Queen Penelope has ruled since the loss of her husband... uh...your father, at sea. Yet you speak of him as though he lives."

"He was long delayed in returning from Troia," Telemakos said. "He was blown off course many times."

"I've heard of that. Was he held in slavery, then?"

I gloated inside. The man who had exhorted Pyrrhos to send my son to his death, the man who would have enslaved Queen Hekabe, himself a captive! Ah, sweet Justice!

Pyrrhos went on, "The waters are as full of pirates as waves these days, I hear."

"He was not captured by men but by wayward winds, for Troia fell at a time of year not good for sailing," the young man said. "We know he meant to reopen Achaian trade routes begun by Herakles and Jason. But travelers reported to my mother that he was lost at sea."

"Indeed both Agamemnon and Meneláos wanted those roads reopened," Pyrrhos said thoughtfully.

"Just so. My father was ordered by Agamemnon to restore trade with peoples of the Herkynian Forest. But I digress." He recounted what he knew of his father's epic adventures.

When he finished, Pyrrhos asked, "But what has this to do with the problem of blood-guilt?"

"That is another story, my lord. When my father failed to return, my mother's family urged her to remarry after the old way. They were besieged by nobles from many places who came courting her. But she, being as independent as your lady mother, Helen," and he deferred to Hermione, "insisted on ruling the island herself. By the time my father returned, his goods were wasted and destroyed by this mob of men. He killed them all during a feast." Telemakos sobered. "These men had relatives, who demand my father's punishment by law. But since there are various laws from place to place, my lord Pyrrhos, you are asked to arbitrate between my father and these people."

"When must I be there?"

"As soon as possible. Rebellion is already fomenting in Ithaka and all nearby lands."

"Odysseus has not the forces to put them down?"

"They demand more than recompense; according to the old way the Ithakans want my father's death and that my mother choose a new king.

416

A truce has been agreed to last until a judgment is made. You, Pyrrhos Neoptolemos, have been chosen to arbitrate. No less than a son of Akhilles is acceptable to the satisfaction of all concerned."

Pyrrhos glanced at Hermione. "What reward is offered?"

"The customary choice between land or gold."

"What land is offered? I have much gold from my conquests."

"My father is overlord of Kephallenia, a goodly island."

"But a long way south." Pyrrhos glanced at his wife again, and she smiled encouragingly.

For some reason, Hermione's smile made me uneasy.

"That is not too far from Mykene," she said.

Pyrrhos turned to Telemakos. "Fine. I can depart soon, as I already have trained men ready. Tell your sages I will hear both sides at their leisure."

The Ithakan left and Pyrrhos ordered Tereos to go to Pharsalos. "Ligyron will soon be as old as I was when I left Skyros," he told the herald. "You are to represent me in keeping peace for King Peleos. Helenos will come here and act as regent. He is also to study here with the Suliot priests, and, later, become their chief. Their practices must be better organized, against the time when Molossos succeeds me. Helenos will fulfill these duties—I know—with honor."

When Tereos had gone, Pyrrhos left soon afterward.

Helenos and I could lead a revolt! The time was at hand. With Peleos remaining in Pharsalos and Pyrrhos off in Ithaka, we would only have Hermione to be concerned about. The queen had not endeared herself to the household, what with her inconsiderate treatment of them. In addition, she had managed to drive Lycosa away completely, and Xanthos had taken off in search of her. However, many people believed that these two animals were under the divine protection of the gods, and feared that their disappearance would bring blight upon the land.

In contrast, I had been kind to those captives from Asia forced into menial tasks. They were skilled potters, unguent-boilers, charcoal-burners; there were sun-scorched men who spread grapes for drying into raisins from which wine was made. There were gatherers and storers of grain, wine, beer, cheese, as well as scribes and inventory-keepers.

I was well into spinning my plans when a runner announced the imminent arrival of Helenos' party. Hermione found me with Briseis and Thalpia in the storerooms, where jars of wine and grain were sunk into the earth.

The queen's eyes were hostile, her tone sharp, "You are not needed here, Āndrōmakhê. Pyrrhos appointed Briseis to see after household matters. Get back to your weaving which is more suitable of a woman your age. Helenos will be here before night and I need you, and you." She looked from Thalpia to Briseis. "Get rooms ready. He's to stay here, not in the dormitory."

"Which room, my lady?" Briseis asked quietly.

"I said, *rooms.* He is bringing two novices. Fix up that big one in back and two small ones next to it. The largest is for him, of course."

"Very well." The two women went out.

I moved to follow, but Hermione caught my arm, "Not you. I know about you and Helenos, as who doesn't? Pyrrhos says he is through with you, but you are still mine. *My personal property.* I will not have any more of your bastards running around here, especially not Trojan ones. Keep to your room of nights!"

I gave her a cold stare and flung out of the series of small rooms. Soon…so soon now! Helenos and I would have other captives on call to rise up and win our freedom. Ten years! Yes, years ago, Helenos had said something about ten years that were needed to wait. And was this not the tenth year? Yes! Pyrrhos would come home to a shambles! I almost laughed aloud as triumph already soared through me. No, I did not need to quarrel with that woman; the sweetness of success was already honeyed in my mouth.

Light-footed I went to prepare the rooms for Helenos. I smoothed the rolled bed linens so that no hollows could attract evil spirits. I straightened the plundered Sidonian rug that had been in the house Helen had shared with Alexis, in Troia. After him, Deiphobos had walked here. Deiphobos, Hektôr's dear brother, his best man of the twinkling eyes, at our wedding….

Arrival noises sounded below. Hermione was escorting her guests up the stairs. At the doorway, her eyes passed over me, and she indicated the two novices behind Helenos. "Look after these men." She went back down the stairs.

Thalpia and Briseis came behind the novices and invited them to their rooms. Helenos entered. My throat tight, I welcomed him to Passaron in formal words. He strode to stare from the window. When he turned, there was a strange, dark passion in his eyes.

Moving swiftly, he caught me in his arms. His voice was tight with control. "I will talk with you when we are alone."

He freed me and I left the room silently.

On the gallery, Hermione stood at the doorway. She stepped to the entrance, her voice spitting-sharp. "I sacrifice and pray to Ilythia every day; I wear charms against that woman's evil-eye. You, with your powers, must intercede for me with the Goddess."

Helenos remained motionless in the center of the room.

"I will show Pyrrhos a full womb, whether it be his or yours, Trojan priest!" She ran along the gallery and into her room.

I walked slowly toward the stairs, and then turned at the sound of Helenos' steps. When he joined me at the head of the stairs, his eyes were bleak.

"You have another son?"

"Yes. Pergamos."

"Ah, I did not know about him because Pyrrhos did not name him." A strangeness came over him as if seeing beyond me, and he stepped back, keeping a space between us. "He is a Trojan! You will one day bless the hour of his birth." I saw in his eyes knowledge beyond his words. "His name will spread from Achaia to Troia." A glow shone on his face. "I know something of all your sons."

"Then you are giving prophecy? For all three of them?"

"All five."

"Five? If you had said four, I would have known you speak of Skamandrios, but...five?"

"I see their names written in the light of Phobus Apollo; indeed their names will spread throughout the kingdom of Epirus. The last one shines beyond us against the sea. As for Pergamos...his name covers Troia. He is the Chosen One."

His eyes held an inward look, and his face glowed as he spoke.

While I waited expectantly, there came a terrifying change in him; like one long dead, tight skin sharply outlined against his skull.

"Helenos!" I cried, rushing to him.

"Don't touch me now. I love you more than life, but now the Goddess is in me, the time has not come for Her to free me. I will know when. We will both know it."

"Oh Helenos, Helenos!"

There were no words. Healing tears came, and now he held me, kissing them away. His rigid chest against my soft breasts was blissful, and I felt him shudder with rising desire.

A hiss broke the spell and sharp nails dug into my shoulders. Helenos let me go, keeping an arm about me.

I turned and Hermione was standing behind me. She stepped back and spat squarely in my face.

Helenos, with a stony look at the queen, lifted a corner of my veil and cleaned my face. "My lady," and his voice was like stone, "you are blind. We were one family in Troia, and are still."

"Yes, I can see that." Her eyes raked us sharply and her laugh was a screech. "There'll be no rutting between you two in this house."

Chapter 34: Pyrrhos

First snow had fallen before Pyrrhos returned from Ithaka. He gave his report standing near the altar in his hall, my father Êetiôn's scepter in his hand. The Suliot priests and elders of the city sat on benches along the wall. Hermione stood beside him, noting where I sat with Helenos, Briseis and Okyone.

Lifting the scepter crested with Êetiôn's orb, Pyrrhos concluded, "I found Odysseus guilty under the taboo of blood. He is exiled for ten years to the court of Queen Kallidike in Thesprotia. I have seen to the crowning of Telemakos as King of Ithaka. It is inappropriate that his mother Penelope continues ruling when she has a male heir. As for my reward, the island of Kephallenia is now mine. A son of ours will one day possess it."

Pyrrhos motioned for Helenos to stand. "He, Helenos Priamides, not only fulfilled my trust, but accomplished more than I asked! Few men can be trusted with such power as I delegated to him."

Pyrrhos then turned to the priest. "Ten years ago, you saved me from destruction at sea, and have served me well ever since. Now I return to find a loyal people, where I could have faced rebellion." He looked to the elders on their benches. "You have been governed in my absence by a slave. Troia was conquered by the wisdom of Athené, who rewarded the victors with Trojan captives. This man, as dual Priest of Apollo and Athené, was a prince in his own land. He has proven to me and to you, honorable chiefs, the nobility of his heritage. He held my land for me, and was fair to you. Because of this, he is now a free man."

The intense silence broke into a mighty cheer when the gathering stood, clattering their staves upon the floor. Pyrrhos embraced his former slave. "Henceforth, Helenos, son of Priam, is Chief Hierophant in Passaron. He has mastered in the healing-temple at Trikka, such arts of health as have never been known before, in body and of the spirit."

I held my breath. My heart thundered throughout my whole body.

Pyrrhos repeated with emphasis, "Helenos, Chief Hierophant of Passaron, rejoice, you are no longer my slave, but a free man!"

I waited as the Suliots spoke briefly with Helenos, then left singly. My body was filled with sensations that came and went like comets, slipping away and bursting, within me again and again.

When everyone had gone except for Helenos, Hermione, and myself Pyrrhos' voice filled the room again. "You will have your own house, land, a wife, and slaves. You will be honored for your services. When your initiation into the Suliot Mysteries is completed, I want you to make whatever changes in their teachings that you deem necessary."

"You give me the *temenos* of an equal, my lord."

"So you would have been in Troia." He clapped his former slave on the shoulder. "Come, man, it's not every captive who is so well earned in his freedom! I said rejoice! Choose any wife you wish."

"Do you give me your oath on that?"

"You have it, friend, witnessed by Zeus and Apollo. I bind my word with libations before their altars. Speak up."

"I ask for Ãndrõmakhê."

Pyrrhos' face turned purple, his breath quickened. "You presume again on the privilege I give you, Priest. This very morning I could have had you whipped for such presumption. How dare you demand the mother of my three sons? Have I freed you before witnesses so that you can lead an uprising against me after all?"

"I have not, and never will be, traitor to any man," Helenos roared. "You know it is customary among my people, as with yours, for a man to marry his brother's widow."

When Pyrrhos spoke again, his words were laden with ice, "She is no longer mine to give, for she belongs to my wife, Hermione."

Hermione sprang to her feet. "I don't want that snake in my house! She is plotting to kill me!"

For an instant, Pyrrhos seemed to be taken aback by her fury. His face deeply flushed, his gaze swung between his wife and me.

She pressed, "You don't want Helenos to have her, because you still want her for yourself! I do not want her freed from slavery; neither do I want to give her to Helenos! I just want her *out of my house!* I will give her as slave to a Spartan of my choosing."

Pyrrhos bit his lips, drew a deep breath, and then turned to Helenos. "Fine, Helenos. Ãndrõmakhê may come to you as concubine. Since I have a wife, she will bear me no more children. You may get sons on her, sons of your house to be brought up as free men."

"You have sworn an oath." Helenos' voice was commanding. "But I will *not* take a queen to my bed as slave. I will not shame the memory of my brother, the noble Hektôr! You have got to free her."

Pyrrhos rose in fury and sprang at the priest, grasping him on the shoulder. "I have asked you before and still wonder: Are you man, god or eunuch, that your control is so unbreakable?"

"You have sworn a most sacred oath, Pyrrhos, son of Akhilles."

"Before Zeus, Keeper of Oaths, I will not break my word." His body shook with rage and his face shone red.

Hermione grasped Pyrrhos' arm. "You are letting him get the best of you, Pyrrhos! Do not trust this man!"

"But I do! He has proven his wisdom and value many times over; else he would not be a free man now."

Hermione looked at Helenos with burning eyes as she pointed her finger at him. "My father told of how it was *you, Helenos,* who helped Odysseus to take Troia's protective image, the Palladium. No betrayer, are you?" She faced her husband again. "We owe him much, indeed! I know he left his city in a rage because Priam gave my mother to Deiphobos, and not to him. Helenos, betrayer of his people, was snared by Odysseus when he went sulking to Thymbra."

I feared I would explode. It had not been like that at all!

As I opened my mouth to defend him, Pyrrhos thundered, "That's enough!" He glanced at the ashen-faced Helenos, and his tone remained firm. "I know from my father that Helenos spied on us and meant to report back; he'd spotted our crafty wooden horse by the shore."

Hermione spewed saliva as she shouted, "My mother was forced into Deiphobos' bed! It was my father who avenged her on him. My father hacked him to pieces in his bed, and Deiphobos bled to death while my mother rejoiced." She gave a shrieking laugh.

"No! Helen could not have been so cruel!" Helenos turned his back and strode to the stairs. Pausing at the bottom step, he looked back, his face a death mask. Silent words moved his lips. Then he went up the stairs, the hall behind him thick with silence.

It was much later when Pyrrhos, brooding over his wine, was roused by the arrival of guests. He had not allowed me to leave, and overruled Hermione's order that I depart the premises.

"I am Pylados Strophides from Phokis," the more presentable of the two announced. "My companion is noble Orestes Agamemnonides of Mykene."

The room was silenced as if a huge stone had fallen from the sky.

The two men were given seats of honor near Pyrrhos.

Pylados, seated next to Pyrrhos, was deep in conversation while Orestes, a hunk of roast lamb in both hands, was biting from it when Hermione's shocked voice rose, "Your finger!"

Orestes laid down his food and stared at the hand. There was only a diseased stump where a finger belonged. "The Erinyes ate it," Orestes muttered.

Pylados, a smooth man, explained, "The Furies forced him to bite it off. He would have eaten himself if I had not found him in time." He looked apologetically at Pyrrhos. "We heard that amazing cures are made at Trikka, and are on our way there."

"I have a priest here who was trained at Trikka," Pyrrhos reassured him. "I will send you to him."

"We will be most grateful," Pylados said. "It is urgent that he return to Mykene soon. Aletes has usurped the throne."

"I must free Erigone and save our son from that man," Orestes said, his confusion clearing shortly. He glared at Hermione. "I expected to marry you." He erupted into a fit of hysterical laughter.

Pylados quieted him, and then turned to Pyrrhos. "The sickness is still on him." He let out a heavy sigh. "He has been like this since he avenged his father's death on his mother." Pylados gave his cousin a tender look. "The old and the new laws are tearing him apart. He has been absolved at Dodona, but must have final purification at Delphi."

Pyrrhos emptied his cup in one long pull and motioned for Demos to unwrap his lyre. "I will send him to Helenos tomorrow for a cure."

* * * *

Hermione could not be persuaded to free me. Pyrrhos and Helenos did not elevate the issue to the point of all-out battle with her. However, Pyrrhos thwarted her attempts to give me to men of her choosing. They quarreled often, and on occasions when he slammed his way to camp at the barracks with his sons, I dreaded her renewed attempts on my life.

Helenos had moved into his own house, two-storied with a paved courtyard, near the sacred precinct.

Orestes remained in Helenos' care.

* * * *

Pyrrhos' hunters brought in the corpses of Xanthos and Lycosa. As the account went, Lycosa had been wounded during a hunt, and then ensnared in a trap in the nearby forest. Xanthos had found her, and from the look of things, had tried hard, unsuccessfully, to loosen the spiked chain cutting into her leg, which had been tied to a stake hammered into a rock. Gnawed carcasses around the trap showed that Xanthos had hunted and brought food to Lycosa. But then Lycosa had died of her wounds, and from Xanthos' emaciated condition, it was clear he had starved himself to death rather than leave her side.

The pain of losing them, my two, close friends, was ferocious, intensely unbearable. However, I managed to keep it locked in my heart. Not once did Hermione's eyes, gleefully following me at every opportunity, catch me shedding tears.

Pyrrhos took the news of Xanthos and Lycosa's death, stoically. However, often I caught him brooding over his wine. He would look from Hermione to me, his eyes troubled. He would be particularly morose after training sessions with the boys, for at such times she made poison-sharp comments. Then she stirred up his fury even more by taunting him for his swearing that Helenos could marry me, when, after all, I was not *his* property to give.

I seldom saw Molossos and Peleos. They seemed less and less like my own children, for their lives were wholly bound up with matters of warfare. Molossos would soon be old enough to join a group of younger neophytes and receive the Club of Recognition. When he came home, he talked of little else, always looking to his father for approval, not acknowledging his mother's existence beyond mere courtesy.

At midsummer, Orestes returned from Helenos' care, a new man. His preparations for departure to Delphi completed, he left his room early that morning and paused on the gallery, hands resting on the rail. Hermione joined him, laying a hand on his. "Why must our lives be so complicated?" she asked.

I had pressed myself into a doorway, and held my breath.

He turned and pulled her to himself. "Not for long," he said. "Pylados will raise troops for me in Argos while I'm at Delphi. Wait for me." His lips curled in a meaningful smile.

"Pyrrhos is going with you!" She laughed. "He thinks to quicken my womb by sacrifices to Apollo."

Orestes grinned. Without another word, he kissed her fully on the mouth and bounded down the stairs to where Pyrrhos and their chariots waited. Hermione's eyes lit with secret knowledge, and she slowly followed him out into the courtyard.

I stepped back into the shadows, flush with the importance of what I had overheard. I needed to consult with Helenos first, and ask him to open Pyrrhos' eyes.

That night at the table, Pyrrhos made an announcement that might have led the way to his doom.

"Āndrōmakhê," he declared, holding his hand out to me.

"My lord." Taking his hand, I rose from my seat.

"It is unfitting that the mother of my three sons be kept there with the other slaves."

His fingers were strong around mine as I went with him to a chair beside the double one he shared with his wife. Hermione stared with lethal intensity as her husband paused before Orestes.

"Honored guest, this is Ãndrõmakhê, the wife of Hektôr! She has given me three sons. After me, there will be strong rulership, combining the best of Troia and Achaia."

Orestes laughed. "My father brought home Kassandra, princess of Priam's House, and she gave him twin boys. But they are in Hades and will not inherit the kingdom at Mykene."

* * * *

Pyrrhos threw himself into preparations to leave for Delphi. His first act was to be the gathering of rich tithes he had owed the shrine ever since his return from Troia, ten years ago. He sent for Helenos, meeting him in the courtyard where I sat spinning in the sunlight with Thalpia.

"Helenos, you will live in the palace until I return," Pyrrhos declared. "You should also work with my men in the barracks; I cannot have you soften among those sedentary priests when military affairs need attention."

"I am dedicated to Asklepios and Apollo," Helenos replied. "My house is sanctified as a shrine in the service of pilgrims. It would be best to send for King Peleos, for he will be needed here before your oracle is made."

"What insolence is this, Priest? Would you betray my trust and refuse obedience?"

"My lord, I am a free man by your own decree."

Helenos does not get it, I thought with a sinking heart, *Pyrrhos wants him to stay in the palace to watch over the boys and me and thwart a possible coup by Hermione.*

"Yes you are a free man." Pyrrhos sighed. "Ah, the habit of years! I have been accustomed to your obedience. Perhaps it would be a mistake indeed to leave such power to freedmen. King Idomenos was betrayed by his trusted friend Lukas and his wife Meda when he returned to Knossos from the war."

"But you would do well to have Old Peleos here as guardian over your wife, while you are away," Helenos advised.

I was wrong, I thought, *he DOES get it.*

426

Pyrrhos scowled. "Hermione is no Meda, but are you Lukas to usurp my kingdom?"

"Of course you can trust me! But this is not a propitious time for you to visit the oracle at Delphi."

"I have put off this duty too long already. Now that I can travel with a friend, my journey should be safe." He looked sharply at the priest. "Do you plan to leave this land?"

"Not until Āndrōmakhê is my wife."

"You plague me with that oath! It shall be honored, but not yet."

Helenos was silent, and his eyes turned opaque. When he spoke, it was as if the words were forced from him, "Pyrrhos Akhilleides, there is anger against you among the Immortals. The Thread of Fate spins slow and sure, reaching the Knot of Retribution for you, and your people. It follows all who break Divine Law, and you will be overtaken in the full strength of your life."

Helenos turned slowly away and moved to the gate and out.

I watched him go, my spinning stopped with the thread half-twisted between forefinger and thumb.

Pyrrhos was still standing frozen when Orestes came to him from within the palace, accompanied by Hermione.

"What is it, dear, are you ill?" she asked solicitously. "You cannot be sick now—so close to your time of leaving! Your tithes are already loaded in wagons by the slaves."

"Oh, no." He shook his head, then smiled at her and kissed her on her cheek, holding her hand within his own. "Helenos gave me a bad turn—an unfavorable omen, just now. Perhaps I should reconsider."

"After all these years? Can you trust him so much, now that he is free? You have Orestes to travel with—what harm can come of that?"

"I will assuredly see after you," Orestes said. "There is nothing wrong with me now, and I never liked traveling alone."

Pyrrhos looked from him to Hermione, then turned back and looked at me. After a silent moment, he spoke, "Āndrōmakhê, I will have a word with you."

I rose and went with him into the palace. He walked ahead of me until he reached his throne, sat down, and then motioned me to sit by his side, on Hermione's chair.

"You know I loved you," he said with a tight voice.

"So you have said, my lord."

"Now I love Hermione."

"I have seen this, and I am happy for you. I hope you will put aside your differences, and—"

"Ãndrõmakhê! Listen. That I love Hermione does not mean I have stopped loving you. You know you could have been my first wife, and custom be damned. I do not need Hermione to attain the throne of Sparta. But I erred in trying to get back at you for not loving me."

At this moment, his expression was so open, so sincere, that I felt I could not look in his eyes. Nevertheless, I held firm and did not avoid his gaze. "I love Hektôr. I always will."

"Yes, of course. In addition, I admit, there is too much blood between us. But perhaps... if I hadn't been so... cautious...and told you about..."

"Yes, my lord? Told me about what?"

"Skamandrios."

I swallowed hard. My convulsing hands grasped the arms of the chair on each side.

He continued, "I had sent Kiron to gather his body from the bottom of the walls, for a decent funeral rite. When Kiron found him, he did seem dead. Kiron wrapped him in purple cloth, covered him with flowers, and we showed him to the rest of the chiefs. Later we realized that he was breathing, albeit barely. The piled up bodies of those who fell before him, had cushioned his fall. None but the keen and wise Kiron could have known how to look for such shallow signs of life! You remained unconscious for a long time. I decided to substitute the corpse of another boy, of Skamandrios' age, for the pyre, and burial. So, as far as everyone else on that beach, Skamandrios, Hektôr's son by Ãndrõmakhê, is no more. However, by the time my ships left Troia for Skyros, he was still alive, cared for by Kiron, and on another ship bound for Krete."

Breath caught in my throat and I had a violent coughing fit. Still coughing, I left the seat, kneeled in front of him, whispering, "My lord, why did you not tell me of this before?"

"Because I resented your bottomless hatred of me. But more importantly, this was a highly sensitive, political issue. And make no mistake, it still is. If I had let you in on the secret, you would have never ceased demanding more of me, unleashing trouble. Agamemnon and the rest of the kings and chiefs feared your little boy. I did not care to have them unite against me for having saved his life. As you well know, I had other, more important battles to fight."

From the corner of my eye, I caught a movement in the shadows to my left. He had seen it too, and drew back as I rose to my feet.

Leaning toward him, I whispered, "What of him now? Where is he? How is he? Can I find him?"

"After Krete, Kiron took him to Sicily, and died there. After that, I lost track of the boy."

I stared at Pyrrhos, trembling all over.

He bit his lips and sighed. "All right, Āndrōmakhê. When I return from Delphi, I will send fresh inquiries about him."

Hermione stepped forward from the shadows, and Pyrrhos turned to her, staring at her fixedly.

* * * *

When King Peleos' caravan approached us from along the riverside, our fields were rich with harvest, the ripe grain falling before blades and the grain falling from winnowing-fans as chaff dusted the air.

As the old king strode into the great hall, I noticed that he seemed younger than his years. The white of his hair and beard, together with the ruddiness of his face sharpened the sapphire of his eyes as he looked about, missing nothing.

"I could not choose a lovelier wife for my grandson," he said at greeting as he raised Hermione from respectful touching of his knees. He ceremonially kissed her face and shoulders. "You are a credit to your noble parents, and I welcome you to the Aiakid family."

"I trust I will be an honor to your house."

"You are a jewel, my dear. An alliance between the houses of Aisakos and Pelops is vital to the future of our Achaian homeland. You will honor both families with great sons."

"Such is my continual prayer." She flashed hatred toward me, who had come down the stairs to welcome the old king. "But evil forces are keeping my womb empty."

"May Zeus grant that I hold your son in my arms before I die."

They sat together for the evening meal.

Peleos turned to me. "Pyrrhos should have freed you along with Helenos." He turned back to Hermione. "What am I to think of Pyrrhos, having a concubine in his home with you? I see no reason to keep Hektôr's widow in service."

"Oh, no, she is no concubine; I have her watched at all times. Besides, she does not belong to Pyrrhos anymore, but to me. Yet I need to give her to one of my Spartan commanders, so he takes her far away. You see, she has the Evil Eye! She is preventing me from conception! Of course so that her own sons will inherit everything."

Peleos chuckled, "Come now! I am king here while Pyrrhos is away, and I decree that Āndrōmakhê does not have the Evil Eye."

Hermione began to weep, rather charmingly. "Pyrrhos swore *her* sons will he kings after him! This very land is named for Molossos. Everything has been unsettled since the war. Invaders from up north, and now Trojan refugees are making trouble. Even our own kings fight each other!"

"You must not worry, my daughter. This is indeed a time of great change, but also a time of great opportunity. Pyrrhos will not deny any sons of his."

"But Ãndrõmakhê is using spells against me! Why else am I still not pregnant?"

Peleos chuckled. "You will be pregnant from the first night of your husband's return. I will get Helenos to verify this. By the way, where is Helenos? Also, I have not seen the boys...."

"They live in the barracks. Helenos has his own house."

"Good, I am pleased to hear that." Peleos summoned one of the servants. "Send for the boys; I want to see them."

When Molossos came clattering through the doorway, he stopped a second, his eyes scanning the room.

The old man looked at him through tear-dimmed eyes. "You are a true son of Pyrrhos, a second Akhilles!"

Peleos ran in then, and the old man drew both boys to him. Mixed emotions soared through me as I watched. I, a slave, mother to the heirs of Akhilles. A tragic irony that I should bring joy to the father of the man who had killed my father, brothers, and husband.

Okyone came in with Pergamos, who climbed onto my lap and stared boldly at the stranger. I shook with the sensation of memory, this had happened once before: Skamandrios, and the old man, Priam.

Peleos was holding something toward his younger brother, and Pergamos scrambled from my lap, grabbed the offered raw marrowbone, and went back to me sucking on it noisily.

Peleos' face was abeam with delight. "This must be Pergamos."

"Yes. Pyrrhos allows me to keep him." I pulled him back onto my lap and hushed him. He squealed, waving his bone.

Peleos looked at the raw bone with approval. "He knows how to draw his future strength from that." He smiled at me. "They are all beautiful, strong boys, but the youngest is most like you."

"He is all Trojan," I said. A shock flashed through me as I spoke; indeed, he was very like Skamandrios in looks and temperament.

Words hissed from Hermione, *"Bastards!* Can I never escape them? Bastard brothers at home, bastards here..."

Peleos placed a hand over hers. "My dear, forgive my honoring these boys so much in your presence; but they are so like my lost son! In due time you will bring true heirs to the house of Aisakos."

* * * *

"I tell you, Helenos, something terrible is going to happen here." Peleos and the priest were strolling along the narrow road of beaten earth toward the palace from the shrine. Peleos had gone to see Helenos about my ailing son, Pergamos. "Hermione is not the woman I first thought her; there are times when I fear she might kill Ãndrõmakhê."

I continued to follow them, under cover in the shadows of trees along the road.

Helenos spoke, "I warned Pyrrhos not to go to Delphi at this time. The man he went with, though I cured him, is dangerous." Helenos was carrying a silver box of medications.

"But Orestes was cleansed of matricide at Dodona! It is his wife's possession by evil spirits that concerns me."

"There is no more than plain jealousy troubling Hermione," Helenos said. "I will of course see to Ãndrõmakhê's safety. But I assure you there are no evil spirits involved."

"You might be right, but fear of evil is very strong in the people of these mountains," Peleos said. "Is it true that Hermione had Xanthos and Lycosa killed?"

"So it is claimed. By those she gave the task to."

"Ah-ha. Then I know whence the curse upon Hermione comes! Xanthos was a gift to Ãndrõmakhê by Kallichora. I was there, in the shrine with Ãndrõmakhê when the kitten appeared on Her altar."

Helenos drew in a sharp breath. "I did not know of this."

"Kallichora won't forgive those who trespass against her charges." After a silence, "Hermione talks too much, publicly, of the Evil Eye."

"Yes, add that to the death of those two animals, believed by some folks to be of divine origin because of their unique qualities…you know how terrified the populace can be, and how mob action has destroyed a king before now."

"This cannot be true!"

"Belief and fear are strong forces, my lord."

"How is it that Pyrrhos freed only you?"

"Reward for regency. I thought you knew. I am also required to control certain excesses in the priests here."

"I see the seal of rebirth tattooed on your forehead, showing your initiation as Chief Hierophant. And you have made your house a shrine of healing."

"Yes. The first temple in this part of the world dedicated to Apollo-Healer. When Asklepeios made his own house a shrine in Epidoros, he had not yet visited the older one at Trikka. When he did go, he enlarged the place and improved healing methods."

They were near the courtyard gate and Helenos stopped. "The Suliots here have become so disorganized that I am able to take over easily. I am developing the teachings and practices of Asklepeios as much like those at Trikka as possible."

"Then the Suliots have lost their divine support? And do you train these men also in Trojan lore?"

"My training began during my childhood at Thymbra, as a servant of Apollo-Belen-Agdistis. I bring all of that special knowledge which strengthens the Trikkan methods. I am interested only in the spiritual and physical welfare of people."

"I know you were also a notable warrior at Troia."

"I can be a soldier at need, my lord."

"Were you ever given the club to bloody with your totem animal's death, or did you wear its hide?"

"Such is not a Trojan custom. Our training of leaders involves horse taming and mastery of the war-chariot. And Hektôr excelled."

Helenos went through the gate.

I waited the span of a few breaths, and then slipped in as well.

"Why," the old man was asking, "do you, a free man, spend your energies serving my people, and not return home to Troia? I know of survivors there awaiting your leadership."

"The Fates order my future. But self respect and the welfare of others concern me most."

"I see." Peleos retraced his steps and closed the gate. "You cannot leave without Ãndrõmakhê." He sighed. "Pyrrhos should have given you Ãndrõmakhê when he married Hermione. There is no place in any house for a wife *and* a concubine. It was a mistake to give her as a slave to Hermione."

"Pyrrhos swore that Ãndrõmakhê will become my wife, and by the gods, he will keep that promise! She is my brother's widow and finally he acknowledges my right to her. But I won't take her as my concubine; I would not so outrage Hektôr's shade."

"The queen should be glad to let you have her."

"I believe she fears the sons we would have."

"Hah! Scarcely as much as those Pyrrhos trains to rule after him, flaunting them before his wife! My grandson still has much to learn." He paused, and then added with a solemn tone, "I will give you both justice if Pyrrhos does not. You were born a prince, and are now Chief Hierophant of all Phthiotis. I owe you my assistance. The gods are on the side of justice, and I shall be their agent. My grandson has until the Feast of New Life to make things right with you."

When the two men passed me by, they noticed me quietly sitting in the garden, Pergamos on my lap. Smiling, I acknowledged them with a courteous nod.

Peleos then went into the palace and Helenos set his medical box on the bench beside me.

"There now, stand for me like a warrior," he spoke, setting the boy on his feet. Pergamos whimpered in protest, but stood straight while Helenos palpated his rounded abdomen. "How long since he emptied himself?"

"Not since yesterday, but he was hurting for two days before then."

Helenos opened his box and retrieved a few green leaves. "Have Thalpia boil these and give him their liquor in honey. In addition, from now, do not feed him any meat, bread, or sweets other than what I will provide, for both of you! I suspect Hermione's hand in his illness. You were lucky the dose used was not strong enough to kill him."

I took the leaves from him and our eyes locked in silent communion. A delicate breeze lifted our hair, moving the folds of our clothing. The incense of lilies from Hermione's garden rose about us like an invisible mist. A shift in Helenos' gaze made me glance away and see Hermione coming toward us.

"From now on," her voice slashed through the air, "you and this priest will have Passaron to yourselves." She broke off a crimson bloom, her eyes riveted on me. "I'll soon have my last look at you!"

She turned her back, colliding with Thalpia, who was bringing a cup, the gold one Skamandrios had learned to drink from, and offered it to the child. It was astringent with the medicine.

As he drank, Hermione studied us with glittering eyes. "Orestes and Pylados have returned from the trip, they are at the city gate," she announced then. "Pyrrhos has remained behind, waiting for the oracle to speak to him."

* * * *

Autumn was tarnishing the green valleys and reddening rock-boned mountains when Hermione went off on a hunting expedition with Orestes and their attendants. Peleos wondered aloud why they needed so much baggage for only two days in the mountains. "This looks to be a greater hunt than that for the Kaledonian boar," he said as they clattered away from the city.

It was several days later, when they had not returned, that Peleos sent scouts after them. "She has to be here when Pyrrhos returns."

The chief scout came back, distraught. "My lord, the hunters have not been seen in the mountains, but reports are that they have been seen on the road to Mykene."

* * * *

The following weeks were a time of dread and hope for me and of anguish for Peleos. Unusually heavy snows and inclement weather had closed off most of the roads, isolating us from the rest of the world. Helenos could give no comfort to the old man. I saw from his eyes that he knew Pyrrhos would never return, but kept silent to spare the old king the ultimate sorrow as long as possible.

As for me, I felt saddened by the prospect of this golden young man's death. His revelation of his complicity in my little son's survival had healed my hatred of him. True, he had been wrong in his cruel slaying of Priam. Regardless of what Old King Peleos had said about my father doing the same if he had stood in Pyrrhos' boots, the fact was that Priam had been in the sanctuary, a place sacred to the gods and off-limit to bloodshed. Driven by bloodlust in the heat of the battle, Pyrrhos had disregarded the divine laws. Same as Ajax the Lesser, also known as Ajax of Lokris, who had raped Kassandra, as she clung desperately to Athené's statue, and then had been killed by Agamemnon. In his case, divine justice had manifested itself faster than on some of the others.

Had Pyrrhos been granted more time—perhaps due to his kindness to Skamandrios?

* * * *

It was not until the first thaw had muddied roads and avalanched into valleys that Peleos' men returned from their mission to the oracle of Delphi. The messenger announced, "The Lady Queen and Lord Orestes are safely in Mykene. The people rejoice in the end of a cruel usurper's reign and the enthronement of King Orestes and Queen Hermione."

434

"Hermione and Orestes! But she is my grandson's wife."

"No longer," was the laconic reply. "The lord Pyrrhos lies in his grave beside the Delphic oracle."

"No, this cannot be true!" The words keened from Peleos and he collapsed, groveling, to the floor.

"How did he die, and when?" I asked, bending to lift the old man.

"The priests say he was bitten by the sacred python when he stepped too near the enclosure. The people of the village say Orestes attacked and killed him during prayer."

"Murdered by his own guest-friend! A man who was here after killing the son of my son, who ate my bread! And Hermione gone with her husband's murderer! Oh Zeus, Zeus! Oh, Pyrrhos, Pyrrhos!"

I found myself weeping for Peleos' grief. Then I had to ask, "You say he is buried at the shrine?"

"In a sacred place which could not be disturbed; under the threshold to the shrine itself," the man replied.

I said no more. Nevertheless, I remembered all too well Hermione's odd behavior, and words, that time in the garden.

Briseis, running from where she had been when the news reached her, fell to the floor beside Peleos. "Oh my beautiful love, son of my beloved Akhilles!"

Peleos spoke faintly. "To have died in the sacred place of the oracle! Such an honor for him! I will send yearly offerings to appease his soul."

He slew Priam in a place sacred to the gods, I thought, *and in turn lost his life in another sacred place. Same as his father, Akhilles, who slew Hektôr's young brother brave Troilos at the Thymbran shrine of Apollo, later crawled back there asking for His forgiveness, and died.*

Oh, Golden Pyrrhos! Tempestuous, ambitious, yet often kind and generous son of the equally tempestuous demi-god, Akhilles!

You showed mercy to my little son, Pyrrhos, and the gods rewarded you with three of your own, by his mother. Indeed, they knew in advance that I would be grateful to you for this, and gladly raise them to honor your memory.

Towers Across the Plain
"I advance, and recognize a little Troia, with a copy
of great Pergamos and embrace the portals of a Skaian gate..."
Virgil: Aeneid, Book III
H. R. Fairclough, translator

Chapter 35: Helenos

For the Festival of New Life, Thalpia dressed me in flowing lavender, honoring celestial and infernal powers.

I found King Peleos sitting alone, in the great hall. Helenos was just leaving by the courtyard doorway. Kneeling before him, I rested my forearms on his knees. "Old Father, come out with me. Set up a memorial where you can make libations and honor Pyrrhos' shade. I will help you."

"Briseis is seeing to that. I go soon to my own land and will honor him with a tumulus there. I have delegated Helenos to rule here on behalf of Molossos." He urged me to rise. "Few years are left to me and you are a young woman still. I know of the devotion you share with Helenos. As Trojans, you do belong together. It is not fitting that the mother of kings be a slave. My dear child, you are a free woman from this moment on."

"Free! Oh, my lord!" My head went down on his lap and my arms encircled his knees.

"I give you to Helenos as his wife, and to help him in wisely governing this land."

Great sobs of joy racked my body. I was reborn!

* * * *

I joined the ceremonies walking as if in a dream-mist, out into the fields away from Passaron. Everything was fresh and green, more beautiful than for a long while. My mind was a haze of disbelief and happiness. The freedom I had been born into and lost was now returned to me as a precious gift. How many years ago was it since my unencumbered,

436

rambunctious girlhood in Thebe? Oh, my dear brothers! And you, Iris, my beautiful, beloved star-sister, born at the same hour as me. Dear Mother and Father! How I love you, still! Your memory crowns my heart.

My parents had worked so hard to save me from that curse within my birth-horoscope; had they succeeded finally?

A cuckoo called from far away, harbinger of spring. Swallows were swinging in the air overhead, and in trees around me, dove calls softly repeated. Though snows had barely begun melting from the mountaintops, small flowers at my feet peeped from brown leaves.

Spring around me, and within myself.

It was truly time to celebrate Dionysos-Apollo; Dionysos the Guardian of Souls awaiting conception and rebirth.

I must find Helenos and with him make restitution for those years when, as slaves, we had been unable to properly honor our own dead, whose neglected tombs cried out to be remembered. No one had been there to pour libation or otherwise propitiate those restless wanderers in the western Land of Asphodel.

Now, as free man and woman, we could build memorials and, perhaps, summon the lonely spirits to rejoice.

Helenos was in the Labraunda, the Place of the Ax, preparing for that night's ceremonies of rebirth. I sat on a bench and waited. It was dusk when he came to me. I stood up to tell him of my being freed at last, but could only look at him, his figure faintly glimmering in the shadow of a great oak. Tears of joy spilled down my cheeks. "I have something to tell you. Peleos is giving me my freedom!"

"I know, beloved. This is our festival of new life."

His words hung in the air like an echo that would last forever.

"Come," he said at last, and moved beyond the altar.

Our long path led up a recently piled mound of earth, where fresh flowers and leaves were scattered like an offering. We stopped beside a crudely cut stone, a phallus, signaling that death was also life.

Faint writing showed in the moonlight, and I made out Trojan words. "Dedicated to Ate and Zeus Bronton by Helenos, in memory of horse-taming Hektôr, son of Priam."

The new moon rode high above the mound, the thin circle of its orb a thread of electron weighed by a narrow crescent of palest amber.

I looked at Helenos, a dark silhouette in astral light from new moon and stars. His hand took mine and I felt the warm moisture of his palm pressing my fingers down upon the monument as he spoke low words of prayer, "Now we call Hektôr to witness that we are free and give him honor in the land of his enemies."

"May his spirit protect us and guide the future of his people," I added, "the gods have proved the strength of our Trojan blood."

Helenos drew me into his arms and I rested my head upon his breast. His voice was a wind-whisper against my ear, "Now we will carry forward Priam's House and the same of godlike Êetiôn."

"Hektôr Astyanax, son of Priam," I continued, "rest easy, my beloved, our son Skamandrios is still alive. Men will be dispatched to Krete and Sicily, in search of him. One day, he will return home, to Troia."

I breathed in deeply of the fresh air. Here was the power of life and devotion in the presence of death, and at the same moment, I knew what my Goddess had prepared me to appreciate so long ago: Life comes from Death, and is stronger than Death.

Helenos' hard body molded to mine. Resonant, shaken, I knew his urgent embrace released his pained and long unappeased, love. There was fever in his strong fingers built during those terrible years of denial. Above us, the sky spilled stars in all directions around the high-riding moon. In my heart of hearts, the man gently holding me in his arms was Hektôr.

* * * *

The jingling sistra slowed and silenced as Helenos emerged through the trees. He paused before me as I stood tall in my long sheath of yellow linen.

King Peleos gently thrust me toward him, speaking ritual words:

"Helenos Priamides, accept your bride. Today I redeem the pledge made by Pyrrhos Neoptolemos, son of Akhilles, late king of Molossia."

Helenos, his white robe vibrating to an inner excitement, gave the ritual answer. "I will cherish and protect my one and only wife, Andrõmakhê Êetiôneis, with my own life."

My breathing became ragged as well, and, forgetting the ritual words, I cried as I went into his arms, "Helenos!"

Peleos joined our hands and a burst of song and music signaled the ceremony's conclusion. The slow walk began back into Passaron.

In the market place, the smell of roasting lamb and poultry testified that citizens had already begun their own celebration. Many were refugees from our shores, some Trojan, others from dependencies. Each house had set up a table where wheat simmered in gravy over charcoal pans. Small, nutty wedding cakes moistened in rose water, dipped in honey and dried, were presented to the bridal party as they passed.

In my room, Thalpia prepared me for that afternoon's festivities. Stepping out of my clothing, I stood while Thalpia drew over my head a diaphanous loose-flowing robe of finest red Egyptian cotton, settling it with a whisper over my full breasts and thighs.

Okyone brought a collar woven of yellow and white horsehair taken from Hektôr's golden Xanthos. Thalpia bound my strawberry blond hair with two strands of blue Egyptian beads Hermione had given her on a day of sudden generosity.

Something about the veil Thalpia tossed over me...

Ah! I had worn it for my marriage to Hektôr!

The Veil of Aphrodite, a gift to me by Helen.

I pressed a length of it to my lips. "After this—swear, Thalpia, that you will wrap my ashes in this veil at my death."

"By the Goddess, yes, if you want it so. But rejoice now, my lady. You are free, and greatly loved."

Downstairs in the great hall oil-bowls along the walls exuded flowery scents from burning wicks. When Helenos came in with King Peleos and my three sons, I watched him walk toward me. His manner was commanding, and he seemed taller and fuller of figure, a giant compared to his former leanness. A bloom flushed his face, a look I had not seen on him since Sipylos. Robed in the purple of a Trojan Priest-King, he moved toward me with loving triumph in his eyes.

Lyrists and sistra-shakers twanged and clinked lively rhythms while Briseis seated us and served us with half a pigeon each to ensure long life and lasting love.

King Peleos rose when the meal ended, lifting the scepter of Pyrrhos—my father Êetiôn's—in one hand, his own in the other.

His announcement concluded, "You know Helenos as a just representative of my son. He and his wife will rule under my suzerainty until young Molossos is of an age to take the throne."

Dusk had long yielded to the gentle wooing of night when the women escorted me to the bridal chamber. I mounted the three steps of the bed-dais, looked down at the coverlet, and gasped.

"Who found this?" I remembered times I had been with Hektôr under that cover, quiet hours after lovemaking. "No! Take it away! It shall join me on my funeral pyre, but not now."

First the veil, and now the bedspread.

My love for Hektôr was a living shrine in my heart. However, the love I was to share with Helenos was a doorway to new life, with new duties to fulfill. This bringing of the past into my future was more than I could endure.

Briseis removed the spread, folded it, and placed it in one of the chests. Briseis, Thalpia, and I joined holding hands in a circle. How far had we all traveled from home, leaving so many loved ones behind!

Briseis and Thalpia left. I stood beside the bed, my gaze shifting to the window. Stars were garlanding the sky with argent lights. Within the room, a dim glow from one small lamp flickered on shadowed tapestries. I felt old and young, experienced and innocent. My eyes stung and I blinked away tears.

There was a sudden whiteness around me, first a chill, and a delicate substance. A faint stirring like the wafting of a breath in the shadowed pearlescent light.

A man's figure, translucent yet clearly recognizable, glimmered. The face was white as moonlight, the eyes glowed large and dark, hair misted away like a nimbus.

Words formed in my mind, "My brother will care for you and give you joy. You will make him happy, dear one, my love! My wife and my brother, forever united as three by the kindly Fates."

The sense faded and the figure melted away. A little breeze touched my forehead like caressing kisses that Hektôr used to give long ago in late nights, when he wished not to waken me, returning late from working or training with his men.

I burst out in tears and sat on the floor, rocking on my knees.

I did not hear the laughter and ribald singing outside until his comrades thrust Helenos into the room.

He bolted the door and I went from the dais into his arms, a haven from past and future. He caressed my hair and kissed away the tears, the breath of his tenderness not the ghostly phantom of Hektôr, but the strong devotion of his living brother.

Incredibly, that night, our passion soared like an eagle in flight.

Indeed, we were three, moving together on the bed and finding our own special union where all pain was left behind.

* * * *

Within a month, Peleos sent messengers to summon his vassal kings into Passaron. On a day Helenos found propitious, they assembled for council in the market place. Peleos arrived leaning heavily on. Helenos' arm, accompanied by me.

Peleos addressed the restive groups, "You demand I be sole regent for Molossos. My lords, the gods have spared me overlong."

The eldest Councilman stepped forward. "My lord king, these Trojans you would put over us are slaves taken at the fall of Troia. We, though vassals of the Aiakids, are free men."

Peleos, holding Pyrrhos' scepter, surveyed the group. "All is going well. You have made no complaint, knowing that Helenos ruled justly while Pyrrhos was away. Helenos is the son of kings and Āndrõmakhê is daughter and wife to royals."

Helenos lifted his head and spoke softly, "Give them a vote, my lord, as is customary."

Molossos strode forward with a man's assurance—and a man's height—and stopped before the speakers' stone.

King Peleos looked at him, then back to the hundred men again. "You have your right; a vote will be taken."

He sent Peleos the Younger for the sack of round pebbles, and bowls for the casting of them. "Know, my lords, that in due time, if you choose him, Regent Helenos will give the scepter to Molossos."

Peleos returned with the voting materials and, leaving the bowls for Molossos to hold, passed the sack for each man to take his token.

Molossos followed with the bowls, one of silver for the negative, of gold for positive votes. When he presented the bowls afterward to King Peleos, the gold was so much fuller that a count was not needed.

Peleos' voice rang with renewed strength, "The rightful heir, Molossos Pyrrhosides, stands before us all, with Helenos Priamides as his regent."

Molossos took his place on the stone between the two men. "Every man who acknowledges fealty to the house of Aisakos, hear this! From now onward, all captives from Troia, from all of Anatolia, are free. Each is to reimburse his master in assessing the price of manumission."

A stunned silence mixed with scattered shouts, questions, and disputes filled the air.

The oldest Councilman stepped forward again, "My lord king, this will destroy us. How many free women will choose flax-beating, water-carrying...?" Other voices broke in, shouting agreement.

"There will be other slaves to replace them. Until then, they will work harder for you and produce more, because they will do so willingly, for wages."

Helenos handed the scepter to me and assisted Peleos from the rock. He virtually carried the old man into the palace.

Molossos, following along, reached for the wand.

I held it away from him, smiling. "Not for a while yet." I kept my voice gentle. "You *will* have it soon enough." I touched the sphere that had been so prized by my father, and told my son of the rare sacred iron that had once been the stem.

That night, I took a sheaf of papyrus and a stylus, filled it with my handwriting, stamped it, and handed it to Thalpia.

"What is this, my lady?"

"Your freedom. Leave me if you wish, and be assured that I will give you a goodly purse to allow you a comfortable living for the end of your days; or stay with me if you wish. If you stay, you will stay as my cherished companion. But keep this in case of my death."

Thalpia did what I knew she would do, stayed on as my cherished, loyal companion.

"Call me Ãndrõmakhê, instead of Lady," I told her one day, "in proof of friendship."

"Ãndrõmakhê!"

I noticed that the name was strange on the older woman's lips, trembling in utterance, softly sounded.

Rising, I embraced her. For all her formidable strength of character, she really was a small woman, the top of her head barely reaching my nose.

Thalpia began to weep. "No, it is not fitting, my Lady! From the day you came to Troia as a young bride and smiled at me, you have been *my lady*. I want nothing more in life than remain your loyal companion-servant, the nurse of your children, and now, once more the nurse of your child from Priam's family, sent by the Goddess in merciful justice."

"Did you notice that Pergamos is very like Skamandrios?"

"Yes. Molossos is a veritable Akhilles, and Peleos is his father—a new Pyrrhos, and perhaps luckier, blest with a longer life."

My gaze rolled over to Pergamos, and I smiled. Indeed, he was such an affectionate child! Nonetheless, athletic too, and showed signs of great courage. Peleos, good-natured as well, deferred to Molossos, though to Molossos, only. Molossos was fractious and loved contests, whether in sport or anger. He talked much and boasted much, yet, interestingly, in truth he was a loner and kept his inner thoughts to himself. As time passed, he made no effort to conceal his resentment toward Helenos, obeying him grudgingly.

As news of manumission reached Trojan captives throughout the land, many came to Passaron. They swore fealty to King Peleos, and brought thank-offerings to the shrine. To be ruled by Trojans made it easier for them to accept Achaian citizenship. Peleos himself mixed the eagles' blood with holy water for their anointing as Molossians. They left Passaron with the sacred liquid dripping from their hair, joy alighting their faces.

Festivals throughout the land celebrated marriages between many whose owners had kept them apart. Among these last was Briseis, who married a freed man, a Trojan. His name was Andros, tall with curly brown hair and soulful brown eyes, and his disposition kind as that of his namesake, my brother. He bought his own hives and was beekeeper to the royal household, and they lived in a house fit for the highborn.

Not long afterward King Peleos prepared to leave.

On the last day, he went with Helenos and I to the mound dedicated to Hektôr. "I will be at Methone on the coast. That is where Thétis had promised to meet me when my time came to depart this world." He soothed my objections. "I will never return to Pharsalos. Ligyron is a man now; he has bloodied his club and laid it on the altar. He wears a lion's skin, and has his heritage." Peleos looked at me tenderly. "The boys that you and Lanassa gave my grandson are the hope of my old age. The blood of Aisakos is still strong in the land. I am old and the gods are just, but I will live on in these boys. Know that I will protect your memory as though you were my own daughter."

Peleos then spoke to Helenos, "Because of your good and honorable service, there are no more Trojan slaves under Aiakid rule. I commend you both to Zeus the Protector, now and forever."

"We will meet again, Old Father, in the Elysian Fields," Helenos said, his eyes glistening with moisture.

"In that world where there is no war," replied the old king, "where Priam and I, fathers of such heroic sons as Akhilles and Hektôr, may boast without enmity." He added after a pause, "When you are done here, Helenos, I give you land freehold, forever. Pelasgis on the coast of Epirus is in fief to my family. I will bestow this kingdom to you, as reward for faithful service."

It was early morning when King Peleos got into his chariot and lifted an arm in blessing and farewell.

At that moment, the thought occurred to me that there must be justice for Pyrrhos. Indeed, it might have been the Fates' will that he surrender his life in a temple, for he had slain Priam in a temple. Nonetheless, his slayer had not been motivated by doing the gods' bid. No! Orestes had killed him for his own ends. Yet Pyrrhos had shown him kindness and trusted him. Hermione, he had loved. Divine Justice ought to avenge Pyrrhos' murder in due time.

His charioteer slapped reins across the horses' backs. Helenos saluted, tears on his cheeks. I pressed my face against his chest. Yet I could not drown out the clatter and thump of chariot and wagon, with caravan, crossing the market place, leaving the city, separating me from Peleos, a second-father to my heart as had been Priam.

* * * *

Now that he was King-regent, Helenos had many duties beyond the care of pilgrims in his House of Healing. As Chief Lawgiver and Judge, he sat on the throne daily to hear petitions. As Head Farmer, he spent earliest mornings in the fields and orchards. Soon enough I took much of the civil burden from him. My skills as a scribe were of priceless use now, and I sat to hear petitions.

I also learned much about Helenos that I had not known before. He was to have been called Skamandrios, but received the name of Helenos from a Thracian fortune-teller who foresaw his destiny as one of the best seers, ever. He liked to explore and gain knowledge, dig deep into the source of things, and truly reveled in poetry and music. He owned a faithful steed, which he called Athanasios, meaning noble, who had been among Hektôr's colts rescued from the fires of The Fall.

At midsummer, I led the women's seasonal rites assuring plentiful harvests. On the night of solstice Helenos and I, the royal pair, as examples to others, lay together in the field.

Soft and warm after lovemaking, I sensed within myself an ember of life. I moved my arm across his broad chest and his went under my shoulders so that our bodies blended, turning to shield my womb so the baleful moonlight would not harm what I hoped already nestled there. "Our son will be born a free Trojan in this Achaian land." My voice held the joy of hope.

Helenos' quick gasp of joy shivered ecstasy through me as he encircled me with both arms. "He will be king where our enemies rule." He drew me across his body, my hair mingling with the pale fuzz on his chest.

"No!" I sat up with a sudden move. "He should rule where your father Priam ruled!"

Helenos pulled me back down. Gathering a handful of earth, he dribbled it slowly over me. "I will never see Troia again, nor will our son rule there."

"What are you saying, Helenos...?"

"The war is long ended now, my dearest love. Here, on the coast of Epirus by the sea, we will crown a younger kingdom. Yes, I know that there is a future for our bloodline, here. The gods will not permit another great fortress on Ancient Ate's Hill. It was told in times before Ilion went down from mountain-fast Dardania that a city on the Plain would be ill omened. Our people struggled heroically against the prophecy, and lost. We had a beautiful dream, but it will be fulfilled here. New Life is in the Future, not the Past."

"We both have found strength in hope," I sobbed.

"I gave my word to Peleos, and I owe it to your son, to keep Molossia for the oldest and to see the others settled."

He sat up with a sudden move, his gaze fixed on the horizon. "Athené is not forgiving the rape of Kassandra at Her altar. To defile Kassandra was to defile Athené. I see Her setting in motion a long chain of sacrifices by the Lokrians, kin of Ajax. To expiate for his sin, they will be obliged to send two maidens to Troia every year for a thousand years, to serve as slaves in Her temple, if the inhabitants catch them before reaching the temple, they will be executed. In addition, She was so incensed by the defilement of her temple that she had Zeus bring down a storm upon the victorious fleet, destroying half the men. As a result, this one thoughtless act by Ajax causes the downfall of their entire world, as they have known it. Kassandra's rape was not an act of passion, neither a crime that caused pain to one woman and her family, but a horrendous act that resulted in the deaths of many thousands of men."

"Athené never forgave Alexis' judgment favoring Aphrodite," I sighed. "This is so unbecoming for an all-mighty goddess!"

"This was not the only grievance she had against our people."

"Oh?"

"She had heard of a decree of the Fates that a race descended from us, the Trojans, will one day erase a city dear to Her. Its destruction is still in the distant future, by about a thousand years. *Kartaj? Karthaja?* I am not sure of its exact name. However, it's to be a city in which She will be worshipped with much honor, and therefore will regard it with great affection. Thus She hates Aeneas, for through him, as the ancestor of the founders of a city that will be called Rome, the capital of an empire of unimaginable greatness, the downfall of her beloved Karthaja is to be brought about."

"Ah. That's why Athené set about to kill so many of us in order to eliminate a not-yet born race of people?"

"Yes."

"But she is a *goddess!* Goddess of Wisdom, at that! I hold her to a higher standard than the rest of the pantheon. Last I knew of him, Aeneas was still alive. The Achaians had given him, his father, and his son safe passage out of Troia."

"He will stay alive until he succeeds in what the Fates have decreed for him. He will found the city of Rome."

"Despite Athené's will to the contrary."

"Even the gods are subject to the Fates."

I felt a headache coming on. "You mean even the gods are puppets in the hands of other forces."

"But those forces, the Fates, are just. Sooner or later, they reward or punish you according how you behaved as you walked the road they ordained for you before your birth."

- *The life I have given you, bear with courage; and take upon yourself the sufferings I see fit to bestow upon you; and in the end, your sorrows will lift you upon a pillar.*

- *What am I going to do on a pillar, Goddess, after you have taken all my loved ones from me?*

"Why are you laughing, Ãndrōmakhê?"

I sighed. "At the irony of it all, Helenos. Of course, you are right about Athené and Aeneas. I recall a time in Her temple, when I was beseeching Her to lift Her curse from us, and I heard the names Aeneas and Kartaj whispered. But if She knows of the future, as all gods do, then She also knows that Aeneas will succeed. Then why go these lengths and destroy us, anyway?"

"Because Troia's fall too was ordained by the Fates."

"And Athené's rage merely an agent of their decree?"

Helenos smiled and reached to take me in his arms. "Better stop questioning the logic of the Gods and the Fates. Let us enjoy the reward they have given us, today."

* * * *

We had just dismissed the last of several cases when Molossos stamped in from the courtyard. Helenos called the boy to him, who stood defiantly waiting. "You are ready for initiation into the Rams. Your father wanted you sent to the Kentaurs."

"My father! How do I know this?"

Helenos gave him a stern look. "The man who will teach you is kindred to him who taught Akhilles, before he went to Skyros."

446

I reached for Molossos' hand, but he snatched it away. "Your teacher is also named Kiron," I said. "You will have to earn your totem club in this way if your people are to accept you."

Molossos stared at me, dark redness burning his cheeks. He looked at his feet, shuffled them, then back at Helenos. He moved away. "I'll not owe anything to a Trojan slave."

Helenos motioned him back, but the boy stood stolidly.

Helenos said, "You remain under *my* control until you wear the ram's fleece on your back."

The boy started a protest, but Helenos continued, "Pyrrhos named you for Zeus the Ram. No other group will accept you."

"Fine. Then I'll go since my father wanted it." He slammed from the room, and not long afterward set out for the mountain caves.

It was an evening when first buds swelled on trees and snowdrops whitened among blades of grass that I felt uneasiness. I leaned my head on Helenos' shoulder. "I think it's time."

"Go with Thalpia. I'll send the Great Mother's priestesses to you."

He helped me rise and Thalpia came to help. I motioned her to step back. "I'll walk alone! I could bear this child singing."

Hours later, soft linen was under me when I awoke. Thalpia's face loomed over me. "You have a son, my lady."

Helenos came in, holding a laurel branch and round shield.

Thalpia placed the infant in the shield, then dipped the branch into a lustral basin and shook drops of holy water over the baby, chanting charms against evil.

Helenos, holding the shield with the infant still lying in its hollow, fixed his eyes on me, a smile curving his bearded lips, "We will name him for our Phrygian kindred, and our son will father Trojans in this Achaian land."

I reached out and he lifted the child, placing him at my breast. "He has got strength from my shield now, and one day our Trojan people will rally to support our son. But the name will not be spoken before his day of oracle, that nothing evil takes it from him."

I smiled across the room at Helenos. "I'll give him tigress' milk at his weaning."

* * * *

"Kestrinos!"

After the name-feast ended, I savored my baby. For only the second time in my life, I nursed a wanted child. I touched my cheek to the little

447

head, and whispered his name like an endearment, "Kestrinos Helenosides."

Perhaps *he* would be the beacon guiding lost Skamandrios home.

* * * *

As he developed, Kestrinos outgrew my care sooner than the others did. It was Pergamos who needed my reassurance and love; it was Pergamos who wanted to hear tales of Troia at evening. Peleos the Younger, eagerly awaiting his puberty initiation, kept to himself and associated with older boys, making a club of his own to carry.

Often Helenos, watching Kestrinos march around after his older brother, observed with pride, "My son! There were long years when I thought I would never know a son at all. He is a good, earnest son, and will make us proud. However, my dearest, it is Pergamos who is all Trojan. He will build a New Troia for you."

Helenos had no more to say to me, and I kept the prophecy secure in my heart. It must be Kestrinos, I determined, not a son of Pyrrhos, who would restore Trojan power.

Not long afterward, Tereos strode into the shadowed hall from outer light and stood before Helenos and me.

"My lord and lady Regents," he said, "I am sent by King Ligyron with words of sorrow." He lifted his hands in a gesture of mourning. "King Peleos has gone to the Land of Shadows; he is with Thétis."

Peleos had spent his last months haunting the groves of Mount Pelion where he and Thétis had married. Then, his last days found him by the sea-shrine Thétis had tended. Day after day, he had wandered the shore, at times standing motionless on a great boulder high above the water. Then, on an evening when the sun shone an unusual crimson over the water, Peleos had seemed to grow larger. He had reached both arms seaward and strode off into the air, dropping onto the embrace of a swelling wave.

Tereos paused in his story. "The priestesses say he lives with his wife in a green palace under the sea."

* * * *

Molossos was the startling image of Pyrrhos with that golden hair, cheeks and lips shadowed by the down of manhood.

"He will make a great name for himself," Helenos said. "The blending of two great families shows in everything he does."

448

We watched the boy as he strode masterfully to his place for the evening meal, and I was filled with affection. Passaron faded from my mind, and the towers of Troia rose before my memory: tall, sending shadows across the plain. Yet this was not Hektôr's son, though I looked at him with pride trembling on my lips.

He was a man now, and later, in the public market place, I watched him receive the scepter of Êetiôn from the hands of Helenos.

Shortly after, Molossos came, his face dark, making a declaration that shocked us as well as broke our hearts, "It will be a service to me if you take every Trojan malcontent, and leave. I will not have unrest or revolt in my kingdom. I know how well liked you are among these former slaves." He looked at me. "But you, Mother, may stay if you so wish."

Without waiting for my reply, he turned to Peleos, "And you! Find your own kingdom to rule. You've tagged after me long enough."

Helenos spoke, "You have known I have a duty to your brothers."

Peleos pushed his face against his brother's. "When I have my own land, I will never trust you, Molossos!" He strode away.

Molossos stood a moment, then wheeled and followed Peleos.

Helenos turned to me. "He has only hastened our plan. As soon as I get enough colonists together, we shall leave for Pelasgis."

"To be rejected by my son!" But no, he had wanted me to stay here, only *without* my husband. Moreover, it was clear it never occurred to him that I might choose my husband over him.

I leaned toward Helenos. "I know. Our future is not here."

Going upstairs, I told Thalpia and Okyone of my decision.

Helenos instructed Tereos to send around, offering all Trojans the chance for colonization and new homesteads.

* * * *

The rest of that summer was filled with the coming and going of messengers and the arrival of would-be colonists, making camp around the city. It appeared there would be a continuous migratory assembling of colonists anxious to leave for the Pelasgian coast. I realized that there would perhaps be not one Trojan left in Molossia; only those who had married local people would choose to remain behind.

Winter saw the building of ships, and by spring, all was ready.

Then news came from the south. Travelers told of Menelãos' death at Sparta, and of the usurpation by his slave-born sons.

449

Helen was driven to refuge with Queen Polyxo of Rhodes, whose husband Tlepolemos had died in the war at Troia. Meneláos' sons were now fighting among themselves for full control of Lakedaimon.

"They will destroy each other and all they have," Helenos said, shaking his head. "The day will come when Sparta's people will live in shame, serving cruel masters."

"Retribution!" I cried out.

"It always comes," Helenos nodded. "Individuals pay and peoples pay. The Akaians will pay for Agamemnon, the Lakedaimonians for Helen. Alexis paid, also, and now Helen pays." He gave me a smile. "Don't go back to your loom today. We leave here soon. This may be our last free time to pour libation at Hektôr's memorial. His spirit must be told we will carry his memory with us."

* * * *

By midsummer, our ten-ship fleet was loaded, and manned. Many more vessels would add to their number along the route.

I clung to Molossos aboard the pilot ship. A stiff breeze arose and men scurried to adjust the sail. Molossos moved impatiently, pushing me away, and Helenos gave him a last blessing.

The hawser was untied and cast aboard before my son, the young king of Molossia, leapt ashore. Anchor weighed, the sail bellied and the little fleet scudded down the rushing river to quieter waters.

At the rail, I looked at Molossos, my golden son, firstborn of Pyrrhos whose memory I now respected for the mercy he had shown to Skamandrios, with tears in my eyes.

Helenos came and I buried my face on his shoulder.

"Be glad of heart! Your son Molossos' name will last forever, and his sons will rule the earth," he told me softly.

During the long voyage, Pergamos followed the men in their work, sometimes being allowed to help. Peleos had a regular assignment at watch, and it was he who spotted a gigantic boulder blocking the river at a wide bend. Helenos strode to the poop, Pergamos tagging after him, and shouted instructions to the captain, who passed them along to the ship behind them. By now, we numbered twenty vessels, having increased from rivers along the way that emptied into the Acheron.

A terrible shock and scraping shuddered the ship. The mast creaked under the straining sail. I saw that we had not actually struck the rock; the waterway was not completely blocked.

"Sandbars!" Shouted the captain, and men leapt to both shores. Ropes were hauled out, attached at either side of the bow, and looped around the chests of men on either bank. Others seized thong ropes and heaved, assisted by men from other ships.

At last, the vessel slid across and the remainder of the day was spent in getting the rest of the fleet across.

At dusk, camp was set up on shore and Helenos conferred with the fisher-folk living nearby. "We are in Thesprotia," he announced upon returning. "We should reach the river's mouth before dark on the day after next."

At dawn, a great eagle glided from the forest and soared ahead, keeping to our right. "An excellent omen," Helenos announced. "Zeus sends His eagle to guide us."

I recalled the time when the eagle had flown on our left, and Hektôr laughed, and turned around to make it appear on his right.

Each ship ran out twenty-four oars; from then on, the navigating was easy. And indeed, before dark of the second day, the river opened out into a wide bay. The jagged gulf was gnawed by angry hills. It seemed as if the entire fleet had been vomited through the jaws of some vast creature. Around us, the air was a luminous void of silver-blue, so tangible with light that I almost reached to feel its texture. Small ripples sparkled like crystals on the slate-blue water so like undiluted wine.

Helenos made augury, found it favorable, and gave the order to proceed. Through the shallows of the Pelasgian Sea, we made it safely to the Channel of Scheria. Helenos gave orders to anchor in a cove of an island to our left. He came to stand beside me, pointing landward:

"Look! There lays our future home, Āndrõmakhê, where I will build New Troia."

The low-lying coast was thick with willow and tamarisk. In the distance I could see wooded hills and beyond them rough mountains. Then I spotted a black form on a leafless tree at the brink.

"Look there!" I pointed into the incurving bay. "Isn't that the very same eagle which led us here?"

I heard his gasp of realization; the black blob was indeed a resting eagle. "Our guide from Zeus-Badogios! This is the land Peleos gave us. It was a gift from his heart. Behind that eagle, I will build our city."

* * * *

Chapter 36: Phaekis to Chaonia

We were in a huge sheltered bay when the sky turned black and the wind died. A harbor guarded by bollards along the seawall was backed by what looked like long warehouses. Helenos gave landing orders, and then sent a messenger to investigate the seemingly deserted quay. Carrying a small torch lit from the one hoarded from Passaron, the man leapt onto the smooth stones of the wharf. While he was gone, the little fleet hove to and dropped anchor.

Hawsers were secured on land by the time the man returned. He was in a chariot with another man, clad in heraldic dress, who announced when he had exchanged greetings with Helenos, "You are on the island of Phaekis. My lord Alkinoos Nausotheides bids you welcome in his house. Your people will have shelter here." He indicated two large buildings, "The nearer one is filled with goods, but he keeps the other as a shelter for anyone who might need it."

Soon their men, escorted into the vacant building, took the women and children from the ships. I found the place fitted with pallets, covers, and eating utensils. The herald sent for maids and food, seeing to light and warmth.

A handsome chariot preceded the supply wagon, which drew up near the building's entrance. A young man in princely garb leapt from the chariot and approached Helenos. "I am Klytoneos Alkinosides," he answered when Helenos had given his own name and origin. The two men clasped arms in friendship.

"You do me great honor with such provision for my people," Helenos thanked him. By now, the herald was overseeing unloading of the wagon, and had sent maids to help the visitors settle.

"We keep constant watch for distressed travelers, and are prepared to offer hospitality," Klytoneos said with a smile. "We grow extra crops and breed larger herds than are needed here. Our island is fruitful enough to share. Hundreds of refugees have passed by this way since that war around your city so long ago. There is famine now in Achaia and Anatolia."

"I will, of course, pay you for what stores we require. We will be settling the opposite shore and will need commerce with you until our colony is in order," Helenos said.

"Those who are able, buy from us. Those who are unable to, never leave here empty." Klytoneos turned back to his chariot, and then paused. "We wage war with no one here. Such trade as comes our way is sufficient." He motioned Helenos to join him. "Ride with me, my lord." He pointed to a second wagon that had come down from the citadel. "A cushioned carriage for your family."

The city of Drepane stood on high ground between the bay and a lagoon beyond, walled by well-fitted stones.

King Alkinoos and Queen Arête stood to greet us in their outer courtyard. Alkinoos strode to Helenos, clasping arms with him in welcome. Arête greeted me warmly, and led me into the palace. Klytoneos remained outside to see after the horses and vehicles.

Arête spoke while leading me toward the stairs. "You and I will talk later, but first let my maids see to your comfort." She motioned to a boy and young woman nearby, their eyes agleam with interest. "My youngest son, Helios. Helios, will you show these boys to their bath," and she looked at Peleos and Pergamos. "Naosikaa, my only daughter, soon to be married." She smiled at the girl. "Will you see after these ladies, and the baby?"

Naosikaa took Okyone's hand and led her away, followed by Thalpia carrying Kestrinos. Four maids assigned to our bath took Helenos and me in charge.

"We will soon leave for Pelasgis," Helenos said during the meal. "King Peleos bequeathed me the land, assuring us that the Pelasgians there are loyal to him and will be to me."

"When you go," Alkinoos cautioned, "better leave all women and children here. There is famine across there. Lykian settlers arrived some years ago and now Getae are destroying the land."

"Lykians? They were among our strongest allies during the war," Helenos wondered.

"Their leader is Tyrsenos Atysidos; he may perhaps ally with you, then. His father Atys is still in Lykia, but Tyrsenos seeks new land."

Arête offered me a pot of honey for my slab of cheese. "Come now, lady Āndrōmakhê, we must have cheerful talk of our own." She glanced across the hall. "Are those your children?"

And the conversation shifted to families and plans for the future.

* * * *

During days when Helenos made ready to cross to the mainland, I walked with Arête in her garden. On a bench under the grape arbor, I looked out to where two seas joined in gleams of sunlight.

"On our left is the Pelasgian Sea," Arête pointed, "and beyond on your right, is the land where Tyrsenos plans to colonize."

"Do you hear anything of Troia?"

Arête hesitated. "Agamemnon's forces left a land and people destroyed, from Ilion, the capital, all the way south to Lykia. Almost half the population died of famine and plague before most of the survivors left with Tyrsenos. Some of those who survived were reduced to..." Arête sighed, finishing in a lower tone, "to eating their own children."

Numbly, I stared into the queen's face. *The gods are just,* Helenos spoke not too long ago.... *Just?* Starving people reduced to consume their own children? My stomach flooded my mouth. In an instant, I was leaning into a thick arbutus shrub. The sickness spewed among white flowers and green leathery leaves.

Arête offered me a handful of bay flowers and I held the rosy-white petals to my nose. "We will walk a while," Arête said. "I should not have told you."

We left the garden and passed into the courtyard where Alkinoos and Helenos were discussing the imminent departure of his Trojan guests. The king was saying, "Your Pelasgis is rich in soil, but poorly cultivated. I will keep you supplied until your crops come in."

We began walking toward the stables. Alkinoos continued, "In building your new city, you will have much to work with, because an older town once stood there. And those fishermen's huts along the shore can be developed into a port town for your workers. They call the place Onchesmos; and where you will build, has long been known as Buthroton. Beyond there, is a good lake, well stocked with fish."

The sound of approaching hooves and wheels grabbed our attention. Klytoneos sprang from his chariot and went to his father. "A man who calls himself Mylas Termilosidos is at the harbor with ships from Buthroton."

"Make them welcome." Alkinoos went to order a feast prepared.

It was during the meal that Okyone first locked eyes with Mylas.

I noted that the stranger seemed to forget his drink when Okyone refilled his cup, and their hands touched before she moved away.

I bit back a smile. Had my little niece found her future husband?

The twang of strings interrupted talk. Mylas had brought his own minstrel, and now the man chanted the story of how his people, the Chonians, had tried to settle in Pelasgis but been driven out by Tyrsenos.

When Okyone came to me a few days later, the girl's eyes were brilliant as she talked of Mylas. I nodded, resolving to have Helenos look into the young man's lineage.

* * * *

Nearly two summers passed before Helenos returned, bringing ships to Phaekis, and began assembling families for their new home on the mainland. As he strode into Alkinoos' hall, he seemed more royal than I had ever seen him, now more warrior than priest.

Our laden ships sailed eastward on light winds. I appreciated that life under the rule of Priam's son would, for the migrants, be almost like returning home.

I stood tall at the bow with Okyone and Thalpia. The craggy land before me was fringed with pilings where fishermen kept their traps. The landing was a deeply cut opening into the land as if a Titan's spoon had scooped it out.

Other colonists' ships rocked in the gentle tide, secured at dock, sails furled around crossbeams. Willow and tamarisk swayed along the steep bank down to the water. On my right, a river emptied into the bay.

"Another Skamander," I murmured to myself.

"I think it small enough to be called Simois," Helenos said, startling me as he came up. "Or perhaps, even the little Thymbra. It comes from a lake larger than this bay, beyond our city. Rivers fill it from the mountains north and eastward from us."

"What about the famine I had heard of?"

He urged me to the gangplank. "All is well," he reassured me. "There was also plague—you weren't to know. My training at Trikka helped me save many and stopped the disease. There is no more hunger and the land is rich. But we will not feast as long as others starve."

Farther inland, I observed yellowing fields of grain on the lower ground. "I have grapevines on the southern hillsides as well as orchards starting. The Chonians will stay with us. Milyas may govern territories for me."

We landed and he filled a hand with soil. He took one of mine and let the grains fall into my palm. "Behold! New Troia has risen here. This is our land."

I touched the grains to my brow with reverence.

He lifted me into his chariot and climbed in beside me.

The city was on a high strip of land. It was partly under construction, echoing flatly to the sounds of breaking stones and chopping of wood. Men worked in small groups around unfinished houses, while before the completed ones women and children stood or ran out to look at and greet their savior, brave and noble Helenos, son of Priam, brother of Hektôr.

We drew up before square towers flanking the city gate. These were Trojan towers, and that gate the Skaian, above it the figure of a giant eagle across the lintel; at each end, reared a Trojan horse's head.

"The eagle that led us here is the city's protective totem."

The eagle of Badogios Papas!

He helped me to the pavement. Leaning heavily on him, I thought of my long-ago entry into Ilion, capital of Troia, through a similar gate, as Hektôr's loving, happy, young bride.

He sent the chariot ahead and walked with me up the terraced street. From the market place, the citadel could be seen above, with its shrines and noble houses.

"Helenos, I can't bear it! All the familiar places..."

"See, in every direction a lookout can spot invaders long before they reach us." His enthusiasm could not be stopped. "You can almost see the farther shore of Lake Plakia."

"Lake Plakia!" I savored the name. The name of those many springs that watered Thébé.

He moved toward the citadel with me. "Three tribes worked with us. In building, we used brick where stones failed, just as at home."

In the royal courtyard, I saw that, though on a much smaller scale, the building resembled Priam's. Smooth wooden columns supported porticoes, and ornamented beam-ends marked three upper floors. Inside, doors and frames gleamed with bronze plating. Frescoes in the great hall told the Trojan story, with one wall devoted to tales of Thebe and Mysia, my home. The sleeping-rooms were hung with skins and cloths, and on the tiled floors, straw mats silenced footsteps. We waited at the fireless hearth pit until Thalpia came in with the boys. She kept Kestrinos with her and the older boys joined me.

"Peleos, my boy." Helenos turned to him.

I saw that almost overnight, the boy had become a man. Fourteen years had passed since Peleos' birth.

Really? *That* many years?

Still fleshy but tall, he was a young King Peleos with light hair, strong-boned face and sharp, light blue eyes. Helenos was speaking to him, "You will bring in the hearthfire, my son."

He leapt to his task, face alight with pride at this acknowledgement of his newly achieved manhood.

Helenos turned to Pergamos, "Bring the torch from Passaron."

The boy raced along to where handsome Milyas, Okyone's beloved, kept guard over the light.

The log was ceremonially laid over twigs and leaves already piled. Helenos gave the invocation while Pergamos held the torch. "From the heavens Prometheus brought fire to man. Just as now, he opened a new hearth on Eternal Mother's Hill, and so I establish a New Troia with the flame of this log."

Peleos took the torch from his brother and gave it to Helenos, who plunged it into the pit. I trembled as the flames sank, and then caught from tender twigs to branches to the great log.

Milyas brought a jug of wine, followed by Okyone with cups. Thalpia joined them with Kestrinos, and Helenos poured libations into the flames as sizzling smoke rose heavenward.

Milyas filled the cups, Okyone passed them around, and all of us drank in honor of our new home.

Helenos' blue eyes met mine as we set our cups on the hearth-wall. "Troia lives again in this land. From now on this is the kingdom of Chaonia [1]." His tone lowered to sadness. "Do you remember my little brother Chaon?"

"Yes, of course. Chaon, the brother whom you had accidentally killed in that hunting accident. And once upon a time, my intended, as per agreement between our respective fathers." I placed my arms about his waist. "And now, Helenos Priamides, I speak an oracle: You are to be a great and just ruler."

"You know that at first, I was to be named Skamandrios." Helenos spoke up abruptly, "Even after they had changed my name as told by the oracle, in my heart I had remained Skamandrios, believing myself to be a brave huntsman and warrior. But your son, your son by Hektôr, was the true Skamandrios, for in him I knew the seed of greatness! Hektôr told me one night at campfire around the walls, that he thought of me as his son's namesake along with our ancient god-king. After that, I fought with greater courage than before, and was a better warrior despite my lack of training."

"So your true role in life was distorted," I said thoughtfully. "You were born to be a warrior—and a great king, as you will be here."

He shook his head. "All has turned out for the best. If I had been a warrior at first, I would have struggled against the Fates and destroyed myself. My father was wise to send me to Merops, a friend of old, father of his first wife, Arisbe. My training was long and in many ways terrible, because I was willful and not submissive to the gods. Had I not taken hold of my willfulness and managed to learn so well, we would not have freedom now."

"Chaonia," I whispered, "A new land, an old grief."

"Chaon has become the cornerstone of our success. My grief for him is paid, and now I give him honor. My brother will be remembered as though he had lived to earn a warrior's fame."

"Will the people here accept this?"

"Be it as the Moira wills; the world will know Chaonia, for the people do call me their Savior. As for the city, it shall keep the name it had from the beginning, Buthroton, forever. They will be satisfied, knowing this is still a Pelasgian land."

I stood close to him beside the glowing fire as we crossed our hands over our breasts while he prayed for peace in his brother's spirit. Buthroton, a second Ilion, Chaonia, another Troia!

* * * *

At harvest, the fields and vines overflowed with grain and grapes. The annual assembly of Councilmen gathered, this year to confirm Helenos as their ruler. In joint session, the Getae and Pelasgians formally chose him, together with me as co-regent. Feasting was held throughout the city and sacrificial smoke darkened the sky. Arête and Alkinoos were over from their island. During the feast, I turned to Arête, asking, "Your sons are here, but where is Naosikaa?"

"She is preparing for her marriage with Odysseus' son, Telemakos. They will rule Kephallenia."

It was dusk when the newly built thrones were placed at the head of the great hall. Arête, seated beside me, motioned to the bard, Kyathos. He drew fulsome chords from his kithara and announced he would sing for us the Molossiad.

"The Molossiad?! Oh, about my son! Word from him at last—after so long?"

"Much better than from him, my lady, but of him."

My heart thudded and I sat up straight. The minstrel sang first of his heritage and his unusual wisdom for so young a king. Then he told of alliances with Ligyron and how he became overlord of his half-brother, yet kept him for strongest ally. Colonists from their northern neighbors in Dolopeia had first come to settle peacefully in Molossia, but soon were followed by outright seizures of land. Ligyron, son of Lanassa and Pyrrhos, and Molossos, son of Pyrrhos and Āndrōmakhê, united and counter-invaded, conquering all northern kingdoms, thus doubling their original holdings. To seal the conquest Molossos brought home as bride the princess of Dolopeia, while Ligyron married a younger sister. Aglow with the blood of his enemies, Molossos now stood greatest among the northern kings. In future years, the minstrel foretold, Molossos was destined to increase his power and renown.

I looked about, at the jovial faces. It seemed as though my heart would burst for the wonderful freedom and fame that was mine at last. One son already a great warrior, a second, soon to be. Nevertheless, a part of me yearned for young Peleos. He, like his older brother, must earn his own future.

Then the chords shifted to a minor scale and Kyathos chanted a horrifically tragic tale. Helen of Sparta sought protection at the hands of Queen Polyxo of Rhodes. There, she took part in spring rituals with the other women, but afterwards, when the celebrants were gone...terrible sacrilege! I shuddered and trembled, hearing how the Spartan Queen had not been released from her ritual tying against the tree, and was found, later, slashed beyond recognition, dead. It was whispered that Polyxo had exacted this vengeance upon the woman whose escape to Troia with Alexis-Paris had brought King Tleptolemos from Rhodes to die beneath the walls of Troia. Then the citizens rose up in revolt against a queen who could use the Mysteries for vengeance and many left to form colonies far from the island.

As tears ran down my cheeks, Kyathos' tale changed again, this time to warlike drumming as he told of Orestes' march against Sparta. Hermione must have revenge against her brothers who had driven her mother from the throne and to her death. Nikostratos and Megapenthes had ruled jointly but with bickering, keeping the Lakedaimonians in disunity and near famine during the months after Helen's exile. It was with comparative ease that Orestes conquered the feuding land, slew Menelaos' sons, and joined Lakedaimon and Mykene under him and Hermione. Their young son, Tisamenos, would inherit a vast land.

Tisamenos! I was alerted at the name. Hermione had born no son for Pyrrhos, but with Orestes, she was fertile!

* * * *

When Kestrinos was ten, Helenos took him in charge. His growing independence required strict oversight, and Helenos put him under the tutelage of a military instructor. It was Pergamos, three years his senior, and last of Pyrrhos' sons on whom my eyes rested fondly as time passed. Intent like the others, yet he would look at me as if he planned some secret game, a game that would please me one day.

Repeated inquiries we sent out for Skamandrios continued to return with no clue of his whereabouts. Yet I felt no lack of hope, only impatience. By the grace of my Goddess, the mercy of Pyrrhos, and devotion of Kiron, Skamandrios, son of Hektôr, had survived so much; it was clear he was being primed for an important destiny. The Goddess would not forsake him, I had faith in Her.

Young Peleos went off on a distant military expedition with Milyas, and when he returned, he was a stranger to me. Proud and confident, his head was full of grand ideas.

Milyas, even more impatient and eager, told Helenos one evening as they stabled the horses after that day's hunting,

"We leave before winter. I have won my own land now at ancient Phoinike. It is a place rich in timber. Caravans meet ships there in trade with amber and the transport of rare iron. The sea is broad there, and Zeus often strikes our high promontory with bolts of lightning and thunder. This protects our city, where we have safe harborage."

And so it was that dear Okyone, spirited daughter of Andros and Lanassa, married Milyas, and sailed away with her husband.

* * * *

When it was time for the Feast of All Souls, I asked Helenos to find a suitable location for Hektôr's memorial mound. He located a conical hill near the city that had the look of a tumulus. "I will dig a chamber there for our offerings," he promised.

When it was finished, we brought miniature jars of honey, grain and wine. We recited a ritual that would seal the place against evil and bless the dead with food, beauty, and music. When I stepped back, Helenos set up a phallic shaft he had carved with Hektôr's cartouche and a scene representing Hektôr's famed duel with Akhilles.

Then he lifted a pink-and gold-lipped conch shell he had brought and put it to his lips. He blew one great, long blast. The sound pierced my ears and shuddered throughout my whole being, echoing among inland hills and rising to the cloudless sky, letting Hektôr's spirit know he was forever honored and remembered here.

In the market place was a shrine where artistically painted terracotta figures were placed, representing local heroes. It was a custom I liked, reading the names painted in Pelasgian pictographs across the stand of each. But on this wondrous day, one more figure stood there: in Trojan symbols at its feet, I read the name of Hektôr.

[1] Chaonia. The names Chaonia and Molossia are ancient proto-Hellenic Era names that have survived to the Present Era. Here too History and persistent Mythology complement each other. According to Myth, the Chaonians were the descendants of Molossos, one of the three sons of Neoptolemus, son of Achilles and Hector's wife Andromache. Following the sack of Troy, Neoptolemus and his armies settled in Epirus (present day Albania) where they intermixed with the local population.
Molossos/Molossus inherited the kingdom of Epirus after the death of Helenos, son of Priam and Hecuba of Troy, who had married Andromache after Neoptolemus' death.

Chapter 37: The Two Princes

Brothers of the Soul

Helenos joined his new kingdom to the commerce that dealt with Phaekis. The town prospered as Helenos' fame as a Healer-King, who was a truthful seer and wise ruler, attracted rich caravans, and his merchants bartered with them. Chaonia became known in lands far from the western shore. He sent Peleos to work with shepherds, herdsmen and vintners around the city, so that he would learn all aspects of managing a kingdom. At other times, he had the boy learn from artisans as they improved the city. Lasting peace saw to the increasing importance of Buthroton. Industry and trade flourished, and soon luxuries were imported, and then imitated for export.

A sports field and track near the city encircled a large oak where a Pelasgian altar to Dione had stood since time immemorial. Rededicated to Zeus-Dionysos, it became the center of all outdoor activities. On a side sloping up to the city, terraces were dug and stones laid for benches so that spectators watched sports and dances during major festivals. Kyathos would chant an epic there, interpreted by dancers.

Hektôr's memorial was a beautiful, private place where I could take my spinning, or tablets for writing or reading. I tended a small garden of flowers and shrubs that gave garlands to drape around the stone. I had planted pomegranates, fig and mulberry trees so that when they matured, I could place the fruit as refreshment for Hektôr's spirit. At first, my visits to this place renewed my grief, so that sometimes Helenos would come for me and lead me home, supported by his arm around my waist.

"You must not come here often if it makes you suffer," he told me, "don't lose sight that you have another life now. Sadness is due more properly at festivals for the dead. You must not cause his spirit grief by your own grief, my dearest."

I did not know what to say to him. Of course, he was right, but ah, my heart. While together, Hektôr and I had been one soul, and bereft of his half, I would always be only one half seeking the other.

We stopped midway between the mound and the sports field, and he held me more closely against him, kissing my cheeks. "Would it help if I were to show him to you in the Twilight Land?"

"Oh, Helenos..."

"It's difficult for me also," he said, "but I will share what I can with you. I never loved my brother any less because of you."

"Helenos! I do love you. Oh, so very much. I don't understand how it can be—for I love you both, so completely."

"Ãndrõmakhê, I meant what I said before. If we were to come here of a night, I might call his spirit so that you would see him and feel the better for it."

"Perhaps—some time—but not now, I could not bear it."

We walked along together, then paused a while to watch the sport. Peleos was in the field with Pergamos and Kestrinos, lording it over his younger brothers, challenging them to throw the discus farther than he. After a short time, Helenos joined them, dropping his robe as he strode along. Catching the disc when Kestrinos threw it, he shouted happily to them and changed the contest into a lesson. I sat on a marble seat, enjoying the beauty of those four shining bodies bending and twisting and leaping, my thoughts freed from grief.

After this day, I found peace again at Hektôr's memorial, as though his spirit waited there to give reassurance. I felt so close to him that there were days when I experienced great joy, even as I watched the mountains darken before the setting sun.

* * * *

It was on such an evening in early summer that Helenos came toward me followed by another man. The man was not a stranger, nor a native Pelasgian. I looked to Helenos, but something unusual in his attitude and silence caused me to glance again at the man behind him, shadowy in the twilight, and I knew the manner of his walk, his height, his big-boned body. For one flaming instant, I saw Hektôr come to life.

"Ãndrõmakhê!" That voice, the Trojan accent...

I staggered back and Helenos leapt to catch me. The other man was looking at me, turned now so that I could see his profile.

"I am Aeneas, come with my father and son."

The man held out a hand to me and I touched it, trembling. Waves of emotion sent shuddering sensations through my nerve-ends. Fighting back tumultuous feelings, my lips formed whispered words, "Praised be Ma-Kybele, the Great Kind Mother!"

463

We went down the mound together. "Tell me about Troia, Aeneas! Please. Everything."

Helenos silenced me with a soft reminder, "He will tell us all after he has rested."

When our guests returned from the bathing room, Helenos was spitting roasts over the firepit, with Kestrinos watching.

Aeneas strode forward, and then led me to where a young man stood near the throne-chairs conversing with Peleos and Pergamos.

"You remember Ãndrõmakhê, Hektôr's wife," Aeneas said, and the young man turned to me.

My heart went into spasms, he was so like Hektôr, the age he had been when I first met him—and yet not like. Hmm, the difference was that he was not Hekabe's, but Kreusa's son. I reached and seized him in my arms—Askanios, less than a year older than Skamandrios. My fingers dampened from the wetness of his own cheek when I caressed his face, speechless.

Then Helenos came forward with Anchises. When I embraced him, the old king was bony in my arms, a wisp of his former self.

Seated and served their food, I heard Aeneas answer a question from Helenos. A word caught my attention; the word had been my son's name. "What of him?" I demanded.

"Oh, I spoke of another Skamandrios, the son of Sigeia."

A sword pierced my heart.

"He claims the city." Aeneas shifted uneasily, and then went on, "My efforts of rebuilding the fortress proved impossible. Although we were given safe passage from the city, we had returned with some of the survivors, trying to salvage at least some things. We found the streets hopelessly choked with rubble. As we cleared, we buried what dead we found. We had too much work in rebuilding shelter to repair the walls— much of the stone was useless, burned."

"Stone—burned? What terrible, unholy heat!"

"Yes. The stones were pitted and blackened, porous—we left much of it where it had fallen and beat it into the streets for paving. Swords, arms, jewelry—everything of metal was melted into blobs of nothing. It was an impossible task, though we managed to clear the Pergama and cover it with fresh earth, and built upon it."

Pergamos asked, "In the south, then—there is no place you could find alliances? What about the old friends of Priam? The Hittites?"

"Insurrection there, and attack from without. Their King has been disposed, and the Vans have invaded Hittite holdings. The Kassite dynasty barely holds its own, while Tutulti-Ninurta claims Karduniash

464

and Assyria. The fine roads that Memnon had built around shining Susa made the destruction of his own kingdom easy. Kimmerians from the north bypassed Troia, but only because of its poverty. Even well established Egypt has a new king, Merenptha, who is forced to expend troops defending his coast. Our own people have crossed that sea and joined others from many places, escaping famine, plague, invasion..."

Pergamos glanced at me, and then pressed, "But surely something worthy fighting for must remain there."

"You cannot believe, without seeing it, the horror and destruction everywhere." Askanios looked at me, then at Pergamos. "Cousin, we are well away from there."

"Indeed so," Aeneas spoke now, "I had hoped to rebuild the great fortress and restore Dardanian power in the land. But to no avail." He glanced uneasily at Helenos. "We are united now in the brotherhood of our heritage; all rivalries are no more."

Helenos replied, "And the House of Priam is dead there. If we had defeated the Achaians—who knows what internecine strife would have developed between you and Hektôr? My father was quite wary of your ambitions, and thought to bind you to him with my sister Kreusa. If Hektôr had died with no male heir, you would have succeeded him instead of Alexis or Deiphobos, for you were the better warrior."

"Truly spoken," said Aeneas.

"But the House of Priam *does* exist there," spoke up Askanios. "We left Hektôr's son claiming the rulership. He expects to restore not only Ilion, but to rebuild Dardania as well. Impossible task though."

"Conquered but not defeated." I shot the words at him. Then I had to know. "Is that other boy... is he like Hektôr?"

"Very like." Aeneas' words were careful, "We decided to leave when Sigeia's son brought colonists from Thrakia, under the patronage of Polymestor."

"He lives...that murderer of Polydoros, lives?" I demanded.

"No longer. He lived a few years after Hekabe had blinded him, planning overlordship of a restored Trojan kingdom. Sigeia is queen in his place there now, or was those long months ago."

I choked back my outrage. That woman, daughter of Priam's discarded first wife Arisbe and her lover Hyrtakos, queen where Priam's daughter Ilione had ruled.

"What of Ilione?"

"We do not know." The mumbling came from Anchises. "Aeneas was meant to follow Hektôr as king. The house of Dardanos is far older than that of Ilos, who broke away from his Teukrian forebears."

"Forget all that now," Askanios said. "If that Skamandrios wants to struggle with those ruins, he is welcome. I am more inclined toward priesthood than kingship."

Helenos smiled. "You are wise not to fight the Inevitable."

Askanios moved nearer to Helenos. "I ask that while we are here, you instruct me in augury."

"I will initiate you into Trojan Mysteries and the lore of Trikka." He turned to Aeneas. "Do you intend to settle near us?"

"We follow our ancestral trail along the route taken by Dardanos, to Hesperia. I am told that his land is across your sea. The river Oryx at Drepanum where the Sikel people live, is the area."

Helenos gave him a long, thoughtful look. Then, "I will give you precise directions when you go. You will sail to the land where you will build a new city, and sow the seeds of an empire of such greatness that today, we cannot even envision it."

* * * *

During the winter while Askanios huddled in a cushioned chair near the hearthfire, Pergamos was often with him. He continued to ask at length about Dardania and Troia, his eyes intent, firm purpose growing in him.

By spring, the Dardanian ships were repaired and well stocked for another long voyage. I stood on the quay with my sons while Helenos made augury. Face to the sky and holy black stone in his fist, he spoke in another voice, "Hera, Star of the Sea, and great Ilian Ate! Guide these Trojans who will remember you always with prayer and sacrifices." He lowered his head and his look was darkly solemn as it met Aeneas' awed stare. "Go, Aeneas, honoring Troia and Dardania, to win victories for the sons of Dardanos and Ilos. However, you will reach the land safely only in the manner that I tell you, for I have taken augury. You *will* reach Hesperia. Enroute to Hesperia, you must sail around Sikeliot Island, avoiding the strait between there and the mainland. Evil origin curses that water where once land was. One day, the sea will dry again and the land rise as it sank, with fire and smoke and sulfurous fumes. Even here, there is record of how old Kentaur tribesmen were driven into the mountains by walls of water along the coast. Before that time, Scheria was joined to the mountain chain, not an island. Therefore, my cousin, avoid all dangerous places and heed my warnings! What happened once, will happen again."

"A saying of the Initiates, I know," Aeneas acknowledged.

"Follow my advice, and greatness awaits you."

Just before they embarked, Helenos brought out a linked mailcoat and plumed, large helmet. "You will need these in Hesperia," Helenos told Aeneas. "They once belonged to Pyrrhos, fashioned from armor Hephaistos had made for Akhilles. I know they will serve you well."

Then Thalpia stepped forward with an armload of fine garments, and from them I chose a large cloak woven with figures of Hektôr. "For you, Askanios, near twin to my son," I spoke as I draped it across his shoulders, "this is my best work. May the design of Hektôr protect you from ill health!"

Our guests embarked, anchors were weighed, and oars ran out to splash and sparkle as they lifted and dipped southward. I watched until all the sails unfurled, fading at last beyond the morning mists. Trojan vessel of Ida timber, the last I would ever see of my homeland....

* * * *

Four more years totaled twelve peaceful rounds of Trojan rule in Epirus. During that time, Aeneas sent back messages, the first being that Anchises had died on Sikel's island. A year later, Aeneas married a princess of Hesperia, through whom he inherited the kingdom of Latium. Askanios founded the Trojan Mysteries there and was Chief Hierophant of the territory.

One day, a minstrel reported the death of Odysseus, murdered by a son of whose existence he had not known, born during his wanderings.

Many pilgrims for Dodona stopped at Buthroton to visit Hektôr's memorial. Helenos had built for them a large caravan-stop in Apollo's grove, together with a religious compound that included shrines and caves, a House of Healing, and dormitories for priests and priestesses. His liberal hospitality was soon rewarded by tales of great wealth and power. Trade routes by land and sea exchanged local produce, mainly fish, for goods from other lands.

Then merchants trading between north and sough brought sudden rumblings of trouble. From the northern forestlands, the direction whence Erik the Great had marched down, homeless migrants and marauders swept southward. Big blond men driving oxen that hauled women, children and goods in high-wheeled wagons came in ever-increasing number due to a sudden shift in weather that made eking out a living from the earth impossible. Those who settled peacefully in Chaonia told of floods driving out the Forest People, and of invaders besetting them from the east, escaping burning drought. They came southward looking for those rich kingdoms that sent such fine pottery and glass in exchange for amber, iron, and pelts.

After this, ambassadors and messengers came to Buthroton in increasing numbers to confer secretly with Helenos.

I was sitting quietly atop Hektôr's mound one warm summer evening when Pergamos rushed to me, alight with urgency.

"Mother! Aeneas' visit settled my mind on something I have thought of for a long time."

"Oh? Tell me about it, son."

"Askanios had told me of important things I could only learn from someone who had been in Troia after the war. I do not belong here, dear Mother. As Hektôr's spirit is my witness, I am a Trojan! Your blood is strong in me, my father's is weak. I was born Trojan—I know this now."

"King of Troia," I smiled indulgently. "My son. Restorer of Troia on the Straif of Dardanos, in Anatolia, Land of the Morning."

Pergamos went on excitedly, "Last night, I dreamed of my brother Skamandrios again. He looks just like Askanios."

I jumped up, looking at him intently.

"Skamandrios said to tell you that he is still wandering, but one day soon he will land in Messina, on the island of Sicily, and will build his own kingdom there."

"What? What did he tell you? He is going to land *where?"*

"Messina, in Sicily. In addition, he has a betrothed, her name is Kupra. They met while he was on Sardinia, last year."

I found myself hyperventilating. "Shardana! Skamandrios was in Shardana! And his betrothed's name is Kupra!"

"Not Shardana, *Sardinia,"* Pergamos corrected with a smile. "This is not the first time I've dreamt of Skamandrios," he went on, "but it was the first time that he spoke to me so clearly."

I collapsed on my knees, my lips trembling, unable to speak.

"This morning, I consulted Helenos; he foresaw a Trojan throne for me. He said he had always known that Skamandrios' destiny lay in or around Hesperia, like Aeneas'. They were born to enter new lands, and forge new kingdoms. And I am to bring Tomorrow, to Yesterday." He stood up. "Mother! You will go with me."

"Pergamos, this is my home now..." *And not all that far from Hesperia,* the thought crossed my mind. "Besides, I could not leave Helenos, and he will not leave me."

Pergamos' laugh was light-hearted. "Oh, Mother! I did not say we go now. Nevertheless, later on, yet soon enough. What is here for any of us? What the invaders are not destroying, the Achaian chiefs ruin with quarrels and land-grabbing."

"The victors, vanquished." I smiled wryly.

He put an arm about my waist. "I needed some word to anchor me, and Skamandrios gave it. The destruction at Troia, that *other* Skamandrios trying to rebuild it! Ah, let him. Thébé, your home, is south of there. We will build a New Troia around Thébé, Mother!"

My heart was too full for speech. This dreamy boy, the one among my sons who had shown least interest in military affairs—how often had I worried when he came to me more often than the others did, for help or comfort, seeming too tender to ever become a warrior.

Pergamos put his arm about me as we rose together and went back to the palace. My son from Pyrrhos, who communicated with my son from Hektôr, in the Land of Dreams. Pergamos, who wanted to return to Troyland, and resurrect it around Thébé!

Oh, Ma-Kybele, surely it is your hand guiding him?

* * * *

Messengers came into Buthroton with more secret, urgent words for Helenos. Leaving Peleos and Kestrinos to complete the cutting and spitting of the evening sacrifice, Helenos motioned me to a bench near the house door. He hesitated, and then said, "Our borders are being attacked and I must go to the aid of my vassals. King Xystes of the Hylleans threatens Chaonia by hiring wandering tribesmen to help his invasion. I must prepare."

I cried out, "Another war? No! You cannot go!"

Three days later Helenos set up the kettle of stones in the market place and sent Herald Oxylos to summon all men of military age. For five days, they poured in from the countryside and villages to draw lots, each taking a pebble, its color deciding his fate. Nobles came first, who must equip and lead their men, and after them citizens and compatriots. Kestrinos and Peleos whooped with joy when they drew the dark pebbles for service.

Pergamos followed his brothers in determined silence.

Messengers and heralds continued arriving, begging assistance against attacking tribes. In the midst of all this, King Polypoites sent his man from where he lived on the Ambrakian Gulf near the reedy river Arethon. "The Phrygians are attacking us," the man reported when he had been welcomed and fed. "A large tribe of Bryges has also attacked

Thesprotia, coming from the north and east. New migrants are settling their land, driving them out."

"My ally, Milyas of the Chones, recently drove out a band of Hylleans under Xystos," Helenos said. "They claim descent from Herakles, an ancient enemy of my people."

The herald spoke urgently, "King Polypoites sends me to beg your assistance against these invaders."

Helenos spoke with grim determination, "The Phrygians are close kindred of my people, and I must know whether your enemies are refugees from my shores."

"Help us hold them back, or they will invade you, too," the man warned. "Our scouts report that another group of Bryges are headed our way, crossing the Akrokeraunian Mountains. Temnos, another man calling himself a son of Herakles, has brought warriors from Athens and is building a fleet at Naupaktos. If all these Herakleians form into one group, they will destroy us all."

"What is this about Herakleids?" Kestrinos demanded, having come from the stables and taken a cup of wine from one of the tables. He looked at Peleos over its rim. "You look ready for battle, brother."

"Indeed I am." Peleos kept his cold gaze on Helenos. "You will not defend your land, Mother's Husband?"

Distress thinned the messenger's face when King Peleos continued, "My father never allowed marauders to attack his allies. These Phrygians and Bryges are a greater threat to us than Akastos was to him."

"Enough!" Helenos took out his holy stone and held it between them. "I must take augury, and you will have my answer before your leave." He gave the herald a hard look, and the man bowed.

I went with Helenos to Hektôr's mound where he laid our offerings of wine and grain. Holding his holy stone in both hands, he lifted it above his head while I waited, my arms crossed in deference to the dead. When he lowered his hands, he was in a trance as he walked thrice around the memorial-stone.

An eagle floated against the sky, drifting southward.

Helenos' eyes were fixed on the bird.

"Zeus-Belen sends his eagle where I must take my warriors."

"Do not go!" I trembled, a chill wind of warning brushing me.

He swaddled the stone and put it into my hands. "Close your eyes, beloved Ãndrõmakhê, and see with your third eye. Do you find anything for me?"

In the pink darkness behind my lids, I saw golden spirals and small silver balls merging. The opal resting between my breasts burned, singing the skin around, heating its companion, Hektôr's cartouche ring. My fingers began to tingle and a life force seemed to move from the stone into my body. For an instant, the stone moved in my hands like the flutter of a child in my womb. My fingers spasmed and I dropped it, my eyes snapping open with fright.

Helenos smiled, the stone back in his hands.

"I felt life!" I breathed.

"This stone has acquired new life which I awakened during these last days. Everything lives after its own fashion, for no man can put life into nothingness." He returned it to its bag at his belt. "The gods send powers from above and below, giving life and death. But you felt nothing for *me.*"

Then I knew he would go, he would be at war, defending the homeland of strangers. "You will ally yourself with Polypoites against the Phrygians and Bryges?"

"I have no choice. Do not be afraid. The Fates guide me and I must protect our son's inheritance." He touched my cheek tenderly. "There is a time of action for everyone. Hektôr knew that, and I know it. There are turnings where only the Fates have control, my dear one—the noble queen of my heart, my life-long love."

Then, silently holding each other, we strolled back to the city. The towers of Buthroton rose darkly above us, tipped with morning sunlight, and beyond, the citadel.

* * * *

They all went to war. All three sons, with Helenos, southward into spring, and horror.

As summer progressed, there was scant news from my warriors. The Chaonian fleet divided in the Gulf of Ambrakia, so that Young Peleos could join Polypoites against the Bryges. Helenos sailed farther south with Pergamos. And Kestrinos? Nothing from him.

It was early autumn when a runner told me of Peleos' return.

I was at a window when my son drove into the courtyard with a few companions. I rushed downstairs and fell against him as he dismounted from his chariot. "Where are the others?"

"They were fine when I saw them last. Temenos' fleet was wrecked, a total loss."

"What of Helenos? Kestrinos? Pergamos?"

"All in good time."

When he had bathed and taken wine, he replied to my questions. "Helenos and Pergamos are in Delphi for the festival."

"Festival?" And no more war, I hoped.

"Every eight years they honor my father Pyrrhos there," he said. "His tomb is a holy place; and this is an eighth year."

"This attracted Helenos to Delphi? Is the war over?" I clenched my fists and stamped my feet. "Peleos, you drive me wild! Helenos would not go just to honor Pyrrhos, except to humor Pergamos."

"The war is merely interrupted, Mother. We heard the Herakleids were building another fleet in the gulf at Ephyre; they now call the place Korinth. We had to know how far north they might sail, and Helenos went for advice from Apollo's oracle."

I heaved a sigh. "Where, then, is Kestrinos?"

"He won a throne by right of single combat, and now rules the Kammanians and Kassopeians. And I married the princess Sthenele."

"You did *what?*"

Peleos grinned, vastly pleased with his news. "Soon you will meet my wife when the wagons arrive. She travels with my guardsmen."

I was speechless for a long time.

Finally, I said, "Then you, not Kestrinos, will inherit here and build a Troia in this land."

He shrugged. "Troia is dead, Mother. I have listened to your Trojan litany all my life. I am no necromancer to summon up ghosts, but a man whose sons will rule in Akhilles' name. From now on Kyathos will tune his lyre to songs honoring the glory of Pyrrhos' *sons,* the *protégés* of Helenos." He drew in a deep breath. "Helenos is king here now, but understand and accept that the future is mine."

I searched his eyes. "What about your wife?"

"Sthenele is not like other women. You have heard of Echetes."

"That torturer? She is of his family?"

"His daughter's child. The old man destroyed Metope, his daughter. Blinded her for bearing a child. My wife is that child, whom he also tried to destroy."

I watched him resume his pacing. The scraping rumble of a wagon and clopping of hooves interrupted them. Peleos dashed out into the courtyard. I waited, and when he returned, he was holding the hand of a poorly dressed girl. "Mother, this is my wife."

She was beautiful! The aura of her pure heart emanated from every inch of her body.

I embraced the princess. "Welcome home, my daughter."

Taking the girl's hand, I led her up the stairs, where faithful Thalpia met them at the bathing-room door. "This is your home now, Sthenele," I spoke warmly, leaving her with instructions that she be properly clothed and coifed.

Later, when we had eaten, Peleos told his story. "Her mother's father forced her to live in a cave with a cruel hag to guard her. When I found Sthenele, she was terrified of me. It was only when the fighting ended that I learned who she was. An oracle had told him that he would die because of a daughter. When his wife died in childbirth, he sent the baby to that evil woman. When she also died bearing an infant, Sthenele was left at the cave in hopes she would die young." He drew his wife close and she smiled, nestling into his embrace.

* * * *

Kestrinos sent word that he had conquered the Bryges, and had been duly elected king by the elders. With a heavy heart, I realized I would probably never again see my son of Helenos.

Sthenele and I were spinning by the well one autumn day when Peleos strode in. "A messenger is here with Pergamos. He asks to see you, Mother. I will bring in the sacrifice."

I rushed into the great hall and met Pergamos, a wide-shouldered, big blond man now, who lifted me in his arms, and held me a long time, his chest heaving as if with sobs. When he set me down, I saw his expression.

"Helenos?" The name stuck in my throat. "Tell me!"

When he did not speak, I had to scream, "Helenos! Oh great Mother, indeed it's Helenos!"

Silence answered me and I flung away from him, arms flailing as I tore my clothing and hair, screaming and screaming. No one needed to put in words that I would never see him again in my lifetime.

The evening meal became a funeral feast; I ate for his spirit without knowing what I did or tasted. Brave, noble, loyal Helenos was destroyed by another war that would only lead to more devastation.

It was late morning when, rigid and exhausted from lack of sleep, I reached out my arms and Thalpia was there. She drew me, her former mistress, close. My arms ached for Helenos; my heart broke over this new, great loss. There was no other way to live now, except one day at a time. Until it was my turn to cross into the Elysian Fields.

Sudden energy got me to my feet, dressed, and off to find Pergamos. I must know who had killed Helenos and how, against who to send troops. I was queen now! I could drive my own chariot, and draw my own sword. I would direct an attack if I could not join.

I found my sons on the roof where benches and pots of shrubs and flowers made a garden. "You must tell me everything," I challenged. "Since you did not bring his ashes... Why?"

"He was wounded at Delphi." It was Peleos, looking at his brother for confirmation.

Pergamos' voice was hoarse from his own grief, "We had to wait several days for our turn to consult the Pythoness. During that time, he left offerings outside the priestess' enclosure and I paid respects at my father's tomb. It is protected by his own python, which lives in a passage leading to the death-chamber. I brought milk and honey in his honor." He paused, whitened, and slowly continued, "Helenos would meet me there and... but the serpent never came out except... until... until that last time."

"What does this mean?" My voice was shrill. How could I avenge my noble husband's death on a holy python?

"I mean that time of respect for my father' Pyrrhos' spirit. Helenos had set down the food; his right foot was near the hole when the snake struck. I sucked out the poison and he used salves he had with him. We thought it would be all right. But before our turn at the oracle, he was fevered. The pain..."

A cry from me silenced him, "Pyrrhos sent that serpent! That was no sacred python but his spine-marrow!"

Peleos was angry. "My father's ethereal spine would not attack the protector of his sons. Besides, he was as fond of Helenos as if he were his own uncle."

I looked at him blindly, and then turned back to Pergamos. "Did he die at Delphi?"

"No. He would not rest. He insisted on coming back to you. He wanted to die in your arms. We were at Mykene where I had to get a ship built. He died there, waiting."

"And you did not bring him to me...not a single ash." My words were a howl.

"I could not! The poison, the swelling..." He gulped and steadied his voice. "The Thesprotians, where this city of Mykene is, gave him a hero's burial. He has a noble tumulus there."

"So far away." I began pacing, and then whirled on him. "Did the pain ever leave him?"

"At first the juice of poppies helped, but later on...no. He never complained, and I know it was terrible."

I clenched my hands in the tangles of my hair, tearing out strands while I screamed. Wordless despair at the Fates who had robbed me a second time of a noble-hearted husband tore out from my throat. Everything seemed remote even as I myself suffered the pain that had killed Helenos.

My sons seated me on the bench, one on either side of me, and held me until my agony stilled somewhat.

Then Pergamos tried to reassure me, "He had visions, Mother; Apollo Agdistis came to him. He spoke to the Goddess, Ma-Kybele, and he seemed to be back in Troia. Could it be that somewhere…everything is still the same…as if nothing had been destroyed? Is there an Ilion where you and Hektôr might rule in peace, where Helenos is Chief Hierophant? Perhaps he saw such a place."

"*What* did he say, Pergamos? His last words?" I whispered.

"He spoke of going with Kassandra to Thymbra when they were children. He said the Delphic python's poison was leading him to the Bright God, just as that serpent at Thymbra had dripped knowledge into their ears."

"Did he ask for me?"

"He said he would be with you. He said Kestrinos would establish a whole people, namely, the Kestrines. Peleos is to have Chaonia, and my name is written across Asian Anatolia."

"These were his last words?" I lowered my voice in awe.

"No. He did not seem to know he was dying, he thought himself being reborn. He looked at me with great happiness and said, 'So much light… and all the flowers!'"

A pain like the lash of a thousand whips sliced through me.

Oh, Helenos. Weeping tears of gall, I shuddered uncontrollably. Not once had I held a dying loved one in my arms, nor seen the spirit slip away with Hermes….

* * * *

In the spring, Sthenele presented my son Peleos, son of Pyrrhos, with a daughter. My numb state wakened in the pleasure of this child. Then, at midsummer, the Council formally elected Peleos the Younger, king.

On his own prompting, Pergamos sailed to Sicily, which we told everyone was just a simple mission for new trade opportunities. It was not exactly a fool's errand, for Pergamos felt confident he would recognize his half-brother from his dreams and from his resemblance to

Askanios. From Sicily, he took ship to Sardinian ports too, inquiring about a woman named Kupra.

He returned four months later, having clashed with storms and pirates, but with no news of Skamandrios.

Heart-breaking news whipped across from Phaekis: both Alkinoos and Arête had died from sickness brought by pest-ships. If only Helenos the Healer were here, I wept, he could have saved them all!

Klytoneos had long gone to rule some land of his own.

Eurymedon and Rhexenor were away on colonization, leaving Laodamos to rule Phaekis with their younger brother Helios as herald.

Nothing was the same. I consoled myself thinking how these Achaians of Molossia, Chaonia, and Kestrine, were ruled by Trojans. All my sons were settled except Pergamos. By the time his new ships were ready, he would also be leaving me.

Still not a word of Skamandrios, not even in dreams.

Though tormented by notions of taking ship on my own, to scour all the lands of Hesperia, Helenos' death had left me weaker in body, and I did not dare tackle the unknown.

Surely, it was time for me too to depart this world!

However, how could I bear to die here, so far from home? I ought to return to the shores I was born. Yes, I would refuse to die like an old rag, in these foreign lands.

"Mother." Pergamos' voice beat on my ears. Stepping back from the roof-wall I turned to him, shoulders erect, head up, eyes wide.

His gaze was bright, his face flushed. "I have something important to tell you."

"Yes?"

"My colony is here, and my ships supplied."

"Where do you take your colony?"

"Where else but Anatolia? Those tales you told me all my life were not wasted on my ears, Mother! Helenos saw my name spread across there. And you are going with me to Troialand."

"Oh, Goddess in All Names!" A deep sob wrenched me and I leaned on him, my stiff pride melting like snow in the sun.

"You will be queen of all the Trojans yet."

Oh, Skamandrios, I thought, *you are indeed given a brother in Pergamos, this youngest son of Pyrrhos.*

* * * *

476

It was late summer when Pergamos' ships tacked bravely outward, sails unfurling to southward winds. The six ships floated smartly down the Channel of Scheria as far as the two mouths of the Thyamis River. I went on deck where Pergamos was directing the furling of sails and rowing inland.

"This land was called Kimmeria, only now it is Kestrine," he said.

My heart leapt. "Then, I will see your brother Kestrinos!"

"He was in Athens at last report, but we will wait for him. I had hoped to reach the Acheron before dark, but this is better."

We dropped anchor and tied up. The colonists disembarked to set up camp on shore. Pergamos led me from the ship, followed by Thalpia who carried minimal needs in a sack. The river road was a rude track overhung by enormous trees. After the long day on board, invigorating odors of pine and myrtle refreshed me.

Kestrino's palace—*my son's palace!*—rose above the village of New Ilion, of roughhewn stones roofed in thatch and only of two stories. Kestrinos met us at the door. My heart was swollen with pride. He seemed older than his years, a man and king in his own right. When he led me into the hall, it was smoke-filled, extending over the entire ground floor, with an upper gallery along the back wall. Through the smoke, I saw box-like enclosures along the walls.

"My unmarried men sleep there," he explained. "Everything here is primitive but I am improving the town every day, bit by bit."

He took us to small rooms along the gallery, each with a single large window.

"How can he live like this, and still call himself a king?" I asked Thalpia when he had gone. I sat down on the hard bed.

"It *belongs* to him, Lady." Thalpia opened our bags and began tossing clothes over a rail at one end of the room.

"Hand me that sack, Thalpia. I have something for him."

I reached in and found the small gold cup I had hoarded for so many years.

After the evening meal, I took Kestrinos aside, and presented the cup to him. "From my first son, Skamandrios Hektôrides, to my last son, Kestrinos Helenosides. This is a Trojan talisman for *your* son, and all future kings of this land."

"Mother! Beloved Mother! Nothing I could treasure more."

Kestrinos held it in his hands reverently. "I used to covet this when I saw it on your table."

"You don't remember, but all my sons, including you, of course, learned to drink from this cup."

"Was your mission to Athens successful?" Pergamos asked then.

"I met with chiefs assembled there. We signed a treaty of mutual assistance against these Herakleian invaders." Kestrinos looked at me. "Orestes was there. His son Penthilos took a colony to the Troad; settled at Daskylion on the coast east of Troia."

"Orestes' son? Then Hermione has given him two?"

"No, only Tisamenos. Penthilos is his by his sister, his mother's daughter by Aigisthos." He turned back to his brother. "Temenos' fleet was destroyed at Naupaktos, but he has a new one now. We were at Trikorythos north of the Marathon Plain when we set our seals. That's near Athens." Kestrinos held his cup for the bearer to refill. "Tell me your plans. Do you actually think you can rebuild the city of Troia after what Aeneas told us?"

"Troia has many cities. I will find a suitable place."

* * * *

Pergamos took ship at dawn, and we passed the Acheron River late. At the Ambrakian Gulf, camp was set up on the north shore where the Arachthos emptied.

"This is where I stopped with Helenos." His voice was low and sad. "Tomorrow we pay honor at his mound."

The memorial stone was a rough shaft with a small altar beside it. Round of heaps of vegetables and flowers lay there in testimony to the veneration given his spirit by local people.

Pergamos laid offerings on the altar while I, moaning and lifting my arms in prayer, repeated my ritual dirge memorializing his deeds.

Pergamos, son of Pyrrhos, raising his arms also, gave praise to the man who had cared so well for the sons of an enemy.

Then Pergamos handed his short sword to me. I cut a long thick stretch of hair, still resolutely strawberry-blond as in defiance of time, and placed it on the altar. I spoke to the spirit, assuring him he was remembered, and telling him of my plans. The moon rose, shedding soft light over the mound and meadow around it, like the Fields of Elysion.

PART VI: The PILLAR

...To Āndrōmakhê... there is still a shrine in the city.
Pausanias: Attica, XI, 3 W. S. Jones, translator

Chapter 38: Troialand

Around the Peloponnesos and up the coast to Attika from where Menesthos had captained ships against Troia, we crossed the sea to pass Andros and other islands northward until winds blew us to Tenos; from there to Samos off the coast between Karia and Moesia, giving me my first sight of my homeland. With faithful Thalpia by my side, I sunk to my knees, wept, and gave thanks to the Great Mother, for allowing me to live long enough to see this day.

After that, our little fleet sailed north along the Trojan coast to Issan Lesbos. We camped overnight near the ruined harbor at Bresa where, so long ago, Diomede's father King Phorbas had ruled.

I wept as I watched the once beautiful island recede, and then crossed the deck to see the emergence of the land of my birth. The waters around the ship, slate-blue and opaquely clear, like none elsewhere, my own, waves that I saw from my window as a girl. This land, this earth, precious with memories, and sealed to my heart forever by the ashes of my beloved dead.

Then I noticed that we were edged the Adramyttion Gulf to land at Chryse. I glanced questioningly at Pergamos, but he strode forward to the captain's deck where to oversee the tethering. I looked again toward land and observed that the wharves were unchanged except for improvements. The village had grown into a town, seeming prosperous despite the terrible stories Aeneas had brought us.

Landing orders, ships heaving to, ropes cast landward, men leaping ashore and tethering to firm-set bollards.

I began to tremble. I was going down the gangplank and setting foot on ground—the earth of home. Slipping down from Pergamos' supporting arm I flattened myself on the paving stones, scrabbling my fingers between them to bits of soil to hold against my lips, to smear over my tear-wet face.

Strength rose from the earth and entered me, the silenced voices and unseen movements of my people whose centuries of habitation imbued this land and air with my heritage.

At last, my son lifted me up, gently, and led me into the town. It was like and yet unlike, for strangers lived there now, and so many new houses enlarged it.

However, the temple of Apollo was still surrounded by its own field and garden, and the house of Chryses was there.

But a strange priest emerged from it to greet me with the formal politeness all pilgrims received. He was a tall, red-blond man, strangely familiar. I looked at him sharply, reminded of Agamemnon.

"Could you tell me of the priest Chryses, and his daughter, Astynome?" I asked.

"*I* am Chryses Agamemnonides, and my mother is Astynome Chryseides," he said, surprised out of his formality.

"You!" Then I remembered what Aeneas had told. "The priest I knew would be your grandfather," I explained. "I am Āndrōmakhê Êetiôneis, your mother's girlhood friend."

Pergamos spoke up too, giving his name and lineage.

"Welcome, son of Pyrrhos Neoptolemos." Chryses' greeting was hearty now, and he led us to the house. "You will honor me as guests in my home and not as pilgrims in the dormitory. Our fathers were allied. We will keep that friendship."

In the vestibule an old woman with a deeply lined face, approached us, stopping to stare. I stared back, knowing but not accepting that this was my friend...so old, so different.

"Yes, Mother, this is Āndrōmakhê Êetiôneis," Chryses declared.

We rushed forward and clung together.

"So many years!" Astynome's blue eyes glistened. "I can't believe it. You are here, and with a son not Skamandrios."

"One of three by Pyrrhos, son of Akhilles," and as we went into the reception area, we began exchanging our stories.

* * * *

There days of feasting, sacrifices and oracular questionings passed before Astynome escorted me to a quiet bench where we could sit undisturbed in the herb garden.

"Astynome, we are going to rebuild Troia."

"Impossible. We are Achaians here now. The future is for them. Your son is an Achaian."

481

"Pergamos is *Trojan!*" I bristled.

"My father was a seer, you know that. He understood and accepted the inevitable when Odysseus brought me back to him from Agamemnon's tent. Agamemnon. My own son is an Achaian, and a priest. This shrine has been greatly honored and respected by them."

"What was Agamemnon to you but a cruel master?"

"He was a *loving* husband, Āndrōmakhê. He was a kindly man and I did not want to leave him. I loved him with all my heart, and am proud to have his son." She breathed a deep sigh. "Let us not speak of these things. Why should we quarrel at this time of reunion? The Fates lead us now, as they did then." She took my hand and drew me up. We walked amid the flowers beside a row of blooming peonies. I smiled at her, but knew that things would never be the same between us.

* * * *

Pergamos went with Chryses the Younger to the site of Thébé, having forcefully persuaded me to remain at the shrine. I was on the roof, looking for his return when he returned with the priest. When he joined me on the roof, he placed a small skin of earth in my hands.

"From the mound of your father and brothers."

I lifted the bag to my lips.

"This earth holds the tears I wept for you today, dearest Mother," he went on softly. "But do take comfort in that Akhilles did honorably by them; he did raise a heroic tomb over their ashes."

I squeezed the sack against my heart. "For all their bustling lives, I have only this." I looked up at him, moonlight dewing my tears. "My good son, my precious, loyal son. Tell me of Thébé."

"Don't ask. Keep your memories."

"Oh Pergamos!" I swallowed my tears. "My noble father was honored there like a god, and his city was the pride of Mysia."

I pushed the sack into the bosom of my dress and ran both hands through my hair, keening. My son sat down and gathered me against his strong young chest.

"Please ask no more, Mother. It is all gone. I saw that the Fates have closed their eyes on Thébé."

On the next day, the priest Chryses, grandson of Chryses and son of Agamemnon, took augury under the great oak tree as his grandfather had done. When he rejoined us, his manner was grave

"The Simoeis is dry, the Thymbrios a swamp, and the Skamander feeble. Your future sleeps on a rock beside the rushing Kaikos River. Allow the dead in Troia, their peace."

I felt strangely flat and breathless, rejecting the veracity of the oracle outright. I could not trust a son of Agamemnon!

"I need to sail to Troia," I said to Pergamos, "I owe homage to Hektôr, Priam, Hekabe, and Alexis! Just take me there, and I will always bless you for this, be the oracle of Chryses right or wrong."

When next we rounded the Sigeian promontory, I was overpowered with emotion so great that I could scarcely see for the tears.

Crimson sun hung low over Imbros Island when we reached the tremendous Skamandrian curve and hove to where the Achaian fleet had rocked and rotted beside their camp. No remnant of the enemy camp remained except for scattered rocks and boulders left by torrential rains that had sluiced over the plain every season.

Then at last, I dared to look inland, to see in the dimming light that high rock, a mound across the plain, with one tall tower still standing hollow-sided against the sky.

We set up camp that night where the thousand enemy ships had waited for many years, but today, no vestige of them remained. I was dazed and silent in the torchlight as Thalpia led me to our small tent, scarcely knowing when I lay down to sleep. My rest was heavy yet uneasy, for I could almost hear the tramp of men and shout of voices with the clash of arms throughout the night. The battles were fought allover in my sleep.

"This is a haunted place," Thalpia muttered in the morning. "These Achaian ghosts threaten us."

When we broke camp, Pergamos said he would not spend another night at this place. We must go inland to the Trojan mounds. I kept silent, for I could sense he too had not slept well last night.

"Those of you who cannot sleep on land, keep to your ships for safety," he told the captains. "I will scout around and let you know whether to colonize here."

Pergamos fastened a dagger and a knife around his waist, set up a wagon driven by two horses, added an axe, pick, shovel, leather bags and a clay jar of water. Thalpia went inland with us on the long ride to Hektôr's tomb.

As we approached it, I saw that the wall had been crudely repaired at that place near the fig tree, the place where Hektôr and Akhilles had dueled, and close to where Pyrrhos had dropped Skamandrios to his presumed death. Fields of grain, already harvested, were in stubble around the broken city. We passed the Skaian Gate where the enormous bronze-plated doors were replaced by ones of rough logs half-falling from the dowels.

"You don't want to go in there," Pergamos spoke softly, "but I will investigate. I never saw the city well built, but I know it was never like *this!* Nonetheless, I say Aeneas and his ilk did not really try hard to rebuild it. Not with the jealousy he and Anchises felt toward Priam and his power. Aeneas would rule from Troia as it was in its glory days, or leave altogether—and he did."

I turned to look at Ida Mountains where Dardania had once stood among the trees. Then I glanced aside, and screamed.

He sat on a high boulder of stones, looking at me from blue eyes.

I blinked, and blinked again, to clear my sight. But no, there could be no mistake. Here he was, white coat, black mask, black tail, and black boots.

Thalpia and I exclaimed at the same time, "Nefru!"

Nefru leapt down, and began running in the direction that I knew led to my home with Hektôr.

"Stop!" I cried out, and he paused, looking back at me over his shoulder.

"Come."

He did, and I lifted him up, pressing him to my breast.

"Nefru? Are you really Nefru?"

The cat purred. "Nefru," I repeated, "Nefru."

- *Yes, my friend.*

- *Oh, this time you can talk!* I replied.

Turning to Thalpia and Pergamos, "First we have to visit Hektôr," I said, "and then we make our way home. Thalpia, remember, we left something there. We forgot all about it, but as you can see, Nefru came telling us that he has been guarding it all along, with his bones, just as he had promised long ago."

Pergamos, clearly bursting with the need to know more, remained silent, watching me through shining eyes. Then he asked, "Where did you say Dardania was? The place to where Ilos came when he first settled Ate's Hill?"

"Inland." I pointed toward the Ida Mountains. "Akhilles destroyed it completely. They took stones from there to build their camp wall."

"And you said Akhilles' tomb was near the camp?"

"We were not far last night; you must have seen the mound."

"All right, I'll return there later to pay homage to my grandfather. But now I shall go with you to Hektôr's sleeping place."

Hektôr's sleeping place! What a delicate manner of speech he had, this son of mine from Pyrrhos.

At the foot of Hektôr's tomb I dropped to the earth, put Nefru aside, my fingers scrabbling up bits of soil. Holding the grains against my lips, I sensed the silenced voices of my people whose centuries of habitation had imbued the ground and air with presences. On my feet again, I almost fell over a small barrow apparently dug from the large mound. It was like a thumb against a fist. Was this where the boy who was made to take Skamandrios' place, lay?

A stone shaft on the small mound was half buried from neglect, and I collapsed beside it. Smoothing my hands over the pitted surface, I made out Achaian symbols. 'Astyanax,' I read, his title, King of the City. Hektôr's title, the name our people had used for Skamandrios.

Pergamos offered me a sacrificial knife and I hacked off half my hair. I held the swatch a long time, remembering how Skamandrios' little fingers had played with it while nursing. Whispering loving words to him, I wound it around the base of the stone. Half chanting, I uttered a dirge, giving this unknown child, loved by parents who must have died at The Fall, the last rites.

The sun was low when at last I climbed the big mound. The stone atop here was still erect, and garlanded with flowers. I caressed my hands across Hektôr's cartouche, moaning my grief for him. Again, I took the knife from Pergamos and cut the rest of my hair, those from the sides of my head that he had spread tenderly around our pillow before he made love to me.

Pergamos took one of the horses, and left me there with Thalpia keeping watch, going to explore the city.

I lay down upon the earth as close as possible to the memorial stone. Nefru curled up next to me. Not sleeping nor waking, I watched the large shiny stars come out close above. I seemed to whirl into space and look down upon the mound, seeing within it Hektôr. Not ashes and burnt bones but whole as I had known him, Hektôr in his prime as he had died. With him came a vision of the future that was continuing, of victories and tragedies, and the line of kings that would descend from his two sons, my Skamandrios as well as Sigeia's.

When Pergamos returned, the sun was considering to dawn. I made one last prayer and kissed the stone, and joined my son.

We entered the wagon, turned the horses onward to Troia, and saw the man. The figure striding toward us was a giant, flooded gold with the rising sun before him. Hektôr! "Oh God of Light!"

When he spoke the voice was Hektôr's as well, "Take your ships and go." It was an order; he was no apparition.

Pergamos confronted him with quiet dignity, "I have a right to this land by conquest *and* heritage. I am Pergamos, son of Pyrrhos Neoptolemos, Conqueror of Troia. My mother here is Ãndrõmakhê Êetiôneis, widow of Hektôr, Troia's rightful queen. Who are you?"

The man laughed derisively. "I am Skamandrios Hektôrides, heir to Troyland." He locked eyes with Pergamos. "You are not the first puny, upstart claimant. I will send you off like the others if you are still here by sundown. Pyrrhos' name is of no consequence to me. His father Akhilles is still less."

He turned, coldly staring at me. "As for you, Ãndrõmakhê, whore to my father's murderers: This is my father's mound, and I alone pay him honor here."

He turned and strode back toward the Hill of Ancient Ate.

I was suffocating. To have seen this other Skamandrios—strong, self-important—while my own son was a wanderer in strange lands.

I looked at Pergamos, noting the grim line of his jaw.

"Hadn't we better leave?" Thalpia asked cautiously.

"No, not yet," I said, lifting Nefru in my arms.

Resolutely I pointed the way into the Pergama, and then to the remnants of the house I had lived with Hektôr, still deserted, not even occupied by stragglers.

I closed my heart against the pain of seeing it destroyed, boulders, columns, cracked pavement in the courtyard, torn out trees. At first, I could not find the fountain either. So, I put Nefru down, and he scurried to a spot filled high with stones and wild rose bushes.

Giving me a strange look, Pergamos returned to the wagon and brought out the axe, pick, and two shovels. The three of us dug around for a long time.

Then, we found it.

The treasure chest, as intact as on the day Thalpia and I had sunk it here, more years ago than I was willing to count now.

When I turned to look for Nefru, he was gone. I could not accept losing him again and we spent an hour searching for him in the rubble.

Finally, Thalpia said, "We must leave now, Lady. He is not of this world; he only came to show that he knew you would return, and watched over your treasure."

I knew this was the truth. Yet my legs would not carry me. I sank down, feeling forlorn.

"Let's go, Mother," Pergamos said lightly, "I want another oracle. Thymbra is that way, yes?"

"It is."

We lifted the chest into the wagon and trotted the neglected Sacred Way along the river.

Nothing had remained of the village but a few foundation stones and part of the temple walls which had fallen in about the altar, but still stolid, unbroken. The surrounding grove still sheltered the precinct, though showing neglect and ravage from floods. I did not dismount but stood in the wagon while Pergamos went to say a prayer before the altar. While he was there, I looked up through the trees and saw an eagle floating against the sky, unmoving above the lone Skaian Tower that sent shadow across the plain.

I pointed, "Badogios guides us."

As I spoke these very words, the bird's wings dipped for a turn and drifted southward.

"That's an omen that we should go immediately," Thalpia said.

"On the right, and moving south," Pergamos said. "Now I know Chryses' prophecy was an honest one. Southward, he had said."

As we sailed away from Troia, I looked back from the ship until the mountains faded away. The jagged coastline went steadily by, and our ships turned southward.

My son came to stand by me, and spoke reassuringly, "I left a lock of my hair on an altar I found there. The altar was dedicated to them both, *Akhilles and Hektôr.*"

Chapter 39: King of Pergama

The Elaitic Bay was not large, just an inlet edged by rocky shores and trees to the water's edge. As we entered, the Kaikos river estuary, I realized we had arrived at the part of Teuthrania where Priam's sister Astyoche had ruled with Telephos.

I looked at Pergamos, pointing shoreward, "This land Pyrrhos son of Akhilles made heirless when he killed Eurypylos, brother of Lanassa, at the walls of Troia."

His eyes lit up with interest. "There is no heir? Indeed the oracle at Chryse speaks the truth! This is the land where I will rule."

He left me and directed the man who tested depths. The river would not take more than a flat barge at this time of year; Pergamos must be content to anchor at the ruined quay.

The captain approached, "Shall I drop anchor here?" He pointed to a ragged fisherman on shore with his catch.

"Yes. Have all the captains tie up," Pergamos ordered.

"Tie up?" The man pointed to the ruined quay and its cracked paving and slanted bollards.

Pergamos went with him to oversee docking while I remained at the rail. The once fine port of Kidainis was now only a rude village. The one public building seemed intact on its small akropolis. Around this, huddled tiny houses of mud and stone separated by twisting, path-like streets. The fields I could see were harvested and dry. Beyond them, dust-powdered trees dropped limply or seemed to reach thirstily for the heavy sky. The river eddied lazily into the bay.

Pergamos returned from the village when the sun was seeding strips of gold across the sky. He sent word to the other ships that no one was to land. They must all sleep on board.

"This land is ruled now by Arios, a harsh man much hated here, with no right to rule but by marriage," he told me. "In the morning I will challenge him to single combat for the right to rule."

I did not know how to react to this news. My swashbuckling son thinks he can take over a kingdom just by single combat. True, Kestrinos had achieved that, and Pergamos certainly did have the physique and the skills for it. Nonetheless, he did not know enough of his would-be opponent's ability to fend off his challenge.

After morning sacrifices, Pergamos mounted his chariot and, accompanied by men in two others, set out for the inland city. He did not return until dusk. Only when we had eaten did he answer my questions.

"The city has many Achaian settlers, who call it Berge because it is still a good fortress. There is overcrowding by refugee Lydians, Treres and Taurians as well as families of Trojans. A few years back a band of Kimmerians wrecked what was left after the war. They have also fought among themselves. Arios is a despot, and cannot control the disorder except by cruel repression."

"What is he like? How did he take your bid?"

"I did not see him; he was out on a hunt. However, I talked to his herald. Arios took the land by invasion. Kassite lord ousted by troubles at Karduniash. He forced the heiress, a daughter of Eurypylos, to marry him. Dead now, she left a child, a daughter. So, I might be able to get the throne by marriage."

"Marriage, huh? Hmm, so what did you hear about this heiress?" I smiled at him even while worry dug at me.

He continued thoughtfully, "They've had almost no peace since Queen Astyoche's death. Their disorganization is total. The people wait: for anyone at all to free them of him. I was surprised by the frankness of his herald."

I retired to my deck-tent. As age brought me nearer death, I was also closer to rebirth. But how old was I now? Had I been twenty-three, or twenty-four, when Pyrrhos had thrown me into his ship bound to his lands? I must be almost fifty now. The years had been kind to me though, perhaps because of my stubbornness to yield to their passing. In my heart, I had stayed young, still with not a single strand of white daring to enter my hair, so that Hektôr could recognize me upon his return to the flesh. I laughed to myself. Upon leaving this world, I would, for a sweet spell, rest in the company of those I loved. Then the quickening urge for sunlight and earth would lead me to drink the waters of Lethe in a new womb, refreshed for one more lifetime on earth. The peace of aging was like the shadow of youthful play.

I was late abed next morning for the aching of my body. Yet my mind was clear and eager, pulling like a young girl against the dragging weight of clay that held me. I was determined not to let Pergamos leave without my blessings.

By the time I stepped out of my cabin, the quiet morning was raucused by strident noises along the shore. Armed men in chariots spattered with mud and dust were lining up along the quay. Wrapping myself in woolen cloth, I went on deck. A cold wind swept over me, and I shivered. Rain was in the air.

Shortly, a heavy-set, hawk-nosed man, perhaps of Hittite origin, mounted and took stance near the pilot ship. "I am Arios Herakleides, king of Teuthrania." He clattered sword against shield. "Who are you to camp unasked by my port?"

Pergamos shouted back his lineage going back eight generations, as it was custom, and invited the man aboard.

Arios sheathed his weapon but did not move. "Strangers are not welcome here. You have until dawn tomorrow to leave my shore."

"Is this a bid to war?" Pergamos demanded.

"Since the war at Troia, there has been little else in this land," Arios spat. "We will burn your ships and set upon your people by night if you are still here at noon tomorrow. I don't wish to subject the people to another war."

Pergamos shrugged. "I see no need for war, if you don't."

"Oh? Where is your army, your weapons? To the south of us famine and plague have raged for years, brought by marauders from the west, men claiming Atros as their leader."

Pergamos broke out laughing. "Atros has been dead for a very long time! Where have you been?"

"So has the great Herakles, but I am still his son."

"Oh, not another one!" I murmured, "How did Herakles find the time to be a Hero if he was so busy fathering all these sons?"

Arios remounted his chariot and drove with his men back to the city. Pergamos swore. He summoned his captains on land for consultation. Then he turned to me. "We will stay here. The rainy season is due and we would have mutiny if we left now."

He ordered disembarkation. We formed groups for negotiating the narrow alleyways of the little town, and by evening were settling into the large building on the akropolis. I remained on deck with Thalpia, for I would go last in my son's chariot. The moon was full, saving us the use of torches. A shout from the lookout shifted my attention inland. A large dark mass moved along the river road to the village. The moon glinted on metal, alerting me to danger.

Armed men!

But silent; ghosts of warriors killed during past invasions?

Pergamos' warning shout told me they were real as he raced about ordering the families to stay in their refuge ashore, and their men to defend the ships. The clanging and stamping of their return, frantic hands digging among stores for weapons on every ship, and another command from him, stopped all movement.

I retrieved my old dagger, securing it around my waist, proud of that I was still a strong woman with wrists steady enough to swing a weapon. Thalpia empowered herself with two sharp butcher's knives and an axe.

Pergamos slammed aboard and spoke to his captain, who pounded aft to pass orders along to the other captains. Silence spread from ship to ship. The men began lying down on deck, clustering with their weapons at the head of each gangplank. Pergamos strode to me.

"Flat on deck, *now!"* His tone allowed no argument.

There was no sound from the fleet or on shore. The silence was eerie, broken only by the light slapping of waves against planks.

Pergamos looked around, and then whispered more orders as he raced among his men. They half-rose to place what shields they had in rows along the bulwarks. The women were called upon to hold them there, with me like the rest hanging onto the straps of a heavy round shield that my son placed for me.

Then I felt the stamp of enemy feet vibrate on the gangway.

Pergamos clanged his spear against his shield for attack and sprang down to the gangplank. An unearthly cry reverberated from him: "For Troia! For our wives and children!"

Hektôr's cry for battle!

Pandemonium raged as more battle cries ripped through the air and feet scuffled. Weapons clashed. The besiegers were halfway onboard when the defenders hurled themselves upon them from the deck. The enemy was tossed into the water. Others pushed backward onto the broken stones of the wharf. Thrashing in the water and struggling to get footage under the momentum of those behind them, the besiegers broke into confusion and rout. Some fought comrades in their madness to escape, while at the rear, men simply turned and fled into the twisted ways of Kidainis.

Pergamos, at the foot of his plank, brandished his sword while howling derision in the madness of victory.

I swept the scene from behind the protection of my shield. It was the disorderly breakup of a sneak attack. Not a single duel, not a drop of blood, I noted. My whole being was alight with pride in my son's swiftly executed strategy.

Then I saw a clump of men on shore, knotted around the burly figure of Arios. Men from the ships lined up along the water's edge while Arios' guards backed into the village.

Pergamos, shield lifted and sword at the ready, strode to him.

The battle around the two leaders stopped as if by silent command, craggy-faced warriors giving space, ringing them for the inevitable duel that would decide the conflict. Water was behind them, for Arios and Pergamos had met upon the uneven quay-stones near the ships. This paving was not only uneven but also slippery from water and blood. Jars and baskets heaped under sailcloth made their contest more hazardous.

All waited silently as Arios prepared his own shield of bronze and drew his long sword. Then he sprang, clashing against the shield of Pergamos, held by him with almost contemptuous ease.

The old king, enraged, flailed and feinted while Pergamos parried light-footed, danced aside, thrust and withdrew. How well he fought, this son of mine! I saw Akhilles in his body, and in his moves, Pyrrhos, and for some eerie reason, Hektôr, also.

The young man and the older one battled on with berserk fury, avoiding or climbing over obstacles as best they might, while stamping among broken crockery and unraveling bales of straw.

I could not always tell the two apart, but as dawn lightened the east I saw that Pergamos had cornered Arios among the bales.

Then Arios, despite his age and weight, made a lightning fast lunge striking Pergamos' sword from his hand. Pergamos slammed his shield against the other's sword, seized the man's shield and wrenched it from his arm. In a flash, he had his adversary by the throat. Arios dropped his sword and Pergamos grabbed it, releasing his grip on the king's neck. When the Teuthranian lurched forward to seize his attacker's neck, Pergamos forced an upward thrust with the sword he had taken.

Howling, holding his chest, Arios fell heavily, and lay groveling on the stones as blood spurted between his hands.

His words, screaming into the first gray of dawn, rattled in his throat, "You are victor—take it all. But my daughter—protect her! Don't leave any of the women to the mob."

The words choked and gurgled as he lay still.

"Shade of Arios, rest!" Pergamos cried, facing the sky, "I shall protect your daughter and all your women."

Pergamos then knelt and quickly removed the breastplate, dark with blood, and the helmet. He took away the bronze-studded abdominal belt, and last, the arm and leg greaves.

As he got to his feet, holding aloft the armor to show his victory, the rainy season broke upon us with a sheeting downpour. Even as he shouted his triumph, a flash of golden-red broke through. I looked up and observed the furled sail taking fire from a hurled torch caught in the rigging. Screaming and stamping surrounded me, and from all the other ships, pandemonium broke as each caught flame in its sail.

I rushed back to snatch a few things from the tent, and pulled the treasure chest roughly toward the gangplank. Stampede to the land was increasing all around us. Neighing horses and bellowing cattle struggled onto land amidst screaming children and their mothers.

Some of the Teuthranians now joined the Chaonians in pulling them ashore, while terrified animals charged among those still fighting, ending that abortive war.

Pergamos, continuing to announce the death of Arios and holding high the king's empty breastplate, raced to the pilot-ship. Together with the captain, he pulled out a few things, but they had to leap down as crossbeam and halyard crashed heavily behind them.

Thalpia and I managed to push the treasure chest overboard, and then flung ourselves after it.

Most of the besiegers began to retreat, though a small number cast an occasional torch onto a ship not burning as rapidly as the others.

The chest, although heavy, buoyed and Thalpia and I managed to pull it ashore.

Others of the king's guardsmen took up their lord's body and raced inland with it. Stores were dragged by desperate hands away from the conflagration.

Pergamos led us into Kidainis where the simple fisherfolk merely stood and stared blankly. He brought us into the one large building that crowned the acropolis, where he had already prepared for his people during the proposed siege of Telephon.

"It belongs to King Arios," a fisherman told us, "for use the few times he visited the port."

Then the headman came to Pergamos where he was supporting me in his arms. "You are welcome here," he shouted above the din of screaming, bleating and lowing.

"I claim this land in the name of Troia!" Pergamos shouted back.

"You have earned that right by freeing us from a tyrant," the man hollered. He pointed toward the low citadel. "Your people will find shelter there until you can take them into Berge."

* * * *

It was three days later when Pergamos brought his people into the city. Dressed in a royal purple outfit that had once belonged to Hekabe, I rode with him in his chariot, with Thalpia behind to hold an umbrella over us. However, the rain held up during this important trek. Behind us followed a cavalcade of wagons harnessed to local onegers and bullocks, as well as foot marchers, all the sixteen miles to the city. Plane trees and willows bent above us as we followed the Kaikos River. The encircling hills were dimly outlined through the fog-steamed air, while below us the earth rutted in dark richness as we passed. The broad plain ascended inland, revealing at last Telephon along a high ridge. It stood on a lofty hill within a rounded triangle between the Kaikos and Kteios rivers, inland from where they converged to flow as one into the bay. At first sight, the gate-towers of Telephon tipped against the sky and for a moment, I saw the diadem of Troia welcoming me across the plain.

"This land is truly ours now," my son told me now, "I've given our colonists freedom of choice on whether to follow me, or find homesteads elsewhere. Tomorrow we go in peace to Arios' palace."

"So the city gave in to us with no more struggle?"

"They locked the gates at first, but I explained that I will enter peacefully, and my men will not touch their women. The truth is we are colonists, comprised of families, and not warriors or bandits."

I smiled with relief. "I am glad Teuthrania will not suffer from our arrival. They were loyal allies of Troia. But are you sure they will accept you as king?"

"They already have! I told you, Arios was a despotic ruler, hated by most of the people. I am their rescuer. We enter Telephon as victors, Mother, yet with so little bloodshed. Just as the Fates ordained before my birth." His eyes shone.

Pergamos stopped the cavalcade to pay respects at a high, rounded tumulus crested by the stone image of a woman. He alighted and lifted me down, then started up the mound with me by his side.

"This is the tomb of Queen Ague," I told him, "she was patroness of the city and mother of King Telephos, father of Lanassa."

"I know the story," he acknowledged. "Her father sold her to King Tetras when he learned she was pregnant by Herakles. But Tetras married her and left the kingdom to her son Telamon."

At the top he added, "It is unusual to honor a woman as if she were a goddess." He examined the statue.

"Oh, not so unusual in the old days. The tomb of Batieia at Ilion was always as holy as that of Ilos, the Founder." I placed my hand on the rude sculpture. "Many women, such as Myrina the Amazon, founded cities in the old days."

"Then, my dear Mother, you shall be honored here, along with Queen Ague. You may name the city."

"New Ilion." I savored the name. I looked toward the city, just within sight. Telephon stood on a high ridge, its Lower City spread down over terraces. My first visit here had been during childhood. Just as then, I was overwhelmed by its lofty isolation rising within a triangle formed by the two converging rivers.

I breathed a heavy sigh. "No, not Ilion. I named you for the holy Pergama there, and that is enough." I rested my hand on his, which grasped the image. "Spirit of Ague, be my witness!" I held my son's fingers firmly in mine. "The past has gone, and this will be a new life in a new city. There is no more Telephon. For I name this city Pergamon! Yes, not Ilion, but Pergamon—for you, my brave and gallant son."

I bent and kissed his hand, then pressed my lips to the stone. Sudden tears moistened the rough surface. "May you be a just and beloved king, my son, live long, and may you and your people enjoy peace and prosperity, always."

"I accept your gift of this city at this sacred place of oaths where three roads meet. However, the town fathers must vote on renaming the city. For you and me, this is Pergamon."

When we continued along, he chose the western road as nearest. *Ah, my son looks and acts every inch the king,* I thought, smothering a smile while my heart fluttered with pride.

The towers lowered against their mountain fastness and then enlarged as we approached. The city showed clear through drifting mists upon its stony mountain. Natural divisions formed four long terraces and below them was the marketplace. North of the western road, a gurgling stream sparkled into marble basins where women stood at laundering. Taking advantage of the lessened rain, they had come out, escorted by older men, all staring as their new rulers passed.

The marketplace was just inside the southern gate, and as I went into it, I looked up at the high watchtowers on either side where I could see guardsmen looking down. The lintel here was no sarcophagus, but one big stone carved with a horse in gallop reaching from end to end.

A horse in gallop.

So symbolic of Hektôr.

Oh my husband, are we coming home together?

Below that, and intertwining, were tendrils of a vine, seeming as though cut into the stone later than the original work.

Crowds waited silently, staring as the Chaonians crossed the bare trachyte rock, its smooth unbroken surface dressed to look like paving-stones. Pergamos's face was set and impervious as he drove the horses steadily along. The sky was so clear, mists and fog blown away. A good omen that the rain held away so long for us!

The second terrace was beautiful with stately buildings and shrubs, obviously homes of nobles and ambassadors. Above this, rose the terrace of altars and rich temples with their large gardens and sacred trees.

At last, we reached the fourth level, acropolis and royal compound. The palace stood at the northern end in aloof grandeur surrounded by medicinal gardens. From the gateway, I looked back and saw the narrow street twisting its way throughout the Lower City. Around me, the terraced hill was fortified with towers and walls that once again reminded me of Troia.

"Incredible that you just walked in here and took the city," I said.

He laughed. "Truly Arios was so hated that anyone would have been welcome. The soldiers who came with him against us, swore fealty to me as soon as his burial pyre was lit. They had been so hard-pressed for years with no imports from neighboring lands that our settlers with their supplies are very much appreciated."

Nobles welcomed us cautiously in the citadel's marketplace before the palace. Their representative came forward and gave formal welcome. He was about the same age as my son, tall and wiry, his brown hair dressed in Trojan moon horns, his eyes piercingly alert in his square face as he spoke the ceremonial words.

Pergamos turned to me, "This is Zakis, my herald. His family has served the kings of Teuthrania in this capacity for generations." He now faced Zakis, "Rest assured that you will be duly honored in my house. Let it be known throughout Telephon that I wish only to make of this place a seat of empire. I am enemy to no one here."

"It is done, my lord," Zakis answered. "We knew when you crossed our gates without bloodshed, than you were divinely ordered."

Pergamos clasped arms with him, and then presented me. "Here is your queen. Widow of the Trojan hero Hektôr, and again, widow of Helenos, Priest of the Oracle at Thymbra. I am her son by Pyrrhos, Son of Akhilles. We were sent by Apollo's oracle at Chryse. As Trojan and Achaian, I will protect the rights of both peoples."

In the great hall, we were met by a statuesque woman younger than me, her black hair in thin plaits down her back. Stiffly formal, she was faintly hostile.

"I am Galena, nurse to Princess Klytie, and keeper of this house." She glanced at Pergamos. "You, my lord, may browse the building. I will show these ladies to their rooms."

He bristled. "This is my mother, Queen Ãndrõmakhê. I have not yet seen the princess."

"Nor will you, except in the company of myself and the lady, uh, Queen Ãndrõmakhê, as is proper." Galena turned with a swirl of her robe and started for the stairs at the rear of the hail.

I suppressed a smile; she had reminded me of my mother's bossy but well-meaning nurse, Mykale. Then, followed by Thalpia, I accompanied Galena up and along the short gallery. Exhausted as I was by all this excitement, I only noticed that the palace was large, somewhat after the style of my father's in Thébé.

Galena paused at one door, pushed it, and looked at Thalpia. "This is yours." When Thalpia entered, Galena moved to the adjoining doorway and pushed open the door.

She preceded me into the room, and then turned. "Who is that woman? She is no relation, or your son would have told me."

"What woman? Oh, you mean Thalpia? She was a present from Priam's queen Hekabe when I married Hektôr. She was nurse to all my sons and is free now; my cherished companion."

"So, my mistake, not your maid. We are equals, then, for I too was a slave until ..." Her face clouded and when she spoke again her voice was strained, "This was her majesty's room, my lady, and your friend has that of her chief attendant."

"I thank you for your courtesy." I liked what I saw, and went around the room examining the furnishings. "If I should make changes later, I will consult you."

Galena smiled, friendliness emanating from her. She stepped back to the doors. "Call on me at any time. You will find me at the end of the gallery next to the workroom." She went out and pointed. "I keep the princess with me, for I do not know your son. She is heiress to this land."

I smiled. "He has heard of her, and would marry her. All in good time, Galena."

When she left, I stepped to the bed, glad that the bedding had been unrolled and covers spread invitingly.

Home, at last....

* * * *

497

When I awoke next morning, I listened to water sluicing from the projecting roof, and knew that the rainy season had commenced full force. I snuggled deeper under the covers. I was safe and warm listening to the drum and patter on the roof. Journey's end, and I was at last back in my own part of the world, never to leave again.

A light scratch at the door barely preceded Pergamos. He bounced in, flushed with excitement. "Good morning, Queen Āndrōmakhê!"

I sat up and reached my arms to him. "I am your most loyal subject, King Pergamos."

He bent and embraced me. "Early this morning Zakis set up the voting pot in our hall and the Council cast in their pebbles. They had heard so much about you! Indeed you are chosen queen, with me as your regent."

"No! You are king. You are King Pergamos. I am queen-mother. Your wife will be queen. I will not take away the princess' right."

"Ah, you mean Klytie? I've heard that she is lovely, but Galena, the old gorgon, will not let me see her until we pay respects at her father's tomb."

"I trust you gave him honorable rites."

"But of course! His men raised a noble barrow over his ashes. I have seen to it that his shade will never want for honor and memory. This place is to be our kingdom and I'll not risk hauntings."

"The daughter must learn not to hate you."

"How could she hate me? Galena told me he was not a kind father. Besides, I have done everything properly. Moreover, everyone knows the fortunes of war. Zakis is already sending word through the city that I will marry her. It is only proper that as victor, I marry the heiress."

"Be kind to her, son." I knew very well the dread of subjugation to a man who had killed a loved one.

As if reading my thoughts, he said, his voice gentle, "I am more considerate than that. I have been chosen even without this marriage. However, I will follow through, for I will not violate custom. The girl is lucky not to be enslaved by me." He gave a chuckling laugh.

Ah, you cocky young bull, I thought with an inward smile.

* * * *

On a day of intermittent rain, Thalpia went with me to the shrine of healing. I meant to set up a memorial statue of Helenos there, with Pergamos' approval. The place was behind a low stone fence opening into a sacred grove extending to the terrace below. The small wooden building was open along the front, its roof supported by inverted tree trunks.

Hermos, chief of the physician-priests, met me at the altar of Apollo Paian. After I had offered up prayers to Him, I sat on a bench beside Hermos, and explained my wish.

He was a small-boned, dark, muscular man, whose brown eyes met mine with a kindly smile. He indicated votive figures near the altar, "We will place a figure of your husband there. As you may know, not all the physicians honored here are native. I myself was born at Klaros in Karia. My father brought his family here to Telephos when Merops invaded Karia. Alas, I am the last of my family."

Sympathy stirred in me; but for my sons, I was also the last of my family. He stood up, raised my hand to his lips, and then silently went away. I remained sitting, planning how I might improve this place and name it for Helenos.

A soft sound diverted me and I saw, for the first time, a small niche near the altar where a young woman knelt, arms uplifted to a wooden figure there.

"That's Klytie paying respects to Telephos," Thalpia muttered in my ear, startling me. I had forgotten her presence.

The girl, pale and delicately freckled, seemed weighted by the luxuriance of her auburn hair. A movement from Thalpia startled her and she lowered her arms, turned, and gasped.

Before I could move, the girl's arms were about my knees, the young voice wobbling with fear, "Lady, by your knees I beg mercy for the daughter of Arios. I have no man to protect me; I only have Galena, my faithful nurse."

I leaned down, urging her to rise. "I know you are Klytie Arioseis, and I have no quarrel with you. You are heiress to this land and will be treated as my equal."

"Galena says I have to marry your son, who killed my father."

"Such is the custom. But there is no taint of blood on my son, for he won in an agreed duel." I touched the girl's shoulder. "There is to be no vengeance here, Klytie. Come, my dear, sit beside me under the protection of Telephos. He and my father, Êetiôn, were lifelong friends, and fought in many campaigns to defend our homeland, together. So, now allow me to get to know you."

Klytie obeyed, her blue eyes still dark with the dread coursing through her. "I am so afraid!" She shuddered. "Terrible things have happened for as long as I can remember."

I put an arm about her. "My son will respect you and protect you." Then I added with a smile, "My brother Andros had married Lanassa, the younger sister of Eurypylos, your grandfather, and they had a daughter, Okyone. We spent our time in captivity, together. So you can consider me a relative."

Pergamos came in clad in his best finery, followed by Galena who lay a hand on the girl's shoulder, "Klytie Arioseis, I give you into the care of Pergamos Pyrrhosides."

I felt the soft body tremble beside me before she stood up.

Standing straight, Klytie waited as Pergamos took her hand, "For your protection, I must make you my wife at once. I have word that our southern neighbors need help against an Assyrian revolt."

He turned as Zakis pounded in, "My lord! More urgency! Marduk-apal-iddina is about to take Karduniash. Ashur-dan is raising his Assyrians against him."

Pergamos addressed Zakis, "Bring Hermos to seal my agreement with Princess Klytie." The man went out by the door through which Hermos had left.

Pergamos turned to Galena, "I will have to go at once to the border. You understand that Klytie, as my lawfully wedded wife, will be better protected than if she is not."

The nurse bowed her head in acceptance. Hermos returned with Zakis, and Pergamos stated his demand for an immediate marriage.

Placing themselves before the shrine, Hermos intoned, "Telephos, witness! This man and this woman will rule Teuthrania. Klytie, daughter of Herakles through you; Pergamos, son of Pyrrhos through Akhilles, I unite them in your sight as husband and wife."

At last, when locks of hair from the two lay mingled on the altar, Hermos joined their hands, while my eyes misted.

The young couple left the shrine together.

Rain was falling in a light, feathery spray, which had not kept a small crowd from gathering outside the gate. As the pair walked across the long plaza children ran ahead with branches of evergreen to sweep clear the pavement, leaving fine streaks of muddied dust to mark their path. Younger adults from the crowd began to sing and walk along beside he engaged couple, their voices sweet and clear in the damp air as they sang.

* * * *

When Pergamos returned from his southern expedition with slaves and cattle, he reported the settling by Hittite refugees beyond the mountains. Among his booty was a herd of pure white horses.

"Sacred Laomedons!" he boasted. "I found them this side of the southern mountains."

"I thought the Achaians had taken all of Priam's herds," I said. "No other white horses were ever known. How would they be so far south?"

"They could have been herded there after the war," he reminded me. "But also, this could mean that the excuse he had told Herakles, the one about not being able to find the horses, because frightened by the noise of the battle between Drako and Herakles, the horses had trampled down the stable doors and galloped off like the wind, was the truth."

I reached to pet one of the mares, which swung away and trotted off. Klytie, her pregnancy showing, came out from behind Pergamos. Arms wound around each other, they watched the beautiful animals graze like white sails on the green Selinos Plain. Somewhere in the forest, an early nightingale began a flow of song. Farther away, a late cuckoo called from some stolen nest. I put an arm about them both, pleased by the affection shared by the young couple.

* * * *

When it was winter, our family sat in the great hall one pleasant evening while Minstrel Oiagros sang ballads and dirges.

"Has he no heroic tales?" Pergamos asked his wife.

"Yes," and her eyes lit. "My father chose Oiagros from contestants at the School of Ialemos; he knows tales of Tantalos and the white shoulder of Pelops, of Attis' death and rebirth, and of how Tyrsenos led away the Lydians."

As I listened to these songs, I helped Klytie make swaddlings for the baby. I cherished these quiet times, looking across the firepit where Pergamos carved posts for his child's bed. I truly loved these quiet evenings, for as I looked at my son across the flames, I saw shadows of my father, my husbands, and my master, all doing the same work. Now I could think of the past without bitterness. Everything was beautiful for me as the past blended into the present. I began to think more often of my future life in the Elysian Fields and took to speaking of it.

"No more tears there, children," I would say. "It has been a long time since I saw my parents, brothers, and Hektôr."

"Why are you so impatient to leave us?" Pergamos asked.

"I'll be near you also, Son. When you are old, you will understand. Death is not an end, for, after a time of rest, we return." Folding my hands in my hands, I stared into the fire.

"You are so beautiful now, Mother," Pergamos said tenderly.

"No more!" I laughed. "You flatter me needlessly."

"You glow in this light like a jewel," Klytie said suddenly. "It must be the firelight—there's crimson and gold and orange in your hair, Husband's Mother, and you gleam like a goddess."

She rose and stepped over in quick little movements despite her heaviness and knelt, hands folded on my knees. I laid a hand on her head, its shining tresses reflecting the firelight that glinted with the rhythm of her breath and the blaze.

"Dear one," she said, "you don't truly want to leave the sunlight."

"Oh, it will not be too dark for me there, Klytie. I will be basking in the light of my loved ones. But bless you for your sensitive heart, dear child. You truly are beautiful." I leaned over and as the girl looked up, kissed her on the brow.

If only…I could see Skamandrios before I crossed over….

* * * *

When it was spring and clouds no longer loomed over the plain, Klytie was delivered of a healthy infant. The fragile mother lay for days as if dead, while the lusty-voiced boy howled and was fed fig-milk because his mother had no milk. They tended the somnolent mother until the day when it was necessary that Pergamos accept and name the child.

He waited at the hearthfire with the shield he had taken from Arios, and it was here that I laid the baby. He lifted him up with pride.

"My son! You are Endeion Pergameides," he announced, then carried him to the outer door where citizens crowded to see.

Screams from upstairs brought me rushing back to the birth-room. A second labor was destroying the feeble mother!

It was a long night before the priestess was able to extract this child, a wizened little girl, and long dead.

Klytie never moved nor made a sound, the breath scarcely lifting her chest. At dawn, she opened her eyes. "The baby." Her head rolled on the pillow. I smoothed the matted hair and laid cool compresses on her forehead. Pergamos, defying taboo, entered with the baby and laid it on her breast. A smile flickered in her eyes and faded into emptiness.

The outer door, where he had proudly hung a laurel wreath announcing a son, was now covered with symbols of death. He hung a red leather phallus to show that his wife would live again, and below it a garland of early white lilies to invoke the protection of Ate-Athené, Guardian of Women, Lady of Lilies.

Klytie's pyre was set near the tomb of Ague, attended by mourners in grayish-brown linen. Pergamos hacked off most of his hair and laid it on the white-robed body atop the heaped-up timbers.

When flames had purified the body, her ashes were put into a large urn together with the stillborn infant. Sealed, they were buried under the pavement in the great hall near the firepit so that fertility would bless other marriages in that house.

Chapter 40: Glory

Young Endeion grew into a vigorous child with his mother's looks, and his father's height and strength. Galena was appointed his attendant, who found a suitable wet-nurse in the city.

When the child was three, Pergamos taught him wrestling and took him to plantings and harvestings. Pergamos, carrying Endeion on his shoulder, became a looked for sight in Pergama.

I was with Hermos when Pergamos laid the cornerstone for the House of Healing honoring Helenos and Asklepeios.

Afterward, holding my hand, Pergamos strolled back to the palace. We stopped beside a stone block in the public area before the building, and I brushed a hand across it.

"I will raise a statue there," he said, and pulled me along. "This was a shrine at one time, and will be again."

The people of Pergamos began looking upon me not only as Foundress but also as Patroness-Mother. I went about among the women of the city and countryside, helping with family needs and showing them better ways of home economy, raising of children, and just importantly, how to read and write. I learned to know the poorer women and went with them to consult Hermos on matters of health. Gladly I led the sacred lustrations of women in the murmuring Kaikos or turbulent Kteios Rivers.

By now, Thalpia was growing weaker and no longer accompanied me; Galena took her place on these visits. At such times that Pergamos did not take Endeion to the fields or sports area, Thalpia played nurse. I was increasingly concerned about my friend, and arranged that a servant be in constant attendance upon her.

One evening after I had been in the Lower City later than usual, I met Hermos leaving Thalpia's room. Followed by Galena, he was giving low-voiced instructions.

The woman went away, and Hermos turned to me. "My lady queen, your good friend is dying. She will need constant care and Galena knows what to do."

"Dying! Thalpia? How did this happen?"

"She fell. Your slave girl is not at fault; you know Thalpia's willfulness. They were in the public square with Endeion. When he climbed onto that old stone base out there, Thalpia tried to get him down. She stumbled over her stick and fell, striking her back first and then her head on a corner of the stone base." He paused, then went on; "She sleeps, and may never wake. I have left soothing potions that Galena knows how to give her. She is to do the heavy lifting, my lady; this you must not do. You are not young yourself and must let others help you with her."

I flew into the room to find my friend flat on her back, covered with a tapestry spread, eyes closed. Bending down, I was gladdened that she still breathed. So I settled in the one chair.

Pergamos found me there later, and urged me to take a bite to eat.

"I am not leaving her," I stated firmly.

"You can see she's sleeping. You need strength for this."

I looked at him, not answering, and then turned back to the unconscious Thalpia.

"Forgive me, Mother, but you are coming with me. You can do nothing much here." His strong arms thrust under my knees and shoulders and he carried me from the room.

He laughed. "You are so little and light! To see you walking around, I've always thought you an impressive woman." We had come to the head of the stairs.

"All right—just put me down before we fall."

Giddiness made me feel as if we were already tumbling to the floor below. "I'll eat with you."

"Galena will call if you are needed." He set me on my feet and I glanced back to see Galena enter the sickroom.

I had a small bed set up and kept constant watch lest Thalpia wake and ask for me. Hermos came daily with salves and soothing drinks. Tears, prayers, and offerings to Apollo Healer availed nothing. Thalpia slept on with only faint rousings for medication.

One autumn night, however, she did rouse, the faint sounds waking me. The dim oil lamp showed the sick woman's wide eyes. When I bent over her, she seemed to quiet down. Her lips moved and after a supreme effort she whispered, "Lady, don't worry over me."

"Thalpia, I must help you. How can I ever repay you?" Sobs burst from me and I hid my face on Thalpia's breast.

"Dear Lady, I will always belong to you. When the old queen had ordered me to serve you, she gave me the gift of a new and better life. Yes, to be in your service, was a reward for all my sufferings in the past! There is nothing else or better for me, Lady Āndrõmakhê, but to serve you as best I can."

"All right, but now it's my turn to serve you." I lifted her head and pushed tendrils of hair from the older woman's forehead.

"When Hektôr brought you from Thébé…you were so beautiful and so happy." Her eyes searched mine, yet seemed to look beyond. "And always kind."

"And those countless times when Hektôr had to stay away nights at camp…you were with me, or slept at my door." I kissed my faithful friend's forehead. "You were with me at the Skaian Tower by night, and helped me locate his watch-fire. Afterward, you'd put me to bed… my nurse, and me a little child."

"Those were good days, Lady."

"You were with me when Skamandrios first wakened in me and I couldn't sleep for joy of him. You were with me all those times, Thalpia. Even those horrible years after the war."

"Yet the worst brought you fine sons, Lady. The Goddess was so merciful. Are they not worth the price?"

"I would not pay it again, nor would I be without them."

"In my dream, I saw Skamandrios, Lady. He said that soon, you will hear of him."

"Oh, Thalpia!"

She gasped and moved her hands over the coverlet as if searching. "Lady, go fetch Pergamos!"

Fear pursued me along the gallery to the room my son shared with his new wife, Kloris. I opened the door cautiously, calling his name in a sibilant whisper. When I heard his answering grunt, I rushed back to Thalpia's room and was holding her hand in both of mine when he came in with a lit torch, stuck it into a holder at the door, and joined me at the bedside.

Thalpia gasped. Her voice was a croak, "Please leave now, Lady, I must see him alone."

The dying woman's eyes were emptying. She seemed to wait for me to go, breathing shallowly.

I stepped back into the shadows.

506

"Pergamos, I've nursed you. Swear to me that you will do what...what I...can... not..." She paused, inhaling shakily.

I did not move.

"I swear, Nurse Thalpia," and his fervent voice was firm.

"Your mother—I promised when she married Helenos – I would wrap her ashes...in the veil...the veil of Hektôr's bride...the veil worn for two brothers..." She stopped again.

"I *will* do this for you, and for her, Thalpia." My son's voice was unsteady, his own tears brimming.

"I'm sorry I couldn't...but I can't! My lady, my lady, I am ... Where are you, Lady Āndrōmakhê?" It was clear she was blinded, blinded by the approaching White Light. She was feeling around on the bed again. I gripped her hands and kissed them, unrestrained sobs breaking from me. "Sorry, Lady, I couldn't..." and her voice faded into a faint rattle.

One last rise of strength as she opened her eyes wide and cried, "How beautiful!"

Then, silence.

Weeping uncontrollably, I bent over and kissed the departing soul through her lips, then raised myself and found myself staring. A delicate whiteness as of frosted breath, etherealized from Thalpia, dissipating through the ceiling.

* * * *

Thalpia's funeral pyre was royal, but her ashes were not put under a mound. "She grew up without freedom nor did she want it when given to her," I told Pergamos. "She could never find peace alone in the Elysian Fields. When my time comes to leave the sunlight, please place her ashes in the mound with that of mine."

"I promise, but may that day be long in the future."

Thalpia's ashes were placed in a delicately painted urn, sealed, and brought to my sleeping room. It was too large for the votive niche I kept above my head where I maintained a little shrine to Dea Madre and Ma-Kybele, the Great Kind Mother.

"There's a loose block here," Pergamos said, testing the wall at my bed's foot. He reached over and tapped an oblong flat stone that did not quite match the others. It gave a hollow sound. "I can get this moved. There should be enough space here."

He called in two men and when the stone was wrestled from its place, dust and bits of rock filtered onto the bedroll. A faint glitter reflected the lamplight, and I gasped.

Something was in there. I leaned to look, "Pergamos, those are jewels!" I peered more closely into the dark space. "Oh, holy Ate! That's the Vine of Zeus."

"The *what?*" He reached in and drew out the treasure by its base. He set it on the dressing table beside the lamps.

"The family heirloom that Priam gave to Astyoche," I said, touching it with a finger. "He sent it to his sister as a reward for dispatching her son, Eurypylos, to lead Troia's forces after Hektôr." I could not go on.

Pergamos dismissed the workers, and then turned to me. "Endeion has the blood of Laomedon," he said in wonder. "I will see that he treasures this heritage from his Trojan forebears."

I remained a speechless statue. I could not see enough of the treasure, given to old Laomedon by Zeus in return for his stolen son, Ganymedes. I had seen it only once, but could not mistake it. Almost a tree, the gold stems grew from a crystal-white rock, sprouting leaves and blossoms of many-colored gems. I touched the small leaves and they trembled, hanging on threadlike gold wires. A treasure, a jewel, but most of all a divine gift, a talisman of royal Trojans. An exchange for the life of Eurypylos, whose delicate granddaughter had died bearing Pergamos' son. A talisman of death, but also a symbol of life. How had it survived? Had Astyoche entombed it here to save it from marauding hands? No one would ever know.

Galena came in and I turned to her. At the woman's amazed stare I said, speaking as if before a conjured spirit, "Galena, see that the niche is cleaned and the vine put back." I told its history. "And I will have Thalpia's urn in there, beside it."

The royal treasure must go to Pergamos, thence to Young Endeion as scion of Eurypylos, kindred of my second father Priam, and on down the generations after him.

That night, as I lay in bed with my night lamp lit, I looked at the vine and the urn above my feet. I knew that in no sense would Thalpia ever leave me now, and that the royal treasure was secured to the oldest son of Pergamos. I was resigned at last, even happy, to think that my life would soon end, no, change; for, growing more feeble as the years passed, I was already partly in two worlds.

I lay a long while, half-dreaming, remembering Thalpia, and how I had always been with her from the first day of my marriage to Hektôr. She had been the one continuity in my life. Thalpia, alone of all my loved ones, had died in my presence. Hektôr, whose bravery had defied pity, his profound fulfillment of duty rejecting death in his loving wife's arms, had given his life in dust and blood, before the walls of his home. I had not even seen that last duel, just as I had been so far away when Helenos died yearning for me.

Oh, Helenos! Not to have held his head in my lap, he who had starved so many years for my love. "Oh Dea Madre, Mother Ate, hold him close to your breast for me."

I moaned the words aloud. To have lived alone so long, and to die alone, initiate into a higher wisdom, slave and king, seer always.

"Did Hektôr meet you when Hermes wakened you beyond Lethe?' I whispered.

The dirge I had uttered for him in Buthroton was word-clear in my mind, and as I whispered it, changed here and there for Thalpia, my eyes drooped until I slept.

* * * *

One day, a wandering minstrel arrived. He was born in Hesperia, he said, Hesperia, Land of the West, the place Aeneas had sailed to, and Skamandrios still wandered. When the minstrel gave his name as Nurziu, I sat up and took notice. He had been taken captive by Spartan pirates, but traded with them along the Tirenean Sea, and the islands of Sardinia and Sicily.

Then he sang the tale of a Titan, a blond warrior of heroic stature, by the name of Astyanax, who had been tossed onto Hesperia after the fall of Troia, via Krete. Though having lost an eye and part of his leg, Astyanax was swordsman with no equal and his beauty such that women laughed and wept at the sight of him. Astyanax was eighteen when he fell in love with a princess named Kupra, who was a devotee of the goddess Kupra, and when she fell in the hands of marauders from Keltia, he went on a long quest to find and free her. He succeeded after many years, the couple ended up in Sicily, and together they founded the Kingdom of Messina. Their realm lay on the lower slopes of the Peloritani Mountains, on the Strait of Messina, and its harbor was shaped like a sickle.

"The oracles foresee that," concluded Minstrel Nurziu his tale, "from Astyanax [1] and Kupra, will derive two branches of royal families. One will be known as the royal race of Pepin and Charlemagne, and the other, that of Reggio."

Yes, dear Thalpia, just as you had told me, today I have heard word of Skamandrios Astyanax.

Hektôr! Did you hear this, too, my husband?

* * * *

It was some time later that sounds from outside wakened me. During several nights, there had been stirrings in rooms near and below mine. A growing sense of surprise and pleasant anticipation pervaded the palace, not like any I had known before. Mysterious glances and evasive answers had been the only responses to my questioning.

I pushed off my covers and moved carefully from the bed, being rather stiff in the joints as was usual these days. Wrapping a linen cloth around myself, I went to the window; not the one toward distant hills, but the small one that looked onto the public square.

The block of stone in its center was gone ... no, that tall shaft was in its place. Covered with a cloth—a sail? It was attracting a crowd already, so early. The rising sun edged dark towers of the citadel.

I looked toward the temple of Athené-Ate, its polished stone ornamented in a new way with sculptures. Opposite, the glooming Grove of Telephos and Asklepeios where was also the House of Healing, dedicated to Helenos. Had I missed an important festival?

I went to the clothes chest and tried to raise the heavy carved lid. Galena came in and found me seated there, the cloth bunched around my hips, otherwise naked as I had slept. The woman was festively dressed in a rust-colored side-slit sheath bordered in white. "This is a special day for you," she spoke.

"What festival is it? I forget so much these days." I stood up so the woman could open the chest. "My childhood is clearer to me than yesterday." I moved aside.

"This is the first day of a new celebration to be held every year from now on." Galena lifted out several items, and a fleecy wool shawl that she wrapped around me.

When we left the bathing room, Galena dressed me in white linen, drifting from pleats at each shoulder held by silver clasps. My strawberry blond hair was finally being streaked with white strands, barely reaching my ears after I had shorn it for Thalpia, and it was held in place by a veil of silver threads under a circlet of gold leaves.

No one was in the hall below, and Galena brought me my first meal of the day.

Pergamos came in while I was still eating. Breaking off a hunk of sesame bread and pouring himself a cup of watered wine, he sat with me while I finished. His manner was mysterious, ebullient and partly teasing. "Hasn't Galena told you, Mother? This is the name-day of our city. You are to call Telephon by any name you choose."

"I already named the city for you." I tapped him on his wrist with a chunk of sesame bread, and then ate it with a sip of wine.

When we finished he helped me to my feet and I stood with hands behind my neck. The chain I always wore came loose in my hands and I held it out to him. The opal as well as a heavy ring dangled from it. "My son, this has never left my neck." I swung the chain a little. "The opal will go on the pyre with me, but this… this is Hektôr's cartouche ring and has never been on any hand but his. It carries the royal cartouche of Troia, and you, as bearer of future fame in Trojan lands, are next to wear it." I tried to hook it behind his neck but he was too tall, and he bent so I could fasten it.

"Mother, the seal of Hektôr will be the seal of all future rulers here after me." He held me to his chest, and then stood back from me. He was magnificent in long Trojan purple edged in gold, and tears dimmed my eyes, tears of joy and pride.

Galena called from outside. "My lord, my lady, it is time."

We went out to where the festive crowd milled and talked. Children ran about scattering flowers and leaves. Near that shaft before me, lyrists and flutists strummed and whistled to the rhythms beaten out by sistra. They stopped at the covered shaft. I looked up to see beyond it the dark citadel towers, squared against the sunlit sky.

Inos, eldest of the Councilmen and Chief Citizen, approached with a chain of gold and silver owl-eyes and goat-horns in his hands.

He bowed low, and then spoke to me, "The citizens of Pergamon, formerly Telephon, choose to honor you, Āndrōmakhê Êetiônis. Those of us who remember King Priam's wisdom and power, and the always-just rule of godlike Êetiôn, salute you. Today, the peoples of Mysia once ruled by your father, join us in honoring you."

He held high the necklace so all could see. "On behalf of all Teuthrania! I present you with the sacred chain of Athené-Ate-Ma, Lady of Women, Mother of the Mountains, Protectress of Wild Animals. Wear this as Patroness of our city."

He placed the necklace around my throat, and Galena attached the clasps under my veil.

Wordless with emotion, I lifted my arms in prayer and gratitude. My voice failed at the glory of this moment. All around me were quiet, sharing my emotions.

My noble son Pergamos stepped forward and slowly pulled away the cloth from the shaft before me. It fell with a rush of air. The rhythmic strum of lyres and shrill of flutes rose from the musicians, and the bard Oiagros led a melodious chant,

"Queen of Kilikia and Troia, Queen of Chaonia and Teuthrania, praise to Ãndrõmakhê!"

The crowd joined in choral unison. "Patroness of all the people, forever honored as divine!"

My throat full, I looked up at the enormous statue before me. Made of white marble, it sat upon a pillar.

A woman ...

Myself?

Yet not myself as I was now. No, the statue was youthful and beautiful. Thus I would be remembered, not only as the mother of the city's namesake, but as the faithful wife of Hektôr and loving daughter of Êetiôn and Latmia.

I was hurled back in time, to a night in my bedchamber in my father's Theban palace.

"The life I have given you," declared a woman's voice, *"bear with courage; and take upon yourself the sufferings I will see fit to bestow upon you. In the end, your sorrows will lift you upon a pillar."*

I smiled, blinking in the brilliant sun.

Lo! I stood in front of a statue that sat on a pillar, built in my name as my Goddess had ordained, and I could see my parents, and my seven brothers, and Helenos, Thalpia, Iris, Nefru, and now... looking as he did during the night of the Maze Dance, Hektôr.

Hektôr, my husband. Forever.

* * * *

[1] Astyanax' death is actually only mentioned in Ovid's *Metamorphoses* (XIII, 399-428) while the *Aeneid* only refers to "lost Astyanax (II, 457). Other sources, such as Bullfinch's *Mythology,* say that Astyanax founded the kingdom of Messina in Sicily,

ĀNDRÕMAKHÊ © KRISTINA O'DONNELLY

Cast of Characters (alphabetically)

- **Aeneas:** Prince of Dardania; son of King Anchises; said to be a contender for the Trojan throne
- **Agamemnon:** High King of the Mykene on mainland Achaia (today's Greece); descendant of the House of Atros, also called Agamemnon Atrides, which means 'son of Atros' [Possible roots of the name: Very Steadfast, Admirable for Staying the Course.]
- **Akamas:** Prince, son of King Theseus of Athens; his love for Laodike, daughter of Priam, does not prevent him from fighting against Troia
- **Akhilles:** Prince of Phthia in Thessaly; son of the mortal King Peleos, leader of the Myrmidons in Phthia, and Thétis, the Nereid. [Tracing the roots of the name Achilles: Achilles' name can be analyzed as a combination of ἄχος (akhos) "grief" and λαός (laos) "a people, tribe, nation, etc." Thus, Achilles is an embodiment of the grief of the people, grief being a theme raised numerous times in the Iliad—often by Achilles himself. His role as the hero of grief forms a juxtaposition with the conventional view of Achilles as the hero of kleos (glory, usually glory in war).]
- **Alexander/Alexis** (a.k.a. Paris): Prince of Troia, brother of Hektôr, Aphrodite's pawn, and lover/husband of Helen of Sparta [Alexandros is the name Homer used for him in the Iliad]
- **Anchises:** King of neighboring Dardania, cousin of King Priam
- **Āndrõmakhê** (Andromache): Daughter of King Êetiôn and Queen Latmia; wife of Hektôr; later on Queen of Kilikia, Epirus, and Pergama; mother of four sons; [Āndrõmakhê is a Greek name, meaning 'battle of a man' from the Greek elements ανδρος (andros) 'of a man' and μαχη (mache) 'battle', or in short, 'Man Fighter.' There was an Amazon queen named Andromache, who fought against Herakles.]
- **Antenor:** Trojan noble, powerful brother of Queen Hekabe; arch enemy of Prince Alexis (Paris), leader of the Council of Elders and head of the Trojan faction that secretly negotiates with the enemy
- **Astynome:** daughter of **Chryse,** Priest of Apollo, at Thébé; best friend of Āndrõmakhê.
- **Briseis:** daughter of **King Brisos** of Pedasos, who is Chief-priest of Zeus; friend of Āndrõmakhê.
- **Deiphobos:** Prince of Troia; Hektôr's loyal, younger brother
- **Diomede:** daughter of **King Phorbas** of Lesbos; friend of Āndrõmakhê.
- **Êetiôn:** King of Kilikia, overlord of Mysinia, a ruler as good with the plow as with the sword; loving husband and father, staunch ally of Troia
- **Hekabe:** Queen, Priam's devoted wife, mother of nineteen of his children
- **Hektôr:** Prince of Troia, renowned as Horse Tamer and Defender of Troia. [The name Hektôr is the Latinized form of Greek Εκτωρ (Hektôr), which was derived from 'εκτωρ (Hektôr) 'holding fast', ultimately from εχω (echo) meaning 'to hold, to possess'. Hektôr held fast to his duty as Defender.]
- **Helen:** Queen of Sparta; wife of King Meneláos; her face launched a 1,000 ships, but in fact she was a pawn of kings who battled to extend their dominions around Greece and Asia. [The name Helen: Possibly from either

Greek ελενη *(Helene)* 'torch' or 'corposant', or Greek σεληνη *(selene)* 'moon'.]

- **Helenos:** Prince; Hektôr's younger brother; Ãndrõmakhê's first love, respected seer, Priest of Apollo, later King of Chaonia, in Epirus
- **Helikaon:** Son of Antenor and Theano; husband of Princess Laodike
- **Hermione:** Daughter of Meneláos and Helen of Sparta; Ãndrõmakhê's mortal enemy
- **Kassandra:** Hektôr's full sister by Priam and Hekabe; Princess of Troia; Priestess of Apollo; the prophetess whose predictions everyone ignores—as ordained by Apollo. [Kassandra is a Greek name and means 'helper of man' as well as 'disbelieved by man']
- **Kebriones:** Hektôr's half-brother and trusted charioteer
- **Kreusa:** Hektôr's full sister; wife of Aeneas, son of King Anchises
- **Lanassa:** Daughter of Teuthranian King Telephos; friend of Ãndrõmakhê
- **Laodike:** Hektôr's full sister; wife of Helikaon, son of Antenor
- **Latmia**: Queen; King Êetiôn's wife, daughter of King Nomion of Miletos; Priestess of Kybele, mother of Ãndrõmakhê and seven sons
- **Memnon:** King of Ethiopia; legendary warrior, called the handsomest man alive; son of Priam's brother Tithonos, and Eos, Goddess of the Morning
- **Meneláos:** King of Sparta; brother of Agamemnon; husband of Helen
- **Odysseus (a.k.a. Ulysses):** King of Ithaka, an island on the Ionian Sea; well-versed and cunning, he is credited as the one who thought of building the famous Trojan horse {Possible original root of his name: Giver/Sufferer of Pain.]
- **Peleos:** King, Father of Akhilles; friend of Ãndrõmakhê
- **Penthesilea:** Warrior Queen of the Amazons; ally of Troia; [Meaning of the name, Penthesilea: Compelling Men to Mourn.]
- **Polydoros:** Brother of Hektôr; youngest son of Priam and Hekabe
- **Polydamas:** Hektôr's trusted second-in-command
- **Polymestor:** King of Thrakia (Thrace); husband of **Ilione,** oldest daughter of Priam and Hekabe; betrayer of trust
- **Priam**: King of Troia; Overlord of Dardania, the Troad, and twelve other cities; Father of fifty sons and twelve daughters
- **Pyrrhos Neoptolemos**: Warrior-prince; son of Akhilles of Thessaly and Princess Deidameia of Skyros; later, King of Epirus
- **Sigeia:** Princess of Thrakia, Hektôr's lover before his marriage to Ãndrõmakhê, mother of his son who is a contender for the Trojan throne
- **Somer, Olivia, Hakan Berk,** and **Rosemary Thompson:** four of the modern-era descendants of the 13th Century B.C.E Trojans; **Viktor Berk:** Patriarch of the Berk family
- **Thalpia:** Ãndrõmakhê's loyal servant and friend during her long exile
- **Theano:** Priestess of Pallas Athené; wife of Antenor, shares her husband's enmity of Prince Alexis, supports betrayal of Troia
- **Xanthos, Lampos, Aithos** and **Podarkes:** Hektôr's favorite four chariot horses, as named in the *Iliad*

Lands of the Morning™ Series

Kaleidoscopic, exotic, and international, Lands of the Morning™ Series is Michenesque in scope. The trials, tribulations and triumphs of three respective families are traced from their roots in the mists of pre-history. They are the **Berks,** Trojans, the **Alkibiades',** Achaians, and the **Kayhans,** Turks.

This series of ten novels is an arabesque of culturally/ethnically diverse history, mythology, sociology, politics, consuming passions, suspense/thrillers, ambition, triumph and tribulation, woven on a rich tapestry.
Skeins of exotic people, places and customs rooted in Anatolia, and branching out to Greece, Italy, Ireland, Israel, Sardinia, Illyria, and the United States of America, interlace the subplots with the fast-growing scheme of events, which always climax in unexpected denouements.
The fruit of lifetime of research and writing, this series is fiction based upon authentic contemporary/historical backgrounds and events.
Although woven upon a timeline, each novel can be read independently.

The series' titles:

1: The Horseman (winner of two awards) **2:** Clarion of Midnight/Megali Idea,
3: The Scorpion Child/Defy Eternity, **4:** Morgana – Poseidon Unbound
5: Trojan Enchantment (award-winner), **6:** Āndrõmakhê, **7:** Korinna –
Daughter of the Fire **8:** Constantinople, My Love (2007)
9: Battle of the Wolf and Falcon (2007), **10:** Shardana (2008)

About the Author:

Author of exotic, internationally plotted novels, Kristina O'Donnelly was born in Rome, Italy, from an Austrian mother and Italian father, and raised in Istanbul, Turkey, until the threesome relocated to the United States.
Married to her soulmate, Michael, native of Co. Armagh, in Northern Ireland, Kristina feels at
home in Turkey, Ireland, as well as the United States of America. O'Donnelly is known for offering novels described as "imbibing exotic cocktails on the Orient Express."
Her multi-cultural plots include sizzling love affairs, yes, but also controversial socio/political issues that are current, as well as ancient philosophies, no-holds barred human emotions, and far-flung and beguiling locales.
O'Donnelly is a firm believer in the can do, will do, spirit, and that one should never give up the good fight as every person's effort, counts.
Her diversified rucksack of professional experiences span 25 + years and include acting, writing (journalist, columnist, editor, publisher), and advertising (12 years with the New York Daily News), union activism (The Newspaper Guild of America), even real estate sales.
Her novels have received four awards and been published in the USA as well as Canada, Spain, England, New Zealand and Turkey.
She is a Founder of Florida Writers Association, Inc.

Kristina's novels are available at:

http://www.amazon.com
http://www.authorsden.com
http://www.fictionwise
http://www.booksforabuck.com
http://www.kristinaodonnelly.com

ĀNDRŌMAKHĒ © KRISTINA O'DONNELLY

Dateline March 3, 2003, University of Delaware website:

Combining an interest in the classics with expertise in the sedimentary geology that defines coastlines, a University of Delaware researcher has discovered that Homer's "Iliad" presents an accurate account of the geography of ancient Troy. John C. Kraft, H. Fletcher Brown Professor of Geology, writes in the February 2003 issue of the journal Geology, which is published by the Geological Society of America, that the area's sedimentology and geomorphology do indeed complement the features described in Homer's "Iliad."
"The reality of Homer's description of place, event and topography correlated with geologic investigation helps show that the 'Iliad' is not just a legend but regularly consistent with paleogeograhic reconstruction," concluded the research team, which also included George Rapp of the University of Minnesota, Ilhan Kayan of Ege University in Izmir, Turkey, and classical scholar John V. Luce of Trinity College in Dublin, Ireland. Kraft has been studying the ancient coastlines of the eastern Mediterranean Sea for over two decades and has always been interested in the classics, and particularly in their descriptions of geography.
Citation: *Sedimentology and geomorphology complement Homer's Iliad. By: Kraft, John C.; Rapp, George; Kayan, Ilhan; Luce, John W.. Geology, Feb.2003, Vol. 31 Issue 2, p163, 4p, 1 graph, 5 maps*

Gallery les Arts Turcs

In the heart of old Istanbul

Dear Reader/Traveler…

One of my favorite places in Istanbul, Turkey, is Gallery Les Arts Turcs, headed by my Dervish friend, Nurdoğan Şengüler.

When you arrive in Istanbul, and hurry over to the Old City, you can find the entrance; walk through a narrow doorway, then up three flights of curving stairs. You ring the bell, and hear voices. After a moment or two, the heavy wooden door opens, and someone, perhaps one of the young boys who make tea, or get sandwiches, dust, study English and work on computers, will be standing there, holding open the door, looking at you brightly and smiling, *"Hoş geldiniz." "Bienvenue." "Welcome."*

Stepping inside you are immediately enfolded in color, light, and music. Directly in front of you are shelves and tables heaped with Turkish arts and crafts, clothes, and jewelry. Prominently displayed on a large easel is a beautifully colored drawing of the hoopoe, the mystical bird from Farid ud-Din Attar's. The Conference of the Birds, which functions as the sheikh like guide for a group of birds traveling in search of Simorgh.

On the left is a serious workspace—six computers, a printer, a fax machine, two desks, and several telephones. On the right, your eye is caught by a large room lined with shelves filled with an enormous collection of CD's. You can select Turkish folk music from east Turkey, the Black Sea region, and the middle of Turkey. There is Çerkez music, Kurdish music, sanat music (art music), tasavvuf music (Sufi music), Gypsy music, you name it, as well as music from all the neighboring countries—Azerbaijan, Romania, Bulgaria, Russia, etc. The walls are covered with original paintings and drawings, and the light pours in. The renowned Hagia Sophia and trees seem to fill the windows, making them look like paintings too.

Gallery Les Arts Turcs is a unique meeting place for local and international artists, journalists, writers, photographers, painters, and travelers. The aim is to help visitors to Turkey appreciate all that this country has to offer in terms of history and culture. They provide guides to the Sufi community in Turkey and offer a chance to see an authentic whirling dervish ceremony. By the way, they also offer classes in painting, ebru, calligraphy, Oriental dance, guided tours for individuals and small groups, and more. Throughout the years they have developed a truly international network. There was even a story about the activities of Les Arts Turcs Gallery and its owner, Nurdoğan Şengüler, in a recent issue of the Paris-based newspaper, Le Figaro.

Les Arts Turcs is located in Sultanahmet, the old town of Istanbul, Turkey. The Aya Sophia and Blue mosques are their neighbors. If you look out the windows, over the park covering the underground cistern, you can see both of these treasures, the Topkapi palace, and the sea of Marmara beyond.

You are welcome in their gallery/office anytime. Just stop by to browse and to sit down for a cup of tea. They are open everyday from 10:00 until 22:00.

Address

Les Arts Turcs
Incili Çavus Sok. No: 37 Kat:3
Alemdar Mahallesi, Sultanahmet 34400
Istanbul, Turkey
Talk to us
Tel: 90 (212) 520 77 43
Tel: 90 (212) 511 22 96
Tel: 90 (212) 511 75 56
Fax: 90 (212) 511 22 96
Fax: 90 (212) 511 21 98

Printed in the United States
53755LVS00001B/1-4